A TEXT BOOK OF

# STRENGTH OF MATERIALS

(S. I. UNITS)

28th REVISED AND ENLARGED EDITION

COMMON FOR ALL COURSES IN MECHANICAL ENGINEERING GROUP

COURSE CODE : ME / PG / PT / AE / MH / FE / MI / PS

FOR SECOND YEAR DIPLOMA IN ENGINEERING AND TECHNOLOGY

SEMESTER III

AS PER M.S.B.T.E.'s REVISED ('G'-SCHEME) SYLLABUS, w.e.f. 2013-2014

By

## SUNIL S. DEO

M. E. Civil (Structures)
Principal,
Pune District Education Association's,
Institute of Technology,
Hadapsar, Pune - 411 028.

Price ₹ 350.00

N1943

## STRENGTH OF MATERIALS (MECHANICAL ENGINEERING GROUP)  ISBN : 978-93-83073-28-3

| | | |
|---|---|---|
| **Twenty-Eighth Edition** | : | **June, 2015** |
| Co-Author | : | **Sou. Sangita S. Deo** |
| © | | **Shri. S. S. Deo, Sou. Sangita S. Deo** |

**Published By :**                                           CPT
**NIRALI PRAKASHAN**
Abhyudaya Pragati, 1312, Shivaji Nagar,
Off J.M. Road, PUNE – 411005
Tel - (020) 25512336/37/39, Fax - (020) 25511379
Email : niralipune@pragationline.com

## ☞ DISTRIBUTION CENTRES

**PUNE**

**Nirali Prakashan** : 119, Budhwar Peth, Jogeshwari Mandir Lane, Pune 411002, Maharashtra
Tel : (020) 2445 2044, 66022708, Fax : (020) 2445 1538
Email : bookorder@pragationline.com, niralilocal@pragationline.com

**Nirali Prakashan** : S. No. 28/27, Dhyari, Near Pari Company, Pune 411041
Tel : (020) 24690204 Fax : (020) 24690316
Email : dhyari@pragationline.com, bookorder@pragationline.com

**MUMBAI**

**Nirali Prakashan** : 385, S.V.P. Road, Rasdhara Co-op. Hsg. Society Ltd.,
Girgaum, Mumbai 400004, Maharashtra
Tel : (022) 2385 6339 / 2386 9976, Fax : (022) 2386 9976
Email : niralimumbai@pragationline.com

## ☞ DISTRIBUTION BRANCHES

**JALGAON**

**Nirali Prakashan** : 34, V. V. Golani Market, Navi Peth, Jalgaon 425001,
Maharashtra, Tel : (0257) 222 0395, Mob : 94234 91860

**KOLHAPUR**

**Nirali Prakashan** : New Mahadvar Road, Kedar Plaza, 1st Floor Opp. IDBI Bank
Kolhapur 416 012, Maharashtra. Mob : 9850046155

**NAGPUR**

**Pratibha Book Distributors** : Above Maratha Mandir, Shop No. 3, First Floor,
Rani Jhanshi Square, Sitabuldi, Nagpur 440012, Maharashtra
Tel : (0712) 254 7129

**DELHI**

**Nirali Prakashan** : 4593/21, Basement, Aggarwal Lane 15, Ansari Road, Daryaganj
Near Times of India Building, New Delhi 110002
Mob : 08505972553

**BENGALURU**

**Pragati Book House** : House No. 1, Sanjeevappa Lane, Avenue Road Cross,
Opp. Rice Church, Bengaluru – 560002.
Tel : (080) 64513344, 64513355, Mob : 9880582331, 9845021552
Email:bharatsavla@yahoo.com

**CHENNAI**

**Pragati Books** : 9/1, Montieth Road, Behind Taas Mahal, Egmore,
Chennai 600008 Tamil Nadu, Tel : (044) 6518 3535,
Mob : 94440 01782 / 98450 21552 / 98805 82331,
Email : bharatsavla@yahoo.com

niralipune@pragationline.com   |   www.pragationline.com

Also find us on  f  www.facebook.com/niralibooks

Dedicated to,

My Loving Daughter

**"SHRIYA"**

# PREFACE TO THE TWENTY-EIGHTH EDITION

'A text book of Strength of Materials' is specifically written for the benefit of Second Year Diploma Course (Semester III) in Mechanical Engineering Group. The book is written according to the revised semester pattern ('G'-scheme) syllabus introduced in June 2013 by the Board of Technical Examinations, Maharashtra State. Though the book is written for diploma students, it is very informative to degree and A.M.I.E. students as well.

The salient features of this edition are :

1.  A core Text-book for class room teaching and self-study.

2.  Simple language with 'Explanations to the point'.

3.  A large number of solved examples and theory questions of various types, from B.T.E. papers upto Summer 2015.

4.  Practice questions along with answers and important hints.

5.  Important points for revision of each topic.

I am thankful to the Publisher **Shri. Dineshbhai Furia, Shri. Jignesh Furia** and staff of **Nirali Prakashan**, for publishing this book in the short span of time. My Sincere thanks are due to my wife Sou. S. S. Deo (M. Sc. Statistics) who has done the tiring work of proof correction with utmost care.

Any suggestions for the improvement of the book brought to my notice will be highly appreciated and incorporated in the subsequent edition of the book.

**Pune, June 2015**                                                        **Sunil S. Deo**

# SYLLABUS

## 1. MECHANICAL PROPERTIES OF MATERIALS, SIMPLE STRESSES AND STRAINS (10 Hours, 16 Marks)

**1.1 Mechanical Properties and Concept of Simple Stresses and Strains** (8 Marks)

- Elasticity, Plasticity, Plastic flow, Ductility, Malleability, Stiffness and Strength.
- Types of loads, Stresses-Tensile, Compressive, Shear, Single and Double shear, Concept of plain strain-Tensile, Compressive, Direct shear strain, Torsional shear strain, Lateral strain, Hooke's law.
- Poission ratio, Common values for C.I. and M.S., Relation between stress-strain. Stress-strain diagram for tensile and brittle materials, Important points on the stress-strain diagram.
- Modulus of elasticity and Modulus of rigidity, Volumetric strain, Bulk modulus, Relation between Modulus of elasticity and Modulus of rigidity.
- Thermal stresses – Temperature stresses and strains of uniform section.

**1.2 Composite Section** (4 Marks)

- Stress and Strains in bars of stepped and uniformly varying sections subjected to axial load at ends only, Composite sections having same length.

**1.3 Buckling of Long Columns** (4 Marks)

Euler's theory, Rankine's theory- Equivalent length of the column for the cases below :

- Both end hinged, One end fixed and other free, Both ends fixed, One end fixed and other end hinged (Simple numericals only).

## 2. PRINCIPAL STRESSES AND PLANES (5 Hours, 8 Marks)

**2.1 Concept of Principal Stresses and Principal Planes**

Stresses on an oblique section of a body subjected to (4 Marks)

- Direct stresses on one plane.
- Direct stresses on mutually perpendicular planes
- Direct and Shear stress on one plane.
- Direct and Shear stress on mutually perpendicular plane (No derivations).
- Mohr's circle method for finding principal stresses and planes (only simple numericals)

**2.2 Thin Cylindrical Shell** (4 Marks)

- Stresses in thin closed cylindrical vessels subjected to Internal pressure, Hoop stress, Radial and Axial stress. (Simple numericals only)

## 3. BENDING MOMENT AND SHEAR FORCE (8 Hours, 16 Marks)

**3.1 Concept and Definition of Shear Force and Bending Moment**

- Relation between Rate of loading, Shear force and Bending moment.
- Shear force and Bending moment diagrams for Cantilevers, Simply supported beam and Overhanging beam subjected to point loads and uniformly distributed load. Location of point of contraflexure.

## 4. MOMENT OF INERTIA (6 Hours, 16 Marks)

**4.1 Concept and Definition of Moment of Inertia, Parallel and Perpendicular Axes Theorem**

- (No derivation).

- Moment of inertia of Solid sections - Square, Rectangular, Circular, Semicircular, Triangular. Hollow sections – Square, Rectangular and Circular cross-sections only.

- Moment of inertia of Angle section, Channel section, Tee-section, I-section about centroidal axis and any other axis parallel to centroidal axis.

- Polar moment of inertia.

## 5. BENDING STRESSES (6 Hours, 12 Marks)

**5.1 Theory of Simple Bending** (6 Marks)

- Assumptions in the Theory of bending, Moment of resistance, Section modulus, Neutral axis, Stress distribution diagram for Cantilever and Simply supported beam. Equation of bending (Simple numericals based on formula).

**5.2 Concept of Direct and Transverse Shear Stress** (6 Marks)

- Transverse shear stress equation (No derivation).

- Shear stress distribution diagrams : Average shear stress and Maximum shear stress for rectangular and circular sections.

## 6. DIRECT AND BENDING STRESSES (7 Hours, 16 Marks)

**6.1 Concept of Axial Load, Eccentric Load, Direct Stresses, Bending Stresses, Maximum and Minimum Stresses** (4 Marks)

- Stress distribution diagram.

- Problems on the above concepts for strut, machine parts such as Offset links, C-clamp, Bench vice, Drilling machine frame etc. (8 Marks)

- Condition for no tension in the section, Core of section. (4 Marks)

## 7. TORSION (6 Hours, 16 Marks)

**7.1 Concept of Pure Torsion**

- Assumptions in the theory of Pure torsion, Torsion equation for solid and hollow circular shafts, Stress distribution across solid circular shaft. (No derivation).

- Power transmitted by a shaft. (10 Marks)

**7.2 Comparison between Solid and Hollow Shafts subjected to Pure Torsion (No Problems on Composite and Non-Homogeneous Shaft)** (6 Marks)

# CONTENTS

1. Mechanical Properties of Materials, Simple Stresses and Strains    1.1 – 1.122

2. Principal Stresses and Planes    2.1 – 2.54

3. Bending Moment and Shear Force    3.1 – 3.86

4. Moment of Inertia    4.1 – 4.76

5. Bending Stresses    5.1 – 5.58

6. Direct and Bending Stresses    6.1 – 6.46

7. Torsion    7.1 – 7.38

M.S.B.T.E. Question Papers as per G Scheme Syllabus with Answers    P.1 – P.22

●●●

# MECHANICAL PROPERTIES OF MATERIALS, SIMPLE STRESSES AND STRAINS

| Weightage of Marks = 16, Teaching Hours = 10 |
| --- |

## *Objectives*

Specific Objectives :

* Acquire elementary knowledge of stresses, strains and material properties.
* Study and apply Euler's theory.

## *Contents*

1.1  Mechanical properties and Concept of simple stresses and strains.  **(8 Marks)**

* Elasticity, Plasticity, Plastic flow, Ductility, Malleability, Stiffness and Strength.
* Types of Loads, Stresses – Tensile, Compressive, Shear, Single and Double shear, Concept of Plain Strain – Tensile, Compressive, Direct shear strain, Torsional shear strain, Lateral strain, Hooke's law.
* Poisson ratio, Common values for C.I. and M.S., Relation between stress-strain. Stress-strain diagram for Tensile and Brittle materials, Important points on the stress-strain diagram.
* Modulus of elasticity and Modulus of rigidity, Volumetric strain, Bulk modulus, Relation between Modulus of elasticity and Modulus of rigidity.
* Thermal stresses : Temperature stresses and strains of uniform section.

1.2  Composite Section  **(4 Marks)**

* Stresses and Strains in bars of stepped and uniformly varying sections subjected to axial load at ends only, Composite sections having same length.

1.3  Buckling of Long Columns  **(4 Marks)**

* Euler's theory, Rankine's theory – Equivalent length of the column for the cases below.
* Both ends hinged, one end fixed and other free. Both ends fixed, one end fixed and other end hinged. (Simple Numericals only)

## SUB-TOPIC 1.1 : MECHANICAL PROPERTIES AND CONCEPT OF SIMPLE STRESSES AND STRAINS  (8 Marks)

## (A) BASIC CONCEPTS AND MECHANICAL PROPERTIES OF MATERIALS

### Synopsis

Introduction, Deformation, Concept of elastic, plastic and rigid body, Materials, Classification of materials, Mechanical properties of materials.

## 1.1 INTRODUCTION

The subject 'Strength of Materials' or 'Mechanics of Structures' or 'Materials and Structures' deals with the study of strength and mechanical properties of materials and the behaviour of structural members under the action of an externally applied loads. Before going into the details of the subject matter, it is very necessary to understand the following basic concepts.

## 1.2 DEFORMATION

When an external force is applied to a body of an elastic material, there will be some change in its size and shape due to change in the dimensions of a body. *This change in the size and shape of a body due to an externally applied load is called as deformation.*

## 1.3 CONCEPT OF ELASTIC, PLASTIC AND RIGID BODY

**Elastic Body :** A body which possesses the property of elasticity is called an elastic body. *A body is said to be elastic if it regains its original size and shape when an externally applied load causing deformation is entirely removed.*

**Plastic Body :** *If a body does not regain its original size and shape on removal of an externally applied load and gets permanently deformed, it is called a plastic body.*

**Rigid Body :** *If a body does not undergo any deformation under the action of external loads, it is called a rigid body.* The distance between any two particles of a rigid body remains unchanged even after applying an external load to it. Rigid body is an imaginary concept. In fact, no body is perfectly rigid.

## 1.4 MATERIALS

Mild steel, tor steel, cast iron, brass, aluminium, copper, concrete, bricks, tiles, stone, timber, glass, etc. are some commonly used materials for engineering purposes. The important properties of materials are mechanical, thermal, magnetic, electrical, chemical, physical, etc. From this subject point of view, here we shall discuss only mechanical properties of materials. Before going into the details of these properties, it is necessary to understand the classification of materials.

## 1.5 CLASSIFICATION OF MATERIALS

The materials generally used for structural purposes, machine parts or electronic devices can be classified as (i) elastic, (ii) plastic, (iii) ductile and (iv) brittle.

**Elastic Material :** *A material is said to be perfectly elastic when the deformation produced under the action of external loads vanishes completely on the removal of the load.*

**Plastic Material :** *If a material does not regain its original size and shape on the removal of the load and gets permanently deformed, it is called a plastic material.* A perfectly plastic material is that in which the material shows a phenomenon of flow with comparatively less load. For example, clay and lead are the plastic materials.

**Ductile Material :** *If a material can undergo a considerable deformation without rupture or can be drawn into wires, it is called a ductile material.* A ductile material has a large tensile strain upto the point of rupture. For example, mild steel (low carbon steel), copper, gold, platinum, silver etc. are the examples of ductile materials. A ductile material must be both strong and plastic. A ductile material gives prior warning before its failure.

**Brittle Material :** *If a material cannot undergo any deformation under the action of external loads and it fails by rupture, it is called a brittle material.* A brittle material fails suddenly upon attaining its maximum load and has a small tensile strain upto the point of rupture. Cast iron, concrete, glass, stone, etc. are the examples of brittle materials.

## 1.6 MECHANICAL PROPERTIES OF MATERIALS

Some important mechanical properties are :

(i)     Strength (in tension, compression, shear, bending and torsion),

(ii)    Elasticity,          (iii)  Plasticity,          (iv)  Ductility,

(v)     Brittleness,         (vi)   Malleability,        (vii)  Impact strength,

(viii)  Hardness,           (ix)   Fatigue,             (x)   Creep,

(xi)    Stiffness.

**(i) Strength :** *The strength of a material is its ability to sustain loads without undue distortion, collapse or rupture.* A material should have adequate strength when subjected to tension, compression, shear, bending or torsion as per the intended use. For example, a beam of a building should have a proper bending strength, a column should have adequate compressive strength, a shaft of an automobile should have proper torsional strength. The maximum stress that any material will withstand is called *ultimate strength or tenacity.*

**(ii) Elasticity :** *It is the property of a material by virtue of which it regains its original size and shape after deformation, when the loads causing deformation are removed.*

**(iii) Plasticity :** Lack of elasticity is called plasticity. *The plasticity of a material is the ability to change its shape without destruction under the action of external loads and to regain the shape given to it when the forces are removed.*

| 1.   Define elasticity and plasticity. | **(B.T.E. S-2013/2 Marks)** |
| --- | --- |

**(Most Likely and Asked in Previous B.T.E. Exam.)**

**(iv) Ductility :** *It is the property of a material to undergo a considerable deformation under tension before rupture.* A body possessing ductility can be reduced from large sections to thinner and thinner sections i.e. it can be drawn into wires. This is a tensile quality of a material.

The usual measures of ductility are the percentage elongation in gauge length of the test piece upto fracture and percentage reduction in cross-sectional area upto fracture in the tension test.

In a laboratory, in addition to tension test, cold bend test is also performed to measure the ductility of metals. In this test, ductility is judged by non-cracking of metals under the conditions of test. Generally, mild steel and tor steel bars of different diameters are tested for ductility. If the cracks are observed on the bend portion, the bar is said to have lost its ductility.

**(v) Brittleness :** Lack of ductility is called brittleness. *The brittleness of a material is the property of breaking, fracturing or shattering without prior warning or without much permanent distortion under load.* There are many materials which shatter before much deformation takes place. e.g. cast iron, glass, concrete, stone, etc. These materials are suitable for resisting compressive loads but usually less suitable for resisting tensile and impact loads. The compression test is generally performed for testing the brittleness of a material. Brittleness is a compressive *quality* of a material.

| 1. Define brittleness. Name two brittle materials. | **(B.T.E. W-2011/2 Marks)** |

**(Most Likely and Asked in Previous B.T.E. Exam.)**

**(vi) Malleability :** *It is the property of a material by virtue of which it gets permanently deformed by compression without rupture.* It is the ability of a material to be rolled or beaten up into thin sheets without cracking by rolling and hammering. This is also a compressive quality of a material. Gold is the most malleable of all metals. Silver, aluminium, copper, tin are also malleable materials.

| 1. Define malleability and state the names of any two malleable materials. |
| **(B.T.E. S-2015, 2014, W-2004, S-2003/2 Marks)** |

**(Most Likely and Asked in Previous B.T.E. Exam.)**

**(vii) Impact Strength :** *The amount of shock energy absorbed by a specimen before it fractures is called its impact strength or toughness.* Izod and charpy impact tests are generally conducted to measure the toughness of a material. The energy required to break the given specimen is measured in joules (N - m).

**(viii) Hardness :** The ability of a material to resist wear, abrasion, scratching or indentation (penetration) by harder bodies is called hardness. Tests such as Brinell, Rockwell, Vickers are generally performed to measure the hardness of a material.

| 1. Define hardness and brittleness. | **(B.T.E. S-2011/2 Marks)** |

**(Most Likely and Asked in Previous B.T.E. Exam.)**

**(ix) Fatigue :** Some of the machine parts such as axles, shafts, springs, connecting rod, pinion teeth, etc. vibrate as they run and this is known as repetition of loading. A material may fail under fluctuating or repeated loads (or stresses) eventhough the maximum applied stress is considerably less than the tensile strength of the material under steady loads. *This phenomenon of failure of a material under fluctuating or repeated loading is called fatigue or endurance.* Fatigue fracture is progressive, and starts as minute cracks at the centres of stress concentration within the material or on the surface. These cracks go on extending more and more under the action of fluctuating stresses causing the failure.

The maximum stress that a material can sustain without failure for a specific large number of cycles of stresses is known as its fatigue value or *endurance limit.*

| | |
|---|---|
| 1. What is fatigue ? Mention one situation where it occurs. | |
| | **(B.T.E. W-2014, 2011, S-2004/2 Marks)** |
| 2. A metal repeatedly stressed for a sufficiently long time to stresses less than static breaking stress. Will this cause failure of the material ? State reason for your answer. | |
| | **(B.T.E. W-2003/2 Marks)** |

**(Most Likely and Asked in Previous B.T.E. Exam.)**

**(x) Creep :** Many structural members and machine parts sustain steady loads for long periods of time. For example, beams in a R.C.C. building, plastic mountings for the parts of electronic devices, blades of turbine rotor, etc. Under such conditions, the material may continue to deform and will ultimately break. Creep continues as long as the load is applied. Therefore, it is a time dependent phenomenon. The greater the time, the more will be the creep. *The continuous deformation with time which the material undergoes due to application of external steady loads is called creep or time yield or plastic flow.*

| | |
|---|---|
| 1. Define creep. Give one example. | **(B.T.E. W-2012/2 Marks)** |
| 2. Define creep and fatigue. | **(B.T.E. S-2015, 2011/2 Marks)** |

**(Most Likely and Asked in Previous B.T.E. Exam.)**

**(xi) Stiffness :** *The ability of a material to resist elastic deformation is called stiffness.* Mathematically, it is the load required to produce unit deformation. A material which deforms by a lesser amount under a given load possesses a high degree of stiffness. For identical cross-sections, the stiffness is proportional to the modulus of elasticity.

Mechanical properties of materials define the behaviour of materials under the action of applied forces, called loads. These are usually expressed in terms of *stress, strain* or *both.* The knowledge of mechanical properties of materials is very essential to construct a mechanically sound, stable and durable structure. These properties can be determined by conducting laboratory tests on the material specimen.

## *Practice Questions*

### Questions of 2 marks

1. Define elasticity and plasticity.    **(B.T.E. S-2013)**
2. Define creep. Give one example.    **(B.T.E. W-2012)**
3. Define brittleness. State any two names of brittle materials.    **(B.T.E. W-2011)**
4. What is fatigue ? Mention one situation where it occurs.    **(B.T.E. W-2011, S-2004)**
5. A metal is repeatedly stressed for a sufficiently long time to stresses less than static breaking stress. Will this cause failure of the material ? State reason for your answer.
    **(B.T.E. W-2003)**
6. Define hardness and brittleness.    **(B.T.E. S-2011)**
7. Define creep and fatigue.    **(B.T.E. S-2011, W-2010)**

8. Define malleability and state the names of any two malleable materials.

**(B.T.E. W-2004, S-2003)**

9. Define ductility. State any two names of ductile materials.
10. Define impact strength.
11. What do you understand by endurance limit ?

### Questions of 4 marks

12. State and explain classification of materials.
13. Explain concept of elastic, plastic and rigid body.
14. State important mechanical properties of materials and explain any two.

**Important Points**

1. The materials generally used for structural purposes, machine parts or electronic devices can be classified as (i) Elastic, (ii) Plastic, (iii) Ductile, (iv) Brittle.
2. Some important mechanical properties of materials are : (i) Strength, (ii) Elasticity, (iii) Plasticity, (iv) Ductility, (v) Brittleness, (vi) Malleability, (vii) Impact strength, (viii) Hardness, (ix) Fatigue, (x) Creep, (xi) Stiffness.

## (B) SIMPLE STRESSES AND STRAINS

### *Synopsis*

Introduction, Loads, Types of loads, Effects of load on a member, Concept of stress, Concept of strain, Member axis, Concept of axial load, Axial stresses and axial strains, Types of axial stresses and strains, Concept of shear load, Shear stress and strain, Definition of single shear and double shear, Torsional shear strain, Punching shear, Elastic limit, Permanent set, Hooke's law, Change in length of a body due to force acting on it, Deformation of a body subjected to axial forces, Principle of superposition, Behaviour of ductile materials under tension, Definitions, Behaviour of brittle materials under tension (stress-strain curve for brittle materials).

## 1.7 INTRODUCTION

In Engineering Mechanics, we have studied the effects of external forces on rigid bodies. But in fact no body is perfectly rigid. When a force acts on a body, it undergoes some deformation. In this topic we shall study the internal effects produced and the deformations of bodies caused by externally applied loads.

## 1.8 LOADS

*External forces and moments (or couples) acting on a body are called loads.* Dead loads, live loads, wind loads, impact loads, seismic loads, snow loads are some of the loads to be considered in the design of a structure.

## 1.9 TYPES OF LOADS

Basically, there are three types of loads or forces, as shown in Fig. 1.1.

**(i) Tensile force :** *The force which acts away from the point of application is called tensile force, pulling force or pull.*

**(ii) Compressive force :** *The force which acts towards the point of application is called compressive force, pushing force or push.*

Tensile and compressive forces are also called *normal forces* since they act normal (i.e. perpendicular) to the plane.

**(iii) Shear force (Tangential force) :** *A force which acts parallel or tangential to the plane under consideration is called shear force, tangential force or shearing force.*

Fig. 1.1 shows normal and shear forces acting on the horizontal plane.

Here   $P_1$ = Compressive force

     $P_2$ = Tensile force (Normal forces)

$q_1$ and $q_2$ = Shear force or tangential force

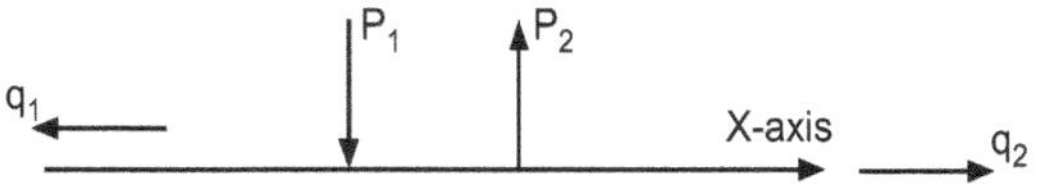

**Fig. 1.1**

## 1.10 EFFECTS OF LOAD ON A MEMBER

1. It may pull the member on which it acts to produce the tensile stress and tensile strain. (See Fig. 1.2) In this case, a member is said to be under tension. A member under tension is called a *tie member*.

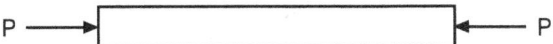

**Fig. 1.2 : A member under tension**

2. It may push the member on which it acts to produce the compressive stress and compressive strain. (See Fig. 1.3). In this case, a member is said to be under compression. A member under compression is called as column or *strut*.

**Fig. 1.3 : A member under compression**

3. It may shear the member on which it acts to produce the shear stress and shear strain. (See Fig. 1.4). Pins, rivets and bolts are known as shear members.

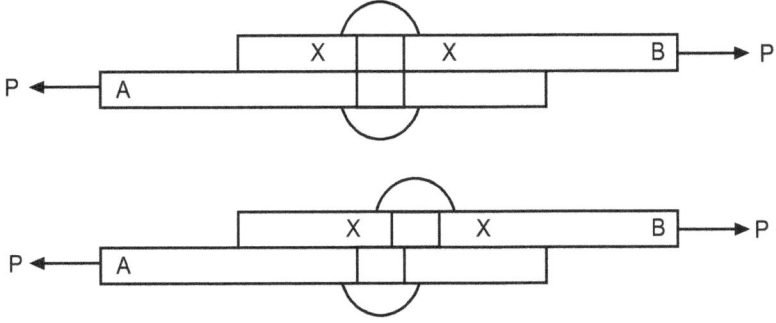

**Fig. 1.4 : A rivet under shear**

4. It may bend the member on which it acts to produce the bending stress and strain. (See Fig. 1.5) *A beam is a bending member or flexural member.* (Bending action in a beam is called flexure).

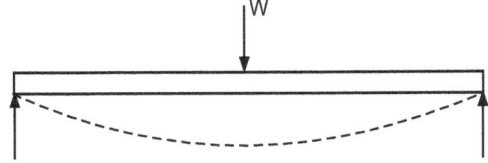

**Fig. 1.5 : A beam under flexure**

5. It may twist the member on which it acts to produce the torsional stress and strain. In this case, a member is said to be under *torsion*. A *shaft* is a twisting member. (See Fig. 1.6).

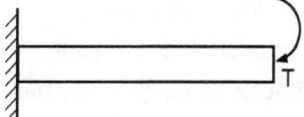

**Fig. 1.6 : A shaft under torsion**

## 1.11 CONCEPT OF STRESS

Consider a bar of elastic material having length L and cross-sectional area A subjected to an axial tensile load P as shown in Fig. 1.7.

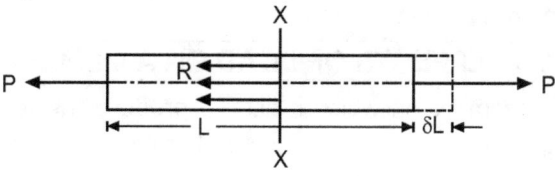

**Fig. 1.7**

Under the action of the tensile load P, the bar will deform and its length increases to δL. This deformation (i.e. increase in length) is resisted by the internal force R which is uniformly distributed over any cross-section X-X. The process of deformation is continued till the internal resistance R is equal to an externally applied load P. If the internal force R is unable to resist this deformation fully, the deformation continues till the failure takes place. *The internal resistive force to deformation per unit cross-sectional area is called as stress, intensity of stress or unit stress. It is denoted by σ.*

$$\therefore \qquad \sigma = \frac{R}{A}$$

In the equilibrium condition, the internal resistance R is equal to an external load P i.e. R = P.

$$\therefore \qquad \sigma = \frac{P}{A}$$

where  σ = Stress

    P = Load acting on the body

    A = Cross-sectional area of the body

Mathematically, *stress may be defined as the force per unit area.*

**S.I. Unit :** S.I. unit of stress $= \dfrac{\text{S.I. unit of force}}{\text{S.I. unit of area}} = \dfrac{\text{N}}{\text{m}^2}$

$\dfrac{\text{N}}{\text{m}^2}$ is called *Pascal* and is denoted by Pa. Therefore, S.I. unit of stress is *Pascal*.

$$\boxed{1 \text{ Pa } = 1 \text{ N/m}^2}$$

Other units of stress are kilo Pascal (kPa), Mega Pascal (MPa), Gega Pascal (GPa) etc.

$$1 \text{ kPa } = 10^3 \text{ Pa} = 10^3 \text{ N/m}^2$$

$$1 \text{ MPa } = 10^6 \text{ Pa} = 10^6 \text{ N/m}^2 = \frac{10^6 \text{ N}}{10^6 \text{ mm}^2} = 1 \text{ N/mm}^2$$

$$1 \text{ GPa } = 10^9 \text{ Pa} = 10^9 \text{ N/m}^2 = \frac{10^9 \text{ N}}{10^6 \text{ mm}^2} = 10^3 \text{ N/mm}^2 = 1 \text{ kN/mm}^2$$

**(Note :** k = kilo= $10^3$, M = Mega = $10^6$, G = Gega = $10^9$)

## 1.12 CONCEPT OF STRAIN (PLAIN STRAIN)

When a load is applied to a body of elastic material, its shape is altered. This alternation in member is called strain. Strain is simply a measure of deformation produced in a member by the loads acting on it. *It is defined as the ratio between change in length and the original length.* It is denoted by e or ε.

∴          $\text{Strain } = \dfrac{\text{Change in length}}{\text{Original length}}$

∴          $e = \dfrac{\delta L}{L}$

where  e = Strain, δL = Change in length of the body, L = Original length of the body

**Unit :** Strain being the ratio of two similar quantities, *it has no unit.*

**Note :** **(1) *Stress is induced in the material of the body while the load / force is applied on the body.***

**(2) *The stress calculated by using the equation $\sigma = \dfrac{P}{A}$ is also called direct stress, longitudinal stress, axial stress or normal stress.***

**(3) *The strain calculated by using the equation $e = \dfrac{\delta l}{L}$ is also called direct strain, longitudinal strain, axial strain, linear strain or primary strain.***

## 1.13 MEMBER AXIS

*A line joining the centroids of all cross-sections of a member is called a member axis (or axis of a member).*

## 1.14 CONCEPT OF AXIAL LOAD

*A load whose line of action coincides with the axis of a member, is called an axial load.* An axial load may be either tensile (pull) or compressive (push).

Fig. 1.8 shows a bar of length L subjected to an axial tensile load.

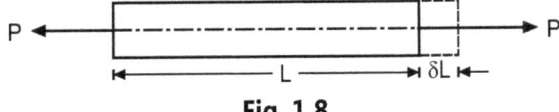

**Fig. 1.8**

Under the action of the tensile load P, the original length L of the bar increases by δL.

Fig. 1.9 shows a bar of length L subjected to an axial compressive load.

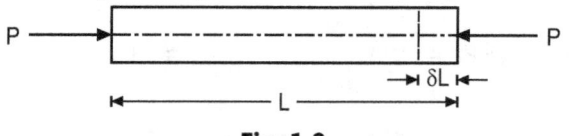

**Fig. 1.9**

Under the action of the compressive load P, the original length L of the bar decreases by $\delta L$.

**Note :** *(1) Since the line of action of the load is along the length of the bar, an axial load is also called as longitudinal load.*

*(2) Sometimes an axial load is also called as direct load.*

## 1.15 AXIAL STRESSES AND AXIAL STRAINS

*The stresses produced due to axial loads are called as axial stresses and the corresponding strains are called as axial strains.*

### 1.15.1 Types of Axial Stresses and Strains

There are two types of axial stresses and strains.

**1. Tensile stress and strain :**

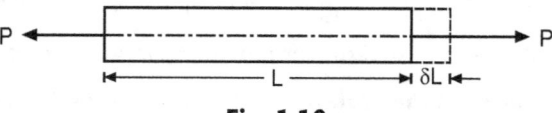

**Fig. 1.10**

*When two equal and opposite pulls applied to a body tend to elongate it, the body is said to be under tension and the stress induced in it is called as tensile stress and the corresponding strain is called tensile strain.*

Consider a bar of length 'L' and uniform cross-sectional area A subjected to an axial tensile load P as shown in Fig. 1.10.

Here tensile stress, $\qquad \sigma_t = \dfrac{p}{A} \quad$ and $\quad$ tensile strain $e_t = \dfrac{+\,\delta L}{L}$

**2. Compressive stress and strain :**

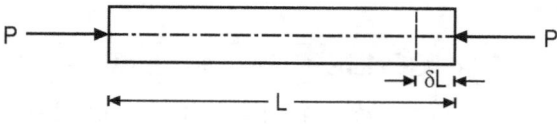

**Fig. 1.11**

*When two equal and opposite pushes applied to a body tend to shorten it, the body is said to be under compression and the stress induced in it is called compressive stress and the corresponding strain is called compressive strain.*

Consider a bar of length L and uniform cross-sectional area subjected to an axial compressive load P, as shown in Fig. 1.11.

Here compressive stress, $\quad \sigma_c = \dfrac{P}{A}$

and compressive strain, $\quad e_c = \dfrac{\delta L}{L}$

**Sign Convention :** Generally tensile stress and tensile strain are taken as positive whereas compressive stress and compressive strain as negative.

---

1. Sketch the behaviour of member under axial pull and axial push.

**(B.T.E. W-2006/2 Marks)**

---

**(Most Likely and Asked in Previous B.T.E. Exam.)**

## 1.16 CONCEPT OF SHEAR LOAD

*A load / force which acts parallel or tangential to the plane under consideration is called shear load, shear force or shearing force.* Normal forces (i.e. tensile or compressive) act across the area whereas a shear force acts along the area.

## 1.17 SHEAR STRESS AND STRAIN

*When the section of a body is subjected to two equal and opposite forces acting tangentially to the section, tending to slide its one part over the other at that section, the body is said to be in a state of shear; the stress induced in it is called shear stress and the corresponding strain is called shear strain. The force acting tangentially along the section is called shear force.*

Shear stress is generally denoted by 'q' or 'τ' and shear strain by 'ϕ'.

### 1.17.1 Shear Stress

Fig. 1.12 shows a rivet of diameter 'd' connecting two plates A and B and subjected to two shear forces P acting tangentially to the plane XX. In this case, the rivet may shear along the plane XX.

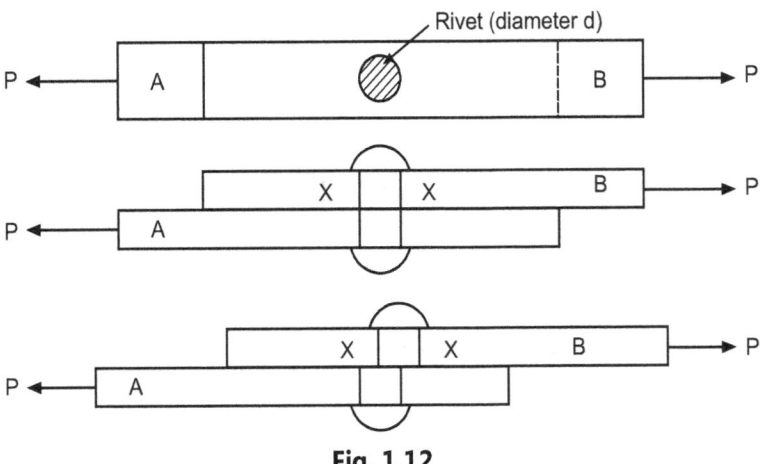

**Fig. 1.12**

If 'd' is the diameter of the rivet, then the area of the cross-section of the rivet subjected to single shear is

$$A = \frac{\pi}{4}d^2$$

∴    Shear stress, $q = \dfrac{P}{A} = \dfrac{P}{\frac{\pi}{4}d^2}$

| 1.  Define shear load and shear stress. | **(2 Marks)** |
|---|---|

**(Most Likely and Asked in Previous B.T.E. Exam.)**

### 1.17.2 Shear Strain

Consider a cube of side L subjected to two equal and opposite forces P on the top and bottom faces. If the bottom face AB is fixed, the cube ABCD will be distorted to ABC'D' through an angle φ as shown in Fig. 1.13.

Let x = shear deformation at right angles to length L.

Now,        $\tan\phi = \dfrac{DD'}{AD} = \dfrac{x}{L}$

∴  Shear strain,      $\phi = \dfrac{x}{L}$

Here φ is the angular deformation produced in a member and is the measure of shear strain.

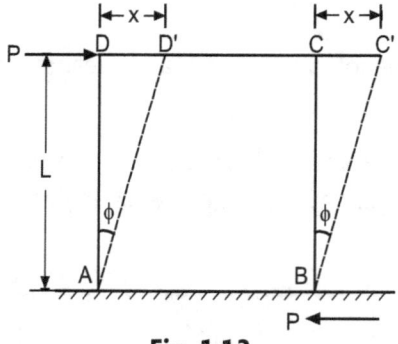

**Fig. 1.13**

| 1.  Define shear strain and show it on a diagram. | **(2 Marks)** |
|---|---|

**(Most Likely and Asked in Previous B.T.E. Exam.)**

## 1.18 DEFINITION OF SINGLE SHEAR AND DOUBLE SHEAR

A rivet is a shear member. The rivets fail by shearing if the shearing stress exceeds their shearing strength.

*Let us consider failure of a lap joint as shown in Fig. 1.14. Since a rivet connects two plates there will be only plane of shear failure and the cross-sectional area subjected to shear is $\frac{\pi}{4}d^2$, where d is the diameter of a rivet. This is called single shear failure.*

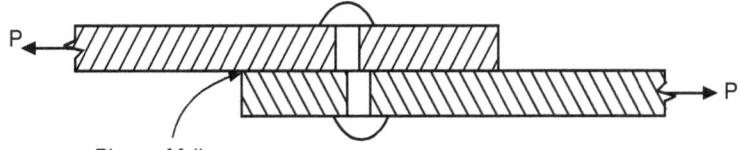

**Fig. 1.14 : Single shear failure of lap joint**

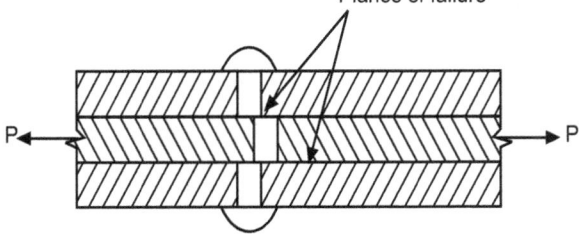

**Fig. 1.15 : Double shear failure of butt joint**

$$\text{Single shear stress} = \frac{\text{Shear load}}{\text{Area subjected to shear}} = \frac{P}{\frac{\pi}{4}d^2}$$

*Let us consider failure of a butt joint as shown in Fig. 1.15. Since a rivet connects three plates, there will be two planes of shear failure and the cross-sectional area subjected to shear is $2 \times \frac{\pi}{4}d^2$. This is called double shear failure.*

$$\text{Double shear stress} = \frac{\text{Shear load}}{\text{Area subjected to shear}} = \frac{P}{2 \times \frac{\pi}{4}d^2}$$

1. Differentiate between single shear and double shear. **(B.T.E. S-2013/2 Marks)**
2. What is meant by double shear ? **(B.T.E. W-2012/2 Marks)**

**(Most Likely and Asked in Previous B.T.E. Exam.)**

## 1.19 TORSIONAL SHEAR STRAIN

Consider a solid shaft of length L and radius R fixed at one end and subjected to a torque T at the other end as shown in Fig. 1.16.

As a resultant of the application of the torque T, the shaft will get twisted and every cross-section of the shaft will be subjected to some shear stress.

Let the line AB on the surface of the shaft is deformed to AB' and OB to OB'.

∠ BAB' = $\phi$ = BB'/AB is called torsional shear strain and is equal to ratio of shear stress q to the modulus of rigidity G.

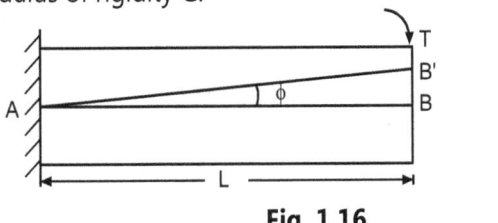

**Fig. 1.16**

For details of torsional shear strain, refer to chapter 7, derivation of torsional formula.

**Definition :** When a body is loaded within its elastic limit, the ratio of shear stress and shear strain is constant. This constant is known as shear modulus or modulus of rigidity. It is denoted by C, G or N.

Mathematically,

$$\frac{\text{Shear modulus}}{\text{(or modulus of rigidity)}} = \frac{\text{Shear stress}}{\text{Shear strain}}$$

$$\therefore \qquad G = \frac{q}{\phi}$$

$$\therefore \qquad \phi = \frac{q}{G}$$

*Hence torsional shear strain is equal to the ratio of shear stress q to the modulus of rigidity G. It has no unit.*

| | |
|---|---|
| 1.   Define torsional shear strain. | **(2 Marks)** |

**(Most Likely and Asked in Previous B.T.E. Exam.)**

## 1.20  PUNCHING SHEAR

As the punch penetrates into the plate, the circumference of the punch encounters shear resistance from the plate.

Surface area of the plate to resist shear = $\pi d \times t$                           … for circular hole

where,      d  =  diameter of the hole, t = thickness of the plate

Force required to punch the hole

= Circumferential area of the hole × Shear stress of the material at failure

= $\pi \, d \, t \times f_S$

where,      $f_S$  =  ultimate shear stress in the material

## 1.21  ELASTIC LIMIT

*For every material there is a limiting (maximum) value of load for a given resisting section upto and within which the strain (or deformation) entirely disappears on removal of the load. The value of intensity of stress corresponding to the limiting load is known as elastic limit of the material.*

| | |
|---|---|
| 1.   Define elasticity and elastic limit. | **(B.T.E. S-2012/2 Marks)** |

**(Most Likely and Asked in Previous B.T.E. Exam.)**

## 1.22  PERMANENT SET

If a material is loaded beyond elastic limit, it loses to some extent its property of elasticity and it will be in a *plastic stage*. In this stage, the material will not regain its original size and shape even after removal of the load and the structure of the material may get changed or damaged. *The strain produced by the corresponding load will not disappear completely on removal of the load and the residual or the remaining strain is called as a permanent set.*

Generally we handle a member in its elastic stage. Structural members or machine parts are generally designed so as to remain in the elastic stage under the action of working loads.

| | | |
|---|---|---|
| 1. | What is a permanent set ? | **(2 Marks)** |

**(Most Likely and Asked in Previous B.T.E. Exam.)**

## 1.23 HOOKE'S LAW

It states, *'when a material is loaded within its elastic limit, the stress produced is directly proportional to the strain.'*

Mathematically,     Stress $\propto$ Strain

$$\sigma \propto e$$

∴          $\sigma = \text{constant} \times e$

∴          $\dfrac{\sigma}{e} = \text{constant}$

*The ratio of stress and strain which is a constant within the elastic limit, is called modulus of elasticity or Young's modulus.* It is denoted by E.

∴          $E = \dfrac{\sigma}{e}$     i.e. Young's modulus $= \dfrac{\text{Stress}}{\text{Strain}}$

∴   S.I. unit of E is same as that of stress i.e. *N/m² or Pascal.*

| | | |
|---|---|---|
| 1. | State Hooke's law. | **(B.T.E. W-2013, 2012, 2009, 2000/2 Marks)** |
| 2. | Define modulus of elasticity and state its S.I. unit. | **(B.T.E. S-2000/2 Marks)** |

**(Most Likely and Asked in Previous B.T.E. Exam.)**

## 1.24 CHANGE IN LENGTH OF A BODY DUE TO FORCE ACTING ON IT

We know that, Stress   $\sigma = \dfrac{P}{A}$, Strain $e = \dfrac{\delta L}{L}$ and Young's modulus $E = \dfrac{\sigma}{e}$

Substituting the values of $\sigma$ and $e$ in this equation,

$$E = \dfrac{\dfrac{P}{A}}{\dfrac{\delta L}{L}}$$

∴          $E = \dfrac{P}{A} \cdot \dfrac{L}{\delta L}$

∴          $\boxed{\delta L = \dfrac{PL}{AE}}$

This is the expression for the change in length of a body due to force acting on it.

## SOLVED EXAMPLES

**Type 1 : Examples based on simple formulae :**

| Important Formulae |
| --- |
| Stress $\sigma = \dfrac{P}{A}$,  Strain $e = \dfrac{\delta L}{L}$ |
| Young's modulus $E = \dfrac{\sigma}{e}$, Deformation (change in length) $\delta L = \dfrac{PL}{AE} = \dfrac{\sigma L}{E}$ |

**Example 1 :** *A bar 500 mm long and 22 mm in diameter is elongated by 1.2 mm under the effect of axial pull of 105 kN. Calculate the intensities of stress, strain and the modulus of elasticity of the bar.* **(B.T.E. S-2013, W-2000/4 Marks)**

**Data**     : L = 500 mm, d = 22 mm, $\delta L$ = 1.2 mm, P = 105 kN = $105 \times 10^3$ N.

**To find**   : (i) $\sigma$, (ii) e, (iii) E

**Concept :** Use of standard formulae.

**Solution :** (i) Stress,     $\sigma = \dfrac{P}{A} = \dfrac{105 \times 10^3}{\dfrac{\pi}{4}(22)^2} = \mathbf{276.22\ N/mm^2}$

(ii) Strain,     $e = \dfrac{\delta L}{L} = \dfrac{1.2}{500} = \mathbf{0.0024}$

(iii) Modulus of elasticity,   $E = \dfrac{\sigma}{e} = \dfrac{276.22}{0.0024} = \mathbf{115091.67\ N/mm^2}$

**Answer :** (i) $\sigma$ = 276.22 N/mm², (ii) e = 0.0024, (iii) E = 115091.67 N/mm²

**Example 2 :** *A steel rod 800 mm long and 60 mm × 20 mm in cross-section is subjected to an axial push of 89 kN. If the modulus of elasticity is 2.1 × 10⁵ N/mm², calculate the stress, strain and reduction in the length of the rod.* **(B.T.E. S-2000/4 Marks)**

**Data**     : Length L = 800 mm, Area A = 60 × 20 = 1200 mm²,

          Pull P = 89 kN = $89 \times 10^3$ N, Young's modulus E = $2.1 \times 10^5$ N/mm²

**To find**   : (i) $\sigma$, (ii) e, (iii) $\delta L$.

**Concept :** Use of standard formulae.

**Solution :** (i) Stress,     $\sigma = \dfrac{P}{A} = \dfrac{89 \times 10^3}{1200} = \mathbf{74.17\ N/mm^2}$

(ii) Strain,     $e = \dfrac{\sigma}{E} = \dfrac{74.17}{2.1 \times 10^5} = \mathbf{0.00035319}$

(iii) Reduction in length, $\delta L = \left(\dfrac{P}{A}\right)\dfrac{L}{E} = \dfrac{\sigma L}{E}$

          $= \dfrac{74.17 \times 800}{2.1 \times 10^5} = \mathbf{0.2825\ mm}$

**Answer :** (i) $\sigma$ = 74.17 N/mm², (ii) e = 0.00035319, (iii) $\delta L$ = 0.2825 mm

**Example 3 :** *A steel rod 500 mm long and 20 mm $\times$ 10 mm in section is subjected to an axial pull of 300 kN. If the modulus of elasticity is 2 $\times 10^5$ MPa, calculate the stress, strain and elongation of the rod.* **(B.T.E. S-2008/4 Marks)**

**Data     :**     Length L = 500 mm, Area = 20 $\times$ 10 = 200 mm$^2$,
            Pull P = 300 kN = 300 $\times 10^3$ N,
            Young's modulus E = 2 $\times 10^5$ MPa = 2 $\times 10^5$ N/mm$^2$.

**To find  :**     (i) Stress $\sigma$, (ii) Strain e, (iii) Elongation $\delta L$.

**Concept :**     Use of basic formulae.

**Solution :**     (i)  **Stress, $\sigma = \dfrac{P}{A} = \dfrac{300 \times 10^3}{200} =$ 150 N/mm$^2$**

            (ii)  **Strain, e $= \dfrac{\sigma}{E} = \dfrac{150}{2 \times 10^5} =$ 0.00075**

            (iii) **Elongation, $\delta L = \left(\dfrac{P}{A}\right)\dfrac{L}{E} = \dfrac{\sigma L}{E} = \dfrac{150 \times 500}{2 \times 10^5} =$ 0.375 mm**

**Answer  :**     (i) $\sigma$ = 150 N/mm$^2$ = 150 MPa, (ii) e = 0.00075, (iii) $\delta L$ = 0.375 mm

**Example 4 :** *Calculate the safe axial load in tension for a steel bar of cross-section 75 mm $\times$ 12 mm, if allowable maximum stress is 155 MPa.* **(B.T.E. W-1997/4 Marks)**

**Hint :** $\sigma = \dfrac{P}{A}$ i.e. P = $\sigma \times$ A = 155 $\times$ 900 = 139500 N = 139.5 kN

**Answer :**     P = 139.5 kN

**Example 5 :** *A load of 6 kN is to be raised with the help of steel cable. Find the minimum diameter of steel cable if stress is not to exceed 110 N/mm$^2$.*

**(B.T.E. W-2006, 2004; S-2004/4 Marks)**

**Data :** Load W = 6 kN = 6 $\times 10^3$ N, stress $\sigma$ = 110 N/mm$^2$.

**To find :** Diameter of steel cable (d).

**Concept :** $\sigma = \dfrac{W}{A}$, A = $\dfrac{\pi}{4} d^2$

**Solution :**          Stress, $\sigma = \dfrac{W}{A}$

$\therefore$              $110 = \dfrac{6 \times 10^3}{A}$

$\therefore$              $A = \dfrac{6 \times 10^3}{110}$ = 54.54 mm$^2$

Now,              $A = \dfrac{\pi}{4} d^2$

$\therefore$              $54.54 = \dfrac{\pi}{4} d^2$

**Answer :**     d = 8.33 mm

**Example 6 :** *Find the required diameter of steel rod that has to carry axial pull of 40 kN if the permissible stress is 150 MPa.* **(B.T.E. S-2015, W-1998/4 Marks)**

**Hint :**  $\text{Stress, } \sigma = \dfrac{P}{A} = \dfrac{P}{\dfrac{\pi}{4} d^2}$

$\therefore \qquad d^2 = \dfrac{4P}{\pi\sigma} = \dfrac{4 \times (40 \times 10^3)}{\pi \times 150} = 339.53$

**Answer :**  $\boxed{d = \sqrt{339.53} = \textbf{18.43 mm}}$

---

**Example 7 :** *A bar of cross-sectional area 200 mm² is axially pulled by a force 'P' kN. If the maximum stress induced in the bar is 30 MPa, determine 'P'. If elongation of 1.2 mm is observed over a gauge length 3 m, determine Young's modulus.* **(B.T.E. S-2004/4 Marks)**

**Data :** A = 200 mm², Axial pull = P, $\sigma_{max}$ = 30 MPa = 30 N/mm²,

Elongation $\delta L$ = 1.2 mm, Gauge length L = 3 m = $3 \times 10^3$ mm.

**To find :** P, E.

**Concept :** Use of standard formulae.

**Solution :**  $\text{Stress, } \sigma = \dfrac{P}{A}$

$\therefore \qquad 30 = \dfrac{P}{200}$

$\therefore \qquad \textbf{P} = 30 \times 200 = 6000 \text{ N} = \textbf{6 kN}$

$\text{Strain, } e = \dfrac{\delta L}{L} = \dfrac{1.2}{3 \times 10^3} = \textbf{0.4} \times \textbf{10}^{\textbf{-3}}$

$\text{Young's modulus, } E = \dfrac{\sigma}{e} = \dfrac{30}{0.4 \times 10^{-3}} = \textbf{7.5} \times \textbf{10}^{\textbf{4}} \textbf{ N/mm}^2$

**Answer :**  $\boxed{\text{(i) P = 6 kN, (ii) E} = 7.5 \times 10^4 \text{ N/mm}^2}$

---

**Example 8 :** *A rod having diameter 20 mm is subjected to an axial pull of 60 kN. The length of the member is 2 meters. If E = $2 \times 10^5$ N/mm², find the deformation of the rod.*

**(B.T.E. S-1994/4 Marks)**

**Hind :** $\delta L = \dfrac{PL}{AE} = \dfrac{60 \times 10^3 \times 2000}{\dfrac{\pi}{4} (20)^2 \times (2 \times 10^5)} = \textbf{1.91 mm}$

**Answer :**  $\boxed{\delta L = 1.91 \text{ mm}}$

---

**Example 9 :** *A copper wire of length 500 mm is subjected to an axial pull of 5.5 kN. Find the minimum diameter if the stress is not to exceed 70 N/mm². Also calculate the elongation if E = 100 kN/mm².* **(Imp./4 Marks)**

**Hint :** $\sigma = \dfrac{P}{A} = \dfrac{P}{\dfrac{\pi}{4}d^2} = \dfrac{4P}{\pi d^2}$

Knowing $\sigma$ and P, find d. From $\delta L = \dfrac{PL}{AE}$, find $\delta L$.

**Answer :** $\boxed{\text{d = 10 mm, } \delta L = 0.35 \text{ mm}}$

### Type 2 : Examples based on shear stress.

**Example 10 :** *Calculate the force required to punch a hole of 30 mm diameter in a metal plate of 20 mm thickness. The permissible shear stress in the material and corresponding factor of safety is 400 MPa and 3 respectively.*          **(B.T.E. S-2004, 2003; W-2003/4 Marks)**

**Solution :** Shearing area $= \pi d \times t = \pi \times 30 \times 20 = 1884.95 \text{ mm}^2$

Force required
to punch a hole $= $ Ultimate shear stress $\times$ area

$= $ (Permissible stress $\times$ f.s.) $\times$ area

$= 400 \times 3 \times 1884.95$

$= 2261940 \text{ N} = \textbf{2261.94 kN}$

**Answer :** $\boxed{\text{Force required to punch a hole = 2261.94 kN}}$

**Example 11 :** *A 12 mm diameter M.S. bar when tested for single shear carries a load of 8.16 kN. Determine the shear stress induced.*          **(V.V. Imp./2 Marks)**

**Data :** d = 12 mm, F = 8.16 kN $= 8.16 \times 10^3$ N.

**To find :** q.

**Concept :** Shear stress $q = \dfrac{\text{Shear force (load)}}{\text{Area}} = \dfrac{P}{\dfrac{\pi}{4}d^2}$

**Solution :** Since a bar is subjected to a single shear, the area subjected to shear is,

$$A = \frac{\pi}{4}d^2 = \frac{\pi}{4}(12)^2 = 113.09 \text{ mm}^2$$

$\therefore$  Shear stress induced,

$$\mathbf{q} = \frac{\text{Force}}{\text{Area}} = \frac{8.16 \times 10^3}{113.09} = \textbf{72.154 N/mm}^2$$

**Answer :** $\boxed{q = 72.154 \text{ N/mm}^2}$

**Example 12 :** *A 12 mm diameter circular pin in double shear carries a force of 12 kN. Determine the stress induced.*          **(V.V. Imp./2 Marks)**

**Data :** d = 12 mm, F = 12 kN $= 12 \times 10^3$ N.

**To find :** q.

**Concept :** Since a pin is in a double shear, the area subjected to shear is

$$A = 2\frac{\pi}{4}d^2 = 2\frac{\pi}{4}(12)^2 = 226.195 \text{ mm}^2$$

When a body is in a double shear, the stress induced in it is called double shear stress.

**Solution : q** = Double shear stress = $\dfrac{\text{Force}}{\text{Area}}$ = $\dfrac{12 \times 10^3}{226.195}$ = **53.05 N/mm²**

**Answer :** $\boxed{q = 53.05 \text{ N/mm}^2}$

---

**Example 13 :** *Two plates 12 mm and 10 mm thick respectively are connected by means of lap joint by a rivet of 16 mm diameter. Find the strength of the joint in shearing if the ultimate shearing strength of the rivet is 300 N/mm².* **(B.T.E. W-1994/4 Marks)**

**Data :** As shown in Fig. 1.17, diameter of rivet d = 16 mm, shear stress, $f_S$ = 300 N/mm².

**To find :** Strength of the joint, P.

**Concept :** $P = f_S \times \dfrac{\pi}{4} d^2$.

**Solution :**

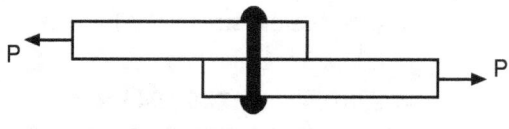

**Fig. 1.17**

Strength of the joint = Shear stress × Area subjected to shear
(Strength)

∴ $\quad$ **P** $= 300 \times \dfrac{\pi}{4} d^2 = 300 \times \dfrac{\pi}{4} (16)^2 = 60318.58$ N **= 60.318 kN**

**Answer :** $\boxed{P = 60.318 \text{ kN}}$

---

**Example 14 :** *Two plates 100 mm × 10 mm are joined by 2 rivets as shown in Fig. 1.18. Determine the stress induced in each rivet.* **(B.T.E. W-2009/4 Marks)**

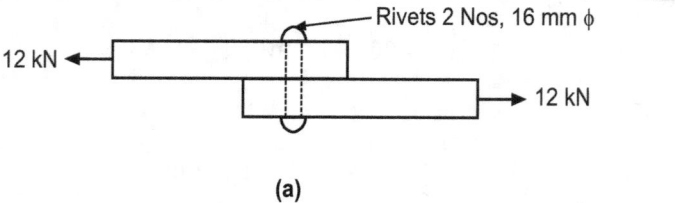

**Fig. 1.18**

**Data :** As shown in Fig. 1.18, shear force P = 12 kN = 12 × 10³ N, diameter of rivet d = 16 mm.

**To find :** Shear stress q.

**Concept :** $q = \dfrac{P}{A}$ and $A = 2 \times \dfrac{\pi}{4} d^2$.

**Solution :** Due to a shear force of 12 kN, the stress induced in each rivet will be a shear stress.

In this case, area subjected to shear is given by,

$$A = 2 \times \frac{\pi}{4} d^2 = 2 \times \frac{\pi}{4} (16)^2 = 402.124 \text{ mm}^2$$

∴     Shear stress induced in each rivet,

$$q = \frac{P}{A} = \frac{12 \times 10^3}{402.124} = \textbf{29.84 N/mm}^2$$

**Answer :** $\boxed{q = 29.84 \text{ N/mm}^2}$

## 1.25 DEFORMATION OF A BODY SUBJECTED TO AXIAL FORCES

### 1.25.1 Principle of Superposition

**Statement :** *"When a number of forces are acting on a body, the resulting strain will be the algebraic sum of strains caused by individual forces."*

**Note :** If an elastic body is subjected to a number of direct forces (tensile or compressive) at different sections along the length of the body, the deformation of individual sections can be very easily found by drawing free body diagrams for the individual sections. **According to principle of superposition, the total deformation of the body will be equal to the algebraic sum of deformations of the individual sections.**

## SOLVED EXAMPLES

**Type 3 : Examples based on change in length of the bar having uniform cross-section (principle of superposition for bars/members of uniform cross-sectional area.)**

---

**Important steps and formulae**

**Step 1 :** Starting from free end, draw F.B.D. of each member and find force in each member.

**Step 2 :** Find deformation ($\delta L$) of each member.

**Step 3 :** Find algebraic sum of deformations of each member so as to get the net deformation of the body.

$$\delta L = \delta L_1 + \delta L_2 + \delta L_3 + ...$$

$$\delta L = \frac{P_1 L_1}{AE} + \frac{P_2 L_2}{AE} + \frac{P_3 L_3}{AE} + ... = \sum \frac{PL}{AE}$$

**Note :** The net deformation of the body i.e. $\sum \frac{PL}{AE}$ or $\delta L$ may be positive or negative.

(1)   If $\sum \frac{PL}{AE}$ i.e. $\delta L$ is positive, it indicates that the body elongates, as positive sign is associated with tensile forces.

(2)   If $\sum \frac{PL}{AE}$ i.e. $\delta L$ is negative, it indicates that the body shortens, as negative sign is associated with compressive forces.

---

The following examples will illustrate the application of principle of superposition.

**Example 15 :** *A bar of uniform cross-sectional area 100 mm² is subjected to the forces as shown in Fig. 1.19 (i). Calculate the change in the length of the bar. Take E = 2 × 10⁵ N/mm².*

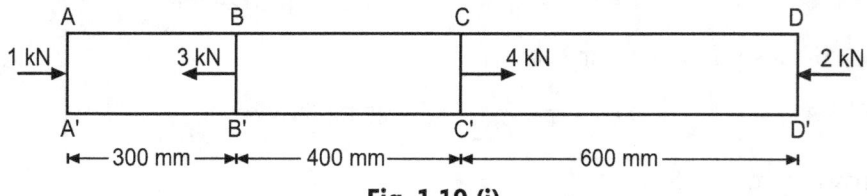

**Fig. 1.19 (i)**

**Data :** A bar of uniform cross-sectional area as shown in Fig. 1.19 (i), A = 100 mm²,

$E = 2 \times 10^5$ N/mm².

**To find :** $\delta L$.

**Concept :** (i) Drawing free body diagrams of the individual sections.

(ii) Applying principle of superposition, $\delta L = \delta L_1 + \delta L_2 + \delta L_3$.

**Solution :** Fig. 1.19 (ii) shows the F.B.D.s for the parts AB, BC and CD.

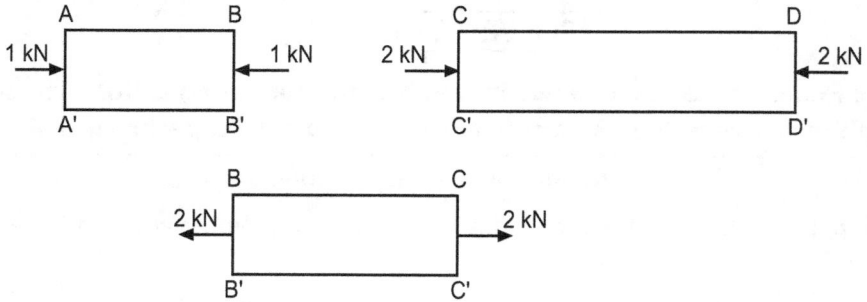

**Fig. 1.19 (ii) : Free body diagrams**

**Steps :**

1. Initially draw a free body diagram for the portion AB. Mark the given external force (1 kN →) at the outer edge AA'. For the equilibrium of part AB, mark the equal and opposite force (i.e. 1 kN ←) at the inner edge BB'.

2. Then draw a free body diagram for the portion CD. Mark the given external force (2 kN ←) at the outer edge DD'. For the equilibrium of part CD, mark the equal and opposite force (i.e. 2 kN →) at the inner edge CC'.

3. Then draw the free body diagram for the middle portion BC.

For the portion BC, force at BB' = $\overset{\leftarrow}{3} - \overset{\leftarrow}{1}$ = 2 kN ←

For the equilibrium of part BC, mark the equal and opposite force (i.e. 2 kN →) at CC'.

**Check :**

$$\begin{bmatrix}\text{Force at inner section}\\ \text{CC' in a given bar}\end{bmatrix} = \begin{bmatrix}\text{Sum of the forces at CC'}\\ \text{in F.B. diagrams}\end{bmatrix}$$

i.e.          4 kN → = (2 kN → + 2 kN →)

Section 'AB' is under compression. Therefore, there will be a decrease in the length of section AB.

Compressive force on AB, $P_1$ = 1 kN = 1000 N

Section 'BC' is under tension. Therefore, there will be an increase in length of section BC.

Tensile force on BC,    $P_2$ = 2 kN = 2000 N

Section 'CD' is under compression. Therefore, there will be a decrease in the length of section CD.

Compressive force on CD, $P_3$ = 2 kN = 2000 N

Here                     $L_1$ = 300 mm,

                         $L_2$ = 400 mm, $L_3$ = 600 mm, A = 100 mm², E = 2 × 10⁵ N/mm²

Let                      $\delta L_1$ = Change in the length of section AB,

                         $\delta L_2$ = Change in the length of section BC,

and                      $\delta L_3$ = Change in the length of section CD.

Now,                     $\delta L_1 = -\dfrac{P_1 L_1}{AE} = \dfrac{-1000 \times 300}{100 \times 2 \times 10^5} = -0.015$ mm (decrease)

                         $\delta L_2 = +\dfrac{P_2 L_2}{AE} = \dfrac{2000 \times 400}{100 \times 2 \times 10^5} = 0.04$ mm (increase)

                         $\delta L_3 = -\dfrac{P_3 L_3}{AE} = -\dfrac{2000 \times 600}{100 \times 2 \times 10^5} = -0.06$ mm (decrease)

∴   Change in the length of the bar,

$$\delta L = \delta L_1 + \delta L_2 + \delta L_3 = -0.015 + 0.04 - 0.06$$

$$= -\mathbf{0.035 \ mm}$$

Negative sign indicates the decrease in the length of the bar.

**Answer :** | Decrease in the length of the bar = 0.035 mm |

---

**Example 16 :** *A circular bar having 200 mm² area is subjected to the axial loads as shown in Fig. 1.20. Find the value of 'P' and the total elongation. Take E = 2 × 10⁵ N/mm².*

**(B.T.E. W-2011, 2010; S-1987)**

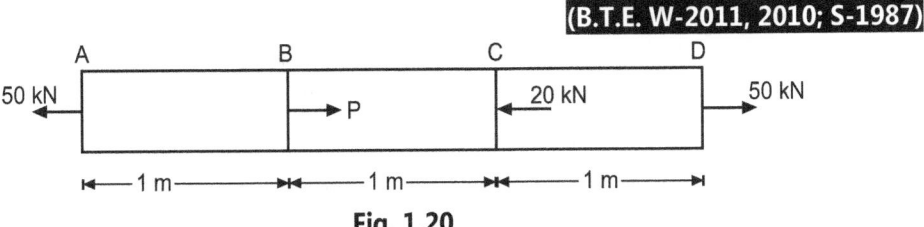

**Fig. 1.20**

**Data :** A circular bar as shown in Fig. 1.20, A = 200 mm², E = 2 × 10⁵ N/mm².

**To find :** (i) P and (ii) δL.

**Concept :** Same as the above example.

**Solution :** For the equilibrium of the entire bar,

$$\sum F_X = 0 \ (\rightarrow +, \leftarrow -)$$

$\therefore$      $-50 + P - 20 + 50 = 0$

$\therefore$      **P = 20 kN ($\rightarrow$)**

F.B.D's for each section are as shown in Fig. 1.21.

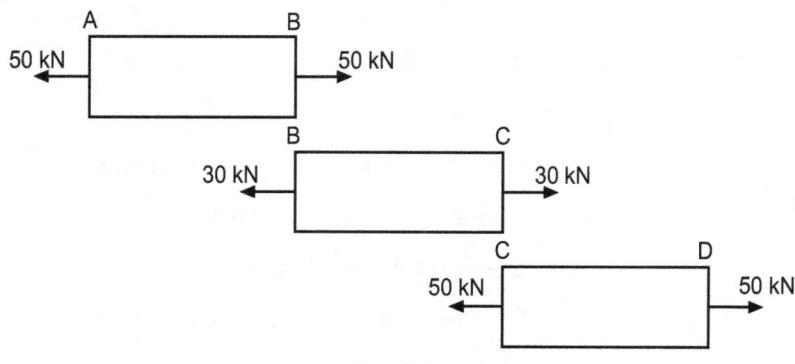

**Fig. 1.21**

In this case, each section AB, BC and CD is under tension. Therefore, there will be an increase in length of each section.

Here,      $P_1 = 50 \text{ kN} = 50 \times 10^3 \text{ N (tensile)}$

              $P_2 = 30 \text{ kN} = 30 \times 10^3 \text{ N (tensile)}$

and      $P_3 = 50 \text{ kN} = 50 \times 10^3 \text{ N (tensile)}$

     $L_1 = L_2 = L_3 = 1 \text{ m} = 1000 \text{ mm},$

     $A = 200 \text{ mm}^2, E = 2 \times 10^5 \text{ N/mm}^2$

Now,      $\delta L_1 = \delta L_{AB} = \dfrac{P_1 L_1}{AE} = \dfrac{50 \times 10^3 \times 1000}{200 \times 2 \times 10^5} = 1.25 \text{ mm (increase)}$

              $\delta L_2 = \delta L_{BC} = \dfrac{P_2 L_2}{AE} = \dfrac{30 \times 10^3 \times 1000}{200 \times 2 \times 10^5} = 0.75 \text{ mm (increase)}$

              $\delta L_3 = \delta L_{CD} = \dfrac{P_3 L_3}{AE} = \dfrac{50 \times 10^3 \times 1000}{200 \times 2 \times 10^5} = 1.25 \text{ mm (increase)}$

$\therefore$      $\delta L = \delta L_1 + \delta L_2 + \delta L_3 = 1.25 + 0.75 + 1.25$

              **= 3.25 mm (increase)**

$\therefore$  **Total elongation of the bar is 3.25 mm.**

**Answer :** | (i) P = 20 kN ($\rightarrow$), (ii) $\delta L$ = 3.25 mm (increase) |

## 1.26 BEHAVIOUR OF TENSILE (DUCTILE) MATERIALS UNDER TENSION

When a ductile material like mild steel bar (of uniform cross-sectional area) is subjected to a gradually increasing tensile load upto fracture using universal testing machine, the relationship between stress and strain is generally of the form as shown in Fig. 1.22.

The following are the salient points on the curve :

(i)　　Limit of proportionality (A)　　(ii)　Elastic limit (B)

(iii)　Upper yield point (C)　　(iv)　Lower yield point (D)

(v)　　Ultimate (maximum) load point (E)　(vi)　Breaking point (F)

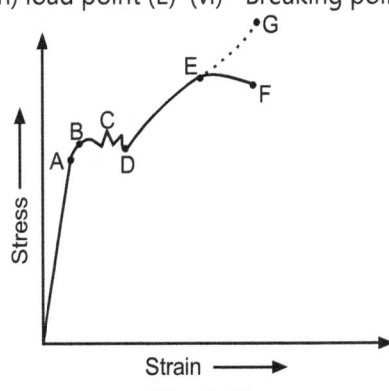

**Fig. 1.22**

**Limit of proportionality :** In the range OA, the strain (or elongation) is proportional to the stress (or load) and the graph is a straight line. Point A is called *limit of proportionality. It is the value of stress upto which stress and strain has a constant ratio and Hooke's law is obeyed.*

**Elastic limit :** At point A, the curve deviates from the straight line and the stress-strain graph from A to B is non-linear. If the load is increased beyond A upto the point B, the material behaves in elastic manner i.e. on removal of the load, the whole deformation will vanish. *The value of stress corresponding to point B upto which the material behaves in an elastic manner is called the elastic limit. The specimen if stressed beyond this limit will not return back to its original position when the load is removed and there will be a permanent deformation of the body called permanent set.* Upto point B, the material will be in its elastic range and beyond B it will be in the plastic range. The two points viz. proportional limit and elastic limit are very close to each other and in some cases they may coincide also.

**Upper yield point :** *Point C is called upper yield point.* At this point there is an increase in strain even though there is no increase in stress (load).

A formation of creep makes the specimen plastic and the material begins to flow. The value of stress corresponding to point C is called *yield stress or yield strength. The yield stress is defined as that unit stress which will cause an increase in length without an increase in load.*

**Lower yield point :** A load may rise and fall while yielding occurs. This is indicated by *wavy appearance* of the stress-strain graph between C and D. *Point D corresponds to the lower yield point.* After yielding has ceased at D, further stresses and strains can be obtained by increasing the load.

**Ultimate load point :** After increasing the load beyond the yield point, the stress-strain curve rises till the point E is reached which is called *ultimate (or maximum) load point. The stress corresponding to this point is also maximum and is called ultimate stress* or *ultimate tensile strength or tenacity.*

**Breaking load point :** Upto point E, the cross-sectional area of the specimen goes on uniformly decreasing forming a neck or waist and the load required to cause further extension is also reduced. As the elongation continues, cross-sectional area becomes smaller and smaller and ultimately the specimen is broken at F into two pieces giving cup cone type of ductile fracture. *Point F is called breaking load point and the stress corresponding to this point is called breaking stress or rupture stress or breaking strength of the material.*

## 1.26.1 Definitions

**1. Nominal Stresses :** *The stresses which are calculated by dividing the respective loads by the original cross-sectional area are called nominal stresses.* From the stress-strain curve, it is clear that the nominal breaking stress is less than the ultimate stress.

**2. Actual Stresses :** *The stresses which are calculated by dividing the respective loads by the reduced cross-sectional area at that point are called actual stresses.*

The actual breaking stress is the ratio of load at breaking point and the reduced cross-sectional area of the specimen at fracture. From the stress-strain curve, it is clear that the actual breaking stress is considerably higher than the ultimate stress as shown by dotted curve EG.

Thus,

$$\text{Nominal breaking stress} = \frac{\text{Load at breaking point}}{\text{Original cross-sectional area}}$$

$$\text{Actual breaking stress} = \frac{\text{Load at breaking point}}{\text{Reduced cross-sectional area at fracture}}$$

**3. Yield Stress :** *It is defined as the ratio of the load at yield point and the original cross-sectional area of the specimen.*

$$\therefore \quad \text{Yield stress} = \frac{\text{Yield load}}{\text{Original cross-sectional area}}$$

It is the nominal stress corresponding to the yield load.

**4. Ultimate Stress :** The ratio of the maximum load that the specimen is capable of withstanding and its original cross-sectional area is called the ultimate stress of the material.

$$\therefore \quad \text{Ultimate stress} = \frac{\text{Maximum load}}{\text{Original cross-sectional area}}$$

It is the nominal stress corresponding to the maximum load.

**5. Working Stress :** *It is defined as the ratio of the actual axial load and the original cross-sectional area of the specimen.*

$$\text{Mathematically, Working stress} = \frac{\text{Actual axial load}}{\text{Original cross-sectional area}}$$

Working stress is the maximum allowable stress to which a material is subjected during its service period. For the safety of a structure, it is very essential that the working stress should be within the elastic limit of the material. This stress is generally determined by dividing the yield stress or ultimate stress by a number called *factor of safety.*

**6. Factor of Safety :** *The ratio of the ultimate stress and the working stress for a material is called factor of safety.*

$$\therefore \qquad \text{Factor of safety } = \frac{\text{Ultimate stress}}{\text{Working stress}}$$

**Measurement of ductility :** In a tension test, both the percentage reduction in area upto fracture and the percentage elongation in gauge length of the specimen upto fracture are considered to be measures of the ductility of a material.

$$\text{Percentage reduction in area } = \left(\frac{\text{Original area} - \text{Final area}}{\text{Original area}}\right) \times 100$$

$$\text{Percentage elongation } = \frac{\text{Final length} - \text{Initial length}}{\text{Initial length}} \times 100$$

---

1.  Draw a stress-strain diagram for M.S. and show salient points on it.

    **(B.T.E. S-2013, 1998; W-2008/2 Marks)**

2.  Draw stress-strain curve for ductile material and explain the term ultimate stress.

    **(B.T.E. W-2012/4 Marks)**

3.  Sketch the nature of stress-strain curve showing behaviour of ductile material under tensile load. Also show important points on the curve.

    **(B.T.E. S-2011, 2006, 2005/2 Marks)**

4.  Draw stress-strain diagram for mild steel and show different limits on it.

    **(B.T.E. W-2010, S-2010/2 Marks)**

5.  Draw stress-strain curve for mild steel and explain the terms.

    **(B.T.E. S-2009/2 Marks)**

6.  Explain the behaviour of mild steel under axial tension. Draw its stress-strain graph.

    **(B.T.E. S-2008/2 Marks)**

7.  Sketch the stress-strain curve for mild steel and show elastic limit and ultimate stress on the curve.    **(B.T.E. S-2004, W-1997/2 Marks)**

8.  Define factor of safety.    **(B.T.E. W-2007/2 Marks)**

9.  Define limit of proportionality.    **(2 Marks)**

---

**(Most Likely and Asked in Previous B.T.E. Exam.)**

## 1.27 BEHAVIOUR OF BRITTLE MATERIALS UNDER TENSION (STRESS-STRAIN CURVE FOR BRITTLE MATERIALS)

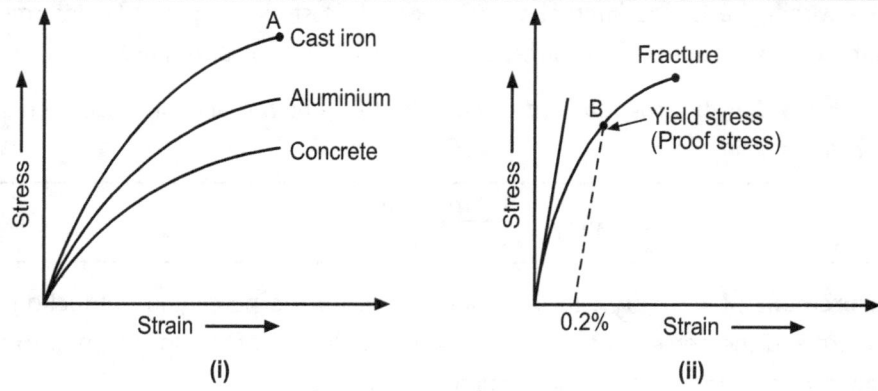

**Fig. 1.23**

Fig. 1.23 shows a graph of stress against strain for brittle materials when subjected to tension. As already seen, mild steel (low carbon steel) is the only material that shows a well defined yield point. Brittle materials like concrete, aluminium, cast iron has very low proportional limit and do not show the yield point. In such a case where the yield point is not clearly defined, it is taken as the point of some definite amount of permanent strain, generally 0.2%. It is obtained by the offset method as shown in Fig. 1.23 (ii). The stress corresponding to the point B is called yield stress or proof stress. For brittle materials the stress-strain graph is a continuous curve from the beginning itself as shown in Fig. 1.23 (i). The ultimate stress is not well defined but the breaking stress at the point A is well defined. A brittle material has a relatively small tensile strain upto the point of rupture.

> 1. Sketch a stress-strain curve for brittle material and give the salient points on it.
> **(B.T.E. S-1998/2 Marks)**

**(Most Likely and Asked in Previous B.T.E. Exam.)**

## SOLVED EXAMPLES

**Type 4 : Examples based on stress-strain curve :**

**Example 17 :** *The following observations were made during a tensile test on a mild steel specimen 40 mm in diameter and 200 mm long.*

*Elongation with 40 kN load (within limit of proportionality) $\delta l$ = 0.0304 mm, yield load = 161 kN, maximum load = 242 kN, length of specimen at fracture = 249 mm. Determine (i) Young's modulus, (ii) Yield stress, (iii) Ultimate stress, (iv) Percentage elongation.*

**(B.T.E. S-2012, W-2003/4 Marks)**

**Solution :** (i) Young's modulus,

$$E = \frac{PL}{A \cdot \delta l} \qquad \left( \because \delta l = \frac{PL}{AE} \right)$$

$$= \frac{40 \times 10^3 \times 200}{\frac{\pi}{4} \times 40^2 \times 0.0304} = \mathbf{2.09 \times 10^5 \, N/mm^2}$$

(ii)  $\text{Yield stress} = \dfrac{\text{Yield load}}{\text{Area}} = \dfrac{161 \times 10^3}{\dfrac{\pi}{4} \times 40^2} = \mathbf{128.12 \ N/mm^2}$

(iii)  $\text{Ultimate stress} = \dfrac{\text{Ultimate load}}{\text{Area}} = \dfrac{242 \times 10^3}{\dfrac{\pi}{4} \times 40^2} = \mathbf{192.58 \ N/mm^2}$

(iv)  $\% \text{ elongation} = \dfrac{\text{Increase in length}}{\text{Original length}} \times 100 = \dfrac{249 - 200}{200} \times 100$

$= \mathbf{24.5 \ \%}$

**Answer :**  (i) E = $2.09 \times 10^5$ N/mm$^2$, (ii) Yield stress = 128.12 N/mm$^2$,
(iii) Ultimate stress = 192.58 N/mm$^2$, (iv) % Elongation = 24.5 %

## (C) ELASTIC CONSTANTS

### Synopsis

Linear strain, Lateral strain, Poisson's ratio, Modulus of elasticity, Shear modulus or Modulus of rigidity (C, G or N), Relation between modulus of rigidity and modulus of elasticity, Volumetric strain, Concept of uni-axial loading, Concept of bi-axial loading, Concept of tri-axial loading, Bulk modulus, Relation between modulus of elasticity and bulk modulus, Relation between three elastic constants E, G and K.

## 1.28 LINEAR STRAIN

As already seen, *the strain in the direction of applied force is known as linear strain, longitudinal strain, primary strain or simply strain.* It is denoted by e.

$\therefore$  Linear strain, $e = \dfrac{\delta L}{L}$

## 1.29 LATERAL STRAIN

*Strain in a direction at right angles to the direction of applied force is known as lateral strain or secondary strain.*

Mathematically,      $\text{Lateral strain} = \dfrac{\text{Change in lateral dimension}}{\text{Original lateral dimension}}$

**For a rectangular bar :**      $\text{Lateral strain} = \dfrac{\delta b}{b} \ \text{ or } \ \dfrac{\delta t}{t}$

where      $\delta b$ = Change in width and b = Original width
$\delta t$ = Change in thickness and t = Original thickness

**For a circular bar :**      $\text{Lateral strain} = \dfrac{\delta d}{d}$

where      $\delta d$ = Change in diameter, d = Original diameter

1. Define lateral strain and longitudinal strain.      **(B.T.E. W-2014, 2010/2 Marks)**
2. Differentiate between linear strain and lateral strain.      **(2 Marks)**

**(Most Likely and Asked in Previous B.T.E. Exam.)**

## 1.30 POISSON'S RATIO

*When a homogeneous material is loaded within its elastic limit, the ratio of the lateral strain to the linear strain is constant and is known as Poisson's ratio.* It is denoted by $\mu$ or $\dfrac{1}{m}$.

The value of Poisson's ratio varies from 0.1 to 0.5. The extreme low value, 0.1 is for concrete and high value of 0.5 is for rubber. [For most metals value of m lies between 3 and 4 i.e. $\mu$ lies between $\dfrac{1}{3}$ to $\dfrac{1}{4}$ i.e. 0.33 to 0.25].

$$\text{Poisson's ratio} = \frac{\text{Lateral strain}}{\text{Linear strain}}$$

$\therefore$
$$\mu \text{ or } \frac{1}{m} = \frac{\text{Lateral strain}}{e}$$

$\therefore$
$$\boxed{\text{Lateral strain} = \mu \times e \text{ or } \frac{1}{m} \times e}$$

Consider a metallic bar of length L, width b and thickness t subjected to an axial tensile force P as shown in Fig. 1.24. Due to tensile load P, the length of the bar increases by amount $\delta L$. This increase in length is associated with the decrease in lateral sides b and t. Therefore, the linear strain is positive and the lateral strains are negative.

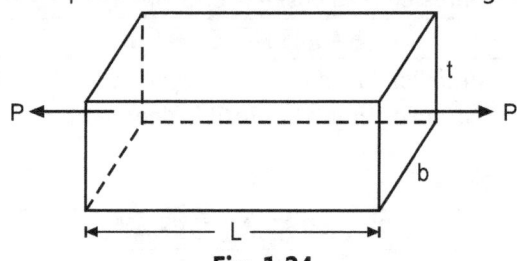

**Fig. 1.24**

In this case, linear strain,  $e = \dfrac{+\delta L}{L}$

and  lateral strain $= \dfrac{-\delta b}{b} = \dfrac{-\delta t}{t}$

The linear strain e is positive and the lateral strains are negative.

$\therefore$  $\boxed{\text{Lateral strain} = -\mu \times e}$

**Note :** *If the same bar is subjected to an axial compressive load P, there will be decrease in length which will be followed by increase in lateral dimensions b and t. In this case, the linear strain is negative and the lateral strains are positive.*

**Conclusion :** Lateral strain is of opposite nature to that of the linear strain.

**Sign convention :** If the linear strain is taken as positive, the lateral strains are taken as negative and vice a versa.

1.  What is Poisson's ratio ?                                   **(B.T.E. S-2009/2 Marks)**
2.  Define Poisson's ratio.                                     **(B.T.E. S-2011, W-1999/2 Marks)**
3.  State the relationship between lateral strain and linear strain.
                                                                **(B.T.E. S-1999/2 Marks)**
4.  State Hooke's law and define Poisson's ratio.              **(B.T.E. S-2010/4 Marks)**
5.  State Hooke's law and define the terms elasticity and Poisson's ratio.
                                                                **(B.T.E. W-2008/2 Marks)**

**(Most Likely and Asked in Previous B.T.E. Exam.)**

## 1.31 MODULUS OF ELASTICITY (E)

When the body is loaded within its elastic limit, the ratio of stress and strain is constant. This constant is known as Modulus of Elasticity or Young Modulus.

$$\therefore \quad E = \frac{Stress}{Strain}$$

S.I. unit of Young's modulus is same as that of stress i.e. *N/m² or Pascal*

## 1.32 SHEAR MODULUS OR MODULUS OF RIGIDITY (C, G OR N)

*When a body is loaded within its elastic limit, the ratio of shear stress and shear strain is constant. This constant is known as shear modulus or modulus of rigidity.* It is denoted by C, G or N. In this book, a letter G is used to denote shear modulus.

Mathematically,

$$\left[\begin{array}{c} \text{Shear modulus} \\ \text{or Modulus of rigidity} \end{array}\right] = \frac{Shear\ stress}{Shear\ strain}$$

$$\therefore \quad G = \frac{q}{\phi}$$

**S.I. Unit :** S.I. unit of G is same as that of stress i.e. N/m² or Pascal.

## 1.33 RELATION BETWEEN MODULUS OF RIGIDITY AND MODULUS OF ELASTICITY

$$E = 2\,G\,(1 + \mu)$$

where     E = Modulus of elasticity

G = Modulus of rigidity and

$$\mu = \frac{1}{m} = \text{Poisson's ratio}$$

Young's modulus (E), bulk modulus (K) and shear modulus (G) are known as *Elastic Constants.*

1.  Define Young's modulus and modulus of rigidity. Also write their equations.
                                                                **(B.T.E. W-2012/4 Marks)**
2.  State the relation between Young's modulus and shear modulus (or modulus of rigidity).                                      **(2 Marks)**
3.  A material has elastic modulus of $2 \times 10^5$ MPa and Poisson's ratio of 0.25. Calculate the modulus of rigidity.        **(B.T.E. W-1999/2 Marks)**

**(Most Likely and Asked in Previous B.T.E. Exam.)**

## 1.34 VOLUMETRIC STRAIN

When a body is subjected to external forces on its face, there will be a change in its volume. *The ratio of change in volume to the original volume is known as volumetric strain. It is denoted by $e_v$.*

$$\therefore \qquad e_v = \frac{\delta V}{V}$$

where $\delta V$ = Change in volume, and V = Original volume.

Volumetric strain is the algebraic sum of all axial or linear strains.

i.e. $\qquad e_v = e_x + e_y + e_z$

where $e_x$ = strain in X-direction, $e_y$ = strain in Y-direction and $e_z$ = strain in Z-direction

1.   What is volumetric strain ?                **(B.T.E. S-2009/2 Marks)**

**(Most Likely and Asked in Previous B.T.E. Exam.)**

## 1.35 CONCEPT OF UNI-AXIAL LOADING

For calculating volumetric strain of a body, we have to consider three principal axes X, Y and Z mutually perpendicular to each other. *If the force is applied in any one direction, say X-direction, it is called uni-axial and the body is said to be under the action of uni-axial stress system.*

**Volumetric strain of a rectangular bar :**

Consider a rectangular bar of length L, width b and thickness t subjected to a tensile force P along X-direction as shown in Fig. 1.25.

This is a case of uni-axial loading.

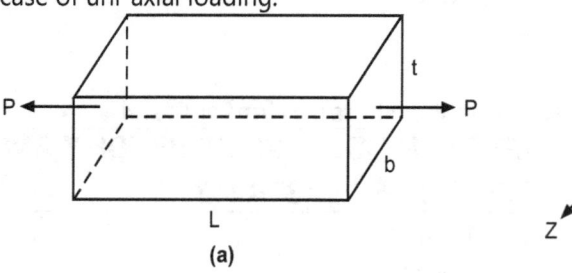

**Fig. 1.25**

Here stress in X-direction, $\qquad \sigma_x = \frac{P}{A} = \frac{P}{b \times t}$

Since there is no load in Y and Z directions, stresses in Y and Z directions are zero.

i.e. $\qquad \sigma_y = \sigma_z = 0$

**Strains :**

Strain in X-direction due to P is linear strain.

$$e_x = \frac{\sigma_x}{E}$$

Strain in Y-direction and strain in Z-direction are lateral strains.

$$e_y = e_z = -\mu \times \text{linear strain} = -\mu \times e_x$$

$$\therefore \qquad e_y = e_z = -\mu \cdot \frac{\sigma_x}{E}$$

∴   Volumetric strain of a rectangular bar,

$$\frac{\delta V}{V} = e_x + e_y + e_z = \frac{\sigma_x}{E} - \mu\frac{\sigma_x}{E} - \mu\frac{\sigma_x}{E} = \frac{\sigma_x}{E}(1 - 2\mu)$$

But                    $\dfrac{\sigma_x}{E} = e_x = $ linear strain, say e.   ∴   $\boxed{\dfrac{\delta V}{V} = e\,(1 - 2\mu)}$

This is the expression for volumetric strain of a rectangular bar subjected to an axial force P. From this expression, the change in volume ($\delta V$) of a rectangular bar due to an axial load P can be calculated.

**Note : *A circular bar having diameter 'd' and length 'L' subjected to an axial tensile force P, is also a case of uni-axial loading and its volumetric strain can also be calculated by using the relation $\dfrac{\delta V}{V} = e\,(1 - 2\mu)$.***

## 1.36 CONCEPT OF BI-AXIAL LOADING

*If the forces are applied in two mutually perpendicular directions, say X and Y, they are called bi-axial forces and the body is said to be under the action of bi-axial stress system.*

The definition of Poisson's ratio as seen earlier applies only to strains caused by uni-axial loading. The resulting strains in the required directions can be obtained by the principle of superposition i.e. by adding algebraically the strains in each direction due to each individual stress.

Consider a piece of material subjected to the two direct tensile stresses along the two mutually perpendicular axes as shown in Fig. 1.26.

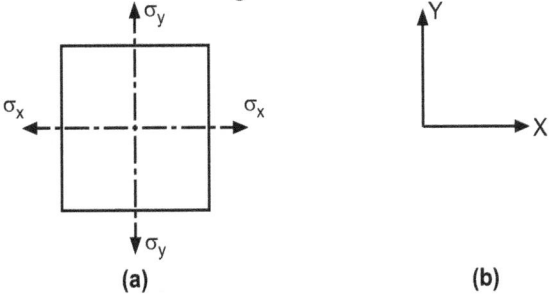

| (a) | (b) |

**Fig. 1.26**

Let     $\sigma_x = $ Stress in X-direction,   $\sigma_y = $ Stress in Y-direction

$e_x = $ Total strain in X-direction, $e_y = $ Total strain in Y-direction

**Strain in X-direction :**

(i)  Due to $\sigma_x$ alone,      $e_x = \dfrac{\sigma_x}{E}$

(ii) Due to $\sigma_y$ alone,      $e_x = -\mu\dfrac{\sigma_y}{E}$

∴   Total strain in X-direction,

$$\boxed{e_x = \frac{\sigma_x}{E} - \mu\frac{\sigma_y}{E}}$$                    ... (I)

**Strain in Y-direction :**

(i)　Due to $\sigma_x$ alone,　$e_y = -\mu\dfrac{\sigma_x}{E}$

(ii) Due to $\sigma_y$ alone,　$e_y = \dfrac{\sigma_y}{E}$

∴　Total strain in Y-direction,

$$\boxed{e_y = \dfrac{\sigma_y}{E} - \mu\dfrac{\sigma_x}{E}}$$　　... (II)

*These equations taken together give the generalized Hooke's law for an elastic body subjected to a bi-axial loading.*

**Note :** ***While calculating the strains $e_x$ and $e_y$ by using the above equations, tensile stresses are taken as positive and compressive stresses as negative.***

## 1.37　CONCEPT OF TRI-AXIAL LOADING

If the forces are applied in three mutually perpendicular directions X, Y and Z, they are called tri-axial forces and the body is said to be under the action of tri-axial stress system.

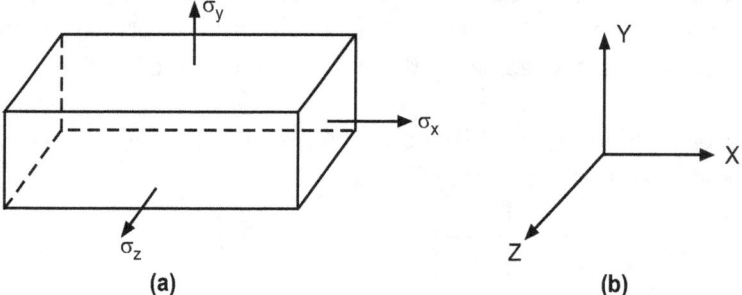

**(a)**　　　　　　　　　　**(b)**

**Fig. 1.27**

Consider a rectangular body subjected to the three direct tensile stresses along the three mutually perpendicular axes as shown in Fig. 1.27.

Let　$\sigma_x$ = Stress in X-direction　　　$\sigma_y$ = Stress in Y-direction

$\sigma_z$ = Stress in Z-direction　　　$e_x$ = Total strain in X-direction

$e_y$ = Total strain in Y-direction　　$e_z$ = Total strain in Z-direction

**Strain in X-direction :**

(i)　Due to $\sigma_x$ alone,　$e_x = \dfrac{\sigma_x}{E}$

(ii) Due to $\sigma_y$ alone,　$e_x = -\mu\dfrac{\sigma_y}{E}$

(iii) Due to $\sigma_z$ alone,　$e_x = -\mu\dfrac{\sigma_z}{E}$

∴　Total strain in X-direction,

$$e_x = \dfrac{\sigma_x}{E} - \mu\dfrac{\sigma_y}{E} - \mu\dfrac{\sigma_z}{E}$$　　... (I)

Similarly, total strain in Y-direction,

$$e_y = \frac{\sigma_y}{E} - \mu\frac{\sigma_x}{E} - \mu\frac{\sigma_z}{E} \qquad \ldots \text{(II)}$$

and total strain in Z-direction,

$$e_z = \frac{\sigma_z}{E} - \mu\frac{\sigma_x}{E} - \mu\frac{\sigma_y}{E} \qquad \ldots \text{(III)}$$

*Equations (I), (II), (III) taken together give the generalized Hooke's law for an elastic body subjected to a tri-axial loading.*

The volumetric strain can be calculated by the relation,

$$\frac{\delta V}{V} = e_x + e_y + e_z \qquad \ldots \text{(A)}$$

Substituting the values of $e_x$, $e_y$ and $e_z$ in equation (A),

$$\frac{\delta V}{V} = \frac{\sigma_x}{E} + \frac{\sigma_y}{E} + \frac{\sigma_z}{E} - 2\mu\frac{\sigma_x}{E} - 2\mu\frac{\sigma_y}{E} - 2\mu\frac{\sigma_z}{E}$$

$$= \left(\frac{\sigma_x + \sigma_y + \sigma_z}{E}\right) - 2\mu\left(\frac{\sigma_x + \sigma_y + \sigma_z}{E}\right)$$

$$\boxed{\frac{\delta V}{V} = \left(\frac{\sigma_x + \sigma_y + \sigma_z}{E}\right)(1 - 2\mu)} \qquad \ldots \text{(IV)}$$

This is the expression for the volumetric strain of a rectangular body subjected to a tri-axial loading.

**Note :** (i) If a rectangular body as shown in Fig. 1.27, is subjected to bi-axial loading, $\sigma_z = 0$.

Therefore, substituting $\sigma_z = 0$ in equation (IV), the volumetric strain can be written as,

$$\boxed{\frac{\delta V}{V} = \left(\frac{\sigma_x + \sigma_y}{E}\right)(1 - 2\mu)}$$

## This formula can be proved as under.

In case of bi-axial loading, the strains in X, Y and Z directions can be written by substituting $\sigma_z = 0$ in the general equations (I), (II) and (III) corresponding to tri-axial loading.

$$e_x = \frac{\sigma_x}{E} - \mu\frac{\sigma_y}{E} \qquad \ldots \text{(V)}$$

$$e_y = \frac{\sigma_y}{E} - \mu\frac{\sigma_x}{E} \qquad \ldots \text{(VI)}$$

$$e_z = -\mu\frac{\sigma_x}{E} - \mu\frac{\sigma_y}{E} \qquad \ldots \text{(VII)}$$

Note that even though there is no stress in Z-direction, there will be a strain in Z-direction due to $\sigma_x$ and $\sigma_y$. Equation (VII) represents the strain in Z-direction due to $\sigma_x$ and $\sigma_y$.

Adding the equations (V), (VI) and (VII), we have

$$e_x + e_y + e_z = \frac{\sigma_x}{E} - \mu\frac{\sigma_y}{E} + \frac{\sigma_y}{E} - \mu\frac{\sigma_x}{E} - \mu\frac{\sigma_x}{E} - \mu\frac{\sigma_y}{E}$$

$$= \frac{\sigma_x}{E} - 2\mu\frac{\sigma_x}{E} + \frac{\sigma_y}{E} - 2\mu\frac{\sigma_y}{E} = \frac{\sigma_x}{E}(1-2\mu) + \frac{\sigma_y}{E}(1-2\mu)$$

$$= (1-2\mu)\left(\frac{\sigma_x + \sigma_y}{E}\right)$$

$\therefore$

$$\boxed{\frac{\delta V}{V} = \left(\frac{\sigma_x + \sigma_y}{E}\right)(1-2\mu)}$$

Using this equation, the volumetric strain of a rectangular body subjected to a bi-axial loading can be calculated.

**Note :** (ii) If $\sigma_y = 0$ and $\sigma_z = 0$, then it is a case of *uni-axial loading*.

Now,

$$\frac{\delta V}{V} = \left(\frac{\sigma_x + \sigma_y + \sigma_z}{E}\right)(1-2\mu)$$

Substituting $\sigma_y = \sigma_z = 0$ in this equation, we have

$$\frac{\delta V}{V} = \frac{\sigma_x}{E}(1-2\mu)$$

$\therefore$

$$\boxed{\frac{\delta V}{V} = e(1-2\mu)}$$

$$\left(\because \frac{\sigma_x}{E} = \text{linear strain} = e\right)$$

## 1.38 BULK MODULUS (K)

*When a body is subjected to three mutually perpendicular like stresses of same intensity then the ratio of direct stress and the corresponding volumetric strain of the body is constant and is known as bulk modulus. It is denoted by K.*

**Note : *Like stresses means all the three stresses should be of the same nature i.e. either tensile or compressive.***

Consider a cube of length L subjected to three mutually perpendicular tensile stresses of intensity $\sigma$ as shown in Fig. 1.28.

Now, Bulk modulus $= \dfrac{\text{Direct stress}}{\text{Volumetric strain}}$  $\therefore$  $\boxed{K = \dfrac{\sigma}{\dfrac{\delta V}{V}}}$

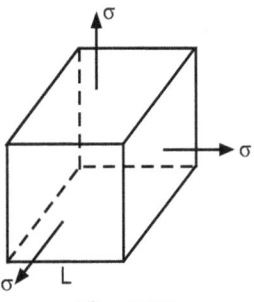

**Fig. 1.28**

**S.I. Unit :** Since $\dfrac{\delta V}{V}$ has no unit, S.I. unit of bulk modulus is same as that of stress

i.e. N/m² or Pascal.

| 1. What is bulk modulus ? | (B.T.E. W-2007/2 Marks) |
|---|---|

**(Most Likely and Asked in Previous B.T.E. Exam.)**

## 1.39 RELATION BETWEEN MODULUS OF ELASTICITY AND BULK MODULUS

We know that when a body is subjected to a tri-axial stress system, its volumetric strain is given by

$$\frac{\delta V}{V} = \frac{\sigma_x + \sigma_y + \sigma_z}{E}(1 - 2\mu)$$

Here     $\sigma_x = \sigma_y = \sigma_z = \sigma$

$\therefore$     $$\frac{\delta V}{V} = \frac{\sigma + \sigma + \sigma}{E} = \frac{3\sigma}{E}(1 - 2\mu)$$

But     $$K = \frac{\sigma}{\dfrac{\delta V}{V}} = \frac{\sigma}{\dfrac{3\sigma}{E}(1 - 2\mu)}$$

$$K = \frac{E}{3(1 - 2\mu)}$$

$\therefore$     $$\boxed{E = 3K(1 - 2\mu)}$$

This is a relation between modulus of elasticity (E) and bulk modulus (K).

1. Explain the relation between modulus of elasticity and bulk modulus and Poisson's ratio.                    **(B.T.E. S-2014, W-2012/4 Marks)**

2. State the relation between Young's modulus and bulk modulus.

**(B.T.E. S-2012, W-2007/2 Marks)**

3. Define bulk modulus. State the relationship between Young's modulus and bulk modulus giving meaning of each term used in it.     **(B.T.E. W-2008/2 Marks)**

**(Most Likely and Asked in Previous B.T.E. Exam.)**

## 1.40 RELATION BETWEEN THREE ELASTIC CONSTANTS E, G AND K

We know that,     $E = 2G(1 + \mu)$     ... (i)

and     $E = 3K(1 - 2\mu)$     ... (ii)

From equation (i),     $1 + \mu = \dfrac{E}{2G}$

$\therefore$     $\mu = \dfrac{E}{2G} - 1$     ... (iii)

Substituting the value of $\mu$ in equation (ii),

$$E = 3K\left[1 - 2\left(\frac{E}{2G} - 1\right)\right] = 3K\left[1 - \frac{E}{G} + 2\right]$$

$$E = 3K\left[3 - \frac{E}{G}\right] = 3K\left[\frac{3G - E}{G}\right]$$

$\therefore$     $EG = 3K(3G - E) = 9KG - 3KE$

$\therefore$     $EG + 3KE = 9KG$

$\therefore$     $E(G + 3K) = 9KG$   $\therefore$   $\boxed{E = \dfrac{9KG}{G + 3K}}$

1. Write down the relationship among E, G and K.     **(B.T.E. S-2015, 2011/2 Marks)**
2. Derive the relationship between E, G and K.     **(V.V. Imp./4 Marks)**
3. Define Poisson's ratio and state the relation between three elastic constants E, G and K.     **(B.T.E. W-2007/4 Marks)**

**(Most Likely and Asked in Previous B.T.E. Exam.)**

## SOLVED EXAMPLES

**Type 5 : Examples based on elastic constants.**

### Important Formulae

Young's modulus, $E = \dfrac{\sigma}{e}$

Linear strain, $e = \dfrac{\delta L}{L}$

Poisson's ratio, $\dfrac{1}{m} = \mu = \dfrac{\text{Lateral strain}}{\text{Linear strain}}$

$E = 2G(1 + \mu)$

$E = 3K(1 - 2\mu)$

$K = \dfrac{\sigma}{\dfrac{\delta V}{V}}$

Volumetric strain of a square, rectangular and circular bar, $\dfrac{\delta V}{V} = e(1 - 2\mu)$

Volumetric strain of a cube subjected to the three like stresses of same intensity,

$$\frac{\delta V}{V} = \frac{3\sigma}{E}(1 - 2\mu)$$

## Type 5.1 : Examples on relationship between E, G and K.

**Example 18 :** *For a certain material, the modulus of elasticity is 2.8 times its bulk modulus. Calculate the Poisson's ratio. Also calculate the ratio of modulus of elasticity to modulus of rigidity.* **(B.T.E. S-2011; W-2014, 2010, 2000/4 Marks)**

**Data**    : E = 2.8 K

**To find**    : (i) μ, (ii) E/G.

**Concept :** (i) Relation between E and K i.e. E = 3 K (1 − 2μ)

(ii) Relation between E and G i.e. E = 2G (1 + μ)

**Solution :** We know that,    E = 3K (1 − 2μ)

∴                            $2.8 K = 3K (1 - 2\mu)$

∴                            $2.8 = 3 (1 - 2\mu)$

∴                      $1 - 2\mu = \dfrac{2.8}{3} = 0.93$

∴                        $2\mu = 1 - 0.93 = 0.07$

∴                          $\mu = \dfrac{0.07}{2} = \mathbf{0.035}$

We know that,                $E = 2G (1 + \mu)$

∴                          $\dfrac{E}{G} = 2 (1 + \mu) = 2 (1 + 0.035) = \mathbf{2.07}$

**Answer :** $\boxed{(i) \; \mu = 0.035, \; (ii) \dfrac{E}{G} = 2.07}$

---

**Example 19 :** *For a certain material, E = K. Calculate E/G and Poisson's ratio.*

**(B.T.E. S-2011/4 Marks)**

**Data**    : E = K

**To find**    : (i) $\dfrac{E}{G}$, (ii) μ.

**Concept :** (i) Relation between E and K, (ii) Relation between E and G.

**Solution :** We know that,    E = 3K (1 − 2μ)

∴                            $K = 3K (1 - 2\mu)$

∴                            $1 = 3 (1 - 2\mu)$

∴                      $1 - 2\mu = \dfrac{1}{3} = 0.33$

∴                        $2\mu = 1 - 0.33 = 0.67$

∴                          $\mu = \mathbf{0.33}$

We know that,                $E = 2G (1 + \mu) = 2G (1 + 0.33)$

∴                          $\dfrac{E}{G} = 2 \times 1.33 = \mathbf{2.66}$

**Answer** : $\boxed{(i) \dfrac{E}{G} = 2.66, \; (ii) \; \mu = 0.33}$

**Example 20 :** *For a material for which E is 2 K, determine the Poisson's ratio and find E/G.* **(V.V. Imp./4 Marks)**

**Answer :** $\mu = 0.165, \quad \dfrac{E}{G} = 2.33$

---

**Example 21 :** *For a certain material, modulus of elasticity is 169 MPa. If Poisson's ratio is 0.32, calculate the values of modulus of rigidity and bulk modulus.*

**(B.T.E. S-2012, 2000/4 Marks)**

**Data**       : E = 169 MPa = 169 N/mm², $\mu$ = 0.32.

**To find** : (i) G, (ii) K.

**Concept :** (i) Relation between E and G, (ii) Relation between E and K.

**Solution :** We know that,   E = 2G (1 + $\mu$)

$\therefore$                                  169 = 2G (1 + 0.32) = 2G × 1.32

$\therefore$                                  169 = 2.64 G

$\therefore$                                  $G = \dfrac{169}{2.64} = \textbf{64.015 N/mm}^2$

We know that                 E = 3K (1 – 2$\mu$)

$\therefore$                                  169 = 3K (1 – 2 × 0.32) = 3K × 0.36 = 1.08 K

$\therefore$                                  $K = \dfrac{169}{1.08} = \textbf{156.48 N/mm}^2$

**Answer :** (i) G = 64.015 N/mm², (ii) K = 156.48 N/mm²

---

**Exactly similar examples for practice :**

**Example 22 :** *For a certain material, modulus of elasticity is 170 MPa. If Poisson's ratio is 0.32, calculate the values of modulus of rigidity and bulk modulus.* **(B.T.E. S-2013/4 Marks)**

**Answer**     : (i) G = 64.39 N/mm² = 64.39 MPa, (ii) K = 157.40 N/mm² = 157.4 MPa

---

**Example 23 :** *For a certain material the modulus of elasticity is 189 MPa. If Poisson's ratio = 0.35, calculate the values of modulus of rigidity and bulk modulus.*

**(B.T.E. W-2007/4 Marks)**

**Answer :** (i) G = 70 MPa = 70 N/mm², (ii) K = 210 MPa = 210 N/mm²

---

**Example 24 :** *For a certain material, E = 2 × 10⁵ MPa and G = 8 × 10⁴ MPa. Find the values of $\dfrac{1}{m}$ and K.* **(B.T.E. W-2009/4 Marks)**

**Data :** E = 2 × 10⁵ MPa = 2 × 10⁵ N/mm², G = 8 × 10⁴ MPa = 8 × 10⁴ N/mm².

**To find :** (i) $\dfrac{1}{m}$ or $\mu$, (ii) K.

**Hint :** Use relation between E and G to find $\mu \Rightarrow \mu = 0.25$ and use relation between E and K to find K.

**Answer :** $\boxed{(i) \dfrac{1}{m} = \mu = 0.25, (ii) \; K = 1.33 \times 10^5 \; MPa = 1.33 \times 10^5 \; N/mm^2}$

---

**Example 25 :** *Young's modulus for a certain metal is 120 kN/mm². If Poisson's ratio is 0.29, find the value of other two modulli.* **(B.T.E. S-2008/4 Marks)**

**Data**      : $E = 120 \; kN/mm^2 = 120 \times 10^3 \; N/mm^2$, $\mu = 0.29$

**To find**   : (i) G and (ii) K.

**Concept**  : (i) Relation between E and G, (ii) Relation between E and K.

**Solution :** (i) Using the relation between E and G, we have

$$E = 2G \, (1 + \mu)$$
$$120 \times 10^3 = 2G \, (1 + 0.29) = 2.58 \; G$$

$\therefore$  $$\mathbf{G} = \frac{120 \times 10^3}{2.58} = \mathbf{46.512 \times 10^3 \; N/mm^2 = 46.512 \; kN/mm^2}$$

(ii) Using the relation between E and K, we have

$$E = 3 \, K \, (1 - 2\mu)$$

$\therefore$  $$120 \times 10^3 = 3 \, K \, (1 - 2 \times 0.29) = 1.26 \; K$$

$\therefore$  $$\mathbf{K} = \frac{120 \times 10^3}{1.26} = 95.238 \times 10^3 \; N/mm^2 = \mathbf{95.238 \; kN/mm^2}$$

**Answer :** $\boxed{(i) \; G = 46.512 \; kN/mm^2, (ii) \; K = 95.238 \; kN/mm^2}$

---

## Type 5.2 : Examples on calculating $\mu$ and E.

**Example 26 :** *A bar of 30 mm diameter is subjected to a pull of 60 kN. The measured extension on gauge length of 200 mm is 0.09 mm and the change in diameter is 0.0039 mm. Calculate the Poisson's ratio and modulus of elasticity.* **(B.T.E. S-2005/4 Marks)**

**Data**    : $d = 30 \; mm$, $P = 60 \; kN = 60 \times 10^3 \, N$, $L = 200 \; mm$, $\delta L = 0.09 \; mm$,

$\delta d = 0.0039 \; mm$

**To find** : $\mu$, E.

**Concept :** $\mu = \dfrac{\text{Lateral strain}}{\text{Linear strain}}$

**Solution :** Linear strain,

$$e = \frac{\delta L}{L} = \frac{0.09}{200} = 0.00045$$

$$\text{Lateral strain} = \frac{\delta d}{d} = \frac{0.0039}{30} = 0.00013$$

$\therefore$  Poisson's ratio, $\mu = \dfrac{\text{Lateral strain}}{\text{Linear strain}} = \dfrac{0.00013}{0.00045} = \mathbf{0.29}$

We know that,        $\delta L = \dfrac{PL}{AE}$

$\therefore$        $E = \dfrac{PL}{A \cdot \delta L} = \dfrac{60 \times 10^3 \times 200}{\dfrac{\pi}{4}(30)^2 \times 0.09} = \mathbf{1.88628 \times 10^5 \ N/mm^2}$

**Answer :** $\boxed{\text{(i) } \mu = 0.29, \text{ (ii) } E = 1.88628 \times 10^5 \ N/mm^2}$

---

**Example 27 :** *For a tension test on 20 mm diameter bar, the following observations were recorded for an axial pull of 100 kN.*

*(i)  Elongation of 0.29 mm over 100 mm gauge length.*

*(ii) Reduction in diameter of 0.016 mm.*

*Calculate Poisson's ratio and modulus of elasticity.*        **(B.T.E. W-1997/4 Marks)**

**Hint**        : d = 20 mm, P = 100 kN = 100 × 10³ N,

        $\delta L = 0.29$ mm, L = 100 mm, $\delta d = 0.016$ mm.

**To find :** $\mu$ and E.

**Answer :** $\boxed{\text{(i) } \mu = 0.276, \text{ (ii) } E = 109762.02 \ N/mm^2}$

---

**Example 28 :** *A metal bar, 50 mm × 50 mm section, is subjected to an axial compressive load of 500 kN. The contraction of a 200 mm gauge length is found to be 0.5 mm and increase in thickness 0.04 mm. Find the value of Young's modulus and Poisson's ratio.*

**(B.T.E. S-2009/4 Marks)**

**Data**        : Square bar : width b = thickness t = 50 mm,

        Area of bar A = 50 × 50 = 2500 mm²,

        Axial compressive load P = 500 kN = 500 × 10³ N.

        Original length L = 200 mm, contraction i.e. decrease in length $\delta L$ = 0.5 mm;

        increase in thickness $\delta t$ = 0.04 mm.

**To find**        : (i) E and (ii) $\mu$.

**Concept**        : (i) $E = \dfrac{\sigma}{e}$, (ii) $\mu = \dfrac{\text{Lateral strain}}{\text{Linear strain}}$

**Solution**        : (i)    Stress $\sigma = \dfrac{P}{A} = \dfrac{500 \times 10^3}{2500} = 200 \ N/mm^2$

        (ii)    Linear strain, $e = \dfrac{\delta L}{L} = \dfrac{0.5}{200} = 0.0025$

        (iii)    Young's modulus $\mathbf{E} = \dfrac{\sigma}{e} = \dfrac{200}{0.0025} = \mathbf{80000 \ N/mm^2}$

        (iv)    Lateral strain $= \dfrac{\delta t}{t} = \dfrac{0.04}{50} = 0.0008$

        (v)    We know that, $\boldsymbol{\mu} = \dfrac{\text{Lateral strain}}{\text{Linear strain}} = \dfrac{0.0008}{0.0025} = \mathbf{0.32}$

**Answer :** $\boxed{\text{(i) } E = 80000 \ N/mm^2 = 80000 \ MPa, \text{ (ii) } \mu = 0.32}$

**Example 29 :** *A bar of 12 mm diameter is tested on U.T.M. and the following observations are noted. Gauge length = 200 mm, Load at proportional limit = 20 kN, Change in length at proportional limit = 0.2 mm, Change in diameter at proportional limit = 0.0025 mm. Calculate the value of* $\dfrac{1}{m}$ *and E.* **(V.V. Imp./4 Marks)**

**Hint :** d = 12 mm, L = 200 mm, P = 20 kN = 20 × 10³ N, δL = 0.2 mm, δd = 0.0025 mm

**To find :** $\dfrac{1}{m}$ (i.e. Poisson's ratio) and E.

**Answer :** (i) $\dfrac{1}{m}$ = μ = 0.21, (ii) E = 176.84 kN/mm²

---

**Example 30 :** *Modulus of rigidity of a material is 0.8 × 10⁵ N/mm². When a 6 × 6 mm² rod was subjected to an axial pull of 3600 N, it was found that the lateral dimension changed to 5.9991 × 5.9991 mm². Find Poisson's ratio and modulus of elasticity.*

**(B.T.E. S-2011/4 Marks)**

**Data :** G = 0.8 × 10⁵ N/mm², b = t = 6 mm, A = 6 × 6 = 36 mm², P = 3600 N,
δb = 6 − 5.9991 = 0.0009 mm, δt = 6 − 5.9991 = 0.0009 mm.

**To find :** (i) μ, (ii) E.

**Concept :** Solution of two simultaneous equations in μ and E.

**Solution :** (i)     Stress, σ $= \dfrac{P}{A} = \dfrac{3600}{36}$ = 100 N/mm²

(ii)     Lateral strain $= \dfrac{\delta b}{b} = \dfrac{0.0009}{6}$ = 0.00015

(iii) But,     lateral strain = μ × e

$$= \mu \times \dfrac{\sigma}{E} \qquad \left( \because e = \dfrac{\sigma}{E} \right)$$

(iv)     $\mu \times \dfrac{\sigma}{E}$ = 0.00015

$$\mu \times \dfrac{100}{E} = 0.00015$$

∴     $\mu = \dfrac{0.00015}{100} E = 1.5 \times 10^{-6} E$     ... (A)

(v)     E = 2G (1 + μ) = 2 × (0.8 × 10⁵) [1 + μ]

E = 1.6 × 10⁵ (1 + μ)     ... (B)

Substituting the value of E from equation (A) in equation (B), we have

$$E = 1.6 \times 10^5 [1 + (1.5 \times 10^{-6} E)]$$
$$= 1.6 \times 10^5 + 1.6 \times 10^5 \times 1.5 \times 10^{-6} E$$
$$= 1.6 \times 10^5 + 2.4 \times 10^{-1} E$$
$$= 1.6 \times 10^5 + 0.24 E$$

$$E - 0.24\,E = 1.6 \times 10^5$$
$$0.76\,E = 1.6 \times 10^5$$
$$\therefore \quad E = \frac{1.6 \times 10^5}{0.76} = \textbf{2.1} \times \textbf{10}^5 \textbf{ N/mm}^2$$

∴ From equation (A),

$$\mu = 1.5 \times 10^{-6}\,E = 1.5 \times 10^{-6} \times 2.1 \times 10^5 = \textbf{0.315}$$

**Answer :** $\boxed{\text{(i) } \mu = 0.315, \text{ (ii) } E = 2.1 \times 10^5 \text{ N/mm}^2}$

---

**Example 31 :** *The modulus of rigidity for a material is 40 GPa. A 10 mm diameter rod of the material was subjected to an axial pull of 5 kN and the change in diameter was observed to be 0.00195 mm. Calculate the value of modulus of elasticity of the material and Poisson's ratio.* **(V.V. Imp./4 Marks)**

**Hint :** Solve two simultaneous equations in E and μ.

**Answer :** $\boxed{\text{(i) } E = 104.5 \text{ kN/mm}^2, \text{ (ii) } \mu = 0.32}$

---

## Type 5.3 : Examples on calculating K and δd.

**Example 32 :** *For a given material, Young's modulus is $1 \times 10^5$ N/mm² and modulus of rigidity $0.4 \times 10^5$ N/mm². Find the bulk modulus and lateral contraction of a round bar of 50 mm diameter and 2.5 m long, when stretched 2.5 mm. Take Poisson's ratio as 0.25.* **(B.T.E. S-1997/4 Marks)**

**Data** : $E = 1 \times 10^5$ N/mm², $G = 0.4 \times 10^5$ N/mm², d = 50 mm, L = 2.5 m = $2.5 \times 10^3$ mm, δL = 2.5 mm, μ = 0.25

**To find** : (i) K, (ii) δd.

**Concept :** (i) Relation between E and K, (ii) Lateral strain = $\mu \times e = \dfrac{\delta d}{d}$.

**Solution :** **(i) To find bulk modulus (K) :**

Using the relation, $E = 3K(1 - 2\mu)$
$$1 \times 10^5 = 3K(1 - 2 \times 0.25) = 3K \times 0.5 = 1.5\,K$$

$$\therefore \quad K = \frac{10^5}{1.5} = \textbf{0.67} \times \textbf{10}^5 \textbf{ N/mm}^2$$

**(ii) To find lateral contraction (δd) :**

$$\because \quad \mu = \frac{\text{Lateral strain}}{\text{Linear strain}}$$

$$\text{Lateral strain} = \mu \times \text{Linear strain} = \mu \times \frac{\delta L}{L}$$

$$= 0.25 \times \frac{2.5}{2.5 \times 10^3} = 0.00025 \qquad \text{... (i)}$$

But, lateral strain $= \dfrac{\delta d}{d}$ $\qquad$ ... (ii)

Equating (i) and (ii), $\dfrac{\delta d}{d} = 0.00025$

$$\therefore \qquad \frac{\delta d}{50} = 0.00025$$

$$\therefore \qquad \delta d = 50 \times 0.00025 = \textbf{0.0125 mm}$$

**Answer :** $\boxed{\text{(i) } K = 0.67 \times 10^5 \text{ N/mm}^2, \text{(ii) } \delta d = 0.0125 \text{ mm}}$

**Example 33 :** *For a round bar of 50 mm diameter and 2.5 m long a certain material has Young's modulus of 1.10 × 10⁵ N/mm² and modulus of rigidity is 0.45 × 10⁵ N/mm². Find the bulk modulus and the lateral contraction of the bar when stretched by 3 mm.*

**(B.T.E. S-2003/4 Marks)**

**Data** : $d = 50$ mm, $L = 2.5$ m $= 2.5 \times 10^3$ mm, $E = 1.10 \times 10^5$ N/mm²,

$G = 0.45 \times 10^5$ N/mm², $\delta L = 3$ mm

**To find** : K, δd.

**Concept :** (i) Relation between E and G, (ii) Relation between E and K,

(iii) Lateral strain $= \mu \times e = \dfrac{\delta d}{d}$.

**Solution** : Using the relation,

$$E = 2G (1 + \mu)$$

$$1.10 \times 10^5 = 2 \times 0.45 \times 10^5 (1 + \mu)$$

$$\therefore \qquad 1 + \mu = 1.22$$

$$\therefore \qquad \mu = 1.22 - 1 = \textbf{0.22}$$

Using the relation, $\qquad E = 3K (1 - 2\mu)$

$$1.10 \times 10^5 = 3K (1 - 2 \times 0.22) = 1.68 \, K$$

$$\therefore \qquad K = \textbf{0.65} \times \textbf{10}^\textbf{5} \textbf{ N/mm}^\textbf{2}$$

Now, $\qquad \mu = \dfrac{\text{lateral strain}}{\text{linear strain}}$

$\therefore \qquad$ Lateral strain $= \mu \times$ linear strain

$$= 0.22 \times \frac{\delta L}{L} = 0.22 \times \frac{3}{2.5 \times 10^3} = 0.000264$$

But, $\qquad$ Lateral strain $= \dfrac{\delta d}{d}$

$\therefore \qquad \delta d = $ lateral strain $\times d$

$$= 0.000264 \times 50 = \textbf{0.0132 mm}$$

**Answer :** $\boxed{\text{(i) } K = 0.65 \times 10^5 \text{ N/mm}^2, \text{(ii) } \delta d = 0.0132 \text{ mm}}$

**Try Yourself :**

**Example 34 :** *A bar of steel 25 mm diameter is subjected to an axial tensile force of 200 kN. If E = 2 × 10⁵ N/mm² and μ = 0.3, determine the decrease in the diameter of the bar.*

**(V.V. Imp./4 Marks)**

**Answer :** $\delta d = 0.015$ mm

---

**Type 5.4 : Examples on calculating δL and δd.**

**Example 35 :** *A hollow cylinder has external diameter 100 mm and thickness of metal 10 mm. The length of cylinder is 800 mm. It carries an axial thrust of 240 kN. If E = 2 × 10⁵ MPa and Poisson's ratio is 0.25, find (i) change in length, (ii) change in diameter.*

**(B.T.E. S-2012, W-2008/4 Marks)**

**Data**          : Hollow cylinder D = 100 mm, t = 10 mm, L = 800 mm,

                   P = 240 kN = $240 \times 10^3$ N, E = $2 \times 10^5$ MPa = $2 \times 10^5$ N/mm², μ = 0.25

**To find**    : (i) δL, (ii) δD.

**Concept**  : (i) $\delta L = \dfrac{PL}{AE}$, (ii) Lateral strain = $\mu e = \dfrac{\delta D}{D}$

**Solution**  : (i)    $A = \dfrac{\pi}{4}(D^2 - d^2) = \dfrac{\pi}{4}(100^2 - 80^2) = 2827.43$ mm²

(ii)    $\delta L = \dfrac{PL}{AE} = \dfrac{240 \times 10^3 \times 800}{2827.43 \times 2 \times 10^5} = \textbf{0.34 mm (decrease)}$

(iii)   Linear strain, $e = \dfrac{\delta L}{L} = \dfrac{0.34}{800} = 0.000425$

(iv)   Lateral strain = $\mu \times e = 0.25 \times 0.000425 = 0.00010625$

(v)    $\dfrac{\delta D}{D} = 0.00010625$                    $\ldots \left( \because \text{Lateral strain} = \dfrac{\delta d}{d} \right)$

(vi)   $\delta D = 100 \times 0.00010625 = \textbf{0.010625 mm (increase)}$

**Answer :** (i) δL = 0.34 mm (decrease), (ii) δD = 0.010625 mm (increase)

---

**Example 36 :** *A steel rod 4 m long and 20 mm diameter is subjected to an axial tensile load of 45 kN. Find the change in length and diameter of the rod. $E_s = 2 \times 10^5$ N/mm².*

*Poisson's ratio = $\dfrac{1}{4}$.*

**(B.T.E. S-2005/4 Marks)**

**Data :** Steel rod L = 4 m = 4000 mm, d = 20 mm, P = 45 kN = $45 \times 10^3$ N,

E = $2 \times 10^5$ N/mm², $\mu = \dfrac{1}{4} = 0.25$.

**To find :** (i) δL, (ii) δd.

**Concept :** (i) $\delta L = \dfrac{PL}{AE}$, (ii) Lateral strain = $\mu e = \dfrac{\delta d}{d}$.

**Solution :** $\qquad A = \dfrac{\pi}{4} d^2 = \dfrac{\pi}{4} \times (20)^2 = 314.16 \text{ mm}^2$

$$\delta L = \frac{PL}{AE} = \frac{(45 \times 10^3) \times 4000}{314.16 \times (2 \times 10^5)} = \textbf{2.86 mm (increase)}$$

**Note :** Since the rod is subjected to an axial tensile load, there will be increase in the length of the bar and decrease in the diameter.

**Linear strain, e** $= \dfrac{\delta L}{L} = \dfrac{2.86}{4000} = \textbf{0.000715}$

Lateral strain $= \mu \times e = 0.25 \times 0.000715 = 0.00017875$

$\therefore \qquad \dfrac{\delta d}{d} = 0.00017875 \qquad\qquad \left( \because \text{lateral strain} = \dfrac{\delta d}{d} \right)$

$\therefore \qquad \dfrac{\delta d}{20} = 0.00017875$

$\therefore \qquad \delta d = 20 \times 0.00017875 = \textbf{0.003575 mm (decrease)}$

**Answer :** $\boxed{\text{(i) } \delta L = 2.86 \text{ mm (increase), (ii) } \delta d = 0.003575 \text{ mm (decrease)}}$

---

### Type 5.5 : Examples on calculating δL, δt, δb, δV.

**Example 37 :** *A mild steel flat 150 mm wide by 20 mm thick, 6 m long, carries an axial pull of 300 kN. If the modulus of elasticity of steel is 200 kN/mm² and Poisson's ratio = 0.25, calculate the change in length, width, thickness and volume of the flat.*

**(B.T.E. W-2011, 2005/4 Marks)**

**Data** : Width b = 150 mm, thickness t = 20 mm, length L = 6 m = 6000 mm,

pull P = 300 kN = $300 \times 10^3$ N, $\mu$ = 0.25,

E = 200 kN/mm² = $200 \times 10^3$ N/mm²,

**To find** : δL, δb, δt and δV.

**Concept :** (i) $\quad e = \dfrac{\delta L}{L}$, (ii) Lateral strain $= \mu \times e = \dfrac{\delta b}{b} = \dfrac{\delta t}{t}$,

(iii) Volumetric strain, $\dfrac{\delta V}{V} = e (1 - 2\mu)$

**Solution :** $\quad$ Area A = b × t = 150 × 20 = 3000 mm².

$\qquad\qquad$ Volume V = A × L = 3000 × 6000 = $18 \times 10^6$ mm³

Now, $\qquad\qquad \delta L = \dfrac{PL}{AE} = \dfrac{300 \times 10^3 \times 6000}{3000 \times (200 \times 10^3)} = \textbf{3 mm (increase)}$

$\qquad$ Linear strain, e $= \dfrac{\delta L}{L} = \dfrac{3}{6000} = 5 \times 10^{-4}$

$\qquad$ Lateral strain $= \mu \times e = 0.25 \times 5 \times 10^{-4} = 1.25 \times 10^{-4}$

$\qquad$ Lateral strain $= \dfrac{\delta b}{b}$

$\therefore$ $\qquad$ $\delta b$ = Lateral strain × b

$\qquad$ = $1.25 \times 10^{-4} \times 150$ = **0.01875 mm (decrease)**

Also, $\qquad$ Lateral strain = $\dfrac{\delta t}{t}$

$\therefore$ $\qquad$ $\delta t$ = Lateral strain × t

$\qquad$ = $1.25 \times 10^{-4} \times 20$ = **0.0025 mm (decrease)**

Volumetric strain, $\qquad$ $\dfrac{\delta V}{V}$ = $e\,(1 - 2\mu)$

$\therefore$ $\qquad$ $\delta V$ = $V \cdot e\,(1 - 2\mu) = (18 \times 10^6) \times (5 \times 10^{-4})\,(1 - 2 \times 0.25)$

$\qquad$ $\delta V$ = **4500 mm³ (increase)**

**Answer :** (i) $\delta L$ = 3 mm (increase), (ii) $\delta b$ = 0.01875 mm (decrease), (iii) $\delta t$ = 0.0025 mm (decrease), (iv) $\delta V$ = 4500 mm³ (increase)

---

**Example 38 :** *A steel bar 50 mm × 50 mm in section, 3 m long is subjected to an axial pull of 20 kN. Calculate the change in length and side of bar. Take E = 200 GPa, and Poisson's ratio = 0.3.* **(B.T.E. S-2013, W-2006/4 Marks)**

**OR**

*A steel bar 50 mm × 50 mm in section and 3 m long is subjected to an axial pull of 20 kN. Take E = $2 \times 10^5$ N/mm² and μ = 0.3. Calculate the alternations in length, side and volume of a bar.*

**Data :** b = t = 50 mm, L = 3 m = 3000 mm, P = 20 kN = $20 \times 10^3$ N,

$\qquad$ E = $2 \times 10^5$ N/mm², μ = 0.3.

**To find :** $\delta L$, $\delta b$, $\delta V$.

**Concept :** (i) $\delta L = \dfrac{PL}{AE}$, (ii) Lateral strain = $\mu e = \dfrac{\delta b}{b} = \dfrac{\delta t}{t}$, (iii) $\dfrac{\delta V}{V} = e\,(1 - 2\mu)$

**Solution :** Area, $\quad$ A = b × t = 50 × 50 = 2500 mm²

$\qquad$ Volume, $\qquad$ V = A × L = 2500 × 3000 = $75 \times 10^5$ mm³

Now, $\qquad$ $\delta L = \dfrac{PL}{AE} = \dfrac{20 \times 10^3 \times 3000}{2500 \times 2 \times 10^5}$ = **0.12 mm (increase)**

$\qquad$ e = $\dfrac{\delta L}{L} = \dfrac{0.12}{3000} = 4 \times 10^{-5}$

$\qquad$ Lateral strain = $\mu \times e = 0.3 \times 4 \times 10^{-5} = 1.2 \times 10^{-5}$

But, $\quad$ Lateral strain = $\dfrac{\delta b}{b}$

$\therefore$ $\qquad$ $\delta b$ = Lateral strain × b = $1.2 \times 10^{-5} \times 50$

$\qquad$ = **$6 \times 10^{-4}$ mm (decrease)**

Since $\quad$ b = t, $\quad$ $\delta t$ = $\delta b$ = $6 \times 10^{-4}$ mm (decrease)

Volumetric strain of a square bar,

$$\frac{\delta V}{V} = e\,(1 - 2\,\mu)$$

$\therefore \qquad \delta V = V \cdot e\,(1 - 2\,\mu)$

$\therefore \qquad \boldsymbol{\delta V} = 75 \times 10^5 \times 4 \times 10^{-5}\,(1 - 2 \times 0.3) = \boldsymbol{120\ mm^3\ (increase)}$

**Answer :** (i) $\delta L = 0.12$ mm (increase), (ii) $\delta b = 6 \times 10^{-4}$ mm (decrease), (iii) $\delta V = 120$ mm$^3$ (increase)

---

**Example 39 :** *A steel bar 20 mm wide and 15 mm thick and 2 m long is subjected to an axial pull of 35 kN. If E = 2 × 10$^5$ N/mm$^2$ and μ = 0.3, calculate the alternation in length, width and thickness of the bar.* **(B.T.E. S-2013/4 Marks)**

**Data :** Width b = 20 mm, Thickness t = 15 mm, Length L = 2 m = 2000 mm,

Axial pull P = 35 kN = 35 × 10$^3$ N, E = 2 × 10$^5$ N/mm$^2$, μ = 0.3.

**To find :** (i) $\delta L$, (ii) $\delta b$, (iii) $\delta t$.

**Concept :** (i) $\delta L = \dfrac{PL}{AE}$, (ii) Lateral strain = $-\mu \times e$ i.e. $\dfrac{\delta t}{t} = -\mu \times e$, $\dfrac{\delta b}{b} = -\mu \times e$.

**Solution : (i) To calculate increase in length due to axial pull,**

$$\delta L = \frac{PL}{AE} = \frac{35 \times 10^3 \times 2000}{(20 \times 15) \times 2 \times 10^5} = 1.167 \text{ mm (increase)}$$

### (ii) To calculate decrease in width and thickness :

**Note :** Since the bar is subjected to axial pull, there will be increase in length of the bar and decrease in width and thickness.

$$\text{Linear strain, } e = \frac{\delta L}{L} = \frac{1.167}{2000} = \boldsymbol{5.83 \times 10^{-4}}$$

**Change in width ($\delta b$) :**

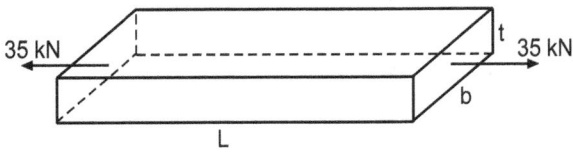

**Fig. 1.29**

$$\text{Lateral strain, } \frac{\delta b}{b} = -\mu \times e$$

$\therefore \qquad \dfrac{\delta b}{20} = -0.3 \times 5.83 \times 10^{-4}$

$\therefore \qquad \delta b = -3.498 \times 10^{-3}$ mm

Negative sign indicates decrease in width.

$\therefore \qquad \boldsymbol{\delta b = 3.498 \times 10^{-3}\ mm\ (decrease)}$

Also, lateral strain, $\dfrac{\delta t}{t} = -\mu \times e$

$$\therefore \qquad \frac{\delta t}{15} = -0.3 \times (5.83 \times 10^{-4})$$

$$\therefore \qquad \delta t = -2.62 \times 10^{-3} \text{ mm}$$

Negative sign indicates decrease in thickness.

$$\therefore \qquad \boldsymbol{\delta t = 2.62 \times 10^{-3} \text{ mm (decrease)}}$$

**Answer :** (i) $\delta L = 1.167$ mm (increase), (ii) $\delta b = 3.498 \times 10^{-3}$ mm (decrease), (iii) $\delta t = 2.62 \times 10^{-3}$ mm (decrease)

---

**Example 40 :** *A steel bar 1.2 m long, 40 mm wide and 20 mm thick is subjected to an axial tensile load of 50 kN in the direction of its length. Find the change in length and thickness of the bar. Take E = 2 ×10⁵ N/mm² and Poisson's ratio = 0.26.* **(B.T.E. S-2003/4 Marks)**

**Answer :** (i) $\delta L = 0.375$ mm (increase), (ii) $\delta t = 1.625 \times 10^{-3}$ mm (decrease)

---

**Example 41 :** *A steel bar 2 m long, 20 mm wide and 10 mm thick is subjected to an axial load of 20 kN in the direction of its length. Find the change in length, breadth, thickness and volume of a bar. Take E = 2 ×10⁵ N/mm² and m = 4.* **(V.V. Imp./4 Marks)**

**Hint :** $\frac{\delta V}{V} = e\,(1 - 2\mu)$

**Answer :** (i) $\delta L = 1$ mm (increase), (ii) $\delta b = 2.5 \times 10^{-3}$ mm (decrease), (iii) $\delta t = 1.25 \times 10^{-3}$ mm (decrease), (iv) $\delta V = 100$ mm³ (increase)

---

## Type 5.6 : Examples on calculating elastic constants μ, E, G and K.

**Example 42 :** *A metal bar of 40 mm × 40 mm in section is subjected to an axial compressive load of 500 kN. The contraction of 200 mm gauge length is found to be 0.6 mm and the increase in thickness is 0.04 mm.*

*Find the value of Poisson's ratio and the three elastic constants.* **(V.V.Imp./4 Marks)**

**Data :** Width b = thickness t = 40 mm, Area of bar, A = 40 × 40 = 1600 mm²

Axial compressive load, P = 500 kN = 500 × 10³ N

Original (Gauge) length L = 200 mm, Contraction i.e. decrease in length, δL = 0.6 mm, Increase in thickness δt = 0.04 mm

**To find :** μ, E, G and K.

**Concept :** Use of standard formulae, relation between E and G, relation between E and K.

**Solution :** Stress $\sigma = \dfrac{P}{A} = \dfrac{500 \times 10^3}{1600} = 312.5$ N/mm²

Linear strain $e = \dfrac{\delta L}{L} = \dfrac{0.6}{200} = 0.003$

**Young's modulus** $E = \dfrac{\sigma}{e} = \dfrac{312.5}{0.003} = 104166.67$ N/mm² **= 104.17 kN/mm²**

Lateral strain $= \dfrac{\delta t}{t} = \dfrac{0.04}{40} = 0.001$

We know that, $\mu = \dfrac{\text{Lateral strain}}{\text{Linear strain}} = \dfrac{0.001}{0.003} =$ **0.33**

Now, $E = 2G (1 + \mu)$

∴ $104.17 = 2G (1 + 0.33) = 2.66 \, G$

∴ $G = \dfrac{104.17}{2.66} =$ **39.16 kN/mm²**

Using the relation, $E = 3K (1 - 2\,\mu)$

∴ $104.17 = 3K (1 - 2 \times 0.33) = 1.02 \, K$

∴ $K = \dfrac{104.17}{1.02} =$ **102.12 kN/mm².**

**Answer :** (i) $\mu = 0.33$, (ii) $E = 104.17 \text{ kN/mm}^2$, (iii) $G = 39.16 \text{ kN/mm}^2$, (iv) $K = 102.12 \text{ kN/mm}^2$

**Example 43 :** *In a tension test on a certain specimen 20 mm diameter, 200 mm long, an axial pull of 100 kN produces an elongation 0.32 mm and reduction in diameter is observed to be 0.0085 mm. Find the value of Poisson's ratio and the three modulii.*

**(B.T.E. W-2007/4 Marks)**

**Data :** Diameter d = 20 mm, length L = 200 mm, Axial pull P = 100 kN = $100 \times 10^3$ N, Elongation $\delta L$ = 0.32 mm, Reduction in diameter $\delta d$ = 0.0085 mm.

**To find :** $\mu$, E, G and K.

**Concept :** Same as the above example.

**Solution :** Stress $\sigma = \dfrac{P}{A} = \dfrac{100 \times 10^3}{\dfrac{\pi}{4} \times (20)^2} = 318.3 \text{ N/mm}^2$

Linear strain $e = \dfrac{\delta L}{L} = \dfrac{0.32}{200} = 0.0016$

Young's modulus $\mathbf{E} = \dfrac{\sigma}{e} = \dfrac{318.3}{0.0016}$

$= 198937.5 \text{ N/mm}^2 =$ **198.94 kN/mm²**

For a circular specimen of diameter d,

Lateral strain $= \dfrac{\delta d}{d} = \dfrac{0.0085}{20} = 0.000425$

We know that, $\mu = \dfrac{\text{Lateral strain}}{\text{Linear strain}} = \dfrac{0.000425}{0.0016} =$ **0.265**

Now, $E = 2G (1 + \mu)$

$198.94 = 2G (1 + 0.265) = 2.53 \, G$

∴ $G = \dfrac{198.94}{2.53} =$ **78.63 kN/mm²**

Using the relation, $E = 3K (1 - 2\mu)$

$\therefore$                          $198.94 = 3K(1 - 2 \times 0.265) = 1.41\ K$

$\therefore$                          $K = \dfrac{198.94}{1.41} = \textbf{141.09 kN/mm}^2$

**Answer :** | (i) $\mu = 0.265$, (ii) $E = 198.94$ kN/mm$^2$, <br> (iii) $G = 78.63$ kN/mm$^2$, (iv) $K = 141.09$ kN/mm$^2$ |

---

**Example 44 :** *A metal rod of 20 mm diameter and 2 m long when subjected to a tensile force of 60 kN showed an elongation of 2 mm and reduction in diameter 0.006 mm. Calculate the modulus of elasticity and modulus of rigidity.* **(Imp./4 Marks)**

**Answer :** | (i) $E = 190.98$ kN/mm$^2$, (ii) $G = 73.45$ kN/mm$^2$ |

---

**Type 5.7 : Examples on bulk modulus and volumetric strain :**

**Example 45 :** *A cubical element is subjected to uniform tensile force of 320 kN along three mutually perpendicular directions. Determine the volumetric strain. Consider the side of cube as 20 mm.* **(B.T.E. S-1999/4 Marks)**

**Data**     : Direct tensile force $P = 320$ kN $= 320 \times 10^3$ N, Side of cube $L = 20$ mm.

**To find**  : $e_v$.

**Concept :** $e_v = \dfrac{\text{Direct stress}}{\text{Bulk modulus}} = \dfrac{\sigma}{K}$.

**Solution :**                **Direct stress** $= \dfrac{P}{A} = \dfrac{320 \times 10^3}{20 \times 20} = \textbf{800 N/mm}^2$

We know that, bulk modulus,   $K = \dfrac{\text{Direct stress}}{\text{Volumetric strain}}$

$\therefore$  Volumetric strain,          $\mathbf{e_v} = \dfrac{\text{Direct stress}}{\text{Bulk modulus}} = \dfrac{\textbf{800}}{\textbf{K}}$

**Answer :**     | $e_v = \dfrac{800}{K}$ | . Knowing K, $e_v$ can be calculated.

---

**Example 46 :** *A cube of 200 mm side is subjected to a compressive force of 3.6 MN on each face. The change in the volume of the cube is observed to be 5000 mm³. Compute the bulk modulus. If $\mu = 0.28$, find the Young's modulus.* **(V.V. Imp./4 Marks)**

**Data :** Side of cube = 200 mm, Area subjected to compression,

                    $A = 200 \times 200 = 4 \times 10^4$ mm$^2$

Compressive force    $P = 3.6$ MN (Mega Newton) $= 3.6 \times 10^6$ N,

Change in volume,   $\delta V = 5000$ mm$^3$, $\mu = 0.28$.

**To find :** K and E.

**Concept :** $K = \dfrac{\sigma}{\delta V/V}$

**Solution :** Direct compressive stress,

$$\sigma = \frac{P}{A} = \frac{3.6 \times 10^6}{4 \times 10^4} = 90 \text{ N/mm}^2$$

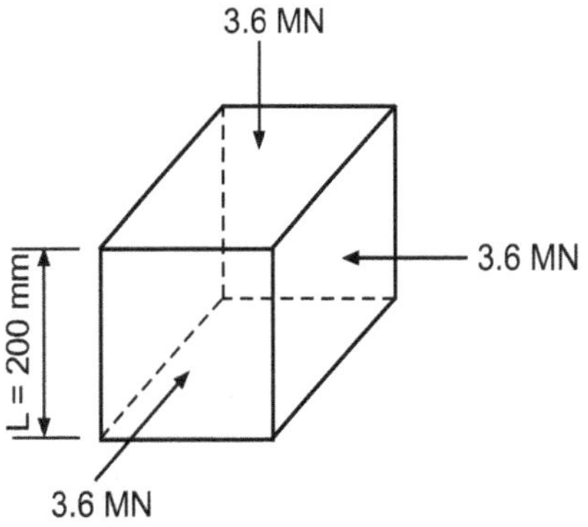

**Fig. 1.30**

Original volume,     $V = (200)^3 = 8 \times 10^6 \text{ mm}^3$

∴          Volumetric strain $= \dfrac{\delta V}{V} = \dfrac{5000}{8 \times 10^6} = 625 \times 10^{-6}$

By definition, bulk modulus, $\mathbf{K} = \dfrac{\sigma}{\dfrac{\delta V}{V}} = \dfrac{90}{625 \times 10^{-6}} = \mathbf{0.144 \times 10^6 \text{ N/mm}^2}$

Using the relation,     $E = 3K(1 - 2\mu) = 3 \times 0.144 \times 10^6 (1 - 2 \times 0.28)$

∴          $\mathbf{E = 0.190 \times 10^6 \text{ N/mm}^2.}$

**Answer :** (i) $K = 0.144 \times 10^6 \text{ N/mm}^2$, (ii) $E = 0.190 \times 10^6 \text{ N/mm}^2$

---

**Example 47 :** *A circular bar 200 mm long and 25 mm diameter is subjected to an axial pull od 50 kN. The change in diameter was observed to be 0.0047 mm. If the Young's modulus for the material is 135 kN/mm² and Poisson's ratio is 0.25, calculate the change in volume of a bar.* **(V.V. Imp./4 Marks)**

**Data :** L = 200 mm, d = 25 mm, P = 50 kN = $50 \times 10^3$ N,
     $\delta d = 0.0047$ mm, E = 135 kN/mm² = $135 \times 10^3$ N/mm², $\mu = 0.25$.

**To find :** $\delta V$.

**Concept :** For a circular bar, $\dfrac{\delta V}{V} = e(1 - 2\mu)$.

**Solution :** Stress in X-direction,

$$\sigma_X = \frac{P}{A} = \frac{50 \times 10^3}{\dfrac{\pi}{4} \times (25)^2} = 101.86 \text{ N/mm}^2$$

Strain in X-direction,

$$e = e_X = \frac{\sigma_X}{E} = \frac{101.86}{135 \times 10^3} = 0.0007545$$

Volume of bar,     $V = A \times L = \dfrac{\pi}{4} \times (25)^2 \times 200 = 98174.77 \text{ mm}^3$

We know that volumetric strain of a circular bar is given by,

$$\frac{\delta V}{V} = e\,(1 - 2\,\mu)$$

$\therefore$ $\qquad\qquad\qquad \delta V = V \cdot e\,(1 - 2\,\mu)$

$\therefore$ $\qquad\qquad\qquad \boldsymbol{\delta V} = 98174.77 \times 0.0007545\,(1 - 2 \times 0.25) = \boldsymbol{37 \text{ mm}^3}$

**Answer :**   $\boxed{\delta V = 37 \text{ mm}^3}$

---

**Example 48 :** *A cube of 100 mm side is subjected to a uniform tensile stress of 40 N/mm² on all faces. Calculate the increase in volume of the cube.*

*Take E = 1.9 × 10⁵ N/mm² and Poisson's ratio = 0.33.*

**(B.T.E. S-2006, 2003; W-2006/4 Marks)**

**Data :** Side of cube L = 100 mm, $\sigma$ = 40 N/mm² (tensile) on all faces,

E = $1.9 \times 10^5$ N/mm², $\mu$ = 0.33.

**To find :** $\delta V$.

**Concept :** $\dfrac{\delta V}{V} = \dfrac{3\sigma}{E}\,(1 - 2\mu)$

**Solution :** Volume of cube,

$$V = L^3 = (100)^3 = 1 \times 10^6 \text{ mm}^3$$

Volumetric strain of a cube subjected to three like stresses of equal intensity is given by,

$$\frac{\delta V}{V} = \frac{3\sigma}{E}\,(1 - 2\mu)$$

$\therefore$ $\qquad \boldsymbol{\delta V} = V \cdot \dfrac{3\sigma}{E}\,(1 - 2\mu) = (1 \times 10^6) \times \left(\dfrac{3 \times 40}{1.9 \times 10^5}\right)(1 - 2 \times 0.33)$

$\qquad\qquad = \boldsymbol{214.74 \text{ mm}^3}$

**Answer :**   $\boxed{\delta V = 214.74 \text{ mm}^3}$

---

**Example 49 :** *A cube of 300 mm side is subjected to a uniform tensile stress of 80 N/mm² on all faces. Calculate the increase in volume of the cube. Take E = 2 × 10⁵ N/mm² and Poisson's ratio = 0.3.*   **(B.T.E. W-2004/4 Marks)**

**Answer :** $\boxed{\delta V = 4320 \text{ mm}^3}$

---

**Type 5.8 : Miscellaneous examples :**

**Example 50 :** *A metal rod of 700 mm long, 28 mm in diameter is pulled with an axial tensile force of 52 kN. A uniform lateral pressure of 36 MPa is maintained over the entire surface of the rod. Calculate the change in length of a rod. Take E = 200 GPa, μ = 0.28.*

**(B.T.E. W-2012/4 Marks)**

**Data :** Metal rod d = 28 mm, L = 700 mm, P = 52 kN = $52 \times 10^3$ N,

Lateral pressure p = 36 MPa = 36 N/mm²,

E = 200 GPa = $200 \times 10^3$ N/mm² = $2 \times 10^5$ N/mm², $\mu$ = 0.28

**To find :** $\delta L$.

**Concept :** (i) Change in length due to axial pull P,

$$\delta L_1 = \frac{\text{Stress} \times L}{E} = \frac{\sigma L}{E} = \left(\frac{P}{A}\right)\frac{L}{E} = \frac{PL}{AE}$$

(ii) Change in length due to lateral pressure p,

$$\delta L_2 = \mu \times \frac{\text{Lateral pressure} \times L}{E} = \mu \left(\frac{p \times L}{E}\right)$$

**Solution :** (i) $\delta L$ due to force P,

$$\delta L_1 = \frac{PL}{AE} = \frac{52 \times 10^3 \times 700}{\frac{\pi}{4}(28)^2 \times (2 \times 10^5)} = \textbf{0.2956 mm}$$

(ii) $\delta L$ due to lateral pressure p,

$$\delta L_2 = \mu \times \frac{p \times L}{E} = 0.28 \times \frac{36 \times 700}{(2 \times 10^5)} = \textbf{0.0353 mm}$$

(iii) $\qquad \delta L = \delta L_1 + \delta L_2 = 0.2956 + 0.0353 = \textbf{0.3309 mm}$

**Answer :** $\boxed{\text{Change in length } \delta L = 0.3309 \text{ mm}}$

---

## SOLVED EXAMPLES

### Type 6 : Examples based on bi-axial and tri-axial stress system :

**Important Formulae**

For a bi-axial stress system,

$$e_x = \frac{\sigma_x}{E} - \mu\frac{\sigma_y}{E}$$

$$e_y = \frac{\sigma_y}{E} - \mu\frac{\sigma_x}{E}$$

$$e_z = -\mu\frac{\sigma_x}{E} - \mu\frac{\sigma_y}{E}$$

For a tri-axial stress system,

$$e_x = \frac{\sigma_x}{E} - \mu\frac{\sigma_y}{E} - \mu\frac{\sigma_z}{E}$$

$$e_y = \frac{\sigma_y}{E} - \mu\frac{\sigma_x}{E} - \mu\frac{\sigma_z}{E}$$

$$e_z = \frac{\sigma_z}{E} - \mu\frac{\sigma_x}{E} - \mu\frac{\sigma_y}{E}$$

Volumetric strain of a rectangular body subjected to a tri-axial loading is given by,

$$\frac{\delta V}{V} = e_x + e_y + e_z = \left(\frac{\sigma_x + \sigma_y + \sigma_z}{E}\right)(1 - 2\mu)$$

### Type 6.1 : Examples on bi-axial stress system :

**Example 51 :** *In a bi-axial stress system, the stresses along the two perpendicular directions are 100 N/mm² tensile (along X-direction) and 200 N/mm² compressive (along Y-direction). Calculate the magnitude and the nature of strains developed along these two directions. Assume μ = 0.25 and E = 2 × 10⁵ N/mm².*     **(B.T.E. S-2013, W-2000/4 Marks)**

**Data**     : $\sigma_x$ = + 100 N/mm², $\sigma_y$ = – 200 N/mm²

**To find**    : $e_x$, $e_y$ and their nature.

**Concept :** Formulae for bi-axial stress system.

**Solution :**     (i) $e_x = \dfrac{\sigma_x}{E} - \mu \dfrac{\sigma_y}{E} = \dfrac{1}{E}(\sigma_x - \mu \, \sigma_y) = \dfrac{1}{2 \times 10^5}[100 - 0.25 \times (-200)]$

$$= \dfrac{1}{2 \times 10^5} \times 150 = \mathbf{0.00075}$$

Since $e_x$ is positive, it is **tensile.**

$$e_x = \mathbf{0.00075 \ (tensile)}$$

(ii) $e_y = \dfrac{\sigma_y}{E} - \mu \dfrac{\sigma_x}{E} = \dfrac{1}{E}[\sigma_y - \mu \, \sigma_x] = \dfrac{1}{2 \times 10^5}[-200 - 0.25 \times 100]$

$$= \dfrac{1}{2 \times 10^5}[-200 - 25] = \mathbf{-0.001125}$$

Since $e_y$ is negative, it is **compressive.**

$$e_y = \mathbf{0.001125 \ (compressive)}$$

**Answer :** (i) $e_x$ = 0.00075 (tensile), (ii) $e_y$ = 0.001125 (compressive)

**Example 52 :** *In a bi-axial stress system, the stresses along the two perpendicular directions are 70 N/mm² (tensile) and 40 N/mm² (compressive). Calculate the strains along these two directions. Take E = 2.1 × 10⁵ N/mm² and Poisson's ratio = 0.28.*

**(B.T.E. S-2004, W-2004/4 Marks)**

**Data :** Bi-axial stress system, $\sigma_x$ = + 70 N/mm² (tensile), $\sigma_y$ = –40 N/mm² (compressive), E = 2.1 × 10⁵ N/mm², μ = 0.28.

**To find :** $e_x$ and $e_y$.

**Concept :** Formulae for bi-axial stress system.

**Solution :**

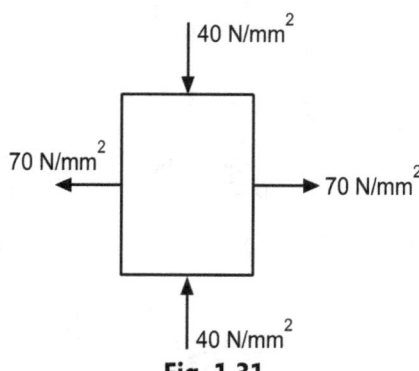

**Fig. 1.31**

(i)   Strain in X-direction, $e_x = \dfrac{\sigma_x}{E} - \mu\dfrac{\sigma_y}{E} = \dfrac{1}{E}(\sigma_x - \mu\sigma_y)$

$$= \dfrac{1}{2.1 \times 10^5}[70 - 0.28 \times (-40)] = \mathbf{38.66 \times 10^{-5}} \textbf{ (tensile)}$$

(ii)   Strain in Y-direction,

$$e_y = \dfrac{\sigma_y}{E} - \mu\dfrac{\sigma_x}{E} = \dfrac{1}{E}(\sigma_y - \mu\,\sigma_x)$$

$$= \dfrac{1}{2.1 \times 10^5}[-40 - 0.28 \times 70]$$

$$= \mathbf{-28.38 \times 10^{-5}} \textbf{ (compressive)}$$

**Answer :** $\boxed{\text{(i) } e_x = 38.66 \times 10^{-5} \text{ (tensile), (ii) } e_y = -28.38 \times 10^{-5} \text{ (compressive)}}$

**Example 53 :** *In a bi-axial stress system, the stresses along the two directions are* $\sigma_x = 50$ *N/mm²* *and* $\sigma_y = 30$ *N/mm²* *both tensile. Determine the strains along these two directions.* $E = 2 \times 10^5$ *N/mm², Poisson's ratio = 0.3.* **(B.T.E. S-2005/4 Marks)**

**Answer :** $\boxed{\text{(i) } e_x = 20.5 \times 10^{-5} \text{ (tensile), (ii) } e_y = 7.5 \times 10^{-5} \text{ (tensile)}}$

**Example 54 :** *Fig. 1.32 shows bi-axial stress system. Find the change in PQ and QR. Take* $E = 200$ *kN/mm²* *and* $\mu = 0.25.$ **(V.V. Imp./4 Marks)**

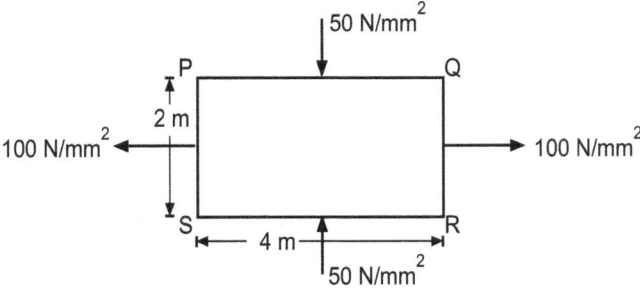

**Fig. 1.32**

**Hint :** Find $e_x$ and $e_y$. PQ = 4 m and QR = 2 m (Given)

From $e_x = \dfrac{\delta L_{PQ}}{PQ}$, find $\delta L_{PQ}$. From $e_y = \dfrac{\delta L_{QR}}{QR}$, find $\delta L_{QR}$.

**Answer :** $\boxed{\text{(i) } \delta L_{PQ} = 2.25 \text{ mm (increase), (ii) } \delta L_{QR} = 0.75 \text{ mm (decrease)}}$

**Example 55 :** *A steel flat is subjected to bi-axial tensile stresses. The tensile stress along X-direction is 42 N/mm². Determine the value of tensile stress along Y-direction if the strain in that direction is zero. What will be the strain in the X-direction if* $E = 2 \times 10^5$ *N/mm² and* $\mu = 0.3$ ? **(B.T.E. S-1985/4 Marks)**

**Data :** $\sigma_x = 42$ N/mm², $E = 2 \times 10^5$ N/mm², $\mu = 0.3$. If $e_y = 0$, $\sigma_y = ?$, $e_x = ?$

**Solution :** This is a case of bi-axial stress system.

For a bi-axial loading,

$$e_y = \frac{\sigma_y}{E} - \mu \frac{\sigma_x}{E} = \frac{1}{E}(\sigma_y - \mu\,\sigma_x)$$

$$\therefore \quad 0 = \frac{1}{2 \times 10^5}[\sigma_y - 0.3 \times 42]$$

$$\therefore \quad 0 = \sigma_y - 12.6$$

$$\therefore \quad \boldsymbol{\sigma_y = 12.6\ N/mm^2\ \textbf{(tensile)}}$$

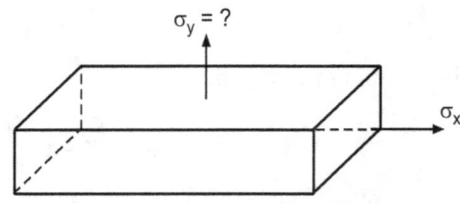

**Fig. 1.33**

Now, $e_x = \dfrac{\sigma_x}{E} - \mu\dfrac{\sigma_y}{E} = \dfrac{1}{E}(\sigma_x - \mu\,\sigma_y) = \dfrac{1}{2 \times 10^5}[42 - 0.3 \times 12.6]$

$$= 0.5 \times 10^{-5} \times 38.22 = \mathbf{1.911 \times 10^{-4}}\ \textbf{(tensile)}$$

**Answer :** $\boxed{\text{(i) } \sigma_y = 12.6\ N/mm^2 \text{ (tensile), (ii) } e_x = 1.911 \times 10^{-4} \text{ (tensile)}}$

**Example 56 :** *A steel plate having dimensions 360 mm × 220 mm × 30 mm is subjected to bi-axial normal stress as shown in Fig. 1.34. Assuming E = 204 GPa and μ = 0.27, calculate*

*(i)  Strain in the X-direction and (ii) Bulk modulus (K).*    **(B.T.E. W-2012/4 Marks)**

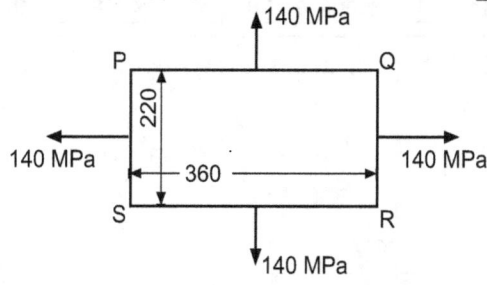

**Fig. 1.34**

**Data :** $\sigma_x = +140$ MPa $= 140$ N/mm$^2$, $\sigma_y = +140$ MPa $= 140$ N/mm$^2$,

       $E = 204$ GPa $= 204 \times 10^3$ N/mm$^2$, $\mu = 0.27$.

**To find :** (i) $e_x$, (ii) K.

**Concept :** (i) By definition,

$$\text{Bulk modulus, K} = \frac{\text{Direct stress}}{\text{Volumetric strain}} = \frac{\sigma}{(\delta V/V)}$$

(ii)  Strain in z-direction due to $\sigma_x$ and $\sigma_y$,

$$e_z = \frac{\sigma_z}{E} - \mu\frac{\sigma_x}{E} - \mu\frac{\sigma_y}{E} = -\mu\frac{\sigma_x}{E} - \mu\frac{\sigma_y}{E} \qquad \dots (\because \sigma_z = 0)$$

Though there is no stress in z-direction, there will be strain in z-direction due to $\sigma_x$ and $\sigma_y$.

**Solution :** (i)       $e_x = \dfrac{\sigma_x}{E} - \mu\dfrac{\sigma_y}{E} = \dfrac{1}{E}(\sigma_x - \mu\,\sigma_y)$

$$= \frac{1}{204 \times 10^3}(140 - 0.27 \times 140) = \mathbf{5.01 \times 10^{-4}}$$

(ii)  $\qquad e_y = \dfrac{\sigma_y}{E} - \mu \dfrac{\sigma_x}{E} = \dfrac{1}{E}(\sigma_y - \mu\,\sigma_x)$

$\qquad\qquad = \dfrac{1}{204 \times 10^3}(140 - 0.27 \times 140) = \mathbf{5.01 \times 10^{-4}}$

(iii)  $\qquad e_z = -\mu \dfrac{\sigma_x}{E} - \mu \dfrac{\sigma_y}{E}$

$\qquad\qquad = -\dfrac{\mu}{E}(\sigma_x + \sigma_y) = -\dfrac{0.27}{204 \times 10^3}(140 + 140) = \mathbf{-3.71 \times 10^{-4}}$

(iv) Volumetric strain,  $\quad e_v = e_x + e_y + e_z$

$\qquad\qquad = 5.01 \times 10^{-4} + 5.01 \times 10^{-4} - 3.71 \times 10^{-4} = \mathbf{6.31 \times 10^{-4}}$

(v)  $\qquad$ Bulk modulus, $\mathbf{K} = \dfrac{\sigma}{e_v} = \dfrac{140}{6.31 \times 10^{-4}} = \mathbf{2.22 \times 10^5 \ N/mm^2}$

**Answer :** $\boxed{\text{(i) } e_x = 5.01 \times 10^{-4}, \text{ (ii) } K = 2.22 \times 10^5 \ N/mm^2}$

## Type 6.2 : Volumetric strain of a rectangular body subjected to tri-axial loading :

**Example 57 :** *A steel bar 200 mm long, 40 mm × 30 mm in cross-section is subjected to a stress of 100 MPa along the length and 40 MPa on other two faces. All the stresses are tensile. The change in the volume of the bar was 125 mm³ under the tri-axial stress system. If E = 120 GPa, find Poisson's ratio.* **(B.T.E. S-2001/4 Marks)**

**Data**  $\quad$ : L = 200 mm, b = 40 mm, t = 30 mm, $\sigma_x$ = + 100 N/mm²

$\qquad\qquad \sigma_y = \sigma_z$ = + 40 N/mm², $\delta V$ = 125 mm³, E = 120 GPa = 120 × 10³ N/mm².

**To find** : $\mu$.

**Concept :** Volumetric strain of a rectangular bar subjected to tri-axial stress system.

$$\dfrac{\delta V}{V} = e_x + e_y + e_z = \left(\dfrac{\sigma_x + \sigma_y + \sigma_z}{E}\right)(1 - 2\mu)$$

**Solution :** (i) Volume of bar,

$\qquad\qquad \mathbf{V}$ = Area × Length

$\qquad\qquad$ = (b × t) × L = (40 × 30) × 200 = **240000 mm³**

(ii)  The volumetric strain of a rectangular bar subjected to tri-axial loading is given by,

$$\dfrac{\delta V}{V} = \dfrac{\sigma_x + \sigma_y + \sigma_z}{E}(1 - 2\mu)$$

$\therefore \qquad \dfrac{125}{240000} = \dfrac{100 + 40 + 40}{120 \times 10^3}(1 - 2\mu) = \dfrac{180}{120 \times 10^3}(1 - 2\mu)$

$\therefore \qquad 1 - 2\mu = \dfrac{125}{240000} \times \dfrac{120 \times 10^3}{180} = 0.3472$

$\therefore \qquad 2\mu = 1 - 0.3472 = 0.6528$

$\therefore \qquad \mu = \dfrac{0.6528}{2} = \mathbf{0.3264}$

**Answer :** $\boxed{\mu = 0.3264}$

**Example 58 :** *A cylindrical bar is 30 mm in diameter and 2000 mm long. The bar is subjected to uniform stress of 100 N/mm$^2$ in all directions. Calculate the modulus of rigidity and bulk modulus, if the modulus of elasticity is $1 \times 10^5$ N/mm$^2$ and Poisson's ratio 0.2.*

**(B.T.E. W-2006/4 Marks)**

**Data**     :   d = 30 mm, L = 2000 mm, $\sigma_x = \sigma_y = \sigma_z = \sigma$ = 100 N/mm$^2$, E = $1 \times 10^5$ N/mm$^2$,

$\mu$ = 0.2

**To find :**   (i) G, (ii) K.

**Concept :** When a body is subjected to a tri-axial stress system, its volumetric strain is given by,

$$\frac{\delta V}{V} = \frac{\sigma_x + \sigma_y + \sigma_z}{E} (1 - 2\mu)$$

Here          $\sigma_x = \sigma_y = \sigma_z = \sigma$

$\therefore$          $$\frac{\delta V}{V} = \frac{\sigma + \sigma + \sigma}{E} (1 - 2\mu) = \frac{3\sigma}{E} (1 - 2\mu)$$

**Solution :** (i)     $$\frac{\delta V}{V} = \frac{3\sigma}{E} (1 - 2\mu) \text{ gives,}$$

$$\frac{\delta V}{V} = \frac{3 \times 100}{1 \times 10^5} (1 - 2 \times 0.2) = 0.0018$$          ... (i)

(ii) **Bulk modulus,**     $K = \dfrac{\sigma}{\delta V/V} = \dfrac{100}{0.0018}$ = **55555.55 N/mm²**

(iii) Now,          E = 2G (1 + $\mu$)

$1 \times 10^5$ = 2G (1 + 0.2) = 2.4 G

$\therefore$          **G = 0.42 $\times$ 10⁵ N/mm²**

**Answer :** $\boxed{\text{(i) K = 55555.55 N/mm}^2\text{, (ii) G = } 0.42 \times 10^5 \text{ N/mm}^2}$

---

**Type 6.3 : Examples on a cube subjected to tri-axial stress system (calculating $e_x$, $e_y$, $e_z$ and $\delta V$).**

**Example 59 :** *A steel cube of 50 mm side is subjected to a force of 6 kN (tensile), 8 kN (compressive) and 4 kN (tensile) along x, y and z directions respectively. Determine the change in volume of the block. Take E as 200 GPa and m as 10/3.* **(B.T.E. W-2010, 4 Marks)**

**Data :** Side of cube L = 50 mm, Tensile force in x-direction, $P_x$ = 6 kN = $6 \times 10^3$ N,

Compressive force in y-direction, $P_y$ = $- 8$ kN = $- 8 \times 10^3$ N.

Tensile force in z-direction, $P_z$ = 4 kN = $4 \times 10^3$ N.

E = 200 GPa = $200 \times 10^3$ N/mm$^2$,  m = $\dfrac{10}{3}$,  $\mu = \dfrac{1}{m} = \dfrac{3}{10} = 0.3$

**To find :** $\delta V$.

**Concept :** (i) $\sigma_x = \dfrac{P_x}{A}$,   $\sigma_y = \dfrac{P_y}{A}$,   $\sigma_z = \dfrac{P_z}{A}$. (ii) Formulae for $e_x$, $e_y$, $e_z$.

(iii) $\dfrac{\delta V}{V} = e_x + e_y + e_z$.

### Solution : (i) Stresses in z-directions :

$$\sigma_x = \frac{P_x}{A} = \frac{6 \times 10^3}{50 \times 50} = +2.4 \text{ N/mm}^2 \text{ (tensile)}$$

$$\sigma_y = \frac{P_y}{A} = \frac{-8 \times 10^3}{50 \times 50} = -3.2 \text{ N/mm}^2 \text{ (compressive)}$$

$$\sigma_z = \frac{P_z}{A} = \frac{4 \times 10^3}{50 \times 50} = +1.6 \text{ N/mm}^2 \text{ (tensile)}$$

### (ii) Strains in three directions :

$$e_x = \frac{\sigma_x}{E} - \mu \frac{\sigma_y}{E} - \mu \frac{\sigma_z}{E} = \frac{1}{E} [\sigma_x - \mu (\sigma_y + \sigma_z)]$$

$$= \frac{1}{200 \times 10^3} [2.4 - 0.3 (-3.2 + 1.6)] = 1.44 \times 10^{-5}$$

$$e_y = \frac{\sigma_y}{E} - \mu \frac{\sigma_x}{E} - \mu \frac{\sigma_z}{E} = \frac{1}{E} [\sigma_y - \mu (\sigma_x + \sigma_z)]$$

$$= \frac{1}{200 \times 10^3} [-3.2 - 0.3 (2.4 + 1.6)] = -2.2 \times 10^{-5}$$

$$e_z = \frac{\sigma_z}{E} - \mu \frac{\sigma_x}{E} - \mu \frac{\sigma_y}{E} = \frac{1}{E} [\sigma_z - \mu (\sigma_x + \sigma_y)]$$

$$= \frac{1}{200 \times 10^3} [1.6 - 0.3 (2.4 - 3.2)] = 9.2 \times 10^{-6}$$

### (iii) Volumetric strain of a cube is given by

$$\frac{\delta V}{V} = e_x + e_y + e_z$$

$$\frac{\delta V}{(50)^3} = 1.44 \times 10^{-5} - 2.2 \times 10^{-5} + 9.2 \times 10^{-6} = 1.6 \times 10^{-6}$$

$$\delta V = 0.2 \text{ mm}^3$$

**Answer :** $\boxed{\delta V = 0.2 \text{ mm}^3}$

---

**Example 60 :** *A cube of 300 mm side is acted upon by stresses along the three directions as 70 N/mm² tensile, 10 N/mm² compressive, 70 N/mm² tensile.*

*Calculate the strains in all the three directions and change in volume of the cube.*

*Take E = 2 ×10⁵ N/mm², μ = 0.27.*                    **(B.T.E. W-2005/4 Marks)**

**Data :** Side of cube L = 300 mm, $\sigma_x$ = + 70 N/mm² (tensile),

$\sigma_y$ = −10 N/mm² (compressive), $\sigma_z$ = +70 N/mm² (tensile),

E = 2 × 10⁵ N/mm², μ = 0.27.

**To find :** $e_x$, $e_y$, $e_z$, $\delta V$.

**Concept :** Same as the above example.

**Solution :** (i)  $e_x = \dfrac{1}{E} [\sigma_x - \mu (\sigma_y + \sigma_z)]$

$$= \dfrac{1}{2 \times 10^5} [70 - 0.27 (-10 + 70)] = \textbf{26.9} \times \textbf{10}^{-5} \textbf{(tensile)}$$

(ii)  $e_y = \dfrac{1}{E} [\sigma_y - \mu (\sigma_x + \sigma_z)]$

$$= \dfrac{1}{2 \times 10^5} [-10 - 0.27 (70 + 70)] = \textbf{--23.9} \times \textbf{10}^{-5} \textbf{(compressive)}$$

(iii)  $e_z = \dfrac{1}{E} [\sigma_z - \mu (\sigma_x + \sigma_y)]$

$$= \dfrac{1}{2 \times 10^5} [70 - 0.27 [70 + (-10)]] = \textbf{26.9} \times \textbf{10}^{-5} \textbf{(tensile)}$$

(iv) Now,     $V = L^3 = (300)^3 = 9 \times 10^6 \, mm^3$

(v)  $\dfrac{\delta V}{V} = e_x + e_y + e_z$

$\therefore \quad \dfrac{\delta V}{9 \times 10^6} = 26.9 \times 10^{-5} - 23.9 \times 10^{-5} + 26.9 \times 10^{-5}$

$$= (26.9 - 23.9 + 26.9) \times 10^{-5} = 29.9 \times 10^{-5}$$

$\therefore \quad \boldsymbol{\delta V} = (29.9 \times 10^{-5}) \times (9 \times 10^6) = \textbf{2691 mm}^3 \textbf{ (increase)}$

**Answer :** (i) $e_x = 26.9 \times 10^{-5}$ (tensile), (ii) $e_y = -23.9 \times 10^{-5}$ (compressive), (iii) $e_z = 26.9 \times 10^{-5}$ (tensile), (iv) $\delta V = 2691 \, mm^3$ (increase)

**Try Yourself :**

**Example 61 :** *A cube of 150 mm side is acted upon by stresses along the three dimensions 20 N/mm² tensile, 10 N/mm² compressive and 20 N/mm² tensile. Calculate the strains in all the three directions and change in volume of the cube. Take E = 2 ×10⁵ N/mm²,* $\mu$ *= 0.25.*                    **(B.T.E. S-2006/4 Marks)**

**Answer :** (i) $e_x = 8.75 \times 10^{-5}$ (tensile), (ii) $e_y = -10 \times 10^{-5}$ (compressive), (iii) $e_z = 8.75 \times 10^{-5}$ (tensile), (iv) $\delta V = 253.125 \, mm^3$ (increase)

**Example 62 :** *A cube of 100 mm side is acted upon by stresses along the three directions such that $\sigma_x$ = 50 N/mm² (tensile), $\sigma_y$ = 40 N/mm² (compressive) and $\sigma_z$ = 30 N/mm² (tensile). Find*

(i)  *Strains in each direction,*

(ii) *Change in the volume of a cube,*

(iii) *If $\sigma_z$ = 0, what will be the strain along Z-direction ?*

*Take E = 2 ×10⁵ N/mm², $\mu$ = 0.25.*                    **(V.V. Imp./4 Marks)**

**Hint :** (i) Formulae for tri-axial stress system, (ii) $\dfrac{\delta V}{V} = e_x + e_y + e_z$. Refer to Fig. 1.35.

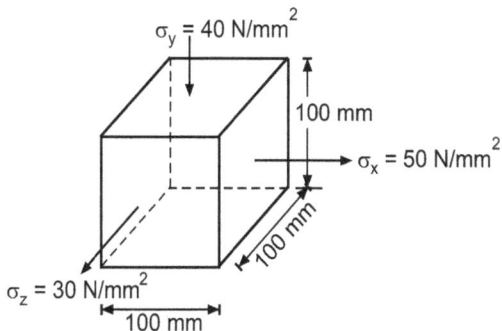

**Fig. 1.35**

**Answer :** (i) $e_x = 0.0002625$ (tensile), (ii) $e_y = -0.0003$ (compressive), (iii) $e_z = 0.0001375$ (tensile), (iv) $\delta V = 100$ mm$^3$ (increase), (v) If $\sigma_z = 0$, $e_z = 0.0000125$ (compressive)

**Example 63 :** *Calculate the strain induced in a cube of 400 mm side in X, Y and Z, if it is subjected to 300 N/mm$^2$ tensile stress in X direction, 500 N/mm$^2$ tensile stress in Y direction and 200 N/mm$^2$ compressive stress in Z direction.* **(B.T.E. S-2011/4 Marks)**

**Data :** Side of cube L = 400 mm, $\sigma_x = +300$ N/mm$^2$ (tensile), $\sigma_y = +500$ N/mm$^2$ (tensile), $\sigma_z = -200$ N/mm$^2$ (compressive).

**Note :** Value of E and $\mu$ is not given here. Hence calculate $e_x$, $e_y$, $e_z$ in terms of E and $\mu$.

**To find :** $e_x$, $e_y$, $e_z$.

**Solution :** (i) $e_x = \dfrac{1}{E}[\sigma_x - \mu(\sigma_y + \sigma_z)] = \dfrac{1}{E}[300 - \mu(500 - 200)] = \dfrac{1}{E}(300 - 300\,\mu)$

... Ans.

(ii) $e_y = \dfrac{1}{E}[\sigma_y - \mu(\sigma_x + \sigma_z)] = \dfrac{1}{E}[500 - \mu(300 - 200)] = \dfrac{1}{E}[500 - 100\,\mu]$

... Ans.

(iii) $e_z = \dfrac{1}{E}[\sigma_z - \mu(\sigma_x + \sigma_y)]$

$= \dfrac{1}{E}[-200 - \mu(300 + 500)] = \dfrac{1}{E}[-200 - 800\,\mu]$     ... Ans.

**Type 6.4 : A rectangular block subjected to tri-axial stress system (calculating $e_x$, $e_y$, $e_z$ and $\delta V$).**

**Example 64 :** *In a tri-axial stress system, the stresses along the three directions are $\sigma_x = 100$ N/mm$^2$ (tensile), $\sigma_y = 60$ N/mm$^2$ (tensile) and $\sigma_z = 30$ N/mm$^2$ (compressive). Find the strains in each direction. Take E = 2 × 10$^5$ N/mm$^2$ and $\mu = 0.25$.* **(V.V. Imp./4 Marks)**

*If x = 400 mm, y = 150 mm and z = 300 mm, calculate the change in volume.*

**Data :** $\sigma_x = 100$ N/mm$^2$, $\sigma_y = 60$ N/mm$^2$, $\sigma_z = -30$ N/mm$^2$,

E = 2 × 10$^5$ N/mm$^2$, $\mu = 0.25$, x = 400 mm, y = 150 mm, z = 300 mm.

**To find :** $e_x$, $e_y$, $e_z$, $\delta V$.

**Solution :**

(i) $\quad\quad\quad e_x = \dfrac{1}{E}[\sigma_x - \mu(\sigma_y + \sigma_z)] = \dfrac{1}{2 \times 10^5}[100 - 0.25(60 - 30)]$

$\quad\quad\quad\quad\quad = \dfrac{1}{2 \times 10^5} \times 92.5 = \textbf{0.0004625 (tensile)}$

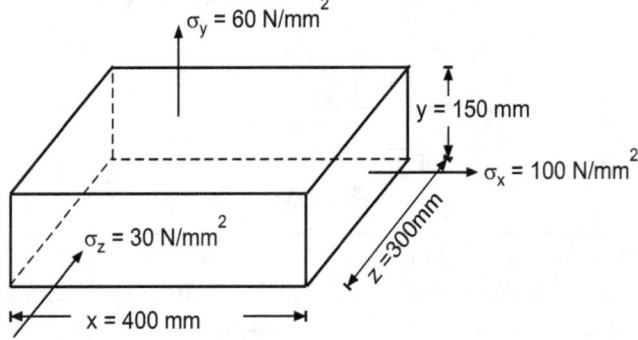

**Fig. 1.36**

(ii) $\quad\quad\quad e_y = \dfrac{1}{E}[\sigma_y - \mu(\sigma_x + \sigma_z)] = \dfrac{1}{2 \times 10^5}[60 - 0.25(100 - 30)]$

$\quad\quad\quad\quad\quad = \dfrac{1}{2 \times 10^5} \times 42.5 = \textbf{0.0002125 (tensile)}$

(iii) $\quad\quad\quad e_z = \dfrac{1}{E}[\sigma_z - \mu(\sigma_x + \sigma_y)] = \dfrac{1}{2 \times 10^5}[-30 - 0.25(100 + 60)]$

$\quad\quad\quad\quad\quad = \dfrac{1}{2 \times 10^5} \times (-70) = -0.00035$

$\therefore \quad\quad\quad e_z = \textbf{- 0.00035 (compressive)}$

(iv) Here,

$\quad\quad$ volume $V = x \times y \times z = 400 \times 150 \times 300 = 18 \times 10^6$ mm$^3$

(v) Now, volumetric strain of a rectangular body subjected to tri-axial loading is given by,

$$\frac{\delta V}{V} = \frac{\sigma_x + \sigma_y + \sigma_z}{E}(1 - 2\mu) = \left(\frac{100 + 60 - 30}{2 \times 10^5}\right)(1 - 2 \times 0.25)$$

$$= 0.00065 \times 0.5 = 0.000325$$

$\therefore \quad\quad\quad \delta V = V \times 0.000325 = 18 \times 10^6 \times 0.000325 = \textbf{5850 mm}^3$

Or volumetric strain can also be calculated by using the relation,

$$\frac{\delta V}{V} = e_x + e_y + e_z = 0.0004625 + 0.0002125 - 0.00035 = 0.000325$$

$\therefore \quad\quad\quad \delta V = V \times 0.000325 = 18 \times 10^6 \times 0.000325 = \textbf{5850 mm}^3 \textbf{ (increase)}$

Hence, the change in volume is 5850 mm$^3$.

**Answer :** | (i) $e_x$ = 0.0004625 (tensile), (ii) $e_y$ = 0.0002125 (tensile),
(iii) $e_z$ = - 0.00035 (compressive), (iv) $\delta V$ = 5850 mm$^3$ (increase)

**Example 65 :** *A rectangular block of size x = 600 mm, y = 800 mm and z = 1000 mm is subjected to a tri-axial stress system. The stresses in the three mutually perpendicular directions are $\sigma_x$ = 100 N/mm² (tensile), $\sigma_y$ = 100 N/mm² (tensile) and $\sigma_z$ = 100 N/mm² (compressive). Find the net strain in each direction and hence the change in the volume of the block. Take E = 200 kN/mm² and m = 3.* **(B.T.E. S-2007/4 Marks)**

**Hint :** $V = x \cdot y \cdot z = 600 \times 800 \times 1000 = 48 \times 10^7$ mm³

**Answer :** | (i) $e_x = e_y = 0.5 \times 10^{-3}$ (tensile), (ii) $e_z = -0.83 \times 10^{-3}$ (compressive), (iii) $\delta V = -8.16 \times 10^4$ mm³ (decrease) |

# (D) THERMAL STRESSES-TEMPERATURE STRESSES AND STRAINS OF UNIFORM SECTIONS

## 1.41 TEMPERATURE STRESSES AND STRAINS IN UNIFORM BAR

Whenever there is an increase or decrease in the temperature of a body, there is corresponding increase or decrease in its dimensions. When a body is free to expand or contract due to rise or fall of the temperature, no stresses are induced in the body. *But, if this expansion or contraction due to temperature variation is wholly or partially prevented by application of external forces, some stresses are induced in the body. Such stresses are known as temperature stresses and the corresponding strains due to temperature stresses are called the temperature strains.*

Let the body of uniform section and length L be heated through t°C. The length of the body will increase depending upon its coefficient of linear expansion $\alpha$ (expressed in /°C). *The increase in length due to increase in temperature when the body is free to expand will be*

$$\delta L = \alpha \cdot t \cdot L$$

Now, if this expansion due to increase in temperature is prevented by applying external compressive force or by fixing the body to rigid supports, then *compressive stress* and *compressive strain* will be induced in the body.

$$\text{Compressive strain } e = \frac{\text{Change in length}}{\text{Original length}}$$

$$\therefore \qquad\qquad e = \frac{\delta L}{L} = \frac{\alpha\, tL}{L}$$

$\therefore$ Temperature strain, $\boxed{e = \alpha\, t}$

From Hooke's law, $\qquad E = \dfrac{\text{Stress}}{\text{Strain}}$

$\therefore \qquad\qquad$ Compressive stress $= E \times$ Compressive strain

$\therefore \qquad\qquad\qquad \sigma = E \times \alpha\, t$

$\therefore$ Temperature stress, $\boxed{\sigma = \alpha\, tE}$

(Conversely, if the body is subjected to decrease in temperature, decrease in the length of the body due to decrease in temperature will be $\alpha tL$. If this contraction is prevented by applying external tensile force or by fixing the body to rigid supports, then tensile stress and tensile strain will be induced in the body.)

**Note :** *Sometimes supports slip (yield) by an amount equal to $\delta$, then the expansion prevented will be $\delta L = \alpha t L - \delta$.*

In this case, temperature strain

$$e = \frac{\delta L}{L} = \frac{\alpha t L - \delta}{L} = \alpha t - \frac{\delta}{L}$$

Temperature stress, $\qquad \sigma = e \cdot E = \left(\alpha t - \frac{\delta}{L}\right) E$

---

1.  A metal rod when heated expands freely. State the nature of stress induced.

    **(B.T.E. W-2009/2 Marks)**

2.  A bar fixed at one end and free at other end is heated through t°C. What is the temperature stress induced in the bar material ? **(B.T.E. S-1999/2 Marks)**

3.  What are temperature stresses ? How are they produced ? **(2 Marks)**

---

## SOLVED EXAMPLES

**Type 7 : Examples based on temperature stresses and strains in uniform bar :**

---

### Important Formulae

Temperature deformation, $\delta L = \alpha t L$

Temperature strain, $e = \dfrac{\delta L}{L} = \dfrac{\alpha t L}{L} = \alpha \cdot t$

Temperature stress, $\sigma = \alpha t \cdot E$

---

**Example 66 :** *A rod 10 m long at 10°C is heated to 70°C. If the free expansion is prevented, find the magnitude and nature of stress induced. Take $E = 2.1 \times 10^5$ N/mm$^2$, $\alpha = 12 \times 10^{-6}$/°C.* **(B.T.E. W-2009, 1998/4 Marks)**

**Data :** L = 10 m = $10 \times 10^3$ mm, $t_1 = 10°C$, $t_2 = 70°C$,

$\qquad$ $E = 2.1 \times 10^5$ N/mm$^2$, $\alpha = 12 \times 10^{-6}$/°C

**To find :** (i) Temperature stress, (ii) Nature of temperature stress.

**Concept :** (i) Increase in length due to increase in temperature when the body is free to expand, $\delta L = \alpha t L$.

(ii) If the expansion due to increase in temperature is prevented then compressive stress and compressive strain will be induced in the body.

**Solution :** (i) Rise in temperature, $t = t_2 - t_1 = 70 - 10 = 60°C$

(ii) Free expansion of the rod, $\delta L = \alpha t L = (12 \times 10^{-6}) \times 60 \times (10 \times 10^3) = 7.2$ mm.

If this expansion is prevented, compressive stress will be induced in the rod.

$\therefore$ **Compressive stress, $\sigma = \alpha t E = (12 \times 10^{-6}) \times 60 \times 2.1 \times 10^5 = $ 151.2 N/mm$^2$**

**Answer :** (i) $\sigma = 151.2$ N/mm$^2$, (ii) Nature of $\sigma$ : compressive

**Example 67 :** *A steel rod 4.5 m long is at a temperature of 28°C. Find the free expansion of the rod when the temperature is raised to 78°C. If this expansion is completely prevented, find the magnitude and nature of temperature stress and strain developed.*

**(B.T.E. S-2012, 2000/4 Marks)**

**Data**       : Steel rod : length L = 4.5 m = 4500 mm, $t_1$ = 28°C, $t_2$ = 78°C.

**To find**   : Temperature, stress, strain and its nature.

**Solution :** Rise in temperature, **t** = $t_2 - t_1$ = 78 – 28 = **50°C**

For steel, since E and $\alpha$ are not given, assume E = $2 \times 10^5$ N/mm² and $\alpha = 12 \times 10^{-6}$/°C.

Free expansion of rod,       $\delta L$ = $\alpha \, t \, L$ = $12 \times 10^{-6} \times 50 \times 4500$ = 2.7 mm

If this expansion is completely prevented by fixing the rod to rigid supports or by applying compressive force at the ends, compressive stress and compressive strain will be induced in the rod.

**Answer :**

> **Compressive stress,**  $\sigma$ = $\alpha \, t \, E$ = $12 \times 10^{-6} \times 50 \times 2 \times 10^5$ = **120 N/mm²**
>
> **Compressive strain,**    e = $\alpha \, t$ = $12 \times 10^{-6} \times 50$ = **$6 \times 10^{-4}$**

**Example 68 :** *A steel rod 20 mm in diameter and 1.2 m long is heated through 120°C and at the same time subjected to a pull 'P'. If the total extension of the rod is 3 mm, what should be the magnitude of P ? Take $\alpha_s = 12 \times 10^{-6}$/°C and $E_s$ = 200 GPa.*

**(B.T.E. S-2011, 2008/4 Marks)**

**Data :** Diameter of steel rod, d = 20 mm, Length L = 1.2 m = $1.2 \times 10^3$ mm,

Temperature rise t = 120°C, Total extension, $\delta L$ = 3 mm, $\alpha_s = 12 \times 10^{-6}$/°C,

$E_s$ = 200 GPa = $200 \times 10^3$ N/mm².

**To find :** P.

**Concept :** Total extension of the rod is the sum of elongation due to P and elongation due to heating i.e. $\delta L = \delta L_1 + \delta L_2$.

**Solution :** (i) **Elongation due to P :**

$$\delta L_1 = \frac{PL}{AE} = \frac{P \times 1.2 \times 10^3}{\frac{\pi}{4}(20)^2 \times (200 \times 10^3)} = 0.000019098 \, P$$

(ii) **Elongation due to heating :**

$$\delta L_2 = \alpha_s \, t \, L = 12 \times 10^{-6} \times 120 \times 1.2 \times 10^3 = 1.728 \text{ mm}$$

(iii) Now,    Total extension $\delta L$ = $\delta L_1 + \delta L_2$

$$3 = 0.000019098 \, P + 1.728$$

∴          $0.000019098 \, P$ = 3 – 1.728 = 1.272

∴          $P = \dfrac{1.272}{0.000019098}$ = **66603.83 N**

**Answer :**    $\boxed{P = 66603.83 \text{ N} = 66.6 \text{ kN}}$

## Similar example for practice :

**Example 69 :** *A rod 300 mm long and 20 mm in diameter is heated through 100 °C and at the same time pulled by a force P. If the total extension is 0.4 mm, what is the magnitude of P ? E = 2 × 10⁵ N/mm² and α = 12 × 10⁻⁶/°C.* **(B.T.E. S-2015, 2010/4 Marks)**

**Answer :**   $P = 8.37 \text{ kN}$

---

**Example 70 :** *A square rod 10 mm × 10 mm in cross-section and 1000 mm long is fixed at both ends. Determine the end reactions due to rise in temperature of 50°C. Take E = 2 × 10⁵ MPa and α = 12 × 10⁻⁶ / °C.* **(B.T.E. S-2013, W-1999/4 Marks)**

**Data**     : A = 10 × 10 = 100 mm², L = 1000 mm, t = 50°C,

E = 2 × 10⁵ MPa = 2 × 10⁵ N/mm², α = 12 × 10⁻⁶/°C.

**To find** : End reactions i.e. force required to prevent the expansion.

**Solution :** Temperature stress,   $\sigma = \alpha \, t \, E = (12 \times 10^{-6}) \times (50) \times (2 \times 10^5)$

= 120 N/mm² (Compressive)

Free expansion of rod,   $\delta L = \alpha \, t \, L = 12 \times 10^{-6} \times 50 \times 1000 =$ **0.6 mm**

**Answer :**
> **Force required to prevent this expansion (end reactions)**
> = Stress × Area = 120 × 100 = 12000 N = **12 kN**

---

**Example 71 :** *A steel bar of 30 mm diameter is heated to 80°C and then clamped at the ends. It is then allowed to cool down to 30°C. During cooling, only 1 mm contraction was allowed. Calculate the temperature stress developed and reactions at the clamps. Take length of the bar = 10 m, α = 12 × 10⁻⁶/°C, E = 200 GPa.* **(B.T.E. W-2010, S-2006/4 Marks)**

**Data :**     Diameter d = 30 mm, fall in temperature t = 80 – 30 = 50°C,

δ = 1 mm, L = 10 m = 10 × 10³ mm, α = 12 × 10⁻⁶/°C,

E = 200 GPa = 200 × 10³ N/mm² = 2 × 10⁵ N/mm².

**Note :**     Since 1 GPa = 1 × 10³ N/mm²,  200 GPa = 200 × 10³ N/mm².

**To find :**  σ, P.

**Solution :**  Actual contraction of bar, $\delta L = \alpha t L - \delta$

∴     Temperature strain  $= \dfrac{\delta L}{L} = \dfrac{\alpha t L - \delta}{L} = \dfrac{12 \times 10^{-6} \times 50 \times 10 \times 10^3 - 1}{10 \times 10^3}$

$= 5 \times 10^{-4}$ (Tensile)

**Answer :**

> **Stress**, σ = strain × E = $5 \times 10^{-4} \times 2 \times 10^5$ = **100 N/mm² (Tensile)**
>
> **Reaction at ends = Pull P** = σ × A = $100 \times \dfrac{\pi}{4}(30^2)$ = **70685.8 N**

---

**Example 72 :** *A hollow circular steel tube is 1000 mm in length. It is rigidly fixed at its ends at 80 °C. If the temperature of the tube is lowered to 40 °C, determine the magnitude and the nature of stresses developed. Take E = 2 × 10⁵ N/mm² and α = 12 × 10⁻⁶/°C.*

**(V.V. Imp./4 Marks)**

**Data :** Length of tube L = 100 mm, Initial temperature $t_1$ = 80°C,

Final temperature $t_2$ = 40°C.

∴   Fall of temperature t = 80 – 40 = 40°C, E = $2 \times 10^5$ N/mm², α = $12 \times 10^{-6}$/°C

**To find :** σ and its nature.

**Solution :** Since the ends of the tube are fixed, this contraction will be prevented, due to which tensile stress will be induced in the tube.

∴   **Tensile stress, σ** = α t E = $12 \times 10^{-6} \times 40 \times 2 \times 10^5$ = **96 N/mm²**

**Answer :** $\boxed{\text{σ = 96 N/mm}^2 \text{ (tensile)}}$

---

**Example 73 :** *A 30 m long rail is prevented from expansion at either end. If the temperature is raised by 30 ℃, what stress will be induced in the rail if the coefficient of linear expansion is $12 \times 10^{-6}$/℃. Take E = $2 \times 10^5$ N/mm².* **(V.V. Imp./4 Marks)**

**Data :** L = 30 m = $30 \times 10^3$ mm, temperature rise t = 30°C,

α = $12 \times 10^{-6}$/°C, E = $2 \times 10^5$ N/mm².

**To find :** σ.

**Solution :** Stress, σ = α t E = $12 \times 10^{-6} \times 30 \times 2 \times 10^5$ = **72 N/mm² (compressive)**

**Answer :** $\boxed{\text{σ = 72 N/mm}^2 \text{ (compressive)}}$

---

**Example 74 :** *A steel rod 10 mm diameter and 2 m in length is at 25 ℃. Find the new length of the rod if the temperature is raised to 70 ℃. Find the magnitude and the nature of the force required to prevent this expansion. Take $E_s$ = $2 \times 10^5$ N/mm² and $α_s$ = $12 \times 10^{-6}$/℃.* **(V.V. Imp./4 Marks)**

**Data :** d = 10 mm, L = 2 m = 2000 mm, $t_1$ = 25°C, $t_2$ = 70°C,

Rise in temperature, t = $t_2 - t_1$ = 70 – 25 = 45°C, $E_s$ = $2 \times 10^5$ N/mm², $α_s$ = $12 \times 10^{-6}$/°C

**To find :** F and its nature.

**Solution :** Area of rod, A = $\frac{\pi}{4} d^2 = \frac{\pi}{4} (10)^2$ = 78.54 mm²

Temperature stress   σ = α t E = $12 \times 10^{-6} \times 45 \times 2 \times 10^5$ = 108 N/mm² (compressive)

Free expansion of the rod,

$$δL = αt L = 12 \times 10^{-6} \times 45 \times 2000 = 1.08 \text{ mm}$$

∴   New length of the rod at 70°C

$$= L + δL = 2000 + 1.08 = 2001.08 \text{ mm}$$

Force required to prevent the expansion,

$$F = \text{Stress} \times \text{Area} = 108 \times 78.54 = 8482.2 \text{ N} = \textbf{8.48 kN}$$

**Answer :** $\boxed{\text{F = 8.48 kN (compressive)}}$

---

**Example 75 :** *A copper bar 16 mm $\phi$ is heated through 50 ℃. If 50% of its elongation is prevented, find the magnitude and the nature of stress induced. Take E = 100 kN/mm², $α_c$ = $18 \times 10^{-6}$/℃, L = 1200 mm.* **(V.V. Imp./4 Marks)**

**Data :** d = 16 mm, t = 50°C, L = 1200 mm, E = 100 kN/mm² = $100 \times 10^3$ N/mm²,

$α_c$ = $18 \times 10^{-6}$/°C.

**To find :** $\sigma$ and its nature.

**Solution :** Free elongation of the rod,

$$\delta L = \alpha_c \, t \, L = 18 \times 10^{-6} \times 50 \times 1200 = 1.08 \text{ mm}$$

$$\text{Elongation prevented } = 50\% \text{ of } \delta L = \frac{50}{100} \times \delta L = \frac{\delta L}{2}$$

$$\delta L_1 = \frac{1.08}{2} = 0.54 \text{ mm}$$

$$\text{Strain induced} = \frac{\delta L_1}{L} = \frac{0.54}{1200} = 0.00045$$

$\therefore$ **Stress induced** $= \text{strain} \times E = 0.00045 \times 100 \times 10^3 = $ **45 N/mm²**

**Answer :** $\boxed{\sigma = 45 \text{ N/mm}^2 \text{ ... Magnitude}}$

Since elongation is prevented, stress induced will be of compressive nature.

**Example 76 :** *A steel rod 1 m long is fixed at the ends and subjected to a pull of 9 kN. Determine the residual stress due to an increase of 20°C. Diameter of bar = 12 mm, E = 200 kN/mm², $\alpha = 16 \times 10^{-6}/°C$.* **(B.T.E. W-1988)**

**Data :** Length of rod L = 1 m = 1000 mm, Pull P = 9 kN = 9000 N,

bar diameter, d = 12 mm, increase in temperature t = 20°C,

E = 200 kN/mm² = $200 \times 10^3$ N/mm², $\alpha = 16 \times 10^{-6}/°C$.

**To find :** Residual (remaining) stress due to increase in temperature of 20°C.

**Solution :** Initial stress in the rod due to a pull of 9000 N is given by

$$\sigma_1 = \frac{P}{A} = \frac{9000}{\dfrac{\pi}{4}(12)^2} = 79.58 \text{ N/mm}^2 \text{ (Tensile)}$$

There will be an increase in length due to rise in temperature and if this elongation is prevented, the compressive stress will be induced in the rod.

$$\sigma_2 = \alpha \, t \, E = 16 \times 10^{-6} \times 20 \times 200 \times 10^3 = 64 \text{ N/mm}^2 \text{ (Compressive)}$$

$\therefore$ **Residual stress** $= \sigma = \sigma_1 \text{ (Tensile)} - \sigma_2 \text{ (Compressive)}$

$$= 79.58 - 64 = \textbf{15.58 N/mm}^2 \textbf{ (Tensile)}$$

**Answer :** $\boxed{\text{Residual stress} = 15.58 \text{ N/mm}^2 \text{ (Tensile)}}$

**Example 77 :** *A metal rod 16 mm diameter, 1500 mm long is loosely held. If the supports slip by 0.5 mm due to rise in temperature of 60°C, find the stress developed in the rod and its nature. Take E = 110 kN/mm², $\alpha = 12 \times 10^{-6}/°C$.* **(B.T.E. W-1994)**

**Data :** Diameter d = 16 mm, length L = 1500 mm, $\delta = 0.5$ mm, t = 60°C,

E = $110 \times 10^3$ N/mm², $\alpha = 12 \times 10^{-6}/°C$.

**To find :** The stress developed and its nature.

**Solution :** Free expansion of the rod is

$$\delta L_1 = \alpha t \, L = 12 \times 10^{-6} \times 60 \times 1500 = 1.08 \text{ mm}$$

Since the supports slip by 0.5 mm, the actual expansion that have taken place will be

$$\delta L_2 = \alpha t\, L - \delta = 1.08 - 0.5 = 0.58 \text{ mm}$$

If the expansion is prevented, compressive stress will be induced in the rod.

$$\text{Compressive strain} = \frac{\delta L_2}{L} = \frac{0.58}{1500} = 3.87 \times 10^{-4}$$

$\therefore$ **Compressive stress** $= \text{Compressive strain} \times E = 3.87 \times 10^{-4} \times 110 \times 10^3$

$$= \textbf{42.53 N/mm}^2$$

**Answer :** $\boxed{\sigma = 42.53 \text{ N/mm}^2 \text{ (Compressive)}}$

---

**Example 78 :** *A steel rod is subjected to a pull of 10 kN and rigidly fixed at the ends at a certain temperature. Find the magnitude of the stress and its nature due to the change in temperature by 20°C (both rise and fall). Area of the bar is 200 mm². E = 200 GPa, $\alpha = 12 \times 10^{-6}/$°C.* **(B.T.E. S-1995)**

**Data :** Pull P = 10 kN = $10 \times 10^3$ N, t = 20°C (increase or decrease), Area A = 200 mm²,
    E = 200 GPa = $200 \times 10^3$ N/mm², $\alpha = 12 \times 10^{-6}/$°C.

**To find :** Magnitude and nature of the stress due to rise and fall of temperature.

**Solution :**

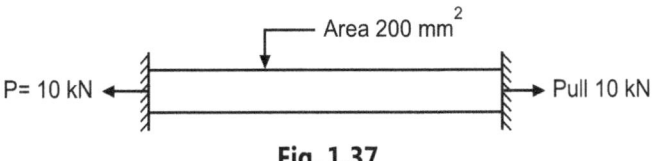

**Fig. 1.37**

Initial stress in the rod due to a pull of 10 kN (if the ends of the rod are not fixed)

$$\sigma_1 = \frac{P}{A} = \frac{10 \times 10^3}{200} = 50 \text{ N/mm}^2 \text{ (Tensile)}$$

If the rod is fixed at both the ends, the stress developed in the rod due to rise or fall in temperature is

$$\sigma_2 = \alpha\, t\, E = 12 \times 10^{-6} \times 20 \times 200 \times 10^3$$
$$= 48 \text{ N/mm}^2 \text{ (Tensile or compressive)}$$

If the rod is subjected to rise in temperature 20°C, there will be a compressive stress in the rod.

i.e.	$$\sigma_2 = -48 \text{ N/mm}^2$$

$\therefore$ **Total stress due to rise in temperature = 50 – 48 = 2 N/mm² (Tensile)**

If the rod is subjected to fall in temperature 20°C, there will be a tensile stress in the rod.

i.e.	$$\sigma_2 = +48 \text{ N/mm}^2$$

$\therefore$ **Total stress due to fall in temperature = 50 + 48 = 98 N/mm² (Tensile)**

**(Sign convention :** Compressive stress is negative, while tensile stress is positive).

**Answer :** $\boxed{\begin{array}{l} \text{(i) } \sigma = 2 \text{ N/mm}^2 \text{ (tensile) due to rise in temperature,} \\ \text{(ii) } \sigma = 98 \text{ N/mm}^2 \text{ (tensile) due to fall in temperature} \end{array}}$

**Example 79 :** *A rolled steel joist 6 metre long is at 15 ℃. Calculate its elongation when the temperature is 40 ℃. If the elongation is prevented, calculate the stress induced in a section and the thrust exerted if the area of the section is 4808 mm².*

$\alpha$ *for steel = 10 × 10⁻⁶ per ℃, E = 200 GPa.*    **(B.T.E. S-1986/4 Marks)**

**Data :** L = 6 m = 6000 mm, $t_1$ = 15°C, $t_2$ = 40°C, A = 4808 mm²,

$\alpha = 10 \times 10^{-6}$/°C, E = $200 \times 10^3$ N/mm²

**To find :** $\delta L$, $\sigma$ and P.

**Solution :**

Free elongation $\delta L = \alpha\, t\, L = 10 \times 10^{-6} \times (40 - 15) \times 6000 =$ **1.5 mm**

Stress $\sigma = \alpha\, t\, E = 10 \times 10^{-6} \times (40 - 15) \times 200 \times 10^3$

$= $ **50 N/mm² (Compressive)**

Thrust (Compressive force),

$P = \sigma \times A = 50 \times 4808 = 240400$ N = **240.4 kN**

**Answer :** (i) $\delta L$ = 1.5 mm, (ii) $\sigma$ = 50 N/mm² (Compressive), (iii) P = 240.4 kN

---

**Example 80 :** *Fig. 1.38 shows a copper rod AB of length 600 mm, when the temperature of the rod is 24 ℃. The gap between B and C is 0.48 mm. Determine :*

*(i) Thermal stress at 40 ℃.*

*(ii) The temperature at which the gap will just close.*

*Take coefficient of expansion $\alpha$ = 16 × 10⁻⁶ per ℃.*    **(B.T.E. W-2012/4 Marks)**

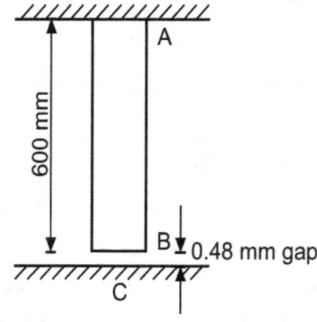

**Fig. 1.38**

**Data :** Copper rod L = 600 mm, gap = 0.48 mm, $\alpha = 16 \times 10^{-6}$/°C,

Change in temperature = 40 − 24 = 16°C.

**To find :** (i) Thermal stress at 40°C.

(ii) The temperature at which the gap will just close.

**Solution :** (i) Free expansion of the rod = $\alpha t L$

$= (16 \times 10^{-6}) \times 16 \times 600$

$= $ **0.1536 mm < 0.48 mm gap**

Hence the gap will not close. Therefore thermal stress will not be developed.

Hence thermal stress at 40°C = 0.

(ii) **To find the temperature at which the gap will just close :**

For closing the gap, $\alpha t L = 0.48$, where t is the change in temperature.

$$\therefore \qquad t = \frac{0.48}{\alpha L} = \frac{0.48}{(16 \times 10^{-6}) \times 600} = \textbf{50°C}$$

$\therefore$ Final temperature required to close the gap = 24 + 50 = **74°C.**

**Answer :** (i) Thermal stress at 40°C = 0, (ii) Final temperature to close gap = 74°C

**Example 81 :** *A copper tube having 10 mm outside diameter, 8 mm inside diameter and 100 mm long is fixed at one end but there is a gap of 0.1 mm at the other end. Determine the temperature at which the gap will close if the temperature of the tube is increased. How much stress will be induced in the tube material due to a total rise of 60 ℃ ?* **(V.V. Imp./4 Marks)**
*Take E = 160 × 10³ MPa, $\alpha$ = 16 × 10⁻⁶/℃*

**Answer :** (i) t = 62.5°C, (ii) $\sigma$ = 153.6 N/mm²

**Example 82 :** *A metal rod 16 mm diameter, 2 m long is held between the two supports at 100 ℃. Find the pull exerted when the temperature falls to 50 ℃, if (i) the supports do not yield, (ii) supports yield by 0.5 mm. Take $\alpha$ = 12 × 10⁻⁶/℃, E = 110 GPa.* **(V.V. Imp./4 Marks)**

**Data :** d = 16 mm, L = 2 m = 2000 mm, $t_1$ = 100°C, $t_2$ = 50°C, $\alpha$ = 12 × 10⁻⁶/°C,

E = 110 GPa = 110 × 10³ N/mm², Fall in temperature, t = $t_1 - t_2$ = 100 – 50 = 50°C.

**To find :** Pull exerted if (i) the supports do not yield, (ii) yield $\delta$ = 0.5 mm.

**Solution : Case (I) : Pull exerted if the supports do not yield :**

Temperature stress     $\sigma = \alpha t E = 12 \times 10^{-6} \times 50 \times 110 \times 10^3 = 66$ N/mm² (Tensile)

**Pull,** $\qquad P = \sigma \times A = 66 \times \dfrac{\pi}{4}(16)^2 = 13270.1$ N = **13.27 kN**

**Case (II) :** Pull exerted if $\delta$ = 0.5 mm

Contraction prevented, $\delta L = \alpha t L - \delta = 12 \times 10^{-6} \times 50 \times 2000 - 0.5 = 0.7$ mm

Temperature strain, $\qquad e = \dfrac{\delta L}{L} = \dfrac{0.7}{2000} = 3.5 \times 10^{-4}$ **(Tensile)**

Temperature stress, $\qquad \sigma = e E = 3.5 \times 10^{-4} \times (110 \times 10^3) = 38.5$ N/mm² **(Tensile)**

**Pull,** $\qquad P = \sigma \times A = 38.5 \times \dfrac{\pi}{4}(16)^2 = 7740.88$ N = **7.74 kN**

**Answer :** (i) P = 13.27 kN, (ii) P = 7.74 kN

**SUB-TOPIC 1.2 : COMPOSITE SECTIONS (4 Marks)**

## 1.42 DEFORMATION OF A BODY OF STEPPED CROSS-SECTION DUE TO AN AXIAL LOAD

**Stresses/strains in bars of varying sections subjected to axial loads at ends only :**

Sometimes a bar is made up of different lengths and of different cross-sections. In such cases, the strain and deformation of each section are worked out separately. The net change in length is equal to sum of changes in lengths of individual sections, but each section is subjected to same axial force as shown in Fig. 1.39.

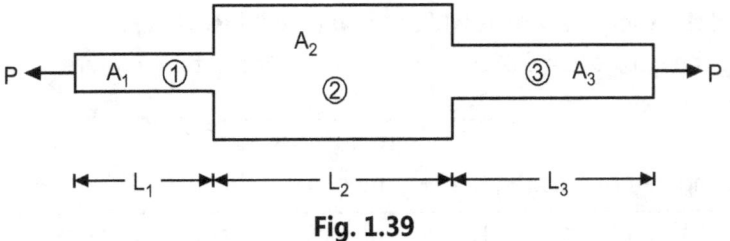

**Fig. 1.39**

Let,                    P = Axial force on the bar

$E_1, E_2, E_3$ = Modulus of elasticity of sections (1), (2) and (3) respectively

$L_1, L_2, L_3$ = Lengths of sections (1), (2) and (3) respectively

$A_1, A_2, A_3$ = Cross-sectional areas of sections (1), (2) and (3) respectively

∴ Change in length of section 1,

$$\delta L_1 = \frac{PL_1}{A_1 E_1}$$

Similarly,         $\delta L_2 = \dfrac{PL_2}{A_2 E_2}$ and $\delta L_3 = \dfrac{PL_3}{A_3 E_3}$

Total change in length,

$$\delta L = \delta L_1 + \delta L_2 + \delta L_3 = \frac{PL_1}{A_1 E_1} + \frac{PL_2}{A_2 E_2} + \frac{PL_3}{A_3 E_3}$$

$$\boxed{\delta L = P\left(\frac{L_1}{A_1 E_1} + \frac{L_2}{A_2 E_2} + \frac{L_3}{A_3 E_3}\right)}$$

**Note :** If the bar is of same material throughout, $E_1 = E_2 = E_3$,

then         $$\delta L = P\left(\frac{L_1}{A_1 E} + \frac{L_2}{A_2 E} + \frac{L_3}{A_3 E}\right)$$

$$\boxed{\delta L = \frac{P}{E}\left(\frac{L_1}{A_1} + \frac{L_2}{A_2} + \frac{L_3}{A_3}\right)}$$

---

1. State how to calculate total elongation for a bar of varying section subjected to axial load P.                                   **(B.T.E. W-2004, 2003/2 Marks)**

---

**(Most Likely and Asked in Previous B.T.E. Exam.)**

## SOLVED EXAMPLES

**Type 8 : Examples on change in length of bar having stepped cross-section**

**(Stresses in bars of varying sections)**

**Example 83 :** *A stepped bar is pulled by 20 kN as shown in Fig. 1.40. Find the total elongation of bar, if E = $1 \times 10^5$ N/mm².*   **(B.T.E. W-2009/4 Marks)**

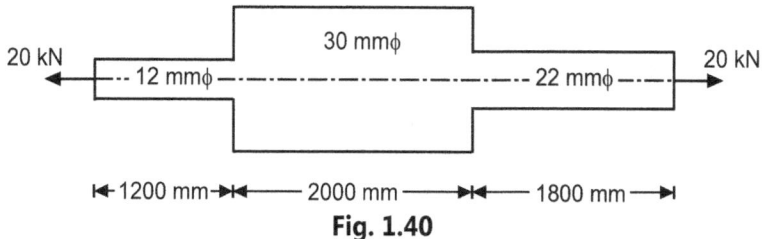

**Fig. 1.40**

**Data :** A stepped bar as shown in Fig. 1.40, E = $1 \times 10^5$ N/mm$^2$.

**To find :** Total elongation of bar, $\delta$L.

**Concept :**  (i)  Principle of superposition i.e. total deformation of the body will be equal to the algebraic sum of deformations of the individual sections.

(ii)  As this is a bar in series, each section is subjected to the same axial pull of 20 kN.

(iii)  E is same for all sections.

(iv)  Due to axial pull, the bar will **elongate**.

**Solution :**  (i)  $P = 20$ kN $= 20 \times 10^3$ N, $L_1 = 1200$ mm, $L_2 = 2000$ mm, $L_3 = 1800$ mm

(ii)  $A_1 = \dfrac{\pi}{4}(12)^2 = 113.1$ mm$^2$

$A_2 = \dfrac{\pi}{4}(30)^2 = 706.86$ mm$^2$

$A_3 = \dfrac{\pi}{4}(22)^2 = 380.13$ mm$^2$

(iii) Total elongation of bar,

$$\delta L = \delta L_1 + \delta L_2 + \delta L_3 = \frac{PL_1}{A_1 E} + \frac{PL_2}{A_2 E} + \frac{PL_3}{A_3 E} = \frac{P}{E}\left(\frac{L_1}{A_1} + \frac{L_2}{A_2} + \frac{L_3}{A_3}\right)$$

$$= \frac{20 \times 10^3}{1 \times 10^5}\left(\frac{1200}{113.1} + \frac{2000}{706.86} + \frac{1800}{380.13}\right) = \textbf{3.63 mm}$$

**Answer :**    $\boxed{\delta L = 3.63 \text{ mm}}$

**Example 84 :** *A member ABCD is subjected to loads as shown in Fig. 1.41 (i). Find the force P and net change in length of the member. Take E = $2 \times 10^5$ N/mm$^2$.*

**(B.T.E. S-2015, W-2003/4 Marks)**

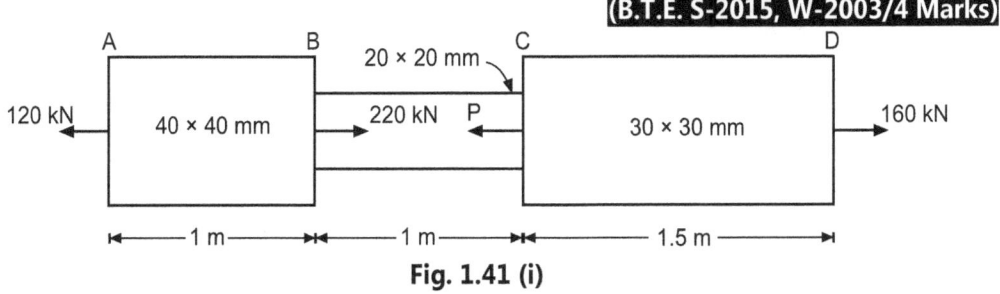

**Fig. 1.41 (i)**

**Data**    :  As shown in Fig. 1.41 (i).

**To find** : P, δL.

**Concept :** (i) Drawing free body diagrams of each section

(ii) Applying principle of superposition.

**Solution :** For the equilibrium of the entire bar,

$\sum$ forces towards left $=\sum$ forces towards right

∴ $120 + P = 220 + 160 = 380$

∴ $P = 380 - 120 = \mathbf{260\ kN}\ (\leftarrow)$

F.B.D.'s for each section are as shown in Fig. 1.41 (ii).

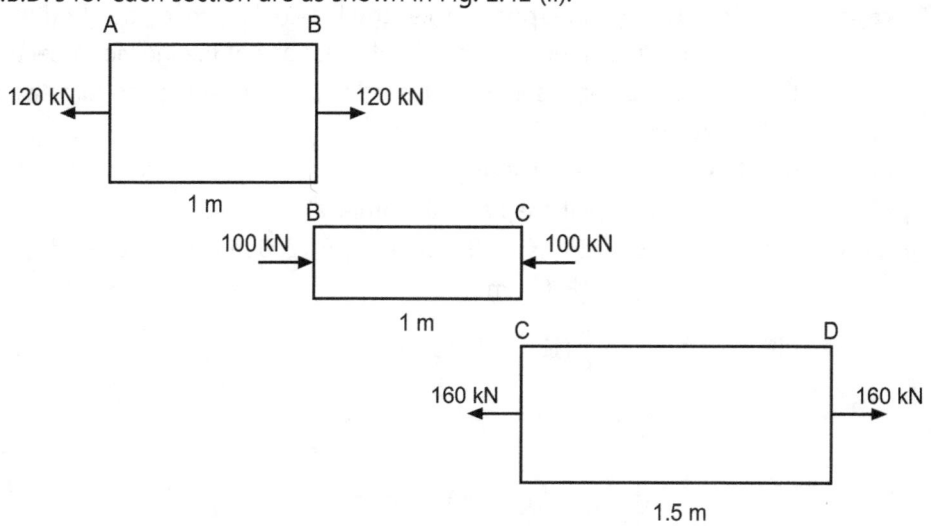

**Fig. 1.41 (ii)**

In this case, sections AB and CD are under tension and section BC is under compression.

Here $P_1 = 120$ kN, $P_2 = 100$ kN, $P_3 = 160$ kN

Now, $\delta L_1 = \delta L_{AB} = + \dfrac{P_1 L_1}{AE} = \dfrac{120 \times 10^3 \times 1000}{(40 \times 40) \times 2 \times 10^5} = 0.375$ mm

$\delta L_2 = \delta L_{BC} = - \dfrac{P_2 L_2}{AE} = - \dfrac{100 \times 10^3 \times 1000}{(20 \times 20) \times 2 \times 10^5} = -1.25$ mm

$\delta L_3 = \delta L_{CD} = + \dfrac{P_3 L_3}{AE} = \dfrac{160 \times 10^3 \times 1500}{(30 \times 30) \times 2 \times 10^5} = 1.33$ mm

∴ $\delta L = \delta L_1 + \delta L_2 + \delta L_3 = 0.375 - 1.25 + 1.33 = \mathbf{+\ 0.455\ mm\ (increase)}$

**Answer :** (i) P = 260 kN ($\leftarrow$), (ii) δL = 0.455 mm (increase)

**Example 85 :** *A brass bar shown in Fig. 1.42 is subjected to a tensile load of 40 kN. Find the total elongation of the bar if E = 1.0 $\times 10^5$ N/mm² and the maximum stress induced.*

**(B.T.E. S-2013, W-2011/4 Marks)**

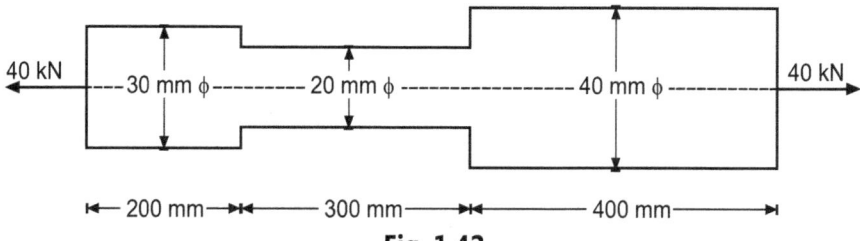

**Fig. 1.42**

**Data :** A brass bar of varying cross-section subjected to tensile load 40 kN as shown in Fig. 1.42, $E = 1 \times 10^5$ N/mm$^2$

**To find :** (i) $\delta L$, (ii) $\sigma_{max}$.

**Concept :** Applying principle of superposition, $\delta L = \delta L_1 + \delta L_2 + \delta L_3$.

**Solution :** In this case, each section is subjected to the same axial pull of 40 kN.

$\therefore$   P = 40 kN = $40 \times 10^3$ N, $L_1$ = 200 mm, $L_2$ = 300 mm, $L_3$ = 400 mm

$$A_1 = \frac{\pi}{4}(30)^2 = 706.86 \text{ mm}^2, \ A_2 = \frac{\pi}{4}(20)^2 = 314.16 \text{ mm}^2, \ A_3 = \frac{\pi}{4}(40)^2 = 1256.64 \text{ mm}^2$$

Since, the bar is made up of same material throughout, E is same for all sections.

$\therefore$          $E_1 = E_2 = E_3 = E = 1.0 \times 10^5$ N/mm$^2$

Now,                $\delta L = \delta L_1 + \delta L_2 + \delta L_3$

$$= \frac{PL_1}{A_1E} + \frac{PL_2}{A_2E} + \frac{PL_3}{A_3E} = \frac{P}{E}\left[\frac{L_1}{A_1} + \frac{L_2}{A_2} + \frac{L_3}{A_3}\right]$$

$$= \frac{40 \times 10^3}{1 \times 10^5}\left[\frac{200}{706.86} + \frac{300}{314.16} + \frac{400}{1256.64}\right]$$

$$= \frac{40 \times 10^3}{1 \times 10^5}[0.283 + 0.955 + 0.318] = 40 \times 10^{-2} \times 1.556$$

$\therefore$                         $\delta L = 0.62$ mm

Naturally, the maximum stress will be induced in the section having smaller cross-sectional area i.e. in the middle portion of 20 mm $\phi$.

$\therefore$        **Maximum stress** $= \dfrac{P}{A_2} = \dfrac{40 \times 10^3}{314.16} = $ **127.32 N/mm$^2$ = 127.32 MPa**

**Answer :** $\boxed{\delta L = 0.62 \text{ mm}, \ \sigma_{max} = 127.32 \text{ MPa}}$

---

**Example 86 :** *A circular bar of 500 mm length has a cross-section as given below.*

*First 100 mm has a diameter 12 mm, second 200 mm has a diameter 20 mm and the last 200 mm has a diameter of 30 mm. Determine the maximum axial pull which the bar may be subjected if the maximum stress is limited to 100 N/mm$^2$. Find the total elongation. Take $E = 2 \times 10^5$ N/mm$^2$.*          **(B.T.E. S-1994/4 Marks)**

**Data :** A circular bar of varying cross-section as shown in Fig. 1.43, $E = 2 \times 10^5$ N/mm$^2$.

**To find :** (i) Axial pull P, (ii) $\delta L$.

**Concept :** (i)  Maximum stress will be induced in the portion AB having minimum cross-sectional area.

(ii) Applying principle of superposition, $\delta L = \delta L_{AB} + \delta L_{BC} + \delta L_{CD}$.

## Solution :

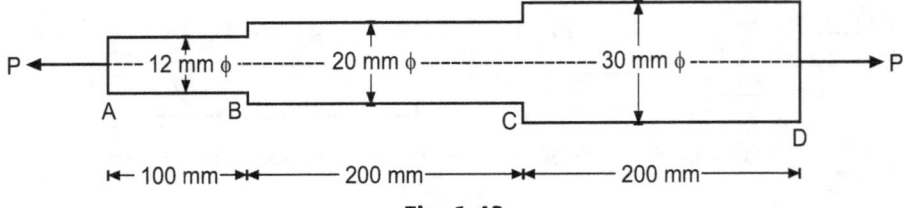

**Fig. 1.43**

Fig. 1.43 shows a circular bar subjected to an axial pull P. The maximum stress will be induced in the portion AB having 12 mm $\phi$ i.e. stress in AB = 100 N/mm$^2$.

Let P be the maximum axial pull.

$$\text{Stress in AB} = \frac{P}{\text{Cross-sectional area of AB}}$$

$$\therefore \quad 100 = \frac{P}{\frac{\pi}{4}(12)^2}$$

$$\therefore \quad \mathbf{P} = 100 \times \frac{\pi}{4} \times 12^2 = \mathbf{11309.73 \ N}$$

Now, total elongation, $\quad \mathbf{\delta L} = \delta L_{AB} + \delta L_{BC} + \delta L_{CD} = \delta L_1 + \delta L_2 + \delta L_3$

$$= \frac{PL_1}{A_1 E} + \frac{PL_2}{A_2 E} + \frac{PL_3}{A_3 E} = \frac{P}{E}\left[\frac{L_1}{A_1} + \frac{L_2}{A_2} + \frac{L_3}{A_3}\right]$$

$$= \frac{11309.73}{2 \times 10^5}\left[\frac{100}{\frac{\pi}{4}(12)^2} + \frac{200}{\frac{\pi}{4}(20)^2} + \frac{200}{\frac{\pi}{4}(30)^2}\right]$$

$$= \frac{11309.73}{2 \times 10^5}[0.8842 + 0.6366 + 0.2829]$$

$$= \frac{11309.73}{2 \times 10^5} \times 1.8037 = \mathbf{0.102 \ mm}$$

**Answer :** $\boxed{P = 11.309 \ kN, \ \delta L = 0.102 \ mm}$

**Example 87 :** *Determine the magnitude of P for equilibrium and the total elongation of the bar shown in Fig. 1.44 (a). E = 210 GPa.*    **(B.T.E. W-2003/8 Marks)**

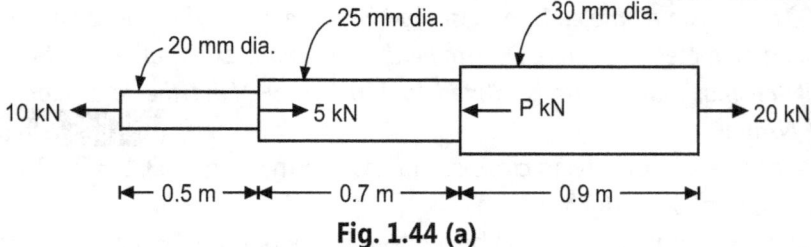

**Fig. 1.44 (a)**

**Data :** A bar as shown in **Fig. 1.44 (a)**, E = 210 GPa = 210 × 10$^3$ N/mm$^2$.

**To find :** (i) P, (ii) $\delta L$.

**Concept :** Applying principle of superposition i.e. $\delta L = \delta L_1 + \delta L_2 + \delta L_3$.

**Solution :** For the equilibrium of the entire bar,

$$\sum F_X = 0 \; (\rightarrow +, \leftarrow -)$$

$\therefore \qquad -10 + 5 - P + 20 = 0$

$\therefore \qquad \qquad \mathbf{P = 15 \; kN} \; (\leftarrow)$

F.B.D.s of each section are as shown in **Fig. 1.44 (b)**.

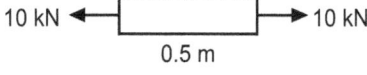

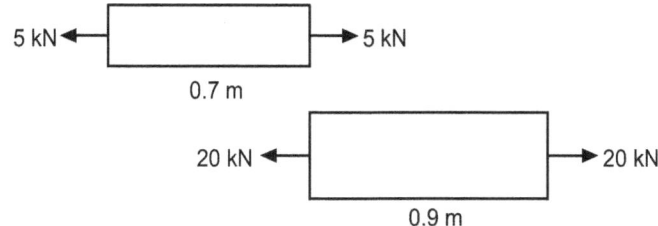

**Fig. 1.44 (b)**

In this case, each section is under tension. Therefore, there will be increase in length of each section.

$$\delta L_1 = \frac{P_1 L_1}{A_1 E} = \frac{(10 \times 10^3) \times (0.5 \times 10^3)}{\frac{\pi}{4} (20)^2 \times (210 \times 10^3)} = 0.076 \text{ mm}$$

$$\delta L_2 = \frac{P_2 L_2}{A_2 E} = \frac{(5 \times 10^3) \times (0.7 \times 10^3)}{\frac{\pi}{4} (25)^2 \times (210 \times 10^3)} = 0.034 \text{ mm}$$

$$\delta L_3 = \frac{P_3 L_3}{A_3 E} = \frac{(20 \times 10^3) \times (0.9 \times 10^3)}{\frac{\pi}{4} (30)^2 \times (210 \times 10^3)} = 0.121 \text{ mm}$$

$\therefore \qquad \mathbf{\delta L} = \delta L_1 + \delta L_2 + \delta L_3 = 0.076 + 0.034 + 0.121 = \mathbf{0.231 \; mm}$

**Answer :** $\boxed{\delta L = 0.231 \text{ mm (increase)}}$

## (E) STRESSES AND STRAINS IN BARS OF UNIFORMLY VARYING SECTION SUBJECTED TO AXIAL LOADS AT ENDS ONLY, COMPOSITE SECTIONS HAVING SAME LENGTH

### Synopsis

Introduction, Solved Examples on Bars of Uniformly Varying Sections Subjected to Axial Load, Stress and Strain in Composite Members Connected Rigidly together in Parallel, Solved Examples based on Stresses in Composite Bars

## 1.43 INTRODUCTION

In such a type of bar, the change in cross-sectional area is not sudden as in case of stepped section. The change is however gradual, uniform and for the entire length of the bar. The evaluation of the elongation requires the help of integration.

## SOLVED EXAMPLES

### Type 9 : Examples on bars of uniformly varying sections subjected to axial load

**Example 88 :** *A flat bar of rectangular cross-section and constant thickness 't' is subjected to an axial tensile force P. The width of the bar varies linearly from $b_1$ at left end to $b_2$ at right end.*

*Derive a formula for elongation $\delta L$ of the bar.*

**Data :** As shown in Fig. 1.45.

**To find :** Change in length '$\delta L$'.

**Concept :** Member of uniformly varying cross-section.

**Solution :**

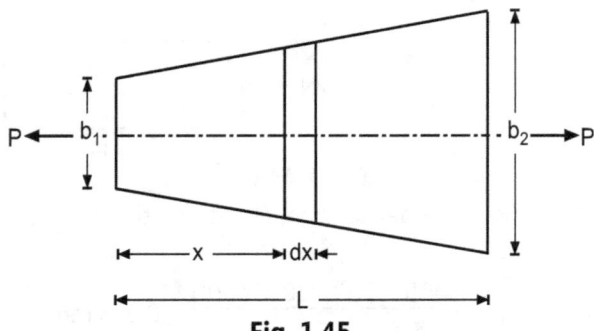

**Fig. 1.45**

(i) Consider an elementary strip of length dx at a distance 'x' from the left end, as shown in Fig. 1.45. Let b be the width of section at x from the left end.

Since, width of bar varies linearly,

$$\frac{b_2 - b_1}{L} = \frac{b - b_1}{x}$$

$\therefore$
$$b - b_1 = \left(\frac{b_2 - b_1}{L}\right) x$$

$\therefore$
$$b = b_1 + \left(\frac{b_2 - b_1}{L}\right) x = b_1 + K \cdot x, \text{ where } K = \frac{b_2 - b_1}{L}$$

Cross-sectional area for strip
$$= A = bt = (b_1 + Kx)\, t$$

Change in length of strip $= \dfrac{PL}{AE} = \dfrac{P\, dx}{(b_1 + Kx)\, t\, E}$

(ii) **Change in length of bar :**

$$\delta L = \int_0^L \frac{P\, dx}{(b_1 + Kx)\, t\, E}$$

$$= \frac{P}{t\, E} \int_0^L \frac{dx}{(b_1 + Kx)}$$

$$= \frac{P}{tE}\frac{1}{K}\left[\log_e(b_1 + Kx)\right]_0^L$$

$$= \frac{P}{tEK}\left[\log_e(b_1 + KL) - \log_e(b_1)\right]$$

$$= \frac{P}{tEK}\left[\log_e\left(b_1 + \frac{b_2 - b_1}{L}\cdot L\right) - \log_e b_1\right]$$

$$= \frac{P}{tEK}\left[\log_e(b_1 + b_2 - b_1) - \log_e b_1\right]$$

$$= \frac{P}{tEK}\left[\log_e b_2 - \log_e b_1\right]$$

$$= \frac{P}{tEK}\,loe_e\left(\frac{b_2}{b_1}\right)$$

$$= \frac{PL}{tE(b_2 - b_1)}\log_e\left(\frac{b_2}{b_1}\right) \qquad\qquad \left(\because \frac{1}{K} = \frac{L}{b_2 - b_1}\right)$$

**Answer :** $\boxed{\delta L = \dfrac{PL}{tE(b_2 - b_1)}\log_e\left(\dfrac{b_2}{b_1}\right) = \dfrac{PL}{tE(b_2 - b_1)}\ln\left(\dfrac{b_2}{b_1}\right)}$

---

**Example 89 :** *A plate of uniform thickness is 50 mm wide at one end and 100 mm wide at other end and 500 mm long. Assuming uniform thickness of 8 mm, find elongation of plate when subjected to axial tensile force of 35 kN. Take E = 200 GPa.* **(V.V. Imp./4 Marks)**

**Data :** As shown in Fig. 1.46.

$b_1$ = 50 mm, $b_2$ = 100 mm, L = 500 mm, t = 8 mm,

P = 35 kN = $35 \times 10^3$ N, E = 200 GPa = $200 \times 10^3$ N/mm$^2$

**To find :** $\delta$L.

**Concept :** Member of uniformly varying cross-section.

**Solution :**

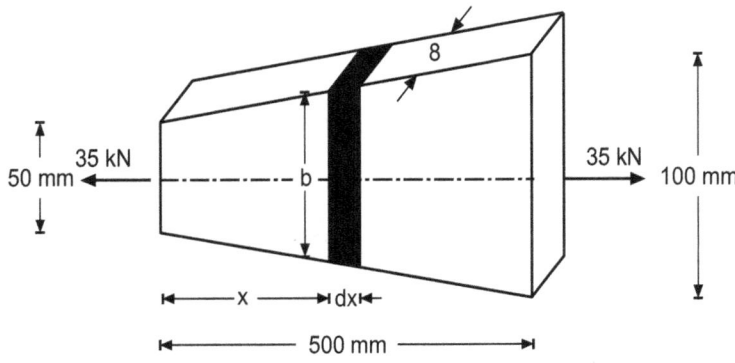

**Fig. 1.46**

For a uniformly tapering plate subjected to axial force P, we have

$$\delta L = \frac{PL}{t\,E\,(b_2 - b_1)} \log_e \left(\frac{b_2}{b_1}\right)$$

$$= \frac{35 \times 10^3 \times 500}{8 \times (200 \times 10^3)\,(100 - 50)} \log_e \left(\frac{100}{50}\right)$$

$$= \mathbf{0.1516 \ mm}$$

**Answer :**    $\boxed{\delta L = 0.1516 \ mm}$

---

**Example 90 :** *For a member having solid circular cross-section, diameter is '$d_1$' at one end and it linearly increases to '$d_2$' at other end over the length 'L'. Show that its change in length under the action of axial force P is given by*

$$\delta L = \frac{4PL}{\pi E\,d_1\,d_2}$$

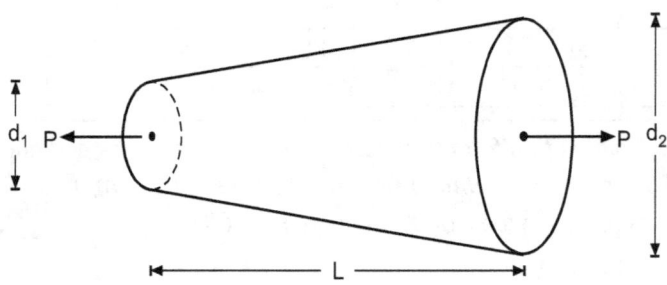

**Fig. 1.47**

**Data :** As shown in Fig. 1.47.

**To find :** Change in length $\delta L$.

**Concept :** Member of uniformly varying cross-section.

**Solution :**

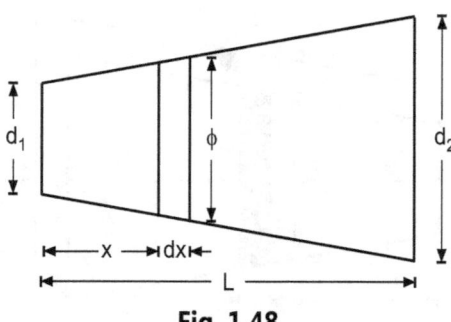

**Fig. 1.48**

(i) Consider an elementary strip of length dx at a distance x from left end.

Let '$\phi$' be the diameter of the section at a distance 'x' from left end as shown in Fig. 1.48.

Since, diameter of bar varies linearly,

$$\frac{d_2 - d_1}{L} = \frac{\phi - d_1}{x}$$

$\therefore$

$$\phi - d_1 = \left(\frac{d_2 - d_1}{L}\right)x$$

$\therefore$

$$\phi = d_1 + \left(\frac{d_2 - d_1}{L}\right)x$$

$$\text{Cross-sectional area of strip} = A = \frac{\pi}{4}\phi^2 = \frac{\pi}{4}\left[d_1 + \left(\frac{d_2 - d_1}{L}\right)x\right]^2$$

$$\text{Change in length of strip} = \frac{PL}{AE} = \frac{P\,dx}{\frac{\pi}{4}\left[d_1 + \left(\frac{d_2 - d_1}{L}\right)x\right]^2 E}$$

(ii) **Change in length of member :**

$$\delta L = \int_0^L \frac{P\,dx}{\frac{\pi}{4}\left[d_1 + \left(\frac{d_2 - d_1}{L}\right)x\right]^2 E}$$

$$= \frac{4P}{\pi E}\left[\frac{-1}{d_1 + \left(\frac{d_2 - d_1}{L}\right)x} \div \frac{d_2 - d_1}{L}\right]_0^L$$

$$= \frac{4P}{\pi E}\left[\frac{-1}{d_1 + \left(\frac{d_2 - d_1}{L}\right)x} \times \frac{L}{(d_2 - d_1)}\right]_0^L$$

$$= \frac{-4PL}{\pi E (d_2 - d_1)}\left[\frac{1}{d_1 + \left(\frac{d_2 - d_1}{L}\right)\cdot L} - \frac{1}{d_1}\right]$$

$$= \frac{-4PL}{\pi E (d_2 - d_1)}\left[\frac{1}{d_1 + d_2 - d_1} - \frac{1}{d_1}\right]$$

$$= \frac{-4PL}{\pi E (d_2 - d_1)}\left(\frac{1}{d_2} - \frac{1}{d_1}\right) = \frac{-4PL}{\pi E (d_2 - d_1)}\left(\frac{d_1 - d_2}{d_1 d_2}\right)$$

$$= \frac{4PL}{\pi E (d_1 - d_2)}\left(\frac{d_1 - d_2}{d_1 d_2}\right) \qquad \cdots \left(\because -\frac{1}{d_2 - d_1} = \frac{1}{d_1 - d_2}\right)$$

$$= \frac{4PL}{\pi E\, d_1\, d_2}$$

**Answer :** $\boxed{\delta L = \dfrac{4PL}{\pi E\, d_1\, d_2}}$

This is the required expression for the elongation of the bar under an axial pull P.

**Note :** If the bar is prismatic i.e. of uniform cross-section,

$$d_1 = d_2 = d$$

$$\delta L = \frac{4PL}{\pi E\, d.d} = \frac{PL}{\left(\frac{\pi}{4} d^2\right) E} = \frac{PL}{AE}$$

---

**Example 91 :** *Find the elongation of a rod tapering uniformly from 105 mm to 55 mm under the action of axial force of 40 kN. Length of the rod is 2 m and E = 2 × 10⁸ kN/m².*

**(B.T.E. S-2012/4 Marks)**

**OR**

*Find the elongation of a rod tapering uniformly from 10.5 cm to 5.5 cm under the action of axial force of 40 kN. Length of the rod is 2 m and E = 2 × 10⁸ kN/m².*

**(B.T.E. W-2012/4 Marks)**

**Data :** A bar of solid circular cross-section tapering uniformly,

$d_1 = 10.5$ cm = 105 mm, $d_2 = 5.5$ cm = 55 mm, P = 40 kN = $40 \times 10^3$ N,

L = 2 m = $2 \times 10^3$ mm,

$E = 2 \times 10^8$ kN/m² $= \dfrac{2 \times 10^8 \times 10^3}{10^6}$ N/mm² $= 2 \times 10^5$ N/mm²

**To find :** $\delta L$.

**Concept :** Bar of uniformly varying cross-section.

**Solution :** Elongation of a rod of solid circular cross-section having diameter $d_1$ at one end and $d_2$ at other end, subjected to axial force P,

$$\delta L = \frac{4PL}{\pi E\, d_1 d_2}$$

$$= \frac{4 \times 40 \times 10^3 \times 2 \times 10^3}{\pi \times 2 \times 10^5 \times 105 \times 55}$$

$$= \mathbf{0.088\ mm}$$

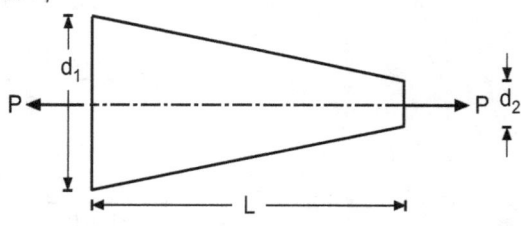

**Fig. 1.49**

**Answer :** | Elongation of a rod is 0.088 mm |

---

## 1.44 STRESS AND STRAIN IN COMPOSITE MEMBERS CONNECTED RIGIDLY TOGETHER IN PARALLEL
### (Composite Sections having Same Length)

**Composite member :** *If two or more members of different materials are connected together and are subjected to loads, then the combination is called a composite member.*

Consider a composite bar of length L made up of two different materials (1) and (2) connected rigidly together in parallel and carrying a compressive load P as shown in Fig. 1.50.

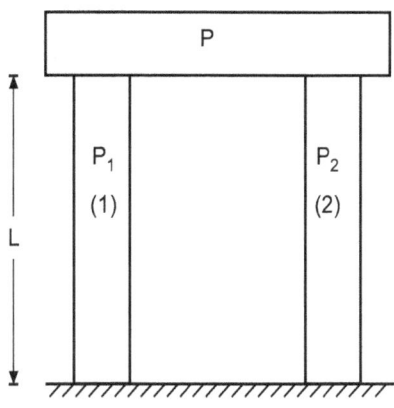

**Fig. 1.50**

Let            $P_1$ = Load shared by bar 1, $P_2$ = Load shared by bar 2 and

             P = Total load on composite bar

Naturally,     $P = P_1 + P_2$

∴            $P = \sigma_1 A_1 + \sigma_2 A_2$                                    ... (I)

Let            δL = decrease in length of the bar

*For a composite bar, decrease (or increase) in length of each bar must be equal i.e. strain in each bar must be equal.*

Strain in bar 1,        $e_1 = \dfrac{\sigma_1}{E_1}$                        ... (II)

Strain in bar 2,        $e_2 = \dfrac{\sigma_2}{E_2}$                        ... (III)

Now, $e_1 = e_2$ gives $\dfrac{\sigma_1}{E_1} = \dfrac{\sigma_2}{E_2}$

∴            $\sigma_1 = \dfrac{E_1}{E_2} \cdot \sigma_2$

∴            $\sigma_1 = m \cdot \sigma_2$                                    ... (IV)

where          $m = \dfrac{E_1}{E_2}$ = modular ratio.

From the equations (I) and (IV), stresses in two bars $\sigma_1$ and $\sigma_2$ can be calculated. Knowing stresses in two bars, strains in bars can be calculated from the equation (II) or (III).

## 1.44.1 Modular Ratio

*It is defined as the ratio of modulii of elasticity of the two different materials.* It is denoted by 'm'.

∴            $m = \dfrac{E_1}{E_2}$

where  $E_1$ = Modulus of elasticity of material-1 and $E_2$ = Modulus of elasticity of material-2

| 1.   Define a composite section and modular ratio.    **(B.T.E. W-2014, 1998/2 Marks)** |
| --- |
| **(Most Likely and Asked in Previous B.T.E. Exam.)** |

## SOLVED EXAMPLES

### Type 10 : Examples based on stresses in composite bars.

**Important Formulae**

$$P = P_1 + P_2 = \sigma_1 A_1 + \sigma_2 A_2 \qquad \dots \text{(i)}$$

$$e_1 = e_2$$

$$\frac{\sigma_1}{E_1} = \frac{\sigma_2}{E_2}$$

$$\therefore \quad \sigma_1 = \frac{E_1}{E_2} \cdot \sigma_2 = m\sigma_2 \qquad \dots \text{(ii)}$$

**Example 92 :** *A steel tube 40 mm inside diameter and 4 mm metal thickness is filled with concrete. Determine the stress in each material due to an axial thrust of 60 kN.*

*Take E for steel = $20 \times 10^5$ MPa*

*E for concrete = $0.14 \times 10^5$ N/mm².*

**(B.T.E. W-2011, 1989; S-2010/4 Marks)**

**Data** : Inside diameter of steel tube, d = 40 mm

$\therefore$ Metal thickness, t = 4 mm

$\therefore$ Outside diameter of steel tube, D = d + 2t = 40 + 2 × 4 = 48 mm

$\therefore$ Area of steel, $A_S = \frac{\pi}{4}(D^2 - d^2) = \frac{\pi}{4}(48^2 - 40^2) = 552.92$ mm²

Area of concrete, $A_C = \frac{\pi}{4}d^2 = \frac{\pi}{4}(40)^2 = 1256.64$ mm²

Axial thrust, $P = 60$ kN $= 60 \times 10^3$ N

**To find :** $\sigma_S$ and $\sigma_C$.

**Concept :** Two equations for composite bars having same length

$$\text{(i) } P = \sigma_S A_S + \sigma_C A_C, \text{ (ii) } \sigma_S = \frac{E_S}{E_C} \cdot \sigma_C = m \sigma_C$$

**Solution :**

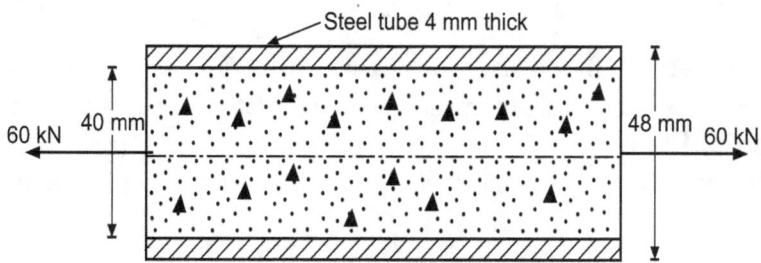

**Fig. 1.51**

Using $\qquad P = \sigma_1 A_1 + \sigma_2 A_2$ we have

$$P = \sigma_S A_S + \sigma_C A_C$$

$\therefore \qquad 60 \times 10^3 = \sigma_S \times 552.92 + \sigma_C \times 1256.64 \qquad \dots \text{(i)}$

Using $\qquad \sigma_1 = \dfrac{E_1}{E_2}\,\sigma_2$

∴ $\qquad \sigma_s = \dfrac{E_s}{E_c}\,\sigma_c = \dfrac{2.1 \times 10^5}{0.14 \times 10^5}\,\sigma_c$

∴ $\qquad \sigma_s = 15\,\sigma_c$ $\qquad\qquad$ ... (ii)

Substituting this value in equation (i),

$$60 \times 10^3 = 15\,\sigma_c \times 552.92 + \sigma_c \times 1256.64$$
$$= (15 \times 552.92 + 1256.64)\,\sigma_c = 9550.44\,\sigma_c$$

∴ $\qquad \sigma_c = \dfrac{60 \times 10^3}{9550.44} = \textbf{6.28 N/mm}^2$

From equation (ii), $\qquad \boldsymbol{\sigma_s} = 15 \times 6.28 = \textbf{94.2 N/mm}^2$

**Answer :** (i) $\sigma_c = 6.28$ N/mm$^2$, (ii) $\sigma_s = 94.2$ N/mm$^2$

---

**Example 93 :** *A copper wire 20 mm² in cross-section and steel wire 30 mm² in cross-section both 1 m long are rigidly connected to plates on either side. They jointly share load of 8 kN. $E_{steel} = 20 \times 10^5$ MPa, $E_{copper} = 1 \times 10^5$ MPa. Find the stresses produced in each material.*

**(B.T.E. S-2013, 2012, 1999/4 Marks)**

**Data** : $A_c = 20$ mm², $A_s = 30$ mm², $L = 1$ m $= 1000$ mm, $P = 8$ kN $= 8 \times 10^3$ N,

$\qquad E_s = 20 \times 10^5$ MPa $= 20 \times 10^5$ N/mm², $E_c = 1 \times 10^5$ MPa $= 1 \times 10^5$ N/mm²

**To find :** $\sigma_c$, $\sigma_s$.

**Concept :** Two equations for composite bar.

**Solution :** Using the relation, $\quad \sigma_1 = \dfrac{E_1}{E_2} \times \sigma_2$

∴ $\qquad \sigma_s = \dfrac{E_s}{E_c} \times \sigma_c = \dfrac{20 \times 10^5}{1 \times 10^5} = 20 \times \sigma_c$ $\qquad$ ... (i)

Using the relation, $\qquad P = \sigma_1 A_1 + \sigma_2 A_2$

we have, $\qquad\qquad P = \sigma_s A_s + \sigma_c A_c$

∴ $\qquad 8 \times 10^3 = 20 \times \sigma_c \times 30 + \sigma_c \times 20 = 600\,\sigma_c + 20\,\sigma_c = 620\,\sigma_c$

∴ $\qquad \boldsymbol{\sigma_c} = \dfrac{8 \times 10^3}{620} = \textbf{12.9 N/mm}^2$

Substituting this value in equation (i),

$$\boldsymbol{\sigma_s} = 20 \times 12.9 = \textbf{258.1 N/mm}^2$$

**Answer :** (i) $\sigma_c = 12.9$ N/mm$^2$, (ii) $\sigma_s = 258.1$ N/mm$^2$

---

**Example 94 :** *A brass rod of 250 mm length and 20 mm diameter is fixed inside a steel tube of 40 mm external diameter and 20 mm internal diameter and of same length. The composite bar is subjected to an axial pull of 150 kN. Find the stress in each metal. Take $E_{steel} = 200$ GPa and $E_{brass} = 110$ GPa.* **(B.T.E. S-2001/4 Marks)**

**Data** : Brass rod (solid) : L = 250 mm, d = 20 mm,

Hollow steel tube : D = 40 mm, d = 20 mm, L = 250 mm,

Pull P = 150 kN = $150 \times 10^3$ N, $E_s$ = 200 GPa = $200 \times 10^3$ N/mm$^2$,

$E_b$ = 110 GPa = $110 \times 10^3$ N/mm$^2$

**To find:** $\sigma_b$ and $\sigma_s$.

**Concept :** Two equations for composite bar.

**Solution :** Area of brass rod,

$$A_b = \frac{\pi}{4} d^2 = \frac{\pi}{4} (20)^2 = 314.16 \text{ mm}^2$$

Area of steel tube, $A_s = \frac{\pi}{4} (D^2 - d^2) = \frac{\pi}{4} (40^2 - 20^2) = 942.48 \text{ mm}^2$

Using $\qquad\qquad P = \sigma_1 A_1 + \sigma_2 A_2$

we have, $\qquad\qquad P = \sigma_s A_s + \sigma_b A_b$

$\therefore \qquad 150 \times 10^3 = \sigma_s \times 942.48 + \sigma_b \times 314.16$ ... (i)

Using $\qquad\qquad \sigma_1 = \frac{E_1}{E_2} \sigma_2$

$\therefore \qquad \sigma_s = \frac{E_s}{E_b} \cdot \sigma_b = \frac{200 \times 10^3}{110 \times 10^3} \times \sigma_b = 1.818 \times \sigma_b$ ... (ii)

Substituting this value in equation (i),

$$150 \times 10^3 = (1.818 \times \sigma_b) \times 942.48 + \sigma_b \times 314.16$$
$$= 1713.43 \times \sigma_b + 314.16 \times \sigma_b$$
$$= (1713.43 + 314.16) \times \sigma_b = 2027.59 \times \sigma_b$$

$\therefore \qquad\qquad \sigma_b = \dfrac{150 \times 10^3}{2027.59} = \mathbf{73.98 \text{ N/mm}^2}$

From equation (ii), $\sigma_s = 1.818 \times 73.98 = \mathbf{134.5 \text{ N/mm}^2}$

**Answer :** $\boxed{\text{(i) } \sigma_b = 73.98 \text{ N/mm}^2, \text{ (ii) } \sigma_s = 134.5 \text{ N/mm}^2}$

**Example 95 :** *Two vertical rods are of steel and the other of copper are rigidly fixed at the top as shown in Fig. 1.52. A horizontal cross bar of copper fixed to the rods at the lower ends carries a load of 6000 N such that the cross bar remains horizontal after loading. Calculate the load shared by each rod.*

*Take $E_s$ = $2 \times 10^5$ N/mm$^2$,*

*$E_c$ = $1 \times 10^5$ N/mm$^2$*

**(B.T.E. S-2004/4 Marks)**

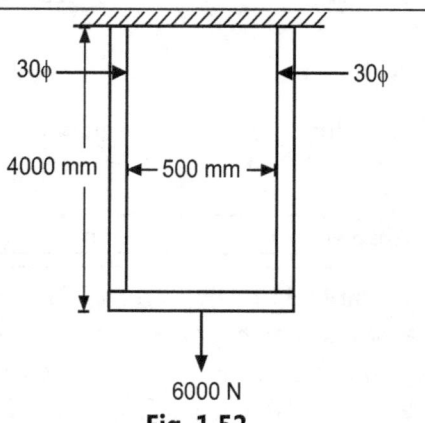

**Fig. 1.52**

## OR

*Two vertical rods are of steel and the other of copper are rigidly fixed at the top, as shown in Fig. 1.52. Calculate the load shared by each rod if $E_s$ = 200 GPa and $E_c$ = 100 GPa.*

**(B.T.E. W-2010/4 Marks)**

**Data**    :   $L = L_s = L_c = 4000$ mm, $A_s = A_c = \frac{\pi}{4}(30)^2 = 706.86$ mm$^2$,

load P = 6000 N, $E_s = 2 \times 10^5$ N/mm$^2$, $E_c = 1 \times 10^5$ N/mm$^2$,

distance between two rods = 500 mm

**To find** :   $P_s$ and $P_c$.

**Concept :** Two equations for composite bar.

**Solution :**   Using $P = P_1 + P_2$, we have

$$P = P_s + P_c = \sigma_s A_s + \sigma_c A_c \qquad \text{... (i)}$$

$$6000 = \sigma_s \times 706.86 + \sigma_c \times 706.86$$

$$\sigma_s + \sigma_c = 8.49 \qquad \text{... (A)}$$

Using                $\dfrac{\sigma_1}{E_1} = \dfrac{\sigma_2}{E_2}$

∴                $\dfrac{\sigma_s}{E_s} = \dfrac{\sigma_c}{E_c}$

∴                $\sigma_s = \dfrac{E_s}{E_c} \cdot \sigma_c = \dfrac{2 \times 10^5}{1 \times 10^5}\sigma_c$

∴                $\sigma_s = 2\sigma_c \qquad \text{... (B)}$

∴ From equation (A),

$$2\sigma_c + \sigma_c = 8.49$$

$$3\sigma_c = 8.49$$

∴                $\sigma_c = 2.83$ N/mm$^2$

Now, from equation (B), $\sigma_s = 2\sigma_c = 2 \times 2.83 = 5.66$ N/mm$^2$

**Loads shared by rods : $P_s$** $= \sigma_s A_s = 5.66 \times 706.86 = $ **4000.83 N = 4 kN**

$\qquad\qquad\qquad$ **$P_c$** $= \sigma_c A_c = 2.83 \times 706.86 = $ **2000.41 N = 2 kN**

**Answer :**   $\boxed{P_s = 4 \text{ kN}, P_c = 2 \text{ kN}}$

**Example 96 :** *Two steel rods and one copper rod each of 20 mm $\phi$ together support a load of 20 kN as shown in Fig. 1.53. Find the stresses in the rod. $E_s$ = 210 GPa and $E_c$ = 110 GPa.*                **(B.T.E. W-2006, S-1991/4 Marks)**

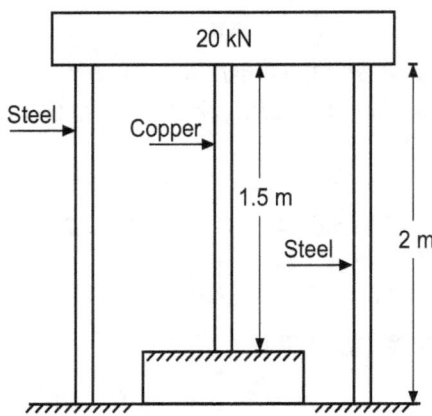

**Fig. 1.53**

**Data :** Length of steel rod = 2000 mm, length of copper rod = 1500 mm, diameter of steel rod = diameter of copper rod = 20 mm, compressive load P = 20 kN = 20 × 10³ N,

$E_s$ = 210 GPa = 210 × 10³ N/mm², $E_c$ = 110 GPa = 110 × 10³ N/mm²

Area of steel,        $A_s = \dfrac{\pi}{4} \times 20^2 = 314.16$ mm²

Area of copper,     $A_c = \dfrac{\pi}{4} \times 20^2 = 314.16$ mm²

**To find :** $\sigma_s$ and $\sigma_c$.

**Concept :** (i) $\delta L_s = \delta L_c$, (ii) $P = 2P_s + P_c$

**Solution :** Compression of each bar will be the same.

$\therefore$        $\delta L_s = \delta L_c$

$\therefore$        $\left(\dfrac{PL}{AE}\right)_s = \left(\dfrac{PL}{AE}\right)_c$

$\therefore$        $\left(\dfrac{P_s}{A_s}\right)\dfrac{L_s}{E_s} = \left(\dfrac{P_c}{A_c}\right)\dfrac{L_c}{E_c}$

$\therefore$        $\dfrac{\sigma_s \times 2000}{210 \times 10^3} = \dfrac{\sigma_c \times 1500}{110 \times 10^3}$

$\therefore$        $\sigma_s = 1.4318\ \sigma_c$                                    ... (i)

The total load P is shared by the two steel rods and one copper rod.

$\therefore$        $P = P_s + P_s + P_c = 2\,P_s + P_c$

$\therefore$        $P = 2\,\sigma_s A_s + \sigma_c A_c$                        ... (ii)

Substituting the values of P, $\sigma_s$, $A_s$ and $A_c$, we have

        $20000 = 2 \times 1.4318\ \sigma_c \times 314.16 + \sigma_c \times 314.16$

        $= 899.63\ \sigma_c + 314.16\ \sigma_c = 1213.79\ \sigma_c$

$\therefore$        $\sigma_c = \mathbf{16.48\ N/mm^2}$

$\therefore$   From equation (i), we have

        $\sigma_s = 1.4318 \times 16.48 = \mathbf{23.6\ N/mm^2}.$

**Answer :** (i) $\sigma_c = 16.48$ N/mm², (ii) $\sigma_s = 23.6$ N/mm²

**Example 97 :** *A rigid body AB of 40 kN hangs from 3 wires of equal lengths. The middle wire is of steel and two outer wires are of copper. If cross-sectional area of each wire is 250 mm², calculate the load shared by each wire.*

$E_s$ = 210 GPa, $E_c$ = 120 GPa.     **(B.T.E. W-2012/4 Marks)**

**Data :** Length of steel rod = length of copper rod = L, area of each rod A = 250 mm²,

$E_s$ = 210 GPa = $210 \times 10^3$ N/mm², $E_c$ = 120 GPa = $120 \times 10^3$ N/mm².

**To find :** $P_s$ and $P_c$.

**Concept :** (i) $\delta L_s = \delta L_c$, (ii) $P = P_s + 2P_c$

**Solution :**     $\delta L_s = \delta L_c$

$$\left(\frac{PL}{AE}\right)_s = \left(\frac{PL}{AE}\right)_c$$

$$\frac{P_s L_s}{A_s E_s} = \frac{P_c L_c}{A_c E_c}$$

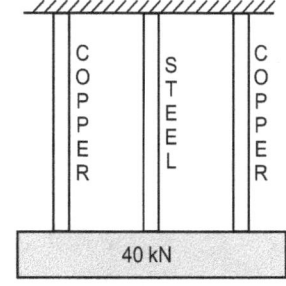

**Fig. 1.54**

Since $L_s = L_c$ and $A_s = A_c$, we have

$$\frac{P_s}{E_s} = \frac{P_c}{E_c}$$

∴     $P_s = \frac{E_s}{E_c}(P_c) = \frac{210 \times 10^3}{120 \times 10^3} \times P_c$

∴     $P_s = 1.75 \, P_c$     ...(i)

The total load P is shared by two copper rods and one steel rod,

$P = 2 P_c + P_s$

$= 2 P_c + 1.75 \, P_c = 3.75 \, P_c$

∴     $40 \times 10^3 = 3.75 \, P_c$

∴     $\mathbf{P_c}$ = 10666.67 N = 10.666 kN = **10.67 kN**

∴ From equation (i),

$\mathbf{P_s}$ = 1.75 × 10.67 = **18.67 kN**

**Answer :** $\boxed{P_s = 18.67 \text{ kN}, \ P_c = 10.67 \text{ kN}}$

---

**Example 98 :** *A concrete column 300 mm × 300 mm is reinforced with 4 bars of 20 mm diameter and carries a load of 400 kN. The modular ratio is 15. Calculate the stresses in steel and concrete. Also calculate the load shared by each material.* **(V.V. Imp./4 Marks)**

**Data :** Column area A = 300 × 300 = $9 \times 10^4$ mm²

Area of steel, $A_s = 4 \times \frac{\pi}{4}(20)^2 = 1256.64$ mm²

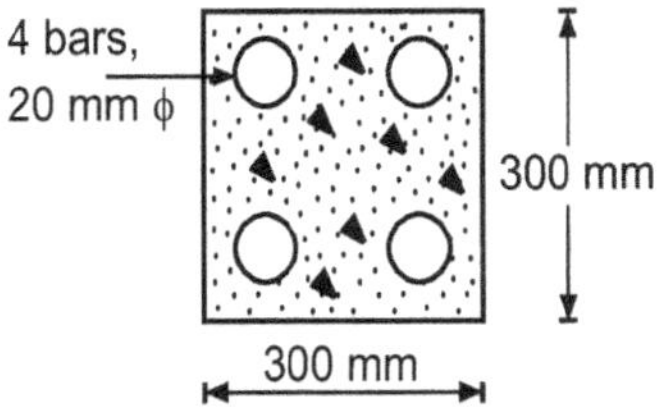

4 bars, 20 mm φ

300 mm

300 mm

**Fig. 1.55**

$\therefore$ Area of concrete, $\mathbf{A_c}$ = $A - A_s$

$$= 9 \times 10^4 - 1256.64 = \mathbf{88743.36 \ mm^2}$$

Axial load, P = 400 kN = $400 \times 10^3$ N

$$m = \frac{E_s}{E_c} = 15$$

**To find :** $\sigma_s$, $\sigma_c$ and $P_s$, $P_c$.

**Concept :** Two equations for composite bar.

**Solution :** Using the relation, $\sigma_1 = m\,\sigma_2$

we have,  $\sigma_s = 15\,\sigma_c$  ... (i)

Using the relation,  $P = \sigma_1 A_1 + \sigma_2 A_2$

we have,  $P = \sigma_s A_s + \sigma_c A_c$  ... (ii)

$\therefore$  $400 \times 10^3 = 15\,\sigma_c \times 1256.64 + \sigma_c \times 88743.36$  ... ($\because \sigma_s = 15\,\sigma_c$)

$\therefore$  $400 \times 10^3 = (15 \times 1256.64 + 88743.36)\,\sigma_c = 107592.96 \times \sigma_c$

$\therefore$  $\sigma_c = \dfrac{400 \times 10^3}{107592.96} = \mathbf{3.72 \ N/mm^2}$

Substituting this value in equation (i),

$\mathbf{\sigma_s} = 15 \times 3.72 = \mathbf{55.76 \ N/mm^2}$

Load shared by steel, $\mathbf{P_s}$ = $\sigma_s A_s = 55.76 \times 1256.64 = 70077.45$ N = **70.08 kN**

Load shared by concrete, $\mathbf{P_c}$ = $\sigma_c A_c = 3.72 \times 88743.36 = 330125.3$ N = **330.12 kN**

**Answer :** | (i) $\sigma_s = 55.76$ N/mm$^2$, (ii) $\sigma_c = 3.72$ N/mm$^2$, (iii) $P_s = 70.08$ kN, (iv) $P_c = 330.12$ kN |

**Example 99 :** *A concrete column 400 mm square reinforced with 4 steel bars of 20 mm diameter carries an axial load of 1000 kN. Determine the stress induced in each material. Take $E_s = 18\ E_c$.*  **(B.T.E. W-2006, 2005/4 Marks)**

**Data :**  Column area, A = $400 \times 400 = 16 \times 10^4$ mm$^2$

Area of steel, $A_s$ = $4 \times \dfrac{\pi}{4}(20)^2 = 1256.64$ mm$^2$

Area of concrete, $A_c$ = $A - A_s = 16 \times 10^4 - 1256.64 = 158743.36$ mm$^2$

Axial load, P = 1000 kN = $1000 \times 10^3$ N

$E_s = 18\ E_c$ i.e. $m = \dfrac{E_s}{E_c} = 18$

**To find :** $\sigma_s$, $\sigma_c$.

**Concept :** Two equations for composite bar.

**Solution :** Using the relation,

$\sigma_1 = m\sigma_2$

we have,  $\sigma_s = 18\,\sigma_c$  ... (i)

Using the relation,  $P = \sigma_1 A_1 + \sigma_2 A_2$

we have,  $P = \sigma_s A_s + \sigma_c A_c$  ... (ii)

$\therefore$    $1000 \times 10^3 = 18\sigma_c \times 1256.64 + \sigma_c \times 158743.36 = 181362.88 \, \sigma_c$

$\therefore$    $\sigma_c = \dfrac{1000 \times 10^3}{181362.88} = \textbf{5.51 N/mm}^2$

$\therefore$ From equation (i), $\boldsymbol{\sigma_s} = 18 \times 5.51 = \textbf{99.25 N/mm}^2$

**Answer :** $\boxed{(i) \; \sigma_c = 5.51 \text{ N/mm}^2, \text{ (ii) } \sigma_s = 99.25 \text{ N/mm}^2}$

---

**Example 100 :** *A R.C.C. column 500 mm in diameter is reinforced with 6 number of 20 mm diameter bars. Find the load carrying capacity of column, if permissible stresses in concrete and steel are 4 N/mm² and 130 N/mm² respectively. Take modular ratio = 18.*

**(B.T.E. S-2006, W-2005/4 Marks)**

**Solution :** Column area,

$$A = \frac{\pi}{4} \times (500)^2 = 196349.54 \text{ mm}^2$$

Area of steel, $A_s = 6 \times \dfrac{\pi}{4} (20)^2 = 1884.95 \text{ mm}^2$

$\therefore$    Area of concrete, $\textbf{A}_c = A - A_s = 196349.54 - 1884.95 = \textbf{194464.59 mm}^2$

Modular ratio, $\dfrac{E_s}{E_c} = 18$

Now,    $\sigma_1 = m\sigma_2$ gives

$\sigma_s = m\sigma_c$

$\therefore$    $\sigma_s = 18\sigma_c$    ... (i)

From equation (i), stress in steel is 18 times stress in concrete.

If    $\sigma_c = 4 \text{ N/mm}^2$, $\boldsymbol{\sigma_s} = 18 \times 4 = \textbf{72 N/mm}^2 < 130 \text{ N/mm}^2$   $\therefore$ O.K.

Load carrying capacity of the column is given by,

$$\textbf{P} = P_1 + P_2 = P_s + P_c$$
$$= \sigma_s A_s + \sigma_c A_c$$
$$= 72 \times 1884.95 + 4 \times 194464.59$$
$$= 913574.76 \text{ N} = \textbf{913.57 kN}$$

**Answer :**    $\boxed{P = 913.57 \text{ kN}}$

---

## Practice Questions

### Questions of 2 marks

1. Differentiate between single shear and double shear.    **(B.T.E. S-2013)**
2. What is meant by double shear ?    **(B.T.E. W-2012)**
3. State Hooke's law.    **(B.T.E. W-2012, 2009; S-2008, 1998, 1997)**
4. State the relation between Young's modulus and bulk modulus.
    **(B.T.E. S-2012, W-2007)**
5. Define elasticity and elastic limit.    **(B.T.E. S-2012)**
6. State the relation between three elastic constants E, G and K.    **(B.T.E. S-2011)**
7. Define Poisson's ratio.    **(B.T.E. S-2011, W-1999)**

8. Sketch the nature of stress-strain curve showing behaviour of ductile material under tensile load. Also show important points on the curve.   **(B.T.E. S-2011; 2006, 2005)**

9. Draw a stress-strain curve for mild steel and give the salient points on it.
**(B.T.E. W-2010, S-2010, 1998)**

10. Draw stress-strain diagram for mild steel rod and show different limits on it.
**(B.T.E. S-2010)**

11. Define lateral strain and longitudinal strain.       **(B.T.E. S-2010)**

12. Define modulus of rigidity.       **(B.T.E. W-2009; S-2008, 1998, 1997)**

13. A metal rod when heated expands freely. State the nature of stress induced.
**(B.T.E. W-2009)**

14. What is Poisson's ratio ?       **(B.T.E. S-2009)**

15. Draw stress-strain curve for mild steel and explain the terms.       **(B.T.E. S-2009)**

16. What is volumetric strain ?       **(B.T.E. S-2009)**

17. Draw a stress-strain diagram for M.S. and give salient points on it.   **(B.T.E. W-2008)**

18. State Hooke's law and define the terms elasticity and Poisson's ratio.**(B.T.E. W-2008)**

19. State the types of loads.       **(Imp)**

20. State the effects of load on a member.

21. Define torsional shear strain.       **(V.V. Imp.)**

22. Define bulk modulus. State the relation between Young's modulus and bulk modulus giving meaning of each term used in it.       **(B.T.E. W-2008)**

23. Explain the behaviour of mild steel bar under axial tension. Draw its stress-strain graph.       **(B.T.E. S-2008)**

24. Define factor of safety.       **(B.T.E. W-2007)**

25. What is bulk modulus ?       **(B.T.E. W-2007)**

26. Sketch the behaviour of member under axial pull and axial push.     **(B.T.E. W-2006)**

27. Sketch stress-strain curve for mild-steel and show elastic limit and ultimate stress on the curve.       **(B.T.E. S-2004, W-1997)**

28. State how to calculate total elongation for a bar of varying section subjected to an axial load P.       **(B.T.E. W-2004, 2003)**

29. Sketch a stress-strain curve for brittle material and give salient points on it.
**(B.T.E. S-1997)**

30. Define a composite section and modular ratio.       **(B.T.E. W-1998)**

31. State the relationship between lateral strain and linear strain.       **(B.T.E. S-1999)**

32. Differentiate between linear strain and lateral strain.

33. Define modulus of elasticity and state its S.I. unit.       **(B.T.E. S-2000)**

34. What are temperature stresses ? How are they produced ?       **(Imp.)**

35. Define limit of proportionality.

36. What is a permanent set ?

37. Define shear strain and show it on a diagram.       **(V.V. Imp)**

38. State the relation between Young's modulus and shear modulus.

39. Define shear load and shear stress.       **(V.V. Imp.)**

40. A bar fixed at one end and free at the other end is heated through t°C. What is the temperature stress induced in the bar material ?     **(B.T.E. S-1999)**

41. A material has elastic modulus of $2 \times 10^5$ MPa and Poisson's ratio of 0.25. Calculate the modulus of rigidity.     **(B.T.E. W-1999)**

## Questions of 4 marks

42. Draw a stress-strain curve for mild steel and show the salient points on it.
**(B.T.E. S-2013)**

43. Draw stress-strain curve for ductile material and explain the term ultimate stress.
**(B.T.E. W-2012)**

44. Define Young's modulus and modulus of rigidity. Also write their equations.
**(B.T.E. W-2012)**

45. Explain the relation between modulus of elasticity and bulk modulus and Poisson's ratio.     **(B.T.E. W-2012)**

46. State Hook's law and Poisson's ratio.     **(B.T.E. S-2010)**

47. Define Poisson's ratio and state the relation between E, G and K.     **(B.T.E. W-2007)**

## Problems of 4 marks

48. A metal rod 24 mm diameter and 2 m long is subjected to an axial pull of 40 kN. If the elongation of the rod is 0.5 mm, find the stress induced and the value of Young's modulus.     (**Ans.** $\sigma$ = 88.42 N/mm², E = 353.68 kN/mm²)

49. A mild steel bar of square cross-section 10 mm × 10 mm is subjected to the forces as shown in Fig. 1.56. Calculate the change in the length of the bar. Take E = 200 kN/mm².     (**Ans.** 0.01 mm (increase))

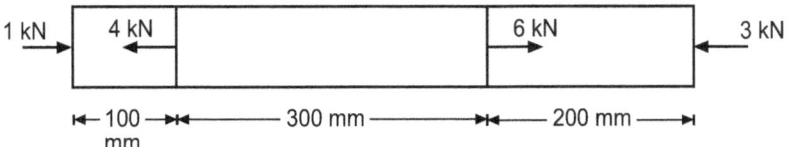

**Fig. 1.56**

50. A solid circular bar of a certain material remains unchanged in volume when subjected to an uni-axial loading. Calculate the Poisson's ratio of the material.

**Hint :** $\dfrac{\delta V}{V}$ = e (1 – 2 $\mu$) = 0 and e ≠ 0     $\left(\text{**Ans.** } \mu = \dfrac{1}{2}\right)$ **(B.T.E. W-2010)**

51. In an experiment on a steel specimen, the values of E and G were found to be $2 \times 10^5$ N/mm² and $0.8 \times 10^5$ N/mm². Determine the Poisson's ratio and bulk modulus for the steel.     (**Ans.** $\mu$ = 0.25, K = 1.33 × 10⁵ N/mm²)

52. A load of 50 kN is applied to a rectangular bar 50 mm × 40 mm in section. Find the percentage change in the volume of the bar.
Take E = 2 × 10⁵ N/mm², G = 0.8 × 10⁵ N/mm².     (**Ans.** 0.00625 %)

**Hint :** Percentage change in volume = $\dfrac{\delta V}{V} \times 100$

53. A metal bar of 20 mm diameter and 1 m long is subjected to an axial pull of 60 kN. If $E = 1.8 \times 10^5$ N/mm$^2$ and $K = 1.2 \times 10^5$ N/mm$^2$, find the change in volume of the bar. Also calculate the change in diameter of the bar.

**(Ans.** $\delta V = 166.67$ mm$^3$, $\delta d = 0.0053$ mm**)**

54. A bar of 22 mm diameter is subjected to a pull of 25 kN. The measured extension on the gauge length of 200 mm is 0.07 mm. If $\mu = 0.29$, find the modulus of rigidity and bulk modulus.     **(Ans.** $G = 0.73 \times 10^5$ N/mm$^2$, $K = 1.49 \times 10^5$ N/mm$^2$**)**

55. A steel bar 20 mm wide, 15 mm thick and 2 m long is subjected to an axial pull of 35 kN. If $E = 2 \times 10^5$ N/mm$^2$ and $\mu = 0.3$, calculate the alternations in length, width and thickness of the bar. Also find the volumetric strain and the change in volume.

**(B.T.E. S-2013)**

**(Ans.** $\delta L = 1.17$ mm, $\delta b = 0.003498$ mm, $\delta t = 0.002623$ mm, $e_v = 0.0002333$, $\delta V = 140$ mm$^3$**)**

56. In a tension test on a certain specimen 20 mm diameter, 200 mm long, an axial pull of 110 kN produced an elongation of 0.35 mm and the reduction in diameter is observed to be 0.00875 mm. Find the value of Poisson's ratio and the three modulii.

**(B.T.E. W-1991)**

**(Ans.** $\mu = 0.25$, $E = 2 \times 10^5$ N/mm$^2$, $K = 1.33 \times 10^5$ N/mm$^2$, $G = 0.8 \times 10^5$ N/mm$^2$**)**

57. A rectangular block of size x = 600 mm, y = 800 mm and z = 1000 mm, is subjected to a tri-axial stress system. The stresses in the three mutually perpendicular directions are $\sigma_x = 100$ N/mm$^2$ (tensile), $\sigma_y = 100$ N/mm$^2$ (compressive), and $\sigma_z = 100$ N/mm$^2$ (tensile).

Find the net strain in each direction and hence the change in the volume of the block. Take $E = 200$ kN/mm$^2$ and m = 3.

**(Ans.** $e_x = 0.0005$, $e_y = -0.00083$, $e_z = 0.0005$ and $\delta V = 81600$ mm$^3$**)**

58. In a bi-axial stress system the stresses along the two directions are $\sigma_x = 60$ N/mm$^2$ (tensile) and $\sigma_y = 40$ N/mm$^2$ (compressive). Find the maximum strain.

Take $E = 200$ kN/mm$^2$ and m = 4.     **(Ans.** $e_x = e_{max} = 0.00035$**)**

59. A steel rod of uniform cross-sectional area is fixed at both the ends which are 2 m apart and the rod is subjected to an initial compressive stress of 40 N/mm$^2$. Determine the temperature drop necessary to make the rod stress-free. Take $E_s = 200$ GPa, $\alpha_s = 12 \times 10^{-6}$ /°C.     **(B.T.E. W-2010) (Ans.** t = 20°C**)**

**Hint :** The rod will be free of stress only if total stress is zero i.e. Initial compressive stress – tensile stress due to fall of temperature = 0. $\therefore$ 48 – $\alpha$tE = 0 OR 48 = $\alpha$tE.

60. A steel rail 10 m long is at a temperature of 23°C. Find the expansion of the rail when its temperature is raised to 70°C. If the expansion is completely prevented, find the magnitude and the nature of the stress developed in the steel rail. Take $E = 200$ kN/mm$^2$ and $\alpha = 12 \times 10^{-6}$ /°C.

**[Ans.** $\delta L = 5.64$ mm, $\sigma = 112.8$ N/mm$^2$ (compressive)**]**

61. A rectangular hole of size 8 mm $\times$ 10 mm is to be punched through a plate 2 mm thick. Find the force required to punch the hole if the shear strength of the plate material is 300 N/mm$^2$. Hence find the compressive stress developed in the punch material.     **(Ans.** F = 21600 N, $\sigma = 270$ N/mm$^2$**)**

62. A bar of steel 4 m long is subjected to a pull (axial) of 80 kN. It is 32 mm diameter for 1000 mm of its length, 28 mm diameter for 2000 mm and 25 mm diameter for the remaining length. Find the elongation of each part and the total elongation. Take $E = 2 \times 10^5$ MPa.

    (**Ans.** $\delta L_1 = 0.49$ mm, $\delta L_2 = 1.29$ mm, $\delta L_3 = 0.815$ mm, $\delta L = 2.61$ mm)

63. A force of 31.68 kN is required to punch a circular hole of 14 mm diameter in a metal plate 2 mm thick. Calculate the compressive stress developed in the punching rod.

    (**Ans.** $f_s = 360.14$ N/mm², $\sigma_c = 205.8$ N/mm²)

## Important Points

- **Stress :** It is the internal resistance set up in a material due to externally applied load. Mathematically, stress is equal to the load divided by the cross-sectional area of the specimen.

  S.I. unit of stress is Pascal. 1 Pa = 1 N/m². Stress $\sigma = \dfrac{P}{A}$.

- **Strain :** Strain in a member is defined as the ratio of change in length to the original length.

  $$\text{Strain, } e = \frac{\delta L}{L}$$

- **Shear stress :** When a section of a body is subjected to two equal and opposite forces acting tangentially to the section, tending to slide its one part over the other at that section, the stress induced in it is called shear stress. It is denoted by q or $\tau$.

- **Shear strain :** It is the ratio of deformation due to shear force to the original length. It is denoted by $\phi$.

- **Volumetric strain :** It is the ratio of change in volume to the original volume and is denoted by $e_v$.

  $$e_v = \frac{\delta V}{V} = e_x + e_y + e_z.$$

  where $e_x$, $e_y$ and $e_z$ are the strains in x, y and z directions respectively.

- **Elasticity :** The property of certain materials by virtue of which it regains its original size and shape after removing the external force is called as elasticity.

- **Elastic limit :** It is the maximum value of stress upto which the material behaves as completely elastic one.

- **Hooke's law :** It states, "when a material is loaded within its elastic limit, the stress produced is directly proportional to the strain."

- **Young's modulus :** If a body is loaded within its elastic limit, the ratio of stress and strain is constant and this ratio is called as Young's modulus or modulus of elasticity.

- **Change in length of a body due to force acting on it :**

  $$\delta L = \frac{PL}{AE}$$

- **Linear strain and lateral strain :** Strain in the direction of applied force is called as linear strain. Strain in a direction at right angles to the direction of applied force is called as lateral strain.

- **Poisson's ratio :** When a homogeneous material is loaded within its elastic limit, the ratio of the lateral strain to the linear strain is constant and this ratio is called as Poisson's ratio. It is denoted by $\mu$ or $\frac{1}{m}$.

- **Shear modulus or Modulus of rigidity :** When a body is loaded within its elastic limit, the ratio of shear stress to the shear strain is called shear modulus or modulus of rigidity. It is denoted by C, G or N.

- **Bulk modulus :** When a body is subjected to three mutually perpendicular like stresses of the same magnitude, the ratio of direct stress to the corresponding volumetric strain of the body is called bulk modulus. It is denoted by K.

- **Relation between Young's modulus and bulk modulus :** $E = 3 K (1 - 2 \mu)$

- **Relation between Young's modulus and shear modulus :** $E = 2 G (1 + \mu)$

- **Relation between E, G and K :** $E = \dfrac{9 \, GK}{G + 3 \, K}$

- **Temperature stresses and strains :** If the expansion or contraction of the body due to temperature variation is wholly or partially prevented by applying external forces, the stresses induced in the body are known as temperature stresses and the strains produced due to temperature stresses are called as temperature strains.

  Deformation of a body due to increase or decrease in the temperature is given by,

  $$\delta L = \alpha \cdot t \cdot L$$

  Temperature stress $= \alpha \, t \, E$, Temperature strain $= \alpha \, t$.

## SUB-TOPIC 1.3 : BUCKLING OF LONG COLUMNS (4 Marks)

### Synopsis

Introduction, Buckling, Radius of gyration, Effective length of column, Slenderness ratio, Column end fixities, Column end conditions, Classification of columns, Buckling of axially loaded compression member, Euler's theory for long columns, Assumptions made in Euler's theory, Euler's formula, Limitations of Euler's formula, Factor of safety, Safe load, Strength of column, Rankine's formula.

## 1.45 INTRODUCTION

*A structural member carrying an axial compressive load is called a column. The vertical compression members in buildings are called columns, posts or stanchions. The compression members in roof trusses are called struts.*

In this topic, we shall study Euler's column theory, limitations of Euler's formula and its applications to design solid and hollow circular sections. Before going into the details of this topic, it is very necessary to understand the following terms.

**(i) Buckling :** *The bending action of a column/strut is called buckling or crippling.* The buckling of the column depends on its own initial curvature, column end conditions and the eccentricity of loading.

**(ii) Radius of gyration :** *It is the property of a section and is denoted by r or K.*

Mathematically,          $I = AK^2$

$\therefore$          $K^2 = \dfrac{I}{A}$

$$\therefore \qquad K = \sqrt{\frac{I}{A}}$$

where,     $K$ = radius or gyration

$I$ = moment of inertia of the column section

$A$ = cross-sectional area of the column section

**(i)   For a solid circular column of diameter D :**

$$I = \frac{\pi}{64} D^4, \text{ and } A = \frac{\pi}{4} D^2$$

Now     $K^2 = \dfrac{I}{A}$

$$\therefore \qquad K^2 = \frac{\frac{\pi}{64} D^4}{\frac{\pi}{4} D^2} = \frac{D^2}{16}$$

$$\therefore \qquad \boxed{K = \frac{D}{4}}$$

**(ii) For a hollow circular column of external diameter D and internal diameter d :**

$$I = \frac{\pi}{64} (D^4 - d^4) \text{ and } A = \frac{\pi}{4} (D^2 - d^2)$$

Now,     $K^2 = \dfrac{I}{A}$

$$\therefore \qquad K^2 = \frac{\frac{\pi}{64} (D^4 - d^4)}{\frac{\pi}{4} (D^2 - d^2)} = \frac{1}{16} \frac{(D^2 - d^2)(D^2 + d^2)}{(D^2 - d^2)}$$

$$\therefore \qquad K^2 = \frac{(D^2 + d^2)}{16}$$

$$\therefore \qquad \boxed{K = \frac{\sqrt{D^2 + d^2}}{4}}$$

*The buckling of the column takes place about the axis having least strength i.e. least moment of inertia. Hence in column problems, we shall always consider least moment of inertia i.e. minimum of $I_{xx}$ and $I_{yy}$. Hence, we have to consider minimum radius of gyration i.e. minimum of $K_{xx}$ and $K_{yy}$. Hence the above formula for radius of gyration can be modified as*

$$K = K_{min} = \sqrt{\frac{I_{min}}{A}}$$

In Euler's formula mostly we require value of $K^2$ and not K.

$$K^2 = \frac{D^2 + d^2}{16}$$   ... for hollow circular section

$$K^2 = \frac{D^2}{16}$$   ($\because$ d = 0, for solid circular section)

Please refer to chapter 4, for details of moment of inertia.

### (iii) Effective length of the column :

*The length of the column which bends or deflects as if it is hinged (pin - jointed) at its ends is called its effective length or equivalent length. It is denoted by $L_e$ or l.*

### (iv) Slenderness ratio :

*It is defined as the ratio between the effective length of a column and its minimum radius of gyration and is generally denoted by $\lambda$.*

Mathematically, $\lambda = \dfrac{L_e}{K}$

where,    $\lambda$ = Slenderness ratio

$L_e$ = Effective length of the column

K = Minimum radius of gyration of the column section

The effective length of the column depends upon the end conditions of the column.

### (v) Column end fixities :

The ends of a column may be hinged (pinned), fixed or free.

**(a) Hinged end :** *An end is said to be hinged if it is not allowed to move from its position but allowed to rotate in any direction i.e. a hinged end allows only rotation but does not allow translation.*

At the hinged end, deflection is zero but slope exists. Mathematically, y = 0 but $\dfrac{dy}{dx} \neq 0$.

(**Note :** y indicates deflection and $\dfrac{dy}{dx}$ indicates slope)

**(b) Fixed end :** *An end is said to be fixed if it is not allowed to move from its position as well as not allowed to rotate in any direction i.e. a fixed end does not allow both translation and rotation.*

At the fixed end, deflection and slope both are zero.

Mathematically, y = 0 and $\dfrac{dy}{dx}$ = 0.

**(c) Free end :** *An end is said to be free if it allows both translation and rotation.*

At the free end, deflection and slope both exist.

Mathematically, $y \neq 0$ and $\dfrac{dy}{dx} \neq 0$.

### (vi)  Column end conditions :

As already seen, the ends of a column may be fixed, hinged or free. A loaded column may have any one of the following four end conditions as given in Table 1.1.

**Table 1.1**

| Sr. No. | End condition | Sketch | Original length | Effective length |
|---|---|---|---|---|
| 1. | Both ends hinged | 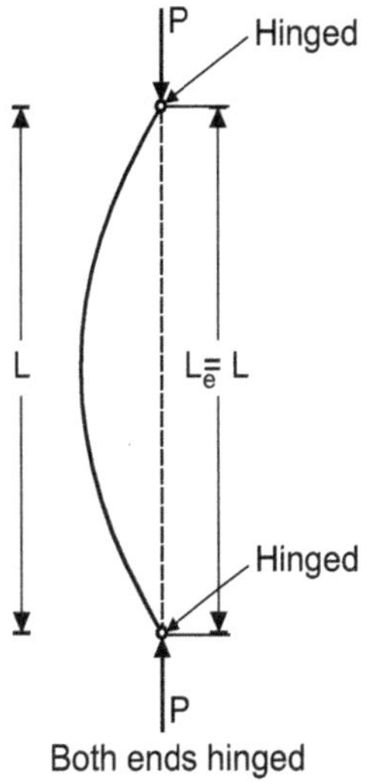  Both ends hinged  **Fig. 1.57** | L | L |
| 2. | Both ends fixed | 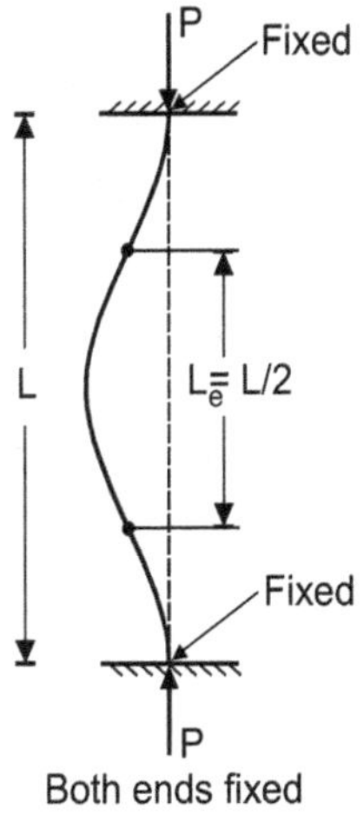  Both ends fixed  **Fig. 1.58** | L | $\dfrac{L}{2}$ |

| | | | | |
|---|---|---|---|---|
| 3. | One end fixed and other end hinged | 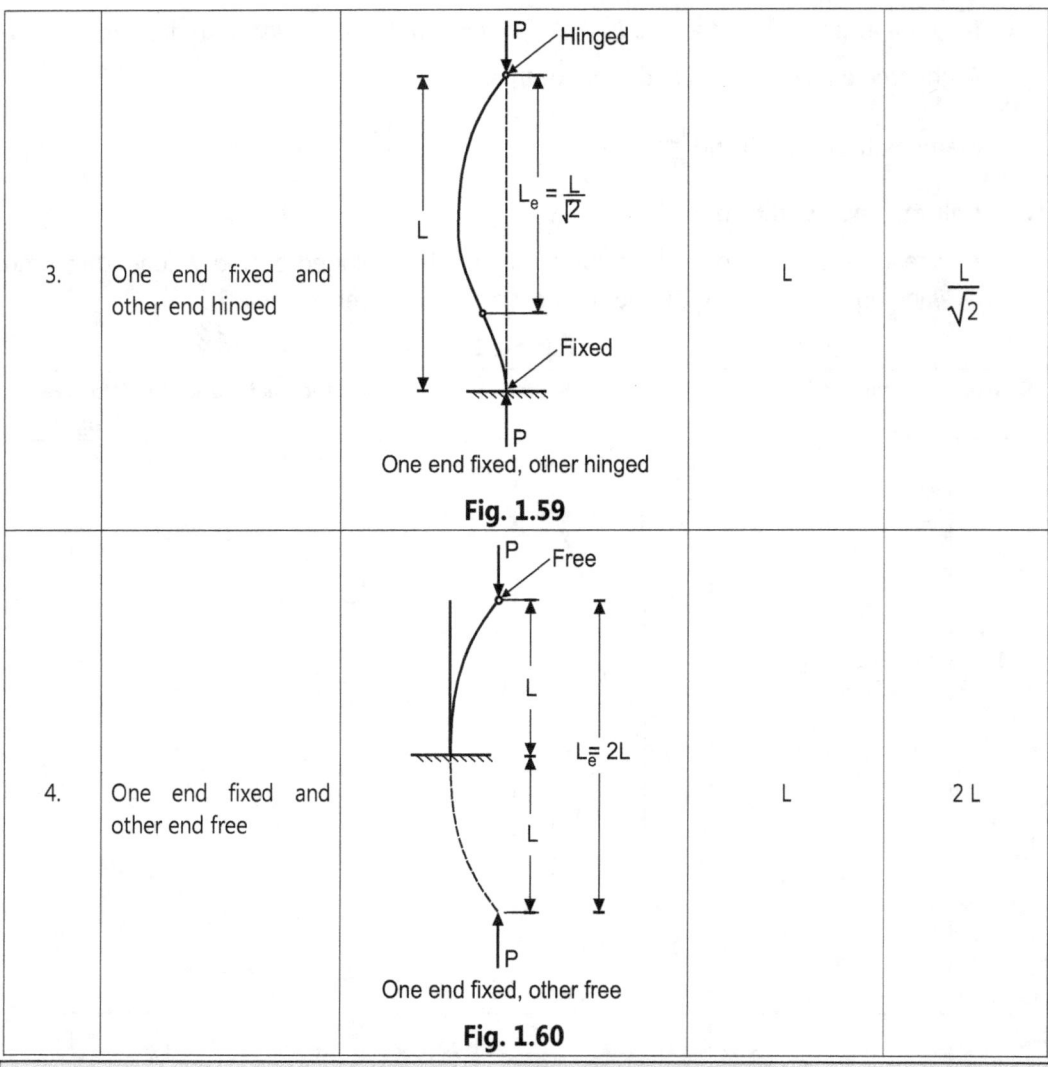 | L | $\dfrac{L}{\sqrt{2}}$ |
| 4. | One end fixed and other end free | | L | 2 L |

$L_e = \dfrac{L}{\sqrt{2}}$

One end fixed, other hinged

**Fig. 1.59**

$L_e = 2L$

One end fixed, other free

**Fig. 1.60**

## 1.46 CLASSIFICATION OF COLUMNS

A column may be classified as short, medium or long depending upon its mode of failure.

**(i) Short column :** *A column in which failure occurs due to crushing* (direct compressive stress) *is called a short column.* Short columns do not buckle under the action of axial compressive load. Therefore in the design of short columns, buckling stresses are neglected and only direct stresses are taken into account.

**(ii) Medium size column :** *A column in which failure occurs both due to direct stress and buckling stress (bending stress) is called a medium size column.*

**(iii) Long column :** *A column in which failure occurs due to buckling (crippling or bending) is called a long column.* Slenderness ratio of such a column is very large. In the design of long columns, direct stresses are neglected and only buckling (bending) stresses are taken into account.

## 1.47 BUCKLING OF AXIALLY LOADED COMPRESSION MEMBER

Let us consider a short column subjected to axial compressive load using compressive testing machine. If the load is gradually increased, it will crush at a certain critical load $P_c$.

Crushing load, $P_c = \sigma_c \times A$

where,        $\sigma_c$ = Ultimate (maximum) crushing stress for the column material.

        A = Cross-sectional area of the column.

The column being short, will not buckle under the action of axial compressive load and will fail due to direct compressive stress only.

Direct stress,   $\sigma_c = \dfrac{P_c}{A}$

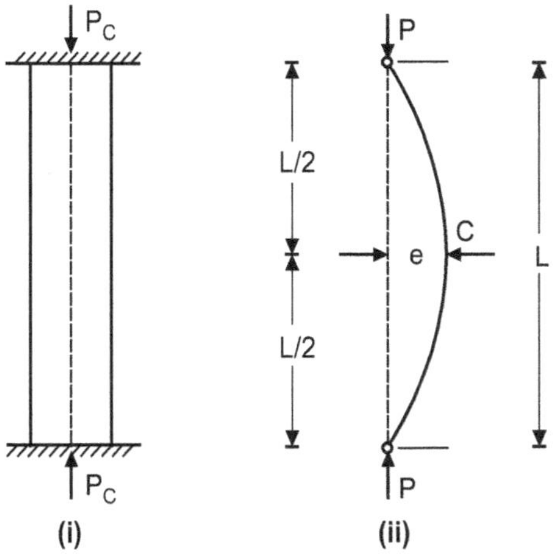

**Fig. 1.61**

Let us consider a long column of length L of the same material subjected to axial gradually increasing compressive load. At a certain load the column starts bending i.e. buckling or crippling. (The minimum load at which the column just buckles or tends to have lateral displacement is known as buckling, crippling or critical load). If the load is increased further, the column will fail at a certain load P which will be less than $P_c$.

In this case, the mid-height point C has the maximum eccentricity if the specimen has both ends hinged.

Moment at C due to P = P × e

The column being long will fail due to combined effect of direct and bending stresses.

$$\text{Direct stress} = \frac{P}{A}$$

$$\text{Bending stress} = \frac{M}{Z}$$

$$\text{Maximum stress, } \sigma_{max} = \frac{P}{A} + \frac{M}{Z}$$

$$\text{Minimum stress, } \sigma_{min} = \frac{P}{A} - \frac{M}{Z}$$

The column will fail at the middle point C when either $\sigma_{max}$ reaches the ultimate crushing stress or when $\sigma_{min}$ reaches the ultimate tensile stress for the column material.

The buckling of the column depends upon its end conditions. A column with both ends hinged will buckle as shown in Fig. 1.62.

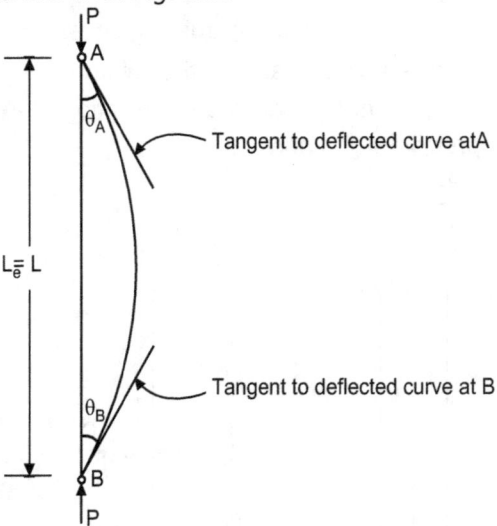

**Fig. 1.62**

Since both the ends of a column are hinged, deflection at A and B are zero. But slope of tangent to the deflected curve at A and B is maximum. *The vertical length of a column between the tangents having maximum slope is known as effective length or equivalent length of a column.* In short the length over which the column buckles is called its effective length.

If the column is hinged at both ends, it buckles over the entire original length L. Hence in this case, effective length and the actual length is one and the same.

Let us consider a column with both ends fixed as shown in Fig. 1.63.

Since the ends A and B are fixed, slope at A and B is zero i.e. the tangent to the deflected curve at A and B will be vertical. The tangents at C and D will have maximum slope. In this case, the vertical length CD between the tangents to the deflected curve at C and D is taken as effective length. The column will buckle for portion CD only. The points C and D are known as points of contraflexure (i.e. points of zero bending moment).

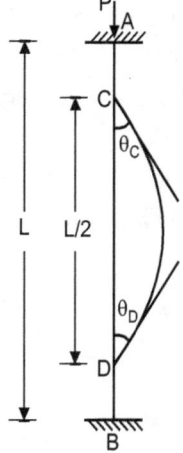

Both ends fixed

**Fig. 1.63**

Since the tangents at C and D has maximum slope, *C and D can be treated as hinged supports.*

In this case, effective length = length CD = $\dfrac{L}{2}$

A column with one end fixed and other hinged will buckle as shown in Fig. 1.64. Since end A is fixed, slope at A i.e. $\theta_A = 0$. The vertical length CB between the tangents to the deflected curve at C and B is taken as effective length and is equal to $L/\sqrt{2}$.

A column with one end fixed and the other free is unstable and has effective length equal to 2 L.

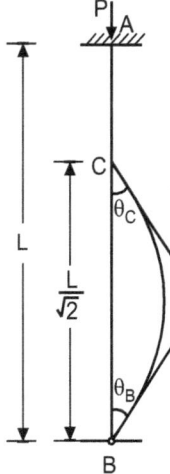

One end fixed and other end hinged

**Fig. 1.64**

## 1.48 EULER'S THEORY FOR LONG COLUMNS

Stability of long columns was first studied by the Swiss Mathematician Leonhard Euler in 1757. He neglected the effect of direct compressive stresses totally and determined critical loads that would cause failure due to buckling (bending) only. Euler's analysis is based on the following assumptions.

### 1.48.1 Assumptions Made in Euler's Theory

(i)    The compressive load is exactly axial i.e. it passes through the centroid of the column section.

(ii)    The material of the column is perfectly homogeneous and isotopic.

(iii)    The column is initially straight and of uniform lateral dimensions.

(iv)    The column is long and fails due to buckling only.

(v)    Shortening of the column due to direct compression is neglected.

(vi)    The self weight of the column is neglected.

(vii)    The stresses do not exceed the limit of proportionality.

### 1.48.2 Euler's Formula

The buckling load for a long column of constant cross-sectional area and length L hinged at both ends and subjected to axial compression is given by the equation

$$P = \frac{\pi^2 E I_{min}}{(L_e)^2} \qquad \text{... (i)}$$

where       P = Euler's buckling load at failure,

E = Modulus of elasticity of column material,

$I_{min}$ = Minimum moment of inertia of column section,

$L_e$ = Effective length of the column which depends upon column end conditions.

## 1.49 LIMITATIONS OF EULER'S FORMULA

Crippling load by Euler's formula is given by

$$P = \frac{\pi^2 E I_{min}}{(L_e)^2}$$

$\therefore$

$$P = \frac{\pi^2 E A K_{min}^2}{(L_e)^2}$$

$\therefore$

$$P = \frac{\pi^2 E A}{\left(\dfrac{L_e}{K_{min}}\right)^2}$$

Euler's crippling stress is given by

$$\sigma_c = \frac{P}{A} = \frac{\pi^2 E}{\left(\dfrac{L_e}{K_{min}}\right)^2} \qquad \text{... (ii)}$$

The value of $\sigma_c$ thus depends only on E and the slenderness ratio $\dfrac{L_e}{K_{min}}$.

The column material cannot withstand compressive stresses more than the yield stress for the material.

For mild steel, yield stress = 320 N/mm$^2$ and Young's modulus = $2 \times 10^5$ N/mm$^2$

Now, maximum value of $\sigma_c$ = 320 N/mm$^2$

i.e.                          $\sigma_c \leq 320$

$\therefore$

$$\frac{\pi^2 E}{\left(\dfrac{L_e}{K_{min}}\right)^2} \leq 320$$

$\therefore$

$$\left(\frac{L_e}{K_{min}}\right)^2 \geq \frac{\pi^2 E}{320}$$

$$\therefore \qquad \frac{L_e}{K_{min}} \geq \sqrt{\frac{\pi^2 \times 2 \times 10^5}{320}}$$

$$\therefore \qquad \frac{L_e}{K_{min}} \geq 80.48$$

*Thus for the Euler's formula to be valid, the slenderness ratio for mild steel column should be greater than or equal to 80.48. Euler's formula cannot be applied if the slenderness ratio for mild steel column is less than 80.48. This is limitation of Euler's formula for a mild steel column/strut.*

## 1.50 FACTOR OF SAFETY

Euler's formula gives the buckling load at failure. To determine the safe working load a suitable factor of safety must be applied. Generally factor of safety for mild steel is taken as 3 and for cast iron as 5.

## 1.51 SAFE LOAD

*It is obtained by dividing buckling load at failure by a suitable factor of safety.*

$$\text{Safe load} = \frac{\text{Buckling load}}{\text{Factor of safety}}$$

## 1.52 STRENGTH OF COLUMN

*It means the load carrying capacity of a column.*

Strength of a column by Euler's formula is given by

$$P = \frac{\pi^2 E I_{min}}{(L_e)^2}, \text{ where the symbols have usual meanings.}$$

The strength of a column depends upon the slenderness ratio. As the slenderness ratio increases, the tendency of buckling increases and hence the compressive strength of the column decreases. The strength of a column also depends upon the column end conditions.

## 1.53 RANKINE'S FORMULA

Rankine suggested the following empirical formula for calculating the strength of a column.

$$\frac{1}{P_R} = \frac{1}{P_C} + \frac{1}{P_e} \qquad \qquad \text{... (i)}$$

where    $P_R$ = Rankine's crippling load

$P_C = \sigma_c \times A$ = Crippling load for short column in which there is no buckling

$P_e = \frac{\pi^2 EI}{(L_e)^2}$ = Euler's crippling load for long column

Substituting the values of $P_c$ and $P_e$ in equation (i), we have,

$$\frac{1}{P_R} = \frac{1}{\sigma_c A} + \frac{1}{\dfrac{\pi^2 EI}{(L_e)^2}} = \frac{1}{\sigma_c A} + \frac{L_e^2}{\pi^2 EI}$$

$$= \frac{1}{\sigma_c A} + \frac{L_e^2}{\pi^2 E (AK^2)} = \frac{1}{\sigma_c A}\left[1 + \frac{\sigma_c}{\pi^2 E}\left(\frac{L_e}{K}\right)^2\right] \qquad \dots (\because\ I = AK^2)$$

$\therefore \qquad P_R = \dfrac{\sigma_c A}{1 + \dfrac{\sigma_c}{\pi^2 E}\left(\dfrac{L_e}{K}\right)^2}$

$\therefore \qquad \boxed{P_R = \dfrac{\sigma_c A}{1 + a\left(\dfrac{L_e}{K}\right)^2}} \qquad \dots \text{(ii) where } a = \dfrac{\sigma_c}{\pi^2 E}$

This is Rankine's formula (also called Rankine Gordon formula) which is valid for all types of columns ranging from very short to very long columns. This formula gives a crippling load which is in between $P_c$ and $P_e$ and takes into account the effect of both direct and bending stresses. *Euler's formula can be used only for long columns whereas Rankine's formula can be used for all lengths of columns.*

**Meaning of symbols used :**

$P_R$ = Rankine's crippling load

$\sigma_c$ = Ultimate crushing stress for the column material

A = Area of cross-section

$a = \dfrac{\sigma_c}{\pi^2 E}$ = Rankine's constant

$L_e$ = Effective length or effective height of the column which depends upon the column end conditions

K = Minimum radius of gyration = $\sqrt{\dfrac{I_{min}}{A}}$ where

$I_{min}$ = Minimum moment of inertia = Least of $I_{XX}$ and $I_{YY}$

For a given column material, the quantity $a = \dfrac{\sigma_c}{\pi^2 E}$ is a constant. Similarly $\sigma_c$ i.e. the ultimate crushing stress is also a constant. Table 1.2 shows the values of $\sigma_c$ and **a** for different column materials.

## Table 1.2

| Material | $\sigma_c$ (or $f_c$) N/mm$^2$ | a |
|---|---|---|
| Mild steel | 320 | 1/7500 |
| Cast iron | 550 | 1/1600 |
| Wrought iron | 250 | 1/9000 |
| Timber | 35 to 50 | 1/750 |

**Note :**

(1) *Generally, the suffix R is omitted while writing the Rankine's formula. Hence the Rankine's formula can be written as,*

$$P = \frac{\sigma_c\, A}{1 + a\left(\dfrac{L_e}{K}\right)^2}$$

(2) *Since f or $\sigma$ indicates the stress, sometimes the notation $f_c$ is used instead of $\sigma_c$. The values of $f_c$ (or $\sigma_c$) are given in MPa i.e. N/mm$^2$ in Table 1.2.*

(3) *The column material and the corresponding values of the two constants i.e. $\sigma_c$ and a are generally given in the problem. If not given, their values should be assumed as per Table 1.2.*

*For example, if a column material is cast iron, '$\sigma_c$' should be assumed as 550 N/mm$^2$ and 'a' should be assumed as $\dfrac{1}{1600}$ .*

(4) *Before applying Rankine's formula, the value of $a\left(\dfrac{L_e}{K}\right)^2$ should be worked out separately for the simplicity of calculations.*

## SOLVED EXAMPLES

**Type 11 : Examples based on Euler's formula :**

**Example 101 :** *A steel rod 3 m long and 40 mm diameter is used as a column, one end fixed and other end free. Find the buckling load by Euler's formula. E = 210 kN/mm$^2$.*

**(B.T.E. S-1986/4 Marks)**

**Data :** Steel rod D = 40 mm, L = 3 m, E = 210 kN/mm$^2$ = 210 × 10$^3$ N/mm$^2$.

**End condition :** One end fixed, other free.

**To find :** Buckling load by Euler's formula.

**Solution :** Since one end is fixed and the other is free,

$$L_e = 2L = 2 \times 3 = 6 \text{ m} = 6000 \text{ mm}$$

For a solid circular section,

$$I = \frac{\pi}{64}\, D^4 = \frac{\pi}{64} \times 40^4 = 125663.71 \text{ mm}^2$$

Using Euler's formula,

$$P = \frac{\pi^2 \, EI}{(L_e)^2} = \frac{\pi^2 \times (210 \times 10^3) \times 125663.71}{(6000)^2}$$

$$= 7234.79 \text{ N} = \textbf{7.23 kN}$$

**Answer :** $\boxed{P = 7.23 \text{ kN}}$

---

**Example 102 :** *A circular steel bar of 10 mm $\phi$ and 1.2 m long is subjected to a compressive load in a testing machine. Assuming both ends hinged, determine Euler's crippling load. E = 2 ×10⁵ N/mm². Also calculate the safe load if factor of safety is 3.*

**(B.T.E. W-2006, 1988/4 Marks)**

**Data :** D = 10 mm, L = 1.2 m = $1.2 \times 10^3$ mm, E = $2 \times 10^5$ N/mm²,

      factor of safety = 3.

**End condition :** Both ends hinged.

**To find :** (i) Euler's crippling load, (ii) Safe load.

**Solution :** Since both the ends of a column are hinged,

$$L_e = L = 1.2 \times 10^3 \text{ mm}$$

(i) Crippling load by Euler's formula is given by,

$$P = \frac{\pi^2 \, E \, I}{(L_e)^2}$$

$\therefore$          $$P = \frac{\pi^2 \times 2 \times 10^5 \times \dfrac{\pi}{64}(10)^4}{(1.2 \times 10^3)^2} = \textbf{672.8 N}$$

(ii)      **Safe load** $= \dfrac{\text{Euler's crippling load}}{\text{Factor of safety}} = \dfrac{672.8}{3} = \textbf{224.3 N}$

**Answer :** $\boxed{\text{(i) P = 672.8 N, (ii) Safe load = 224.3 N}}$

---

**Example 103 :** *A hollow steel tube of 200 mm external diameter and 25 mm thick is 4 m long and used as a column. If one end is fixed and the other end is hinged, find the load the column can carry. Use Euler's formula and factor of safety 2.* **(B.T.E. S-1994/4 Marks)**

**Data :** Hollow steel tube, L = 4 m = $4 \times 10^3$ mm, external diameter D = 200 mm,

      thickness t = 25 mm, internal diameter d = D – 2t = 200 – 2 × 25 = 150 mm,

      factor of safety = 2.

**To find :** Safe load by Euler's formula.

**End condition :** One end fixed, other hinged.

**Solution :** Since one end is fixed and the other hinged,

$$L_e = \frac{L}{\sqrt{2}} = \frac{4 \times 10^3}{\sqrt{2}} = 2828.43 \text{ mm}$$

M.I. of hollow circular section is given by,

$$I = \frac{\pi}{64}(D^4 - d^4) = \frac{\pi}{64}(200^4 - 150^4) = 53689327.58 \text{ mm}^4$$

Assume    E = $2 \times 10^5$ N/mm²

Crippling load by Euler's formula is given by

$$P = \frac{\pi^2 E I}{(L_e)^2} = \frac{\pi^2 \times 2 \times 10^5 \times 53689327.58}{(2828.43)^2}$$

$$= 13247283.66 \text{ N} = 13247.28 \text{ kN}$$

$$\therefore \quad \textbf{Safe load} = \frac{\text{Euler's crippling load}}{\text{Factor of safety}} = \frac{13247.28}{2} = \textbf{6623.64 kN}$$

**Answer :** $\boxed{\text{Safe load} = 6623.64 \text{ kN}}$

**Example 104 :** *A cast iron column with both ends fixed carries safe load of 800 kN with factor of safety 4. If the column is 4 m long, having external diameter of 200 mm, calculate the internal diameter of column cross-section. Use Euler's equation. Take E = 2 × 10⁵ N/mm².*

**(B.T.E. S-2006/4 Marks)**

**Data :** Hollow C.I. column, safe load = 800 kN, factor of safety = 4,
original length L = 4 m = 4000 mm, D = 200 mm, E = 2 × 10⁵ N/mm²

**End condition :** Both ends fixed.

**To find :** d.

**Solution :** Euler's crippling load = safe load × factor of safety

$$P = 800 \times 4 = 3200 \text{ kN} = 3200 \times 10^3 \text{ N}$$

Using Euler's formula,

$$P = \frac{\pi^2 EI}{(L_e)^2}$$

$$= \frac{\pi^2 EI}{\left(\frac{L}{2}\right)^2} \qquad \dots \left(\text{both ends fixed, } L_e = \frac{L}{2}\right)$$

$$= \frac{4\pi^2 EI}{L^2}$$

$$\therefore \quad 3200 \times 10^3 = \frac{4\pi^2 \times 2 \times 10^5 \times I}{(4000)^2}$$

$$\therefore \quad I = 6484555.753 \text{ mm}^4$$

$$\therefore \quad \frac{\pi}{64}(D^4 - d^4) = 6484555.753$$

$$\therefore \quad \frac{\pi}{64}(200^4 - d^4) = 6484555.753$$

$$(16 \times 10^8 - d^4) = 132102285$$

$$\therefore \quad d^4 = 1467897715$$

$$\therefore \quad \textbf{d} = \textbf{195.74 mm}$$

**Answer :** $\boxed{d = 195.74 \text{ mm}}$

**Example 105 :** *A steel bar of rectangular section 40 mm × 50 mm pinned at each end is subjected to axial compression. The bar is 2 m long. Determine the buckling load and the corresponding axial stress using Euler's formula. Also calculate the slenderness ratio if the proportional limit of the material is 200 N/mm². Take E = 2 × 10⁵ N/mm².*

**(B.T.E. S-2004/4 Marks)**

**Data :** Steel bar b = 40 mm, d = 50 mm, L = 2 m, $\sigma_c$ = 200 N/mm², E = 2 × 10⁵ N/mm².

**End condition :** Both ends hinged (pinned).

**To find :** (i) P, (ii) σ, (iii) λ.

**Solution :** $\quad I_{XX} = \dfrac{bd^3}{12} = \dfrac{40 \times 50^3}{12} = 416666.67$ mm⁴

$$I_{YY} = \dfrac{db^3}{12} = \dfrac{50 \times 40^3}{12} = 266666.67 \text{ mm}^4$$

∴ $\quad I = I_{min} = I_{YY} = 266666.67$ mm⁴

$\quad A = bd = 40 \times 50 = 2000$ mm²

Since both ends are hinged, $L_e = L = 2$ m = 2000 mm

(i) Buckling load by Euler's formula,

$$P = \frac{\pi^2 EI}{(L_e)^2} = \frac{\pi^2 \times (2 \times 10^5)(266666.67)}{(2000)^2} = \mathbf{131594.7 \text{ N}}$$

(ii) Axial stress,

$$\sigma = \frac{P}{A} = \frac{131594.7}{2000} = \mathbf{65.79 \text{ N/mm}^2}$$

(iii) Slenderness ratio (λ) :

$$P = \frac{\pi^2 EI}{(L_e)^2} = \frac{\pi^2 EAK^2}{L^2} \qquad \dots (\because I = AK^2, L_e = L)$$

$$\sigma_c \cdot A = \frac{\pi^2 EAK^2}{L^2}$$

∴ $\qquad \sigma_c = \dfrac{\pi^2 E}{\left(\dfrac{L}{K}\right)^2} = \dfrac{\pi^2 E}{\lambda^2} \qquad \dots \left(\because \lambda = \dfrac{L}{K}\right)$

∴ $\qquad \lambda^2 = \dfrac{\pi^2 E}{\sigma_c}$

$$\lambda = \sqrt{\frac{\pi^2 E}{\sigma_c}} = \sqrt{\frac{\pi^2 \times 2 \times 10^5}{200}} = \mathbf{99.35}$$

**Answer :** (i) P = 131594.7 N, (ii) σ = 65.79 N/mm², (iii) λ = 99.35

**Example 106 :** *Find the shortest length L for pin ended steel column having a cross-section of 60 mm × 100 mm for which Euler's formula remains applicable. Take $E_s$ = 2 × 10⁵ N/mm² and critical proportional limit is 250 N/mm².* **(B.T.E. W-2003/4 Marks)**

**Data :** b = 60 mm, d = 100 mm, $E_s$ = 2 × 10$^5$ N/mm$^2$, $\sigma_c$ = 250 N/mm$^2$

**End condition :** Both ends pinned i.e. $L_e$ = L.

**To find :** L.

**Solution :** For a rectangular section,

$$I_{XX} = \frac{bd^3}{12} = \frac{60 \times 100^3}{12} = 5 \times 10^6 \text{ mm}^4$$

$$I_{YY} = \frac{bd^3}{12} = \frac{100 \times 60^3}{12} = 18 \times 10^5 \text{ mm}^4$$

$$\therefore \quad I_{min} = I_{YY} = \frac{db^3}{12} = \frac{100 \times 60^3}{12} = 18 \times 10^5 \text{ mm}^4$$

$$P = \frac{\pi^2 EI_{min}}{(L_e)^2}$$

$$\sigma_c \cdot A = \frac{\pi^2 EI_{min}}{(L_e)^2} \qquad \qquad ... (\because P = \sigma_c \cdot A)$$

$$250 \times 60 \times 100 = \frac{\pi^2 \times 2 \times 10^5 \times 18 \times 10^5}{(L)^2} \qquad \qquad ... (\because L_e = L)$$

$$\therefore \quad L = 1539 \text{ mm} = \textbf{1.539 m}$$

**Answer :** $\boxed{\text{L = 1.539 m}}$

---

**Example 107 :** *A column of timber section 200 mm × 250 mm is 8 m long, both ends being fixed. If the Young's modulus for timber = 17.5 kN/mm$^2$, determine : (A) Crippling load, (B) Safe load for the column if factor of safety = 3.* **(B.T.E. W-2004/4 Marks)**

**Data :** b = 200 mm, d = 250 mm, L = 8 m,

E = 17.5 kN/mm$^2$ = 17.5 × 10$^3$ N/mm$^2$, factor of safety = 3.

**End condition :** Both ends fixed.

**To find :** (i) Crippling load, (ii) Safe load.

**Solution :** Since both ends of column are fixed,

$$L_e = \frac{L}{2} = \frac{8}{2} = 4 \text{ m} = 4000 \text{ mm}$$

For a rectangular section,

$$I_{XX} = \frac{bd^3}{12} = \frac{200 \times 250^3}{12} = 260.41 \times 10^6 \text{ mm}^4$$

$$I_{YY} = \frac{bd^3}{12} = \frac{250 \times 200^3}{12} = 166.67 \times 10^6 \text{ mm}^4$$

$$I = I_{min} = I_{YY} = \textbf{166.67} \times \textbf{10}^6 \text{ mm}^4$$

(i) Crippling load by Euler's formula is given by,

$$P = \frac{\pi^2 EI}{(L_e)^2} = \frac{\pi^2 \times 17.5 \times 10^3 \times 166.67 \times 10^6}{(4000)^2} = 1799.18 \times 10^3 \text{ N}$$

$$= \textbf{1799.18 kN}$$

(ii) **Safe load** $= \dfrac{P}{\text{factor of safety}} = \dfrac{1799.18}{3} = \textbf{599.73 kN}$

**Answer :** (i) P = 1799.18 kN, (ii) Safe load = 599.73 kN

**Example 108 :** *Calculate the safe compressive load on a hollow C.I. column (one end rigidly fixed and the other hinged) of 150 mm external diameter, 100 mm internal diameter and 10 m length. Use Euler's formula with a factor of safety of 5 and consider modulus of elasticity as 95 GPa.* **(B.T.E. S-2005/4 Marks)**

**Data :** Hollow C.I. column, D = 150 mm, d = 100 mm, L = 10 m,
factor of safety = 5, E = 95 GPa = $95 \times 10^3$ N/mm²

**End condition :** One end fixed and other end hinged.

**To find :** Safe compressive load.

**Solution :** For a hollow circular section,

$$I = I_{least} = I_{XX} = I_{YY} = \frac{\pi}{64}(D^4 - d^4) = \frac{\pi}{64}(150^4 - 100^4)$$

$$= 1.9942 \times 10^7 \text{ mm}^4$$

$$A = \frac{\pi}{4}(D^2 - d^2) = \frac{\pi}{4}(150^2 - 100^2) = 9817.48 \text{ mm}^2$$

Since one end is fixed and other hinged,

$$L_e = \frac{L}{\sqrt{2}} = \frac{10}{\sqrt{2}} = 7.071 \text{ m} = 7071 \text{ mm}$$

Buckling load by Euler's formula,

$$P = \frac{\pi^2 EI}{(L_e)^2} = \frac{\pi^2 \times (95 \times 10^3)(1.9942 \times 10^7)}{(7071)^2}$$

$$= 373964.50 \text{ N} = \textbf{373.96 kN}$$

**Safe load** $= \dfrac{P}{\text{factor of safety}} = \dfrac{373.96}{5} = \textbf{74.79 kN}$

**Answer :** (i) P = 373.96 kN, (ii) Safe load = 74.79 kN

**Example 109 :** *A strut 2.4 m long 40 mm diameter, one end of the strut is fixed while the other end is hinged. Estimate buckling load for the member using Euler's formula. Take E = $2 \times 10^5$ N/mm².* **(B.T.E. W-2003, S-2004/2 Marks)**

**Data :** L = 2.4 m, D = 40 mm, E = $2 \times 10^5$ N/mm²

**End condition :** One end fixed and other hinged.

**To find :** Buckling load by Euler's formula.

**Solution :** For a circular strut,

$$I = \frac{\pi}{64} D^4 = \frac{\pi}{64}(40)^4 = 125663.71 \text{ mm}^4$$

Since one end is fixed and the other is hinged,

$$L_e = \frac{L}{\sqrt{2}} = \frac{2.4}{\sqrt{2}} = 1.69 \text{ m} = 1.69 \times 10^3 \text{ mm}$$

Using Euler's formula,

$$P = \frac{\pi^2 EI}{(L_e)^2} = \frac{\pi^2 \times (2 \times 10^5)(125663.71)}{(1.69 \times 10^3)^2} = 86849.28 \text{ N} = \mathbf{86.85 \text{ kN}}$$

**Answer :** $\boxed{P = 86.85 \text{ kN}}$

## Type 12 : Examples based on Rankine's Formula

**Example 110 :** *Find the buckling load for a 16 mm diameter pin ended strut of length 600 mm. Rankine's constants to be used are a = $\frac{1}{7500}$, $\sigma_c$ = 330 N/mm²*

**(B.T.E. W-1992/4 Marks)**

**Data :** Pin ended (hinged) strut diameter D = 16 mm, L = 600 mm, a = $\frac{1}{7500}$,

$\sigma_c$ = 330 N/mm²

**To find :** Rankine's buckling load.

**Solution :** Assuming both the ends as hinged,

$$L_e = L = 600 \text{ mm}$$

For a strut of solid circular section,

$$A = \frac{\pi}{4} D^2 = \frac{\pi}{4} \times 16^2 = \mathbf{201.06 \text{ mm}^2}$$

M.I. of a solid circular section,

$$I_{least} = I_{XX} = I_{YY} = \frac{\pi}{64} D^4 = \frac{\pi}{64}(16)^4 = 3216.99 \text{ mm}^4$$

Now,     $$K^2 = \frac{I}{A} = \frac{3216.99}{201.06} = \mathbf{16}$$

($\therefore$ Radius of gyration K = $\sqrt{16}$ = 4 mm)

Now     $$1 + a\frac{(L_e)^2}{K^2} = 1 + \frac{1}{7500} \times \frac{600^2}{16} = 4$$

Buckling load by Rankine's formula,

$$P = \frac{\sigma_c A}{1 + a\frac{(L_e)^2}{K^2}} = \frac{330 \times 201.06}{4} = 16587.45 \text{ N} = \mathbf{16.58 \text{ kN}}$$

**(Note :** For a solid circular section, $K^2$ can directly be calculated as,

$$K^2 = \frac{D^2}{16} = \frac{16^2}{16} = 16)$$

**Answer :** $\boxed{P = 16.58 \text{ kN}}$

**Example 111 :** *A 250 mm × 200 mm rolled steel section, flanges 9 mm thick, web 6.7 mm thick, is used as a strut, 5 m long, both ends fixed. Estimate the safe axial load that it will carry using a factor of safety of 3. Rankine's constant is 1/7500 and crushing stress is 320 MPa.*

**(B.T.E. W-2005/4 Marks)**

**Data :** A rolled steel section (I section) as shown in Fig. 1.65, L = 5 m, f.s. = 3, $a = \dfrac{1}{7500}$,

$f_c$ = 320 MPa = 320 N/mm²

**End condition :** Both ends fixed.

**To find :** Safe load by Rankine's formula.

**Solution :** Area of cross-section,

$$A = 200 \times 9 + (250 - 9) \times 6.7 = 3414.7 \text{ mm}^2$$

$$I_{min} = I_{YY} = \frac{9 \times 200^3}{12} + \frac{(250 - 9)(6.7)^3}{12} = 6006040.32 \text{ mm}^4$$

$$K = \sqrt{\frac{I}{A}} = \sqrt{\frac{6006040.32}{3414.7}} = \textbf{41.94 mm}$$

Since both ends are fixed,

$$L_e = \frac{L}{2} = \frac{5}{2} = 2.5 \text{ m} = 2500 \text{ mm}$$

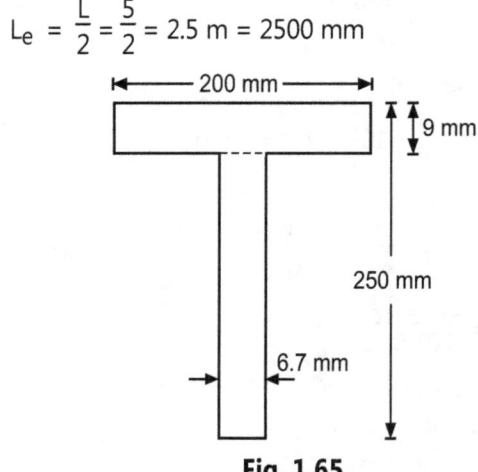

**Fig. 1.65**

Crippling load by Rankine's formula,

$$P = \frac{f_c\,A}{1 + a\left(\dfrac{L_e}{K}\right)^2} = \frac{320 \times 3414.7}{1 + \dfrac{1}{7500}\left(\dfrac{2500}{41.94}\right)^2} = 741437.65 \text{ N} = \textbf{741.44 kN}$$

$$\text{Safe load} = \frac{P}{f.s.} = \frac{741.44}{3} = \textbf{247.15 kN}$$

**Answer :** Safe load = 247.15 kN

**Example 112 :** *Find the crippling load by Rankine's formula for a hollow circular column of 150 mm external diameter and 100 mm internal diameter. Effective length of the column is 5 m. Take $f_c$ = 550 N/mm², a = $\frac{1}{1600}$.*    **(B.T.E. W-1985/4 Marks)**

**Data :** Hollow circular column D = 150 mm, d = 100 mm,

$$L_e = 5 \text{ m} = 5000 \text{ mm}, f_c = 550 \text{ N/mm}^2, a = \frac{1}{1600}.$$

**End condition :** Since effective length of the column is given, it is not necessary to mention the column end condition.

**To find :** Rankine's crippling load.

**Solution :** For a hollow circular section,

$$I_{least} = I_{xx} = I_{yy} = \frac{\pi}{64}(D^4 - d^4) = \frac{\pi}{64}(150^4 - 100^4) = 1.9942 \times 10^7 \text{ mm}^4$$

$$A = \frac{\pi}{4}(D^2 - d^2) = \frac{\pi}{4}(150^2 - 100^2) = 9817.48 \text{ mm}^2$$

$$\mathbf{K^2} = \frac{I}{A} = \frac{1.9942 \times 10^7}{9817.48} = \mathbf{2031.27}$$

(**Check :** For a hollow circular section,

$$K^2 = \frac{D^2 + d^2}{16} = \frac{150^2 + 100^2}{16} = 2031.25)$$

$$1 + a\frac{(L_e)^2}{K^2} = 1 + \left[\frac{1}{1600} \times \frac{(5000)^2}{2031.27}\right] = \mathbf{8.6922}$$

Crippling load by Rankine's formula,

$$\mathbf{P} = \frac{f_c A}{1 + a\dfrac{(L_e)^2}{K^2}} = \frac{550 \times 9817.48}{8.6922} = 621202.2 \text{ N} = \mathbf{621.2 \text{ kN}}$$

**Answer :** $\boxed{P = 621.2 \text{ kN}}$

---

**Example 113 :** *Determine by Rankine's formula the safe load on the column of 6 m length, with both ends fixed, can carry with factor of safety 4. The properties of section are, A = 1777 mm², $I_{xx}$ = 1.16 × 10⁷ mm⁴, $I_{yy}$ = 0.84 × 10⁶ mm⁴, $f_c$ = 320 N/mm², a = $\frac{1}{7500}$.*    **(B.T.E. S-1996/4 Marks)**

**Data :** L = 6 m = 6000 mm, f.s. = 4, A = 1777 mm²,

$$f_c = 320 \text{ N/mm}^2, a = \frac{1}{7500}, I_{xx} = 1.16 \times 10^7 \text{ mm}^4, I_{yy} = 0.84 \times 10^6 \text{ mm}^4.$$

**End condition :** Both ends fixed.

**To find :** Safe load on the column.

**Solution :** For both ends fixed,

$$L_e = \frac{L}{2} = \frac{6}{2} = 3\ m = \mathbf{3000\ mm}$$

$$I_{min} = \text{Minimum of } I_{xx} \text{ and } I_{yy} = 0.84 \times 10^6\ mm^4$$

$$A = 1777\ mm^2$$

Now, $$K^2 = \frac{I}{A} = \frac{0.84 \times 10^6}{1777} = 472.7068$$

$$a\frac{L_e^2}{K^2} = \frac{1}{7500} \times \frac{3000^2}{472.7068} = 2.53857$$

$$\therefore \quad 1 + a\left(\frac{L_e}{K}\right)^2 = 1 + 2.53857 = \mathbf{3.53857}$$

Using Rankine's formula, crippling load

$$P = \frac{f_c\ A}{1 + a\left(\frac{L_e}{K}\right)^2} = \frac{320 \times 1777}{3.53857} = 160697.68\ N$$

$$= \mathbf{160.7\ kN\ (approximately)}$$

Now,    **Safe load** $= \dfrac{\text{Crippling load}}{\text{Factor of safety}} = \dfrac{160.7}{4} = \mathbf{40.175\ kN}$

**Answer :** $\boxed{\text{Safe load} = 40.175\ kN}$

---

**Example 114 :** *An ISHB 300 is used as a column having an effective length of 6 m. Calculate the maximum safe load it can carry taking a factor of safety 3. Take the following Rankine's constant.* $\sigma_c = 320\ MPa,\ a = \dfrac{1}{7500}.$

*Properties of ISHB – 300 : C.S. area = 8025 mm², $I_{xx} = 12.95 \times 10^7\ mm^4$*

*and $I_{yy} = 2.25 \times 10^7\ mm^4$*    **(B.T.E. S-1994/4 Marks)**

**Data :** Effective length $L_e = 6\ m = 6000\ mm$, f.s. = 3, $\sigma_c = 320\ MPa = 320\ N/mm^2$,

$$a = \frac{1}{7500},\ A = 8025\ mm^2,\ I_{xx} = 12.95 \times 10^7\ mm^4,\ I_{yy} = 2.25 \times 10^7\ mm^4.$$

**End condition :** Not necessary to mention since $L_e$ is given.

**To find :** Safe load.

**Solution :** ISHB - 300 means Indian standard heavy beam (I section) having the overall depth equal to 300 mm.

Infact, this depth is not required for the calculation work.

$$I_{min} = I_{yy} = 2.25 \times 10^7\ mm^4$$

$$K^2 = \frac{I}{A} = \frac{2.25 \times 10^7}{8025} = 2803.7383$$

$$a\frac{L_e^2}{K^2} = \frac{1}{7500} \times \frac{6000^2}{2803.7383} = 1.7120$$

$$\therefore \quad 1 + a\left(\frac{L_e}{K}\right)^2 = 1 + 1.7120 = \mathbf{2.7120}$$

Using Rankine's formula, crippling load

$$\mathbf{P} = \frac{\sigma_c A}{1 + a\left(\frac{L_e}{K}\right)^2} = \frac{320 \times 8025}{2.7120} = 946902.65 \text{ N} = \mathbf{946.9 \text{ kN}}$$

$$\therefore \quad \mathbf{Safe\ load} = \frac{\text{Crippling load}}{\text{Factor of safety}} = \frac{946.9}{3} = \mathbf{315.63 \text{ kN}}$$

**Answer :** $\boxed{\text{Safe load} = 315.63 \text{ kN}}$

---

**Example 115 :** *A hollow C.I. column has 200 mm × 150 mm outside dimensions and 150 mm × 100 mm inside dimensions. Height of the column is 6 m, both ends fixed. If E = 1200 N/mm², find buckling load by Euler's formula. Also find crippling load by Rankine's formula, if $f_c$ = 500 N/mm² and a = $\frac{1}{1600}$.* **(B.T.E. W-1987/4 Marks)**

**Data :** Hollow C.I. column having b = 100 mm, d = 150 mm,
B = 150 mm, D = 200 mm, Original length L = 6 m = 6000 mm.

**End condition :** Both ends fixed.

$$E = 1200 \text{ N/mm}^2, f_c = 500 \text{ N/mm}^2, a = \frac{1}{1600}.$$

**To find :** Euler's buckling load, Rankine's crippling load.

**Solution :** Refer to Fig. 1.66.

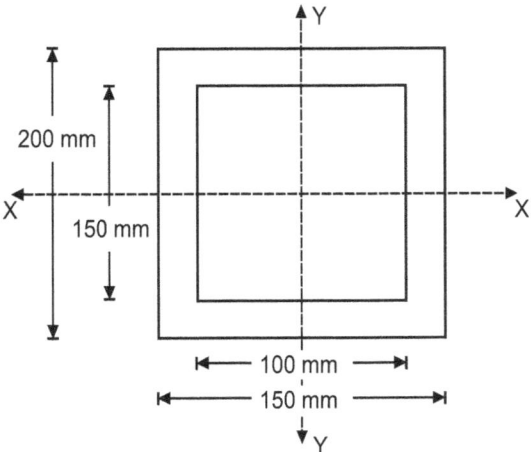

**Fig. 1.66**

Since both the ends are fixed,

$$L_e = \frac{L}{2} = \frac{6}{2} = 3 \text{ m} = 3000 \text{ mm}$$

For a hollow rectangular section,

$$I_{XX} = \frac{1}{12}(BD^3 - bd^3) = \frac{1}{12}(150 \times 200^3 - 100 \times 150^3)$$

$$= 71.875 \times 10^6 \text{ mm}^4$$

$$I_{YY} = \frac{1}{12}(DB^3 - db^3) = \frac{1}{12}(200 \times 150^3 - 150 \times 100^3) = 43.75 \times 10^6 \text{ mm}^4$$

$$\therefore \quad \mathbf{I_{least}} = \mathbf{I_{YY}} = \mathbf{43.75 \times 10^6 \text{ mm}^4}$$

Buckling load by Euler's formula,

$$\mathbf{P_E} = \frac{\pi^2 EI}{(L_e)^2} = \frac{\pi^2 \times 1200 \times 43.75 \times 10^6}{(3000)^2} = 57572.69 \text{ N}$$

$$= \mathbf{57.57 \text{ kN}}$$

Area of section,   $A = BD - bd = 150 \times 200 - 100 \times 150 = 15000 \text{ mm}^2$

Now,        $K^2 = \dfrac{I}{A} = \dfrac{43.75 \times 10^6}{15000} = 2916.67$

$$1 + a\frac{(L_e)^2}{K^2} = 1 + \frac{1}{1600} \times \frac{(3000)^2}{2916.67} = \mathbf{2.9286}$$

Crippling load by Rankine's formula,

$$\mathbf{P_R} = \frac{f_c A}{1 + a\left(\dfrac{L_e}{K}\right)^2} = \frac{500 \times 15000}{2.9286} = 2560950.6 \text{ N} = \mathbf{2560.95 \text{ kN}}$$

**Answer :** | (i) $P_E = 57.57$ kN, (ii) $P_R = 2560.95$ kN |

---

## Practice Questions

### Questions of 2 marks

1. Define column. State the end conditions of column.
2. State and explain the classification of columns.
3. State the values of effective length of column for the following end conditions.

**(2 marks each)**

   (a) Both ends hinged, (b) Both ends fixed, (c) One end fixed and other hinged, (d) One end fixed and other free.
4. Define the following :                                    **(2 marks each)**

   (a) Buckling, (b) Radius of gyration, (c) Slenderness ratio, (d) Effective length, (e) Safe load.
5. State Euler's formula and write the meaning of symbols used.
6. State Rankine's formula and write the meaning of symbols used.        **(W-2014)**
7. State the assumptions made in Euler's column theory.        **(S-2015)**
8. Define strength of a column.
9. State the factors affecting strength of a column.

### Problems of 4 marks

10. A column having diameter 200 mm is of length 3 metres. Both ends of a column are hinged. Find Euler's crippling load. Take E = $2 \times 10^5$ MPa.        **(Ans.** P = 17.19 MN)

11. A steel rod 5 m long and 40 mm diameter is used as a column with one end fixed and other free. Determine the crippling load by Euler's formula. Take E = 200 GPa.

    **(Ans.** P = 2.48 kN)

12. A steel rod 4 m long and 30 mm diameter is used as a column with one end fixed and other hinged. Determine the crippling load by Euler's formula. E = $2 \times 10^5$ MPa.

    **(Ans.** P = 9.81 kN)

13. A hollow steel tube of 30 mm external diameter and 20 mm internal diameter is used as a column 3 m long with both ends hinged. Determine the Euler's load. E = $2 \times 10^5$ MPa.        **(Ans.** P = 7 kN)

14. A hollow circular column having D = 300 mm and d = 200 mm has a length of 5 m. One end of it is fixed and the other is hinged. Using Euler's formula and factor of safety 3, find crippling load.        **(Ans.** Safe load = 16791.5 kN)

15. A column has a hollow symmetrical rectangular section with 140 mm × 60 mm outside dimensions and 120 mm × 40 mm inside dimensions. The column has 3.0 m length. One end of the column is fixed and the other free. Calculate the safe load by Euler's formula taking a factor of safety 3. Take E = 200 GPa.        **(B.T.E. W-1994)**
    **(Ans.** $I_{min}$ = $7.96 \times 10^6$ mm$^4$, Euler's load = 436.45 kN, Safe load = 145.48 kN)

16. Compare the crippling loads by Rankine and Euler's formula for a tubular strut 3 m long. The outer and inner dimensions are 40 mm and 30 mm respectively. The strut is pin jointed at both ends. Take yield stress as 315 N/mm$^2$, a = $\dfrac{1}{7500}$ and E = 200 kN/mm$^2$.        **(B.T.E. S-1988)**
    **(Ans.** Rankine's crippling load is more than Euler's load, $P_R$ = 19.95 kN, $P_E$ = 18.84 kN)

17. A cast iron column is circular in cross-section having external diameter 80 mm and internal diameter 50 mm. It is used as a column of length 3 m with both ends fixed. Using Rankine's formula, determine the crippling load. Take compressive stress = 500 N/mm$^2$ and Rankine's constant = $\dfrac{1}{1600}$.        **(B.T.E. W-1996) (Ans.** P = 434.1 kN)

18. A steel rod 5 m long and 40 mm in diameter is used as a column with one end fixed and the other hinged. Determine the critical load, the column can carry by using Euler's formula. Take E = $2 \times 10^5$ N/mm$^2$.        **(Ans.** P = 19.84 kN)

### Important Points

- **Column :** A structural member carrying an axial compressive load is called column/strut.
- **Buckling :** The bending action of a column is called buckling or crippling.
- **Slenderness ratio :** It is the ratio of effective length of the column and its minimum radius of gyration.
- **Effective length :** The length of the column which bends or deflects as if it is hinged at its ends is called effective length or equivalent length.

- **Radius of gyration :** It is the property of a section and is calculated by the relation

$$I = AK^2$$

$$\therefore \qquad K^2 = I/A$$

Or $\qquad K = \sqrt{I/A}$

For a solid circular column, K = D/4

For a hollow circular column, $K = \sqrt{\dfrac{D^2 + d^2}{16}}$

- **Classification of columns :** A column may be classified as short, medium or long depending on its mode of failure. A short column fails due to crushing (direct stress). A medium column fails due to both direct stress and bending (crippling) stress. A long column fails due to only bending stress.

- **Column end conditions :** The effective length of a column depends on the end conditions of a column. A loaded column may have any one of the following end conditions.

  (i)   Both ends hinged : $L_e = L$

  (ii)  Both ends fixed : $L_e = L/2$

  (iii) One end fixed, other hinged : $L_e = L / \sqrt{2}$

  (iv)  One end fixed, other free : $L_e = 2 L$.

- **Euler's formula :** $\qquad P = \dfrac{\pi^2 \, EI_{min}}{(L_e)^2}$

- **Rankine's formula :** $\quad P = \dfrac{\sigma_c \, A}{1 + a \left(\dfrac{L_e}{K}\right)^2}$

- **Safe load :** It is obtained by dividing the buckling load at failure by a suitable factor of safety.

$$\boxed{\text{Safe load } = \frac{\text{Buckling (or Crippling) load}}{\text{Factor of safety}}}$$

❒❒❒

# Chapter 2

# PRINCIPAL STRESSES AND PLANES

Weightage of Marks = 08, Teaching Hours = 05

## Objectives

Specific Objectives :

Acquire elementary knowledge of hoop stresses and principal stresses.

## Contents

2.1 Concept of Principal Stresses and Principal Planes (4 Marks)

Stresses on an oblique section of a body subjected to

- Direct stresses on one plane.
- Direct stresses on mutually perpendicular planes.
- Direct and shear stress on one plane.
- Direct and shear stress on mutually perpendicular plane (No derivations).
- Mohr's circle method for finding principal stresses and planes (only simple numericals).

2.2 Thin Cylindrical Shell (4 Marks)

- Stresses in thin closed cylindrical vessels subjected to Internal pressure, Hoop stress, Radial and Axial stress (Simple numericals only)

## SUB-TOPIC 2.1 : CONCEPT OF PRINCIPAL STRESSES & PRINCIPAL PLANES (4 Marks)

### Synopsis

Introduction, Different states of stresses, Some important definitions, Location of principal planes and magnitudes of principal stresses for different cases, Mohr's circle (Graphical method).

## 2.1 INTRODUCTION

A body may be subjected to only normal stress, only shear stress or complex stresses (i.e. combination of normal and shear stresses). In this topic, we shall study the analytical and graphical methods to find the stresses acting on an inclined plane of a body subjected to several simultaneous loadings / stresses.

## 2.2 DIFFERENT STATES OF STRESSES

### (i) A state of normal stress :

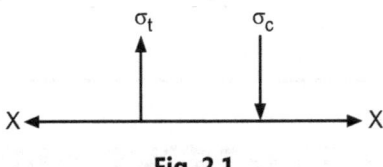

**Fig. 2.1**

Let us consider a plane XX subjected to two stresses $\sigma_t$ and $\sigma_c$ as shown in Fig. 2.1. The stress $\sigma_t$ pulls out the plane XX and hence it is called tensile stress. The stress $\sigma_c$ compresses or pushes the plane XX and hence it is called compressive stress. The two stresses $\sigma_t$ and $\sigma_c$ act normal (i.e. perpendicular) to the plane XX. Hence they are called normal stresses. In this case, a plane XX is subjected to only normal stresses. A normal stress is denoted by $\sigma_n$.

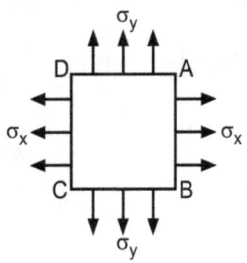

**Fig. 2.2**

Fig. 2.2 shows the tensile normal stresses on the planes AB, BC, CD and AD.

Normal stress on planes AB and CD = $\sigma_x$

Normal stress on planes AD and BC = $\sigma_y$

### (ii) A state of shear stress :

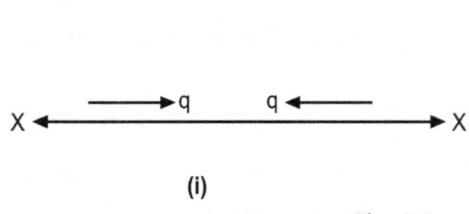

(i)

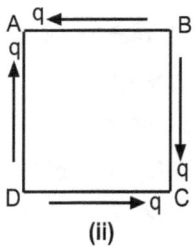

(ii)

**Fig. 2.3**

Fig. 2.3 (i) shows a plane XX subjected to two stresses of magnitude q acting parallel to the plane XX in the opposite directions. Hence, they are called shear stresses or tangential stresses. A shear stress is generally denoted by q or $\tau$. Sometimes a letter $\sigma_t$ is also used for tangential stress or shear stress. (*Here t stands for tangential and not tensile and $\sigma$ stands for stress*).

Fig. 2.3 (ii) shows a state of simple shear (pure shear) of intensity q acting along all the four planes of the element ABCD.

### (iii) An inclined stress :

Fig. 2.4 shows a plane XX subjected to tensile stress $\sigma$ acting at an angle $\theta$ to the plane XX. This stress can be resolved along the plane and normal to the plane XX.

Component of $\sigma$ along the plane = $\sigma \cos \theta$

∴  Shear stress  $\sigma_t$ = q = $\sigma \cos \theta$ ($\rightarrow$)

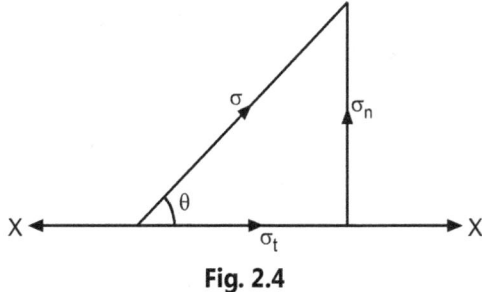

**Fig. 2.4**

Component of σ normal to the plane = σ sin θ

∴   Normal stress $\sigma_n = \sigma \sin \theta$ (↑)

Naturally the given inclined stress is the resultant of q and $\sigma_n$. Thus, an inclined stress σ has always two stress components viz. normal component $\sigma_n$ and a shear component q.

## 2.3 SOME IMPORTANT DEFINITIONS

**Resultant Stress :** *It is the resultant of normal stress and tangential stress and is denoted by $\sigma_r$. Since $\sigma_n$ and $\sigma_t$ act at right angles to each other,*

$$\sigma_r^2 = \sigma_n^2 + \sigma_t^2$$

∴
$$\sigma_r = \sqrt{\sigma_n^2 + \sigma_t^2}$$

**Angle of Obliquity (φ) :** *It is the angle made by the resultant stress with the normal stress and is denoted by φ. Refer to Fig. 2.5.*

$$\tan \phi = \frac{\sigma_t}{\sigma_n}$$

∴
$$\boxed{\phi = \tan^{-1} \frac{\sigma_t}{\sigma_n}}$$

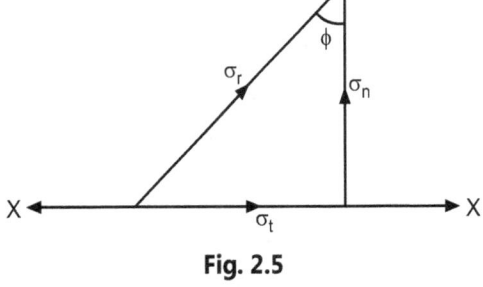

**Fig. 2.5**

**Principal plane :** *A plane which carry only normal stress and no shear stress is called a principal plane.*                                              **(S-2015)**

**Principal stress :** *The magnitude of normal stress acting on the principal plane is called principal stress.*                                              **(S-2015)**

**Major principal stress :** *The maximum value of normal stress acting on the principal plane is called major principal stress or the maximum intensity of direct stress.*

**Minor principal stress :** *The minimum value of normal stress acting on the principal plane is called minor principal stress or the minimum intensity of direct stress.*

**Major principal plane :** *A plane which carries a major principal stress is called a major principal plane.*

**Minor principal plane :** *A plane which carries a minor principal stress is called a minor principal plane.*

## 2.4 LOCATION OF PRINCIPAL PLANES AND MAGNITUDES OF PRINCIPAL STRESSES FOR DIFFERENT CASES

**Case 1 : Location of principal planes and magnitude of principal stresses for a complex stress system : (No derivation is expected to be asked in the examination as per syllabus. The derivation is given here just for understanding the basic concepts of principal stresses and planes.)**

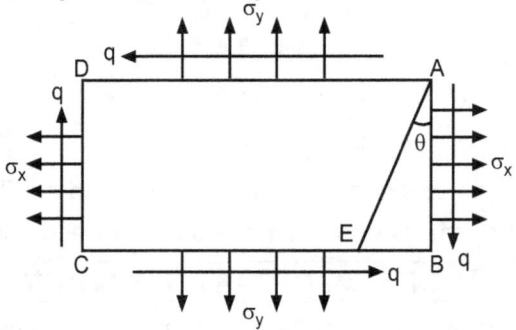

**Fig. 2.6**

Let us consider a rectangular element ABCD of unit thickness (perpendicular to the plane of paper) subjected to all types of stresses $\sigma_x$, $\sigma_y$ and q as shown in Fig. 2.6.

Let　$\sigma_x$ = Tensile stress on the faces AB and CD

　　$\sigma_y$ = Tensile stress on the faces AD and BC

　　q = Shear stress intensity along all the four planes.

Let us consider an oblique section AE inclined at an angle $\theta$ with the plane AB carrying the stress $\sigma_x$. This oblique section is also subjected to some normal and shear stresses. Hence, the plane AE is not a principal plane. Similarly, the planes AB, BC, CD and AD carry shear stresses q. Hence, they are not the principal planes. In such a case, it is very necessary to locate the principal planes and calculate the principal stresses.

**To find :**　(i)　Normal and shear stresses on the plane AE

　　　　(ii)　Principal planes and stresses

　　　　(iii)　Maximum shear stress

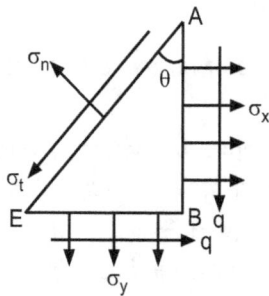

**Fig. 2.7**

Let us assume that a plane element ABE (i.e. wedge) is removed from the body. Consider the equilibrium of the wedge ABE, as shown in Fig. 2.7. Let $\sigma_n$ and $\sigma_t$ be the normal and shear stresses on the plane AE.

The wedge is in equilibrium under the action of the following six forces.

(i)     $\sigma_x \times AB$ and $q \times AB$ on the face AB

(ii)    $\sigma_y \times BE$ and $q \times BE$ on the face BE and

(iii)   $\sigma_n \times AE$ and $\sigma_t \times AE$ on the face AE

Fig. 2.8 shows the forces acting on the wedge ABE.

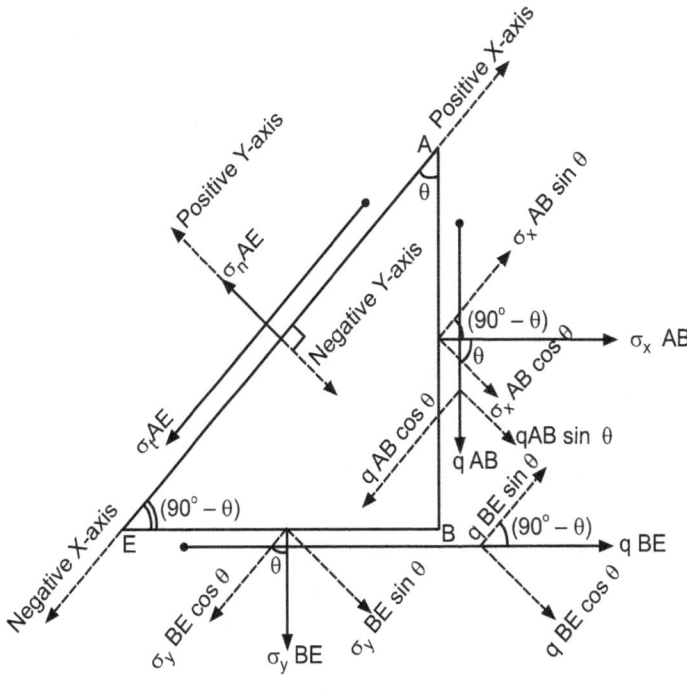

**Fig. 2.8**

Treat the plane AE as X-axis.

## Components of $\sigma_x \cdot AB$ :

Shear component $= \sigma_x AB \cos (90° - \theta) = \sigma_x AB \sin \theta$

Normal component $= \sigma_x AB \sin (90° - \theta) = \sigma_x AB \cos \theta$

## Components of $\sigma_y \cdot BE$ :

Shear component $= \sigma_y BE \cos \theta$

Normal component $= \sigma_y BE \sin \theta$

## Components of $q \cdot AB$ :

Shear component $= q \cdot AB \cos \theta$

Normal component $= q \cdot AB \sin \theta$

## Components of $q \cdot BE$ :

Shear component $= q BE \cos (90° - \theta) = q BE \sin \theta$

Normal component $= q BE \sin (90° - \theta) = q BE \cos \theta$

(**Note :** Shear component = x - Component = Component along AE

Normal component = y - Component = Component perpendicular to AE)

Using the conditions of equilibrium,

$\sum$ Forces along + Y-axis = $\sum$ Forces along – Y-axis

$$\sigma_n\, AE = \sigma_x\, AB \cos\theta + q\, AB \sin\theta + q\, BE \cos\theta + \sigma_y\, BE \sin\theta$$

$\therefore$
$$\sigma_n = \sigma_x \frac{AB}{AE} \cos\theta + q\, \frac{AB}{AE} \sin\theta + q\, \frac{BE}{AE} \cos\theta + \sigma_y \frac{BE}{AE} \sin\theta$$

$$= \sigma_x \cos^2\theta + q \cos\theta \sin\theta + q \sin\theta \cos\theta + \sigma_y \sin^2\theta$$

$$= \sigma_x \cos^2\theta + \sigma_y \sin^2\theta + 2\,q \sin\theta \cos\theta$$

But $\qquad \cos^2\theta = \dfrac{1 + \cos 2\theta}{2}$ and $\sin^2\theta = \dfrac{1 - \cos 2\theta}{2}$ and $2 \sin\theta \cos\theta = \sin 2\theta$

$\therefore$
$$\sigma_n = \sigma_x \left(\frac{1 + \cos 2\theta}{2}\right) + \sigma_y \left(\frac{1 - \cos 2\theta}{2}\right) + q \sin 2\theta$$

$$= \frac{\sigma_x}{2} + \frac{\sigma_x}{2} \cos 2\theta + \frac{\sigma_y}{2} - \frac{\sigma_y}{2} \cos 2\theta + q \sin 2\theta$$

$$\boxed{\sigma_n = \frac{\sigma_x + \sigma_y}{2} + \left(\frac{\sigma_x - \sigma_y}{2}\right) \cos 2\theta + q \sin 2\theta} \qquad \dots\text{(i)}$$

From this equation, the normal stress on the plane AE can be calculated.

Using the condition of equilibrium,

$\sum$ Forces along – X-axis = $\sum$ Forces along + X-axis

$\sigma_t \cdot AE + q\, AB \cos\theta + \sigma_y\, BE \cos\theta = \sigma_x\, AB \sin\theta + q\, BE \sin\theta$

$\therefore \qquad \sigma_t\, AE = \sigma_x\, AB \sin\theta + q\, BE \sin\theta - q\, AB \cos\theta - \sigma_y\, BE \cos\theta$

$\therefore$
$$\sigma_t = \sigma_x \frac{AB}{AE} \sin\theta + q\, \frac{BE}{AE} \sin\theta - q\, \frac{AB}{AE} \cos\theta - \sigma_y \frac{BE}{AE} \cos\theta$$

$$= \sigma_x \cos\theta \sin\theta + q \sin^2\theta - q \cos^2\theta - \sigma_y \sin\theta \cos\theta$$

$$= (\sigma_x - \sigma_y) \sin\theta \cos\theta - q\,(\cos^2\theta - \sin^2\theta)$$

$$= \frac{\sigma_x - \sigma_y}{2} \cdot 2 \sin\theta \cos\theta - q \cos 2\theta$$

$$\boxed{\sigma_t = \frac{\sigma_x - \sigma_y}{2} \sin 2\theta - q \cos 2\theta} \qquad \dots\text{(ii)}$$

**(Note :** $\cos 2\theta = \cos^2\theta - \sin^2\theta$)

From this formula, the shear stress on the plane AE can be calculated.

**Resultant stress on the plane AE :**

$$\sigma_r = \sqrt{\sigma_n^2 + \sigma_t^2} \qquad \dots\text{(iii)}$$

**Angle of obliquity :** $\qquad \tan\phi = \dfrac{\sigma_t}{\sigma_n}$

$\therefore$
$$\boxed{\phi = \tan^{-1} \frac{\sigma_t}{\sigma_n}} \qquad \dots\text{(iv)}$$

## Location of principal planes :

For principal planes, we have $\sigma_t = 0$

$\therefore \quad \dfrac{\sigma_x - \sigma_y}{2} \sin 2\theta - q \cos 2\theta = 0$

$\therefore \quad \dfrac{\sigma_x - \sigma_y}{2} \sin 2\theta = q \cos 2\theta$

$\therefore \quad \dfrac{\sin 2\theta}{\cos 2\theta} = \dfrac{2q}{\sigma_x - \sigma_y}$

$\therefore \quad \boxed{\tan 2\theta = \dfrac{2q}{\sigma_x - \sigma_y}} \qquad \qquad \dots (v)$

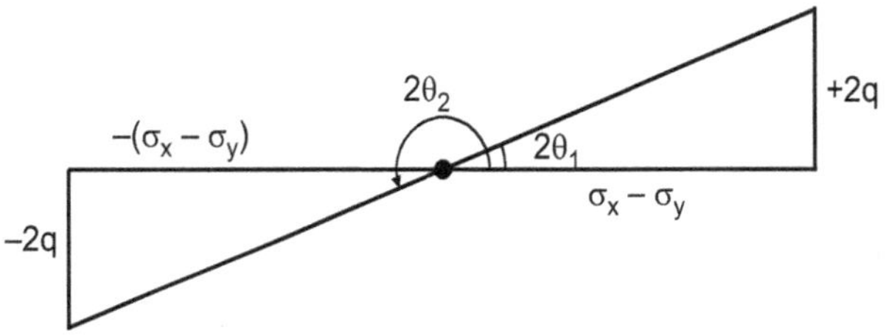

**Fig. 2.9**

Now, from Fig. 2.9, it can be seen that there are two values of $2\theta$ viz. $2\theta_1$ and $2\theta_2$ which satisfy the equation (v).

**[Note :** $\sin(180° + 2\theta) = -\sin 2\theta$ and $\cos(180° + 2\theta) = -\cos 2\theta$]

For the values of $2\theta$, we have

$$\sin 2\theta_1 = \frac{2q}{\sqrt{(\sigma_x - \sigma_y)^2 + 4q^2}}$$

and

$$\cos 2\theta_1 = \frac{\sigma_x - \sigma_y}{\sqrt{(\sigma_x - \sigma_y)^2 + 4q^2}}$$

$$\sin 2\theta_2 = \sin(180° + 2\theta_1) = -\sin 2\theta_1$$

$$= \frac{-2q}{\sqrt{(\sigma_x - \sigma_y)^2 + 4q^2}}$$

and

$$\cos 2\theta_2 = \cos(180° + 2\theta_1) = -\cos 2\theta_1$$

$$= \frac{-(\sigma_x - \sigma_y)}{\sqrt{(\sigma_x - \sigma_y)^2 + 4q^2}}$$

*Note that the angles $2\theta_1$ and $2\theta_2$ differ by 180°.*

*$\therefore \quad \theta_1$ and $\theta_2$ differ by 90° i.e. the two principal planes are always perpendicular to each other.*

## Magnitudes of principal stresses :

Now, the principal stresses can be found by substituting the values of $\sin 2\theta_1$; $\cos 2\theta_1$ and $\sin 2\theta_2$; $\cos 2\theta_2$ in the equation (i).

$$\sigma_n = \frac{\sigma_x + \sigma_y}{2} \pm \left(\frac{\sigma_x - \sigma_y}{2}\right) \frac{(\sigma_x - \sigma_y)}{\sqrt{(\sigma_x - \sigma_y)^2 + 4q^2}} \pm q \cdot \frac{2q}{\sqrt{(\sigma_x - \sigma_y)^2 + 4q^2}}$$

$$= \frac{\sigma_x + \sigma_y}{2} \pm \frac{(\sigma_x - \sigma_y)^2 + 4q^2}{2\sqrt{(\sigma_x - \sigma_y)^2 + 4q^2}}$$

$$= \frac{\sigma_x + \sigma_y}{2} \pm \frac{\sqrt{(\sigma_x - \sigma_y)^2 + 4q^2}}{2}$$

$$= \frac{\sigma_x + \sigma_y}{2} \pm \sqrt{\left(\frac{\sigma_x - \sigma_y}{2}\right)^2 + q^2}$$

Use positive sign for calculating the major principal stress and negative sign for the minor principal stress.

> **Major principal stress :** $\sigma_{n_1} = \dfrac{\sigma_x + \sigma_y}{2} + \sqrt{\left(\dfrac{\sigma_x - \sigma_y}{2}\right)^2 + q^2}$ ,
>
> **Minor principal stress :** $\sigma_{n_2} = \dfrac{\sigma_x + \sigma_y}{2} - \sqrt{\left(\dfrac{\sigma_x - \sigma_y}{2}\right)^2 + q^2}$　　　... (vi)

**Planes of maximum shear :**

The planes of maximum shear will be inclined at $\theta_1 + 45°$ and $\theta_1 + 135°$ to the plane AB.

> $q_{max} = \sigma_{t_{max}} = \dfrac{\sigma_{n_1} - \sigma_{n_2}}{2}$
>
> $q_{max} = \sigma_{t_{max}} = \pm\sqrt{\left(\dfrac{\sigma_x - \sigma_y}{2}\right)^2 + q^2}$

... (vii)

**Case 2 : Location of principal planes and magnitude of principal stresses for a body subjected to normal stress in one direction accompanied by a simple shear stress q :**

Refer to Fig. 2.10.

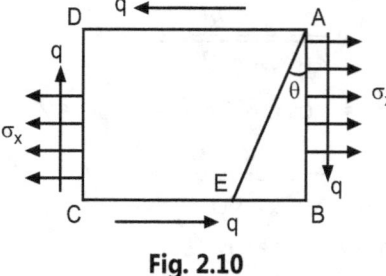

**Fig. 2.10**

The unknowns corresponding to this case can be calculated by substituting $\sigma_y = 0$ in the equations derived in case 1.

**(i) Normal stress on plane AE,**

$$\sigma_n = \frac{\sigma_x}{2} + \frac{\sigma_x}{2}\cos 2\theta + q\sin 2\theta = \frac{\sigma_x}{2}(1 + \cos 2\theta) + q\sin 2\theta$$

**(ii) Shear stress on plane AE,**

$$\sigma_t = \frac{\sigma_x}{2} \sin 2\theta - q \cos 2\theta$$

**Location of principal planes :**

$$\tan 2\theta = \frac{2q}{\sigma_x} . \text{ Find } \theta_1 \text{ and } \theta_2.$$

**(iii) Major principal stress :**

$$\sigma_{n_1} = \frac{\sigma_x}{2} + \sqrt{\left(\frac{\sigma_x}{2}\right)^2 + q^2}$$

**Minor principal stress :**

$$\sigma_{n_2} = \frac{\sigma_x}{2} - \sqrt{\left(\frac{\sigma_x}{2}\right)^2 + q^2}$$

**(iv) Maximum shear stress :**

$$\sigma_{t_{max}} = \pm \frac{\sigma_{n_1} - \sigma_{n_2}}{2} = \pm \sqrt{\left(\frac{\sigma_x}{2}\right)^2 + q^2}$$

**(v) The planes of maximum shear will be inclined at $\theta_1 + 45°$ and $\theta_1 + 135°$ to the plane AB.**

**Case 3 : A body subjected to normal stresses in two mutually perpendicular directions (q = 0) :**

Refer to Fig. 2.11.

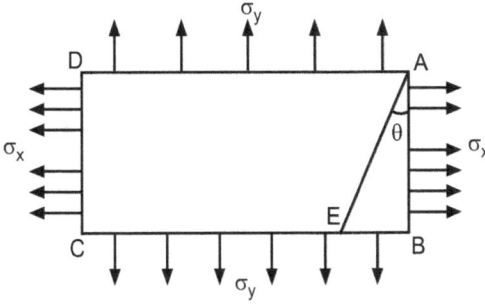

**Fig. 2.11**

**Important note :** In this case, the planes AB and CD carry only normal stress $\sigma_x$ (tensile) and the planes AD and BC carry only normal stress $\sigma_y$ (tensile). Moreover, there is no shear stress on any plane. Hence the planes AB, CD and AD, BC are the principal planes and the stresses $\sigma_x$ and $\sigma_y$ are the principal stresses. The principal planes AB and BC are at right angles to each other. Hence in such a case, it is not necessary to locate the principal planes and find out the principal stresses. In such types of examples, we are interested to calculate normal and shear stresses on the oblique section AE.

The unknowns corresponding to this case can be calculated by substituting q = 0 in the equations derived in case I.

**(i) Normal stress on plane AE :** $\sigma_n = \dfrac{\sigma_x + \sigma_y}{2} + \dfrac{\sigma_x - \sigma_y}{2}\cos 2\theta$

**(ii) Shear stress on plane AE :** $\sigma_t = \dfrac{\sigma_x - \sigma_y}{2}\sin 2\theta$

**(iii) Maximum shear stress :** $\sigma_{t_{max}} = \dfrac{\sigma_{n_1} - \sigma_{n_2}}{2}$

$$= \pm\frac{\text{Difference of principal stresses}}{2} = \pm\frac{\sigma_x - \sigma_y}{2}$$

**(Note :** This can also be calculated by putting $\theta = 45°$ and $135°$ in the equation of $\sigma_t$)

**(iv) Planes of maximum shear will be inclined at 45° to the principal planes.**

**(v) Normal stress on the planes of maximum shear :** This can be calculated by putting $\theta = 45°$ and $135°$ in the equation of $\sigma_n$.

$$\sigma_n = \frac{\sigma_x + \sigma_y}{2} + \frac{\sigma_x - \sigma_y}{2} \times 0 = \frac{\sigma_x + \sigma_y}{2}$$

$$[\because \cos(2 \times 45°) = \cos(2 \times 135°) = 0]$$

**Case 4 : A body subjected to normal stress in one plane ($q = 0$, $\sigma_y = 0$) :**

Refer to Fig. 2.12.

**Note :** The planes AB and CD carry only normal stress $\sigma_x$ (tensile) and no shear stress. There is no normal stress on planes AD and BC.

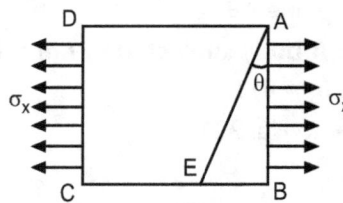

**Fig. 2.12**

In this case, the plane AB (or CD) is a principal plane and the stress $\sigma_x$ acting on it is a principal stress. The unknowns corresponding to this case can be calculated by substituting $\sigma_y = 0$ and $q = 0$ in the equations derived in case 1.

**(i) Normal stress on plane AE :**

$$\sigma_n = \frac{\sigma_x}{2} + \frac{\sigma_x}{2}\cos 2\theta = \frac{\sigma_x}{2}(1 + \cos 2\theta) = \frac{\sigma_x}{2} \cdot 2\cos^2\theta$$

$$= \sigma_x \cos^2\theta \qquad\qquad \dots (\because 1 + \cos 2\theta = 2\cos^2\theta)$$

**(ii) Shear stress on plane AE :**

$$\sigma_t = \frac{\sigma_x}{2}\sin 2\theta$$

**(iii) Maximum shear stress :**

$$\sigma_{t_{max}} = \pm\frac{\sigma_x}{2}$$

**(iv) Planes of maximum shear will be inclined at 45° to the principal plane AB.**

**(v) Normal stress on the plane of maximum shear :** This can be calculated by substituting $\theta = 45°$ in the equation of $\sigma_n$.

$$\sigma_n = \sigma_x \cdot \cos^2(45°) = \sigma_x \left(\frac{1}{\sqrt{2}}\right)^2 = \frac{\sigma_x}{2}$$

## 2.5 MOHR'S CIRCLE (GRAPHICAL METHOD)

Mohr's circle is a graphical representation of all the information contained in equations derived in case 1.

In this method, normal stresses are plotted along the horizontal axis and shearing stresses along the vertical axis.

### Sign conventions :

(i) Tensile stress is positive and compressive stress is negative. Hence tensile stresses are plotted to the right side of the origin and compressive stresses to the left.

(ii) Clockwise shear is positive and anticlockwise shear is negative. Hence positive shear is plotted along positive Y-axis and negative shear along negative Y-axis.

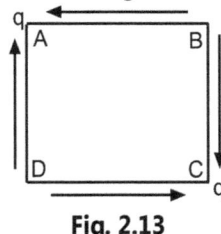

**Fig. 2.13**

q as seen on vertical planes AD and BC is positive because they tend to rotate the element clockwise.

q as seen on horizontal planes AB and CD is negative because they tend to rotate the element anticlockwise.

### Construction of Mohr's Circle :

We shall understand the procedure of construction of Mohr's circle with the help of solved examples.

## SOLVED EXAMPLES

**Type 1 : Examples based on the body subjected to normal stress in one plane only :**

Normal stress on an oblique section, $\sigma_n = \sigma_x \cdot \cos^2 \theta$.

Shear stress on an oblique section, $\sigma_t = \frac{\sigma_x}{2} \cdot \sin 2\theta$

Resultant stress, $\sigma_r = \sqrt{\sigma_n^2 + \sigma_t^2}$

Angle of obliquity, $\tan \phi = \frac{\sigma_t}{\sigma_n} \Rightarrow \phi = \tan^{-1} \frac{\sigma_t}{\sigma_n}$

Plane of maximum shear is inclined at $45°$ to the principal plane.

Maximum shear stress, $\sigma_{t\,max} = \frac{\sigma_x}{2}$

**Example 1 :** *A 12 mm diameter bar is subjected to a pull of 12 kN. Calculate the normal and tangential stresses on planes making angles of 5° and 37° with the axis of the bar.*

**(B.T.E. S-2004/4 Marks)**

**Data**     :     Diameter of bar d = 12 mm, $P_x$ = 12 kN = $12 \times 10^3$ N, $\theta_1$ = 5° and $\theta_1$ = 37°.

**To find**   :    $\sigma_n$ and $\sigma_t$ on 5° and 37° planes.

**Concept :**    (i) $\sigma_n = \sigma_x \cos^2 \theta$, (ii) $\sigma_t = \dfrac{\sigma_x}{2} \cdot \sin 2\theta$

**Solution :**    Cross-sectional area,

$$A = \frac{\pi}{4} d^2 = \frac{\pi}{4} (12^2) = 113.097 \text{ mm}^2$$

∴   Horizontal stress,     $\sigma_x = \dfrac{P_x}{A} = \dfrac{12 \times 10^3}{113.097} = 106.1 \text{ N/mm}^2$

**Case (i) :** When $\theta_1$ = 5°.

Angle made by oblique section with vertical,

$$\theta = 90° - 5° = 85°$$

**Normal stress,**        $\sigma_n = \sigma_x \cdot \cos^2 \theta$

$$= 106.1 \cos^2 85°$$

$$= \mathbf{0.806 \text{ N/mm}^2}$$

**Tangential stress,**   $\sigma_t = \dfrac{\sigma_x}{2} \cdot \sin 2\theta = \dfrac{106.1}{2} \sin(2 \times 85°) = \mathbf{9.212 \text{ N/mm}^2}$

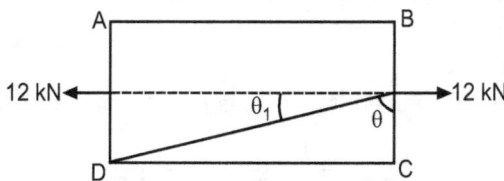

**Fig. 2.14**

**Case (ii) :** When $\theta_1$ = 37°, $\theta$ = 90° − 37° = 53°.

**Normal stress,**        $\sigma_n = \sigma_x \cdot \cos^2 \theta = 106.1 \cos^2 53° = \mathbf{38.43 \text{ N/mm}^2}$

**Tangential stress,**     $\sigma_t = \dfrac{\sigma_x}{2} \cdot \sin 2\theta = \dfrac{106.1}{2} \sin(2 \times 53°) = \mathbf{50.995 \text{ N/mm}^2}$

**Answer :**   | **Case (i) :** $\sigma_n = 0.806 \text{ N/mm}^2$, $\sigma_t = 9.212 \text{ N/mm}^2$ |
| **Case (ii) :** $\sigma_n = 38.43 \text{ N/mm}^2$, $\sigma_t = 50.995 \text{ N/mm}^2$ |

**Example 2 :** *A tension member is subjected to axial stress 10 N/mm² and the plane of oblique is 30° to the axis of stress. Compute the normal and shear stress on an oblique plane.*

**(B.T.E. S-1998/4 Marks)**

**Data**     : Axial stress, $\sigma_x$ = 10 N/mm², $\theta$ = 90° − 30° = 60°.

**To find** : $\sigma_n$ and $\sigma_t$ on an oblique plane BE.

**Solution :**

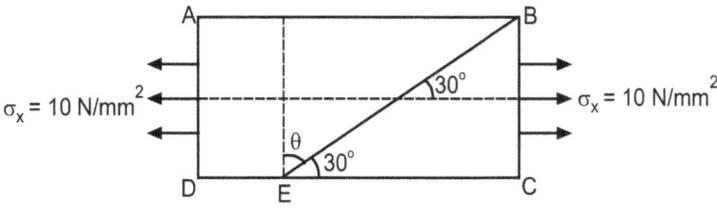

**Fig. 2.15**

Here the oblique plane BE is inclined at 30° to the axis of $\sigma_x$ i.e. with the horizontal.

∴ θ = angle made by oblique plane BE with vertical = 90° − 30° = 60°

$$\sigma_n = \sigma_x \cos^2 \theta = 10 \cos^2 60° = \textbf{2.5 N/mm}^2 \textbf{ (tensile)}$$

$$\sigma_t = \frac{\sigma_x}{2} \sin 2\theta = \frac{10}{2} \sin (2 \times 60°) = 5 \sin 120° = \textbf{4.33 N/mm}^2$$

**Answer :** $\boxed{\sigma_n = 2.5 \text{ N/mm}^2 \text{ (tensile)}, \sigma_t = 4.33 \text{ N/mm}^2}$

---

**Example 3 :** *A straight bar of uniform cross-section has a diameter of 10 mm. It is subjected to an axial pull of 20 kN. Find the normal and tangential stresses on a plane inclined at an angle of 30° to the axis of the bar.* **(B.T.E. S-2015, 1986/4 Marks)**

**Answer :** $\boxed{\sigma_n = 63.66 \text{ N/mm}^2 \text{ (tensile)}, \sigma_t = 110.27 \text{ N/mm}^2}$

---

**Example 4 :** *A bar is subjected to a tensile stress of 100 N/mm². Determine the normal and tangential stresses on a plane making an angle of 60° with the axis of tensile stress.*

**(B.T.E. W-1985/4 Marks)**

**Data** : Here θ = 90° − 60° = 30°, $\sigma_x$ = 100 N/mm² (tensile)

**To find** : $\sigma_n$ and $\sigma_t$ on plane BE.

**Solution :**

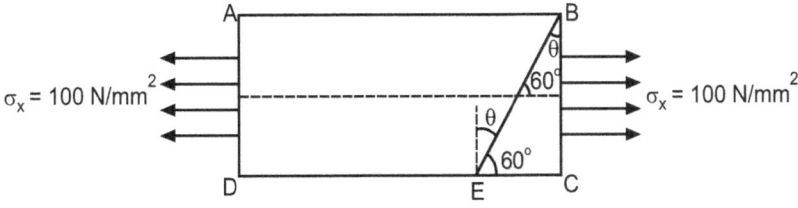

**Fig. 2.16**

$$\sigma_n = \sigma_x \cos^2 \theta = 100 \times \cos^2 30° = \textbf{75 N/mm}^2 \textbf{ (tensile)}$$

$$\sigma_t = \frac{\sigma_x}{2} \sin 2\theta = \frac{100}{2} \sin (2 \times 30°) = \textbf{43.3 N/mm}^2$$

**Answer :** $\boxed{\sigma_n = 75 \text{ N/mm}^2 \text{ (tensile)}, \sigma_t = 43.3 \text{ N/mm}^2}$

**Type 2 :** **Examples based on a body subjected to normal stresses in two mutually perpendicular directions :**

---

**Normal stress on an oblique section :** $\sigma_n = \dfrac{\sigma_x + \sigma_y}{2} + \dfrac{\sigma_x - \sigma_y}{2} \cos 2\theta$

**Shear stress on an oblique section :** $\sigma_t = \dfrac{\sigma_x - \sigma_y}{2} \sin 2\theta$

**Resultant stress :** $\sigma_r = \sqrt{\sigma_n^2 + \sigma_t^2}$

**Angle of obliquity :** $\tan \phi = \dfrac{\sigma_t}{\sigma_n} \Rightarrow \phi = \tan^{-1}\dfrac{\sigma_t}{\sigma_n}$

**Maximum shear stress :** $\sigma_{t_{max}} = \pm \dfrac{\sigma_x - \sigma_y}{2}$

**Planes of maximum shear are inclined at 45° to the principal planes.**

**Normal stress on the plane of maximum shear** $= \dfrac{\sigma_x + \sigma_y}{2}$

---

**Example 5 :** *The principal stresses at a point in the section of a boiler shell are 120 MPa and 30 MPa, both tensile. Find the normal, tangential and resultant stresses across a plane through the point inclined at 50° to the plane carrying 120 MPa stress.*

**(B.T.E. W-2005/4 Marks)**

**Data** : $\sigma_x = 120$ MPa $= 120$ N/mm² (tensile), $\sigma_y = 30$ MPa $= 30$ N/mm² (tensile),
$\theta = 50°$

**To find** : $\sigma_n, \sigma_t, \sigma_r$ on plane BE.

**Solution :**

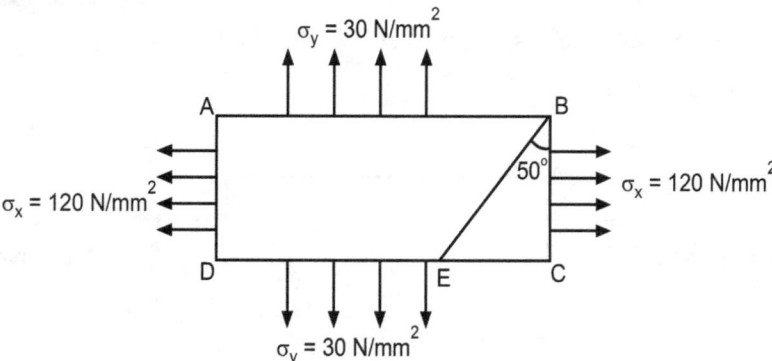

**Fig. 2.17**

**Normal stress,** $\sigma_n = \dfrac{\sigma_x + \sigma_y}{2} + \dfrac{\sigma_x - \sigma_y}{2} \cos 2\theta$

$= \dfrac{120 + 30}{2} + \dfrac{120 - 30}{2} \cos (2 \times 50°)$

$= \textbf{67.18 N/mm² (tensile)}$

**Tangential stress,**   $\sigma_t = \dfrac{\sigma_x - \sigma_y}{2} \sin 2\theta = \dfrac{120 - 30}{2} \sin (2 \times 50°) = \mathbf{44.31 \ N/mm^2}$

**Resultant stress,**   $\sigma_r = \sqrt{\sigma_n^2 + \sigma_t^2} = \sqrt{(67.18)^2 + (44.31)^2}$

$\qquad\qquad\qquad = \mathbf{80.47 \ N/mm^2 \ (tensile)}$

**Answer :** $\boxed{\sigma_n = 67.18 \ N/mm^2 \ (tensile), \ \sigma_t = 44.31 \ N/mm^2, \ \sigma_r = 80.47 \ N/mm^2 \ (tensile)}$

**Example 6 :** *At a point in a strained material, normal stress of 40 MPa (tensile) and $\sigma_y$ (tensile) are acting along 'x' and 'y' directions respectively. If the tangential stress developed on a plane is 8.66 MPa which is making an angle of 30° to the y-direction, calculate '$\sigma_y$' and normal stress.*   **(B.T.E. S-2006/4 Marks)**

**Data**   : $\sigma_x = 40$ MPa $= 40 \ N/mm^2$ (tensile), $\sigma_y$ is tensile,

$\qquad\qquad \sigma_t = 8.66$ MPa $= 8.66 \ N/mm^2, \ \theta = 30°.$

**To find**  : (i) $\sigma_y$, (ii) $\sigma_n$ on plane BE.

**Solution :**

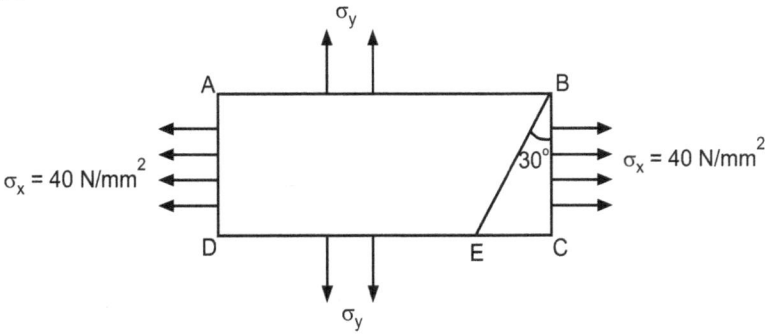

**Fig. 2.18**

**Tangential stress,**   $\sigma_t = \dfrac{\sigma_x - \sigma_y}{2} \cdot \sin 2\theta$

$\therefore \qquad\qquad 8.66 = \left(\dfrac{40 - \sigma_y}{2}\right) \cdot \sin (2 \times 30°)$

$\therefore \qquad 40 - \sigma_y = 2 \times 8.66 \div \sin 60° = 20$

$\therefore \qquad\qquad \sigma_y = 40 - 20 = \mathbf{20 \ N/mm^2 \ (tensile)}$

**Normal stress,**   $\sigma_n = \dfrac{\sigma_x + \sigma_y}{2} + \dfrac{\sigma_x - \sigma_y}{2} \cdot \cos 2\theta = \dfrac{40 + 20}{2} + \dfrac{40 - 20}{2} \cdot \cos (2 \times 30°)$

$\qquad\qquad\qquad = 30 + 5 = \mathbf{35 \ N/mm^2 \ (tensile)}$

**Answer :** $\boxed{\sigma_y = 20 \ N/mm^2 \ (tensile), \ \sigma_n = 35 \ N/mm^2 \ (tensile)}$

**Example 7 :** *At a point in a stressed body the principal stresses are 100 MN/m² (tensile) and 600 MN/m² (compressive). Calculate the normal and the shear stress on a plane inclined at 50° to the axis of the major principal stress.*   **(B.T.E. S-2001/ 4 Marks)**

**Data**   :   $\sigma_x = 100 \ MN/m^2$ (tensile) $= + 100 \ MN/m^2$

$\qquad\qquad \sigma_y = 600 \ MN/m^2$ (compressive) $= - 600 \ MN/m^2$

$\qquad\qquad \theta = 50°$ with the axis of major principal stress (i.e. with horizontal)

**To find** : $\sigma_n$ and $\sigma_t$ on an oblique plane.

**Solution** : We have to calculate $\sigma_n$ and $\sigma_t$ on an oblique plane BE which is inclined at 50° with the axis of major principal stress (horizontal).

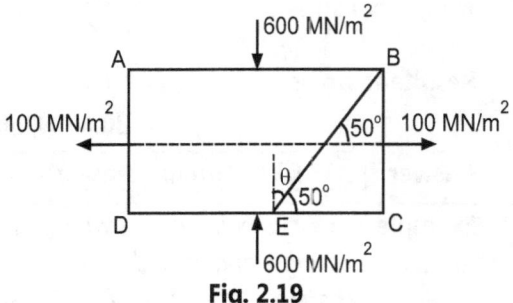

∴   Angle made by BE with vertical

$$\theta \;=\; 90° - 50° = 40°$$

**Fig. 2.19**

(i)  Normal stress on plane BE,

$$\sigma_n \;=\; \frac{\sigma_x + \sigma_y}{2} + \frac{\sigma_x - \sigma_y}{2}\cos 2\theta = \frac{100 + (-600)}{2} + \frac{100 - (-600)}{2}\cos(2 \times 40°)$$

$$=\; \frac{100 - 600}{2} + \frac{100 + 600}{2}\cos 80°$$

$$=\; -250 + 350 \times 0.1736 = \mathbf{-189.22\ N/mm^2\ (compressive)}$$

(ii) Shear stress on plane BE,

$$\sigma_t \;=\; \frac{\sigma_x - \sigma_y}{2}\sin 2\theta = \frac{100 - (-600)}{2}\sin(2 \times 40°)$$

$$=\; 350 \sin 80° = \mathbf{344.68\ N/mm^2}$$

**Answer :** $\boxed{\sigma_n = -189.22\ N/mm^2\ \text{(compressive)},\ \sigma_t = 344.68\ N/mm^2}$

**Example 8 :** *A point in a strained material is subjected to two mutually perpendicular stresses of 200 MPa (compressive) and 350 MPa (tensile). Determine the intensities of normal and tangential stresses on a plane inclined at 38° to the plane carrying 200 MPa stress.*

**(B.T.E. W-2000/4 Marks)**

**Data**     :     $\sigma_x = 200\ \text{MPa (comp)} = -200\ N/mm^2,$

$\sigma_y = 350\ \text{MPa (tensile)} = 350\ N/mm^2,$

$\theta = \text{angle made by oblique plane with vertical} = 38°$

**To find** : $\sigma_n$ and $\sigma_t$ on plane BE.

**Solution :** We have to calculate $\sigma_n$ and $\sigma_t$ on a plane BE which is inclined at 38° to the plane BC carrying 200 MPa stress.

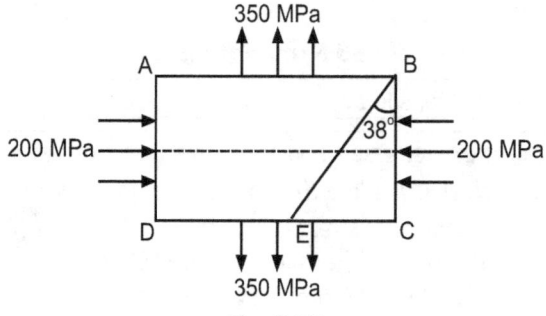

**Fig. 2.20**

(i) Normal stress on plane BE,

$$\sigma_n = \frac{\sigma_x + \sigma_y}{2} + \frac{\sigma_x - \sigma_y}{2} \times \cos 2\theta$$

$$= \frac{-200 + 350}{2} + \frac{(-200 - 350)}{2} \times \cos(2 \times 38°) = \frac{150}{2} + \left(\frac{-550}{2}\right) \times \cos 76°$$

$$= 75 - 275 \times \cos 76° = 75 - 66.53 = \textbf{8.47 N/mm}^2 \textbf{ (tensile)}$$

(ii) Shear stress on plane BE,

$$\sigma_t = \frac{\sigma_x - \sigma_y}{2} \cdot \sin 2\theta = \frac{-200 - 350}{2} \cdot \sin(2 \times 38°)$$

$$= -275 \sin 76° = -275 \times 0.97 = \textbf{-266.75 N/mm}^2$$

**Answer :** $\boxed{\sigma_n = 8.47 \text{ N/mm}^2 \text{ (tensile)}, \sigma_t = -266.75 \text{ N/mm}^2}$

---

**Example 9 :** *At a point in a strained material, the principal stresses are 60 MPa tensile and 10 MPa tensile. Calculate the normal and tangential stresses on a plane at this point inclined at 50° with the major principal plane.* **(B.T.E. S-1999/4 Marks)**

**Answer :** $\boxed{\sigma_n = 30.66 \text{ N/mm}^2 \text{ (tensile)}, \sigma_t = 24.62 \text{ N/mm}^2}$

---

**Example 10 :** *At a point in the cross-section of a loaded beam, the major principal stress is 70 MPa and the maximum shear stress is 40 MPa. Find the major principal stress and the direct stress on a plane of maximum shear stress.* **(B.T.E. S-2003/4 Marks)**

**Data** : Major principal stress, $\sigma_x$ = 70 MPa = 70 N/mm$^2$,

　　　　　Maximum shear stress, $\sigma_{t \, max}$ = 40 MPa = 40 N/mm$^2$

**To find** : (i) Minor principal stress, $\sigma_y$,

　　　　　(ii) Direct stress on the plane of maximum shear stress.

**Solution :** (i) Maximum shear stress,

$$\sigma_{t \, max} = \left(\frac{\sigma_x - \sigma_y}{2}\right)$$

∴ $$40 = \left(\frac{70 - \sigma_y}{2}\right)$$

∴ $$80 = (70 - \sigma_y)$$

∴ $$\sigma_y = \textbf{-10 N/mm}^2 \textbf{ (compressive)}$$

(ii) Direct stress on the plane of maximum shear stress

$$= \frac{\sigma_x + \sigma_y}{2} = \frac{70 - 10}{2} = \textbf{30 N/mm}^2 \textbf{ (tensile)}$$

**Answer :** $\boxed{\begin{array}{l}\sigma_y = -10 \text{ N/mm}^2, \text{ direct stress on the plane of maximum shear stress} \\ = 30 \text{ N/mm}^2 \text{ (tensile)}\end{array}}$

**Example 11 :** *The principal stresses at a point in the section of a member are 100 N/mm² and 50 N/mm² both tensile. Find the normal and tangential stresses across a plane passing through that point inclined at 60° to the plane having 100 N/mm² stress.*

**(B.T.E. W-2014, 1985, S-1992/4 Marks)**

**Data :** $\sigma_x = 100$ N/mm² (tensile), $\sigma_y = 50$ N/mm² (tensile), $\theta = 60°$

**To find :** $\sigma_n$ and $\sigma_t$ on plane BE.

**Solution :**

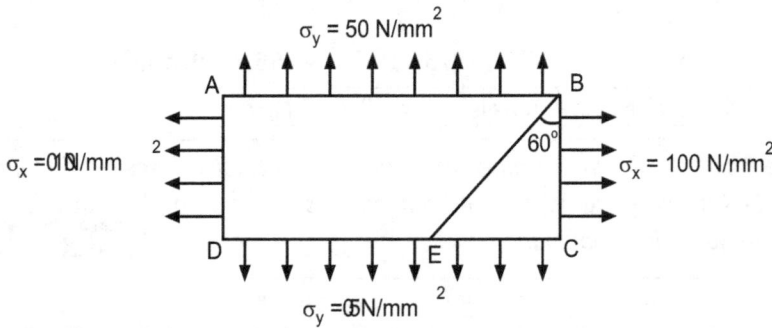

**Fig. 2.21**

$$\sigma_n = \frac{\sigma_x + \sigma_y}{2} + \frac{\sigma_x - \sigma_y}{2} \cdot \cos 2\theta = \frac{100 + 50}{2} + \frac{100 - 50}{2} \cos(2 \times 60°)$$

$$= 75 + 25 \times \cos 120° = \textbf{62.5 N/mm}^2 \textbf{ (tensile)}$$

$$\sigma_t = \frac{\sigma_x - \sigma_y}{2} \cdot \sin 2\theta = \frac{100 - 50}{2} \cdot \sin(2 \times 60°) = \textbf{21.65 N/mm}^2$$

**Answer :** $\boxed{\sigma_n = 62.5 \text{ N/mm}^2 \text{ (tensile)}, \sigma_t = 21.65 \text{ N/mm}^2}$

**Extension to the problem :** Also calculate the resultant stress, angle of obliquity, maximum shear stress and the normal stress on the plane of maximum shear.

Now,
$$\sigma_r = \sqrt{\sigma_n^2 + \sigma_t^2} = \sqrt{62.5^2 + 21.65^2} = \textbf{66.14 N/mm}^2 \textbf{ (tensile)}$$

$$\phi = \tan^{-1}\frac{\sigma_t}{\sigma_n} = \tan^{-1}\frac{21.65}{62.5} = \textbf{19.1°}$$

$$\sigma_{t_{max}} = \pm\frac{\sigma_x - \sigma_y}{2} = \pm\frac{100 - 50}{2} = \pm\textbf{25 N/mm}^2$$

**Planes of maximum shear are inclined at 45° to the principal planes.**

**Normal stress on the plane of maximum shear**

$$\sigma_n = \frac{\sigma_x + \sigma_y}{2} = \frac{100 + 50}{2} = \textbf{75 N/mm}^2 \textbf{ (tensile)}$$

**Answer :** $\boxed{\begin{array}{l}\sigma_r = 66.14 \text{ N/mm}^2 \text{ (tensile)}, \phi = 19.1°, \sigma_{t\ max} = \pm 25 \text{ N/mm}^2, \\ \sigma_n \text{ on plane of maximum shear} = 75 \text{ N/mm}^2 \text{ (tensile)}\end{array}}$

**Example 12 :** *At a point in a strained material the principal stresses are 200 N/mm² (tensile) and 30 N/mm² (compressive). Determine (i) Normal, shear and the resultant stress on a plane inclined at 60° to the major principal plane (or inclined at 30° to the axis of major principal stress), (ii) Maximum shear stress and (iii) Normal stress on the plane of maximum shear.*

**Data :** $\sigma_x$ = 200 N/mm² (tensile), $\sigma_y$ = −30 N/mm² (Compressive),

Angle made by oblique section with vertical, $\theta$ = 60°.

**To find :** $\sigma_n$, $\sigma_t$, $\sigma_r$, $\sigma_{t_{max}}$, $\sigma_n$ on the plane of maximum shear.

**Solution :**

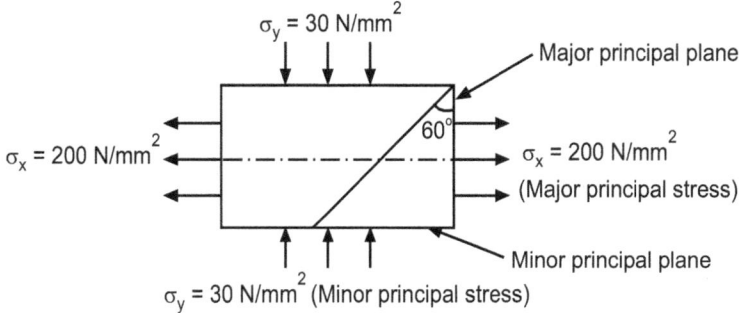

**Fig. 2.22**

$$\sigma_n = \frac{\sigma_x + \sigma_y}{2} + \frac{\sigma_x - \sigma_y}{2} \cos 2\theta = \frac{200 - 30}{2} + \frac{200 - (-30)}{2} \cos (2 \times 60°)$$

$$= 85 + \frac{230}{2} \times \cos 120° = 85 - 57.5 = \textbf{27.5 N/mm² (tensile)}$$

$$\sigma_t = \frac{\sigma_x - \sigma_y}{2} \sin 2\theta = \frac{200 - (-30)}{2} \sin (2 \times 60°)$$

$$= \frac{230}{2} \times \sin 120° = \textbf{99.59 N/mm²}$$

$$\sigma_r = \sqrt{\sigma_n^2 + \sigma_t^2} = \sqrt{27.5^2 + 99.59^2} = \textbf{103.32 N/mm² (tensile)}$$

$$\sigma_{t_{max}} = \pm \frac{\sigma_x - \sigma_y}{2} = \pm \frac{200 - (-30)}{2} = \pm \frac{230}{2} = \textbf{± 115 N/mm²}$$

**Planes of maximum shear are inclined at 45° to the principal planes.**

**Normal stress on the plane of maximum shear :**

$$\sigma_n = \frac{\sigma_x + \sigma_y}{2} = \frac{200 - 30}{2} = \frac{170}{2} = \textbf{85 N/mm² (tensile)}$$

**Answer :**

$\sigma_n$ = 27.5 N/mm² (tensile), $\sigma_t$ = 99.59 N/mm²,
$\sigma_r$ = 103.32 N/mm² (tensile) , $\sigma_{t\,max}$ = ± 115 N/mm²
$\sigma_n$ on plane of maximum shear = 85 N/mm² (tensile)

## Type 3 : Examples based on a body subjected to normal stress in one plane accompanied by a simple shear stress :

Normal stress on an oblique section : $\sigma_n = \dfrac{\sigma_x}{2}(1 + \cos 2\theta) + q \sin 2\theta$

Shear stress on an oblique section : $\sigma_t = \dfrac{\sigma_x}{2}\sin 2\theta - q \cos 2\theta$

Resultant stress : $\sigma_r = \sqrt{\sigma_n^2 + \sigma_t^2}$

Obliquity : $\phi = \tan^{-1}\left(\dfrac{\sigma_t}{\sigma_n}\right)$

Location of principal planes : $\tan 2\theta = \dfrac{2q}{\sigma_x}$.

From this expression, find $\theta_1$ and $\theta_2$.

Magnitude of principal stresses :

Major principal stress : $\sigma_{n_1} = \dfrac{\sigma_x}{2} + \sqrt{\left(\dfrac{\sigma_x}{2}\right)^2 + q^2}$

Minor principal stress : $\sigma_{n_2} = \dfrac{\sigma_x}{2} - \sqrt{\left(\dfrac{\sigma_x}{2}\right)^2 + q^2}$

Maximum shear stress : $\sigma_{t_{max}} = \pm\dfrac{\sigma_{n_1} - \sigma_{n_2}}{2}$

**Planes of maximum shear are inclined at 45° to the principal planes.**

**Example 13 :** *At a certain point in a beam there is a tensile bending stress of 120 N/mm² in the horizontal direction accompanied by a shear stress of 40 N/mm². Find the principal stresses at the point and position of principal planes.* **(B.T.E. W-1988/4 Marks)**

**Data**      : $\sigma_x = 120$ N/mm² (tensile), $q = 40$ N/mm²

**To find**   : Principal stresses and principal planes.

**Solution :**

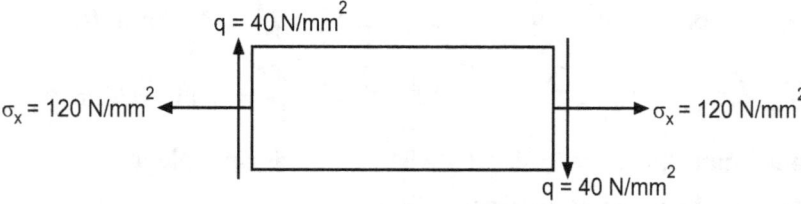

**Fig. 2.23**

**Major principal stress :**

$$\sigma_{n_1} = \frac{\sigma_x}{2} + \sqrt{\left(\frac{\sigma_x}{2}\right)^2 + q^2} = \frac{120}{2} + \sqrt{\left(\frac{120}{2}\right)^2 + (40)^2}$$

$$= 60 + 72.11 = \textbf{132.11 N/mm}^2 \textbf{ (tensile)}$$

**Minor principal stress :**

$$\sigma_{n_2} = \frac{\sigma_x}{2} - \sqrt{\left(\frac{\sigma_x}{2}\right)^2 + q^2} = \frac{120}{2} - \sqrt{\left(\frac{120}{2}\right)^2 + (40)^2} = 60 - 72.11$$

$$= -12.11 \text{ N/mm}^2 \text{ (compressive)}$$

**Location of principal planes :**

Let $\theta$ be the angle made by principal plane with normal to the $\sigma_x$.

Then　　$\tan 2\theta = \dfrac{2q}{\sigma_x} = \dfrac{2 \times 40}{120} = 0.67$

$$2\theta = \tan^{-1} 0.67 = 33.82°$$

$\therefore$　　　　$\theta = \mathbf{16.91°}$ or $16.91° + 90° = \mathbf{106.91°}$

$\therefore$　　　　$\theta_1 = \mathbf{16.91°}$ and $\theta_2 = \mathbf{106.91°}$

**Extension to the problem :**

Also calculate the value of maximum shear stress.

$$\sigma_{t_{max}} = \pm \frac{\sigma_{n_1} - \sigma_{n_2}}{2} = \pm \frac{132.11 - (-12.11)}{2}$$

$$= \pm \frac{132.11 + 12.11}{2} = \pm \mathbf{72.11 \text{ N/mm}^2}$$

**Answer :** $\boxed{\begin{array}{l} \sigma_{n_1} = 132.11 \text{ N/mm}^2 \text{ (tensile)}, \ \sigma_{n_2} = -12.11 \text{ N/mm}^2 \text{ (compressive)}, \\ \theta_1 = 16.91°, \ \theta_2 = 106.91°, \ \sigma_{t_{max}} = \pm 72.11 \text{ N/mm}^2 \end{array}}$

---

**Example 14 :** *A point in a strained material is subjected to stresses as shown in Fig. 2.24. Find the normal and tangential stresses across the plane EF.*

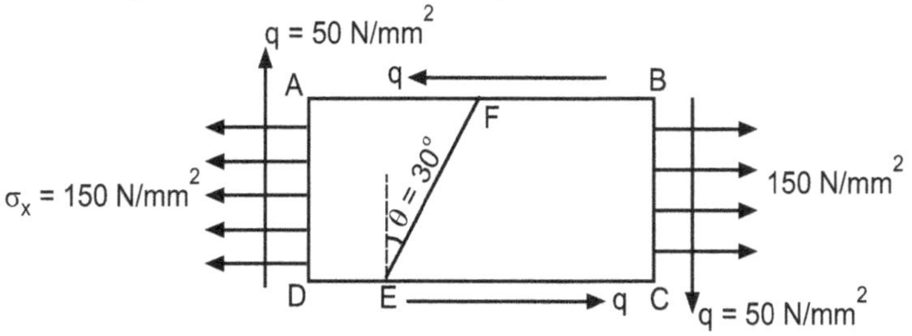

**Fig. 2.24**

**Data**　　: $\sigma_x = 150 \text{ N/mm}^2$, $q = 50 \text{ N/mm}^2$

Angle made by oblique plane EF with the normal to $\sigma_x$ (i.e. with vertical), $\theta = 30°$

**To find**　: $\sigma_n$ and $\sigma_t$ on plane EF.

**Solution :**　　$\sigma_n = \dfrac{\sigma_x}{2}(1 + \cos 2\theta) + q \sin 2\theta$

$$= \frac{150}{2}[1 + \cos(2 \times 30°)] + 50 \sin(2 \times 30°)$$

$$= 75(1 + \cos 60°) + 50 \sin 60° = \mathbf{155.8 \text{ N/mm}^2 \text{ (tensile)}}$$

$$\sigma_t = \frac{\sigma_x}{2} \sin 2\theta - q \cos 2\theta = \frac{150}{2} \sin(2 \times 30°) - 50 \cos(2 \times 30°)$$

$$= 75 \sin 60° - 50 \cos 60° = \textbf{39.95 N/mm}^2$$

**Answer :** $\boxed{\sigma_n = 155.8 \text{ N/mm}^2 \text{ (tensile)}, \sigma_t = 39.95 \text{ N/mm}^2}$

**Example 15 :** *At a point in the web of a girder, the bending stress is $\sigma_b$ and the shear stress is $\tau$. The principal stresses at a point are 80 MPa tensile and 20 MPa compressive. Evaluate the values of $\sigma_b$ and $\tau$. Determine the directions of principal planes.*

**(B.T.E. W-1997/4 Marks)**

**Data :** In this case, there is no stress in y-direction

i.e. $\sigma_y = 0$, $\sigma_x = \sigma_b$ and $q = \tau$, $\sigma_{n_1} = +80$ N/mm², $\sigma_{n_2} = -20$ N/mm².

**To find :** $\sigma_b$, $\tau$, $\theta_1$ and $\theta_2$.

**Solution :** Fig. 2.25 shows the given stress system.

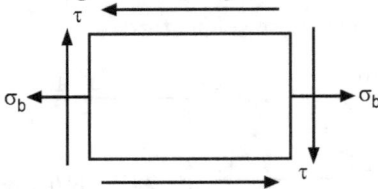

**Fig. 2.25**

**Major principal stress :**　$\sigma_{n_1} = \frac{\sigma_x}{2} + \sqrt{\left(\frac{\sigma_x}{2}\right)^2 + q^2}$

$$80 = \frac{\sigma_b}{2} + \sqrt{\left(\frac{\sigma_b}{2}\right)^2 + \tau^2} \qquad \ldots \text{(i)}$$

**Minor principal stress :**　$\sigma_{n_2} = \frac{\sigma_x}{2} - \sqrt{\left(\frac{\sigma_x}{2}\right)^2 + q^2}$

$$-20 = \frac{\sigma_b}{2} - \sqrt{\left(\frac{\sigma_b}{2}\right)^2 + \tau^2} \qquad \ldots \text{(ii)}$$

Adding the equations (i) and (ii), we have,

$$80 - 20 = 2\left(\frac{\sigma_b}{2}\right)$$

∴　　　　　　$60 = \sigma_b$

∴　**Bending stress $\sigma_b$ = 60 N/mm² (tensile)**

Substituting the value of $\sigma_b$ in equation (i), we have,

$$80 = \frac{60}{2} + \sqrt{\left(\frac{60}{2}\right)^2 + \tau^2}$$

∴　　　　　　$80 = 30 + \sqrt{900 + \tau^2}$

∴　　　　$(80 - 30)^2 = 900 + \tau^2$

$\therefore$          $2500 = 900 + \tau^2$

$\therefore$          $\tau^2 = 1600$

$\therefore$          $\tau = 40 \text{ N/mm}^2$

$\therefore$          **Shear stress $\tau$ = 40 N/mm$^2$.**

### Directions of principal planes :

Let $\theta$ = angle made by principal plane with the normal to $\sigma_x$.

Then,          $\tan 2\theta = \dfrac{2q}{\sigma_x} = \dfrac{2\tau}{\sigma_b} = \dfrac{2 \times 40}{60} = 1.33$

$\therefore$          $2\theta = \tan^{-1} 1.33 = 53.13°$

$\therefore$          $\theta_1 = \dfrac{53.13}{2} = \mathbf{26.56°} \dots$ **Position of 1st plane**

          $\theta_2 = \theta_1 + 90° = \mathbf{116.56°} \dots$ **Position of 2nd plane.**

**Answer :** $\boxed{\sigma_b = 60 \text{ N/mm}^2 \text{ (tensile)}, \tau = 40 \text{ N/mm}^2, \theta_1 = 26.56°, \theta_2 = 116.56°}$

---

**Type 4 : Examples based on a body subjected to normal stresses in two mutually perpendicular directions accompanied by a simple shear stress :**

**Normal stress on an oblique section :**

$$\sigma_n = \frac{\sigma_x + \sigma_y}{2} + \frac{\sigma_x - \sigma_y}{2} \cos 2\theta + q \sin 2\theta$$

**Shear stress on an oblique section :**

$$\sigma_t = \frac{\sigma_x - \sigma_y}{2} \sin 2\theta - q \cos 2\theta$$

**Resultant stress :**     $\sigma_r = \sqrt{\sigma_n^2 + \sigma_t^2}$ and

**Obliquity :**          $\phi = \tan^{-1}\left(\dfrac{\sigma_t}{\sigma_n}\right)$

**Location of principal planes :** $\tan 2\theta = \dfrac{2q}{\sigma_x - \sigma_y}$

From this expression, find $\theta_1$ and $\theta_2$.

**Magnitude of principal stresses :**

**Major principal stress :** $\sigma_{n_1} = \dfrac{\sigma_x + \sigma_y}{2} + \sqrt{\left(\dfrac{\sigma_x - \sigma_y}{2}\right)^2 + q^2}$

**Minor principal stress :** $\sigma_{n_2} = \dfrac{\sigma_x + \sigma_y}{2} - \sqrt{\left(\dfrac{\sigma_x - \sigma_y}{2}\right)^2 + q^2}$

**Maximum shear stress :** $\sigma_{t_{max}} = \pm \dfrac{\sigma_{n_1} - \sigma_{n_2}}{2}$.

**Planes of maximum shear are inclined at 45° to the principal planes.**

**Example 16 :** *At a point in a strained material there are two mutually perpendicular stresses of 600 N/mm² and 400 N/mm² both tensile. They are accompanied by a shear stress of 100 N/mm². Find (i) Principal stresses, (ii) Position of principal planes, (iii) Maximum shear.*

*Refer to Fig. 2.26 (i).*

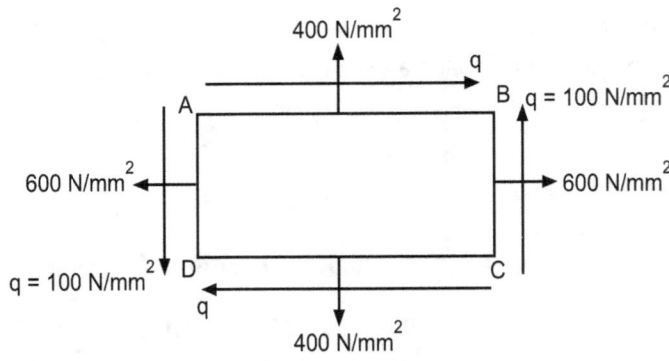

**Fig. 2.26 (i)**

**Data :** $\sigma_x$ = 600 N/mm², $\sigma_y$ = 400 N/mm²,  Shear stress q = –100 N/mm²

**To find :** $\sigma_{n_1}$ , $\sigma_{n_2}$ , $\theta_1$ , $\theta_2$ and $\sigma_{t_{max}}$ .

**Solution : Principal stresses :**

**Major principal stress :** $\quad \sigma_{n_1} = \dfrac{\sigma_x + \sigma_y}{2} + \sqrt{\left(\dfrac{\sigma_x - \sigma_y}{2}\right)^2 + q^2}$

$$= \frac{600 + 400}{2} + \sqrt{\left(\frac{600 - 400}{2}\right)^2 + (-100)^2}$$

$$= 500 + 141.42$$

$$= \textbf{641.42 N/mm}^2 \textbf{ (tensile)}$$

**Minor principal stress :** $\quad \sigma_{n_2} = \dfrac{\sigma_x - \sigma_y}{2} - \sqrt{\left(\dfrac{\sigma_x - \sigma_y}{2}\right)^2 + q^2}$

$$= 500 - 141.42 = \textbf{358.58 N/mm}^2 \textbf{ (tensile)}$$

**Position of principal planes :**

Let θ = angle made by principal plane with the normal to $\sigma_x$ (i.e. with face BC).

Then,  $\qquad \tan 2\theta = \dfrac{2\,q}{\sigma_x - \sigma_y} = \dfrac{2 \times (-100)}{600 - 400} = -1$

∴  $\qquad\qquad 2\theta = \textbf{135}°$

**Position of first principal plane :**

∴  $\theta_1 = \dfrac{135°}{2} = \textbf{67.5}°$

## Position of second principal plane :

Principal planes are at right angles to each other.

$\therefore \qquad \theta_2 = \theta_1 + 90° = 67.5° + 90° = \mathbf{157.5°}$

## Maximum shear stress :

$$q_{max} = \sigma_{t_{max}} = \pm \frac{\sigma_{n_1} - \sigma_{n_2}}{2} = \pm \frac{641.42 - 358.58}{2}$$

$$= \pm 141.42 \text{ N/mm}^2$$

## Planes of maximum shear are inclined at 45° to the principal planes.

## Planes of maximum shear :

$$\theta_3 = \theta_1 + 45° = 67.5° + 45° = \mathbf{112.5°}$$

$$\theta_4 = \theta_2 + 45° = 157.5° + 45° = \mathbf{202.5°}$$

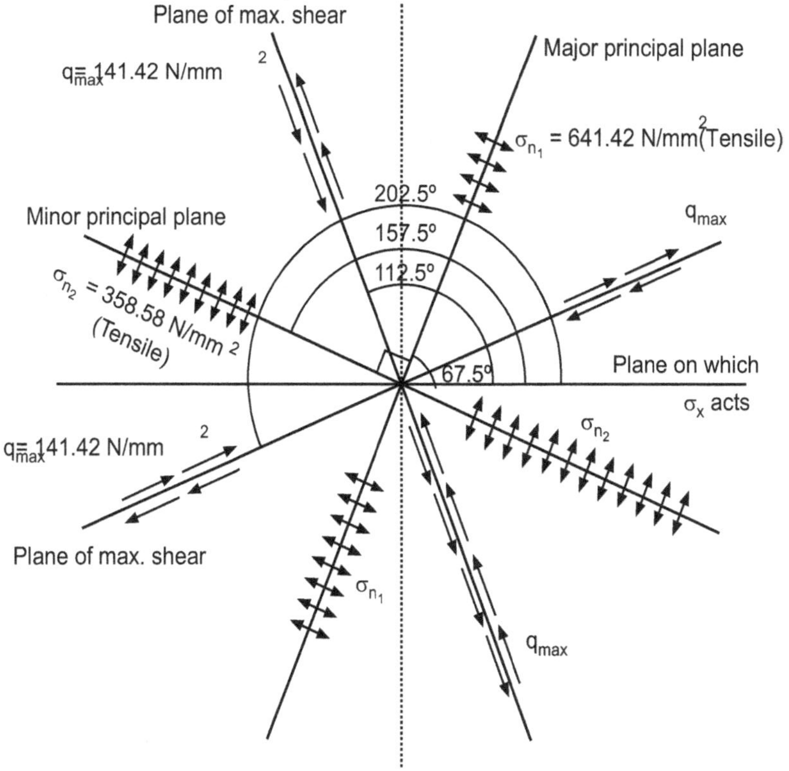

**Principal planes :** $\theta_1 = 67.5°$, $\theta_2 = 157.5°$

**Planes of maximum shear :** $\theta_3 = 112.5°$, $\theta_4 = 202.5°$

### Relationship between major and minor principal planes, the planes of maximum shear stress and the plane on which $\sigma_x$ acts.

**Fig. 2.26 (ii)**

**Answer :** | $\sigma_{n_1} = 641.42$ N/mm$^2$ (tensile), $\sigma_{n_2} = 358.58$ N/mm$^2$ (tensile), $\theta_1 = 67.5°$, $\theta_2 = 157.5°$, $\sigma_{t\,max} = \pm 141.42$ N/mm$^2$, $\theta_3 = 112.5°$, $\theta_4 = 202.5°$

**Example 17 :** *At a point in a strained material there is a tensile stress of 80 MPa upon a horizontal plane and a compressive stress of 40 MPa upon a vertical plane. There is also a shear stress of 48 MPa acting upon each of these planes. Determine the planes of maximum shear stress at the point along with its magnitude.*          **(B.T.E. S-2005/4 Marks)**

**Data**     :   $\sigma_x$ = 80 MPa = 80 N/mm$^2$ (tensile),

$\sigma_y$ = – 40 MPa = – 40 N/mm$^2$ (compressive), q = 48 MPa = 48 N/mm$^2$.

**To find** :   (i) $q_{max}$, (ii) $\theta_3$, $\theta_4$.

**Solution : Principal stresses :**

$$\sigma_n = \frac{\sigma_x + \sigma_y}{2} \pm \sqrt{\left(\frac{\sigma_x - \sigma_y}{2}\right) + q^2}$$

$$= \frac{80 - 40}{2} \pm \sqrt{\left[\frac{80 - (-40)}{2}\right]^2 + 48^2} = 20 \pm 76.84$$

∴   Major principal stress,

$$\sigma_{n_1} = 20 + 76.84 = 96.84 \text{ N/mm}^2 \text{ (tensile)}$$

Minor principal stress,     $\sigma_{n_2}$ = 20 – 76.84 = – 56.84 N/mm$^2$ (compressive)

Maximum shear stress,   **$q_{max}$** $= \pm \dfrac{\sigma_{n_1} - \sigma_{n_2}}{2} = \pm \dfrac{96.84 - (-56.84)}{2} = \pm \mathbf{76.84 \text{ N/mm}^2}$

**Principal planes :**     $\tan 2\theta = \dfrac{2q}{\sigma_x - \sigma_y} = \dfrac{2 \times 48}{80 - (-40)} = 0.8$

∴                           $2\theta = 38.66°$

Position of 1$^{st}$ principal plane,

$$\theta_1 = \frac{38.66}{2} = \mathbf{19.33°}$$

Principal planes are at right angles to each other.

∴   Position of 2$^{nd}$ principal plane,

$$\theta_2 = \theta_1 + 90° = 19.33° + 90° = \mathbf{109.33°}$$

**Planes of maximum shear :** Planes of maximum shear are inclined at 45° to the principal planes.

$$\theta_3 = \theta_1 + 45° = 19.33° + 45° = \mathbf{64.33°}$$

$$\theta_4 = \theta_2 + 45° = 109.33° + 45° = \mathbf{154.33°}$$

**Answer :** $\boxed{q_{max} = \pm 76.84 \text{ N/mm}^2,\ \theta_3 = 64.33°,\ \theta_4 = 154.33°}$

**Example 18 :** *The resultant stresses on two mutually perpendicular planes are as shown in Fig. 2.27 (i). Calculate the principal stresses and their directions.* **(B.T.E. W-2004/4 Marks)**

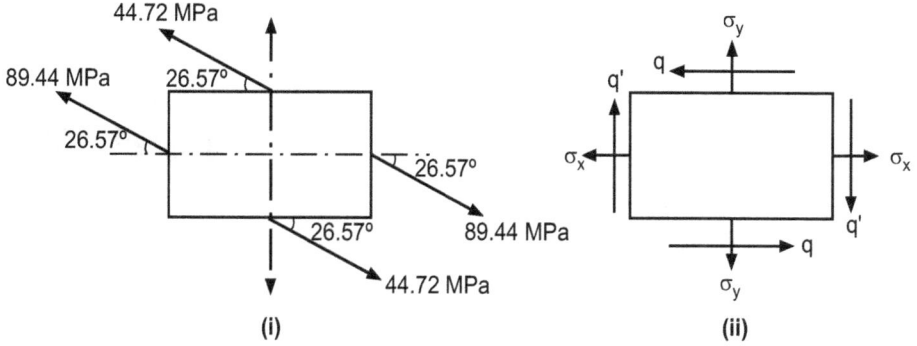

**Fig. 2.27**

**Data** : A stress block as shown in Fig. 2.27 (i).

**To find** : (i) $\sigma_{n_1}$, $\sigma_{n_2}$ (ii) $\theta_1$, $\theta_2$.

**Solution :** By resolving the resultant stresses along and perpendicular to the planes, the stresses obtained are as shown in Fig. 2.27 (ii).

$\sigma_x$ = x-component of 89.44 MPa = 89.44 cos 26.57° = 80 N/mm² (tensile)

$q'$ = y-component of 89.44 MPa = 89.44 sin 26.57° = 40 N/mm²

$\sigma_y$ = y-component of 44.72 MPa = 44.72 sin 26.57° = 20 N/mm² (tensile)

$q$ = x-component of 44.72 MPa = 44.72 cos 26.57° = 40 N/mm²

**Principal stresses :**

$$\sigma_n = \frac{\sigma_x + \sigma_y}{2} \pm \sqrt{\left(\frac{\sigma_x - \sigma_y}{2}\right)^2 + q^2}$$

$$= \frac{80 + 20}{2} \pm \sqrt{\left(\frac{80 - 20}{2}\right)^2 + 40^2}$$

$$= 50 \pm 50$$

**Major principal stress,**

$$\sigma_{n_1} = 50 + 50 = \textbf{100 N/mm}^2 \textbf{ (tensile)}$$

**Minor principal stress,**

$$\sigma_{n_2} = 50 - 50 = \textbf{0}$$

**Directions of principal stresses (Location of principal planes) :**

$$\tan 2\theta = \frac{2q}{\sigma_x - \sigma_y} = \frac{2 \times 40}{80 - 20} = 1.33$$

∴　　　$$2\theta = \tan^{-1} 1.33 = 53.13°$$

∴　　　$$\theta_1 = \frac{53.13°}{2} = \textbf{26.56°} \textbf{ ... 1}^{\textbf{st}} \textbf{ plane}$$

$$\theta_2 = \theta_1 + 90° = 26.56° + 90° = \textbf{116.56°} \textbf{ ... 2}^{\textbf{nd}} \textbf{ plane}$$

**Answer :** $\boxed{\sigma_{n_1} = 100 \text{ N/mm}^2 \text{ (tensile)}, \sigma_{n_2} = 0, \theta_1 = 26.56°, \theta_2 = 116.56°}$

**Example 19 :** *A point is subjected to a tensile stress of 100 MPa and a compressive stress of 60 MPa acting on two mutually perpendicular planes along with a shear stress of 18 MPa on these planes. Locate the principal planes and determine the stresses acting on these planes.*

**(B.T.E. S-2000/4 Marks)**

**Data** : $\sigma_x = 100$ MPa $= 100$ N/mm$^2$,

$\sigma_y = -60$ MPa $= -60$ N/mm$^2$, $q = 18$ MPa $= 18$ N/mm$^2$

**To find** : (i) Principal planes $\theta_1, \theta_2$ and (ii) Principal stresses $\sigma_{n_1}, \sigma_{n_2}$.

**Solution : (i) Principal planes :**

$$\tan 2\theta = \frac{2q}{\sigma_x - \sigma_y} = \frac{2 \times 18}{100 - (-60)} = \frac{36}{100 + 60} = \frac{36}{160} = 0.225$$

$\therefore$      $2\theta = \tan^{-1}(0.225) = 12.68°$

**Position of 1$^{st}$ principal plane :**

$\therefore$      $\theta_1 = \dfrac{12.68}{2} = \mathbf{6.34°}$

**Position of 2$^{nd}$ principal plane :**

$$\theta_2 = \theta_1 + 90° = 6.34° + 90° = \mathbf{96.34°}$$

**(ii) Principal stresses :**

$$\sigma_{n_1} = \frac{\sigma_x + \sigma_y}{2} + \sqrt{\left(\frac{\sigma_x - \sigma_y}{2}\right)^2 + q^2} = \frac{100 + (-60)}{2} + \sqrt{\left(\frac{100 - (-60)}{2}\right)^2 + (18)^2}$$

$$= \frac{40}{2} + \sqrt{\left(\frac{160}{2}\right)^2 + (18)^2} = 20 + \sqrt{(80)^2 + (18)^2}$$

$$= 20 + \sqrt{1600 + 324} = 20 + \sqrt{1924} = 20 + 43.86$$

$$= \mathbf{63.86 \ N/mm^2 \ (tensile)}$$

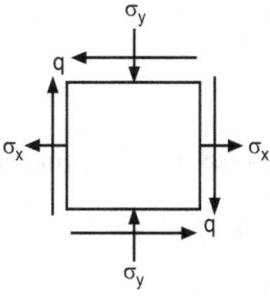

**Fig. 2.28**

$$\sigma_{n_2} = \frac{\sigma_x - \sigma_y}{2} - \sqrt{\left(\frac{\sigma_x - \sigma_y}{2}\right)^2 + q^2} = 20 - 43.86 = \mathbf{-23.86 \ N/mm^2 \ (compressive)}$$

**Ans.** $\theta_1 = 6.34°$, $\theta_2 = 96.34°$, $\sigma_{n_1} = 63.86$ N/mm$^2$ (tensile), $\sigma_{n_2} = -23.86$ N/mm$^2$ (compressive)

**Example 20 :** *At a point in a strained material, the stress in x-direction is 60 N/mm²* *(tensile) and that in y-direction is 40 N/mm² (compressive). The shear stress at the point is* *20 N/mm². What is the principal stress at the point and in which direction it acts ?*

**(B.T.E. W-1986/4 Marks)**

**Data :** $\sigma_x$ = 60 N/mm² (tensile), $\sigma_y$ = – 40 N/mm² (compressive), q = 20 N/mm².

**To find :** Principal stresses and location of principal planes.

**Solution :**

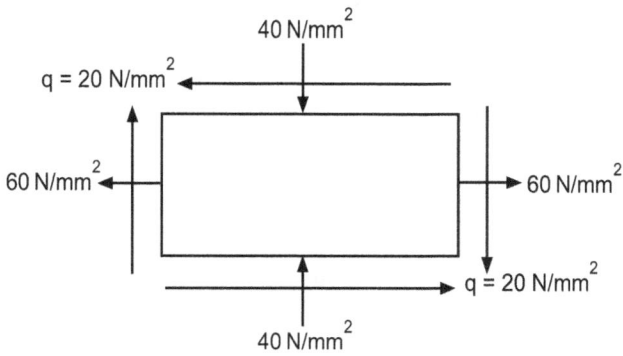

**Fig. 2.29 (i)**

**Principal stresses :**   $\sigma_n = \dfrac{\sigma_x + \sigma_y}{2} \pm \sqrt{\left(\dfrac{\sigma_x - \sigma_y}{2}\right)^2 + q^2}$

$$= \frac{60 - 40}{2} \pm \sqrt{\left(\frac{60 - (-40)}{2}\right)^2 + 20^2} = \mathbf{10 \pm 53.85}$$

**Major principal stress,**

$$\sigma_{n_1} = 10 + 53.85 = \textbf{63.85 N/mm}^2 \textbf{ (tensile)}$$

**Minor principal stress,**

$$\sigma_{n_2} = 10 - 53.85 = -43.85 \text{ N/mm}^2 = \textbf{43.85 N/mm}^2 \textbf{ (compressive)}$$

**Location of principal planes :**

Let θ = angle made by the principal plane with the normal to $\sigma_x$.

Then,   $\tan 2\theta = \dfrac{2\,q}{\sigma_x - \sigma_y} = \dfrac{2 \times 20}{60 - (-40)} = 0.4$

∴   $2\theta = 21.8°$

∴   $\theta_1 = \dfrac{21.8°}{2} = \mathbf{10.9°}$

and   $\theta_2 = 90° + \theta_1 = 90° + 10.9° = \mathbf{100.9°}$

**Extension to the problem :**

Also calculate the maximum shear stress and locate the planes of maximum shear.

**Maximum shear stress :**

$$\sigma_{t_{max}} = \pm \frac{\sigma_{n_1} - \sigma_{n_2}}{2} = \pm \frac{63.85 - (-43.85)}{2} = \pm \textbf{53.85 N/mm}^2$$

**Planes of maximum shear :**

$$\theta_3 = \theta_1 + 45° = 10.9° + 45° = \mathbf{55.9°}$$
$$\theta_4 = \theta_2 + 45° = 100.9° + 45° = \mathbf{145.9°}$$

Planes of maximum shear are at right angles to each other and are inclined at 45° to the principal planes as shown in Fig. 2.29 (ii).

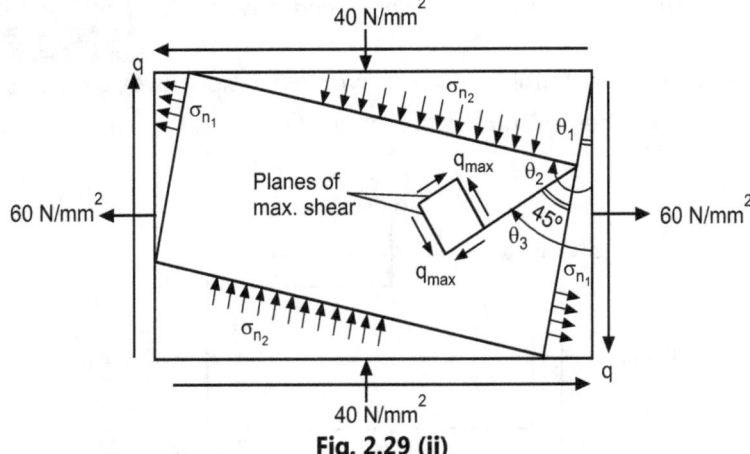

**Fig. 2.29 (ii)**

**Answer :** $\boxed{\begin{array}{l} \sigma_{n_1} = 63.85 \text{ N/mm}^2 \text{ (tensile)}, \sigma_{n_2} = -43.85 \text{ N/mm}^2 \text{ (compressive)}, \\ \theta_1 = 10.9°, \theta_2 = 100.9°, \sigma_{t\,max} = \pm 53.85 \text{ N/mm}^2, \theta_3 = 55.9°, \theta_4 = 145.9° \end{array}}$

**Example 21 :** *A point in a strained material is subjected to stresses as shown in Fig. 2.30. Find the normal, tangential and resultant stresses across the inclined plane, inclined at 25° to the stress of 90 MPa.*          **(B.T.E. S-1994/4 Marks)**

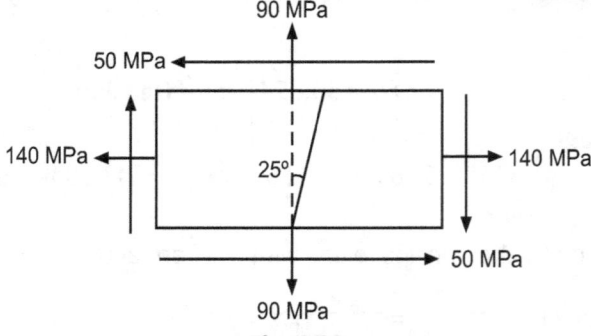

**Fig. 2.30**

**Data :** A stress system as shown in Fig. 2.30.

$\sigma_x = 140$ MPa $= 140$ N/mm² (tensile), $\sigma_y = 90$ MPa $= 90$ N/mm² (tensile),

$q = 50$ MPa $= 50$ N/mm², $\theta$ = angle made by oblique section with vertical = 25°

**To find :** $\sigma_n$, $\sigma_t$ and $\sigma_r$ on an oblique plane inclined at 25° to the stress of 90 N/mm².

**Solution : Normal stress on an oblique section,**

$$\sigma_n = \frac{\sigma_x + \sigma_y}{2} + \frac{\sigma_x - \sigma_y}{2} \cos 2\theta + q \sin 2\theta$$

$$= \frac{140 + 90}{2} + \frac{140 - 90}{2} \cos (2 \times 25°) + 50 \sin (2 \times 25°)$$

$$= 115 + 16.07 + 38.3 = \textbf{169.37 N/mm}^2 \textbf{ (tensile)}$$

**Tangential (shear) stress on an oblique section :**

$$\sigma_t = \frac{\sigma_x - \sigma_y}{2} \sin 2\theta - q \cos 2\theta = \frac{140 - 90}{2} \sin (2 \times 25°) - 50 \cos (2 \times 25°)$$

$$= 19.15 - 32.14 = \mathbf{-12.99 \ N/mm^2}$$

**Resultant stress on an oblique section :**

$$\sigma_r = \sqrt{\sigma_n^2 + \sigma_t^2} = \sqrt{(169.37)^2 + (-12.99)^2} = \mathbf{169.87 \ N/mm^2.}$$

**Answer :** $\boxed{\sigma_n = 169.37 \ N/mm^2 \ \text{(tensile)}, \ \sigma_t = -12.99 \ N/mm^2, \ \sigma_r = 169.87 \ N/mm^2}$

## Type 5 : Examples on Mohr's Circle Method (Graphical Method) :

**Example 22 :** *At a point in a strained material, there are two mutually perpendicular stresses of 30 N/mm² and 70 N/mm² both tensile. They are accompanied by a shear stress of 20 N/mm². Find (i) Principal stresses, (ii) Position of principal planes, (iii) Maximum shear stress. Use Mohr's circle method.*

**Data :** $\sigma_x = +30 \ N/mm^2$, $\sigma_y = +70 \ N/mm^2$, $q = 20 \ N/mm^2$

**To find :** $\sigma_{n_1}$, $\sigma_{n_2}$, $\theta_1$, $\theta_2$, $q_{max}$.

**Solution :**

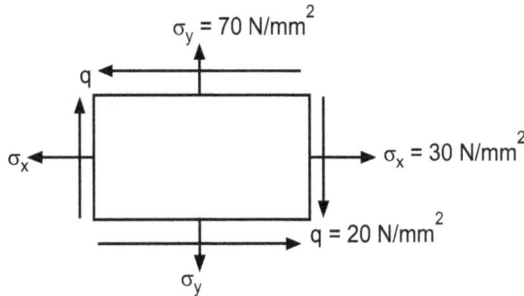

Fig. 2.31 (i)

**Fig. 2.31 (ii)**

## Steps to construct Mohr's circle :

**Step 1 :** Choose a suitable scale. Choose origin O and draw normal stresses $\sigma_x$ and $\sigma_y$ along X-direction.

Taking a scale 1 cm = 10 N/mm$^2$,

$\qquad\qquad$ OA = $\sigma_x$ = 30 N/mm$^2$ shall be drawn 3 cm.

$\qquad\qquad$ OB = $\sigma_y$ = 70 N/mm$^2$ shall be drawn 7 cm.

**Note :** Since $\sigma_x$ and $\sigma_y$ both are tensile, they should be plotted on the right side of O.

**Step 2 :** Plot shear stress along Y-direction from the points where $\sigma_x$ and $\sigma_y$ end.

From A, draw AD along positive Y-direction and from B, draw BE along negative Y-direction, which represents the shear stress.

$\qquad$ AD = BE = q = 20 N/mm$^2$ shall be drawn 2 cm.

**Note :** OA represents $\sigma_x$. Shear stress q on the plane carrying $\sigma_x$ is ↑↓ i.e. positive. Hence AD is drawn above the X-axis representing positive shear stress. OB represents $\sigma_y$.

Shear stress q on the plane carrying $\sigma_y$ is ⇆ i.e. negative. Hence BE is drawn below the X-axis representing negative shear stress.

**Step 3 :** Find the centre of AB as C.

$$\left( \textbf{Note :}\ OC = \frac{OA + OB}{2} = \frac{30 + 70}{2} = 50\ \text{N/mm}^2 = 5\ \text{cm} \right)$$

Join DE. Taking C as centre, CD = CE as radius, draw a circle. This circle is called Mohr's circle.

**Step 4 :** The circle intersects the X-axis at two points, say P and Q.

**Step 5 : Calculations :**

(i) $\qquad\qquad\qquad \sigma_{n_1}$ = Major principal stress = Length OP × Scale = 7.8 × 10

$\qquad\qquad\qquad\qquad$ = **78 N/mm$^2$ (tensile)**

$\qquad\qquad\qquad \sigma_{n_2}$ = Minor principal stress = Length OQ × Scale = 2.1 × 10

$\qquad\qquad\qquad\qquad$ = **21 N/mm$^2$ (tensile)**

(ii) $\qquad\qquad\qquad q_{max}$ = Maximum shear stress = Radius of Mohr's circle × Scale

$\qquad\qquad\qquad\qquad$ = Length CF × Scale = 2.8 × 10 = **28 N/mm$^2$**

**(iii) Position of principal planes :**

Measure $\qquad\qquad \angle$ ECP = 2 $\theta$

We have, $\qquad\qquad$ 2$\theta$ = 45°

∴ $\qquad\qquad\qquad \theta_1 = \dfrac{45}{2}$ = **22.5°** $\qquad\qquad$ ... Position of 1$^{st}$ principal plane

∴ $\qquad\qquad\qquad \theta_2$ = $\theta_1$ + 90° = 22.5° + 90°

$\qquad\qquad\qquad\qquad$ = **112.5°** $\qquad\qquad$ ... Position of 2$^{nd}$ principal plane

**(iv) Normal stress on the plane of maximum shear :**

$\qquad\qquad\qquad \sigma_n$ = Length OC × Scale = 5 × 10 = 50 N/mm$^2$ (tensile)

## Analytical check :

(i) $\qquad\qquad \sigma_n = \dfrac{\sigma_x + \sigma_y}{2} \pm \sqrt{\left(\dfrac{\sigma_x - \sigma_y}{2}\right)^2 + q^2} = \dfrac{30 + 70}{2} \pm \sqrt{\left(\dfrac{30 - 70}{2}\right)^2 + 20^2}$

$\qquad\qquad\qquad$ = 50 ± 28.28

$$\sigma_{n_1} = 50 + 28.28 = \textbf{78.28 N/mm}^2$$

$$\sigma_{n_2} = 50 - 28.28 = \textbf{21.72 N/mm}^2$$

(ii) $\quad \tan 2\theta = \left| \dfrac{2q}{\sigma_x - \sigma_y} \right| = \left| \dfrac{2 \times 20}{30 - 70} \right| = \left| \dfrac{40}{-40} \right| = 1$

∴ $\qquad 2\theta = \tan^{-1}(1) = 45°$

∴ $\qquad \theta_1 = \textbf{22.5°}$ and $\theta_2 = \theta_1 + 90° = \textbf{112.5°}$

(iii) $\quad q_{max} = \dfrac{\sigma_{n_1} - \sigma_{n_2}}{2} = \dfrac{78.28 - 21.72}{2} = \textbf{28.28 N/mm}^2$

**Comparison of values :**

| Sr. No. | | Analytical method | Graphical method |
|---|---|---|---|
| (i) | $\sigma_{n_1}$ | 78.28 N/mm² | 78 N/mm² |
| (ii) | $\sigma_{n_2}$ | 21.72 N/mm² | 21 N/mm² |
| (iii) | $\theta_1, \theta_2$ | 22.5°, 112.5° | 22.5°, 112.5° |
| (iv) | $q_{max}$ | 28.28 N/mm² | 28 N/mm² |

**Example 23 :** *Solve Example 21 by Mohr's circle method.*

**Data :** $\sigma_x = +140$ N/mm², $\sigma_y = +90$ N/mm², $q = 50$ N/mm²

**To find :** $\sigma_n$, $\sigma_t$ and $\sigma_r$ on an oblique plane inclined at 25° to the stress of 90 N/mm².

**Solution :**

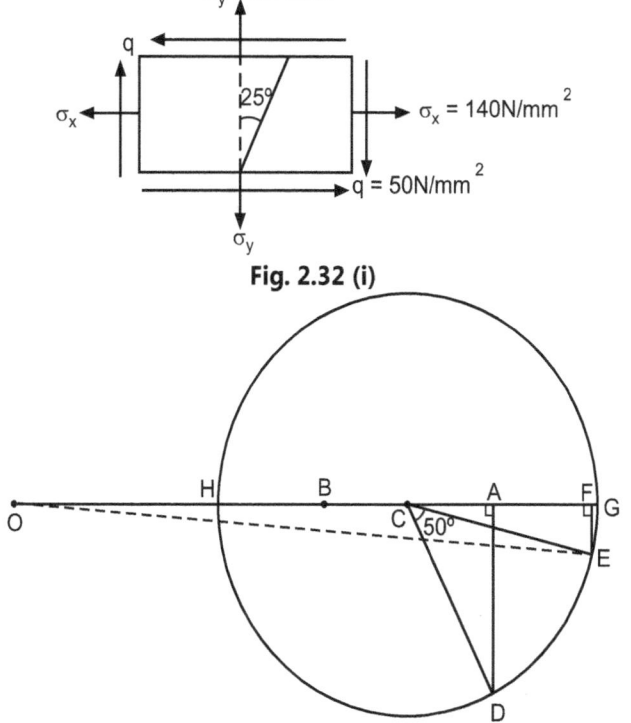

**Fig. 2.32 (i)**

**Fig. 2.32 (ii)**

**Steps :**  (1)  Choose a suitable scale. (1 cm = 20 N/mm²)

       (2)  Draw OA = $\sigma_x$, OB = $\sigma_y$ and at A, draw AD = q.

           (OA = 7 cm, OB = 4.5 cm, AD = 2.5 cm)

       (3)  Bisect AB at C.

       (4)  Taking C as centre and radius equal to CD, draw a circle.

       (5)  On the base CD, draw a line CE at an angle 2θ i.e.

           2 × 25° = 50° cutting the circle at E.

       (6)  From E, draw EF perpendicular to X-axis.

       (7)  The stresses on an oblique plane can be determined as

$$\sigma_n = \text{OF}, \ \sigma_t = \text{EF} \ \text{and} \ \sigma_r = \text{OE}$$

**Calculations :**      $\sigma_n$ = OF × scale = 8.4 × 20 = **168 N/mm² (tensile)**

(**Note :** EF = 7 mm = 0.7 cm)

$$\sigma_t = \text{EF} \times \text{scale} = 0.7 \times 20 = \textbf{14 N/mm}^2$$

$$\sigma_r = \text{OE} \times \text{scale} = 8.5 \times 20 = \textbf{170 N/mm}^2$$

---

**Example 24 :** *Solve Example 13 by Mohr's circle method.*

**Data :** $\sigma_x$ = 120 N/mm² (tensile), q = 40 N/mm²

**To find :** $\sigma_{n_1}$ , $\sigma_{n_2}$ , $\theta_1$, $\theta_2$, $q_{max}$.

**Solution :**

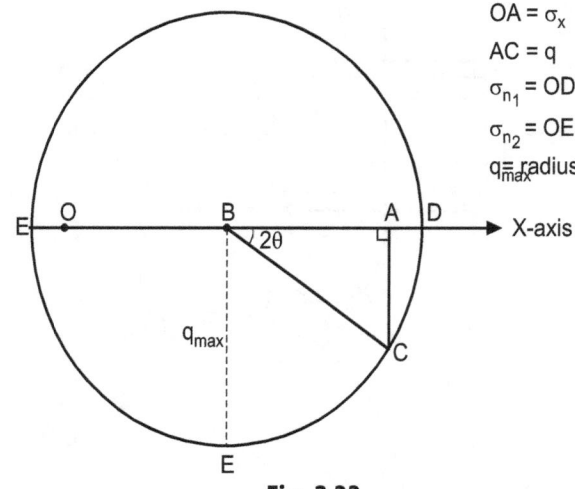

OA = $\sigma_x$
AC = q
$\sigma_{n_1}$ = OD
$\sigma_{n_2}$ = OE
$q_{max}$ = radius

**Fig. 2.33**

**Steps :**

   (1)  Choose a suitable scale. (1 cm = 20 N/mm²)

   (2)  Draw OA = $\sigma_x$. At A, draw AC = q. (OA = 6 cm, AC = 2 cm)

   (3)  Bisect OA at B.

   (4)  Taking B as centre and radius equal to BC, draw a circle.

   (5)  The circle intersects X-axis at two points say D and E.

**(6) Calculations :**

(i) $\qquad \sigma_{n_1}$ = OD × scale = 6.6 × 20 = **132 N/mm² (tensile)**

$\qquad\qquad \sigma_{n_2}$ = OE × scale = –0.6 × 20 = **– 12 N/mm² (compressive)**

**Note :** Since the point E is to the left of O, minor principal stress $\sigma_{n_2}$ is negative.

(ii) $\qquad q_{max}$ = radius of Mohr's circle × scale = BE × scale = 3.6 × 20

$\qquad\qquad\qquad$ = **72 N/mm²**

(iii) Let $\angle$ CBD = 2 θ

$\qquad$ We have, 2 θ = 34°

∴ $\qquad\qquad \theta_1 = \dfrac{34}{2}$ = **17°** $\qquad\qquad\qquad$ ... Position of 1st principal plane

$\qquad\qquad \theta_2 = \theta_1 + 90° = 17° + 90° = $ **107°** $\qquad\qquad$ ... Position of 2nd principal plane

**Example 25 :** *Solve Example 14 by Mohr's circle method.*

**Data :** $\sigma_x$ = 150 N/mm² (tensile), q = 50 N/mm²

**To find :** $\sigma_n$ and $\sigma_t$ on oblique plane which makes an angle 30° with vertical (θ = 30°).

**Solution : Steps :**

(1) Choose a suitable scale (1 cm = 25 N/mm²).

(2) Draw OA = $\sigma_x$ and at A, draw AC = q · (OA = 6 cm, AC = 2 cm).

(3) Bisect OA at B.

(4) Taking B as centre and radius equal to BC, draw a circle.

(5) On the base BC, draw a line BD at an angle 2θ

$\qquad$ i.e. 2 × 30° = 60° cutting the circle at D.

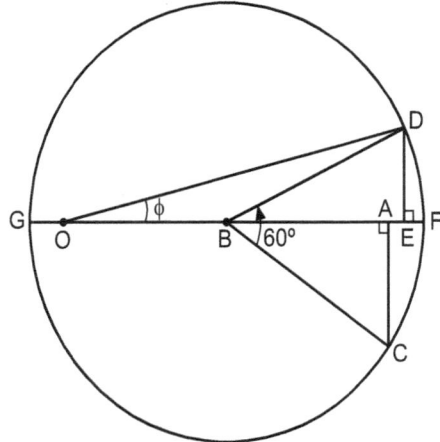

**Fig. 2.34**

(6) From D, draw DE perpendicular to X-axis.

(7) $\qquad\qquad \sigma_n$ = OE × scale = 6.2 × 25 = **155 N/mm² (tensile)**

$\qquad\qquad \sigma_t$ = DE × scale = 1.6 × 25 = **40 N/mm²**

$\qquad\qquad \sigma_r$ = OD × scale = 6.4 × 25 = **160 N/mm²**

$\qquad\qquad \phi$ = angle of obliquity = **14°**

**Example 26 :** *Solve Example 12 by Mohr's circle method.*

**Data :** $\sigma_x = +200$ N/mm$^2$,　$\sigma_y = -30$ N/mm$^2$

**To find :**　(i)　$\sigma_n$, $\sigma_t$, $\sigma_r$ on an oblique plane having $\theta = 60°$

　　　　　　(ii)　$q_{max}$, $\sigma_n$ on a plane of maximum shear.

**Solution : Step 1 :** Choose origin 'O' and draw normal stresses $\sigma_x$ and $\sigma_y$ along X-direction. Taking a scale 1 cm = 20 N/mm$^2$,

　　　　　　OA　=　$\sigma_x$ = 200 N/mm$^2$ shall be drawn 10 cm (to the right of O).

　　　　　　OB　=　$\sigma_y$ = 30 N/mm$^2$ shall be drawn 1.5 cm (to the left of O).

**Step 2 :** Bisect AB at C. Taking C as centre and radius equal to CA or CB, draw a circle.

**Step 3 :** Through centre C, draw a line CD making an angle of $2\theta$

　　　　= $2 \times 60° = 120°$ with X-axis cutting the circle at D

**Step 4 :** Through D, draw DE perpendicular to X-axis. Join OD.

**Step 5 :** Measure the lengths OE, DE and OD.

　　$\sigma_n$ = Length OE × Scale = 1.4 × 20 = **28 N/mm$^2$ (tensile)**

　　$\sigma_t$ = Length DE × Scale = 5 × 20 = **100 N/mm$^2$**

　　$\sigma_r$ = Length OD × Scale = 5.2 × 20 = **104 N/mm$^2$**

　$q_{max}$ = Radius of Mohr's circle × Scale

　　　= Length CD × Scale = 5.7 × 20 = **114 N/mm$^2$**

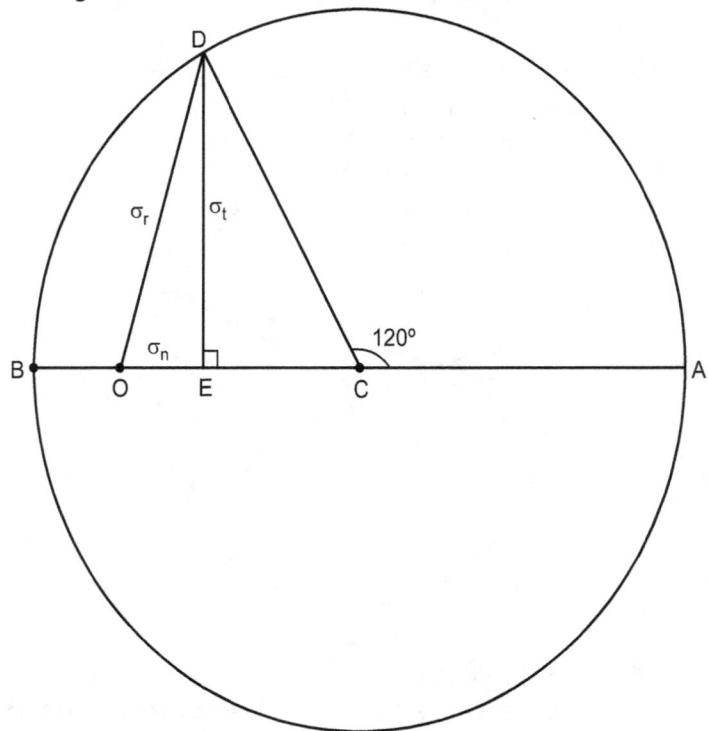

**Fig. 2.35**

**Normal stress on the plane of maximum shear :**

　　　$\sigma_n$ = Length OC × Scale = 4.2 × 20 = **84 N/mm$^2$ (tensile)**

**Example 27 :** *Solve Example 4 by Mohr's circle method.*

**Data :** $\sigma_x$ = + 100 N/mm$^2$

**To find :** $\sigma_n$ and $\sigma_t$ on a plane making an angle 60° with axis of tensile stress i.e. **30°** with vertical. (Here $\theta$ = 30°).

**Solution :**

**Steps :**

   (1)  Choose a suitable scale. (1 cm = 20 N/mm$^2$)

   (2)  Draw OA = $\sigma_x$. (OA = 5 cm)

   (3)  Bisect OA at B.

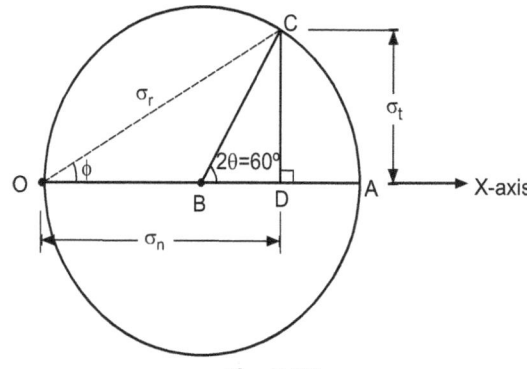

**Fig. 2.36**

   (4)  Taking B as centre and radius BA or BO, draw a circle.

   (5)  On the base BA, draw a line BC at an angle 2$\theta$ i.e. 2 × 30° = 60° cutting the circle at C.

   (6)  From C, draw CD perpendicular to X-axis.

   (7)  $\sigma_n$ = OD × scale = 3.7 × 20 = **74 N/mm$^2$ (tensile)**

        $\sigma_t$ = CD × scale = 2.2 × 20 = **44 N/mm$^2$**

**Additional calculations :**   $\sigma_r$ = OC × scale = 4.3 × 20 = 86 N/mm$^2$

                          $\phi$ = 30°

               $q_{max}$ = radius × scale = 2.5 × 20 = **50 N/mm$^2$**

Normal stress on plane of maximum shear = OB × scale = 2.5 × 20 = **50 N/mm$^2$**

**Example 28 :** *Draw respective Mohr's circles for the elements subjected to state of stress as shown in the following figures.*

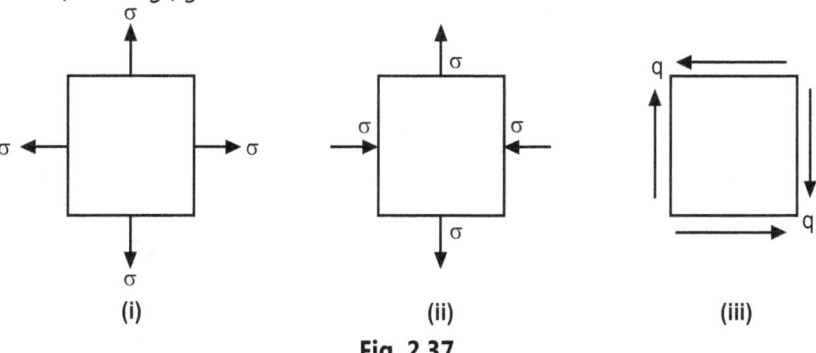

              (i)                       (ii)                (iii)

**Fig. 2.37**

**Solution :** (i) Since $\sigma_x = \sigma_y = \sigma$, both stresses drawn on the right side of origin O will reduce to a point. Hence, Mohr's circle cannot be constructed.

(ii) Here $\sigma_x = -\sigma$ and $\sigma_y = +\sigma$

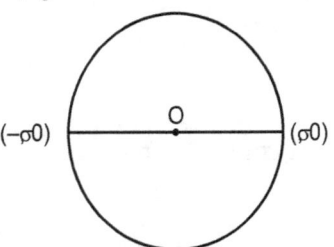

$(-\sigma 0)$      O      $(\sigma 0)$

**Fig. 2.38**

(iii) This is a body subjected to a pure shear.

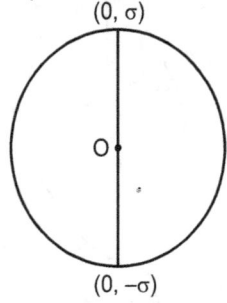

$(0, \sigma)$

O

$(0, -\sigma)$

**Fig. 2.39**

## Practice Questions

### Questions of 2 marks

1. A brass tube is tested in compression, then the fracture line is somewhat inclined. State the theory behind this pattern. **(B.T.E. S-2003, W-2003)**
2. Define principal planes and principal stresses. **(B.T.E. S-1997, 2000; W-1997)**
3. When a plane is designated as the principal plane ? What is the name of stress acting on this plane ? **(B.T.E. W-2000)**
4. Write the equation of tangential stress on an inclined plane making an angle $\theta°$ with the plane subjected to stress (in uniaxial stress system). **(B.T.E. W-1998)**
5. State the values of two different angles of the planes with the principal plane where the tangential stress is maximum. **(B.T.E. S-1999)**
6. Fill in the blanks : Planes of maximum shear make an angle of ............ with the principal plane.
7. Define angle of obliquity.

### Problems of 4 marks

8. At a point in a strained cylindrical shell the principal stresses are 120 N/mm² and 60 N/mm² both tensile. Find normal, tangential and resultant stress and direction of the resultant stress on a plane inclined at 60º to the direction of major principal plane.

    [**Ans.** $\sigma_n$ = 75 N/mm² (tensile), $\sigma_t$ = 25.98 N/mm², $\sigma_r$ = 79.37 N/mm² , $\phi$ = 19.10°]

9. A point in a strained material is subjected to a tensile stress of 100 N/mm$^2$ and a compressive stress of 60 N/mm$^2$. Find the resultant stress on a plane inclined at an angle of 30° with the compressive stress.

   [**Ans.** $\sigma_n$ = 60 N/mm$^2$ (tensile), $\sigma_t$ = 69.28 N/mm$^2$, $\sigma_r$ = 91.65 N/mm$^2$ (tensile), $\phi$ = 49.1°]

10. A point in a strained material is subjected to a compressive stress of 70 N/mm$^2$ and a shear stress of 40 N/mm$^2$. Locate the principal planes and calculate the principal stresses.

    [**Ans.** $\theta_1$ = 65.6°, $\theta_2$ = 155.6°, $\sigma_{n_1}$ = 18.15 N/mm$^2$ (tensile),

    $\sigma_{n_2}$ = – 88.15 N/mm$^2$ (compressive)]

11. At a point in a strained material, there are two mutually perpendicular stresses of 70 N/mm$^2$ (tensile) and 50 N/mm$^2$ (compressive). They are accompanied by a shear stress of 10 N/mm$^2$. Determine the principal stresses and the maximum shear stress.

    [**Ans.** $\sigma_{n_1}$ = 70.83 N/mm$^2$ (tensile), $\sigma_{n_2}$ = – 50.83 N/mm$^2$ (compressive),

    $\sigma_{t_{max}}$ = 60.83 N/mm$^2$]

12. A point in a strained material is subjected to stresses as shown in Fig. 2.40. Find the normal and tangential stresses across the plane BE.

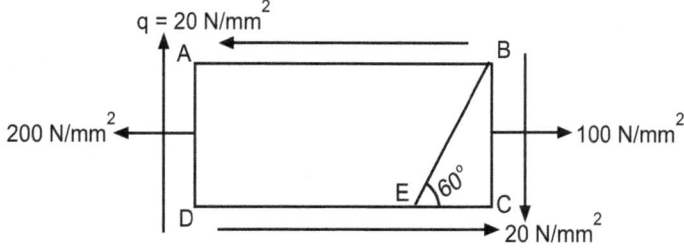

**Fig. 2.40**

[**Ans.** $\sigma_n$ = 92.32 N/mm$^2$ (tensile), $\sigma_t$ = 33.3 N/mm$^2$]

13. A point in a strained material is subjected to stresses as shown in Fig. 2.41. Find the normal and shear stresses on the plane EF.

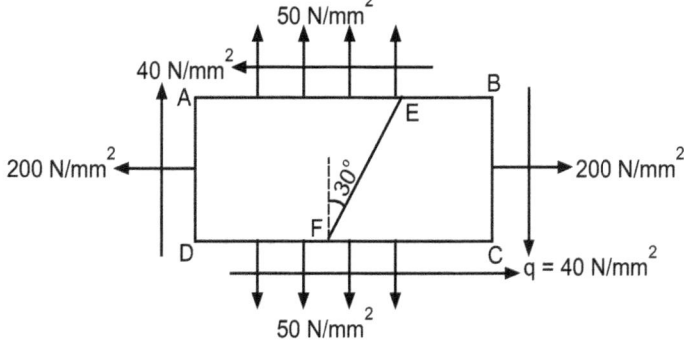

**Fig. 2.41**

[**Ans.** $\sigma_n$ = 197.14 N/mm$^2$ (tensile), $\sigma_t$ = 44.95 N/mm$^2$]

**Important Points**

- **Principal plane :** A plane which carry only normal stress and no shear stress is called a principal plane. The principal planes are always at right angles to each other.
- **Principal stress :** The magnitude of normal stress acting on the principal plane is called principal stress. Principal stresses may be tensile or compressive.

## SUB-TOPIC 2.2 : THIN CYLINDRICAL SHELL (4 Marks)

### Synopsis

Introduction, Expression for hoop stress ($\sigma_C$), Expression for longitudinal stress ($\sigma_L$), Changes in dimensions due to internal pressure, Maximum shear stress.

## 2.6 INTRODUCTION

*When the thickness of the wall of the cylinder is equal to or less than $\dfrac{1}{20}$ th of the diameter of the cylinder, the cylinder is called as thin cylinder. For a thick cylinder, $\dfrac{t}{d} > \dfrac{1}{20}$. Thin cylinders* like tanks, boilers, steam pipes, gas or water pipes, compressed air receivers, etc. are subjected to internal liquid pressure which is uniform over the internal surface area and acts normal or perpendicular to the walls.

When a thin cylinder is subjected to internal liquid pressure, the following three types of stresses are developed.

- **(i)  Hoop stresses :** *The stresses which act in the tangential direction to the perimeter (circumference) of the cylinder are called as hoop stresses or circumferential stresses, and are denoted by $\sigma_c$.*          **(W-2014)**

- **(ii)  Longitudinal stresses :** *The stresses which act parallel to the longitudinal axis of the cylinder are called as longitudinal stresses and are denoted by $\sigma_L$.*          **(W-2014)**

- **(iii) Radial stresses :** *The stresses which act radially i.e. along the radius of the cylinder are called radial stresses and are denoted by $\sigma_r$.*

These three stresses are mutually perpendicular to each other and are called as principal stresses. *Radial stresses are negligible in thin cylinders and hence not considered at all.*

## 2.7 EXPRESSION FOR HOOP STRESS ($\sigma_C$)

Let us consider a thin cylinder of internal diameter d, thickness t and length L subjected to internal liquid pressure 'p'. This pressure causes a bursting force in the material which acts tangential to the circumference of the shell and is called hoop tension. As a result of this, the cylinder has a tendency to split into two troughs (semi-circular portions).

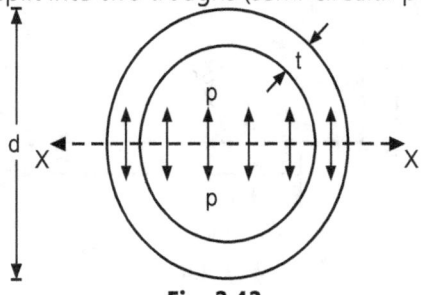

**Fig. 2.42**

**Circumferential stress :** $\qquad \sigma_C = \dfrac{\text{Bursting force}}{\text{Resisting area}} = \dfrac{p \times d \times L}{2 \times (L \times t)}$

$\therefore$

$$\boxed{\sigma_C = \dfrac{pd}{2t}}$$

## 2.8 EXPRESSION FOR LONGITUDINAL STRESS ($\sigma_L$)

Now, let us assume that the cylinder is closed at both the ends by flat plates. As a result of internal pressure 'p' the cylinder has a tendency to split into two small cylinders.

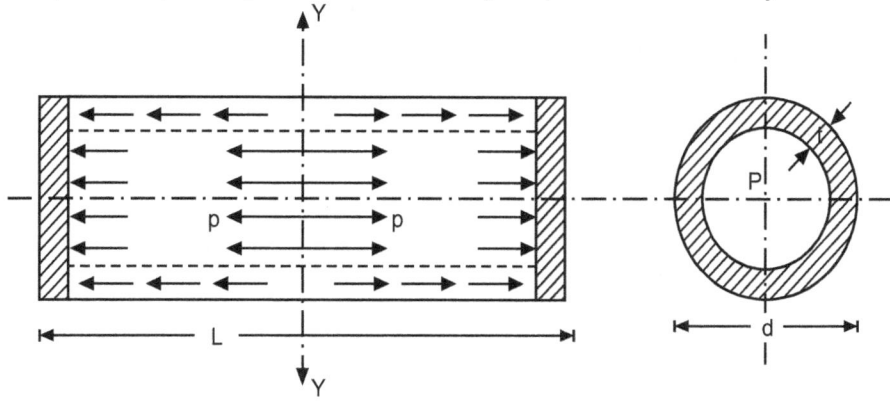

**Fig. 2.43**

Let $\qquad\qquad \sigma_L$ = longitudinal stress produced in the shell

**Longitudinal stress :** $\qquad \sigma_L = \dfrac{\text{Pressure on the ends}}{\text{Resisting area}} = \dfrac{p \times \frac{\pi}{4} d^2}{\pi \times d \times t}$

$\therefore$

$$\boxed{\sigma_L = \dfrac{pd}{4t}}$$

Therefore, *the hoop or circumferential stress ($\sigma_c$) is twice the longitudinal stress ($\sigma_l$).*

**Note :** *In no case should the hoop stress be greater than the permissible stress in the material of the cylinder.*

## 2.9 CHANGES IN DIMENSIONS DUE TO INTERNAL PRESSURE

**Principal stresses :**

Circumferential stress, $\qquad \sigma_C = \dfrac{pd}{2t}$ $\qquad\qquad\qquad$ ... (i)

Longitudinal stress, $\qquad \sigma_L = \dfrac{pd}{4t}$ $\qquad\qquad\qquad$ ... (ii)

**Principal strains :**

**(i) Circumferential strain (strain in diameter) :**

Using generalized Hooke's law for biaxial stress system,

**Circumferential strain,** $\qquad e_C = \dfrac{\sigma_C}{E} - \mu \dfrac{\sigma_L}{E}$

$$\therefore \qquad e_c = \frac{1}{E}[\sigma_c - \mu\,\sigma_L] \qquad \text{... (iii)}$$

But circumferential strain, $\qquad e_c = \dfrac{\text{Change in circumference}}{\text{Original circumference}} = \dfrac{\pi\,\delta d}{\pi d} = \dfrac{\delta d}{d}$    ... (iv)

Equating (iii) and (iv), we have,

**Strain in diameter,** $\qquad \dfrac{\delta d}{d} = \dfrac{1}{E}[\sigma_c - \mu\,\sigma_L] \qquad$ ... (v)

From this equation, the change in diameter of a thin cylindrical shell can be calculated.

### (ii) Longitudinal strain (strain in length) :

Longitudinal strain, $\qquad e_L = \dfrac{\sigma_L}{E} - \mu\,\dfrac{\sigma_c}{E} = \dfrac{1}{E}[\sigma_L - \mu\,\sigma_c] \qquad$ ... (vi)

But longitudinal strain, $\qquad e_L = \dfrac{\delta L}{L} \qquad$ ... (vii)

Equating (vi) and (vii), we have,

Strain in length, $\qquad \dfrac{\delta L}{L} = \dfrac{1}{E}[\sigma_L - \mu\,\sigma_c] \qquad$ ... (viii)

From this equation, the change in length of a thin cylindrical shell can be calculated.

### (iii) Volumetric strain (strain in volume) :

Original volume, $\qquad V = \text{Area} \times \text{Length}$

$$= \frac{\pi}{4}d^2 \times L$$

Differentiating both sides w.r.t. x,

$$\delta V = \frac{\pi}{4}[d^2 \times \delta L + L \times 2d \times \delta d]$$

$$\therefore \qquad \frac{\delta V}{V} = \frac{\frac{\pi}{4}[d^2 \times \delta L + L \times 2d \times \delta d]}{\frac{\pi}{4}d^2 \times L} = \frac{d^2 \times \delta L}{d^2 \times L} + \frac{L \times 2d \times \delta d}{d^2 \times L} = \frac{\delta L}{L} + 2\frac{\delta d}{d}$$

$$\therefore \qquad \boxed{\frac{\delta V}{V} = e_L + 2\,e_c}$$

From this equation, the change in volume of a thin cylindrical shell can be calculated.

**Note :** *When a thin cylindrical shell is subjected to internal pressure, there will be increase in the diameter, increase in the length and hence increase in the volume of the shell.*

## 2.10 MAXIMUM SHEAR STRESS

At any point on the circumference of a thin cylindrical shell there is a set of two mutually perpendicular principal stresses $\sigma_c$ and $\sigma_L$ and the planes on which they act are the principal planes.

We know that,  maximum shear stress = $\dfrac{\text{Difference of principal stresses}}{2}$

$\therefore$

$$\boxed{q_{max} \;=\; \dfrac{\sigma_C - \sigma_L}{2}}$$

Substituting the values of $\sigma_C$ and $\sigma_L$ in the above equation, we have

$$q_{max} \;=\; \dfrac{\dfrac{pd}{2t} - \dfrac{pd}{4t}}{2} = \dfrac{\dfrac{pd}{4t}}{2} \quad \therefore \quad \boxed{q_{max} \;=\; \dfrac{pd}{8t}}$$

## SOLVED EXAMPLES

**Type 1 : Examples on hoop and longitudinal stress and strain, and changes in dimensions of a shell**

> **Stress :** Circumferential (hoop) stress,   $\sigma_C = \dfrac{pd}{2t}$
>
> Longitudinal stress,   $\sigma_L = \dfrac{1}{2}\sigma_C = \dfrac{pd}{4t}$
>
> Maximum shear stress,   $q_{max} = \dfrac{pd}{8t}$
>
> **Strains :** Circumferential (hoop) strain,   $e_C = \dfrac{\delta d}{d} = \dfrac{\sigma_C}{E} - \mu\dfrac{\sigma_L}{E}$
>
> From this equation, $\delta d$ can be calculated.
>
> Longitudinal strain,   $e_L = \dfrac{\delta L}{L} = \dfrac{\sigma_L}{E} - \mu\dfrac{\sigma_C}{E}$
>
> From this equation, $\delta L$ can be calculated.
>
> Volumetric strain,   $e_V = \dfrac{\delta V}{V} = e_L + 2\,e_C$
>
> From this equation, $\delta V$ can be calculated.

**Example 1 :** *Calculate circumferential strain, if longitudinal stress and circumferential stress are 25 MPa and 50 MPa respectively. Take E = 210 kN/mm², $\dfrac{1}{m}$ = 0.3.*

**(B.T.E. W-1997/ 2 Marks)**

**Data**     : $\sigma_L$ = 25 MPa = 25 N/mm², $\sigma_C$ = 50 MPa = 50 N/mm²,

E = 210 kN/mm² = 210 × 10³ N/mm², $\mu = \dfrac{1}{m} = 0.3$

**To find**  : $e_C$.

**Solution :** Circumferential strain,

$$e_C = \dfrac{\sigma_C}{E} - \mu\dfrac{\sigma_L}{E} = \dfrac{1}{E}\left[\sigma_C - \mu\,\sigma_L\right] = \dfrac{1}{210 \times 10^3}\,(50 - 0.3 \times 25)$$

$\therefore$          $$\mathbf{e_C} = \dfrac{42.5}{210 \times 10^3} = \mathbf{0.0002024}$$

**Answer :** $\boxed{e_C = 0.0002024}$

**Example 2 :** *If the hoop stress in a thin cylinder is 200 N/mm², what will be the longitudinal stress ?*

**Data** : $\sigma_C$ = 200 N/mm²

**To find :** $\sigma_L$.

**Solution :**
$$\sigma_L = \frac{1}{2} \times \sigma_C = \frac{1}{2} \times 200 = \textbf{100 N/mm}^2$$

**Answer :** $\boxed{\sigma_L = 100 \text{ N/mm}^2}$

**Example 3 :** *A cylinder shell is 3 m long, 1 m diameter and 15 mm metal thickness. Calculate the circumferential strain and longitudinal strain, if the cylindrical shell is subjected to internal pressure of 1.5 N/mm².*
*Take E = 2 × 10⁵ N/mm², μ = 0.3.*　　**(B.T.E. S-2006/4 Marks)**

**Data** : L = 3 m = 3000 mm, d = 1 m = 1000 mm, t = 15 mm, p = 1.5 N/mm².

**To find :** $e_C$, $e_L$.

**Solution :** Circumferential stress,
$$\sigma_C = \frac{pd}{2t} = \frac{1.5 \times 1000}{2 \times 15} = 50 \text{ N/mm}^2$$

Longitudinal stress,
$$\sigma_L = \frac{1}{2}\sigma_C = \frac{1}{2} \times 50 = 25 \text{ N/mm}^2$$

**Circumferential strain :**
$$e_C = \frac{1}{E}(\sigma_C - \mu\sigma_L) = \frac{1}{2 \times 10^5}(50 - 0.3 \times 25)$$
$$= \textbf{2.125} \times \textbf{10}^{-4}$$

**Longitudinal strain :**
$$e_L = \frac{1}{E}(\sigma_L - \mu\sigma_C) = \frac{1}{2 \times 10^5}(25 - 0.3 \times 50)$$
$$= \textbf{5} \times \textbf{10}^{-5}$$

**Answer :** $\boxed{e_C = 2.125 \times 10^{-4},\ e_L = 5 \times 10^{-5}}$

**Example 4 :** *A cylindrical shell 3 m long has 1.2 m internal diameter and 20 mm metal thickness. Calculate the longitudinal stress induced and change in the length of the shell, if it is subjected to internal pressure of 8 N/mm². Take E = 2.1 × 10⁵ N/mm², Poisson's ratio = 0.32.*
　　**(B.T.E. W-2011, S-2000/4 Marks)**

**Data** : L = 3 m = 3000 mm, d = 1.2 m = 1200 mm, t = 20 mm,
p = 8 N/mm², E = 2.1 × 10⁵ N/mm², μ = 0.32.

**To find :** (i) $\sigma_L$ and (ii) $\delta L$.

**Solution :** Using the relation, $\sigma_L = \dfrac{pd}{4t}$

∴
$$\sigma_L = \frac{8 \times 1200}{4 \times 20} = \textbf{120 N/mm}^2$$

Using the relation,  $\sigma_c = \dfrac{pd}{2t}$

$\therefore$  $\sigma_c = \dfrac{8 \times 1200}{2 \times 20} = \textbf{240 N/mm}^2$

$e_L = \dfrac{1}{E}[\sigma_L - \mu\sigma_c]$

$\therefore$  $\dfrac{\delta L}{L} = \dfrac{1}{2.1 \times 10^5}[120 - 0.32 \times 240]$  $...\left(\because e_L = \dfrac{\delta L}{L}\right)$

$\therefore$  $\dfrac{\delta L}{3000} = \dfrac{1}{2.1 \times 10^5} \times 43.2 = 0.000205714$

$\therefore$  $\delta L = 3000 \times 0.000205714 = \textbf{0.617 mm}$

**Answer :** $\boxed{\sigma_L = 120 \text{ N/mm}^2, \ \delta L = 0.617 \text{ mm}}$

---

**Example 5 :** *The compressed air cylinder 1.4 m internal diameter and 20 mm thick is subjected to internal pressure of 1.6 MPa. Calculate the change in diameter. Take Poisson's ratio = 0.28 and E = 2 $\times 10^5$ MPa.* **(B.T.E. S-1999/4 Marks)**

**Data** : d = 1.4 m = $1.4 \times 10^3$ mm, t = 20 mm, p = 1.6 MPa = 1.6 N/mm$^2$,

μ = 0.28, E = $2 \times 10^5$ N/mm$^2$

**To find** : δd.

**Solution :**  $\sigma_c = \dfrac{pd}{2t} = \dfrac{1.6 \times (1.4 \times 10^3)}{2 \times 20} = 56 \text{ N/mm}^2$

$\sigma_L = \dfrac{1}{2}\sigma_c = \dfrac{56}{2} = 28 \text{ N/mm}^2$

$e_c = \dfrac{1}{E}(\sigma_c - \mu\,\sigma_L) = \dfrac{1}{2 \times 10^5}(56 - 0.28 \times 28) = 0.0002408$

$\therefore$  $\dfrac{\delta d}{d} = 0.0002408$  $...\left(\because e_c = \dfrac{\delta d}{d}\right)$

$\therefore$  $\dfrac{\delta d}{1.4 \times 10^3} = 0.0002408$

$\therefore$  $\delta d = (1.4 \times 10^3) \times 0.0002408 = \textbf{0.337 mm}$

**Answer :** $\boxed{\delta d = 0.337 \text{ mm}}$

---

**Example 6 :** *A cylindrical shell 3 m long and 1 m in diameter is subjected to an internal pressure of 1 MPa. If the thickness of the cylindrical shell is 12 mm, find the change in volume of the cylindrical shell. Take E = 2 $\times 10^5$ N/mm$^2$ and Poisson's ratio = 0.3.*

**(B.T.E. W-1999/4 Marks)**

**Data** : L = 3 m = 3000 mm, d = 1 m = 1000 mm, p = 1 MPa = 1 N/mm$^2$,

t = 12 mm, E = $2 \times 10^5$ N/mm$^2$, μ = 0.3

**To find** : δV.

**Solution :**

$$\sigma_C = \frac{pd}{2\,t} = \frac{1 \times 1000}{2 \times 12} = 41.67 \text{ N/mm}^2$$

$$\sigma_L = \frac{1}{2}\,\sigma_C = \frac{41.67}{2} = 20.83 \text{ N/mm}^2$$

$$e_C = \frac{1}{E}\,(\sigma_C - \mu\sigma_L) = \frac{1}{2 \times 10^5}\,(41.67 - 0.3 \times 20.83) = 0.000177105$$

$$e_L = \frac{1}{E}\,(\sigma_L - \mu\sigma_C) = \frac{1}{2 \times 10^5}\,(20.83 - 0.3 \times 41.67) = 0.000041645$$

$$V = \frac{\pi}{4}\,d^2 \times L = \frac{\pi}{4} \times (1000)^2 \times 3000 = 2356194490 \text{ mm}^3$$

$$\frac{\delta V}{V} = e_L + 2\,e_C$$

$$\therefore \quad \frac{\delta V}{2356194490} = 0.000041645 + 2 \times 0.000177105 = 0.000395855$$

$$\therefore \quad \delta V = 2356194490 \times 0.000395855 = \mathbf{932711.3698 \text{ mm}^3}$$

**Answer :** $\boxed{\delta V = 932711.3698 \text{ mm}^3}$

**Example 7 :** *For the cylindrical shell of 1 m diameter, the circumferential and longitudinal strains are 20 × 10⁻⁵ and 4.5 × 10⁻⁵ respectively. Calculate the change in volume per metre length of the shell.* **(B.T.E. S-2001/4 Marks)**

**Data** : $d = 1 \text{ m} = 1000 \text{ mm}$, $e_C = 20 \times 10^{-5}$, $e_L = 4.5 \times 10^{-5}$, $L = 1 \text{ m} = 1000 \text{ mm}$

**To find** : $\delta V$.

**Solution : We have to find the change in volume per metre length of the shell**
**i.e. L = 1 m = 1000 mm.**

Original volume, 

$$V = \left(\frac{\pi}{4}\,d^2\right) \times L = \frac{\pi}{4} \times (1000)^2 \times 1000 = 785398163.4 \text{ mm}^3$$

$$\frac{\delta V}{V} = e_L + 2\,e_C$$

$$\therefore \quad \frac{\delta V}{785398163.4} = 4.5 \times 10^{-5} + 2 \times (20 \times 10^{-5}) = 44.5 \times 10^{-5}$$

$$\therefore \quad \delta V = 785398163.4 \times 44.5 \times 10^{-5} = \mathbf{349502.18 \text{ mm}^3}$$

**Answer :** $\boxed{\delta V = 349502.18 \text{ mm}^3}$

**Example 8 :** *For the cylindrical shell of 1 m diameter, the circumferential and longitudinal strains are 19 × 10⁻⁵ and 2.9 × 10⁻⁵ respectively. Calculate the volume per metre length of the shell.* **(B.T.E. S-2005/4 Marks)**

**Data** : $d = 1 \text{ m} = 1000 \text{ mm}$, $e_C = 19 \times 10^{-5}$, $e_L = 2.9 \times 10^{-5}$, $L = 1 \text{ m} = 1000 \text{ mm}$

**To find** : $\delta V$.

**Solution :**

$$V = A \times L = \frac{\pi}{4}\,d^2 \times L = \frac{\pi}{4}\,(1000)^2\,(1000)$$

$$= 785398163.4 \text{ mm}^3$$

$$\frac{\delta V}{V} = e_L + 2e_C$$

$\therefore$    $\delta V = V(e_L + 2e_C) = 785398163.4\,(2.9 \times 10^{-5} + 2 \times 19 \times 10^{-5})$

$$= \mathbf{321228.5\ mm^3}$$

**Answer :** $\boxed{\delta V = 321228.5\ mm^3}$

---

**Example 9 :** *A shell 3.25 m long and 1 m diameter is subjected to internal pressure of 1 MPa. If the thickness of the shell is 10 mm, find the change in capacity of the shell. Take E = 200 GPa and μ = 0.25.* **(B.T.E. W-2003/4 Marks)**

**Data    :**    L = 3.25 m = 3250 mm, d = 1 m = 1000 mm,

p = 1 MPa = 1 N/mm², t = 10 mm,

E = 200 GPa = 200 × 10³ N/mm², μ = 0.25

**To find  :**    $\delta V$.

**Solution :**    $\sigma_C = \dfrac{pd}{2\,t} = \dfrac{1 \times 1000}{2 \times 10} = 50\ N/mm^2$

$$\sigma_L = \frac{\sigma_C}{2} = 25\ N/mm^2$$

$$e_C = \frac{1}{E}\,[\sigma_C - \mu\sigma_L] = \frac{1}{200 \times 10^3}\,(50 - 0.25 \times 25) = 0.00021875$$

$$e_L = \frac{1}{E}\,[\sigma_L - \mu\sigma_C] = \frac{1}{200 \times 10^3}\,(25 - 0.25 \times 50) = 0.0000625$$

$$V = \frac{\pi}{4}\,d^2 \times L = \frac{\pi}{4}\,(1000)^2 \times 3250 = 2552544031\ mm^3$$

$$\frac{\delta V}{V} = e_L + 2e_C$$

$$\frac{\delta V}{2552544031} = (0.0000625 + 2 \times 0.00021875)$$

$$\delta V = \mathbf{1276272.02\ mm^3}$$

**Answer :** $\boxed{\delta V = 1276272.02\ mm^3}$

---

**Example 10 :** *A thin cylindrical shell 3 m long is of 1.5 m diameter having 12 mm wall thickness. Determine the changes in length and diameter if the shell is subjected to an internal pressure of 19 N/mm². Take E = 210 kN/mm² and Poisson's ratio = 0.28.* **(B.T.E. W-2000/4 Marks)**

**Answer :** $\boxed{\delta L = 3.73\ mm,\ \delta d = 7.3\ mm}$

---

**Example 11 :** *A hydraulic main of 1 m diameter and 10 mm thick has to carry water under a head of 200 m. Calculate (i) hoop stress, (ii) longitudinal stress.* **(B.T.E. S-1986, W-2014/4 Marks)**

**Data** : $d = 1$ m $= 1000$ mm, $t = 10$ mm, $h = 200$ m

**To find** : $\sigma_C$ and $\sigma_L$

**Solution :** Density of water $\gamma_w = 10$ kN/m$^3$

We know that, maximum water pressure

$$P = \gamma_w \times h = 10 \times 200 = 2000 \text{ kN/m}^2 = \frac{2000 \times 10^3}{10^6} = 2 \text{ N/mm}^2$$

$$\sigma_C = \frac{pd}{2t} = \frac{2 \times 1000}{2 \times 10} = \mathbf{100 \text{ N/mm}^2}$$

$$\sigma_L = \frac{1}{2} \times \sigma_C = \frac{1}{2} \times 100 = \mathbf{50 \text{ N/mm}^2}$$

**Answer :** $\boxed{\sigma_C = 100 \text{ N/mm}^2, \sigma_L = 50 \text{ N/mm}^2}$

**Example 12 :** *A cylinder, 1 m diameter and 25 mm thick contains a fluid under pressure of 'p' N/mm². If the change in volume per metre length of the cylinder is observed to be 6.28 × 10⁵ mm³, calculate the value of 'p'. Take modulus of elasticity as 200 GPa and Poisson's ratio as 0.25.* **(B.T.E. W-2005/4 Marks)**

**Data** : $d = 1$ m $= 1000$ mm, $t = 25$ mm, $\delta V = 6.28 \times 10^5$ mm$^3$,

$\quad\quad\quad L = 1$ m $= 1000$ mm, $E = 200$ GPa $= 200 \times 10^3$ N/mm$^2$, $\mu = 0.25$

**To find** : p.

**Solution :** Volume of cylinder per metre length

$$V = \frac{\pi}{4} d^2 \times L = \frac{\pi}{4} (1000)^2 \times 1000 = 785.39 \times 10^6 \text{ mm}^3$$

Let 'p' be in N/mm².

$$\sigma_C = \frac{pd}{2t} = \frac{p \times 1000}{2 \times 25} = (20p) \text{ N/mm}^2$$

$$\sigma_L = \frac{\sigma_C}{2} = (10p) \text{ N/mm}^2$$

$$e_C = \frac{1}{E}(\sigma_C - \mu \times \sigma_L) = \frac{1}{200 \times 10^3}(20p - 0.25 \times 10p)$$

$$\therefore \quad\quad e_C = \frac{17.5p}{2 \times 10^5} = 8.75 \times 10^{-5} p$$

$$e_L = \frac{1}{E}(\sigma_L - \mu \times \sigma_C) = \frac{1}{200 \times 10^3}(10p - 0.25 \times 20p)$$

$$= \frac{5p}{200 \times 10^3} = 0.025 \times 10^{-3} p$$

$$\frac{\delta V}{V} = e_L + 2e_C$$

$$\frac{6.28 \times 10^5}{785.39 \times 10^6} = (0.025 \times 10^{-3})p + (2 \times 8.75 \times 10^{-5})p = \mathbf{0.0002\ p}$$

$$\mathbf{p = 3.99 \text{ N/mm}^2}$$

**Answer :** $\boxed{p = 3.99 \text{ N/mm}^2}$

## Type 2 : Examples on Design of Thin Cylindrical Shell :

In such type of examples, generally maximum allowable stress in the material of the shell (safe stress in tension for material), internal pressure, diameter of the shell are given and the thickness of the shell is required to be calculated.

> **Hint :** Use the relation $\sigma_c = \dfrac{pd}{2t}$
>
> $\therefore \qquad\qquad\qquad t = \dfrac{pd}{2\sigma_c}$

where $\sigma_c$ = Maximum allowable stress in shell material

= hoop stress or circumferential stress

p = Intensity of internal pressure

d = Diameter of the shell

t = Thickness of the shell

**Note :** *Safe stress in tension for a material is always taken as hoop stress and not longitudinal stress. Hence, the thickness is always calculated by using the formula for hoop stress.*

**Example 13 :** *A seamless pipe 800 mm in diameter contains oil under pressure of 2 N/mm². If the permissible tensile stress is 100 N/mm², find the maximum thickness of pipe.*

**(B.T.E. W-1998/2 Marks)**

**Data**    : d = 800 mm, p = 2 N/mm²,

permissible tensile stress = hoop stress = $\sigma_c$ = 100 N/mm²

**To find**  : t.

**Solution :** Using the relation, $\qquad \sigma_c = \dfrac{pd}{2t}$

$\therefore \qquad\qquad\qquad 100 = \dfrac{2 \times 800}{2 \times t}$

$\therefore \qquad\qquad\qquad \mathbf{t} = \dfrac{2 \times 800}{2 \times 100} = \mathbf{8\ mm}$

**Answer :** $\boxed{t = 8\ mm}$

**Example 14 :** *A boiler of 1 m diameter contains fluid at a pressure of 2.5 N/mm². If the safe stress in tension for the material of the boiler is 100 N/mm², find the thickness of the boiler plate.* **(B.T.E. W-1985/2 Marks)**

**Data**    : d = 1 m = 1000 mm, p = 2.5 N/mm², $\sigma_c$ = 100 N/mm²

**To find**  : t

**Solution :** Using the relation, $\qquad \sigma_c = \dfrac{pd}{2t}$

$\therefore \qquad\qquad\qquad \mathbf{t} = \dfrac{pd}{2\sigma_c} = \dfrac{2.5 \times 1000}{2 \times 100} = \mathbf{12.5\ mm}$

**Answer :** $\boxed{t = 12.5\ mm}$

**Example 15 :** *A seamless pipe of 1 m diameter contains a fluid under a pressure of 1.5 N/mm². If the ultimate tensile stress is 450 N/mm², find the minimum thickness of the pipe. Take factor of safety as 4.5.* **(B.T.E. S-2004, 2003/4 Marks)**

**Data** : $d = 1$ m $= 1000$ mm, $p = 1.5$ N/mm², factor of safety $= 4.5$,
ultimate tensile stress $= 450$ N/mm²

**To find** : t.

**Solution :** Working stress $= \dfrac{\text{Ultimate stress}}{\text{Factor of safety}} = \dfrac{450}{4.5} = 100$ N/mm²

$\therefore$ $\sigma_c = 100$ N/mm²

Now, $\sigma_c = \dfrac{pd}{2t}$

$100 = \dfrac{1.5 \times 1000}{2 \times t}$ $\therefore$ **t = 7.5 mm**

**Answer :** $\boxed{t = 7.5 \text{ mm}}$

---

**Example 16 :** *A cylindrical compressed air drum is 2 m in diameter with plate thickness of 12 mm. If the tensile stress is not to exceed 100 N/mm², find the maximum safe air pressure.*
**(B.T.E. W-1986/2 Marks)**

**Data** : $d = 2$ m $= 2000$ mm, $t = 12$ mm,
Maximum tensile stress $=$ Hoop stress $= \sigma_c = 100$ N/mm²

**To find** : p.

**Solution :** Using the relation, $\sigma_c = \dfrac{pd}{2t}$

$100 = \dfrac{p \times 2000}{2 \times 12}$ $\therefore$ **p = 1.2 N/mm²**

**Answer :** $\boxed{p = 1.2 \text{ N/mm}^2}$

---

**Example 17 :** *A thin cylindrical boiler shell of length 8 m and diameter 3 m is subjected to uniform internal pressure intensity of 2 N/mm². Find the factor of safety of design when the thickness of boiler plate is 15 mm and the ultimate strength of material is 540 N/mm².*
**(B.T.E. S-1987/4 Marks)**

**Data** : $L = 8$ m $= 8000$ mm, $d = 3$ m $= 3000$ mm,
$p = 2$ N/mm², $t = 15$ mm, ultimate strength $= 540$ N/mm²

**To find** : Factor of safety.

**Solution :** Allowable stress $=$ hoop stress $= \dfrac{pd}{2t} = \dfrac{2 \times 3000}{2 \times 15} = 200$ N/mm²

We know that,

**Factor of safety** $= \dfrac{\text{Ultimate (Maximum) strength}}{\text{Allowable stress}} = \dfrac{540}{200} = \mathbf{2.7}$

**Answer :** $\boxed{\text{Factor of safety} = 2.7}$

**Example 18 :** *A water main 1.5 m diameter is required to convey water under a head of 200 m. If the allowable tensile stress in the pipe material is 120 N/mm², find the thickness of the water main.*

**Data** ： $d = 1.5$ m $= 1500$ mm, $h = 200$ m, allowable stress $= \sigma_c = 120$ N/mm²

**To find** : t.

**Solution :** We know that density of water,

$$\gamma_w = 10 \text{ kN/m}^3$$

Maximum water pressure,

$$p = \gamma_w \times h = 10 \times 200 = 2000 \text{ kN/m}^2$$

$$= \frac{2000 \times 10^3}{10^6} = 2 \text{ N/mm}^2$$

We know that, $\quad \sigma_c = \dfrac{pd}{2t}$

∴ $\quad \mathbf{t} = \dfrac{pd}{2\sigma_c} = \dfrac{2 \times 1500}{2 \times 120} = \mathbf{12.5 \text{ mm}}$

**Answer :** $\boxed{t = 12.5 \text{ mm}}$

---

**Example 19 :** *Due to corrosion, the thickness of a thin cylindrical shell is reduced by 3 mm. Due to this reduction in thickness, the hoop stress is increased by 12 % under the same internal pressure. Find the original thickness of the shell.* **(B.T.E. S-1993/4 Marks)**

**Solution :** Let $\quad t =$ Original thickness (before corrosion)

$\quad t_1 =$ Reduced thickness (after corrosion) $= t - 3$

Let $\quad \sigma_c =$ Hoop stress before corrosion $= \dfrac{pd}{2t}$

$\quad \sigma_{c_1} =$ Hoop stress after corrosion $= 1.12 \, \sigma_c$ (Given)

Now, $\quad \sigma_{c_1} = \dfrac{pd}{2(t-3)}$

∴ $\quad 1.12 \, \sigma_c = \dfrac{pd}{2(t-3)}$

∴ $\quad 1.12 \times \dfrac{pd}{2t} = \dfrac{pd}{2(t-3)}$

Dividing both sides by pd, $\quad \dfrac{1.12}{2t} = \dfrac{1}{2(t-3)}$

∴ $\quad 1.12 \times 2(t-3) = 2t$

∴ $\quad 2.24t - 6.72 = 2t$

∴ $\quad 0.24t = 6.72$

∴ $\quad \mathbf{t} = \dfrac{6.72}{0.24} = \mathbf{28 \text{ mm}}$

**Answer :** $\boxed{t = 28 \text{ mm}}$

**(Note :** Hoop stress after corrosion $= \sigma_c + 12\%$ of $\sigma_c = \sigma_c + 0.12 \times \sigma_c = 1.12 \, \sigma_c$**)**

**Practice Questions**

## Questions of 2 marks

1.  Differentiate between thin cylinder and thick cylinder.          **(B.T.E. S-2000, 1998)**

2.  Define hoop stress.          **(B.T.E. S-1997)**

3.  Define longitudinal stress.

4.  Write the equation for circumferential stress and longitudinal stress for thin cylinder.

    **(B.T.E. W-1999)**

5.  Write the equation of circumferential stress in thin cylinder and explain each term.

    **(B.T.E. W-1997)**

6.  Write the equation of longitudinal stress in thin cylinder and explain each term.

    **(B.T.E. W-1998)**

7.  Distinguish between circumferential stress and longitudinal stress in a thin cylinder shell, when subjected to an internal pressure.          **(B.T.E. W-2000)**

8.  Write the relationship between circumferential stress and longitudinal stress for thin cylinder.          **(B.T.E. W-1999)**

9.  Calculate the circumferential strain if the longitudinal stress and circumferential stress are 25 MPa and 50 MPa respectively. Take E = 210 kN/mm$^2$, $\dfrac{1}{m}$ = 0.3.

    **(B.T.E. W-1997)**

10. A seamless pipe 800 mm in diameter contains oil under pressure of 2 N/mm$^2$. If the permissible tensile stress is 100 N/mm$^2$, find the maximum thickness of pipe.

    **(B.T.E. W-1998)**

## Problems of 4 marks

11. Derive the expression to find the change in length and change in diameter of a thin cylindrical shell of diameter 'd' and wall thickness 't'. The cylinder is subjected to internal fluid pressure of 'p' N/mm$^2$.          **(B.T.E. W-2004)**

12. A cylindrical shell 2 m long and 1 m internal diameter is 20 mm thick. Find the circumferential and longitudinal stresses when it is subjected to an internal pressure of 100 N/mm$^2$.          **(B.T.E. S-1998) (Ans.** $\sigma_c$ = 2500 N/mm$^2$, $\sigma_L$ = 1250 N/mm$^2$**)**

13. A cylindrical shell 2.4 long, 600 mm in diameter is made up of 15 mm thick plate. Find the changes in its length and diameter when the shell is subjected to an internal pressure of 200 N/mm$^2$. Take E = 2 × 10$^5$ N/mm$^2$ and 1/m = 0.25.          **(B.T.E. S-1997)**

    **(Ans.** $\delta L$ = 12 mm, $\delta d$ = 10.5 mm**)**

14. A gas cylinder of internal diameter 1.2 m and thickness 24 mm is subjected to maximum tensile stress of 90 N/mm². Find the allowable pressure of the gas inside the cylinder.

    [**Hint :** Maximum tensile stress = $\sigma_c$]                    (**Ans.** p = 3.6 N/mm²)

15. A water tank 8 m in diameter and 12 m in height is completely filled with water. Determine the thickness of the tank if the stress is limited to 40 MPa. Calculate (i) hoop stress, (ii) longitudinal stress, (iii) maximum shear stress, (iv) volumetric strain. Take E = 200 GPa, $\mu$ = 0.3.

    [**Hint :** Maximum stress = Hoop stress = 40 MPa (**Given**), Water pressure p = $\gamma_w \times h$

    where $\gamma_w$ = density of water = 10 kN/m³.

    (**Ans.** $\sigma_c$ = 40 MPa, $\sigma_L$ = 20 MPa, $q_{max}$ = 10 MPa, $e_v$ = 38 × 10⁻⁵)

16. A cylindrical shell is 400 mm internal diameter and 8 mm thick and 1 m long. Find the change in internal diameter and length when the cylinder is charged with an internal pressure of 8 N/mm². Take E = 2 × 10⁵ N/mm², $\mu$ = 0.3.          (**B.T.E. S-1995**)

    (**Ans.** $\delta d$ = 0.34 mm, $\delta L$ = 0.2 mm)

17. A thin cylinder contains fluid at pressure of 3 N/mm². The inside diameter of the cylinder is 500 mm and the tensile stress in the material is to be limited to 80 N/mm². What is the wall thickness required ?

    (**B.T.E. S-1995**) (**Ans.** t = 9.375 mm, say 10 mm)

18. A cylindrical shell is 3 m long and 1 m in internal diameter. It is subjected to an internal pressure of 1.2 MPa. If the thickness of the shell plate is 12 mm, find the circumferential stress, changes in diameter and the length. Assume E = 2 × 10⁵ N/mm² and Poisson's ratio = 0.3.

    (**B.T.E. S-1996**) (**Ans.** $\sigma_c$ = 50 N/mm², $\delta d$ = 0.2125 mm, $\delta L$ = 0.15 mm)

19. A cylindrical shell 3 m long, 60 cm in diameter is made up of 15 mm thick plate. Determine the change in volume when the shell is subjected to an internal pressure of 5 N/mm². Take E = 2 × 10⁵ N/mm², $\dfrac{1}{m}$ = 0.25.          (**B.T.E. W-1994**)

    (**Ans.** $\delta V$ = 848230 mm³)

**Important Points**
─────────────────────────────────────────────

- **Thin cylinder :**

    A cylinder is said to be thin if $\dfrac{t}{d}$ ratio is equal to or less than 20,

    where     t = thickness of cylinder,   d = internal diameter of cylinder

- Longitudinal stress is equal to half the circumferential stress.

$$\sigma_L = \frac{1}{2}\sigma_c = \frac{1}{2} \times \frac{pd}{2t} = \frac{pd}{4t}$$

- $\sigma_c$ and $\sigma_L$ are known as principal stresses in thin cylinder. Using the formulae for bi-axial stress system, principal strains $e_c$ and $e_L$ can be calculated.

Major principal stress = Hoop stress = $\frac{pd}{2t}$

Minor principal stress = Longitudinal stress.

To find the thickness of a thin cylindrical shell, always major principal stress is taken into account.

# Chapter 3

---

# BENDING MOMENT AND SHEAR FORCE

---

Weightage of Marks = 16, Teaching Hours 08

## Objectives

Specific Objectives :

Understand and analyse the basic principles involved in the behaviour of machine parts under load in the context of designing it.

## Contents

3.1 Concept and definition of shear force and bending moment

- Relation between rate of loading, shear force and bending moment.

- Shear force and bending moment diagrams for cantilevers, simply supported beam and overhanging beam subjected to point loads and uniformly distributed load. Location of point of contraflexure.

## Synopsis

Introduction, Types of Beams, Types of Loads, Statically Determinate Structure, Support Reactions of Statically Determinate Beams, Reactions of Simply Supported Beams, Reactions of Cantilever Beams Subjected to u.d.l. and Point Load only, Reactions of Overhanging Beams Subjected to u.d.l. and Point Load, Definition of Shear Force, Sign Convention for Shear Force, Definition of Bending Moment, Sign Convention for Bending Moment, Concept of Shear Force and Bending Moment, Relation between Shear Force and Rate of Loading, Relation between Bending Moment and Shear Force, Shear Force and Bending Moment Diagrams, S.F.D. and B.M.D. for Simply Supported Beams, S.F.D. and B.M.D. for Cantilever Beams, S.F.D. and B.M.D. for Overhanging Beams.

---

## 3.1 INTRODUCTION

We know that a beam is a structural member the length of which is considerably more than the other two dimensions (i.e. width and depth) and is only vertically loaded. In this topic, we are going to study the shear force and bending moment diagrams for statically determinate beams.

## 3.2 TYPES OF BEAMS

**(1) Simply supported beam :** *A beam which is freely supported on the walls or columns at its both the ends is called as a simply supported beam.*

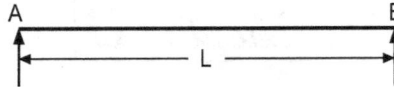

**Fig. 3.1 : Simply supported beam**

**(2) Cantilever beam :** *A beam fixed at one end and free at the other is called as a cantilever beam.*

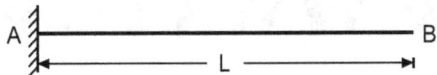

**Fig. 3.2 : Cantilever beam**

**(3) Overhanging beam :** *If the end portion of the beam extends beyond the support, it is called as an overhanging beam.* A beam may be overhanging on one side or on both sides as shown in Fig. 3.3.

A chajja of a room is an example of a overhanging beam.

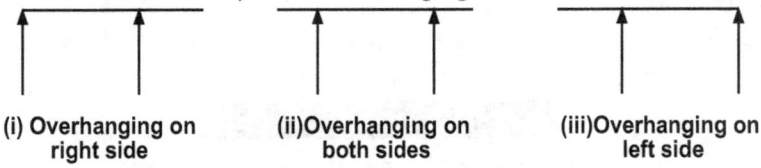

(i) Overhanging on right side     (ii)Overhanging on both sides     (iii)Overhanging on left side

**Fig. 3.3**

**(4) Fixed beam :** *A beam whose both the ends are rigidly fixed in walls is called a fixed beam, constrained beam, built-in beam or an encastre beam.*

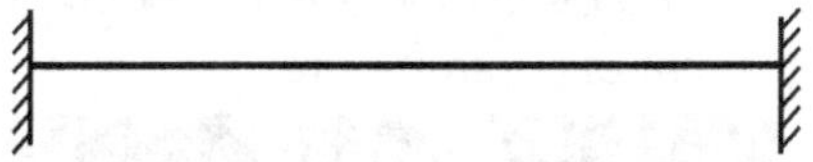

**Fig. 3.4 : Fixed beam**

**(5) Continuous beam :** *A beam which is supported on more than two supports (i.e. at least three supports) is called a continuous beam.* The end supports of a continuous beam may be simply supported or fixed.

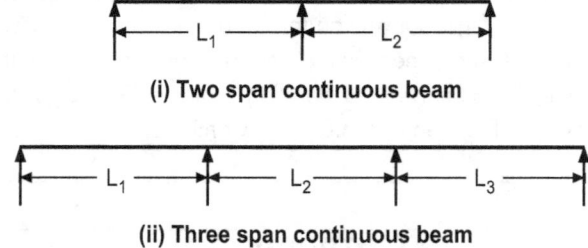

**(i) Two span continuous beam**

**(ii) Three span continuous beam**

**Fig. 3.5**

In this topic, we shall study shear force and bending moment diagrams for simply supported, overhanging and cantilever beams only. The shear force and bending moment diagrams for the fixed beams and continuous beams will be studied in the subject 'Theory of Structures'.

1. What are various types of beam ? Draw neat sketches. **(B.T.E. S-2013/2 Marks)**
2. State the types of beams. Draw a sketch of any one of it. **(B.T.E. W-2012/2 Marks)**

**(Most Likely and Asked in Previous B.T.E. Exam.)**

## 3.3 TYPES OF LOADS

**(1) Concentrated or Point load :** *A load acting at a point on the beam is known as a concentrated load or point load.* In practice, a load distributed over small area is taken as concentrated load. For example, the load from a column is assumed as a point load through the column of size 200 mm × 200 mm.

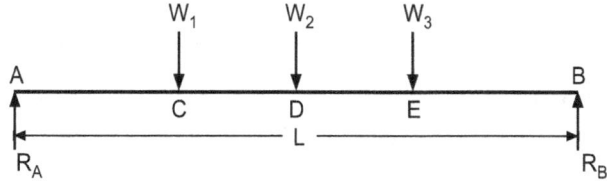

**Fig. 3.6**

Fig. 3.6 shows a simply supported beam of span L subjected to three point loads $W_1$, $W_2$, $W_3$ at C, D and E respectively.

**Note : *Reactions at the ends i.e. $R_A$ and $R_B$ are the point loads acting at A and B respectively.***

**(2) Uniformly distributed load (u.d.l.) :** *A load which is spread up uniformly on the beam i.e. each unit length is loaded to the same extent as shown in Fig. 3.7 (i) and (ii) is known as a uniformly distributed load or rectangular load and is written as u.d.l.* A u.d.l. may act over part of the span also.

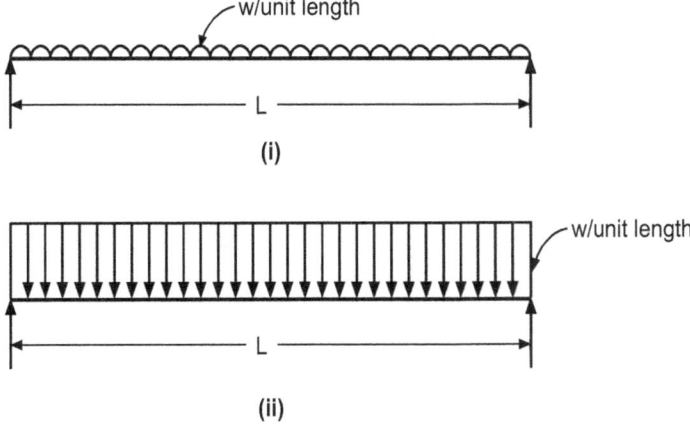

**Fig. 3.7**

`    ` w/unit length is called as intensity of u.d.l. (e.g. 8 N/m, 2 kN/m, etc.)

For example, the load on a beam from the floor or slab is u.d.l.

*For the ease of calculating the beam reactions, u.d.l. is converted into its equivalent point load which is assumed to act at the centre of gravity of the load.*

Refer to Fig. 3.7. In this case, the equivalent point load is nothing but the area of rectangle i.e. wL. This point load is assumed to act at the centre of gravity of the portion on which u.d.l. acts. i.e. at a distance of L/2 from both the ends as shown in Fig. 3.8.

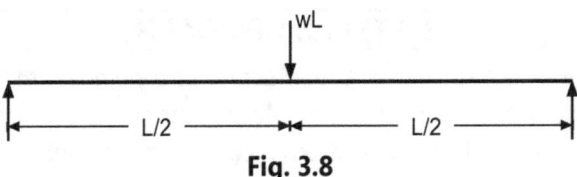

**Fig. 3.8**

---

1.  What is Uniformly Distributed Load; UDL ?

---

**(Most Likely and Asked in Previous B.T.E. Exam.)**

**(3) Uniformly varying load :** *If the load is spread in a non-uniform manner i.e. the intensity of load changes continuously but the rate of change is uniform on each unit length as shown in Fig. 3.9, then it is called a uniformly varying load and is written as u.v.l. A u.v.l. may act over part of the span also.*

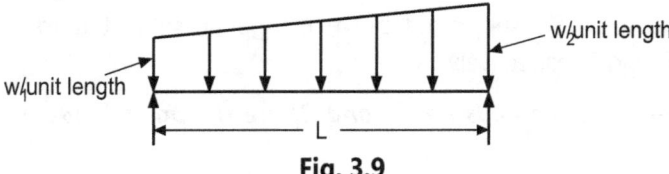

**Fig. 3.9**

A u.v.l. may be a trapezoidal load or a triangular load. If the intensity of u.v.l. as shown in Fig. 3.9 is zero at one end, then a trapezoidal load becomes a triangular load, as shown in Fig. 3.10.

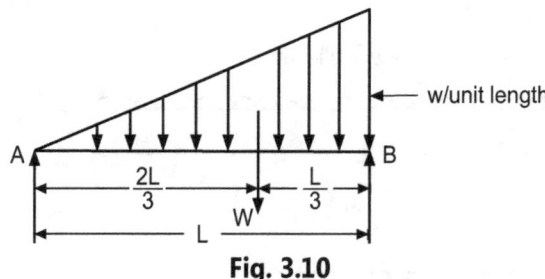

**Fig. 3.10**

W = Total load on AB = Area of triangle = $\frac{1}{2}$ wL.

It acts vertically downwards through the centroid of the triangle i.e. at $\frac{L}{3}$ from B or $\frac{2L}{3}$ from A as shown in Fig. 3.10.

The load coming on a dam wall when it retains water upto a height 'H' is an example of triangular load. Refer to Fig. 3.11.

Water pressure at top = 0

Water pressure at bottom = γH (where γ = density of water)

Total water pressure on dam wall,

$$P = \text{Area of triangular water pressure diagram}$$

$$= \frac{1}{2}\gamma H.H = \frac{1}{2}\gamma H^2$$

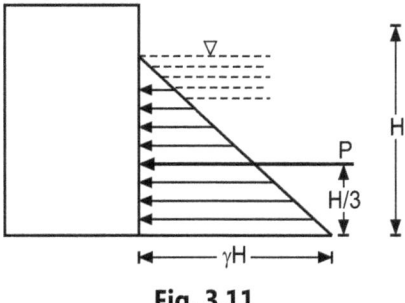

**Fig. 3.11**

| 1. | Explain various types of loading on beams with sketches. | **(B.T.E. S-2009/2 Marks)** |

**(Most Likely and Asked in Previous B.T.E. Exam.)**

## 3.4 STATICALLY DETERMINATE STRUCTURE

*A structure which can be analysed with the help of three equations of statics alone (i.e. $\sum F_x = 0$, $\sum F_y = 0$ and $\sum M = 0$) is known as a statically determinate structure.*

## 3.5 SUPPORT REACTIONS OF STATICALLY DETERMINATE BEAMS

A simply supported beam, cantilever beam, overhanging beam, etc. are some of the examples of statically determinate beams.

### 3.5.1 Reactions of Simply Supported Beams

**Case I : A simply supported beam of span 'L' carrying a central point load 'W' as shown in Fig. 3.12.**

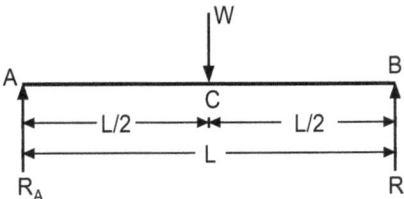

**Fig. 3.12**

Use analytical conditions of equilibrium to find beam reactions $R_A$ and $R_B$.

As there is no horizontal force acting on the beam, sum of all forces in a horizontal direction is zero. Hence the condition $\sum F_x = 0$ is already satisfied.

Using $\sum F_y = 0$, and assuming upward forces positive and downward forces negative, we get

$$R_A + R_B - W = 0$$

$$\therefore \qquad R_A + R_B = W \qquad \qquad \dots (1)$$

Equating sum of moments of all forces about A to zero i.e. $\sum M = 0$, we get

$$R_A \times 0 + W \times \frac{L}{2} - R_B \times L = 0$$

... (Taking clockwise moment positive and anticlockwise moment negative)

$\therefore$ $$\frac{W}{2} = R_B$$

or $$\boxed{R_B = \frac{W}{2}}$$ ... (2)

Substituting the value of $R_B$ in equation (1), we get

$$R_A + \frac{W}{2} = W$$

$\therefore$ $$\boxed{R_A = W - \frac{W}{2} = \frac{W}{2}}$$

**Conclusion :** When a point load 'W' acts at centre of any span 'L', reactions at both ends are equal to $\frac{W}{2}$.

**Case II : A simply supported beam of span 'L' carrying u.d.l. w/unit length over the entire span, as shown in Fig. 3.13.**

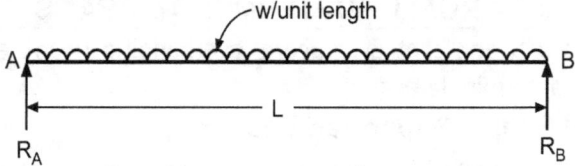

**Fig. 3.13**

Use analytical conditions of equilibrium to find beam reactions $R_A$ and $R_B$.

$\sum F_X = 0$ is of no use to find $R_A$ and $R_B$, since there is no horizontal force acting on the beam.

Using $$\sum F_y = 0, \boxed{\uparrow + , \downarrow -}$$

$$R_A + R_B - w \times L = 0$$

$\therefore$ $$R_A + R_B = w \times L$$ ... (1)

Using $\sum M_A = 0$,

$$R_A \times 0 + (w \times L)\left(\frac{L}{2}\right) - R_B \times L = 0$$

Dividing throughout by L, we get

$$\frac{wL}{2} = R_B$$

or $$\boxed{R_B = \frac{wL}{2}}$$ ... (2)

Substituting the value of $R_B$ in (1),

$$R_A + \frac{wL}{2} = wL$$

$$\therefore \quad R_A = wL - \frac{wL}{2}$$

$$\therefore \quad \boxed{R_A = \frac{wL}{2}}$$

**Case III : A simply supported beam of span 'L' carrying an eccentric point load 'W' as shown in Fig. 3.14.**

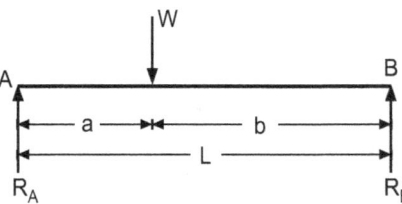

**Fig. 3.14**

To find beam reactions $R_A$ and $R_B$ :

Applying $\qquad \sum F_y = 0$ we get, $\boxed{\uparrow + , \downarrow -}$

$$R_A + R_B - W = 0$$

$$\therefore \qquad R_A + R_B = W \qquad \qquad \qquad \dots (1)$$

Applying $\qquad \sum M_A = 0, \ (\circlearrowleft +, \circlearrowright -)$

$$R_A \times 0 + W \times a - R_B \times L = 0$$

$$\therefore \qquad W \times a = R_B \times L$$

$$\therefore \qquad \boxed{R_B = \frac{Wa}{L}}$$

Substituting the value of $R_B$ in equation (1),

$$R_A + \frac{Wa}{L} = W$$

$$\therefore \qquad R_A = W - \frac{Wa}{L} = W\left(1 - \frac{a}{L}\right) = W\left(\frac{L-a}{L}\right)$$

$$\therefore \qquad \boxed{R_A = \frac{Wb}{L}} \qquad \qquad \dots (\because L = a + b, \therefore L - a = b)$$

## 3.5.2 Reactions of Cantilever Beams
### (Subjected to u.d.l. and Point Load only)

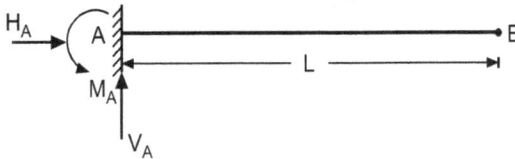

**Fig. 3.15**

Consider a cantilever AB of span L as shown in Fig. 3.15. End A is fixed and B is free. A fixed end of a cantilever has three reaction components $H_A$, $V_A$ and $M_A$.

$$H_A = \text{Horizontal reaction at A}$$

$$V_A = \text{Vertical reaction at A}$$

$$M_A = \text{Fixed end moment at A}$$

If the loads on the beam are purely vertical, $H_A = 0$ and there will be only two reaction components viz. $V_A$ and $M_A$ as shown in Fig. 3.16.

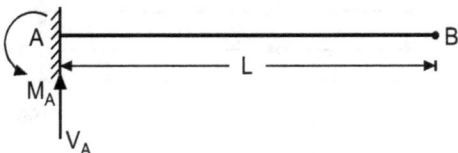

**Fig. 3.16**

**Case 1 :** A cantilever beam of span L carrying a point load 'W' at its free end, as shown in Fig. 3.17.

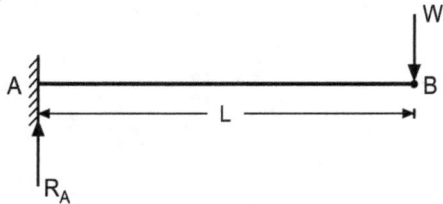

$$\sum F_y = 0 \text{ gives,}$$

$$R_A - W = 0$$

$$\therefore \quad R_A = W$$

**Fig. 3.17**

**Case 2 :** A cantilever of span 'L' carrying a u.d.l. 'w'/unit length over the entire span, as shown in Fig. 3.18.

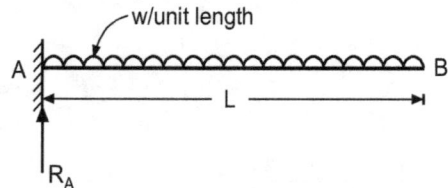

$$\sum F_y = 0 \text{ gives,}$$

$$R_A - wL = 0$$

$$\therefore \quad R_A = wL$$

**Fig. 3.18**

**Other Cases :**

    **Case 3 :**

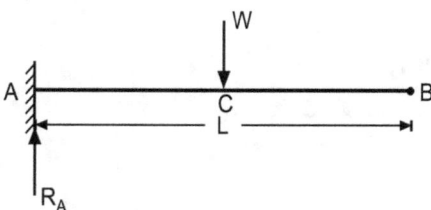

$$\sum F_y = 0 \text{ gives,}$$

$$R_A - W = 0$$

$$\therefore R_A = W$$

**Fig. 3.19**

**Case 4 :**

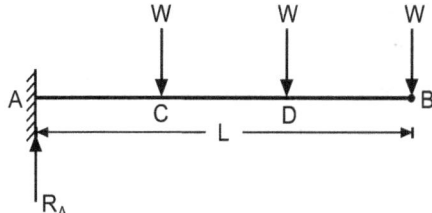

$$\sum F_y = 0 \text{ gives,}$$
$$R_A - W - W - W = 0$$
$$\therefore R_A = 3W$$

**Fig. 3.20**

**Case 5 :**

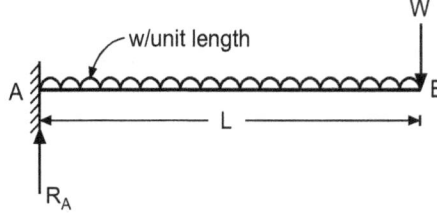

$$\sum F_y = 0 \text{ gives,}$$
$$R_A - wL - W = 0$$
$$\therefore R_A = wL + W$$

**Fig. 3.21**

**Case 6 :**

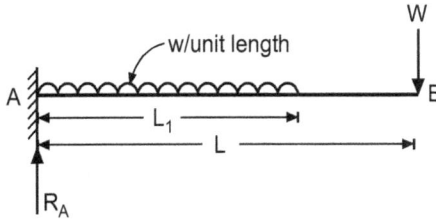

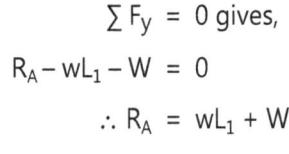

$$\sum F_y = 0 \text{ gives,}$$
$$R_A - wL_1 - W = 0$$
$$\therefore R_A = wL_1 + W$$

**Fig. 3.22**

## 3.5.3 Reactions of Overhanging Beams Subjected to a u.d.l. and Point Load

**Case 1 :**

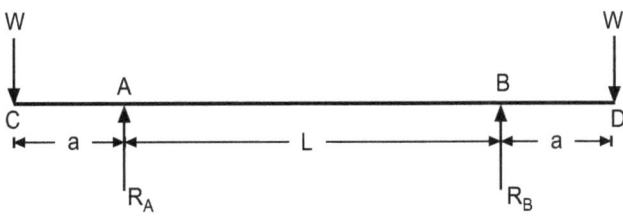

**Fig. 3.23**

As the loading is symmetrical, it is not necessary to use the conditions of equilibrium to find the reactions.

$$R_A = R_B = W$$

**Case 2 :** Since the beam carries a u.d.l. over the entire span and the two supports are equidistant from the ends C and D, therefore the two reactions are equal. (Refer to Fig. 3.24)

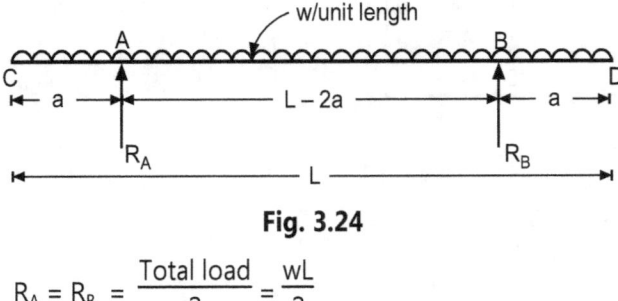

**Fig. 3.24**

$$\therefore \qquad R_A = R_B = \frac{\text{Total load}}{2} = \frac{wL}{2}$$

**Note :** *If the loading is not symmetrical, the reactions of overhanging beam are calculated by using the conditions of equilibrium.*

## 3.6  DEFINITION OF SHEAR FORCE

*Shear force at any cross-section of the beam is the algebraic sum of all vertical forces on the beam acting on the right or left side of the section. In other words, a shear force is the resultant vertical force acting on the either side of a section of a beam.*

### 3.6.1 Sign Convention for Shear Force

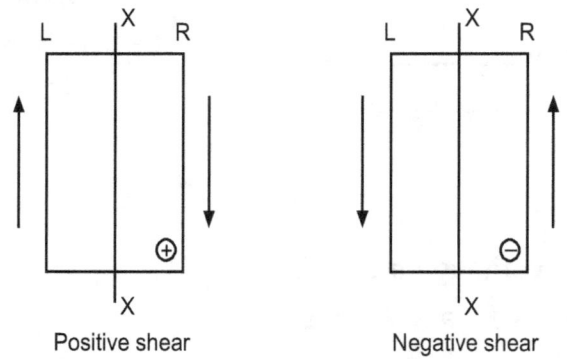

Positive shear      Negative shear

L= Left side of section XX,    R = Right side of section XX

**Fig. 3.25**

An upward force to the left of the section and downward force to the right of the section is taken as positive.

Downward force to the left of the section and upward force to the right of the section is taken as negative.

## 3.7  DEFINITION OF BENDING MOMENT

*Bending moment at any cross-section of the beam is the algebraic sum of the moments of all the forces acting on the right or left side of the section.*

## 3.7.1 Sign Convention for Bending Moment

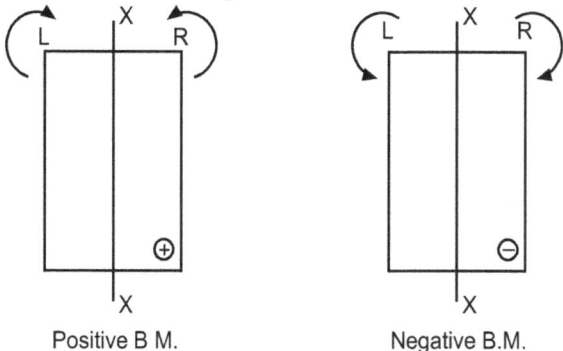

**Fig. 3.26**

Clockwise moment to the left of the section and an anticlockwise moment to the right of the section is taken as positive.

Anticlockwise moment to the left of the section and a clockwise moment to the right of the section is taken as negative.

From Fig. 3.27, it will be seen that upward force to any side of a section produces positive B.M. The portion of the beam deflects in the sagging pattern due to these forces.

Similarly, downward force to any side of a section produces negative B.M. The portion of the beam deflects in the hogging manner due to these forces.

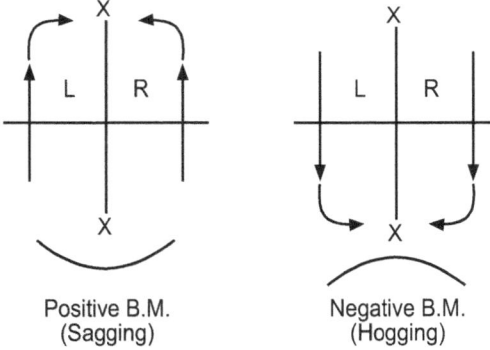

**Fig. 3.27**

*In short, sagging bending moment is taken as positive and hogging bending moment as negative.*

| 1. Define shear force and bending moment. | **(B.T.E. S-2012/2 Marks)** |
|---|---|

**(Most Likely and Asked in Previous B.T.E. Exam.)**

## 3.7.2 Concept of Shear Force and Bending Moment

The following example will illustrate the concept of S.F. and B.M.

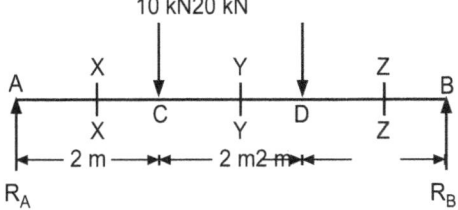

**Fig. 3.28**

Consider a simply supported beam of span 6 m carrying two point loads 10 kN and 20 kN at 2 m and 4 m from left support respectively. (Refer to Fig. 3.28)

**To find support reactions $R_A$ and $R_B$ :**

Using $\qquad\qquad\qquad \sum F_y = 0, \; (\uparrow +, \downarrow -)$

$\qquad\qquad R_A + R_B - 10 - 20 = 0$

$\therefore \qquad\qquad\qquad R_A + R_B = 30$

Using $\qquad\qquad\qquad \sum M_A = 0, (\circlearrowleft +, \circlearrowright -)$

$\qquad 10 \times 2 + 20 \times 4 - R_B \times 6 = 0$

$\therefore \qquad\qquad\qquad 20 + 80 = 6\,R_B$

$\therefore \qquad\qquad\qquad R_B = \dfrac{100}{6} = 16.67 \text{ kN}$

$\therefore$ From (i), $\qquad\qquad R_A = 30 - 16.67 = 13.33 \text{ kN}$

Now, consider a section XX in portion AC.

By considering the forces acting on the left side of section XX, S.F. at section XX,

$\qquad F_X = R_A = 13.33 \text{ kN}$

By considering the forces acting on the right side of section XX, S.F. at section XX,

$\qquad F_X = 10 + 20 - R_B = 30 - 16.67 = 13.33 \text{ kN}$

Now, consider a section YY in portion CD.

By considering the forces acting on the left side of section YY, S.F. at section YY,

$\qquad F_y = R_1 - 10 = 13.33 - 10 = 3.33 \text{ kN}$

By considering the forces acting on the right side of section YY, S.F. at section YY,

$\qquad F_y = +20 - R_B = 20 - 16.67 = 3.33 \text{ kN}$

Now, consider a section ZZ in portion DB.

By considering the forces acting on the left side of section ZZ, S.F. at section ZZ,

$\qquad F_Z = R_A - 10 - 20 = 13.33 - 30 = -16.67 \text{ kN}$

By considering the forces acting on the right side of section ZZ, S.F. at section ZZ,

$\qquad F_Z = -R_B = -16.67 \text{ kN}$

*From this example, it is very clear that the shear force at any cross-section of the beam is the algebraic sum of all vertical forces acting on right or left side of the section.*

**To find bending moments at A, B, C and D : (Sign convention : Sagging +, hogging – )**

**To find $M_C$ :** Take a section XX at C and draw the free body diagram at C, as shown in Fig. 3.29 (i) and (ii).

By considering the moments of all forces acting on the left side of C,

$\qquad M_C = 13.33 \times 2 = 26.66 \text{ kN-m}$

By considering the moments of all forces acting on the right side of C,

$\qquad M_C = -20 \times 2 + 16.67 \times 4 = -40 + 66.68 = 26.68 \text{ kN-m}$

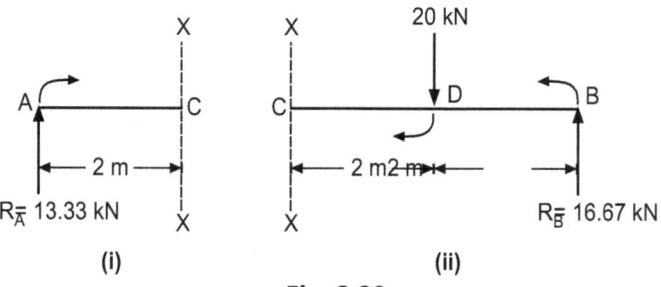

**Fig. 3.29**

**To find M$_D$ :** Take a section XX at D and draw the free body diagram at D, as shown in Fig. 3.30 (i) and (ii).

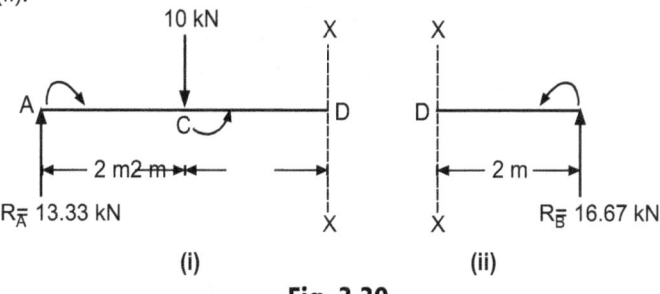

**Fig. 3.30**

By considering the moments of all forces acting on the left side of D,
$$M_D = 13.33 \times 4 - 10 \times 2 = 33.32 \text{ kN-m}$$

By considering the moments of all forces acting on the right side of D,
$$M_D = 16.67 \times 2 = 33.34 \text{ kN-m}$$

**To find M$_A$ :** Take a section XX at A as shown in Fig. 3.31.

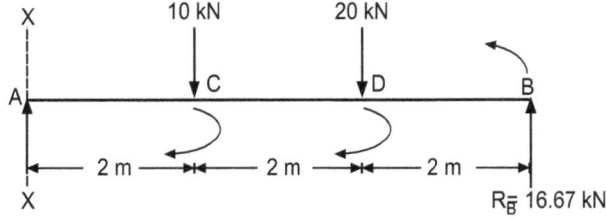

**Fig. 3.31**

By considering the moments of all forces acting on the right side of A,
$$M_A = -10 \times 2 - 20 \times 4 + 16.67 \times 6 = 0$$

Naturally, there is no force acting on left side of A. Hence M$_A$ = 0.

**To find M$_B$ :** Take a section XX at B as shown in Fig. 3.32.

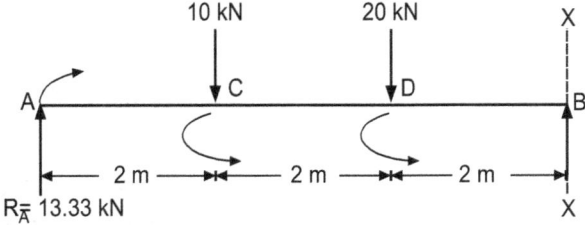

**Fig. 3.32**

By considering the moments of all forces acting on the left side of B,

$$M_B = 13.33 \times 6 - 10 \times 4 - 20 \times 2 = 0$$

Naturally, there is no force acting on right side of B. Hence $M_B = 0$.

**Conclusion :** Bending moment at a simply supported end is always zero.

*From the above example, it is very clear that, the bending moment at any cross-section of a beam is the algebraic sum of moments of all forces, acting on left or right side of the section.*

---

1. Explain in detail the concept of shear force and bending moment.

**(B.T.E. S-2011/4 Marks)**

**(Most Likely and Asked in Previous B.T.E. Exam.)**

## 3.8 RELATION BETWEEN SHEAR FORCE AND RATE OF LOADING

$$\frac{dF}{dx} = w \qquad \qquad \text{... (i)}$$

**The rate of change of shear force with respect to the distance is equal to the intensity of loading.**

## 3.9 RELATION BETWEEN BENDING MOMENT AND SHEAR FORCE

$$\frac{dM}{dx} = F \qquad \qquad \text{... (ii)}$$

**The rate of change of bending moment at any section is equal to the shear force at that section.**

If $F = 0, \dfrac{dM}{dx} = 0$

We know that for a function $y = f(x)$, y will be maximum if $\dfrac{dy}{dx} = 0$.

**Similarly, if $\dfrac{dM}{dx}$ is equal to zero, the bending moment M will be maximum. The point, at which S.F. is zero or S.F. changes the sign from positive to negative, is a point of maximum bending moment.**

---

1. State the relationship between rate of loading, shear force and bending moment.

**(B.T.E. W-2010/2 Marks)**

2. State the relation between B.M., S.F. and rate of loading.

**(B.T.E. W-2008, 2007/2 Marks)**

3. State the relation between shear force and bending moment.

**(B.T.E. S-2015, 2008/2 Marks)**

**(Most Likely and Asked in Previous B.T.E. Exam.)**

## 3.10  SHEAR FORCE AND BENDING MOMENT DIAGRAMS

A shear force diagram is that which shows the variation of shear force along the length of the beam. A bending moment diagram shows the variation of bending moment along the length of the beam. S.F.D. and B.M.D. are generally drawn proportionately and not to the scale.

The following points should be kept in mind while drawing S.F.D. and B.M.D.

(i)   Base of S.F.D. and B.M.D. is equal to the span of the beam.

(ii)  Positive values of S.F. and B.M. are plotted above the base line and negative values below the base line.

(iii) The values of S.F. and B.M. must be calculated at all critical points and written near the respective ordinates. Such critical points are : a point where u.d.l. starts and ends, a point where the concentrated load acts on the beam, a point where S.F. changes its sign (or S.F. is zero).

(iv)  In case of overhanging beam, a point of contraflexure (i.e. a point of zero B.M.) must be located. This point can be located by equating the expression of bending moment to zero and solving it.

(v)   The location of point of zero S.F. and the point of contraflexure must be marked from the supports or from the ends of the beam whichever is convenient.

(vi)  S.F.D. is drawn below the loaded beam and B.M.D. below the S.F.D.

## 3.11 S.F.D. AND B.M.D. FOR SIMPLY SUPPORTED BEAMS

**Case 1 : A simply supported beam of span 'L' carrying a central point load 'W' as shown in Fig. 3.33 (i) :**

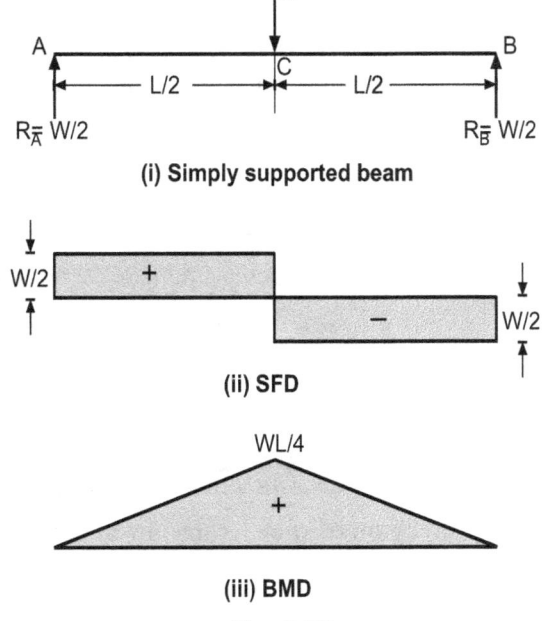

(i) **Simply supported beam**

(ii) **SFD**

(iii) **BMD**

**Fig. 3.33**

**Support Reactions :**

Since the load is at the centre, the reactions at the supports are equal. $\therefore R_A = R_B = \dfrac{W}{2}$

**S.F. calculations :**

S.F. at any section between A and C is

$$F_X = + R_A = \frac{W}{2} \qquad\qquad \text{... (positive since } R_A \text{ is left upward)}$$

This remains constant from A to C.

S.F. at any section between C and B is

$$F_X = - R_B = -\frac{W}{2} \qquad\qquad \text{... (negative since } R_B \text{ is right upward)}$$

This remains constant from C to B.

The complete S.F.D. is as shown in Fig. 3.33 (ii).

**B.M. calculations :**

At simply supported ends, $M_A = M_B = 0$. Since S.F. changes its sign from positive to negative at point C, the maximum B.M. will occur at C.

$$\therefore \qquad M_{max} = M_C = + \frac{W}{2} \times \frac{L}{2} = \frac{WL}{4} \qquad\qquad \text{... (Sagging)}$$

The B.M.D. is as shown in Fig. 3.33 (iii).

**Note :** (i) S.F. at left support   = Positive reaction at that support

i.e. $$\qquad\qquad F_A = R_A = \frac{W}{2}$$

(ii) S.F. at right support   = Negative reaction at that support

i.e. $$\qquad\qquad F_B = - R_B = -\frac{W}{2}$$

---

1. Draw S.F. and B.M. diagrams for a simply supported beam of span L carrying a central point load W. State the values of maximum S.F. and maximum B.M.

   **(B.T.E. S-2015, 2012, W-2008/4 Marks)**

2. In case of simply supported beam, state the point at which B.M. is maximum, when it is carrying full span U.D.L. **(V.V. Imp./2 Marks)**

---

**(Most Likely and Asked in Previous B.T.E. Exam.)**

**Case 2 : A simply supported beam of span L carrying an eccentric point load :**

Consider a simply supported beam AB of span L carrying an eccentric point load at C as shown in Fig. 3.34 (i).

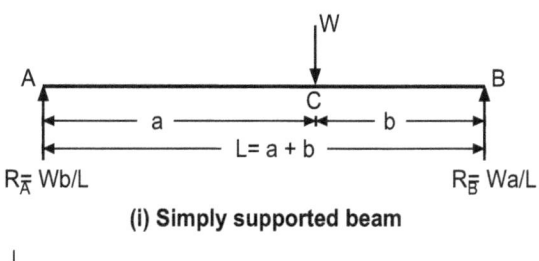

**(i) Simply supported beam**

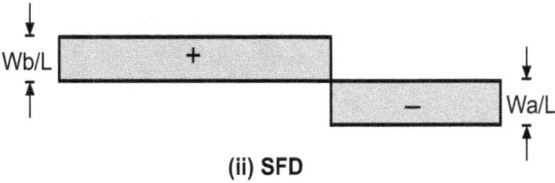

**(ii) SFD**

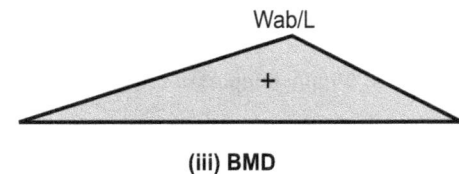

**(iii) BMD**

**Fig. 3.34**

Let span AC = a and span CB = b.

$$\left[\text{Eccentric point load means } a \neq b \neq \frac{L}{2}\right]$$

## Support Reactions :

As already seen, the reactions in this case are,

$$R_A = \frac{Wb}{L} \text{ and } R_B = \frac{Wa}{L}.$$

## S.F. calculations :

S.F. at any section between A and C is,

$$F_X = + R_A = \frac{Wb}{L} \qquad \text{... (positive since } R_A \text{ is left upward)}$$

This remains constant between A and C.

S.F. at any section between C and B is,

$$F_X = -R_B = -\frac{Wa}{L} \qquad \text{... (negative since } R_B \text{ is right upward)}$$

This remains constant from C to B. The complete S.F.D. is as shown in Fig. 3.34 (ii).

## B.M. calculations :

At simply supported ends, $M_A = M_B = 0$.

$$M_C = +\frac{Wb}{L} \times a = \frac{Wab}{L} \qquad \text{... (Sagging)}$$

The B.M.D. is as shown in Fig. 3.34 (iii).

**Note :** (i)　　$F_A = + R_A = + \dfrac{Wb}{L}$

　　　　(ii)　　$F_B = - R_B = - \dfrac{Wa}{L}$

　　　　(iii)　$M_{max} = M_C = \dfrac{Wab}{L}$

**Case 3 :** A simply supported beam of span L carrying a u.d.l. w/unit length over the entire span as shown in Fig. 3.35 (i).

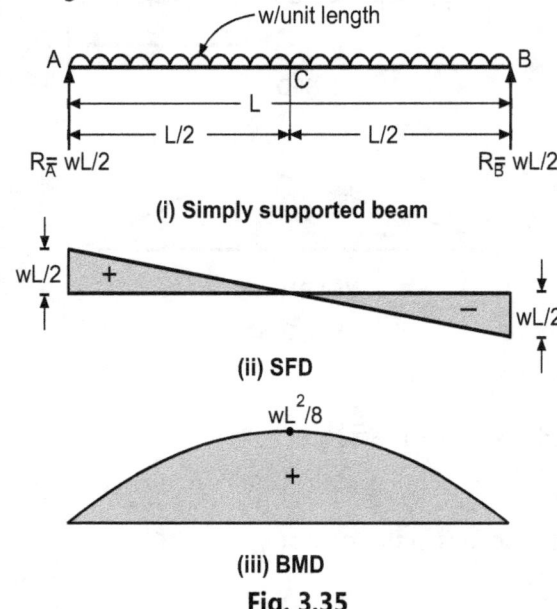

(i) Simply supported beam

(ii) SFD

(iii) BMD

**Fig. 3.35**

### Support reactions :

Since the load is uniformly distributed over the entire length of the beam, the reactions are equal.

$$R_A = R_B = \frac{wL}{2}$$

### S.F. calculations :

Take a section XX at a distance x from A as shown in Fig. 3.35 (iv).

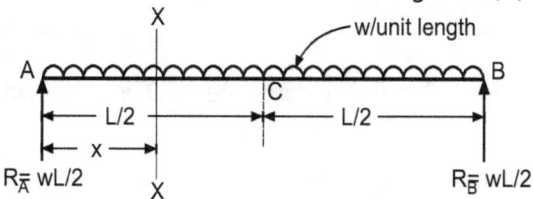

**Fig. 3.35 (iv)**

$$F_X = \text{S.F. at section XX} = \frac{wL}{2} - wx \qquad\qquad \text{... (i)}$$

**Since the power of x is one, the variation of S.F. is linear.**

At A, x = 0. Substituting this value in equation (i),

$$F_A = \frac{wL}{2} - w \times 0 = \frac{wL}{2} = + R_A$$

At B, x = L. Substituting this value in equation (i),

$$F_B = \frac{wL}{2} - w \cdot L = -\frac{wL}{2} = - R_B$$

At the centre of the beam i.e. at C, $x = \frac{L}{2}$

$$F_C = \frac{wL}{2} - w \cdot \frac{L}{2} = 0$$

In this case, the S.F.D. is an inclined straight line as shown in Fig. 3.35 (ii).

**B.M. calculations :** Refer to Fig. 3.35 (iv).

B.M. at a section XX at a distance x from A is given by,

$$M_X = \frac{wL}{2} \times x - wx \cdot \frac{x}{2} = \frac{wL}{2} \times x - \frac{wx^2}{2} \qquad \text{... (ii)}$$

Since the power of x is two, the variation of B.M. is parabolic.

At A, x = 0. Substituting this value in equation (ii),

$$\therefore \qquad M_A = \frac{wL}{2} \times 0 - \frac{w}{2} \times 0^2 = 0$$

At B, x = L. Substituting this value in equation (ii),

$$M_B = \frac{wL}{2} \times L - \frac{w}{2} \times L^2 = \frac{wL^2}{2} - \frac{wL^2}{2} = 0$$

**To find the maximum B.M. :** At the centre C, the S.F. changes its sign and hence the B.M. will be maximum at C.

$$\text{At C, } x = \frac{L}{2}$$

Substituting this value in equation (ii), we have

$$M_C = M_{max} = + \frac{wL}{2} \times \frac{L}{2} - \frac{w}{2} \left(\frac{L}{2}\right)^2 = \frac{wL^2}{4} - \frac{wL^2}{8} = \frac{wL^2}{8} \qquad \text{... (Sagging)}$$

The B.M.D. is as shown in Fig. 3.35 (iii).

1. In case of simply supported beam, state the point at which B.M. is maximum, when it is carrying full span U.D.L. **(B.T.E. S-2012/2 Marks)**

2. Draw S.F.D. and B.M.D. for a simply supported beam of span L carrying u.d.l. w/unit length over the entire span. **(B.T.E. S-2012, W-2007/4 Marks)**

3. Draw S.F.D. and B.M.D. for a simply supported beam of span L and carrying u.d.l. of w/metre. **(B.T.E. S-2009/4 Marks)**

**(Most Likely and Asked in Previous B.T.E. Exam.)**

## 3.12 S.F.D. AND B.M.D. FOR CANTILEVER BEAMS

**Case 1 : A cantilever beam carrying a point load at its free end :**

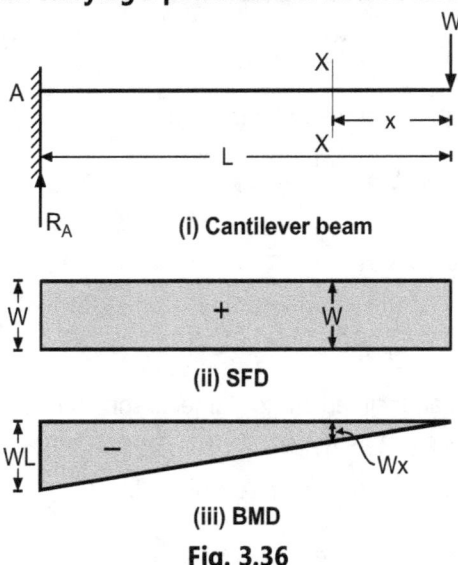

(i) Cantilever beam

(ii) SFD

(iii) BMD

**Fig. 3.36**

Let us consider a cantilever beam AB of span L carrying a point load W at its free end B as shown in Fig. 3.36 (i).

Take a section XX at a distance x from the free end B.

$$F_X = \text{S.F. at section XX} = + W \qquad \text{... (positive since right downward)}$$

Thus, S.F. is constant for all sections between A and B and it is W. Hence S.F. diagram is horizontal as shown in Fig. 3.36 (ii).

Now,        $M_X = \text{B.M. at section XX} = - W \cdot x$

... (negative since clockwise moment to the right i.e. hogging)

Now, since x is measured from B, B is taken as origin.

At B,                $x = 0$

∴                $M_B = - W \times 0 = 0$

At A,                $x = L$

∴                $M_A = - W.L.$

Since in the expression of $M_X$, the power of x is one, therefore the variation of B.M. from 0 to WL is linear i.e. B.M.D. is a straight line as shown in Fig. 3.36 (iii).

**Note : (i) In this case, the maximum bending moment occurs at the fixed end A and the bending moment at the free end B is zero.**

$$M_{max} = M_A = - WL \qquad \text{... (Hogging)}$$

**(ii) From        $\sum F_y = 0$,**

$$R_A - W = 0, \text{ i.e. } R_A = W$$

$$\text{and } F_A = R_A = W$$

**Thus,        S.F. at A = Reaction at A**

*(iii)          S.F. at B  =  Load acting at B*

*(iv) If the S.F. diagram is a horizontal line, the B.M. diagram is an inclined straight line.*

1.  Draw S.F.D. and B.M.D. for a cantilever beam of span L carrying a point load W at the free end. State the maximum S.F. and B.M. values.          **(V.V.Imp./2 Marks)**

**(Most Likely and Asked in Previous B.T.E. Exam.)**

**Case 2 : A cantilever beam carrying a point load not at the free end :**

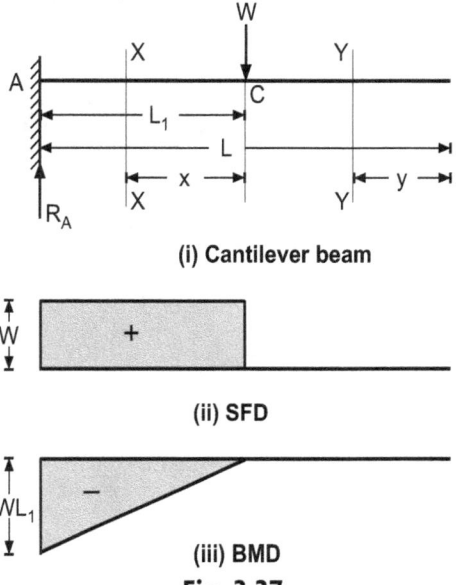

**(i) Cantilever beam**

**(ii) SFD**

**(iii) BMD**

**Fig. 3.37**

Let us consider a cantilever beam AB of span L carrying a point load W at point C at a distance $L_1$ from the fixed end A as shown in Fig. 3.37 (i).

Take a section YY at a distance y from the free end B in portion CB.

$F_y$ = S.F. at section YY = 0 (since there is no force to the right of section YY). Since the section YY is taken in between C and B, **S.F. is zero for all the sections between C and B.**

Take a section XX at a distance x from the point C in portion AC.

Now,          $F_x$ = S.F. at section XX = + W          ... (positive since downward to the right)

i.e. **S.F. for all sections between A and C is constant and it is + W.**

The complete S.F.D. is as shown in Fig. 3.37 (ii).

Now, $M_y$ = B.M. at section YY = 0 (since there is no force to the right of section YY). Since section YY is taken in between C and B, B.M. is zero for all the sections between C and B.

Now,          $M_x$  =  B.M. at section XX at a distance x from C

          = $- W \cdot x$          (minus sign due to hogging)

Since x is measured from C, C is taken as origin.

At C,                $x = 0$

$\therefore$              $M_C = -W \times 0 = 0$

At A,                $x = L_1$

$\therefore$              $M_A = -W \cdot L_1$

Since in the expression of $M_x$, the power of x is one, the variation of B.M. is by a straight line law, as shown in Fig. 3.37 (iii).

---

1. Draw S.F.D. and B.M.D. for a cantilever beam of span L carrying a point load W at a distance '$L_1$' from the fixed end. State the maximum S.F. and B.M. values.

**(V.V.Imp./2 Marks)**

**(Most Likely and Asked in Previous B.T.E. Exam.)**

---

**Case 3 : A cantilever beam carrying a u.d.l. w/unit length over the entire span :**

Let us consider a cantilever beam AB of span L carrying a u.d.l. w/unit length over the entire span AB, as shown in Fig. 3.38 (i).

Take a section XX at a distance x from the free end B.

$F_X =$ S.F. at section XX $= + w.x$          (positive sign since right downward)

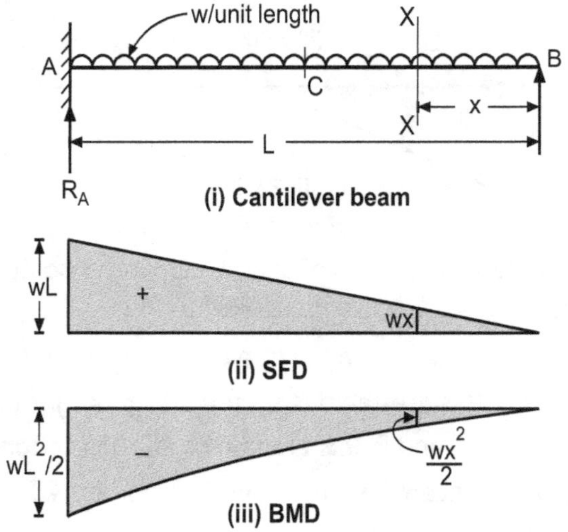

(i) Cantilever beam

(ii) SFD

(iii) BMD

**Fig. 3.38**

Since x is measured from B, B is taken as origin.

At B,                $x = 0$

$\therefore$              $F_B = w \times 0 = 0$

At A,                $x = L$

$\therefore$              $F_A = + w \cdot L$

Since in the expression of $F_X$, the power of x is one, the variation of S.F. from 0 to wL is by a straight line law. The S.F.D. is as shown in Fig. 3.38 (ii).

Now,                 $M_X$ = B.M. at section XX

$$= -wx \cdot \frac{x}{2} \qquad \text{(minus sign due to right clockwise i.e. hogging)}$$

$$= -\frac{wx^2}{2}$$

At B,                 $x = 0$

$\therefore$                 $M_B = -w \times \frac{0^2}{2} = 0$

At A,                 $x = L$

$\therefore$                 $M_A = -\frac{w \cdot L^2}{2}$

Since in the expression of $M_X$, the power of x is two, the variation of B.M. is parabolic. The B.M.D. is as shown in Fig. 3.38 (iii).

**Note** *(i) :*     *From* $\sum F_y = 0$,

$R_A - w \cdot L = 0$ *i.e.* $R_A = w \cdot L$ *Thus, S.F. at A = Reaction at A = w·L*

*(ii)*             $M_{max} = M_A = -\dfrac{wL^2}{2}$ *... ( ∵ Hogging)*

*(iii) If the S.F. diagram is an inclined straight line, the B.M. diagram is a parabolic curve.*

| |
|---|
| 1.  Draw S.F. and B.M. diagrams for a cantilever beam carrying a u.d.l. w/unit length over the entire span. State the maximum S.F. and B.M. values.   **(V.V.Imp./2 Marks)** |

**(Most Likely and Asked in Previous B.T.E. Exam.)**

## 3.13 S.F.D. AND B.M.D. FOR OVERHANGING BEAMS

An overhanging beam is a combination of simply supported beam and a cantilever. The overhanging part behaves like a cantilever and the portion of the beam between the two supports behaves like a simply supported beam. We have already seen that the B.M. in a simply supported beam is positive (sagging) and that in a cantilever beam is negative (hogging). Hence in overhanging beams, there will be a point where the B.M. will change its sign from positive to negative or vice-a-versa. *Such a point where the B.M. changes its sign and is equal to zero is called the point of contraflexure or point of inflection.* The point of contraflexure is located in the simply supported portion of the overhanging beam. For the beam overhanging on one side, we get one point of contraflexure and for the beam overhanging on two sides, we may get two points of contraflexure also. **The position of point of contraflexure is located by finding the expression of $M_X$ and equating it to zero.** The S.F. and B.M. diagrams for the overhanging beams and location of the point of contraflexure will be explained later with the help of solved examples.

| |
|---|
| 1.  Define point of centraflexure of a loaded beam with a sketch.<br>                                                      **(B.T.E. W-2011, 2008/2 Marks)**<br>2.  How is point of contraflexure located for a beam ?          **(B.T.E. S-2008/2 Marks)**<br>3.  Define point of contraflexure.          **(B.T.E. S-2011, 2009/2 Marks)** |

**(Most Likely and Asked in Previous B.T.E. Exam.)**

## SOLVED EXAMPLES

### Type 1 : S.F.D. and B.M.D. for Simply Supported Beam Subjected to a Point Load and u.d.l.

**Example 1 :** *A simply supported beam of span 5 m carries two point loads of 5 kN and 7 kN at 1.5 m and 3.5 m from the left hand support respectively. Draw S.F.D. and B.M.D. showing the important values.* **(B.T.E. S-2013, 2010; W-1985/4 Marks)**

**Solution : (i) Reactions :**

$$\sum M_A = 0 \text{ gives,}$$
$$5 \times 1.5 + 7 \times 3.5 - R_B \times 5 = 0$$
$$\therefore \qquad 5 R_B = 32 \text{ i.e. } R_B = 6.4 \text{ kN} \qquad \text{... (i)}$$
$$\sum F_y = 0 \text{ gives,}$$
$$R_A + R_B - 5 - 7 = 0 \text{ i.e. } R_A + R_B = 12 \qquad \text{... (ii)}$$
$$\therefore \qquad R_A = 12 - 6.4 = 5.6 \text{ kN}$$

**(ii) S.F. calculations :** S.F. at any section between A and C

$$F_X = + R_A = 5.6 \text{ kN}$$

... (positive since left upward and remains constant from A to C)

S.F. at any section between C and D,

$$F_X = 5.6 - 5 = 0.6 \text{ kN and remains constant from C to D.}$$

S.F. at any section between D and B,

$$F_X = 5.6 - 6 - 7 = -6.4 \text{ kN and remains constant from D to B.}$$

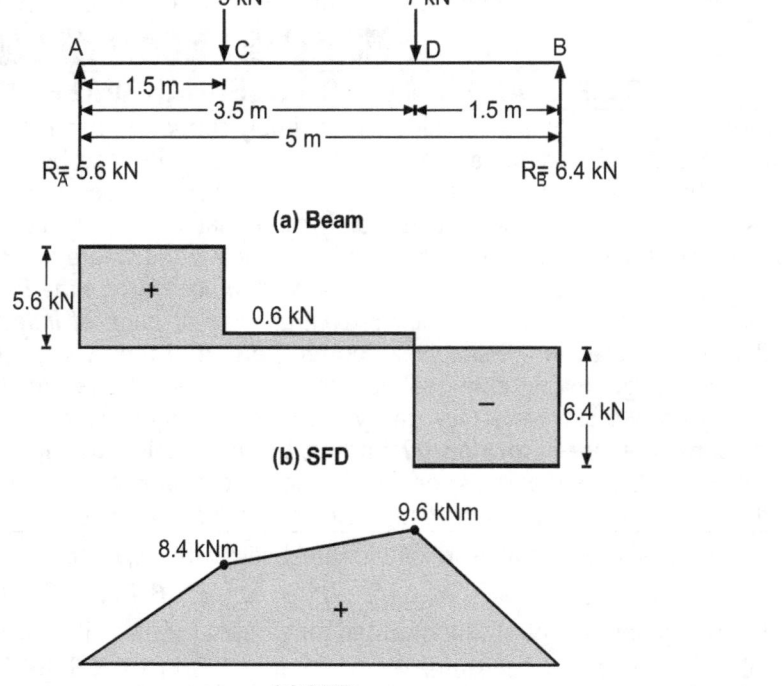

(a) Beam

(b) SFD

(c) BMD

**Fig. 3.39**

(**Note** : Here calculations of S.F. are done from the left support. Upward forces to left are taken positive and downward forces to left are taken as negative).

The S.F.D. is as shown in Fig. 3.39 (b).

### (iii) B.M. calculations :

At simply supported ends, $M_A = M_B = 0$.

By considering the forces acting on left of C,

$$M_C = 5.6 \times 1.5 = 8.4 \text{ kN·m}$$

(positive since clockwise to the left i.e. sagging)

By considering the forces acting on right of D,

$$M_D = 6.4 \times 1.5 = 9.6 \text{ kN·m}$$

(positive since anticlockwise to the right i.e. sagging)

**Note :** (i) B.M. at C can also be calculated by considering the forces acting on right of C.

$$M_C = 6.4 \times 3.5 - 7 \times 2 = 8.4 \text{ kN·m}$$

(ii) B.M. at D can also be calculated by considering the forces acting on left of D.

$$M_D = 5.6 \times 3.5 - 5 \times 2 = 9.6 \text{ kN·m}$$

The B.M.D. is as shown in Fig. 3.39 (c).

**Example 2 :** A simply supported beam of span 7 m carries a u.d.l. of 2 kN/m over 4 m length from the left support and a point load of 5 kN at 2 m from the right support. Draw S.F. and B.M. diagrams.	**(B.T.E. S-2012, 2001, 1999; W-2011/4 Marks)**

**OR**

A simply supported beam of span 7 m carries a u.d.l. of 2 kN/m over 4 m length from L.H.S. and a point load of 5 kN at 2 m from R.H.S. Draw S.F.D. and also calculate the distance of point of contraflexure from L.H.S.	**(B.T.E. W-2010/4 Marks)**

### Solution :

**(i) Reactions :**	$\sum M_A = 0$ gives,

$$2 \times 4 \times \frac{4}{2} + 5 \times 5 - R_B \times 7 = 0$$

$\therefore$	$$R_B = 5.86 \text{ kN}$$

$$\sum F_y = 0 \text{ gives,}$$

$$R_A + R_B - 2 \times 4 - 5 = 0$$

$\therefore$	$$R_A = 13 - R_B = 13 - 5.86 = 7.14 \text{ kN}$$

### (ii) S.F. calculations :

S.F. at any section in AC at a distance x from A is given by

$$F_x = 7.14 - 2x$$

At x = 0, $F_A = 7.14$ kN

At x = 4 m, $F_C = 7.14 - 2 \times 4 = -0.86$ kN

S.F. at any section in CD at a distance x from A,
$$F_X = 7.14 - 2 \times 4 = -0.86 \text{ kN}$$
and it remains constant from C to D.

S.F. at any section in DB,    $F_X = 7.14 - 2 \times 4 - 5 = -5.86 \text{ kN}$

and it remains constant from D to B.

**Check :**    $F_B = -5.86 \text{ kN} = -R_B$

The S.F.D. is as shown in Fig. 3.40 (b).

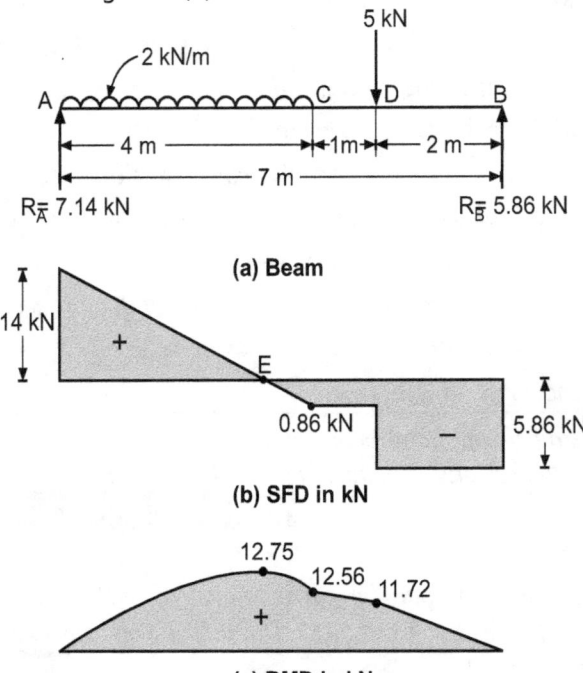

(a) Beam

(b) SFD in kN

(c) BMD in kN-m

**Fig. 3.40**

**(iii) B.M. calculations :**

At simply supported ends,  $M_A = M_B = 0$

$$M_C = 7.14 \times 4 - 2 \times 4 \times \frac{4}{2} = 12.56 \text{ kN·m}$$

$$M_D = 5.86 \times 2 = 11.72 \text{ kN·m}$$

From the S.F.D. it can be seen that, S.F. changes its sign at E in portion AC. Therefore, the maximum B.M. will occur at E. Let 'x' be the distance of E from A.

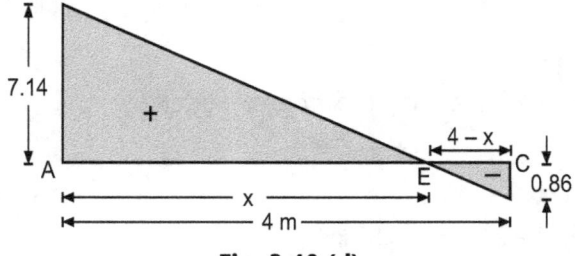

**Fig. 3.40 (d)**

From the similar triangles in S.F.D. as shown in Fig. 3.40 (d),

$$\frac{x}{7.14} = \frac{4-x}{0.86}$$

∴　　　　　　$0.86\,x = (4-x) \times 7.14$

∴　　　　　　$0.86\,x = 28.56 - 7.14\,x$

∴　　　　　　$8\,x = 28.56$

∴　　　　　　$x = 3.57$ m

Therefore B.M. at 3.57 m from A is given by

$$M_E = M_{max} = 7.14 \times 3.57 - 2 \times 3.57 \times \frac{3.57}{2}$$

$$= 25.49 - 12.74 = 12.75 \text{ kN·m}$$

From A to C, there is a u.d.l. and hence B.M.D. is a parabolic curve and the maximum B.M. means the highest point of the parabolic curve. Between the points C and D; D and B there is no load. Hence B.M.D. is a straight line. The B.M.D. is as shown in Fig. 3.40 (c).

**Example 3 :** *Draw S.F.D. and B.M.D. for the beam as shown in Fig. 3.41 (a).*　　(4 Marks)

**Solution :**

**(i) Reactions :** Taking moments about A,

$$2 \times 3 \times \frac{3}{2} + 3 \times 3 + 5 \times 5 = R_B \times 7$$

∴　　　　　　$R_B = 6.14$ kN

∴　　　　　　$R_A = 2 \times 3 + 3 + 5 - 6.14 = 7.86$ kN

**(ii) Shear force calculations :**

S.F. at any section between A and C at a distance x from A,

$$F_x = 7.86 - 2 \times x$$

At x = 0,　　　　　$F_A = 7.86$ kN

At x = 3 m,　　　　$F_C = 7.86 - 2 \times 3 = 1.86$ kN

S.F. at any section in CD,　　$F_x = 7.86 - 2 \times 3 - 3 = -1.14$ kN

and it remains constant from C to D.

S.F. at any section in DB,　　$F_x = 7.86 - 2 \times 3 - 3 - 5 = -6.14$ kN

and it remains constant from D to B. The S.F.D. is as shown in Fig. 3.41 (b).

**(iii) B.M. calculations :**　　$M_A = M_B = 0$

$$M_C = 7.86 \times 3 - 2 \times 3 \times \frac{3}{2} = 14.58 \text{ kN·m}$$

$$M_D = 6.14 \times 2 = 12.28 \text{ kN·m}$$

S.F. changes its sign at C. Hence the maximum B.M. occurs at C. The B.M.D. is as shown in Fig. 3.41 (c).

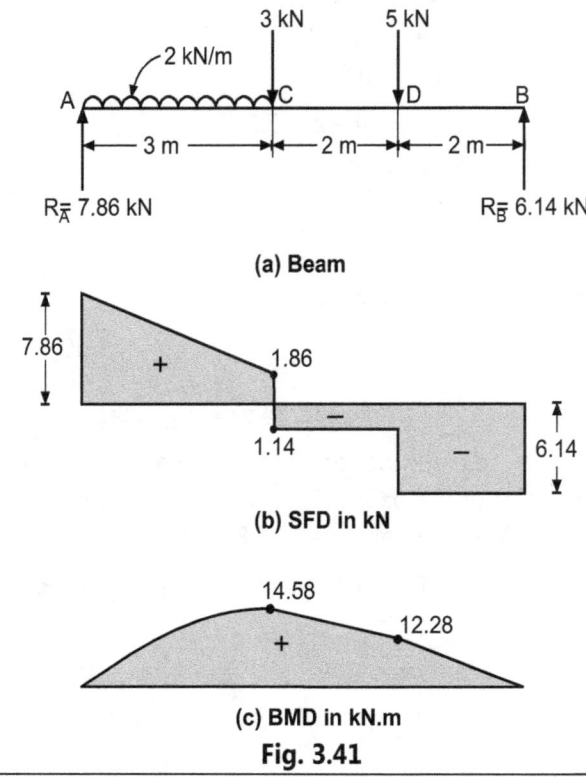

**(a) Beam**

**(b) SFD in kN**

**(c) BMD in kN.m**

**Fig. 3.41**

---

**Example 4 :** *Draw S.F.D. and B.M.D. for the beam as shown in Fig. 3.42 (a).*

**(B.T.E. S-2012/4 Marks)**

**Solution : (i) Reactions :** Taking moments about A,

$$2 \times 3 \times \frac{3}{2} + 3 \times 3 + 1 \times 2 \times \left(3 + \frac{2}{2}\right) + 5 \times 5 = R_B \times 7$$

$$\therefore \qquad\qquad R_B = \frac{51}{7} = 7.28 \text{ kN}$$

$$\therefore \qquad\qquad R_A = (2 \times 3 + 3 + 1 \times 2 + 5) - 7.28 = 8.72 \text{ kN}$$

**(ii) S.F. calculations :** At the points C and D, u.d.l. ends and the point load acts. In such cases, it is convenient to take a section just to the left and just to the right of the point under consideration.

$$F_A = + R_A = 8.72 \text{ kN}$$

$$F_{C_L} = 8.72 - 2 \times 3 = 2.72 \text{ kN}$$

$$F_{C_R} = 8.72 - 2 \times 3 - 3 = -0.28 \text{ kN}$$

$$F_{D_L} = 8.72 - 2 \times 3 - 3 - 1 \times 2 = -2.28 \text{ kN}$$

$$F_{D_R} = 8.72 - 2 \times 3 - 3 - 1 \times 2 - 5 = -7.28 \text{ kN}$$

$$F_B = -R_B = -7.28 \text{ kN}$$

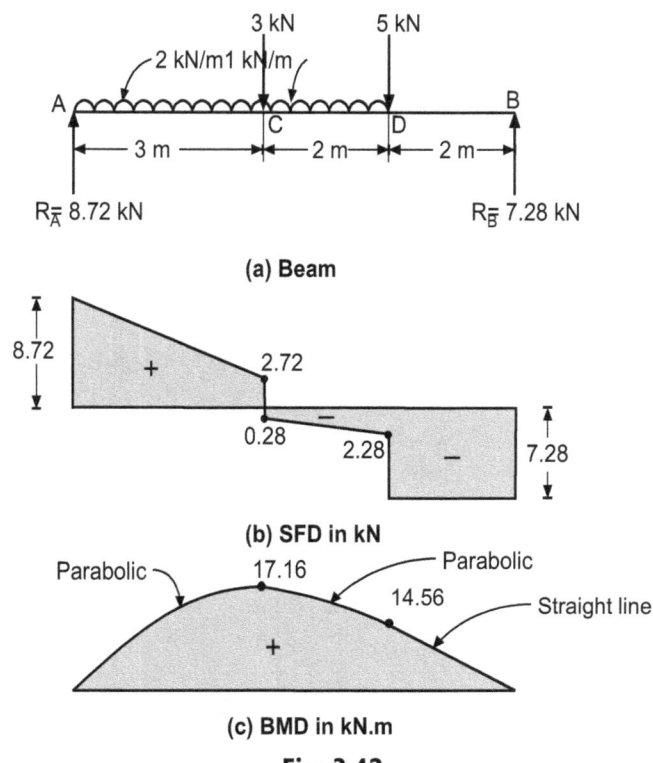

(a) Beam

(b) SFD in kN

(c) BMD in kN.m

**Fig. 3.42**

**Note :** $F_{C_L}$ means S.F. at C assuming that section XX is just to the left of C but very near to C. $F_{C_R}$ means S.F. at C assuming that the section XX is just to the right of C but very near to C.

The S.F.D. is as shown in Fig. 3.42 (b).

**(iii) B.M. calculations :**     $M_A = M_B = 0$

$$M_C = 8.72 \times 3 - 2 \times 3 \times \frac{3}{2} = 17.16 \text{ kN·m}$$

$$M_D = 7.28 \times 2 = 14.56 \text{ kN·m}$$

At C, S.F. changes its sign from positive to negative. Hence the maximum B.M. occurs at C.

The B.M.D. is as shown in Fig. 3.42 (c).

**Example 5 :** *A beam of span 6 m carries a u.d.l. of 1.5 kN per metre run over the entire span and two point loads of 4 kN and 5 kN at 2 m and 4 m from the left hand support. Find the position and magnitude of maximum B.M. Draw S.F. and B.M. diagrams.*

**(B.T.E. S-2011, W-1985/4 Marks)**

**OR**

*Draw S.F.D. and B.M.D. for a simply supported beam as shown in Fig. 3.43 (a).*

**(B.T.E. W-2010/4 Marks)**

**Solution : (i) Reactions :** Taking moments about A,

$$4 \times 2 + 5 \times 4 + (1.5 \times 6) \times \frac{6}{2} = R_B \times 6$$

$\therefore$    $R_B = 9.17$ kN

$\therefore$    $R_A = 4 + 5 + (1.5 \times 6) - 9.17 = 8.83$ kN

**(ii) Shear force calculations :**

$$F_A = + R_A = 8.83 \text{ kN}$$

$$F_{C_L} = 8.83 - 1.5 \times 2 = 5.83 \text{ kN}$$

$$F_{C_R} = 8.83 - 1.5 \times 2 - 4 = 1.83 \text{ kN}$$

$$F_{D_L} = 8.83 - 1.5 \times 2 - 4 - 1.5 \times 2 = -1.17 \text{ kN}$$

$$F_{D_R} = 8.83 - 1.5 \times 2 - 4 - 1.5 \times 2 - 5 = -6.17 \text{ kN}$$

$$F_B = 8.83 - 1.5 \times 2 - 4 - 1.5 \times 2 - 5 - 1.5 \times 2$$

$$= -6.17 - 3 = -9.17 \text{ kN} = -R_B$$

The S.F.D. is as shown in Fig. 3.43 (b).

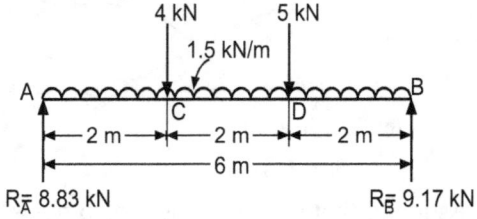

**(a) Beam**

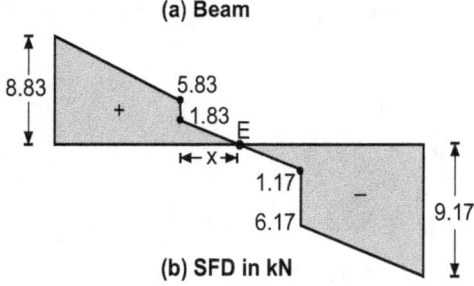

**(b) SFD in kN**

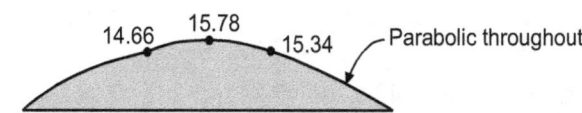

**(c) BMD in kN.m**

**Fig. 3.43**

**(iii) B.M. calculations :**    $M_A = M_B = 0$

$$M_C = 8.83 \times 2 - (1.5 \times 2) \left(\frac{2}{2}\right) = 14.66 \text{ kN·m}$$

$$M_D = 9.17 \times 2 - (1.5 \times 2) \left(\frac{2}{2}\right) = 15.34 \text{ kN·m}$$

**To find $M_{max}$** : At point E in S.F.D., S.F. changes its sign from positive to negative. Hence the maximum B.M. will occur at E. Let x be the distance of E from A. From similar triangles in S.F.D.,

$$\frac{x}{1.83} = \frac{2-x}{1.17}$$

$$1.17x = 1.83\,(2-x) = 3.66 - 1.83\,x$$

$$\therefore \qquad 3x = 3.66 \Rightarrow x = 1.22 \text{ m}$$

$\therefore$ **Distance of E from A** $= 2 + x = 2 + 1.22 = 3.22$ m

$\therefore$ B.M. at 3.22 m from A is given by,

$$M_E = M_{max} = 8.83 \times 3.22 - 4 \times 1.22 - (1.5 \times 3.22)\left(\frac{3.22}{2}\right)$$

$$= 15.78 \text{ kN·m}$$

The B.M.D. is as shown in Fig. 3.43 (c).

---

**Example 6 :** *A simply supported beam of span 3 m is loaded as shown in Fig. 3.44 (a). Draw bending moment diagram for this beam. Indicate all controlling values on it.*

**(B.T.E. S-2013, W-2005/4 Marks)**

**Solution :**

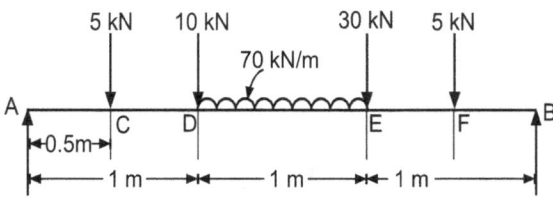

**(a) Beam**

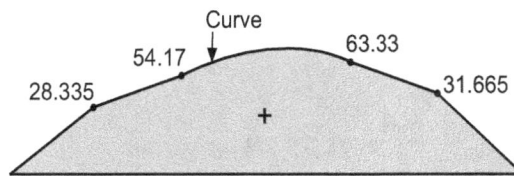

**(b) B.M.D. in kN.m**

**Fig. 3.44**

**(i) Reactions :**  $R_B \times 3 = 5 \times 0.5 + 10 \times 1 + 70 \times 1 \times \left(1 + \frac{1}{2}\right) + 30 \times 2 + 5 \times 2.5$

$$= 2.5 + 10 + 105 + 60 + 12.5 = 190$$

$$R_B = \textbf{63.33 kN}$$

$\therefore \qquad R_A = [5 + 10 + (70 \times 1) + 30 + 5] - 63.33$

$$= 120 - 63.33 = \textbf{56.67 kN}$$

**(ii) B.M. calculations :**

$$M_A = M_B = 0$$

$$M_C = 56.67 \times 0.5 = 28.335 \text{ kN·m}$$

$$M_D = 56.67 \times 1 - 5 \times 0.5 = 54.17 \text{ kN·m}$$

$$M_E = 63.33 \times 1 = 63.33 \text{ kN·m}$$

$$M_F = 63.33 \times 0.5 = 31.665 \text{ kN·m}$$

The B.M.D. is as shown in Fig. 3.44 (b).

### Try Yourself :

**Example 7 :** *Draw the shearing force diagram for the beam as shown in Fig. 3.45 (a).*

**(B.T.E. S-2005/4 Marks)**

**Solution :**

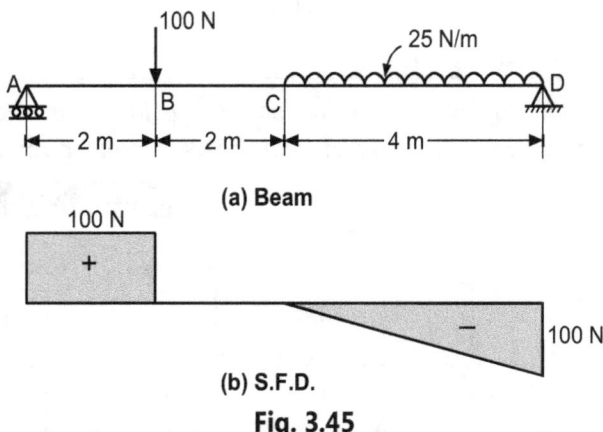

**(a) Beam**

**(b) S.F.D.**

**Fig. 3.45**

**Example 8 :** *For the beam loaded as shown in Fig. 3.46 (a), draw shear force and bending moment diagram locating all important values.* **(B.T.E. S-2008/4 Marks)**

**Solution : (i) Reactions :** Taking moments about A,

$$R_B \times 8 = (22 \times 3) \times \left(2 + \frac{3}{2}\right) + 75 \times 5$$

$$\mathbf{R_B} = \frac{606}{8} = \mathbf{75.75 \text{ kN}}$$

∴　　　　　　$$\mathbf{R_A} = [(22 \times 3) + 75] - 75.75 = \mathbf{65.25 \text{ kN}}$$

**(ii) S.F. calculations :**

$$F_A = R_A = 65.25 \text{ kN (remains constant from A to D)}$$

$$F_D = F_{D_L} = F_{D_R} = 65.25 \text{ kN (since there is no load at D, } F_{D_L} = F_{D_R})$$

$$F_{C_L} = 65.25 - 22 \times 3 = -0.75 \text{ kN}$$

$$F_{C_R} = 65.25 - 22 \times 3 - 75 = -75.75 \text{ kN}$$

Since there is no load between C and B, – 75.75 kN remains constant from C to B.

∴　　　　　　$$F_B = -75.75 \text{ kN} \quad \textbf{(Check :} F_B = -R_B = -75.75 \text{ kN)}$$

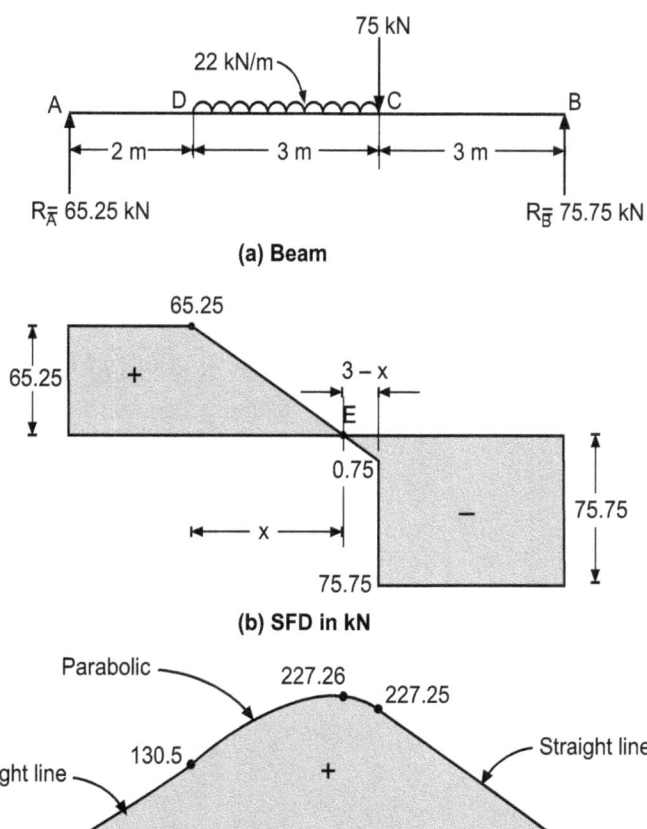

**(a) Beam**

**(b) SFD in kN**

**(c) BMD in kN.m**

**Fig. 3.46**

The S.F.D. is as shown in Fig. 3.46 (b).

The S.F. changes its sign at E.

Let 'x' be the distance of E from D.

From the similar triangles in shear force diagram for portion DC, we have

$$\frac{65.25}{x} = \frac{0.75}{3-x}$$

∴          $0.75\,x = 195.75 - 65.25\,x$

∴          $66\,x = 196.75$

∴          x = 2.96 m from D. The maximum B.M. will occur at 2.96 m from D or 2 + 2.96 = 4.96 m from A.

**(iii) B.M. calculations :**

$$M_A = M_B = 0$$
$$M_D = 65.25 \times 2 = 130.5 \text{ kN.m}$$
$$M_C = 75.75 \times 3 = 227.25 \text{ kN.m}$$

$$\therefore \quad M_E = M_{max} = M_{4.96} = 65.25 \times 4.96 - 22 \times 2.96 \times \frac{2.96}{2} = 227.26 \text{ kN.m}$$

The B.M.D. is as shown in Fig. 3.46 (c).

## Try Yourself :

**Example 9 :** *A simply supported beam is loaded as shown in Fig. 3.47 (a). Draw the S.F. and B.M. diagram indicating the position of maximum bending moment and determine its value.* **(B.T.E. S-2009/4 Marks)**

**Solution :**

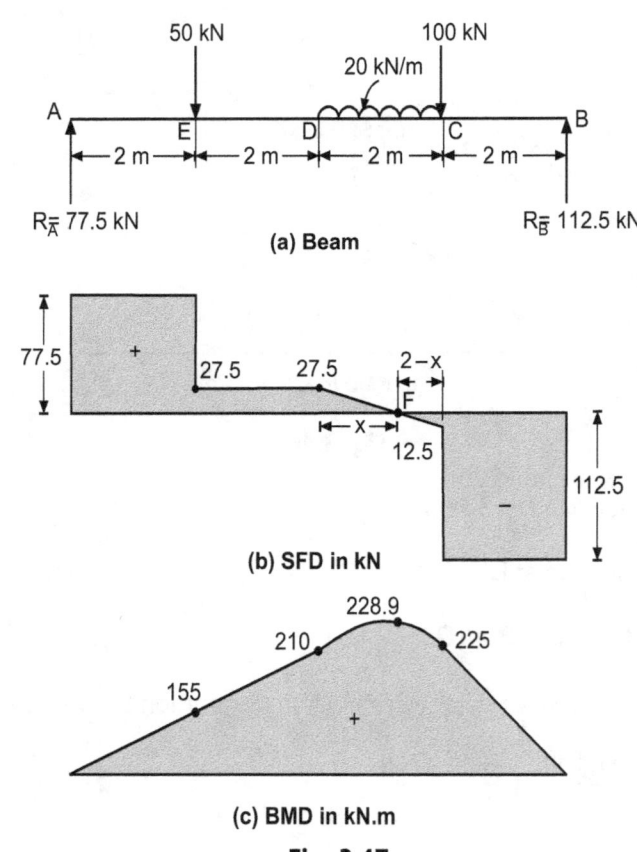

(a) Beam

(b) SFD in kN

(c) BMD in kN.m

**Fig. 3.47**

$$\frac{27.5}{x} = \frac{12.5}{2-x} \quad \therefore \ x = 1.375 \text{ m from D.}$$

**Example 10 :** *A simply supported beam of 6 m span carries two point loads of 20 kN each at 2 m and 4 m from left hand support. It also carries UDL of 30 kN/m between two point loads. Draw SFD and BMD.* **(B.T.E. W-2008/4 Marks)**

**Solution :**

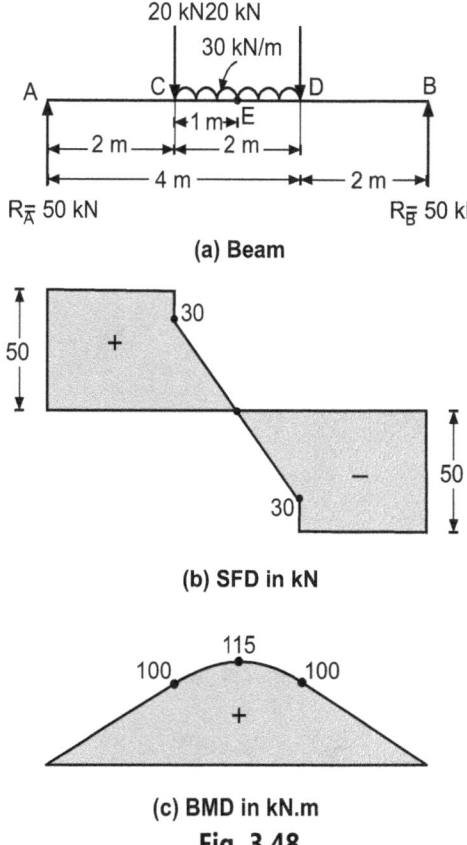

**(a) Beam**

**(b) SFD in kN**

**(c) BMD in kN.m**

**Fig. 3.48**

**Example 11 :** *A simply supported beam carries U.D.L. over entire span. The maximum SF and BM are 10 kN and 10 kN.m respectively. Find the span and intensity of UDL.*

**(B.T.E. W-2009/4 Marks)**

**Solution :** Refer to Fig. 3.49.

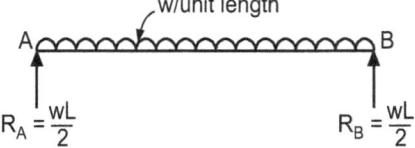

**Fig. 3.49**

We know that, for a simply supported beam carrying u.d.l. over the entire span,

Maximum shear force $= R_A = \dfrac{wL}{2}$        ... (i)

But it is given that,

Maximum shear force $= 10$ kN        ... (ii)

Equating (i) and (ii),

$$\frac{wL}{2} = 10$$        ... (I)

For a simply supported beam carrying u.d.l. over entire span,

$$\text{Maximum B.M.} = \frac{wL^2}{8} \qquad \text{... (iii)}$$

But it is given that, Maximum B.M. = 10 kN.m          ... (iv)

Equating (iii) and (iv),

$$\frac{wL^2}{8} = 10 \qquad \text{... (II)}$$

$$\therefore \qquad \frac{wL}{2} \times \frac{L}{4} = 10$$

$$\therefore \qquad 10 \times \frac{L}{4} = 10 \qquad \ldots \left[ \because \frac{wL}{2} = 10 \text{ from equation (I)} \right]$$

$$\therefore \qquad \boxed{L = 4 \text{ m}}$$

$\therefore$  From equation (I),

$$w \times \frac{4}{2} = 10 \quad \therefore \quad \boxed{w = 5 \text{ kN/m}}$$

**Answer :** $\boxed{\text{(i) Span L = 4 m, (ii) Intensity of u.d.l., w = 5 kN/m}}$

**Example 12 :** *A simply supported beam of span 6 m carries a u.d.l. of 1.5 kN/m over entire span and a point load of 2 kN at 2 m from right support. Draw S.F. and B.M. diagrams.*

**(B.T.E. W-2009/4 Marks)**

**Solution :**

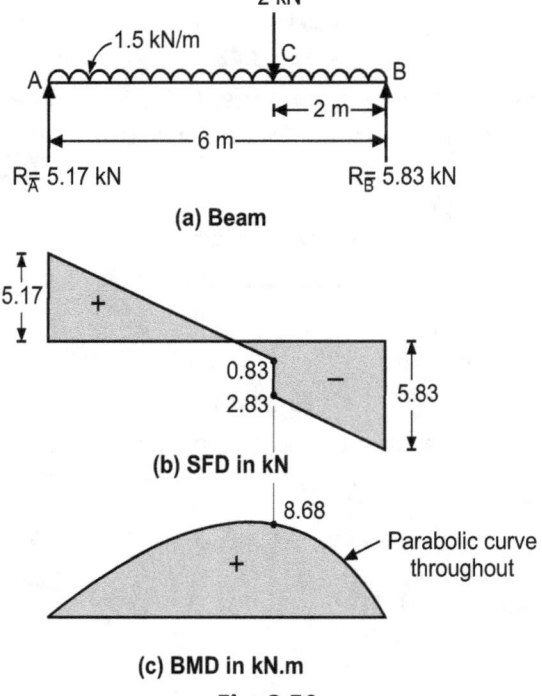

(a) Beam

(b) SFD in kN

(c) BMD in kN.m

**Fig. 3.50**

**(i)** **Reactions :** Taking moments about A,

$$R_B \times 6 = (1.5 \times 6) \times \frac{6}{2} + 2 \times 4 = 27 + 8 = 35$$

$$\therefore \qquad R_B = \frac{35}{6} = 5.83 \text{ kN}$$

$$\therefore \qquad R_A = [2 + (1.5 \times 6)] - 5.83 = 5.17 \text{ kN}$$

**(ii) S.F. calculations :** $F_A = R_A = 5.17$ kN

$$F_{C_L} = 5.17 - (1.5 \times 4) = -0.83 \text{ kN}$$

$$F_{C_R} = [5.17 - (1.5 \times 4)] - 2 = -0.83 - 2 = -2.83 \text{ kN}$$

$$F_B = [5.17 - (1.5 \times 4) - 2] - 1.5 \times 2 = -2.83 - 3 = -5.83 \text{ kN}$$

The S.F.D. is as shown in Fig. 3.50 (b).

**(iii) B.M. calculations :** $M_A = M_B = 0$

$$M_C = 5.17 \times 4 - (1.5 \times 4) \times \frac{4}{2} = 20.68 - 12 = 8.68 \text{ kN.m}$$

or

$$M_C = 5.83 \times 2 - (1.5 \times 2) \times \frac{2}{2} = 11.66 - 3 = 8.66 \text{ kN.m}$$

The B.M.D. is as shown in Fig. 3.50 (c).

## Similar example for practice :

**Example 13 :** *Draw the shear force and bending moment diagrams for the beam shown in Fig. 3.51 (a). Indicate on the diagrams the values of shear force and bending moment at significant points. Find the maximum bending moment.*          **(B.T.E. S-2004/8 Marks)**

**Solution :**

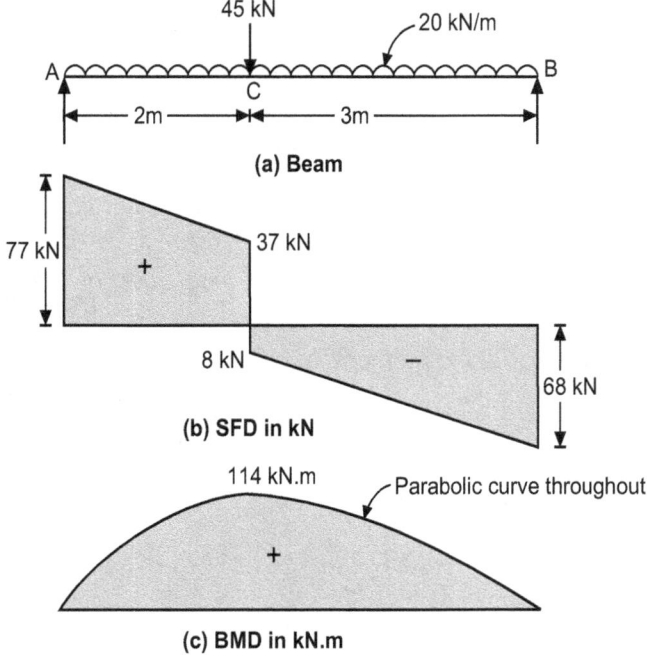

45 kN

20 kN/m

**(a) Beam**

77 kN

37 kN

8 kN

68 kN

**(b) SFD in kN**

114 kN.m          Parabolic curve throughout

**(c) BMD in kN.m**

**Fig. 3.51**

**Try Yourself :**

**Example 14 :** *A simply supported beam of span 6 m carries a u.d.l. of 3 kN/m spread over 2 m from left support and a point load of 6 kN at 4 m from left support. Draw S.F.D. and B.M.D.*

**(B.T.E. S-2010/4 Marks)**

**Solution :**

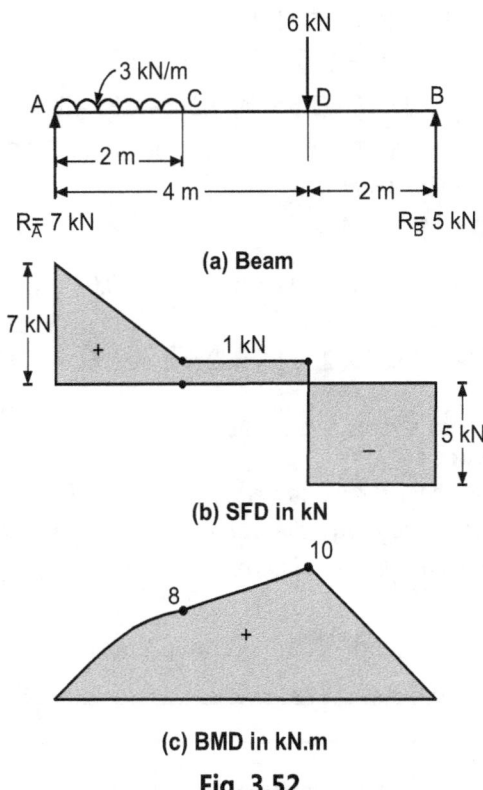

**(a) Beam**

**(b) SFD in kN**

**(c) BMD in kN.m**

**Fig. 3.52**

**Example 15 :** *Draw the shear force and bending moment diagrams for the beam shown in Fig. 3.53 (a). Indicate on the diagrams the values of shear force and bending moment at significant points. Find and show the location and magnitude of the maximum bending moment.*

**(B.T.E. W-2005/8 Marks)**

**Solution : (i) Reactions :** Taking moments about A,

$$R_B \times 4 = (10 \times 2) \times \frac{2}{2} + (20 \times 2) \times \left(2 + \frac{2}{2}\right)$$

$$\therefore \qquad R_B = \frac{140}{4} = 35 \text{ kN}$$

$$R_A = (10 \times 2) + (20 \times 2) - 35 = 25 \text{ kN}$$

**(ii) S.F. calculations :**     $F_A = R_A = 25 \text{ kN}$

$$F_C = 25 - 10 \times 2 = 5 \text{ kN}$$

$$F_B = 25 - 10 \times 2 - 20 \times 2 = -35 \text{ kN} = -R_B$$

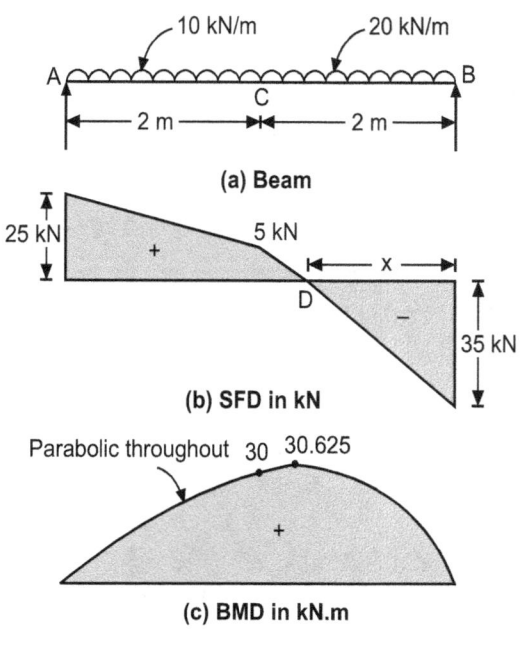

**(a) Beam**

**(b) SFD in kN**

**(c) BMD in kN.m**

**Fig. 3.53**

The S.F.D. is as shown in **Fig. 3.53 (b)**.

At point D, S.F. changes its sign from positive to negative.

Let BD = x. From similar triangles in S.F.D.,

$$\frac{x}{35} = \frac{2-x}{5}$$

∴          $5x = 35(2-x) = 70 - 35x$

∴          $40x = 70$

∴          **x = 1.75 m** (Location of maximum B.M.)

**(iii) B.M. calculations :**

$$M_A = M_B = 0$$

$$M_C = 25 \times 2 - (10 \times 2) \times \frac{2}{2} = \textbf{30 kN.m}$$

Since S.F. changes its sign at point D, $M_{max}$ occurs at point D.

$$\textbf{M}_{\textbf{max}} = \textbf{M}_\textbf{D} = 35 \times 1.75 - (20 \times 1.75) \times \frac{1.75}{2}$$

$$= \textbf{30.625 kN.m} \text{ (Magnitude of maximum B.M.)}$$

The B.M.D. is as shown in **Fig. 3.53 (c)**.

**Example 16 :** *Write the moment equation for the beam simply supported over a span of 8 m and carrying a central point load of 100 kN. State the nature of the curve from BM equation. Draw B.M.D.* **(B.T.E. W-2005/4 Marks)**

**Solution :**

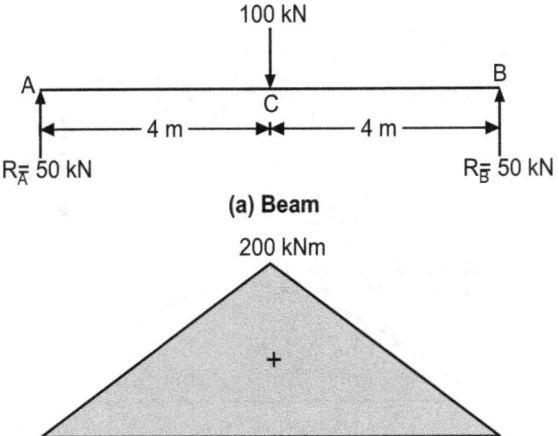

**(a) Beam**

200 kNm

**(b) BMD in kNm**

**Fig. 3.54**

Due to symmetry,          $R_A = R_B = \dfrac{100}{2} = 50$ kN

B.M. at section XX at a distance 'x' from A in portion AC,

$$M_X = 50x \qquad \qquad ... (i)$$

B.M. at section XX at a distance 'x' from A in portion CB,

$$M_X = 50x - 100 (x - 4) \qquad \qquad ... (ii)$$

Hence, the general equation for B.M. at section XX is,

$$M_X = 50x \ \vdots - 100 (x - 4) \qquad \qquad ... (A)$$
$$\text{AC} \ \vdots \ \text{CB}$$

The expression upto first dotted line is valid if section XX is taken in portion AC and the entire expression is valid if section XX is taken in portion CB.

*In equation (A), the power of 'x' is one. Hence, the variation of BM is linear.*

Now, for portion AC,     $M_X = 50x$

At A, x = 0,          $M_A = 50 \times 0 = 0$

At C, x = 4 m,          $M_C = 50 \times 4 = 200$ kN.m

For portion CB,          $M_X = 50x - 100 (x - 4)$

At C, x = 4 m,          **$M_C = 50 \times 4 - 100 (4 - 4) = $ 200 kN.m**

At B, x = 8 m,          $M_B = 50 \times 8 - 100 (8 - 4) = 400 - 400 = 0$

The B.M.D. is as shown in **Fig. 3.54 (b)**.

**Example 17 :** *Write the shear and moment equations for the beam which is simply supported over a span 4 m and carries a central point load of 20 kN. Sketch the shear and moment diagram.* **(B.T.E. S-2003/4 Marks)**

**Solution :**

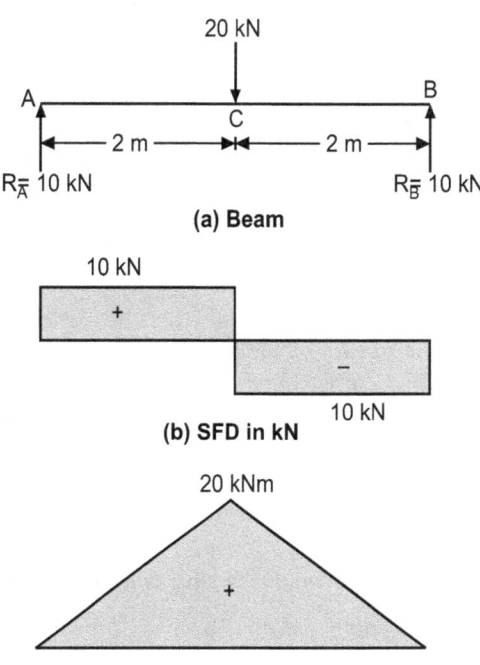

**(a) Beam**

**(b) SFD in kN**

**(c) BMD in kNm**

**Fig. 3.55**

Due to symmetry,  $R_A = R_B = \dfrac{W}{2} = \dfrac{20}{2} = 10$ kN

**Shear equation :** S.F. at section XX at a distance 'x' from A in **portion AC** is given by,

$$F_X = 10 \text{ kN} \text{ (remains constant from A to C)}$$

S.F. at section XX at a distance 'x' from A in **portion CB** is given by,

$$F_X = 10 - 20 = -10 \text{ kN (remains constant from C to B)}$$

The S.F.D. is as shown in **Fig. 3.55 (b)**.

**Moment equation :** B.M. at section XX at a distance 'x' from A in portion AC is given by,

$$M_X = 10 \times x \qquad \qquad \dots \text{(A)}$$

At A, x = 0, hence,     $M_A = 10 \times 0 = 0$

At C, x = 2 m, hence,     $M_C = 10 \times 2 = 20$ kN.m

B.M. at section XX at a distance 'x' from A in **portion CB** is given by,

$$M_x = 10x - 20(x - 2) \qquad \qquad ...(B)$$

At C, x = 2 m, hence,　　$M_C = 10 \times 2 - 20(2 - 2) = 20$ kN.m

At B, x = 4 m, hence,　　$M_B = 10 \times 4 - 20(4 - 2) = 0$

In equations (A) and (B), since the power of 'x' is one, the variation of B.M. is linear.

The B.M.D. is as shown in **Fig. 3.55 (c)**.

## Type 2 : S.F.D. and B.M.D. for a cantilever beam subjected to u.d.l. and point load :

**Example 18 :** *A cantilever beam of span 2.5 m carries three point loads of 1 kN, 2 kN and 3 kN at 1 m, 1.5 m and 2.5 m from the fixed end. Draw S.F.D. and B.M.D.*

(B.T.E. S-2013/4 Marks)

**OR**

*Draw B.M. and S.F. diagrams for the cantilever as shown in Fig. 3.56 (a).*

(B.T.E. W-2011/4 Marks)

**Solution :**

**(i) Calculations of S.F. :**

*In case of cantilever beams, it is convenient to start calculation work from the free end.*

S.F. at any section between D and B,

$$F_x = +3 \text{ kN} \qquad \qquad ... \text{(positive since right downward)}$$

It remains constant from D to B.

S.F. at any section between C and D,

$$F_x = 3 + 2 = 5 \text{ kN and remains constant from C to D.}$$

S.F. at any section between A and C,

$$F_x = 3 + 2 + 1 = 6 \text{ kN and remains constant from A to C.}$$

The S.F.D. is as shown in Fig. 3.56 (b).

**(ii) Calculations of B.M. :**

At the free end B, $M_B = 0$

(Because if we assume section at B, there is no force to the right of B.)

$$M_D = -3 \times 1 = -3 \text{ kN·m}$$

... (minus sign due to clockwise moment to the right i.e. hogging)

$$M_C = -3 \times 1.5 - 2 \times 0.5 = -5.5 \text{ kN·m}$$

$$M_A = -3 \times 2.5 - 2 \times 1.5 - 1 \times 1 = -11.5 \text{ kN·m}$$

The B.M.D. is as shown in Fig. 3.56 (c).

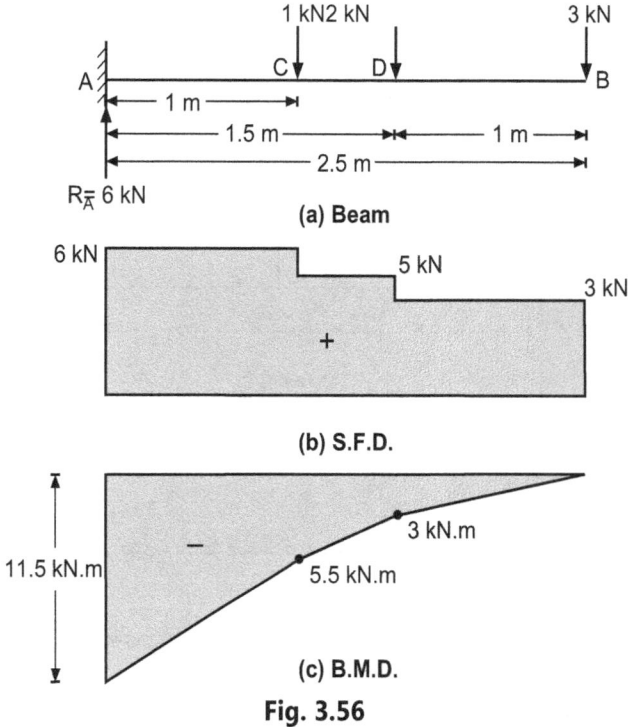

**(a) Beam**

**(b) S.F.D.**

**(c) B.M.D.**

**Fig. 3.56**

**Alternative procedure :** The calculations of S.F. can be done from the left fixed end A. But for this purpose, it is necessary to calculate the reaction at the fixed end A.

$\sum F_y = 0$ gives, $R_A - 1 - 2 - 3 = 0$ i.e. $R_A = 6$ kN

**Check :** $F_A = R_A = 6$ kN

After finding the value of $R_A$, calculate the values of shear forces in the following manner.

S.F. at any section in AC,     $F_X = + R_A = 6$ kN, and remains constant from A to C.

S.F. at any section in CD,     $F_X = 6 - 1 = 5$ kN. It remains constant from C to D.

S.F. at any section in DB,     $F_X = 6 - 1 - 2 = 3$ kN. It remains constant from D to B.

**Example 19 :** *A cantilever is loaded as shown in Fig. 3.57 (a). Draw S.F.D. and calculate B.M. at point A.*                                      **(B.T.E. S-2013, W-2007/4 Marks)**

**Solution :**

**(i)  Calculations of S.F. :**

S.F. just to the left of B,

$$F_B = 3 \text{ kN} \qquad \qquad \text{... (positive since right downward)}$$

(**Note :** S.F. just to the right of B is zero)

$$F_{D_R} = 3 + 2 \times 2 = 7 \text{ kN}$$

S.F. just to the left of D,

$$F_{D_L} = 3 + 2 \times 2 + 2 = 9 \text{ kN}$$

Since there is no load between D and C, 9 kN remains constant from D to C.

S.F. at any section between A and C,

$$F_X = 1 + 2 + 2 \times 2 + 3 = 10 \text{ kN}$$

and it remains constant from A to C.

The S.F.D. is as shown in Fig. 3.57 (b).

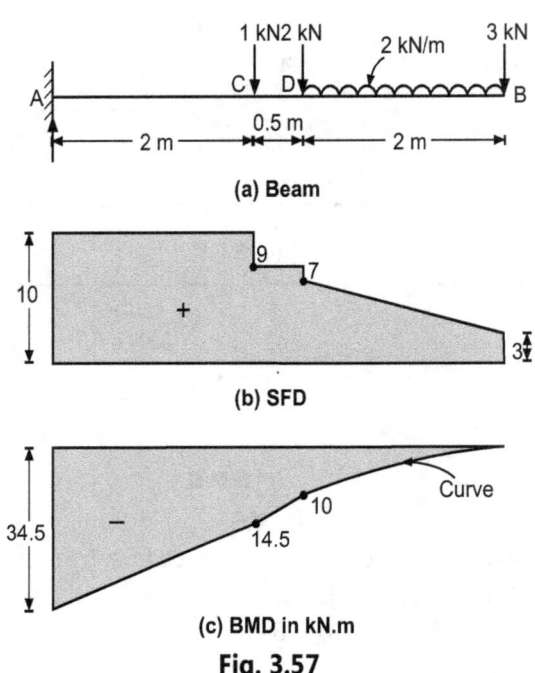

**(a) Beam**

**(b) SFD**

**(c) BMD in kN.m**

**Fig. 3.57**

**(ii) Calculations of B.M. :**

At the free end B,     $M_B = 0$ (since there is no force to the right of B)

$$M_D = -3 \times 2 - (2 \times 2)\left(\frac{2}{2}\right) = 10 \text{ kN·m}$$

$$M_C = -3 \times 2.5 - (2 \times 2)\left(\frac{2}{2} + 0.5\right) - 2 \times 0.5 = -14.5 \text{ kN·m}$$

$$M_A = -3 \times 4.5 - (2 \times 2)\left(\frac{2}{2} + 2.5\right) - 2 \times 2.5 - 1 \times 2 = -34.5 \text{ kN·m}$$

The B.M.D. is as shown in Fig. 3.57 (c).

**Example 20 :** *Draw S.F. and B.M. diagrams for the beam shown in Fig. 3.58 (a).* **(4 Marks)**
**Solution :**
**(i)  Calculations of S.F. :**

S.F. just to the left of B, $F_B = 3$ kN

S.F. just to the right of D, $F_{D_R} = 3 + 2 \times 2 = 7$ kN

S.F. just to the left of D, $F_{D_L} = 3 + 2 \times 2 + 2 = 9$ kN

S.F. just to the right of C, $F_{C_R} = 3 + 2 \times 2 + 2 + 1 \times 0.5 = 9.5$ kN

S.F. just to the left of C, $F_{C_L} = 3 + 2 \times 2 + 2 + 1 \times 0.5 + 1 = 10.5$ kN

Since there is no load between A and C, 10.5 kN remains constant from A to C. i.e. $F_A = 10.5$ kN

[**Check :** $\qquad$ $R_A$ = Total downward load

$\qquad\qquad = 1 + 2 + 3 + 1 \times 0.5 + 2 \times 2 = 10.5$ kN]

The S.F.D. is as shown in Fig. 3.58 (b).

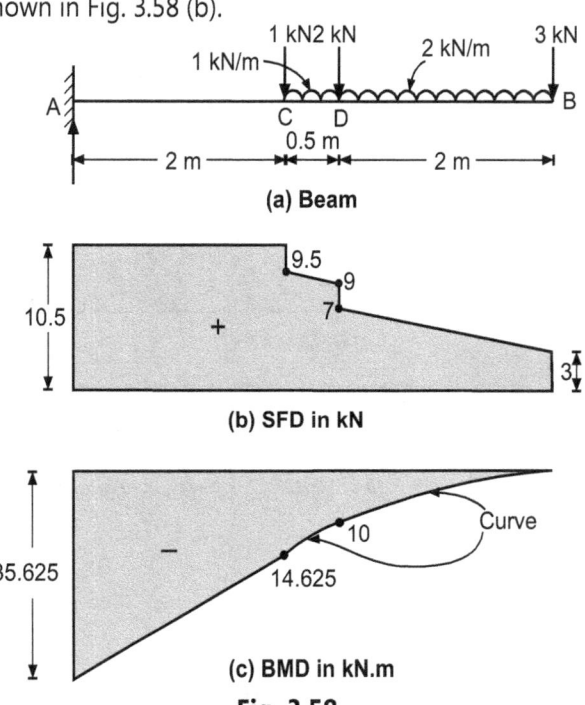

(a) Beam

(b) SFD in kN

(c) BMD in kN.m

**Fig. 3.58**

**(ii) Calculations of B.M. :**

$$M_B = 0$$

$$M_D = -3 \times 2 - 2 \times 2 \times 1 = -10 \text{ kN·m}$$

$$M_C = -3 \times 2.5 - (2 \times 2)\left(\frac{2}{2} + 0.5\right) - 2 \times 0.5 - (1 \times 0.5) \times \frac{0.5}{2}$$

$$= -14.625 \text{ kN·m}$$

$$M_A = -3 \times 4.5 - (2 \times 2)\left(\frac{2}{2} + 0.5\right) - 2 \times 2.5 - (1 \times 0.5) \times \left(\frac{0.5}{2} + 2\right) - 1 \times 2$$

$$= -35.625 \text{ kN·m}$$

The B.M.D. is as shown in Fig. 3.58 (c).

**Example 21 :** *Draw S.F. and B.M. diagrams for the beam shown in Fig. 3.59 (a).* **(4 Marks)**

**Solution :**

**(i) Reaction at the fixed end A :** For the equilibrium of the beam,

$\qquad\qquad R_A$ = Total downward load

$\qquad\qquad\quad = 2 \times 2 + 1 + 1 \times 0.5 + 2 + 2 \times 2 + 3 = 14.5$ kN

**Note :** In this problem, the calculations of shear forces are done from the fixed end. One can do the calculation work from the free end also.

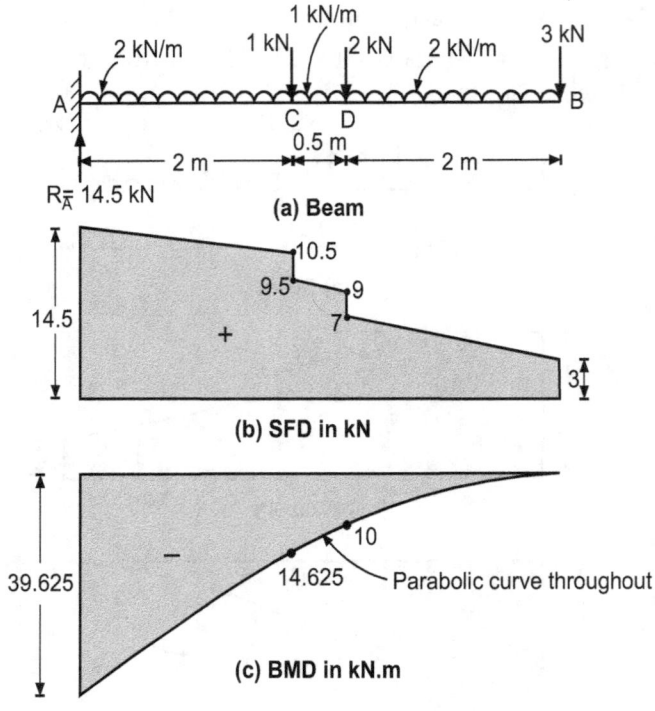

**(a) Beam**

**(b) SFD in kN**

**(c) BMD in kN.m**

**Fig. 3.59**

But note that in case of cantilever beam, the calculations of bending moments are done from the free end only.

**(ii) S.F. calculations :**

$$F_A = + R_A = 14.5 \text{ kN} \quad \text{... (positive since upward to the left)}$$

$$F_{C_L} = 14.5 - 2 \times 2 = 10.5 \text{ kN}$$

$$F_{C_R} = 14.5 - 2 \times 2 - 1 = 9.5 \text{ kN}$$

$$F_{D_L} = 14.5 - 2 \times 2 - 1 - 1 \times 0.5 = 9 \text{ kN}$$

$$F_{D_R} = 14.5 - 2 \times 2 - 1 - 1 \times 0.5 - 2 = 7 \text{ kN}$$

$$F_B = F_{B_L} = 14.5 - 2 \times 2 - 1 - 1 \times 0.5 - 2 - 2 \times 2 = 3 \text{ kN}$$

(**Note :** $F_{B_R} = 0$ and $F_B$ = load at B)

The S.F.D. is as shown in Fig. 3.59 (b).

**(iii) B.M. calculations :**

$$M_B = 0$$

$$M_D = -3 \times 2 - 2 \times 2 \times 1 = -10 \text{ kN·m}$$

$$M_C = -3 \times 2.5 - (2 \times 2)\left(\frac{2}{2} + 0.5\right) - 2 \times 0.5 - (1 \times 0.5) \times \frac{0.5}{2} = -14.625 \text{ kN·m}$$

$$M_A = -3 \times 4.5 - (2 \times 2)\left(\frac{2}{2} + 2.5\right) - 2 \times 2.5 - (1 \times 0.5)\left(\frac{0.5}{2} + 2\right) - 1 \times 2 - (2 \times 2) \times \frac{2}{2}$$

$$= -39.625 \text{ kN·m}$$

The B.M.D. is as shown in Fig. 3.59 (c).

**Example 22 :** *Draw S.F.D. and B.M.D. for the beam loaded as shown in Fig. 3.60 (a).*

**(B.T.E. W-2011, 2007/4 Marks; S-1991/8 Marks)**

**Solution : (i) To find $R_A$ :** For the equilibrium of the beam,

Upward reaction at A = Total downward load

$$R_A = 2 + 0.8 \times 1.5 = 3.2 \text{ kN}$$

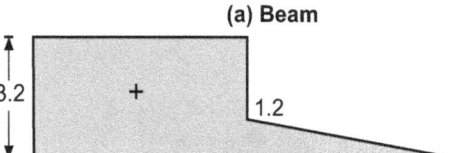

**(a) Beam**

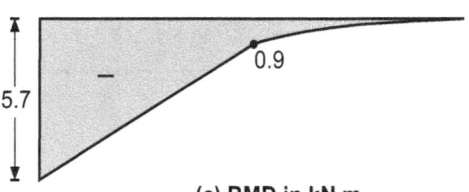

**(b) SFD in kN**

**(c) BMD in kN.m**

**Fig. 3.60**

**(ii) S.F. calculations :**      $F_A = R_A = 3.2$ kN      ... (positive since left upward)

Since there is no load between A and C, 3.2 kN remains constant from A to C.

S.F. just to the right of C,      $F_{C_R} = 3.2 - 2 = 1.2$ kN

(**Note :** S.F. just to the left of C = $R_A$ = 3.2 kN)

S.F. just to the left and right of B,   $F_B = 3.2 - 2 - 0.8 \times 1.5 = 0$

(**Note :** At the free end B, there is no point load.

Hence,                  $F_B = F_{B_L} = F_{B_R} = 0$)

The S.F.D. is as shown in Fig. 3.60 (b).

**(iii) B.M. calculations :**    $M_B = 0$

$$M_C = -(0.8 \times 1.5) \times \left(\frac{1.5}{2}\right) = -0.9 \text{ kN·m}$$

$$M_A = -(0.8 \times 1.5)\left(\frac{1.5}{2} + 1.5\right) - 2 \times 1.5 = -5.7 \text{ kN·m}$$

The B.M.D. is as shown in Fig. 3.60 (c).

## Try Yourself :

**Example 23 :** *Draw S.F. and B.M. diagrams for the beam loaded as shown in Fig. 3.61 (a).*

(V.V. Imp./4 Marks)

**Solution :**

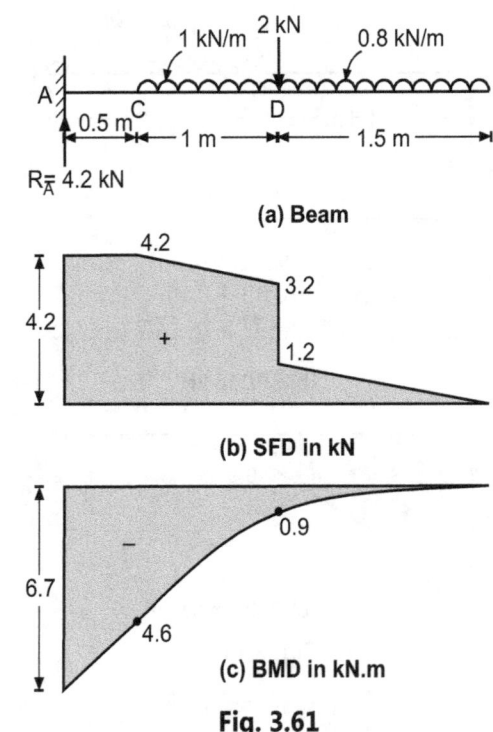

(a) Beam

(b) SFD in kN

(c) BMD in kN.m

**Fig. 3.61**

## Type 3 : Beams subjected to combination of upward and downward loads :

**Example 24 :** *Draw S.F. and B.M. diagrams for a beam shown in Fig. 3.62 (a).*

(B.T.E. W-2010, 1990/4 Marks)

**Solution :**

**(i)  Support reaction :** For the equilibrium of the beam,

$$\sum \text{upward forces} = \sum \text{downward forces}$$

$\therefore$            $R_A + 5 \times 2 = 5 \times 2 + 20$

$$\boxed{R_A = 20 \text{ kN}}$$

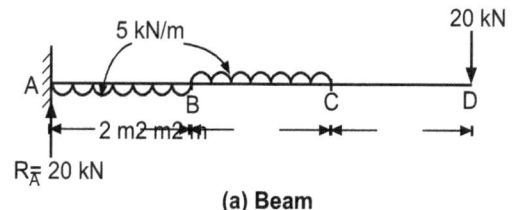

**(a) Beam**

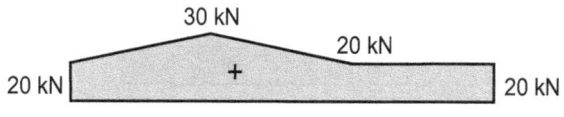

**(b) SFD in kN**

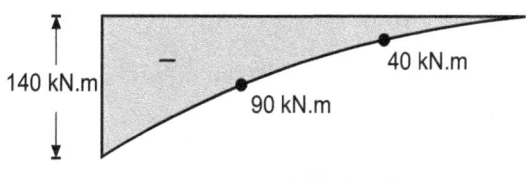

**(c) BMD in kN.m**

**Fig. 3.62**

**(ii) S.F. calculations :**     $F_A = R_A = 20$ kN

$F_B = 20 + 5 \times 2 = 30$ kN

... (positive since there is upward u.d.l. from A to B)

$F_C = 20 + 5 \times 2 - 5 \times 2 = 20$ kN

Since there is no load between C and D, 20 kN remains constant from C to D.

i.e.                    $F_D = 20$ kN

The S.F.D. is as shown in Fig. 3.62 (b).

(**Check :** $F_D$ = load at D = 20 kN)

**(iii) B.M. calculations :**     $M_A = -20 \times 6 - (5 \times 2) \times 3 + (5 \times 2) \times 1$

$= -120 - 30 + 10 = -140$ kN·m

$M_B = -20 \times 4 - (5 \times 2) \times 1 = -80 - 10 = -90$ kN·m

$M_C = -20 \times 2 = -40$ kN·m

The B.M.D. is as shown in Fig. 3.62 (c).

**Example 25 :** *Draw S.F. diagram for a cantilever of span 2 m carrying a point load of 5 kN at the free end.*                    **(B.T.E. W-2011/2 Marks)**

**Solution :**

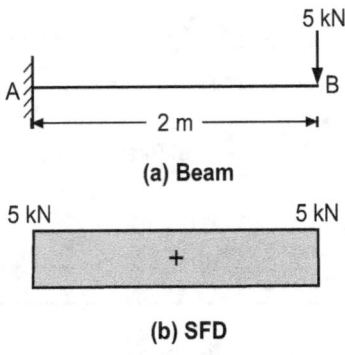

**(a) Beam**

**(b) SFD**

**Fig. 3.63**

(i)  **Reaction :** $R_A$ = Total downward load = 5 kN.

(ii) **S.F. calculations :** S.F. at any section between A and B, $F_x = R_A$ = 5 kN.

It remains constant from A to B. The S.F.D. is as shown in Fig. 3.63 (b).

## Type 4 : Examples from latest B.T.E. papers.

## Try Yourself :

**Example 26 :** *A cantilever beam 3 m span has a point load of 20 kN at 2.5 m from fixed end. Draw S.F. and B.M. diagrams for the beam.*     **(B.T.E. S-2010/2 Marks)**

**Solution :**

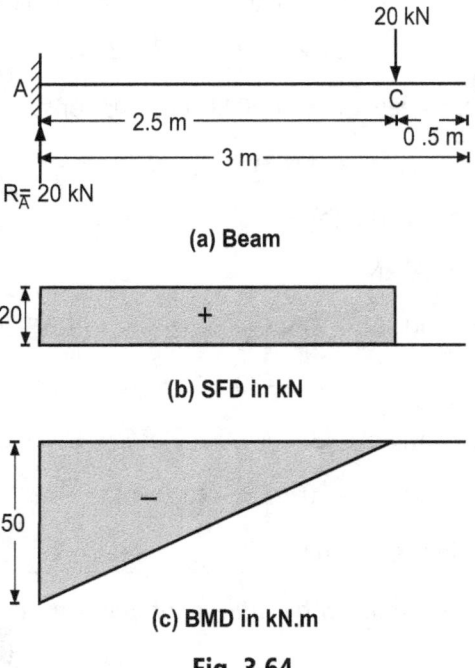

**(a) Beam**

**(b) SFD in kN**

**(c) BMD in kN.m**

**Fig. 3.64**

**Example 27 :** *A cantilever beam 1.5 m long is carrying point loads of 1000 N each at a distance of 0.5 m, 1.0 m and 1.5 m from the fixed end. Draw S.F. and B.M. diagrams for the cantilever beam.* **(B.T.E. W-2012/4 Marks)**

**Solution :** This example is very similar to the solved example **18**. The S.F. and B.M. diagrams are as shown in Fig. 3.65 (b) and (c) respectively.

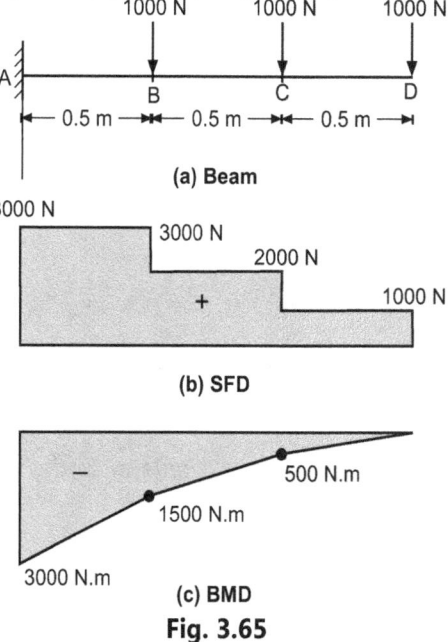

(a) Beam

(b) SFD

(c) BMD

**Fig. 3.65**

**Example 28 :** *Draw B.M. and S.F. diagram for the cantilever beam shown in Fig. 3.66 (a).* **(B.T.E. W-2011/4 Marks)**

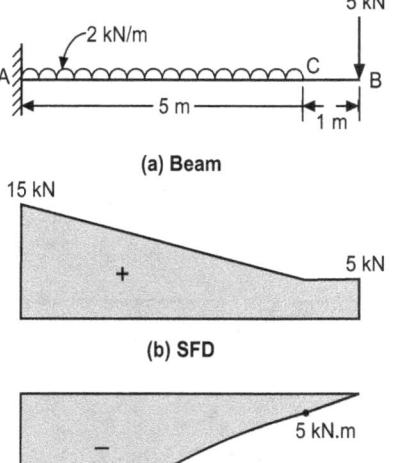

(a) Beam

(b) SFD

(c) BMD

**Fig. 3.66**

**Solution : (i) Reaction :**     $R_A$ = Total downward load

$$= 2 \times 5 + 5 = 15 \text{ kN}$$

**(ii) S.F. calculations :**     $F_A = R_A = 15 \text{ kN}$

$$F_C = 15 - 2 \times 5 = 5 \text{ kN}$$

It remains constant from A to C.

$$F_B = 5 \text{ kN}$$

**(iii) B.M. calculations :**     $M_B = 0$

$$M_C = -5 \times 1$$

$$= -5 \text{ kN.m}$$

$$M_A = -5 \times 6 - 2 \times 5 \times \frac{5}{2} = -55 \text{ kN.m}$$

The S.F.D. and B.M.D. are as shown in Fig. 3.66 (b) and (c) respectively.

## Try Yourself :

**Example 29 :** *Draw S.F.D. and B.M.D. for a cantilever loaded as shown in Fig. 3.67 (a).*

**(B.T.E. W-2009/4 Marks)**

**Solution :**

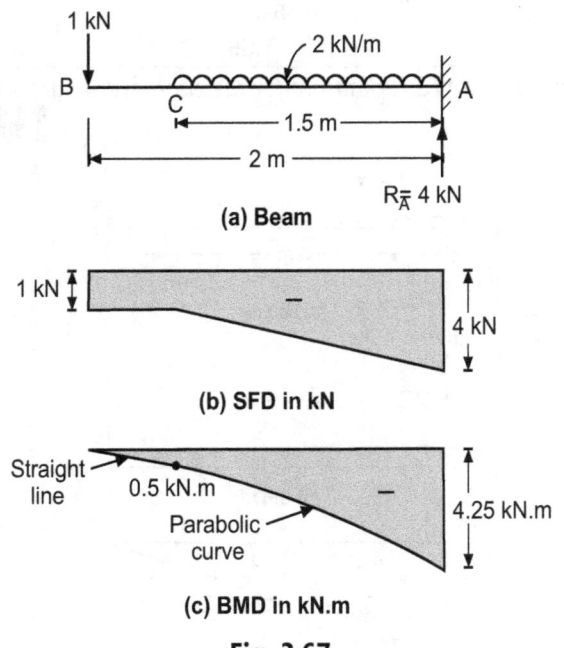

(a) Beam

(b) SFD in kN

(c) BMD in kN.m

**Fig. 3.67**

## Try Yourself :

**Example 30 :** *For the beam shown in Fig. 3.68 (a), draw shear force and bending moment diagram showing all controlling points.*     **(B.T.E. S-2008/4 Marks)**

**Solution :**

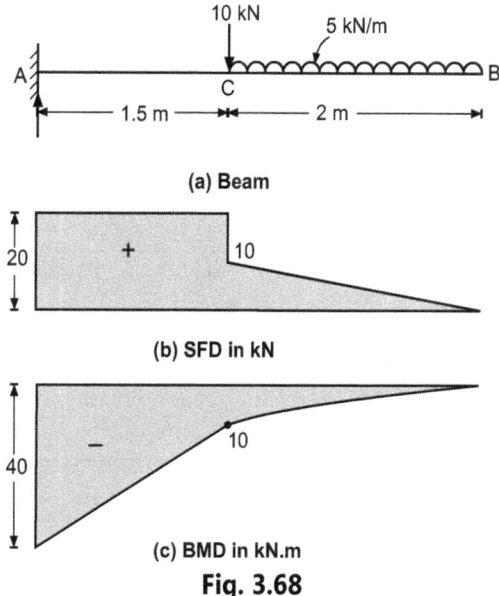

(a) Beam

(b) SFD in kN

(c) BMD in kN.m

**Fig. 3.68**

**Try Yourself :**

**Example 31 :** *Draw bending moment and shear force diagram of a cantilever beam AB 4 m long having its fixed end at A and loaded with a uniformly distributed load of 1 kN/m upto 2 m from B and with a concentrated load of 2 kN at 1 m from A.*

**Solution :**                                        **(B.T.E. S-2009/4 Marks)**

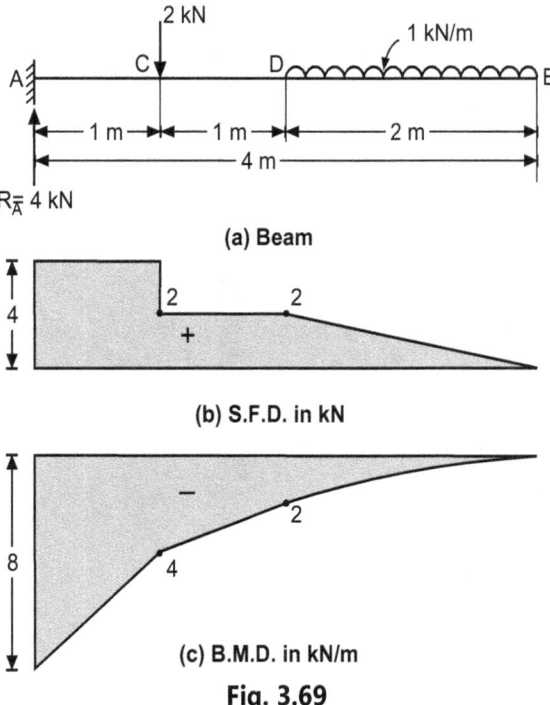

(a) Beam

(b) S.F.D. in kN

(c) B.M.D. in kN/m

**Fig. 3.69**

**Example 32 :** *Draw S.F. and B.M. diagrams for a cantilever beam AB of 4 m long having its fixed end at A and loaded with u.d.l. of 2 kN/m over entire span and point load of 3.5 kN acting upward at the free end of cantilever. Find the point of contraflexure if any.*

**(B.T.E. W-2008/4 Marks)**

**Solution :** Refer to Fig. 3.70.

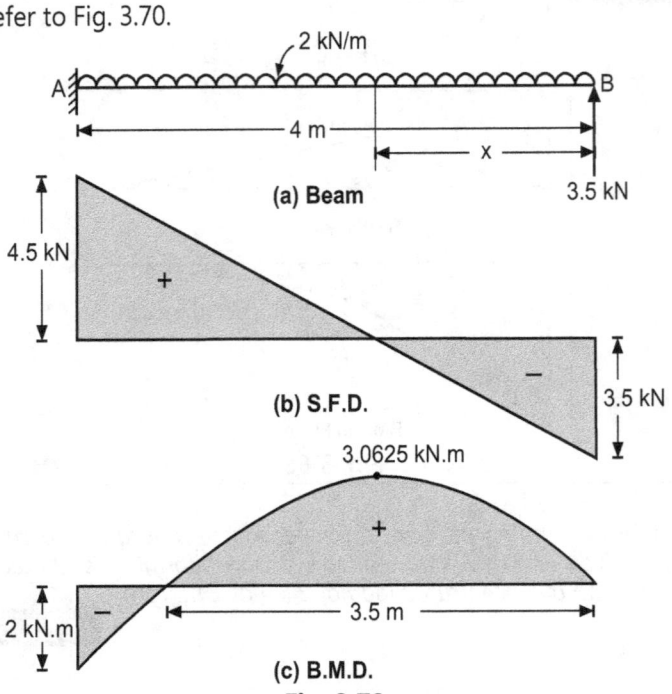

(a) Beam

(b) S.F.D.

(c) B.M.D.

**Fig. 3.70**

**(i)   To find $R_A$ :** The given type of beam is called as propped cantilever.

For the equilibrium of the beam,

$$R_A + 3.5 = 2 \times 4$$

∴                    $R_A = 8 - 3.5 = \textbf{4.5 kN}$

**(ii)  S.F. calculations :**

$$F_A = R_A = 4.5 \text{ kN}$$

$$F_B = 4.5 - (2 \times 4) = -3.5 \text{ kN}$$

S.F. at any section XX at a distance 'x' from B,

$$F_x = -3.5 + 2 \times x \qquad \qquad \text{... (i)}$$

Thus, the variation of S.F. is linear.

**To locate the point of zero S.F. :** Equating $F_x$ to zero, we have

$$-3.5 + 2 \times x = 0$$

$$2x = 3.5$$

∴                  $\boxed{x = \dfrac{3.5}{2} = 1.75 \text{ m}}$

∴    S.F. is zero at 1.75 m from B.

The S.F.D. is as shown in Fig. 3.70 (b).

### (iii) B.M. calculations :

$$M_B = 0$$

$$M_A = 3.5 \times 4 - (2 \times 4) \times \frac{4}{2} = -2 \text{ kN.m}$$

B.M. at any section XX at a distance x from B,

$$M_x = 3.5 \times x - (2 \times x) \times \frac{x}{2} = 3.5\,x - x^2 \qquad \qquad \ldots \text{(ii)}$$

Thus, the variation of B.M. is parabolic, as shown in Fig. 3.70 (c). B.M. is maximum at 1.75 m from B where S.F. changes its sign.

Substituting x = 1.75 m in equation (ii),

$$\mathbf{M_{max}} = M_{1.75} = 3.5 \times 1.75 - (1.75)^2$$
$$= 6.125 - 3.0625 = \mathbf{3.0625 \text{ kN.m}}$$

**To calculate the point of contraflexure :** Equating $M_x$ to zero, we have,

$$3.5x - x^2 = 0$$
$$x^2 = 3.5\,x$$
$$\mathbf{x = 3.5 \text{ m from B}}$$

The B.M.D. is as shown in Fig. 3.70 (c).

**Example 33 :** *Calculate the bending moment at 1 m from the fixed end for the cantilever beam loaded as shown in Fig. 3.71 (a). Draw BMD.* **(B.T.E. S-2004/4 Marks)**

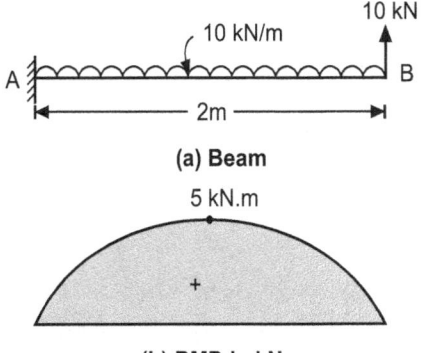

**(a) Beam**

**(b) BMD in kNm**

**Fig. 3.71**

**Solution : B.M. calculations :** B.M. at 1 m from fixed end (at centre)

$$\mathbf{M_C} = +10 \times 1 - (10 \times 1) \times \frac{1}{2} = \mathbf{+5 \text{ kN.m}}$$

$$M_B = 0$$

$$M_A = +10 \times 2 - (10 \times 2) \times \frac{2}{2} = 0$$

The B.M.D. is as shown in **Fig. 3.71 (b)**.

**Example 34 :** *A cantilever beam 2 m span has uniformly distributed load of 10 kN/m throughout the span. Draw SF and BM diagrams.* **(B.T.E. W-2003/4 Marks)**

**Solution :**

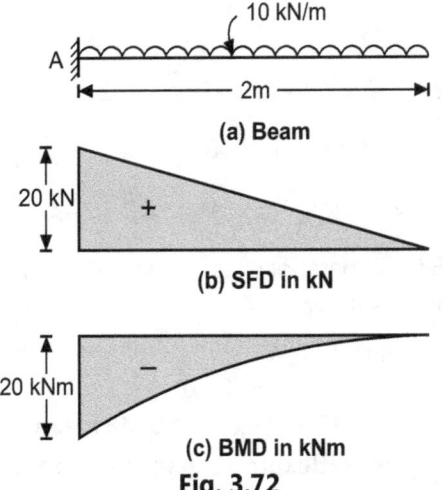

(a) Beam

(b) SFD in kN

(c) BMD in kNm

**Fig. 3.72**

**S.F. calculations :** S.F. at any section XX at a distance x from free end B,

$$F_x = +10 \times x. \text{ The variation of S.F. is linear.}$$

At B,          $x = 0$

∴          $F_B = 10 \times 0 = 0$

At A,          $x = 2$ m

∴          $F_A = 10 \times 2 = 20$ kN

The S.F.D. is as shown in **Fig. 3.72 (b)**.

**B.M. calculations :** B.M. at any section XX at a distance x from free end B,

$$M_x = -10 \times x \times \frac{x}{2} = -5x^2. \text{ The variation of B.M. is parabolic}$$

At B,          $x = 0$

∴          $M_B = -5 \times (0)^2 = 0$

At A,          $x = 2$ m

∴          $M_A = -5 \times (2)^2 = -20$ kN.m.  The B.M.D. is as shown in **Fig. 3.72 (c)**.

**Example 35 :** *A cantilever of 2 m length is subjected to a u.d.l. of 3 kN.m on the entire length. Calculate the maximum bending moment and maximum shear force.*

**(B.T.E. S-2006/2 Marks)**

**Solution :**

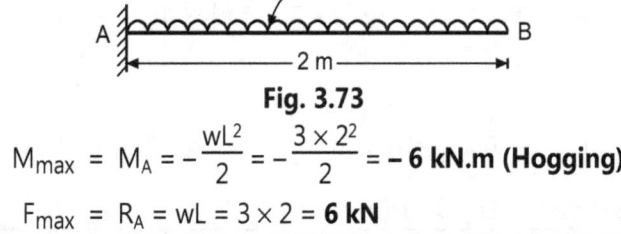

**Fig. 3.73**

$$M_{max} = M_A = -\frac{wL^2}{2} = -\frac{3 \times 2^2}{2} = -6 \text{ kN.m (Hogging)}$$

$$F_{max} = R_A = wL = 3 \times 2 = \textbf{6 kN}$$

**Example 36 :** *Draw S.F. and B.M. diagrams for a cantilever 2 m long subjected to a u.d.l. of 20 kN/m for a distance of 1.5 m from the fixed end.* **(B.T.E. W-1997/4 Marks)**

**Solution : (i)     $R_A$** = Total downward load

= $20 \times 1.5$ = **30 kN** ($\uparrow$)

**(ii)  S.F. calculations :**

$F_A$ = $R_A$ = 30 kN

$F_B = F_{B_L} = F_{B_R}$ = $30 - 20 \times 1.5$ = 0 kN

It remains constant from B to C.

$F_C$ = 0

The S.F.D. is as shown in Fig. 3.74 (b).

**(iii) B.M. calculations :**

$$M_A = -\frac{wL^2}{2}$$

$$= -\frac{20 \times 1.5^2}{2}$$

$$= -22.5 \text{ kN.m}$$

$M_B$ = 0,

$M_C$ = 0

The B.M.D. is as shown in Fig. 3.74 (c).

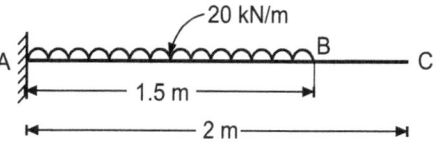

**(a) Beam**

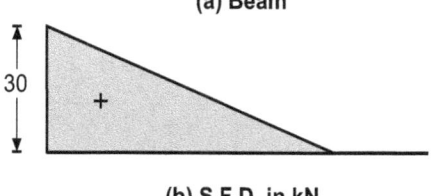

**(b) S.F.D. in kN**

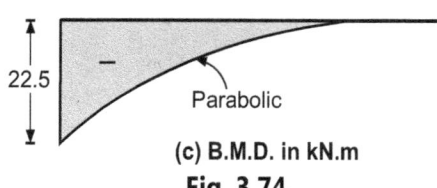

**(c) B.M.D. in kN.m**

**Fig. 3.74**

**Example 37 :** *A cantilever of 2.5 m length carries a point load of 10 kN at free end and u.d.l. of 5 kN/m for a distance of 1 m from free end. Draw S.F. and B.M. diagrams.*

**(B.T.E. W-1999/4 Marks)**

**Solution :**

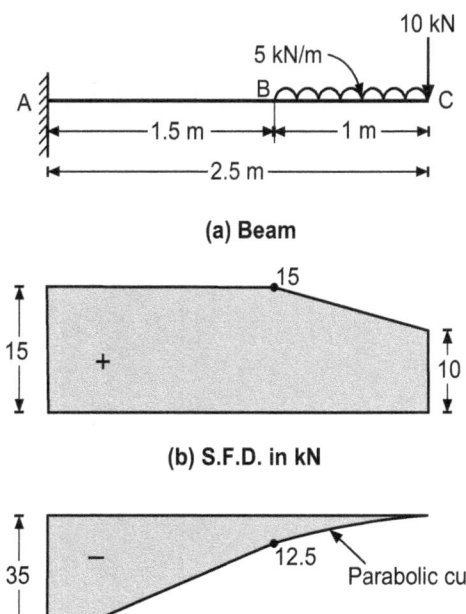

**(a) Beam**

**(b) S.F.D. in kN**

**(c) B.M.D. in kN.m**

**Fig. 3.75**

**Similar example for practice :**

**Example 38 :** *A cantilever beam 4 m long carries a u.d.l. of 2 kN/m over 2 m from free end and a point load of 4 kN at free end. Draw S.F. and B.M. diagrams.* **(B.T.E. S-2010/4 Marks)**

**Solution :**

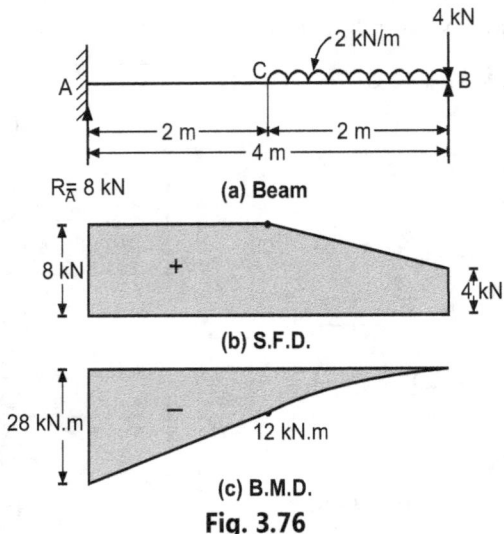

**Fig. 3.76**

**Example 39 :** *For the cantilever as shown in Fig. 3.77 (a), complete the shear force diagram and draw bending moment diagram.* **(B.T.E. W-2003/4 Marks)**

**Solution :**

**(i)  Calculations of S.F. :**

Let us start the calculation work from the free end.

S.F. at any section between A and B,

$F_x = 8$ kN

(It remains constant from A to B)

S.F. at any section between B and C,

$F_x = 8 + 7 = 15$ kN

(It remains constant from B to C)

S.F. at any section between C and D,

$F_x = 8 + 7 + 5 = 20$ kN

(It remains constant from C to D)

The completed S.F.D. is as shown in Fig. 3.77 (b).

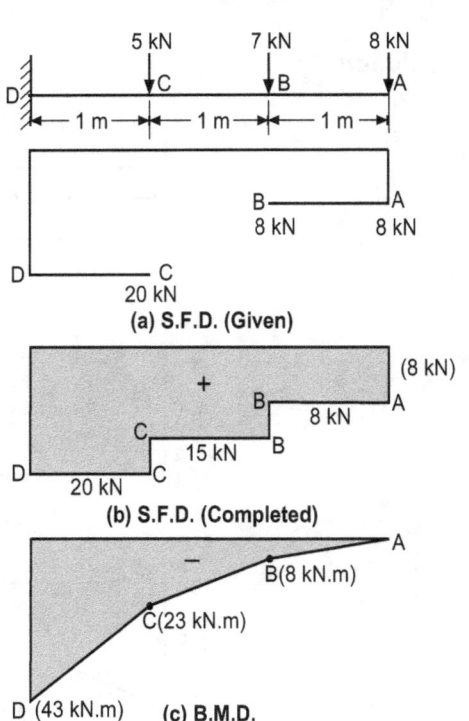

**Fig. 3.77**

**Note :**

(i)  Here positive shear forces are plotted below base line.

(ii)  Negative bending moments are plotted below base line.

**(ii) Calculations of B.M. :** At the free end A, $M_A = 0$.

$$M_B = -8 \times 1 = -8 \text{ kN·m (negative since hogging)}$$

$$M_C = -8 \times 2 - 7 \times 1 = -16 - 7 = -23 \text{ kN·m}$$

$$M_D = -8 \times 3 - 7 \times 2 - 5 \times 1 = -24 - 14 - 5 = -43 \text{ kN·m}$$

The B.M.D. is as shown in Fig. 3.77 (c).

**Example 40 :** *A cantilever 2.4 m long carries point loads of 20 kN and 50 kN at free end and 1.68 m from free end respectively. It also carries uniformly distributed load of 30 kN/m starting from 0.24 m to 1.2 m from free end. Draw S.F.D. and B.M.D.*

**(B.T.E. W-2004, S-2003/4 Marks)**

**Solution :**

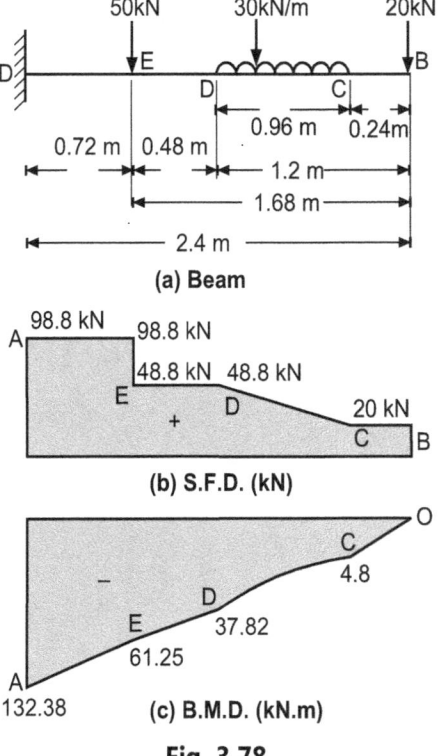

**Fig. 3.78**

**Example 41 :** *Draw B.M. and S.F. diagrams for the beam shown in Fig. 3.79 (a).*

**(B.T.E. W-2011/4 Marks)**

**Solution :**

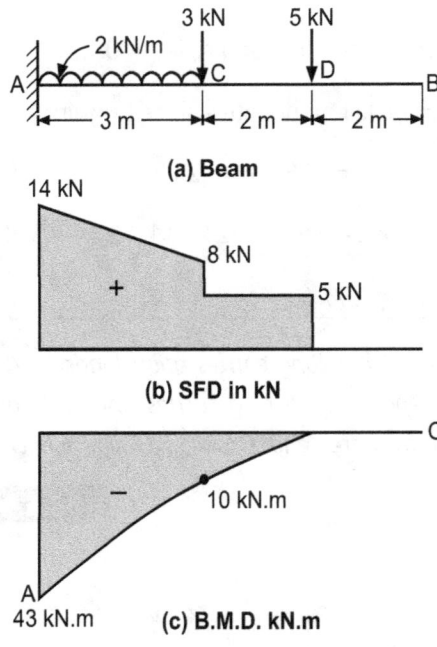

(a) Beam

(b) SFD in kN

(c) B.M.D. kN.m

**Fig. 3.79**

**(i)　To find $R_A$ :**　　　$R_A$ = Total downward load = $2 \times 3 + 3 + 5 =$ **14 kN** ↑

**(ii)　S.F. calculations :**　$F_A = R_A = 14$ kN

$$F_{C_L} = 14 - 2 \times 3 = 8 \text{ kN}$$

$$F_{C_R} = 14 - 2 \times 3 - 3 = 5 \text{ kN. It remains constant from C to D.}$$

∴　　　　　　　　$F_{D_L} = 14 - 2 \times 3 - 3 = 5$ kN

$$F_{D_R} = 14 - 2 \times 3 - 3 - 5 = 0. \text{ It remains constant from D to B.}$$

$$F_B = 0$$

**(iii)　B.M. calculations :**　$M_B = 0$

$$M_D = 0$$

$$M_C = -5 \times 2 = -10 \text{ kN.m}$$

$$M_A = -(2 \times 3) \times \frac{3}{2} - 3 \times 3 - 5 \times 5 = -43 \text{ kN.m}$$

**Example 42 :** *For the beam shown in Fig. 3.80 (a), draw shear force diagram indicating all important values.* **(B.T.E. W-2005/4 Marks)**

**Solution :**

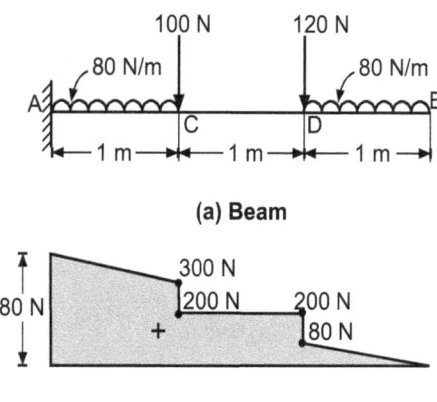

**(a) Beam**

**(b) S.F.D.**

**Fig. 3.80**

**Example 43 :** *A cantilever is loaded as shown in Fig. 3.81 (a). Draw the S.F. diagram and calculate the B.M. at point C.* **(B.T.E. S-2004/4 Marks)**

**Solution :**

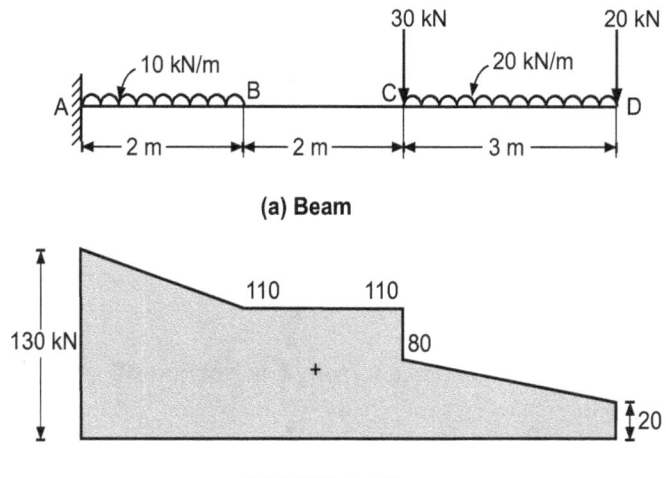

**(a) Beam**

**(b) S.F.D. in kN**

**Fig. 3.81**

The S.F.D. is as shown in **Fig. 3.81 (b)**.

**Answer :** | **B.M. at C :** $M_C = -20 \times 3 - 20 \times 3 \times \dfrac{3}{2} = $ **–150 kN·m (Hogging)**

**Example 44 :** *Draw the bending moment diagram for the cantilever loaded as shown in Fig. 3.82 (a).* **(B.T.E. S-2005/4 Marks)**

**Solution : B.M. calculations :** At free end D, $M_D = 0$.

$$M_C = -30 \times 0.4 - (50 \times 0.4)\left(\frac{0.4}{2}\right) = -16 \text{ N.m}$$

$$M_B = -30 \times 0.6 - (50 \times 0.4)\left(\frac{0.4}{2} + 0.2\right) + 50 \times 0.2 = -16 \text{ N.m}$$

$$M_A = -30 \times 1 - (50 \times 0.4)\left(\frac{0.4}{2} + 0.6\right) + 50 \times 0.6 + 90 \times 0.4$$

$$- (100 \times 0.4)\left(\frac{0.4}{2}\right) = 12 \text{ N.m}$$

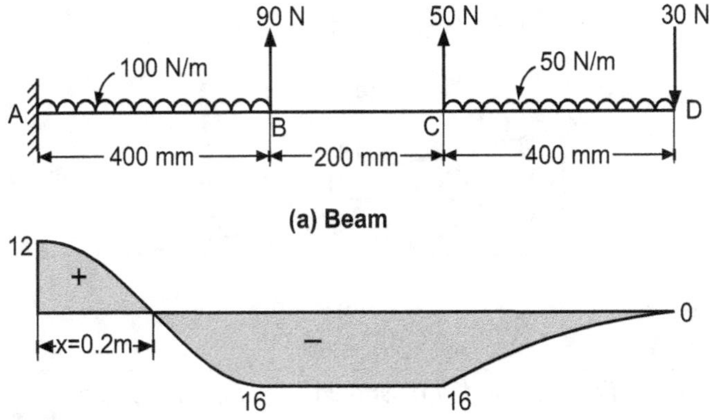

(a) Beam

(b) B.M.D. in N.m

**Fig. 3.82**

**Point of contraflexure in portion AB :** Let us calculate $R_A$. Assume $R_A$ as vertically upwards.

$$R_A + 90 + 50 = 100 \times 0.4 + 50 \times 0.4 + 30$$

$$R_A + 140 = 40 + 20 + 30$$

$$R_A = -50 \text{ N}$$

Negative sign of $R_A$ indicates that, it acts downwards.

$$\therefore \qquad R_A = 50 \text{ N} (\downarrow)$$

**B.M. at any section XX at a distance x from A in portion AB,**

$$M_X = -50 \times x - 100 \times x \times \frac{x}{2} + M_A$$

At point of contraflexure, $M_X = 0$.

$$\therefore \quad -50x - 100\frac{x^2}{2} - 12 = 0$$

Dividing both sides by $-50$,

$$x^2 + x - 0.24 = 0.$$

This is a quadratic in x.

Comparing this equation with $ax^2 + bx + c = 0$, $a = 1$, $b = 1$, $c = -0.24$

$$\therefore \qquad x = \frac{-b \pm \sqrt{b^2 - 4ac}}{2a}$$

$$= \frac{-1 \pm \sqrt{(1)^2 - 4 \times 1 \times (-0.24)}}{2 \times 1}$$

$$= \frac{-1 \pm \sqrt{1 + 0.96}}{2} = \frac{-1 \pm \sqrt{1.96}}{2} = \frac{-1 \pm 1.4}{2}$$

∴          $x = \frac{-1 + 1.4}{2}$ or $x = \frac{-1 - 1.4}{2}$

∴          $x = \frac{0.4}{2}$ or $x = \frac{-2.4}{2}$

∴          $x = 0.2$ m or $x = -1.2$ m

But          $x = -1.2$ m is not possible.

∴          $\boxed{x = 0.2 \text{ m}}$

The B.M. is zero at 0.2 m from A.

The B.M.D. is as shown in **Fig. 3.82 (b)**.

---

**Example 45 :** *A load of 100 kN is placed on a cantilever bracket as shown in Fig. 3.83. If the bracket also has the self weight of 10 kN/m, find loading on the bracket and draw S.F.D. for the bracket. Using S.F.D. find shear force at 0.5 m from fixed end.* **(B.T.E. W-2004/4 Marks)**

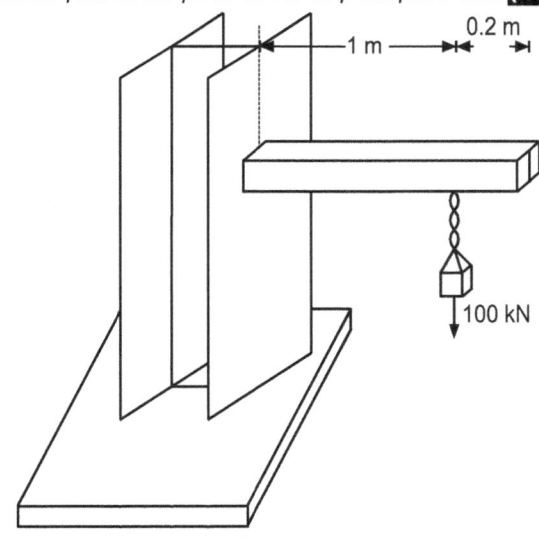

**Fig. 3.83**

**Solution :** The loading on the cantilever beam is as shown in **Fig. 3.84 (a)**.

**(i)  Calculation of $R_A$ :** $R_A = 10 \times 1.2 + 100 = 112$ kN

**(ii)  Calculations of S.F. :**

$$F_A = R_A = 112 \text{ kN}$$

$$F_{C_L} = 112 - 10 \times 1 = 102 \text{ kN}$$

$$F_{C_R} = 112 - 10 \times 1 - 100 = 2 \text{ kN}$$

$$F_B = F_{B_L} = F_{B_R} = 112 - 10 \times 1 - 100 - 100 \times 0.2 = 0$$

(**Check :** $F_B$ = load at B = 0)

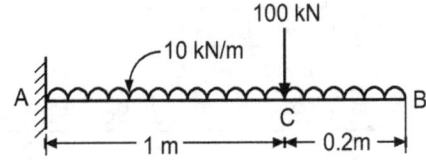

**(a) Loading on the beam**

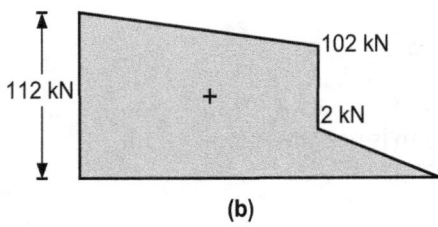

**(b)**

**Fig. 3.84**

### (iii) S.F. at 0.5 m from fixed end A :

$$F_{0.5\ m} = 112 - 10 \times 0.5 = 112 - 5 = \textbf{107 kN}$$

The S.F.D. is as shown in **Fig. 3.84 (b)**.

### Similar example for practice :

**Example 46 :** *A cantilever of 3 m carries a u.d.l. of 4 kN/m over the entire span and a point load of 5 kN at 2 m from the support. Draw S.F. and B.M. diagrams.*

**(B.T.E. S-2011/4 Marks)**

**Solution :**

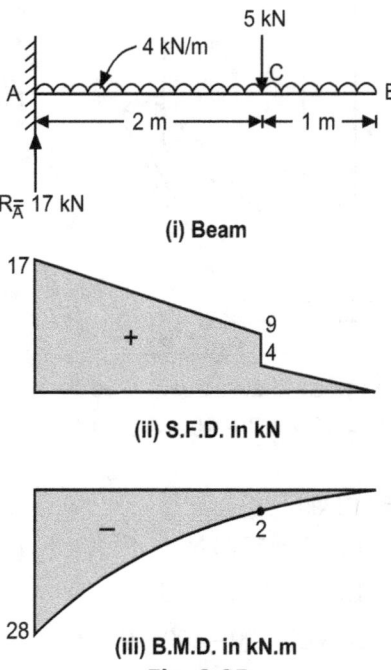

**(i) Beam**

**(ii) S.F.D. in kN**

**(iii) B.M.D. in kN.m**

**Fig. 3.85**

## Type 5 : S.F.D. and B.M.D. for overhanging beams subjected to u.d.l. and point load :

**Example 47 :** *A beam is supported and loaded as shown in Fig. 3.86 (a). Draw S.F. and B.M. diagrams and locate the point of contraflexure if any.* **(B.T.E. S-2013, 2001/8 Marks)**

**Solution :**

**(i) Support reactions :** Taking moments about A,

$$R_B \times 6 = (20 \times 6) \times \frac{6}{2} + 50 \times 7 = 710$$

$$\therefore \qquad R_B = \frac{710}{6} = 118.33 \text{ kN}$$

$$\therefore \qquad R_A = \text{Total load} - R_B = (20 \times 6) + 50 - 118.33 = 51.67 \text{ kN}$$

**(ii) S.F. calculations :**

$$F_A = + R_A = 51.67 \text{ kN}$$

S.F. just to the left of B,

$$F_{B_L} = 51.67 - 20 \times 6 = -68.33 \text{ kN}$$

S.F. just to the right of B,

$$F_{B_R} = 51.67 - 20 \times 6 + R_B = 51.67 - 120 + 118.33 = + 50 \text{ kN}$$

(Since there is no load between B and C, 50 kN remains constant from B to C. i.e. $F_C = 50$ kN) (**Check :** $F_C$ = load at C = 50 kN)

The S.F.D. is as shown in Fig. 3.86 (b).

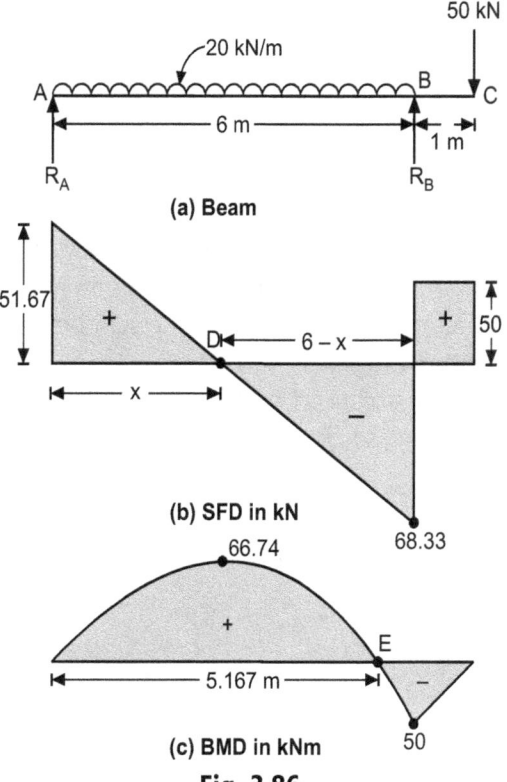

**(a) Beam**

**(b) SFD in kN**

**(c) BMD in kNm**

**Fig. 3.86**

**(iii) B.M. calculations :** At simply supported end A, $M_A = 0$

Overhanging portion BC behaves like a cantilever, as shown in Fig. 3.86 (d).

$\therefore \qquad\qquad M_B = -50 \times 1 = -50$ kN·m (Hogging)

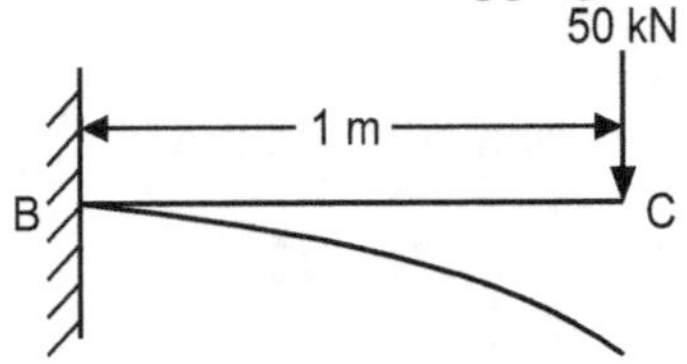

**Fig. 3.86 (d)**

Bending moment at B can also be calculated by considering the moments of all forces acting on left of B.

$$M_B = 51.67 \times 6 - (20 \times 6) \times \frac{6}{2} = -49.98 \cong -50 \text{ kN·m (Hogging)}$$

At free end C, $M_C = 0$          ... (since there is no load to the right of C)

Since there is u.d.l. between A and B, B.M. diagrams for portion AB will be a parabolic curve. Maximum height of the parabolic curve will be $M_{max}$. At point D in S.F. diagram, S.F. changes its sign from positive to negative. Therefore, $M_{max}$ will occur at D. Let 'x' be the distance of D from A.

**To find x :** From similar triangles in S.F.D. as shown in Fig. 3.86 (b),

$$\frac{x}{51.67} = \frac{6-x}{68.33}$$

$\therefore \qquad 68.33\,x = 310.02 - 51.67\,x$

$\therefore \qquad 120\,x = 310.02$

$\therefore \qquad x = 2.583$ m

$\therefore \quad M_D = M_{max} = 51.67 \times 2.583 - (20 \times 2.583) \times \dfrac{2.583}{2} = 66.74$ kN·m

The B.M. diagram is as shown in Fig. 3.86 (c). From the B.M. diagram, it can be seen that the maximum positive (sagging) B.M. takes place at D in simply supported span AB and the maximum negative B.M. takes place at the overhanging support B.

**To locate the point of contraflexure :**

The point of contraflexure occurs in portion AB. Let 'x' be the distance of point of contraflexure 'E' from A. Assuming section XX at E,

$$M_X = M_E = 51.67 \times x - (20 \times x) \times \left(\frac{x}{2}\right) = 51.67 \times x - 20 \times \frac{x^2}{2}$$

At the point of contraflexure, the B.M. is zero.

$\therefore \qquad M_X = M_E = 0$ gives,

$51.67 \times x - 20 \times \dfrac{x^2}{2} = 0$

$\therefore \qquad 51.67 - 10\,x = 0$

$\therefore \qquad\qquad x = 5.167$ m

(**Check :** $0 < x < 6$ m i.e. the point of contraflexure lies between A and B)

**Example 48 :** *A beam ABC, 6 m long is supported at A and B, 4 m apart. BC = 2 m. The beam carries a u.d.l. of 20 kN/m over the entire length alongwith a downward point load of 10 kN at C. Plot S.F.D. and B.M.D. for the beam and locate the point of contraflexure.*

**(V.V. Imp./4 Marks)**

**Solution : (i) Support reactions :** Taking moments about A,

$$R_B \times 4 = (20 \times 6) \times \frac{6}{2} + 10 \times 6 = 420$$

$\therefore$           $R_B = 105$ kN

$\therefore$           $R_A = $ Total load $- R_B = (20 \times 6 + 10) - 105 = 25$ kN

**(ii) S.F. calculations :**

$$F_A = + R_A = 25 \text{ kN}$$

$$F_{B_L} = 25 - 20 \times 4 = -55 \text{ kN}$$

$$F_{B_R} = 25 - 20 \times 4 + 105 = 50 \text{ kN}$$

$$F_C = 25 - 20 \times 4 + 105 - 20 \times 2 = 10 \text{ kN}$$

(**Check :** $F_C = $ load at C)

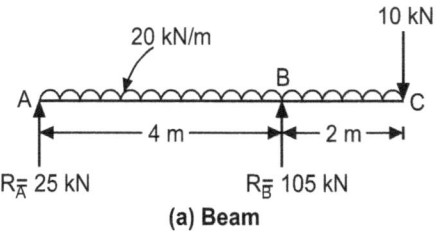

**(a) Beam**

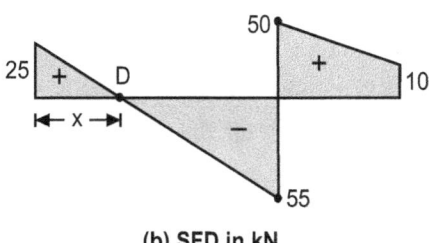

**(b) SFD in kN**

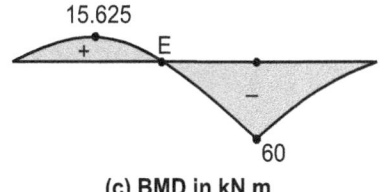

**(c) BMD in kN m**

**Fig. 3.87**

**To locate the point of zero S.F. :**

Let 'x' be the distance of D from A. From the similar triangles in S.F.D., we have

$$\frac{x}{25} = \frac{4-x}{55}$$

$$\therefore \qquad 55\,x = 100 - 25\,x$$
$$\therefore \qquad 80\,x = 100 \text{ i.e. } x = 1.25 \text{ m}$$

The maximum B.M. will occur at D.

The S.F.D. is as shown in Fig. 3.87 (b).

### (iii) B.M. calculations :

$$M_A = 0, \ M_C = 0$$

By considering the cantilever action of portion BC,

$$M_B = -(20 \times 2) \times \frac{2}{2} - 10 \times 2 = -60 \text{ kN-m}$$

$$M_D = M_{max} = 25 \times 1.25 - (20 \times 1.25) \times \frac{1.25}{2} = 15.625 \text{ kN·m}$$

The B.M.D. is as shown in Fig. 3.87 (c).

From the S.F.D., it can be seen that S.F. changes its sign at the points D and B. Therefore, the maximum B.M. will occur at these two points. But note that the maximum positive B.M. occurs at D in simply supported span AB and the maximum negative B.M. occurs at the overhanging support B.

### To locate the point of contraflexure E :

Let x be the distance of E from A.

$$M_X = M_E = 25 \times x - (20 \times x) \times \left(\frac{x}{2}\right) = 25 \times x - 10 \times x^2$$

Equating $M_X$ to the zero, we have

$$25 \times x - 10 \times x^2 = 0$$
$$\therefore \qquad 25 - 10 \times x = 0$$
$$\therefore \qquad 10x = 25 \text{ i.e. } x = 2.5\text{m}$$

(**Check :** 0 < x < 4m i.e. the point of contraflexure lies between A and B)

**Example 49 :** *Write the BM equation for the beam loaded as shown in Fig. 3.88 (a) and draw B.M.D.* **(B.T.E. W-2004/4 Marks)**

### Solution : (i) Support reactions :

$$\circlearrowleft \quad \circlearrowleft$$
$$R_B \times 3 = 15 \times 4$$
$$\therefore \qquad R_B = 20 \text{ kN}$$
$$\therefore \qquad R_A + R_B = 15$$
$$\therefore \qquad R_A = 15 - R_B = 15 - 20 = \textbf{-5 kN} = 5 \text{ kN } (\downarrow)$$

**(ii) B.M. equation :** Let us assume section XX at a distance 'x' from A in portion AB.

$$M_X = \text{B.M. at section XX} = -5x \qquad\qquad \text{... (i)}$$

Now, let us assume section XX at a distance 'x' from A in portion BC.

$$M_X = \text{B.M. at section XX} = -5x + 20\,(x - 3) \qquad\qquad \text{... (ii)}$$

Equation (ii) can be written as,

$$M_X = -5x \ \vdots + 20\,(x - 3)$$
$$(AB) \ \vdots \ (BC)$$

The equation upto first dotted line is valid if section XX is taken in portion AB and the entire expression is valid if section XX is taken in portion BC.

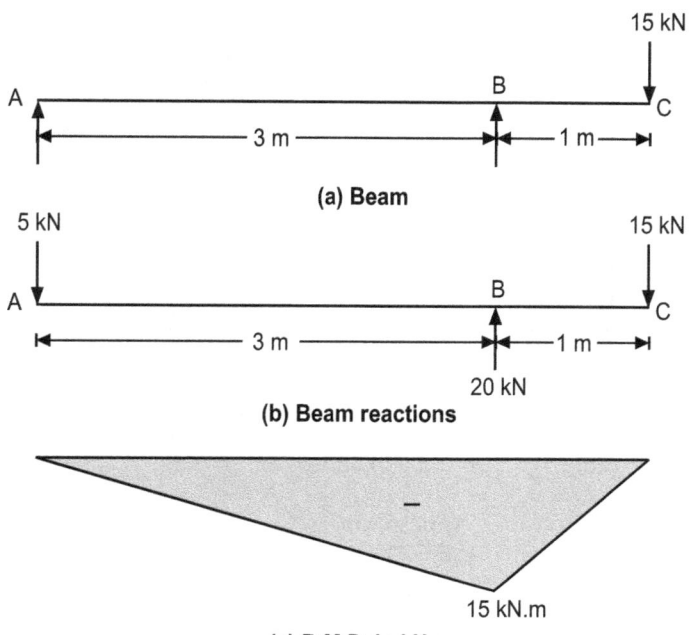

(a) Beam

(b) Beam reactions

(c) B.M.D. in kN.m

**Fig. 3.88**

**(iii) Calculations of B.M. :** For portion AB, $M_x = -5x$

At A, $x = 0$    $\therefore$   $\boxed{M_A = -5 \times 0 = 0}$

At B, $x = 3$ m $\therefore$   $\boxed{M_B = -5 \times 3 = -15 \text{ kN.m}}$

For portion BC,    $M_x = -5x + 20\,(x - 3)$

At C, $x = 4$ m $\therefore$   $\boxed{M_C = -5 \times 4 + 20\,(4 - 3) = 0}$

The B.M.D. is as shown in **Fig. 3.88 (c)**.

---

**Example 50 :** *A simply supported beam having an overhang at one side carry u.d.l. of intensity 10 kN/m as shown in Fig. 3.89 (a). Draw S.F. and B.M. diagrams for the beam.*

**(B.T.E. W-2012/4 Marks)**

**Solution :**

**(i) Support reactions :** Taking moments @ A,

$$R_B \times 4 = 10 \times 5 \times \frac{5}{2} = 125$$

$$\mathbf{R_B = 31.25 \text{ kN}}$$

$\therefore$      $R_A$ = Total load $- R_B = 10 \times 5 - 31.25 = 50 - 31.25 = 18.75$ kN

**(ii) S.F. calculations :** $F_A = 18.75$ kN

$$F_{B_L} = 18.75 - 10 \times 4 = -21.25 \text{ kN}$$

$$F_{B_R} = 18.75 - 10 \times 4 + 31.25 = 10 \text{ kN}$$

$$F_C = 18.75 - 10 \times 4 + 31.25 - 10 \times 1 = 0$$

(**Check :** $F_C$ = load at C = 0)

The S.F.D. is as shown in **Fig. 3.89 (b)**.

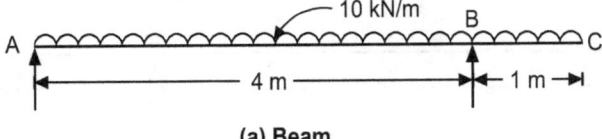

(a) Beam

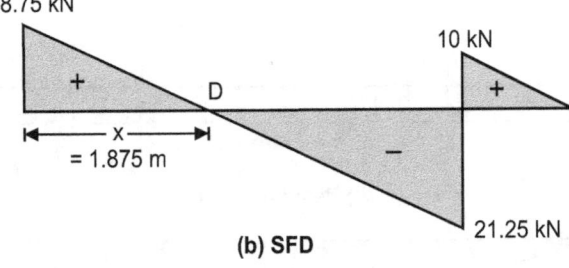

(b) SFD

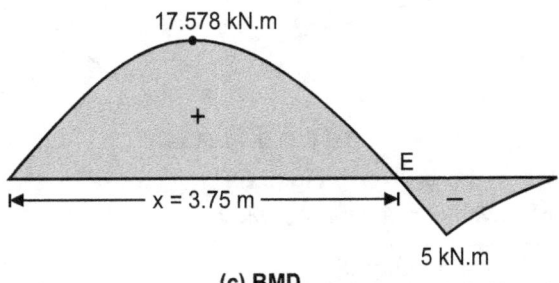

(c) BMD

**Fig. 3.89**

**(iii)** **B.M. calculations :** At simple support A, $M_A = 0$

$$M_B = -(10 \times 1) \times \left(\frac{1}{2}\right) = -5 \text{ kN.m}$$

At free end C, $M_C = 0$.

**(iv)** **Point of zero S.F. (Location of maximum B.M.) :**

Let AD = x.

S.F. at section at a distance x from A,

$$F_x = 18.75 - 10 \times x = 0$$

$$10x = 18.75 \quad \therefore \quad \boxed{x = 1.875 \text{ m (i.e. AD = 1.875 m)}}$$

(x can also be calculated by considering similar triangles in S.F.D. as follows :

$$\frac{18.75}{x} = \frac{21.25}{4 - x}$$

$$18.75 (4 - x) = 21.25 \, x$$

$$75 - 18.75 \, x = 21.25 \, x$$

$$75 = 18.75 \, x + 21.25 \, x = 40 \, x$$

$$\therefore \qquad \mathbf{x = \frac{75}{40} = 1.875 \text{ m}}$$

Hence maximum B.M. occurs at 1.875 m from A.

**(v) Magnitude of maximum B.M. :**

$$\therefore \quad M_{max} = M_{1.875} = R_A \times x - 10 \times x \times \frac{x}{2}$$

$$= 18.75 \times 1.875 - 10 \times 1.875 \times \frac{1.875}{2}$$

$$= \textbf{17.578 kN.m}$$

The B.M.D. is as shown in Fig. 3.89 (c).

**(vi) Point of contraflexure :** Let the point of contraflexure 'E' is at a distance x from A.

$$M_x = 18.75 \times x - 10 \times x \times \frac{x}{2} = 0$$

$$\therefore \quad \textbf{x = 3.75 m from A (i.e. AE = 3.75 m)}$$

## Try Yourself :

**Example 51 :** *Draw the bending moment and shear force diagrams for the beam loaded as shown in Fig. 3.90 (a). Determine the location and magnitude of the maximum bending moment and mark it clearly on the bending moment diagram.* **(B.T.E. S-2006/8 Marks)**

**Solution :**

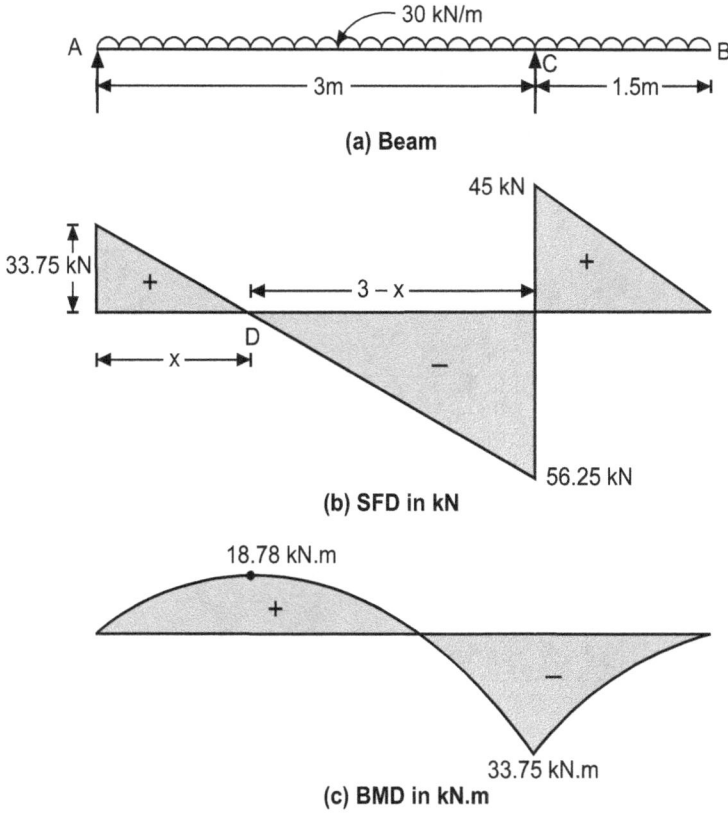

(a) Beam

(b) SFD in kN

(c) BMD in kN.m

**Fig. 3.90**

**Example 52 :** *Draw shear force and bending moment diagram for an overhanging beam as shown in* ***Fig. 3.91 (a).***　　　**(B.T.E. S-2007/8 Marks)**

**Solution :　(i) Support reactions :** Taking moments about A,

$$R_B \times 5 = 5 \times 2 + (8 \times 7) \times \frac{7}{2} + 5 \times 7 = 241$$

$$\therefore \qquad R_B = \frac{241}{5} = 48.5 \text{ kN}$$

$$\therefore \qquad R_A = [5 + (8 \times 7) + 5] - 48.5 = 17.5 \text{ kN}$$

**(ii)　S.F. calculations :**

$$F_A = +R_A = 17.5 \text{ kN}$$

$$F_{D_L} = 17.5 - 8 \times 2 = 1.5 \text{ kN}$$

$$F_{D_R} = 17.5 - 8 \times 2 - 5 = -3.5 \text{ kN}$$

$$F_{B_L} = 17.5 - 8 \times 2 - 5 - 8 \times 3 = -27.5 \text{ kN}$$

$$F_{B_R} = 17.5 - 8 \times 2 - 5 - 8 \times 3 + 48.5 = 21 \text{ kN}$$

$$F_C = 17.5 - 8 \times 2 - 5 - 8 \times 3 + 48.5 - 8 \times 2 = 5 \text{ kN}$$

(**Check :** $F_C$ = load at C = 5 kN)

The S.F.D. is as shown in **Fig. 3.91 (b).**

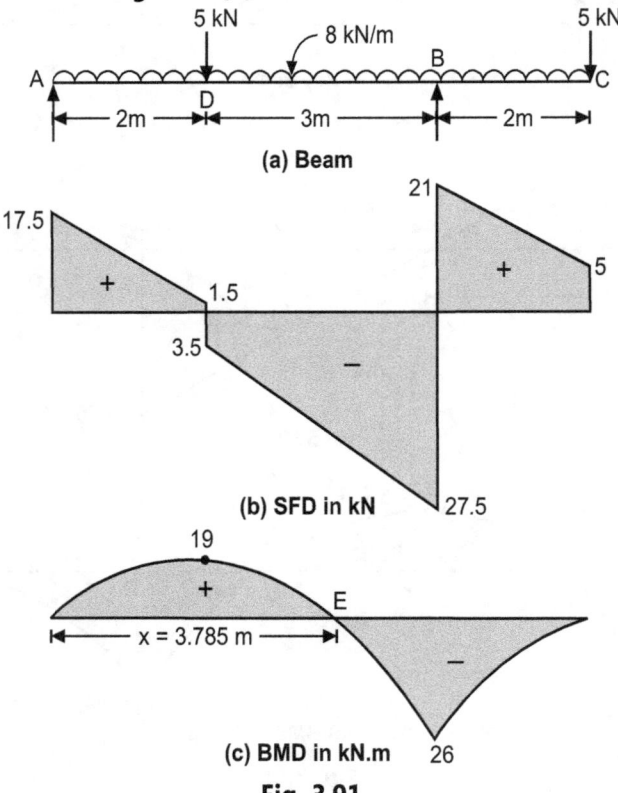

**(a) Beam**

**(b) SFD in kN**

**(c) BMD in kN.m**

**Fig. 3.91**

### (iii) B.M. calculations :

$$M_A = M_C = 0$$

$$M_D = 17.5 \times 2 - (8 \times 2) \times \frac{2}{2} = 19 \text{ kN.m}$$

$$M_B = -5 \times 2 - (8 \times 2) \times \frac{2}{2} = -26 \text{ kN.m}$$

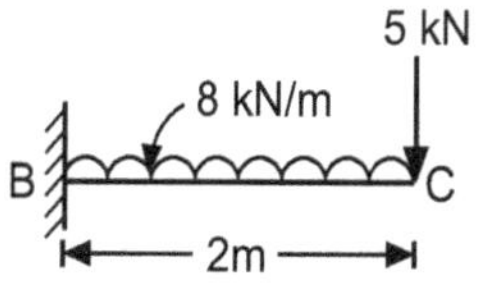

**Fig. 3.91 (d)**

**(iv) Point of contraflexure :** Let 'x' be the distance of point of contraflexure 'E' from A.

$$M_X = M_E = 17.5 \times x - (8 \times x) \times \frac{x}{2} - 5 \times (x - 2)$$

$$= 17.5x - 4x^2 - 5x + 10 = -4x^2 + 12.5x + 10$$

Now,　　　$M_X = M_E = 0$ gives

$$-4x^2 + 12.5x + 10 = 0$$

$$\therefore \quad x = \frac{-12.5 \sqrt{(12.5)^2 - 4 \times (-4) \times 10}}{2 \times (-4)} = \frac{-12.5 \pm 17.78}{-8}$$

$$\therefore \quad x = \frac{-12.5 + 17.78}{-8} \text{ or } x = \frac{-12.5 - 17.78}{-8}$$

$$\therefore \quad x = -0.66 \text{ m} \quad \text{or} \quad x = 3.785 \text{ m}$$

But, x cannot be negative　$\therefore$　x = 3.785 m from A.

(**Check :** 0 < x < 5 m i.e. the point of contraflexure lies between A and B.)

The B.M.D. is as shown in **Fig. 3.91 (c)**.

## Try Yourself :

**Example 53 :** *A beam ABCDEF is supported at B and F. There are two point loads of 40 kN and 45 kN at A and E. There is a load of 50 kN at D. Portion BCD carries a u.d.l. of 30 kN/m. AB = 2 m, BC = 3 m, CD = 1.5 m, DE = 2.5 m, EF = 2 m. Construct S.F. and B.M. diagrams for the beam and find the point of contraflexure.*　　　**(B.T.E. S-1992/8 Marks)**

**Solution :**

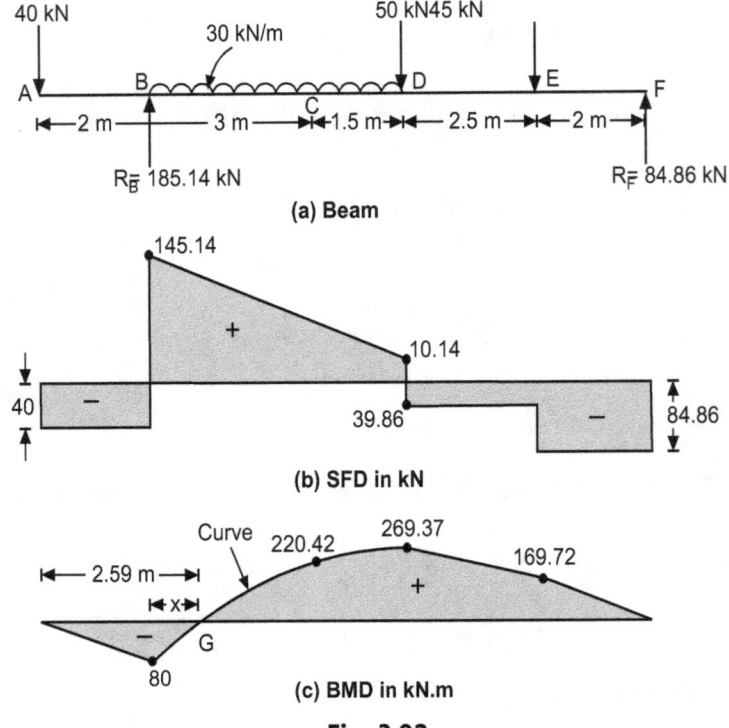

(a) Beam

(b) SFD in kN

(c) BMD in kN.m

**Fig. 3.92**

**Example 54 :** *A simply supported beam having equal overhangs on both sides and carrying point loads is shown in Fig. 3.93 (a). Draw S.F. diagram.* **(B.T.E. W-2012/4 Marks)**

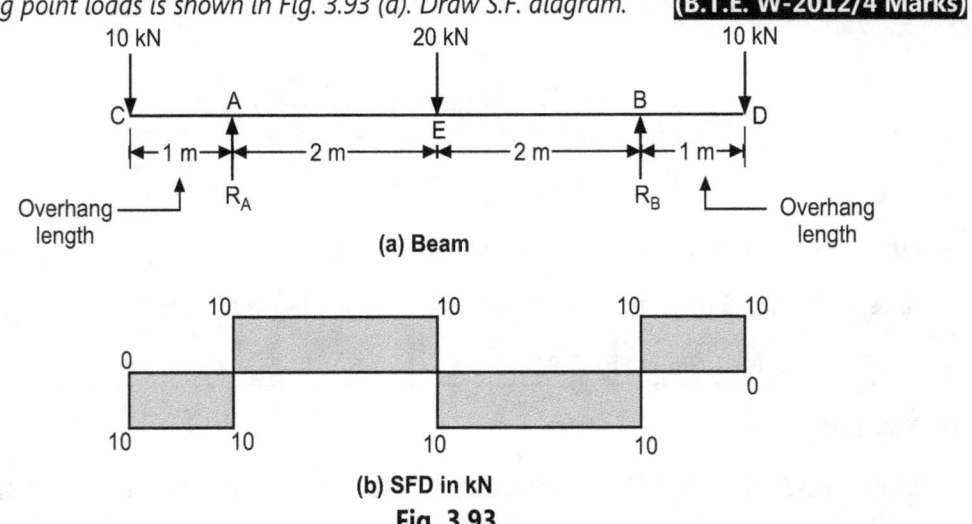

(a) Beam

(b) SFD in kN

**Fig. 3.93**

**Solution :**      $\Sigma M_A = 0$ (**sign convention :** ↻ +, ↺ –)

$$-10 \times 1 + 20 \times 2 + 10 \times 5 - R_B \times 4 = 0$$

∴        **$R_B$ = 20 kN**

$$\Sigma F_y = 0 \quad (\textbf{sign convention :} \uparrow +, \downarrow -)$$

$$R_A + R_B - 10 - 20 - 10 = 0$$

$\therefore \qquad R_A + R_B = 40$

$\therefore \qquad R_A + 20 = 40$

$\therefore \qquad \mathbf{R_A} = 40 - 20 = \mathbf{20\ kN}$

S.F. at any section in C and A = $-10$ kN

S.F. at any section in A and E = $-10 + R_A = -10 + 20 = 10$ kN

S.F. at any section in E and B = $-10 + R_A - 20 = -10 + 20 - 20 = -10$ kN

S.F. at any section in B and D = $-10 + R_A - 20 + R_B = -10 + 20 - 20 + 20 = 10$ kN

The S.F.D. is as shown in **Fig. 3.93 (b)**.

**Example 55 :** *Draw B.M. diagram for the given beam in above question and calculate the point of contraflexure if any. [Refer to Fig. 3.94 (a)].* (B.T.E. W-2012/4 Marks)

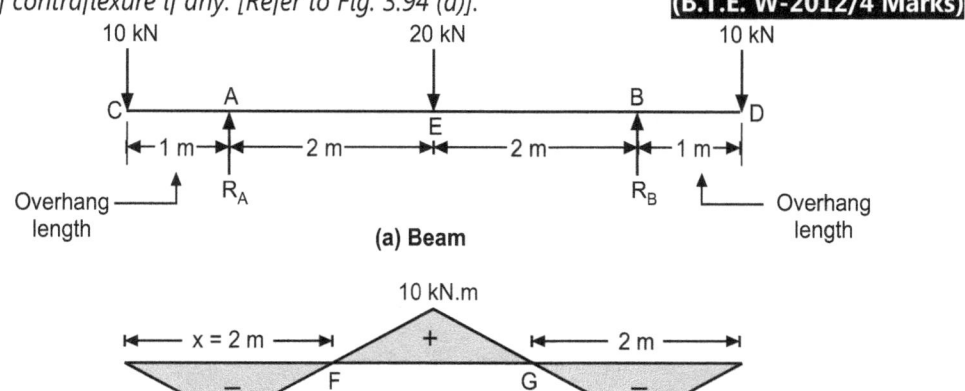

(a) Beam

(b) BMD

**Fig. 3.94**

**Solution : B.M. calculations :**

$$M_C = 0$$

$$M_A = -10 \times 1 = -10 \text{ kN.m (Hogging)}$$

$$M_E = -10 \times 3 + R_A \times 2 = -10 \times 3 + 20 \times 2 = 10 \text{ kN.m (Sagging)}$$

$$M_B = -10 \times 1 = -10 \text{ kN.m (Hogging)}$$

Let the point of contraflexure 'F' be at a distance 'x' from point C. [Refer to Fig. 3.94 (b)].
B.M. at a distance x from C,

$$M_x = -10 \times x + R_A \times (x-1) = -10x + 20(x-1)$$

At point of contraflexure, $M_x$ is zero.

$$-10 \times x + 20(x-1) = 0$$

$$-10x + 20x - 20 = 0$$

$\therefore \qquad 10x = 20$

$\therefore \qquad x = 2$ m from point C.

Due to symmetry, other point of contraflexure 'G' lies at a distance of 2 m from point D.

The B.M.D. is as shown in **Fig. 3.94 (b)**.

**Try Yourself :**

**Example 56 :** *Draw S.F. and B.M. diagrams for the overhanging beam as shown in Fig. 3.95 (a).* **(V.V. Imp./4 Marks)**

**Solution :**

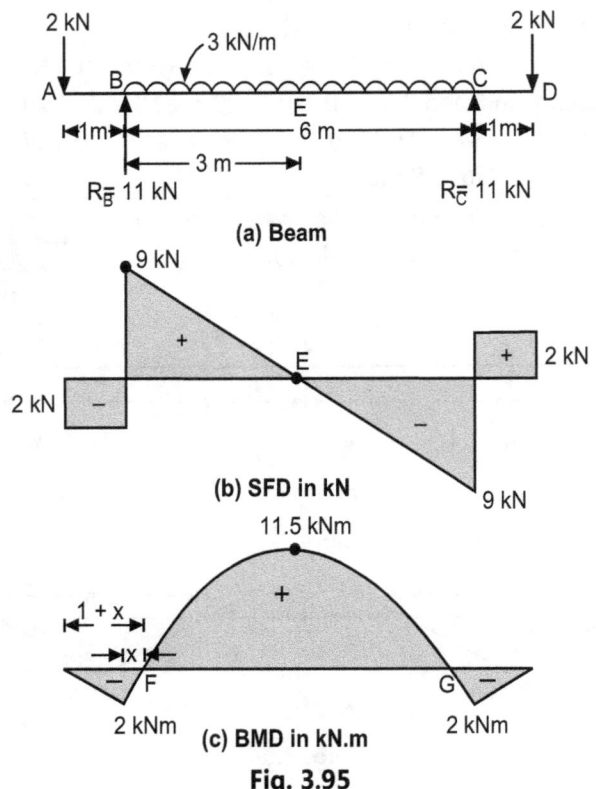

**(a) Beam**

**(b) SFD in kN**

**(c) BMD in kN.m**

**Fig. 3.95**

**Example 57 :** *Draw SF and BM diagrams for simply supported beam with equal overhangs and carrying uniformly distributed load of w per unit run over the whole length [Refer Fig. 3.96 (a)], where L > 2a. Find and mark the maximum B.M.* **(B.T.E. W-2004/8 Marks)**

**Solution :**

**(i)　Support reactions :**

Due to symmetry,　$R_B = R_C = \dfrac{\text{Total load}}{2} = \dfrac{wa + wL + wa}{2} = \dfrac{2wa + wL}{2} = wa + \dfrac{wL}{2}$

**(ii)　S.F. calculations :**

$$F_A = 0$$

$$F_{B_L} = -wa$$

$$F_{B_R} = -wa + R_B = -wa + \left(wa + \dfrac{wL}{2}\right) = \dfrac{wL}{2}$$

$$F_{C_L} = -wa + R_B - wL = -wa + \left(wa + \dfrac{wL}{2}\right) - wL = -\dfrac{wL}{2}$$

$$F_{C_R} = -wa + R_B - wL + R_C$$

$$= -wa + \left(wa + \frac{wL}{2}\right) - wL + \left(wa + \frac{wL}{2}\right) = wa$$

$$F_D = 0$$

The S.F.D. is as shown in **Fig. 3.96 (b)**.

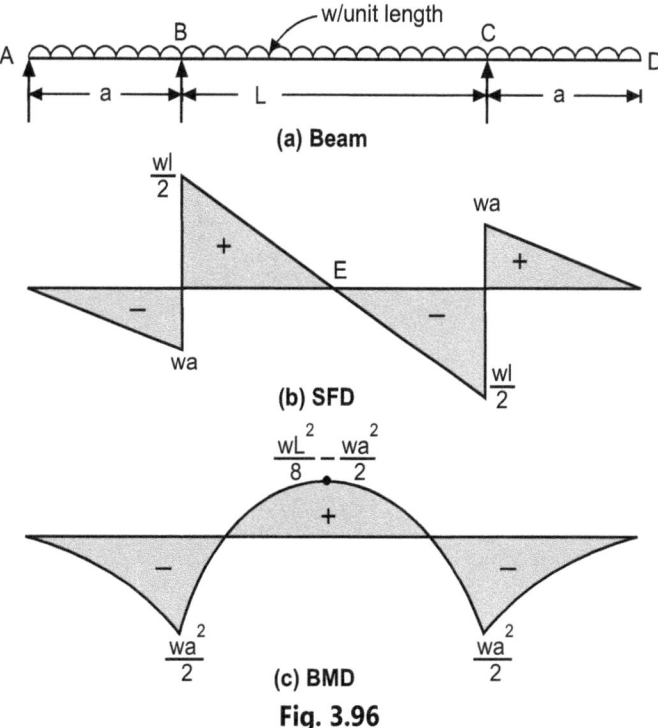

(a) Beam

(b) SFD

(c) BMD

**Fig. 3.96**

**(iii) B.M. calculations :**

$$M_A = M_D = 0$$

$$M_B = M_C = -(wa) \times \frac{a}{2} = -\frac{wa^2}{2}$$

$$\mathbf{M_{max}} = M_E = M_{centre} = -(wa)\left(\frac{a}{2} + \frac{L}{2}\right) + R_B \times \frac{L}{2} - \left(\frac{wL}{2}\right) \times \frac{1}{2} \times \left(\frac{L}{2}\right)$$

$$= -\frac{wa^2}{2} - \frac{waL}{2} + \left(\frac{wL}{2} + wa\right)\frac{L}{2} - \frac{wL^2}{8}$$

$$= -\frac{wa^2}{2} - \frac{waL}{2} + \frac{wL^2}{4} + \frac{waL}{2} - \frac{wL^2}{8}$$

$$= \frac{wL^2}{8} - \frac{wa^2}{2}$$

The B.M.D. is as shown in **Fig. 3.96 (c)**.

**Example 58 :** *Two slings to be used in lifting a newly cast reinforced concrete pole of length 2 m. The pole remains horizontal during its lift. Determine most suitable position for the sling if pole damage would be due to bending under its own weight of 8 kN/m.*

**(B.T.E. W-2010, 2003/4 Marks)**

**Solution :** Refer to **Fig. 3.97**.

**Data :** Pole length L = 2 m, u.d.l. on pole (self weight), w = 8 kN/m.

**To find :** a.

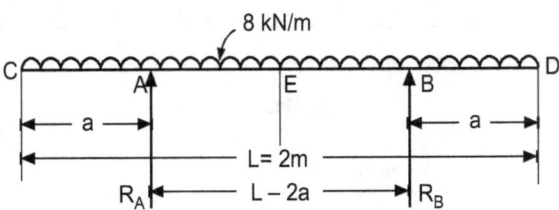

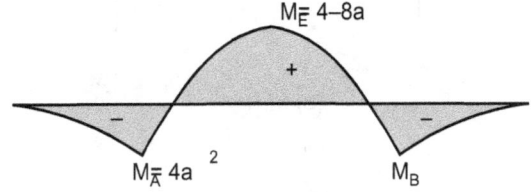

**Fig. 3.97**

Due to symmetry,　　$R_A = R_B = \dfrac{wl}{2} = \dfrac{8 \times 2}{2} = 8$ kN

B.M. at supports A and B,

$$M_A = M_B = -8 \times a \times \frac{a}{2} = -4a^2$$

B.M. at centre of span,

$$M_E = -(w \times 1) \times \frac{1}{2} + R_A \times \left(\frac{L - 2a}{2}\right)$$

$$= -(8 \times 1) \times \frac{1}{2} + 8 \times \left(\frac{2 - 2a}{2}\right)$$

$$= -4 + 4(2 - 2a) = -4 + 8 - 8a = +(4 - 8a)$$

For the most suitable position of the sling, the bending moment should be minimum. This is possible only when negative B.M. at A equals positive B.M. at E i.e. $M_A = M_E$.

$\therefore$　　　　　　$4a^2 = 4 - 8a$

$\therefore$　　　　$4a^2 + 8a - 4 = 0$

$\therefore$　　　　$a^2 + 2a - 1 = 0$

$\therefore$　　　　$a = \dfrac{-2 \pm \sqrt{(2)^2 - 4 \times 1 \times (-1)}}{2} = \dfrac{-2 \pm \sqrt{4 + 4}}{2}$

　　　　　　$= \dfrac{-2 + 2.83}{2}$

Considering positive value of a,

$$a = \frac{-2 + 2.83}{2}$$

∴     $$a = \frac{0.83}{2} = 0.415 \text{ m}$$

**Hence, sling should be at a distance of 0.415 m from the ends.**

**Try Yourself :**

**Example 59 :** *An overhanging beam is as shown in Fig. 3.98. Find the value of $M_{max}$ and locate the point of contraflexure.*          **(B.T.E. S-2012/4 Marks)**

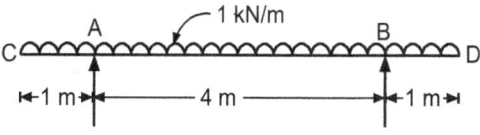

**Fig. 3.98**

**Answer :** $M_{max}$ = 1.5 kN.m, Two points of contraflexure at 1.27 m and 4.73 m from end C.

**Type 6 : Given the shear force diagram. To find loadings on the beam :**

**Example 60 :** *Fig. 3.99 (a) shows a shear force diagram. From this diagram, find the loadings on the beam.*          **(B.T.E. W-1986/4 Marks)**

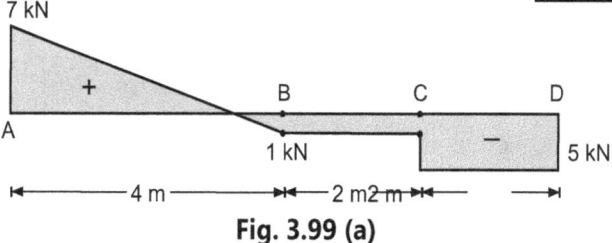

**Fig. 3.99 (a)**

**Solution :** (i) Since S.F. at A is 7 kN, there is a support reaction of 7 kN at A.

(ii) Shear force diagram is an inclined straight line between A and B. Therefore, the beam carries a u.d.l. between A and B. It can be seen that there is a decrease of 7 + 1 = 8 kN. S.F. in 4 m length of beam. Therefore the intensity of u.d.l. is 8/4 = 2 kN/m.

(iii) Shear force diagram is a horizontal straight line between B and C. Therefore, there is no load between B and C.

(iv) At C, S.F. suddenly decreases from – 1 kN to – 5 kN. i.e. decrease in S.F. is –1 – (– 5) = 4 kN. Therefore, there is a point load of 4 kN at C.

(v) At D, shear force diagram has a sudden increase of 5 kN to zero. Therefore, there must be a support reaction of 5 kN at D.

Fig. 3.99 (b) shows loadings on the simply supported beam.

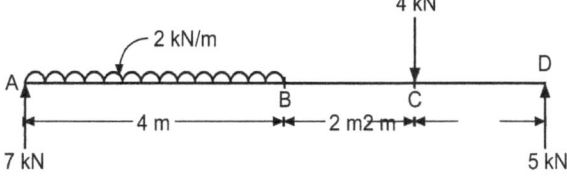

**Fig. 3.99 (b)**

**Example 61 :** *Fig. 3.100 (a) shows S.F.D. for simply supported beam ABCD. Draw its loading diagram and write the values of reactions at supports.*          **(B.T.E. S-2006/4 Marks)**

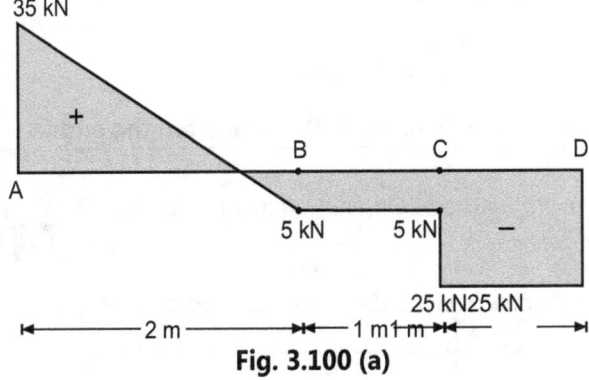

**Fig. 3.100 (a)**

**Solution :**

(i)    S.F. at A = 35 kN, hence $R_A$ = 35 kN

S.F. at D = – 25 kN, hence $R_D$ = 25 kN

(ii)   S.F.D. is an inclined straight line between A and B. Hence, beam carries u.d.l. between A and B.

∴  Intensity of u.d.l. = $\dfrac{35 + 5}{2} = \dfrac{40}{2}$ = **20 kN/m**

(iii)  S.F.D. is a horizontal straight line between B and C. Hence, there is no load between B and C.

(iv)   At C, S.F. suddenly decreases from –5 to –25 kN i.e. decrease in S.F. is – 5 – (–25) = **20 kN.** Therefore, there is a downward point load of 20 kN at C.

Fig. 3.100 (b) shows loadings on the simple supported beam.

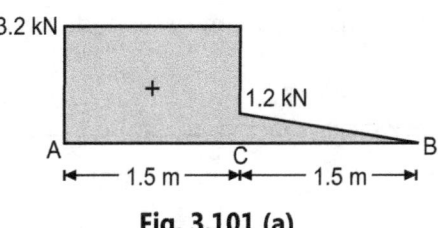

**Fig. 3.100 (b)**

**Example 62 :** *Fig. 3.101 (a) shows a S.F.D. for a beam. Find the loadings on the beam.*

**(V.V. Imp./4 Marks)**

**Fig. 3.101 (a)**

**Solution :**

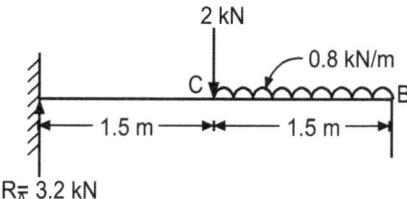

**Fig. 3.101 (b)**

S.F. at A is +3.2 kN. **Therefore the reaction at A is 3.2 kN.** Between A and C, S.F. diagram is a horizontal straight line. Therefore, **there is no load between A and C.** At C, there is a sudden decrease in S.F. from 3.2 to 1.2 kN i.e. decrease in S.F. is 3.2 – 1.2 = 2 kN. Therefore there must be **a downward point load of 2 kN at C.** S.F. diagram is an inclined straight line between C and B. Therefore, there must be a u.d.l. between C and B. There is a decrease of 1.2 kN S.F. in a 1.5 m length of the beam. Therefore, **the intensity of u.d.l. is** $\frac{1.2}{1.5}$ **= 0.8 kN/m.** S.F. at B is zero. Therefore, **there is no load at B.**

From this it is clear that, the given beam is a cantilever having reaction at fixed end equal to 3.2 kN and end B is free.

The loads on the cantilever beam are as shown in Fig. 3.101 (b).

**Example 63 :** *Fig. 3.102 shows shear force diagram for a beam. Interpret from Fig. 3.102,*
*(a)   Value of shear force at 3 m from A. (b) Types of supports and their locations.*
*(c)   Types of loads between AC and BC.*
*(d)   Locate the point of zero shear force.*                  **(B.T.E. W-2006/4 Marks)**

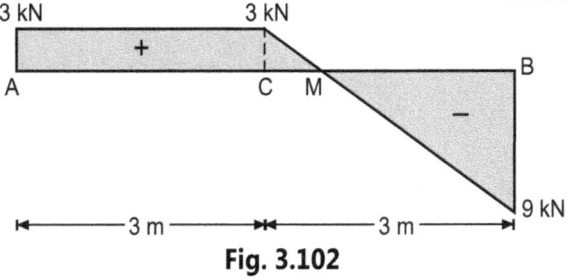

**Fig. 3.102**

**Solution :**

(a)   Since there is a constant S.F. of 3 kN between A and C, S.F. at 3 m from A i.e. $F_C$ = 3 kN.

(b)   Since S.F. at A is 3 kN, there is a support reaction of 3 kN at A. The support at A is simple support. Since S.F. at B is – 9 kN, there is a support reaction of 9 kN at A. The support at B is simple support.

(c)   Since the S.F. is constant (3 kN) between A and C, there is no load between A and C. Shear force diagram is an inclined straight line between C and B. Therefore, the beam carries u.d.l. between C and B. It can be seen that is a decrease of 3 + 9 = 12 kN S.F. in 3 m length of beam. Therefore, the intensity of u.d.l. in BC portion = $\frac{12}{3}$ = 4 kN/m.

(d)  **To locate the point of zero S.F. :**

Let CM = x. From similar triangles in CB portion,

$$\frac{3}{CM} = \frac{9}{MB}$$

$$\therefore \qquad \frac{3}{x} = \frac{9}{3-x}$$

$$\therefore \qquad 3(3-x) = 9x$$

$$\therefore \qquad (3-x) = 3x$$

$$\therefore \qquad 3 = 4x$$

$$\therefore \qquad x = \frac{3}{4} = \mathbf{0.75\ m}\ \text{(Location of point M)}$$

∴  **The point of zero S.F. occurs at 0.75 m from C or 3.75 m from A.**

**Type 7 : Given the bending moment diagram. To find loadings on the beam and draw S.F.D. :**

**Example 64 :** *Fig. 3.103 shows BMD for simply supported beam carrying three point loads at D, E and at mid-point of DE. Find the values of U.D.L. and point load and draw S.F.D.*

**(B.T.E. S-2003/4 Marks)**

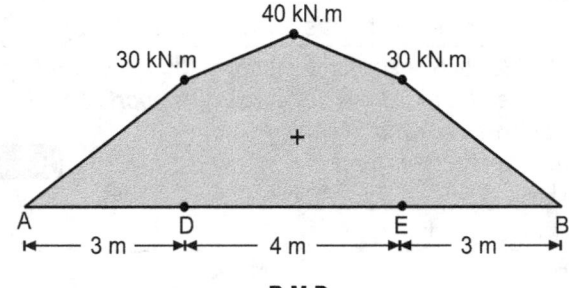

**B.M.D.**

**Fig. 3.103**

**Solution :** Let F be the mid-point of DE.

From B.M.D., we have $M_D = M_E = 30$ kN.m

Now,

| | |
|---|---|
| $M_D = R_A \times 3$ | $M_E = R_B \times 3$ |
| $30 = R_A \times 3$ | $30 = R_B \times 3$ |
| $\therefore \quad R_A = \dfrac{30}{3} = \mathbf{10\ kN}$ | $\therefore \quad R_B = \dfrac{30}{3} = \mathbf{10\ kN}$ |

B.M. at mid-point of DE,

$$M_F = R_A \times (3+2) - \text{load at D} \times \frac{4}{2}$$

$$40 = 10 \times 5 - W_1 \times 2 \qquad\qquad \dots (\because W_1 = \text{load at D})$$

$$40 = 50 - 2W_1$$

$$2W_1 = 10$$

$$\therefore \qquad \mathbf{W_1} = 5\ \text{kN i.e. } \mathbf{W_D = 5\ kN}$$

Due to symmetry,

$$W_2 = W_E = 5 \text{ kN}$$

Now,          $\sum F_y = 0$ gives,

$$R_A + R_B - W_D - W_E - W_F = 0$$

$$\therefore \quad 10 + 10 - 5 - 5 - W_F = 0$$

$$\therefore \quad\quad\quad W_F = 10 \text{ kN}$$

$$W_D = W_E = 5 \text{ kN}, \ W_F = 10 \text{ kN}$$

Fig. 3.104 (a) shows the loadings on the simply supported beam.

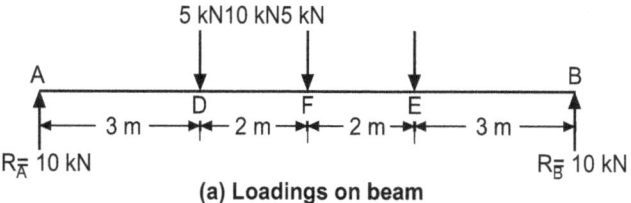

**(a) Loadings on beam**

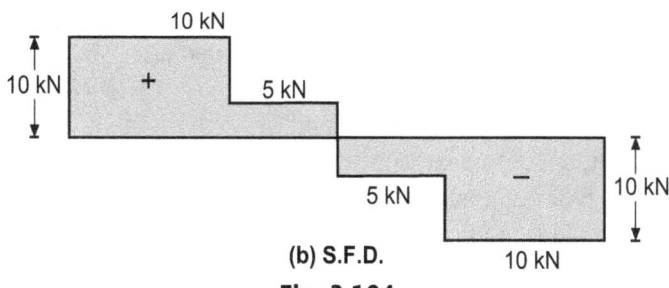

**(b) S.F.D.**

**Fig. 3.104**

Knowing loadings on the S.S. beam, the S.F.D. can be drawn as shown in **Fig. 3.104 (b)**.

S.F. from A to D = 10 kN

S.F. from D to F = 10 − 5 = 5 kN

S.F. from F to E = 10 − 5 − 10 = − 5 kN

S.F. from E to B = 10 − 5 − 10 − 5 = − 10 kN

## Type 8 : Miscellaneous Examples :

**Example 65 :** *Show how the following parts of B.M.D. are related to shear force and loading :*

(1) *The change in B.M. between two points on a beam and area under the shear force curve between the same points.*

(2) *Nature of B.M.D. between two points and load between two points.*

(3) *B.M. maximum at a point in a beam and value or nature of S.F. at that point.*

(4) *Convexity of B.M. curve and S.F. values.*          **(B.T.E. S-2004/4 Marks)**

**Solution :**

(i) The change in B.M. between any two points on a beam is equal to the area under the S.F. diagram between the same points.

(ii) If the B.M.D. is linear, there is no loading between the two points. If the B.M.D. is parabolic curve, the load between the two points is u.d.l.

(iii)  The B.M. is maximum at a point where the S.F. is zero or changes its sign from positive to negative or vice a versa.

(iv)  If the B.M. is hogging, S.F. acts upwards to the left of section. If the B.M. is sagging the S.F. acts downwards to the left of section.

## Practice Questions

### Questions of 2 marks

1.  What are various types of beams ? Draw neat sketches.                   **(B.T.E. S-2013)**
2.  What is Uniformly Distributed Load, U.D.L. ?                            **(B.T.E. W-2012)**
3.  State the types of beams. Draw a neat sketch of any one of it.          **(B.T.E. W-2010)**
4.  Define shear force and bending moment. Also give the sign convention for the same.
    **(B.T.E. S-2012)**
5.  In case of simply supported beam, state the point at which B.M. is maximum, when it is carrying full span U.D.L.                        **(B.T.E. S-2012, W-2000)**
6.  Define point of contraflexure of a loaded beam with sketch. **(B.T.E. S-2008, W-2011)**
7.  Define point of contraflexure.                                **(B.T.E. S-2011, 2009)**
8.  State the relation between B.M., S.F. and rate of loading.
    **(B.T.E. W-2010, 2008, 2007)**
9.  State the relation between shear force and bending moment.       **(B.T.E. S-2008)**
10. How is the point of contraflexure located for a beam ?          **(B.T.E. S-2008)**
11. Explain various types of loading on beams with sketches.        **(B.T.E. S-2009)**
12. Show how the following parts of B.M.D. are related to shear force and loading.
    (i)  Nature of B.M.D. between two points and existence of load between two points.
    (ii) B.M. maximum at a point in a beam and value or nature of shear force at that point.                                            **(B.T.E. W-2010)**
13. State the values of maximum S.F. and B.M. for the following cases.
    (a)  A simply supported beam of span 'L' carrying a central point load.
    (b)  Simply supported beam of span 'L' carrying an eccentric point load.
    (c)  Simply supported beam carrying u.d.l. w/unit length over the entire span.
    (d)  Cantilever beam of span 'L' carrying a point load at its free end.
    (e)  Cantilever beam of span 'L' carrying a u.d.l. w/unit length over the entire span.
14. Draw S.F. diagram for a cantilever of span 2 m carrying a point load of 5 kN at the free end.                                                    **(B.T.E. W-2011)**
15. A simply supported beam of span 9.75 m is carrying full span u.d.l. of 10 kN/m. What is the magnitude and position of maximum bending moment developed ?
    **(B.T.E. S-2000)**
16. A cantilever of 10 m span is carrying a point load of 190 N at its free end. Draw S.F.D. and B.M.D. showing maximum shear force and maximum bending moment respectively.                                              **(B.T.E. S-2000)**
17. A cantilever of span 8 m is carrying a u.d.l. of 12.5 N/m throughout its span. Calculate the values of maximum shear force and maximum bending moment developed.                                                  **(B.T.E. W-2000)**

18. In case of simply supported beam, state the point at which B.M. is maximum when it is carrying full span u.d.l. **(B.T.E. W-2000)**

**Questions of 4 marks**

19. Draw S.F. and B.M. diagrams for a simply supported beam of span 'L' carrying a central point load 'W'. State the values of maximum S.F. and maximum B.M.
**(B.T.E. S-2012, W-2008)**

20. Draw S.F.D. and B.M.D. for a simply supported beam of span L carrying a u.d.l. w/unit length over the entire span. **(B.T.E. S-2012, W-2007)**

21. Explain in detail the concept of shear force and bending moment. **(B.T.E. S-2011)**

22. Draw S.F.D. and B.M.D. for a simply supported beam of span 'L' and carrying a u.d.l. of w/metre. **(B.T.E. S-2009)**

23. Plot the S.F.D. and B.M.D. for a simply supported beam as shown in Fig. 3.105.
**(B.T.E. S-1996)**

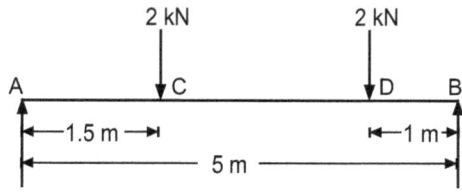

**Fig. 3.105**

(**Ans.** From A to C, S.F. = 2.2 kN; from C to D, S.F. = 0.2 kN; from D to B, S.F. = – 3.8 kN; $M_C$ = 3.3 kN·m; $M_D$ = 3.8 kN-m)

24. Draw the S.F.D. and B.M.D. for a simply supported beam as shown in Fig. 3.106.
**(B.T.E. W-2010)**

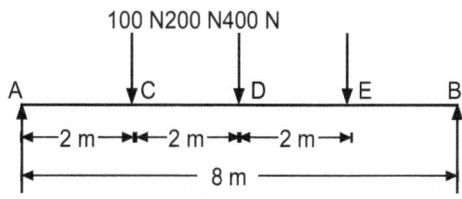

**Fig. 3.106**

(**Ans.** From A to C, S.F. = 275 N; from C to D, S.F. = 175 N; from D to E, S.F. = – 25 N; from E to B, S.F. = – 425 N; $M_C$ = 550 N-m, $M_D$ = 900 N·m, $M_E$ = 850 N-m)

25. A cantilever beam is loaded as shown in Fig. 3.107. Draw the S.F.D. and B.M.D.

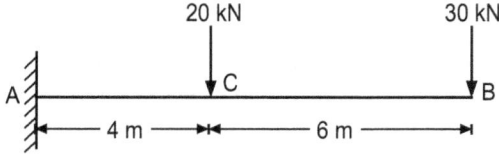

**Fig. 3.107**

(**Ans.** S.F. from A to C = 50 kN, S.F. from C to B = 30 kN, $M_B$ = 0, $M_C$ = – 180 kN-m, $M_A$ = – 380 kN-m)

26. A cantilever beam is loaded as shown in Fig. 3.108. Draw the B.M.D. and S.F.D.

**(B.T.E. S-1996)**

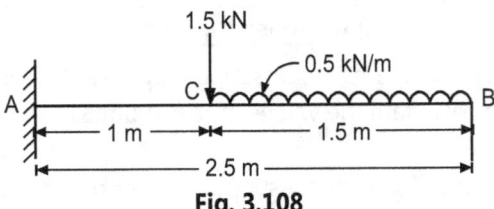

**Fig. 3.108**

(**Ans.** S.F. from A to C = 2.25 kN, $F_{C_R}$ = 0.75 kN, $F_B$ = 0, $M_B$ = 0,

$M_C$ = – 0.5625 kN·m, $M_A$ = – 2.8125 kN·m)

27. An overhanging beam is loaded as shown in Fig. 3.109. Draw S.F. and B.M. diagrams showing the important values.

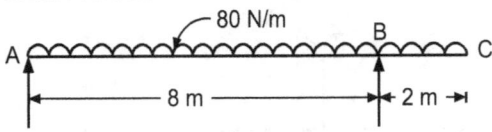

**Fig. 3.109**

(**Ans.** $F_A$ = 300 N, $F_{B_L}$ = – 340 N, $F_{B_R}$ = 160 N, $F_C$ = 0,

$M_{max}$ will occur at 3.75 m from A, $M_{max}$ = 562.5 N·m,

$M_B$ = – 160 N·m, $M_C$ = 0, $M_A$ = 0, point of contraflexure at 7.5 m from left end A)

## Important Points

- **Shear force :** A shear force at the cross-section of a beam is the resultant vertical force acting on the either side of a section of a beam.

- **Bending moment :** Bending moment at the cross-section of a beam is the algebraic sum of the moments of all the forces acting on the right or left side of the section. Generally **sagging** B.M. is taken as **positive** and **hogging** B.M. as **negative.**

- **Relation between shear force and rate of loading :** The rate of change of S.F. with respect to the distance is equal to the intensity of loading.

  Mathematically, $\dfrac{dF}{dx} = w$

- **Relation between B.M. and S.F. :** The rate of change of B.M. at any section is equal to the S.F. at that section. Mathematically, $\dfrac{dM}{dx} = F$.

- **Point of contraflexure (Point of inflection) :** A point in a bending moment diagram where the B.M. changes its sign and is equal to zero is called the **point of contraflexure** or **point of inflection.**

  The position of point of contraflexure can be located by finding the expression of $M_x$ and equating it to zero.

❑❑❑

# MOMENT OF INERTIA

Weightage of Marks = 16, Teaching Hours = 06

## Objectives

Specific Objectives :

Determine area moment of inertia of regular and composite sections.

## Contents

4.1 Concept and definition of Moment of inertia, Parallel and Perpendicular axes theorem (No derivation).

- Moment of inertia of Solid Sections-Square, Rectangular, Circular, Semicircular, Triangular, Hollow sections – Square, Rectangular and Circular cross-sections only.

- Moment of inertia of Angle section, Channel section, Tee-section, I-section about centroidal axis and any other axis parallel to centroidal axis.

- Polar moment of inertia.

## Synopsis

Concept of Moment of Inertia, Moment of Inertia of a Plane Area about the Centroidal Axes, Concept of Radius of Gyration, Centroidal Axes, M.I. of Plane Figures such as Rectangle, Triangle, Circle, Semi-circle and Quarter Circle about the Centroidal Axes, Radius of Gyration of some Standard Sections, Parallel Axis Theorem, Perpendicular Axis Theorem, Polar Moment of Inertia, M.I. of Composite Sections, M.I. of Composite Areas with Cut-out Sections.

## 4.1 CONCEPT OF MOMENT OF INERTIA

In Engineering Mechanics, we have seen that inertia is the property of a body to continue in its state of rest or of uniform motion in a straight line. To change the state of a body, an external agency called force is essential. For bodies in rectilinear motion, the force required to change its state depends upon the mass of the body. Therefore for bodies in rectilinear motion, the mass of a body is the measure of inertia possessed by it.

For bodies in rotation about any axis, the force required to change the state of a body not only depends on the mass of the body but also its distance from the axis around which it is rotating. Therefore for bodies in angular motion, the mass of a body and the distance of the force from the axis of rotation are the true measures of inertia possessed by it. In engineering practice, the mass of a body is replaced by its area.

We know that, the moment of a force about any point is the product of the force and perpendicular distance between the given point and the line of action of the force. Similarly, the moment of area about any axis is the product of the area and the distance of its centroid from that axis. This is called the first moment of area. If we take its moment again about the same axis, it is called the second moment of area. This second moment of area is called moment of inertia and is written as M.I. or I.

## 4.2 MOMENT OF INERTIA OF A PLANE AREA ABOUT THE CENTROIDAL AXES

Let us consider an irregular area A to be divided into small elementary areas $a_1$, $a_2$, $a_3$, ... $a_n$ of known geometric shapes as shown in Fig. 4.1.

Let $x_1$, $x_2$, $x_3$, ... $x_n$ = Respective distances of the centroid of the areas $a_1$, $a_2$, $a_3$, ... $a_n$ from Y-Y axis.

Let $y_1$, $y_2$, $y_3$, ... $y_n$ = Respective distances of the centroid of the areas $a_1$, $a_2$, $a_3$, ... $a_n$ from X-X axis.

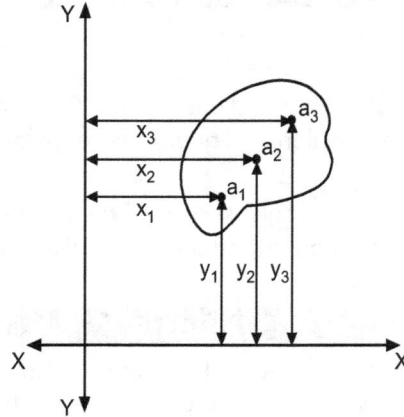

**Fig. 4.1**

Now, first moment of area $a_1$ about Y-Y axis = $a_1 \cdot x_1$

Second moment of area $a_1$ about YY axis = $(a_1 x_1) \cdot x_1$ = $a_1 x_1^2$

Similarly, second moment of area $a_2$ about YY axis = $a_2 x_2^2$

Second moment of area $a_3$ about YY axis = $a_3 x_3^2$

................................................................

................................................................

Second moment of area $a_n$ about YY axis = $a_n x_n^2$

Therefore, the sum of second moment of all elementary areas about YY-axis

$$= a_1 x_1^2 + a_2 x_2^2 + a_3 x_3^2 + ... + a_n x_n^2$$

$$= \sum ax^2$$

Since the moment is taken about Y-Y axis, $\sum ax^2$ denotes the moment of inertia of an area about Y-Y axis and is denoted by $I_{YY}$.

$\therefore$          $I_{YY} = \sum ax^2$

Similarly, the sum of second moment of all elementary areas about X-X axis

$$= a_1 y_1^2 + a_2 y_2^2 + a_3 y_3^2 + ... + a_n y_n^2 = \sum ay^2$$

Since the moment is taken about X-X axis, $\sum ay^2$ denotes the moment of inertia of an area about X-X axis and is denoted by $I_{XX}$.

$$\therefore \qquad I_{XX} = \sum ay^2$$

**Unit of M.I. :**  Naturally unit of M.I. = Unit of area × (Unit of distance)$^2$

$$= m^2 \times m^2, cm^2 \times cm^2, mm^2 \times mm^2$$
$$= m^4, cm^4, mm^4 \text{ etc.}$$

**Definition :** *Moment of inertia of a body about any axis is defined as the sum of second moment of all elementary areas about that axis.*

| 1.  Define moment of inertia. | **(B.T.E. W-2014, S-2013, 2011/2 Marks)** |
|---|---|

**(Most Likely and Asked in Previous B.T.E. Exam.)**

## 4.3 CONCEPT OF RADIUS OF GYRATION

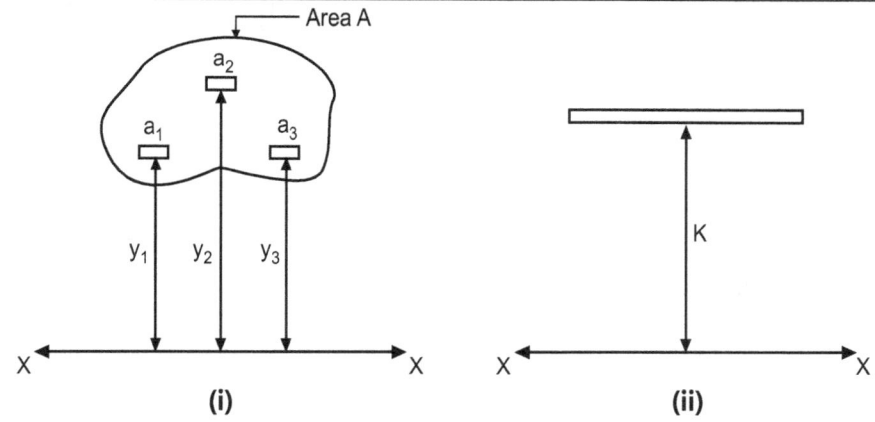

**Fig. 4.2**

Let us consider an irregular area A to be divided into infinite number of small elementary areas $a_1, a_2, a_3, ... a_n$ of known geometric shapes as shown in Fig. 4.2 (i). Let $y_1, y_2, y_3, ... y_n$ be the distances of the centroid of the areas from the X-X axis.

We know that,  $\qquad I_{XX} = \sum ay^2$ ........

$$= a_1 y_1^2 + a_2 y_2^2 + a_3 y_3^2 + ... + a_n y_n^2 \qquad ... (i)$$

Now, let us assume that the entire area A is concentrated into a long narrow horizontal strip as shown in Fig. 4.2 (ii), so that $y_1 = y_2 = y_3 = ... = y_n = K$ (say).

Then from the equation (i),

$$I_{XX} = a_1 K^2 + a_2 K^2 + a_3 K^2 + ... + a_n K^2$$
$$= K^2 (a_1 + a_2 + a_3 + ... + a_n)$$

But  $\qquad a_1 + a_2 + a_3 + ... + a_n = A$

$$\therefore \qquad I_{XX} = K^2 A \qquad ... (ii)$$

where K is known as the radius of gyration about X-X axis.

**Definition :** *The radius of gyration of a given area about any axis is that distance from the given axis at which the entire area is assumed to be concentrated without changing the M.I. about the given axis.* It is denoted by K or r.

Now, from equation (ii), we have

$$K^2 = \frac{I_{XX}}{A}$$

$\therefore$
$$\boxed{K = \sqrt{\frac{I_{XX}}{A}}}$$

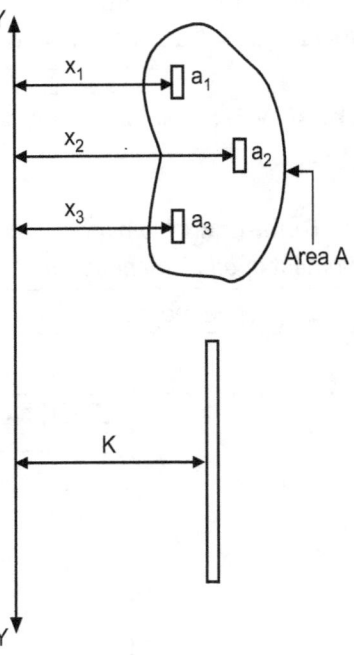

From this expression, the radius of gyration of the area A about X-X axis can be calculated.

Now, let us assume that the entire area A is concentrated into a long narrow vertical strip as shown in Fig. 4.3 so that $x_1 = x_2 = x_3 = ... = x_n = K$ (say)

**Fig. 4.3**

We know that, the M.I. of area A about Y-Y axis is given by,

$$I_{YY} = \sum ax^2$$

$$= a_1x_1^2 + a_2x_2^2 + a_3x_3^2 + ... + a_nx_n^2 \qquad ... \text{(iii)}$$

Substituting $\qquad x_1 = x_2 = x_3 = ... = K$ in equation (iii), we have

$$I_{YY} = a_1K^2 + a_2K^2 + a_3K^2 + ... + a_nK^2$$

$$= K^2 (a_1 + a_2 + a_3 + ... + a_n)$$

$$= K^2A \qquad ... \text{(iv)}$$

where K is known as the radius of gyration about Y-Y axis.

Now, from equation (iv), we have

$$K^2 = \frac{I_{YY}}{A}$$

$\therefore$
$$\boxed{K = \sqrt{\frac{I_{YY}}{A}}}$$

From this expression, the radius of gyration of the area A about Y-Y axis can be calculated.

**Note :** (i) *The radius of gyration about X-X axis is generally denoted by $K_{XX}$ and that about Y-Y axis as $K_{YY}$.*

**Thus,** $\qquad K_{XX} = \sqrt{\dfrac{I_{XX}}{A}} \quad$ and $\quad K_{YY} = \sqrt{\dfrac{I_{YY}}{A}}$

(ii) **In general, $I = AK^2$. The minimum radius of gyration is calculated by the relation**

$$I_{min} = AK_{min}^2 \quad \therefore \quad K_{min} = \sqrt{\dfrac{I_{min}}{A}}$$

(iii) $\qquad$ **Unit of K** $= \sqrt{\dfrac{\text{Unit of I}}{\text{Unit of A}}} = $ **mm, m, cm, etc.**

---

1. Define radius of gyration.

   **(B.T.E. S-2013, 2010, 2009; W-2014, 2008, 2007, 1999, 1998/2 Marks)**

2. Define radius of gyration. State its S.I. unit. **(B.T.E. S-2012/2 Marks)**

---

**(Most Likely and Asked in Previous B.T.E. Exam.)**

## 4.4 CENTROIDAL AXES

*The axes passing through the centre of gravity of a section are called as centroidal axes.* X-X and Y-Y axes are called the horizontal and vertical centroidal axes respectively. The moment of inertia of a body is generally calculated about its centroidal axes. Before finding out the moment of inertia of any plane figure, it is very necessary to locate its centroid. The knowledge of centroid / centre of gravity is essential to understand the concept of M.I.

## 4.5 M.I. OF PLANE FIGURES SUCH AS RECTANGLE, TRIANGLE, CIRCLE, SEMI-CIRCLE AND QUARTER CIRCLE ABOUT THE CENTROIDAL AXES

**(1) M.I. of a solid rectangular section :**

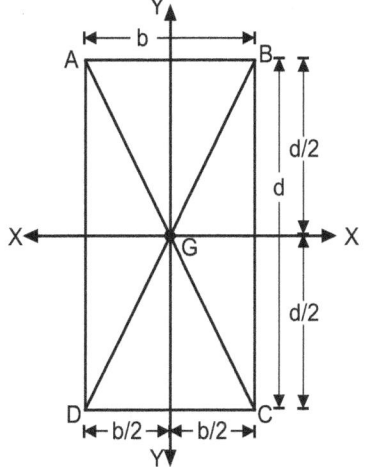

**Fig. 4.4**

Consider a rectangular section ABCD of size b × d as shown in Fig. 4.4.

Let b = Width of the section

d = Depth of the section

Let G be the centroid of the rectangle. The positions of centroidal axes (i.e. X-X and Y-Y axes) are as shown in Fig. 4.4.

M.I. of a rectangle about X-X axis, $I_{XX} = \dfrac{b \cdot d^3}{12}$

M.I. of a rectangle about Y-Y axis, $I_{YY} = \dfrac{d \cdot b^3}{12}$

## (2) M.I. of a hollow rectangular section :

Consider a hollow rectangular section of the outer dimensions B × D and the inner dimensions b × d as shown in Fig. 4.5. ABCD is the main section and PQRS is the cut-out section. The moment of inertia of a shaded area is to be calculated.

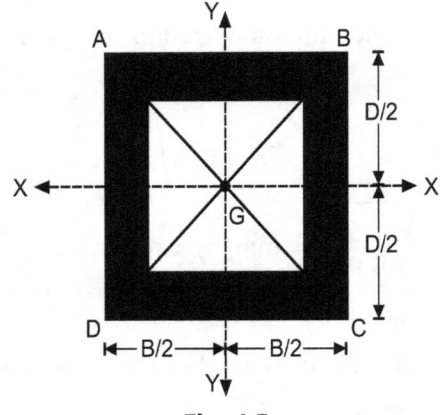

**Fig. 4.5**

Let                  B  =  Width of the outer rectangle

D  =  Depth of the outer rectangle

b  =  Width of the inner rectangle

d  =  Depth of the inner rectangle

In this case, the centroid of both the rectangles is the same i.e. point G.

M.I. of a hollow section  =  M.I. of outer rectangle – M.I. of inner rectangle

In this case,          $I_{XX} = \dfrac{BD^3}{12} - \dfrac{bd^3}{12} = \dfrac{1}{12}(BD^3 - bd^3)$

and                    $I_{YY} = \dfrac{DB^3}{12} - \dfrac{db^3}{12} = \dfrac{1}{12}(DB^3 - db^3)$

## (3)  M.I. of a triangular section :

Consider a triangular section ABC of base b and height h as shown in Fig. 4.6. The centre of gravity of a triangle will be at a distance of $\dfrac{h}{3}$ from the base AB. The position of X-X axis is as shown in Fig. 4.6.

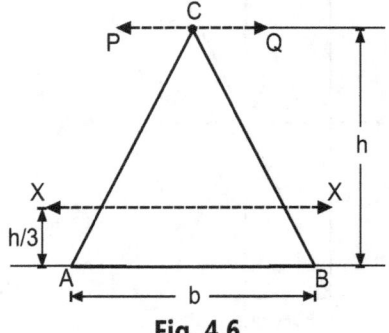

**Fig. 4.6**

In this case,          $I_{XX} = \dfrac{b\,h^3}{36}$

**Note : (i) M.I. of a triangle about base AB,**

$$I_{AB} = \frac{b\,h^3}{12}$$

**(ii) M.I. of a triangle about the horizontal axis PQ passing through its apex C is given by,**

$$I_{PQ} = \frac{b \cdot h^3}{4}$$

## (4) M.I. of a solid circular section of diameter D :

Consider a solid circular section of diameter D as shown in Fig. 4.7. G denotes the centroid of the circle. Since the section is symmetrical about the X-X and Y-Y axes, $I_{XX}$ and $I_{YY}$ are equal.

In this case, $\qquad I = I_{XX} = I_{YY} = \dfrac{\pi}{64}\,D^4$

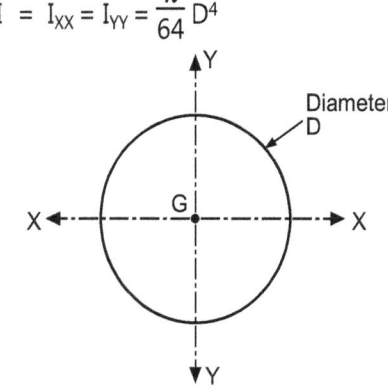

**Fig. 4.7**

## (5) M.I. of a hollow circular section :

Consider a hollow circular section of outer diameter 'D' and inner diameter 'd' as shown in Fig. 4.8. In this case, centroid of both the circles is the same i.e. the point G. The M.I. of the shaded area is to be calculated about the centroidal axes. Since the section is symmetrical about X-X and Y-Y axes, $I_{XX}$ and $I_{YY}$ are equal.

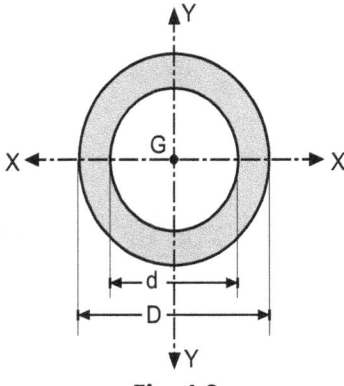

**Fig. 4.8**

$$\begin{bmatrix} \text{M.I. of a hollow} \\ \text{circular section} \end{bmatrix} = \begin{bmatrix} \text{M.I. of a} \\ \text{outer circle} \end{bmatrix} - \begin{bmatrix} \text{M.I. of a} \\ \text{inner circle} \end{bmatrix}$$

$$\therefore \qquad I = I_{XX} = I_{YY} = \frac{\pi}{64}\,D^4 - \frac{\pi}{64}\,d^4$$

$$= \frac{\pi}{64}\,(D^4 - d^4)$$

### (6) M.I. of a semi-circular section :

Consider a semi-circular section ABC of radius 'R' and diameter 'D' as shown in Fig. 4.9. In this case, C.G. will be on the line of symmetry (i.e. on Y-Y axis) at a distance of $\frac{4R}{3\pi}$ from the base AC. The positions of X-X and Y-Y axes are as shown in Fig. 4.9.

In this case,                            $I_{XX} = 0.11\ R^4$

and                            $I_{YY} = \frac{\pi R^4}{8} = \frac{\pi D^4}{128}$

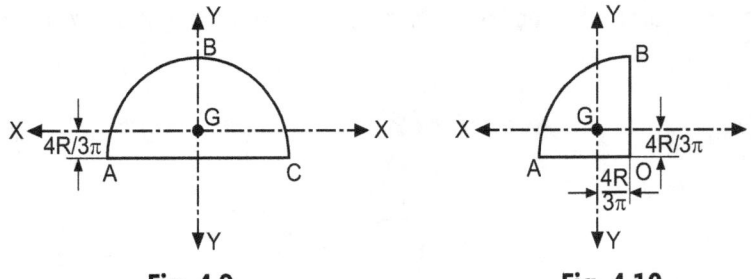

|            Fig. 4.9                           Fig. 4.10            |

### (7) M.I. of a quarter-circle (i.e. quadrant of a circle) :

Consider a quarter-circle OAB of radius 'R' as shown in Fig. 4.10. In this case, c.g. will be at a distance of $\frac{4R}{3\pi}$ from the boundary axes AO and BO.

Naturally, M.I. of a quarter circle is half the M.I. of a semi-circle about X-X axis.

In this case,            $I = I_{XX} = I_{YY} = \frac{1}{2} \times 0.11\ R^4 = 0.055\ R^4$

---

1.  State the value of M.I. of a semi-circle of radius 'R' about centroidal XX and YY axes.

    **(B.T.E. S-2014, W-2008/2 Marks)**

2.  State the value of M.I. of a triangle about its base.        **(B.T.E. W-2007/2 Marks)**

**(Most Likely and Asked in Previous B.T.E. Exam.)**

## 4.6 RADIUS OF GYRATION OF SOME STANDARD SECTIONS

Knowing the values of the M.I. of standard sections and their areas, the radii of gyration of some standard sections are given here for the ready reference.

(i)  For a rectangular section of width b and depth d, we have

$$K_{XX} = \sqrt{\frac{I_{XX}}{A}} = \sqrt{\frac{\frac{1}{12} bd^3}{bd}} = \sqrt{\frac{d^2}{4 \times 3}} = \frac{d}{2\sqrt{3}}$$

$$K_{YY} = \sqrt{\frac{I_{YY}}{A}} = \sqrt{\frac{\frac{1}{12} db^3}{bd}} = \sqrt{\frac{b^2}{4 \times 3}} = \frac{b}{2\sqrt{3}}$$

(ii) For a hollow rectangular section of outer dimensions B and D and inner dimensions b and d, we have

$$K_{XX} = \sqrt{\frac{I_{XX}}{A}} = \sqrt{\frac{\frac{1}{12}(BD^3 - bd^3)}{BD - bd}}$$

and

$$K_{YY} = \sqrt{\frac{I_{YY}}{A}} = \sqrt{\frac{\frac{1}{12}(DB^3 - db^3)}{BD - bd}}$$

(iii) For a solid circular section of diameter D, we have

$$K_{XX} = \sqrt{\frac{I_{XX}}{A}} = \sqrt{\frac{\frac{\pi}{64}D^4}{\frac{\pi}{4}D^2}} = \sqrt{\frac{D^2}{16}} = \frac{D}{4}$$

Since $I_{XX}$ and $I_{YY}$ are equal,

$$K_{YY} = K_{XX} = \frac{D}{4}$$

(iv) For a hollow circular section of external diameter D and internal diameter d, we have

$$K_{XX} = K_{YY} = \sqrt{\frac{I_{XX} \text{ or } I_{YY}}{A}} = \sqrt{\frac{\frac{\pi}{64}(D^4 - d^4)}{\frac{\pi}{4}(D^2 - d^2)}}$$

$$= \sqrt{\frac{1}{16}\frac{(D^2 - d^2)(D^2 + d^2)}{(D^2 - d^2)}} = \frac{\sqrt{D^2 + d^2}}{4}$$

(v) For a triangular section of base b and height h,

$$K_{XX} = \sqrt{\frac{I_{XX}}{A}} = \sqrt{\frac{\frac{1}{36}bh^3}{\frac{1}{2}bh}} = \sqrt{\frac{h^2}{18}} = \frac{h}{3\sqrt{2}}$$

(vi) For a semi-circular section of radius R, we have

$$K_{XX} = \sqrt{\frac{I_{XX}}{A}} = \sqrt{\frac{0.11 R^4}{\pi R^2/2}} = \sqrt{\frac{0.22 R^2}{\pi}} = 0.2646 R$$

and

$$K_{YY} = \sqrt{\frac{I_{YY}}{A}} = \sqrt{\frac{\frac{\pi R^4}{8}}{\frac{\pi R^2}{2}}} = \sqrt{\frac{R^2}{4}} = \frac{R}{2} = 0.5 R$$

(vii) For a quarter circle of radius R, we have

$$K_{XX} = \sqrt{\frac{I_{XX}}{A}} = \sqrt{\frac{0.055 R^4}{\pi R^2/4}} = \sqrt{\left(\frac{0.055 \times 4}{\pi}\right)R^2} = 0.2646 R$$

Since　　　$I_{XX} = I_{YY}$

$$K_{YY} = K_{XX} = 0.2646 R$$

## 4.7 PARALLEL AXIS THEOREM

*It states, "The moment of inertia of a plane section about any axis parallel to the centroidal axis is equal to the moment of inertia of the section about the centroidal axis plus the product of the area of the section and the square of the distance between the two axes."*

Consider an irregular area A as shown in Fig. 4.11. Let G be its centroid.

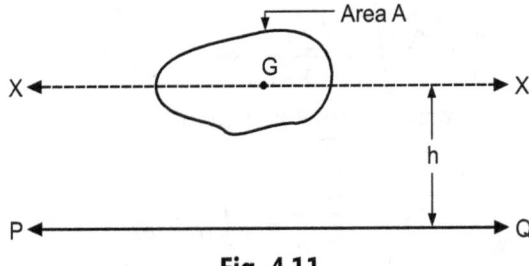

**Fig. 4.11**

Let    $I_G$ = M.I. of the area about its centroidal axis

     $I_{PQ}$ = M.I. of the area about any axis PQ which is parallel to the centroidal axis XX

     A = Area of the section

and    h = Distance between the two axes

Then, by parallel axis theorem,

$$I_{PQ} = I_G + A \cdot h^2$$

In this case,   $I_G = I_{XX}$

∴        $I_{PQ} = I_{XX} + A \cdot h^2$

Now, consider a rectangular section of width b and depth d as shown in Fig. 4.12.

The positions of XX, YY, PQ and AB axes are as shown in Fig. 4.12.

Let      h = Distance between X-X axis and PQ axis

and     h' = Distance between Y-Y axis and AB axis

Now M.I. of a rectangle about the axis PQ is given by,

$$I_{PQ} = I_G + Ah^2$$

$$= I_{XX} + Ah^2$$

$$= \frac{bd^3}{12} + (bd)\, h^2$$

M.I. of a rectangle about the axis AB is given by,

$$I_{AB} = I_G + A\,(h')^2$$

$$= I_{YY} + A\,(h')^2$$

$$= \frac{db^3}{12} + (bd)\,(h')^2$$

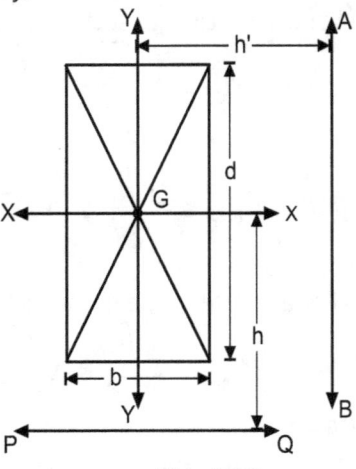

**Fig. 4.12**

**Use :** This theorem is used to find the M.I. of any plane figure about any axis located at some distance away from the centroidal axis.

---

1. State parallel axis theorem. **(B.T.E. S-2014; W-2013, 2012, 2011, 2010)**

2. State parallel axis theorem of moment of inertia.

**(B.T.E. S-2013, 2009, 2008, 1998; W-2008, 2000, 1997/2 Marks)**

---

**(Most Likely and Asked in Previous B.T.E. Exam.)**

## 4.8 PERPENDICULAR AXIS THEOREM

It states, 'If $I_{XX}$ and $I_{YY}$ are the moments of inertia of a plane section about the two mutually perpendicular axes meeting at O, then the moment of inertia $I_{ZZ}$ about the third axis Z-Z perpendicular to the plane and passing through the intersection of X-X and Y-Y is given by,

$$I_{ZZ} = I_{XX} + I_{YY}.$$

Refer to Fig. 4.13. The third axis ZZ is called as polar axis.

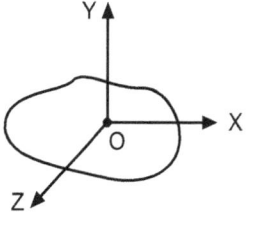

**Fig. 4.13**

Therefore, this theorem is also called as **polar axis theorem.** The moment of inertia $I_{ZZ}$, about the axis Z-Z is called as **polar moment of inertia.** It is denoted by $I_P$.

i.e. $I_{ZZ} = I_P$.

∴ $I_P = I_{XX} + I_{YY}$

**Use :** This theorem is used to calculate the polar moment of inertia of a plane figure.

---

1. State perpendicular axis theorem of moment of inertia.

**(B.T.E. W-2013, 2009; S-2000/2 Marks)**

2. Explain the theorem of mutually perpendicular axis for M.I.

**(B.T.E. W-2014, S-2009/2 Marks)**

3. State parallel axis theorem and perpendicular axis theorem of moment of inertia.

**(B.T.E. S-2014, 2010; W-2007/4 Marks)**

---

**(Most Likely and Asked in Previous B.T.E. Exam.)**

## 4.9 POLAR MOMENT OF INERTIA

**Definition :** The moment of inertia of a plane area about an axis perpendicular to the plane of the figure is called polar moment of inertia with respect to the point, where the axis intersects the plane.

Mathematically, polar moment of inertia is the sum of moments of inertia about the two centroidal axes X-X and Y-Y.

The knowledge of polar M.I. is very important in the torsion of circular shaft. For a solid circular shaft of diameter D,

$$I_P = I_{XX} + I_{YY} = \frac{\pi}{64} D^4 + \frac{\pi}{64} D^4 = 2 \times \frac{\pi}{64} D^4 = \frac{\pi}{32} D^4$$

For a hollow circular shaft of external diameter 'D' and internal diameter 'd',

$$I_P = I_{XX} + I_{YY} = \frac{\pi}{64}(D^4 - d^4) + \frac{\pi}{64}(D^4 - d^4) = 2 \times \frac{\pi}{64}(D^4 - d^4) = \frac{\pi}{32}(D^4 - d^4)$$

---

1. Define the term polar moment of inertia.   **(B.T.E. S-2012, 2008; W-2009/2 Marks)**

2. Find polar moment of inertia of a circle of 50 mm diameter.

   **(B.T.E. W-2012, 1998/2 Marks)**

3. Define radius of gyration and polar moment of inertia.    **(B.T.E. S-2010/4 Marks)**

---

**(Most Likely and Asked in Previous B.T.E. Exam.)**

## 4.10 M.I. OF COMPOSITE SECTIONS

A composite section is a combination of two or more basic plane geometrical figures like rectangle, triangle, circle, semi-circle, quarter-circle, etc.

**Steps to find M.I. of a composite section :**

(i) Divide the composite section into regular plane areas of known geometric shapes and mark these areas as (1), (2), (3), ... etc. Calculate these areas and mark the positions of their centroids. Also mark the positions of their own centroidal axes x-x and y-y.

(ii) Find the C.G. of the composite section by using

$$\bar{x} = \frac{a_1 x_1 + a_2 x_2 + a_3 x_3 + ...}{A}$$

and

$$\bar{y} = \frac{a_1 y_1 + a_2 y_2 + a_3 y_3 + ...}{A}$$

where

$$A = a_1 + a_2 + a_3 + ...$$

$$= \text{Area of the composite section.}$$

Knowing the C.G. of the section, mark the positions of the centroidal axes X-X and Y-Y about which the M.I. of the composite section is generally calculated.

(iii) Find $I_{G_1}$, $I_{G_2}$, $I_{G_3}$, ... etc. i.e. the moments of inertia of the areas about their own centroidal axes X-X and Y-Y.

(iv) Use the theorem of parallel axis and transfer these moments of inertia to the centroidal axes X-X and Y-Y of the composite section or any other required axis.

(v) Use the following formulae to calculate the moment of inertia of a composite figure about the centroidal axes.

M.I. about the horizontal centroidal axis,

$$I_{XX} = I_{XX_1} + I_{XX_2} + I_{XX_3} + ...$$

and M.I. about the vertical centroidal axis,

$$I_{YY} = I_{YY_1} + I_{YY_2} + I_{YY_3} + ...$$

## 4.11 M.I. OF COMPOSITE AREAS WITH CUT-OUT SECTIONS

The moment of inertia of a composite area with cut-out section is found out by deducting the moment of inertia of a cut-out section from the moment of inertia of the main area.

If a composite section is made up of two areas and if area 2 (i.e. $a_2$) is removed from the main area 1 (i.e. $a_1$),

$$I_{XX} = I_{XX_1} - I_{XX_2}$$

and

$$I_{YY} = I_{YY_1} - I_{YY_2}$$

where

$I_{XX_1}$ = M.I. of the main area about X-X axis

$I_{XX_2}$ = M.I. of the removed area about X-X axis

$I_{YY_1}$ = M.I. of the main area about Y-Y axis

$I_{YY_2}$ = M.I. of the removed area about Y-Y axis

**Note : *In this case, the co-ordinates of the c.g. are calculated by using the following equations.***

$$\bar{x} = \frac{a_1 x_1 - a_2 x_2}{a_1 - a_2}$$

$$\bar{y} = \frac{a_1 y_1 - a_2 y_2}{a_1 - a_2}$$

*where  $a_1$ = Main area*

*$a_2$ = Removed area*

*$(x_1, y_1)$ = Co-ordinates of centroid of area $a_1$*

*$(x_2, y_2)$ = Co-ordinates of centroid of area $a_2$*

*$(\bar{x}, \bar{y})$ = Co-ordinates of centroid of the remainder $(a_1 - a_2)$*

## SOLVED EXAMPLES

**Type 1 : Examples on M.I. and radius of gyration of simple plane figures.**

**Type 1.1 : M.I. of square, rectangular, hollow square and hollow rectangular sections.**

| Important Formulae |
|---|
| (i)　For a rectangular section of size b × d, $$I_{XX} = \frac{bd^3}{12}, \quad I_{YY} = \frac{db^3}{12}, \quad A = b \times d.$$ |
| (ii)　For a hollow rectangular section of outer dimensions BD and inner dimensions b, d, $$I_{XX} = \frac{1}{12}(BD^3 - bd^3) \text{ and } I_{YY} = \frac{1}{12}(DB^3 - db^3)$$ $$A = BD - bd$$ |

(iii) For a square section of side b,

$$I_{XX} = I_{YY} = \frac{b \cdot d^3}{12} = \frac{b^4}{12}$$

$$A = b \cdot b = b^2$$

(iv) M.I. about parallel axis = M.I. about centroidal axis + $Ah^2$.

(v) $I_p = I_{XX} + I_{YY}$.

(vi) $K_{XX} = \sqrt{\dfrac{I_{XX}}{A}}$

(vii) $K_{YY} = \sqrt{\dfrac{I_{YY}}{A}}$

**Example 1 :** *Find the moment of inertia of a square of side 'a' about its outer edge.*

**(V.V. Imp./4 Marks)**

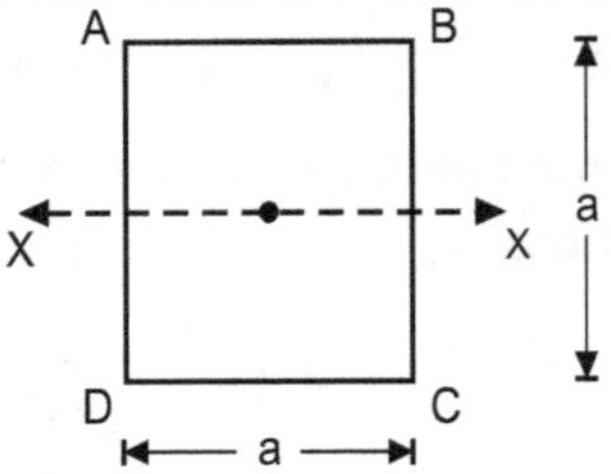

**Data**　　: A square of side 'a' as shown in Fig. 4.14.

**To find**　: $I_{CD}$.

**Concept :** Theorem of parallel axis.

**Fig. 4.14**

**Solution**　: (i) For a square of side 'a',

$$I_{XX} = \frac{a \cdot a^3}{12} = \frac{a^4}{12} \qquad \ldots (i)$$

(ii) Area of section, $\quad A = a \times a = a^2$

(iii) The outer edge CD is parallel to XX axis.

Distance between XX axis and outer edge CD,

$$h = \frac{a}{2}$$

(iv) Using parallel axis theorem,

M.I. about parallel axis = M.I. about centroidal axis + $Ah^2$

∴

$$I_{CD} = I_{XX} + Ah^2$$

$$= \frac{a^4}{12} + a^2 \times \left(\frac{a}{2}\right)^2 \qquad \left(\because h = \frac{a}{2}\right)$$

$$= \frac{a^4}{12} + \frac{a^4}{4} = \frac{a^4 + 3a^4}{12} = \frac{4a^4}{12} = \frac{a^4}{3}$$

**Answer :** $\boxed{I_{CD} = \dfrac{a^4}{3} = \dfrac{(\text{side of square})^4}{3}}$

**Example 2 :** *Calculate polar M.I. of a square section having 200 mm as side.*

(B.T.E. S-2011/2 Marks)

**Data :** A square of side 200 mm.

**To find :** $I_p$.

**Concept :** (i) $I_p = I_{XX} + I_{YY}$, (ii) For a square section,

$$I_{XX} = I_{YY} = \frac{a^4}{12}$$

**Solution :** Refer to Fig. 4.14.

(i)    For a square of side a,

$$I_{XX} = \frac{a \cdot a^3}{12} = \frac{a^4}{12} = \frac{(200)^4}{12} = 1.33 \times 10^8 \text{ mm}^4$$

(ii)   For a square section,

$$I_{YY} = I_{XX} = 1.33 \times 10^8 \text{ mm}^4$$

∴            $\mathbf{I_p} = I_{XX} + I_{YY} = 1.33 \times 10^8 + 1.33 \times 10^8 = \mathbf{2.66 \times 10^8 \text{ mm}^4}$

**Answer :** $\boxed{I_p = 2.66 \times 10^8 \text{ mm}^4}$

---

**Example 3 :** *Find the moment of inertia of a rectangle 60 mm × 200 mm about its 200 mm edge.* (B.T.E. W-2011/4 Marks)

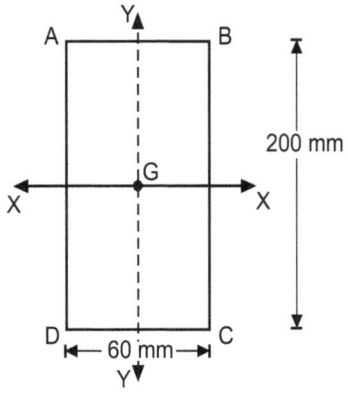

**Fig. 4.15**

**Data :** Here    b = AB = 60 mm

and    d = AD = 200 mm

**To find :** $I_{AD}$

**Concept :** Use of parallel axis theorem.

**Solution :** Fig. 4.15 shows a rectangle of size 60 mm × 200 mm.

(i)    Moment of inertia about Y-Y axis is

$$I_{YY} = I_G = \frac{db^3}{12} = \frac{200 \times 60^3}{12} = 36 \times 10^5 \text{ mm}^4$$

(ii) Area of the section = A = b × d

= 60 × 200

= 12000 mm²

(iii)   Distance between AD and Y-Y axis is h = $\frac{60}{2}$ = 30 mm

(iv)   Using parallel axis theorem,

$\mathbf{I_{AD}} = I_G + Ah^2 = 36 \times 10^5 + 12000 \, (30)^2 = \mathbf{144 \times 10^5 \text{ mm}^4}$

**Answer :** $\boxed{I_{AD} = 144 \times 10^5 \text{ mm}^4}$

**Example 4 :** *A hollow square has inner dimensions a × a and outer dimensions 2a × 2a. Find the moment of inertia about the outer side.*

**(B.T.E. S-2012, 1987; W-2007/4 Marks)**

**Data :** A hollow square as shown in Fig. 4.16.

**To find :** $I_{AB}$.

**Concept :** Use of parallel axis theorem.

**Solution :** Fig. 4.16 shows a square of inner dimensions a × a and outer dimensions 2a × 2a.

We have to find $I_{AB}$.

Here    B = D = 2a and

        b = d = a

(i) In this case,

$$I = I_{XX} = I_{YY}$$

$$= \frac{1}{12}[BD^3 - bd^3]$$

$$= \frac{1}{12}[(2a)(2a)^3 - (a)(a)^3]$$

$$= \frac{1}{12}[16\,a^4 - a^4] = \frac{15a^4}{12}$$

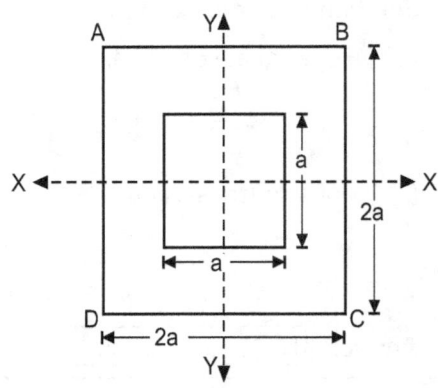

**Fig. 4.16**

(ii)   Now, area of hollow square section,

$$A = 2a \times 2a - a \times a = 4a^2 - a^2 = 3a^2$$

(iii)   Distance between AB and X-X axis,

$$h = \frac{2a}{2} = a$$

**(iv) Moment of inertia about the outer side AB :** Using parallel axis theorem,

$$I_{AB} = I_G + Ah^2 \qquad\qquad \text{... (i)}$$

where    $I_G = I_{XX} = \dfrac{15a^4}{12}$

Substituting these values in equation (i), we have

$$\mathbf{I_{AB}} = \frac{15a^4}{12} + (3a^2)(a)^2 = \frac{15a^4}{12} + 3a^4 = \frac{15a^4 + 36a^4}{12} = \mathbf{\frac{51a^4}{12}}$$

**Answer :**   $\boxed{\mathbf{I_{AB} = \dfrac{51a^4}{12}}}$

---

**Example 5 :** *Calculate the moment of inertia of a hollow rectangle about an axis passing through base 200 mm size. It has the following details :*

*(i)    Internal dimensions = 160 mm × 260 mm*

*(ii)   External dimensions = 200 mm × 300 mm*

**(B.T.E. S-1999/4 Marks)**

**Data :** A hollow rectangle as shown in Fig. 4.17.

    $b = 160$ mm, $d = 260$ mm, $B = 200$ mm, $D = 300$ mm

**To find :** $I_{Base}$.

**Concept :** (i) M.I. of hollow rectangle.

        (ii) Use of parallel axis theorem.

**Solution :** We have to calculate the moment of inertia of a hollow rectangle about the base PQ. Base PQ is parallel to XX axis.

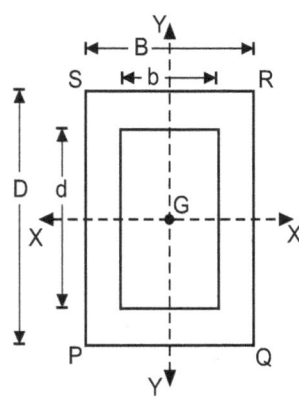

(i)    $I_{XX} = \dfrac{BD^3}{12} - \dfrac{bd^3}{12}$

          $= \dfrac{1}{12}(BD^3 - bd^3)$

          $= \dfrac{1}{12}[200 \times 300^3 - 160 \times 260^3]$

          $= 215653333.3$ mm$^4$

(ii)   $A = BD - bd = 200 \times 300 - 160 \times 260$

          $= \mathbf{18400}$ **mm²**

**Fig. 4.17**

(iii)   Distance between base PQ and XX axis,

          $h = \dfrac{D}{2} = \dfrac{300}{2} = \mathbf{150}$ **mm**

(iv)   Applying the theorem of parallel axis,

    M.I. about parallel axis = M.I. about C.G. axis + A × h²

∴          $\mathbf{I_{PQ}} = I_{XX} + Ah^2$

          $= 215653333.3 + 18400 \times 150^2 = \mathbf{435563333.3}$ **mm⁴**

**Answer :**    $\boxed{I_{PQ} = 435563333.3 \text{ mm}^4}$

---

**Example 6 :** *Calculate M.I. of a hollow rectangle about an axis passing through bottom side. The outer dimensions are 300 mm ×450 mm and inner dimensions are 200 mm ×350 mm.*

**(B.T.E. W-2008/4 Marks)**

**Answer :** $\boxed{I_{bottom} = 4854166667 \text{ mm}^4}$

---

**Type 1.2 : M.I. of circular and hollow circular sections.**

**Important Formulae**

(i)    For a solid circular section of diameter D,

        $I = I_{XX} = I_{YY} = \dfrac{\pi}{64}D^4$

        $A = \dfrac{\pi}{4}D^2$

(ii) For a hollow circular section of external diameter D and internal diameter d,

$$I = I_{XX} = I_{YY} = \frac{\pi}{64}(D^4 - d^4)$$

$$A = \frac{\pi}{4}(D^2 - d^2)$$

(iii) Radius of gyration, $K = \sqrt{\dfrac{I}{A}}$.

(iv) M.I. about tangent = M.I. about centroidal axis + Area $\times \left(\dfrac{D}{2}\right)^2$.

(v) $\qquad\qquad I_p = I_{ZZ} = I_{XX} + I_{YY}$

(vi) For a solid circular section of diameter D,

$$I_p = I_{XX} + I_{YY} = 2 \times \frac{\pi}{64}D^4 = \frac{\pi}{32}D^4$$

(vii) For a hollow circular section of external diameter D and internal diameter d,

$$I_p = I_{XX} + I_{YY} = 2 \times \frac{\pi}{64}(D^4 - d^4) = \frac{\pi}{32}(D^4 - d^4)$$

**Example 7 :** *Calculate polar M.I. of a circular section having 50 mm diameter.*

**(B.T.E. W-2012/2 Marks)**

**Data :** A solid circular section of diameter D = 50 mm.
**To find :** $I_p$.

**Solution :** $\quad \mathbf{I_p} = I_{XX} + I_{YY} = \dfrac{\pi}{64}D^4 + \dfrac{\pi}{64}D^4 = 2 \times \dfrac{\pi}{64}D^4 = \dfrac{\pi}{32}D^4$

$$= \frac{\pi}{32}(50)^4 = \textbf{613592.32 mm}^4$$

**Answer :** $\boxed{I_p = 613592.32 \text{ mm}^4}$

**Example 8 :** *Calculate the moment of inertia about any tangent of a circle having 400 mm radius.*

**(B.T.E. S-2005/2 Marks)**

**Data :** Radius of circle r = 400 mm. Hence, diameter d = 800 mm.
**To find :** $I_{tangent}$ or $I_{AB}$.
**Concept :** Theorem of parallel axis.
**Solution :** Refer to Fig. 4.18. Using theorem of parallel axis, M.I. about the tangent AB parallel to X-X axis can be written as,

$$I_{AB} = I_{XX} + Ah^2$$

$$= \frac{\pi}{64}d^4 + \left(\frac{\pi}{4}d^2\right)\left(\frac{d}{2}\right)^2$$

$$= \frac{\pi}{64}(800)^4 + \frac{\pi}{4}(800)^2\left(\frac{800}{2}\right)^2$$

$$= 2.01 \times 10^{10} + 8.04 \times 10^{10}$$

$$= 10.05 \times 10^{10} \text{ mm}^4$$

**Answer :** $\boxed{I_{AB} = 1 \times 10^{11} \text{ mm}^4}$

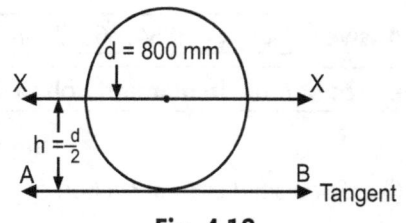

**Fig. 4.18**

**Example 9 :** *Calculate the moment of inertia about any tangent of a circle having 990 mm diameter.* **(B.T.E. S-2002/2 Marks)**

**Answer :** $\boxed{I_{AB} = 2.361 \times 10^{11} \text{ mm}^4}$

**Example 10 :** *Calculate moment of inertia and radius of gyration of 60 mm diameter circle.* **(B.T.E. W-2009/4 Marks)**

**Data :** Solid circular section, D = 60 mm.

**To find :** (i) I, (ii) K.

**Concept :** (i) $I = \dfrac{\pi}{64} D^4$, (ii) $K = \sqrt{\dfrac{I}{A}}$ and $A = \dfrac{\pi}{4} D^2$.

**Solution :** (i) For a solid circular section of diameter D,

$$\mathbf{I} = I_{XX} = I_{YY} = \frac{\pi}{64} D^4 = \frac{\pi}{64} (60)^4 = \mathbf{636172.51 \text{ mm}^4}$$

(ii)  Area of solid circular section,

$$A = \frac{\pi}{4} D^2 = \frac{\pi}{4} (60)^2 = 2827.43 \text{ mm}^2$$

(iii)  Now, radius of gyration,

$$\mathbf{K} = \sqrt{\frac{I}{A}} = \sqrt{\frac{636172.51}{2827.43}} = \mathbf{15 \text{ mm}}$$

**Answer :** $\boxed{\text{(i) } I = 636172.51 \text{ mm}^4, \text{ (ii) } K = 15 \text{ mm}}$

---

**Example 11 :** *A hollow C.I. pipe, with external diameter 100 mm and thickness of metal 10 mm is used as a strut. Calculate the moment of inertia and radius of gyration about its diameter.* **(B.T.E. W-2005/4 Marks)**

**Data :** A hollow C.I. pipe. External diameter, D = 100 mm, thickness, t = 10 mm

Internal diameter, d = 100 – 2 × 10 = 80 mm.

**To find :** (i) I and (ii) K.

**Concept :** M.I. about diameter = $I_{XX} = I_{YY}$.

**Solution : (i) Moment of inertia :**

$$\mathbf{I_{XX}} = I_{YY} = \frac{\pi}{64} (D^4 - d^4) = \frac{\pi}{64} (100^4 - 80^4) = \mathbf{2898119.223 \text{ mm}^4}$$

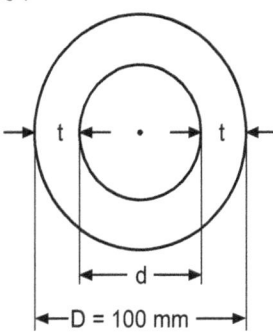

**Fig. 4.19**

**(ii)   Area :**  $A = \dfrac{\pi}{4}(D^2 - d^2) = \dfrac{\pi}{4}(100^2 - 80^2) = 2827.43 \text{ mm}^2$

**(iii)   Radius of gyration :**  $K = \sqrt{\dfrac{I}{A}} = \sqrt{\dfrac{2898119.223}{2827.43}} = \textbf{32 mm}$

**Answer :**  $\boxed{I = 2898119.223 \text{ mm}^4, K = 32 \text{ mm}}$

---

**Example 12 :** *A hollow circular section with 200 mm external diameter and 100 mm internal diameter. Calculate the moment of inertia of the section about any of its tangent.*

**(B.T.E. W-1999/4 Marks)**

**Data :** D = 200 mm,  d = 100 mm

**To find :** $I_{AB}$.

**Concept :** (i)   M.I. of hollow circular section.

(ii)   Use of parallel axis theorem.

**Solution :** (i) M.I. of hollow circular section about XX-axis,

$$I_{XX} = \frac{\pi}{64}(D^4 - d^4)$$

$$= \frac{\pi}{64}(200^4 - 100^4)$$

$$= 73631077.82 \text{ mm}^4$$

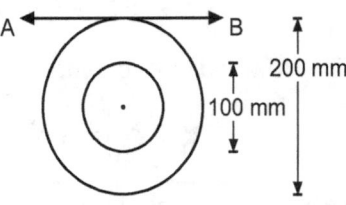

**Fig. 4.20**

(ii)   Distance between tangent AB and XX-axis = h = $\dfrac{200}{2}$ = 100 mm

(iii)   M.I. about tangent AB ($I_{AB}$) : The tangent AB is parallel to XX axis.

Hence we have to use parallel axis theorem,

$$\textbf{I}_{\textbf{AB}} = I_{XX} + Ah^2 = 73631077.82 + \frac{\pi}{4}(200^2 - 100^2)(100)^2$$

$$= 73631077.82 + 235619449 = \textbf{309250526.8 mm}^4$$

**Answer :**  $\boxed{I_{AB} = 309250526.8 \text{ mm}^4}$

---

**Type 1.3 : M.I. of triangular section of base 'b' and height 'h'.**

| Important Formulae |
|:---:|
| $I_{XX} = \dfrac{bh^3}{36}$ , $I_{Base} = \dfrac{bh^3}{12}$ , $I_{Apex} = \dfrac{bh^3}{4}$ |
| $A = \dfrac{1}{2} \times b \times h$ |

**Example 13 :** *State the values of moment of inertia of (i) triangle about its base, (ii) circle about its diameter.* (B.T.E. S-1999/2 Marks)

**Solution :** (i) M.I. of triangle about its base,

$$I_{Base} = I_{BC} = \frac{bh^3}{12}$$

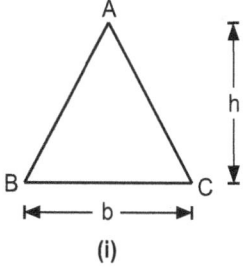

(i)

(ii)　M.I. of circle about its diameter,

$$I_{Diameter} = I_{AB}$$

$$= \frac{\pi}{64} D^4$$

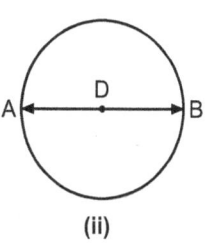

(ii)

**Fig. 4.21**

---

**Example 14 :** *Find M.I. of an equilateral triangle of side 2 m about its base.* (B.T.E. W-2011/2 Marks)

**Solution :** Refer to Fig. 4.22.

In △ ABD,

$$\tan 60° = \frac{AD}{BD} = \frac{h}{(2/2)}$$

∴　　　h = 1.732 m

M.I. of a triangle about its base,

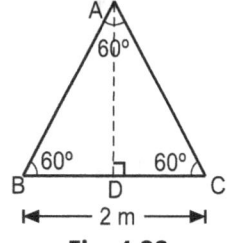

**Fig. 4.22**

$$I_{Base} = I_{BC} = \frac{bh^3}{12} = \frac{2 \times (1.732)^3}{12} = \textbf{0.865949 m}^4$$

---

**Example 15 :** *An equilateral triangle has a side of 150 mm. Find the moment of inertia about its any one of the sides.* (B.T.E. W- 2010, 2005/3 Marks)

**Answer :** $\boxed{I_{Base} = I_{BC} = 27399173.74 \text{ mm}^4}$

---

**Example 16 :** *An isosceles triangular section ABC has base width 80 mm and height 60 mm. Determine the M.I. of the section about the c.g. of the section and the base BC.* (B.T.E. S-2015, W-2012/4 Marks)

**Solution :** $I_{Base} = \frac{bh^3}{12} = \frac{80 \times 60^3}{12} = \textbf{1440000 mm}^4$

$$I_{XX} = \frac{bh^3}{36} = \frac{80 \times 60^3}{36} = \textbf{480000 mm}^4$$

**Answer :** $\boxed{I_{Base} = 1440000 \text{ mm}^4, \; I_{XX} = 480000 \text{ mm}^4}$

**Example 17 :** *Find the moment of inertia of right angled triangle 90 mm height and 120 mm base about an horizontal axis passing through apex.*     **(B.T.E. W-1997/2 Marks)**

**Solution :** M.I. about horizontal axis passing through apex,

$$I_{Apex} = \frac{bh^3}{4} = \frac{120 \times 90^3}{4} = 2187 \times 10^4 \text{ mm}^4$$

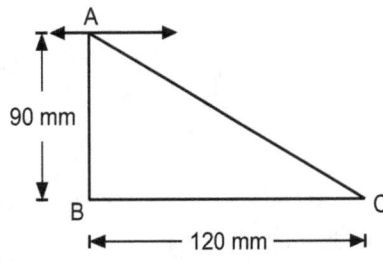

**Fig. 4.23**

**Answer :** $\boxed{I_{Apex} = 2187 \times 10^4 \text{ mm}^4}$

---

**Example 18 :** *Find the M.I. of a right angled triangle 100 mm high and 140 mm base in the following cases :*

1. *About an axis passing through the base.*
2. *About a horizontal axis passing through its C.G.*
3. *About an axis passing through the apex and parallel to the base.*

**(B.T.E. S-2013, W-2003/4 Marks)**

**Data :** A right angled triangle, b = 140 mm, h = 100 mm.

**To find :** (i) $I_{Base}$, (ii) $I_{XX}$, (iii) $I_{Apex}$.

**Concept :** Use of standard formulae.

**Solution :**

(i)     $I_{Base} = I_{BC} = \dfrac{bh^3}{12} = \dfrac{140 \times 100^3}{12} = \mathbf{1.16667 \times 10^7 \text{ mm}^4}$

(ii)     $I_{XX} = \dfrac{bh^3}{36} = \dfrac{140 \times 100^3}{36} = \mathbf{3.88889 \times 10^6 \text{ mm}^4}$

(iii)     $I_{Apex} = I_{PQ} = \dfrac{bh^3}{4} = \dfrac{140 \times 100^3}{4} = \mathbf{3.5 \times 10^7 \text{ mm}^4}$

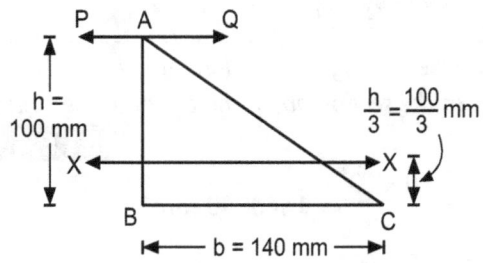

**Fig. 4.24**

**Ans. :** $\boxed{\text{(i) } I_{Base} = 1.16667 \times 10^7 \text{ mm}^4, \text{ (ii) } I_{XX} = 3.88889 \times 10^6 \text{ mm}^4, \text{ (iii) } I_{Apex} = 3.5 \times 10^7 \text{ mm}^4}$

**Example 19 :** *Calculate the moment of inertia for a triangle of height 100 mm about an axis passing through the vertex and parallel to the base, if moment of inertia about the base is $10^4$ mm$^4$.* **(B.T.E. W-2010, 2008; S-1998/4 Marks)**

**Data :** A triangle as shown in Fig. 4.25, h = 100 mm, $I_{Base} = I_{BC} = 10^4$ mm$^4$

**To find :** $I_{vertex}$ i.e. $I_{PQ}$.

**Concept :** Use of standard formulae.

**Solution :** We have to calculate the moment of inertia of a triangle ABC about an axis PQ passing through vertex A and parallel to the base BC.

We know that,

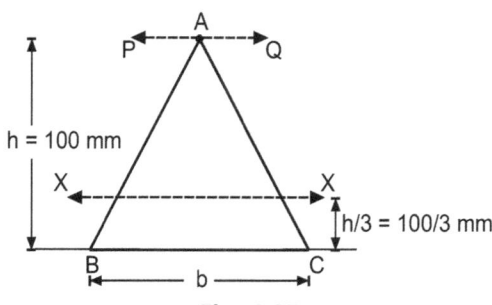

$$I_{Base} = I_{BC} = b \times \frac{h^3}{12}$$

∴ $$10^4 = b \times \frac{100^3}{12}$$

∴ $$b = \frac{10^4 \times 12}{100^3} = 0.12 \text{ mm}$$

**Fig. 4.25**

We know that, $$I_{apex} = \mathbf{I_{PQ}} = b \times \frac{h^3}{4} = 0.12 \times \frac{100^3}{4} = \mathbf{30000 \text{ mm}^4 = 3 \times 10^4 \text{ mm}^4}$$

**Answer :**   $\boxed{I_{PQ} = 3 \times 10^4 \text{ mm}^4}$

---

**Example 20 :** *A base 'b' of an equilateral triangle is horizontal. Show that the centroidal moment of inertia with respect to horizontal and vertical axes are equal. State the value of moment of inertia in terms of 'b'.* **(B.T.E. S-1987/4 Marks)**

**Data :** An equilateral triangle of base = b, height = h (say).

**To find :** $I_{XX}$, $I_{YY}$ and to show that $I_{XX} = I_{YY}$.

**Concept :** (i) $I_{XX} = \dfrac{bh^3}{36}$, (ii) $I_{YY} = 2 I_{BD}$.

**Solution :** Fig. 4.26 (i) shows an equilateral triangle having base 'b' and height 'h'. To show that $I_{XX} = I_{YY}$.

In a triangle ADB,

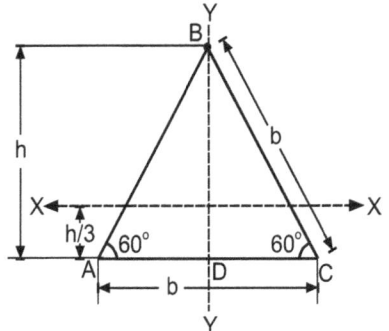

$$\tan 60° = \frac{h}{b/2}$$

∴ $$\sqrt{3} = \frac{2h}{b}$$

∴ $$h = \left(\frac{\sqrt{3}}{2}\right) b$$

**Fig. 4.26 (i)**

The positions of X-X and YY axes are as shown in Fig. 4.26 (i).

In this case, $\quad I_{XX} = \dfrac{bh^3}{36} = \dfrac{1}{36} b \left(\dfrac{\sqrt{3}}{2} b\right)^3 = \dfrac{1}{36} \dfrac{3\sqrt{3}}{8} b^4$

$$= \dfrac{\sqrt{3}}{96} b^4 \qquad\qquad \text{... (i)}$$

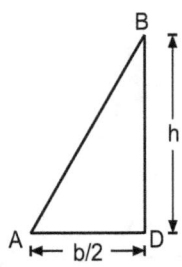

**Fig. 4.26 (ii)**

Now, M.I. of a triangle ADB about YY axis = M.I. of a triangle CDB about YY axis. Consider a triangle ADB as shown in Fig. 4.26 (ii). Treating BD as base and AD as height, we have

$$I_{BD} = \dfrac{1}{12} \text{(base) (height)}^3 = \dfrac{1}{12} (h) \left(\dfrac{h}{2}\right)^3$$

Similarly M.I. of a triangle CDB about BD,

$$I_{BD} = \dfrac{1}{12} (h) \left(\dfrac{h}{2}\right)^3$$

Now, YY axis and BD are coinciding.

∴ M.I. of a complete triangle ABC about YY axis,

$$I_{YY} = 2\, I_{BD} = 2 \times \dfrac{1}{12} (h) \left(\dfrac{b}{2}\right)^3 = \dfrac{hb^3}{48}$$

But $\qquad\qquad h = \dfrac{\sqrt{3}}{2} \cdot b$

∴ $\qquad\qquad I_{YY} = \dfrac{\dfrac{\sqrt{3}}{2} b \cdot b^3}{48} = \dfrac{\sqrt{3}}{96} b^4 \qquad\qquad \text{... (ii)}$

∴ From the equations (i) and (ii),

$$I_{XX} = I_{YY} = \dfrac{\sqrt{3}}{96} b^4$$

**Answer :** $\quad \boxed{I_{XX} = I_{YY} = \dfrac{\sqrt{3}}{96} b^4}$

---

**Example 21 :** *Calculate the ratio of moment of inertia of equilateral triangle about horizontal and vertical centroidal axis. The side of the triangle is $\sqrt{3}$ m.*

**(B.T.E. S-2006/4 Marks)**

**Data**     : An equilateral triangle b = $\sqrt{3}$ m, height = h (say).

**To find**   : $\dfrac{I_{XX}}{I_{YY}}$.

**Concept :** For an equilateral triangle, $I_{XX} = I_{YY} = \left(\dfrac{\sqrt{3}}{96}\right) b^4$.

**Solution : Hint :** Calculate $I_{XX}$ and $I_{YY}$ in terms of b and h as shown in the above example.

For an equilateral triangle of base 'b' and height 'h',

$$I_{XX} = I_{YY} = \frac{\sqrt{3}}{96} b^4$$

$$= \frac{\sqrt{3}}{96} (\sqrt{3})^4 = 0.1623 \text{ m}^4$$

$$\frac{I_{XX}}{I_{YY}} = \frac{\frac{\sqrt{3}}{96} b^4}{\frac{\sqrt{3}}{96} b^4} = \frac{0.1623}{0.1623} = 1$$

**Answer :** $\boxed{\frac{I_{XX}}{I_{YY}} = 1}$

---

### Type 1.4 : M.I. of semi-circle and quarter circle of radius R.

(i)　For a semi-circular section of radius 'R' or diameter 'D',

$$I_{XX} = 0.11 R^4, \ I_{YY} = I_{Base} = \frac{\pi}{128} D^4$$

$$\text{Area A } = \frac{\pi R^2}{2}$$

(ii)　For a quarter circle of radius 'R',

$$I = I_{XX} = I_{YY} = \frac{0.11 R^4}{2} = 0.055 R^4$$

$$\text{Area A } = \frac{\pi R^2}{4}$$

(iii)　　$I_p = I_{XX} + I_{YY}$

(iv)　　$K_{XX} = \sqrt{\frac{I_{XX}}{A}}$

(v)　　$K_{YY} = \frac{I_{YY}}{A}$

**Example 22 :** *A semi-circle of diameter 200 mm is as shown in Fig. 4.27. Find* $I_{AB}$, $I_{XX}$, $I_{YY}$, $I_P$, $K_{XX}$ *and* $K_{YY}$. **(V.V. Imp./4 Marks)**

**Data :** A semi-circle of diameter 200 mm as shown in Fig. 4.27.

**To find :** (i) $I_{AB}$, (ii) $I_{XX}$, (iii) $I_{YY}$, (iv) $I_P$, (v) $K_{XX}$ and (vi) $K_{YY}$.

**Concept :** Use of standard formulae.

**Solution :** Diameter of the semi-circle, D = 200 mm

Radius of the semi-circle,

$$R = \frac{200}{2} = 100 \text{ mm}$$

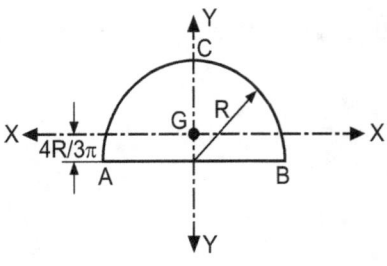

(i) We know that

$$\mathbf{I_{AB}} = \frac{1}{2}\left(\frac{\pi}{64} D^4\right)$$

$$= \frac{\pi}{128} D^4 = \frac{\pi}{128} \times (200)^4$$

$$= \mathbf{39269908.17 \text{ mm}^4}$$

**Fig. 4.27**

(ii) For a semi-circle, $\mathbf{I_{YY}} = I_{AB} = \mathbf{39269908.17 \text{ mm}^4}$

(iii) $\mathbf{I_{XX}} = 0.11 \, R^4 = 0.11 \times (100)^4 = \mathbf{11 \times 10^6 \text{ mm}^4}$

(iv) Now, $\mathbf{I_P} = I_{XX} + I_{YY} = 11 \times 10^6 + 39269908.17 = \mathbf{50269908.17 \text{ mm}^4}$

Area of the semi-circle,

$$A = \frac{\pi R^2}{2} = \frac{\pi \times 100^2}{2} = 15707.96 \text{ mm}^2$$

(v) Now, $\mathbf{K_{XX}} = \sqrt{\frac{I_{XX}}{A}} = \sqrt{\frac{11 \times 10^6}{15707.96}} = \mathbf{26.46 \text{ mm}}$

(vi) and $\mathbf{K_{YY}} = \sqrt{\frac{I_{YY}}{A}} = \sqrt{\frac{39269908.17}{15707.96}} = \mathbf{50 \text{ mm}}$

**Answer :** $\boxed{\begin{array}{l} \text{(i) } I_{AB} = I_{YY} = 32269908.17 \text{ mm}^4, \text{ (ii) } I_{XX} = 11 \times 10^6 \text{ mm}^4, \\ \text{(iii) } I_P = 50269908.17 \text{ mm}^4, \text{ (iv) } K_{XX} = 26.46 \text{ mm}, \text{ (v) } K_{YY} = 50 \text{ mm} \end{array}}$

---

**Example 23 :** *Find $I_P$ of a quadrant of a circle of radius 50 mm.* **(V.V. Imp./4 Marks)**

**Data :** A quadrant of a circle as shown in Fig. 4.28, R = 50 mm.

**To find :** $I_P$.

**Concept :** Use of standard formulae.

**Solution :** Fig. 4.28 shows a quadrant of a circle.

Here　　　　　　R = 50 mm

$$I_{XX} = I_{YY} = 0.055 \, R^4$$

$$= 0.055 \times 50^4$$

$$= 343750 \text{ mm}^4$$

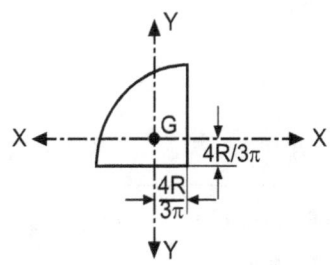

**Fig. 4.28**

Now, $I_P = I_{XX} + I_{YY} = 2I_{XX}$ 　　　　　$\left(\because I_{XX} = I_{YY}\right)$

**Answer :** $\boxed{\mathbf{I_P} = 2 \times 343750 = \mathbf{687500 \text{ mm}^4}}$

## Type 2 : Examples based on M.I. of composite sections.

### Important Formulae

(i)   C.G. of the composite section is calculated by using

$$\bar{x} = \frac{a_1x_1 + a_2x_2 + a_3x_3 + \ldots}{A}$$

$$\bar{y} = \frac{a_1y_1 + a_2y_2 + a_3y_3 + \ldots}{A}$$

where,          $A = a_1 + a_2 + a_3$ = Area of composite section.

(ii)  $I_{G_1}, I_{G_2}, I_{G_3} \ldots$ moments of inertia of the areas 1, 2, 3 about their own centroidal axes.

X-X and Y-Y can be calculated by using standard formulae. (Refer to Section 4.5)

(iii) Knowing $I_{G_1}, I_{G_2}, I_{G_3} \ldots$ M.I. about X-X axis can be calculated by using parallel axis theorem.

$$I_{XX} = I_{XX_1} + I_{XX_2} + I_{XX_3} + \ldots\ldots$$

where          $I_{XX_1} = I_{G_1} + a_1h_1^2$, $I_{XX_2} = I_{G_2} + a_2h_2^2$, $I_{XX_3} = I_{G_3} + a_3h_3^2$,

where,          $h_1$ = distance between $G_1$ and XX axis

                $h_2$ = distance between $G_2$ and XX axis

                $h_3$ = distance between $G_3$ and XX axis

(iv)  Similarly, M.I. about Y-Y axis can be calculated by using parallel axis theorem

$$I_{YY} = I_{YY_1} + I_{YY_2} + I_{YY_3} + \ldots$$

where,          $I_{YY_1} = I_{G_1} + a_1h_1^2$, $I_{YY_2} = I_{G_2} + a_2h_2^2$, $I_{YY_3} = I_{G_3} + a_3h_3^2$,

where,          $h_1$ = distance between $G_1$ and YY axis

                $h_2$ = distance between $G_2$ and YY axis

                $h_3$ = distance between $G_3$ and YY axis

### Type 2.1 : Solved examples on M.I. of symmetrical I section.

Refer to Fig. 4.29.

Since the section is symmetrical about XX axis, its M.I. can be calculated by considering a hollow rectangular section.

$$I_{XX} = \frac{BD^3}{12} - \frac{bd^3}{12} = \frac{1}{12}(BD^3 - bd^3)$$

$$I_{YY} = 2 \times (\text{M.I. of flanges}) + \text{M.I. of web}$$

**Example 24 :** *Find the least M.I. of a symmetrical section having following details.*

*Flanges : 100 mm × 15 mm*

*Overall depth : 280 mm, Thickness of web : 10 mm*          **(V.V. Imp./4 Marks)**

**Data :** A symmetrical I-section as shown in Fig. 4.29.

**To find :** $I_{least}$.

**Concept :** $I_{least} = I_{YY}$.

**Solution :** (i) Divide the section into three areas 1, 2 and 3 as shown in Fig. 4.29.

(ii)  Areas :        $a_1 = a_3 = 100 \times 15 = 1500$ mm², $a_2 = 250 \times 10 = 2500$ mm²

∴ Total area,     $A = a_1 + a_2 + a_3 = 1500 + 2500 + 1500 = 5500$ mm²

(iii)  In this case, we get two lines of symmetry X-X and Y-Y as shown in Fig. 4.29. Hence C.G. is the point of intersection of these two lines of symmetry.

Distance of Y-Y axis from the left face, $\bar{x} = \dfrac{100}{2} = 50$ mm

Distance of X-X axis from the bottom face, $\bar{y} = \dfrac{280}{2} = 140$ mm

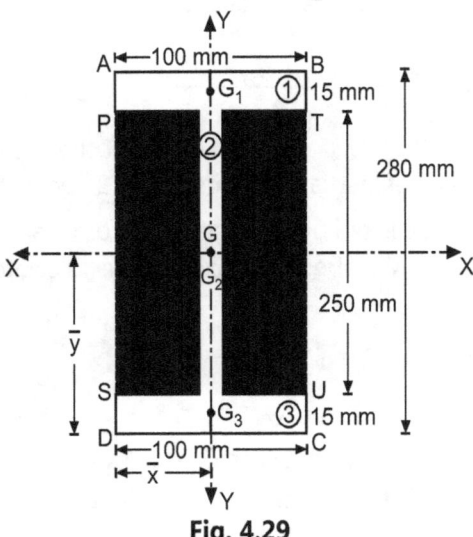

**Fig. 4.29**

(iv) M.I. of I section about X-X axis,

$$I_{XX} = \text{M.I. of rectangle ABCD} - \text{M.I. of rectangle PQRS}$$
$$- \text{M.I. of rectangle WTUV}$$

$$= I_{XX_1} - I_{XX_2} - I_{XX_3}$$

$$I_{XX_1} = \text{M.I. of rectangle ABCD about X-X axis}$$

$$= \dfrac{100 \times 280^3}{12} = 182933333.3 \text{ mm}^4$$

$$I_{XX_2} = I_{XX_3} = \text{M.I. of rectangle PQRS or WTUV about X-X axis}$$

$$= \dfrac{\left[\dfrac{(100-10)}{2}\right](250)^3}{12} = \dfrac{45 \times 250^3}{12} = 58593750 \text{ mm}^4$$

∴　　　$$I_{XX} = 182933333.3 - (58593750 \times 2) = 65.74 \times 10^6 \text{ mm}^4 \text{ (approximately)}$$

(v) **To find $I_{YY}$:** M.I. of the section about the vertical centroidal axis is given by,

$$I_{YY} = I_{YY_1} + I_{YY_2} + I_{YY_3}$$

$$I_{YY_1} = \text{M.I. of rectangle 1 about the vertical centroidal axis Y-Y}$$

$$= \dfrac{15 \times 100^3}{12} = 1250000 \text{ mm}^4 \qquad\qquad \dots \text{(i)}$$

$$I_{YY_2} = \text{M.I. of rectangle 2 about the vertical centroidal axis Y-Y}$$

$$= \dfrac{250 \times 10^3}{12} = 20833.33 \text{ mm}^4 \qquad\qquad \dots \text{(ii)}$$

$I_{YY_3}$ = M.I. of rectangle 3 about the vertical centroidal axis Y-Y

= $I_{YY_1}$ = 1250000 mm⁴                                                         ... (iii)

**Note :** Since $a_3 = a_1$, $I_{YY_3} = I_{YY_1}$

Adding the equations (i), (ii) and (iii),

$I_{YY}$ = 1250000 + 20833.33 + 1250000 = 2520833.33 mm⁴

∴ Least moment of inertia is given by,

$I_{least}$ = $I_{YY}$ = 2520833.33 mm⁴ = **25.2 × 10⁵ mm⁴ (approx.)**

(Least radius of gyration is given by,

$$K_{YY} = \sqrt{\frac{I_{YY}}{A}} = \sqrt{\frac{2520833.33}{5500}} = \sqrt{485.33} = 21.4 \text{ mm})$$

**Answer :** $\boxed{I_{least} = I_{YY} = 25.2 \times 10^5 \text{ mm}^4}$

---

**Example 25 :** *A symmetrical I-section has the following dimensions. Calculate polar M.I. of the section. Flanges = 100 mm × 10 mm, Web = 10 mm × 100 mm.*

**(B.T.E. S-2013, W-2003/4 Marks)**

**Data :** A symmetrical I section as shown in Fig. 4.30.

**To find :** $I_P$.

**Concept :** Calculate $I_{XX}$ and $I_{YY}$. $I_P = I_{XX} + I_{YY}$.

**Solution :** (i) Since the section is symmetrical about XX axis, its M.I. can be determined by considering a hollow rectangular section.

B = 100 mm, D = 10 + 100 + 10 = 120 mm,

b = (100 – 10) = 90 mm, d = 100 mm

(ii)      $I_{XX} = \dfrac{BD^3}{12} - \dfrac{bd^3}{12} = \dfrac{1}{12}(BD^3 - bd)^3$

$= \dfrac{1}{12}[100 \times 120^3 - 90 \times 100^3] = $ **6.9 × 10⁶ mm⁴**

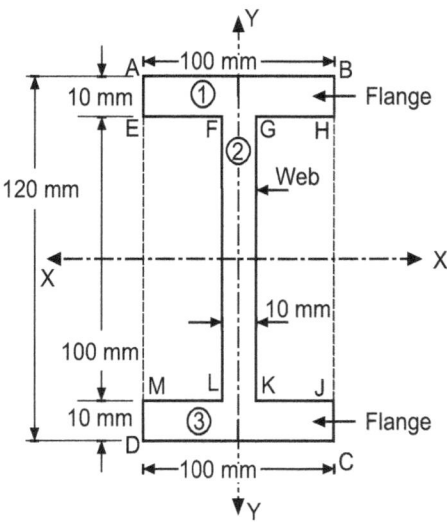

**Fig. 4.30**

**Note :** M.I. about YY axis should not be calculated as $\frac{1}{12}$ (DB$^3$ – db$^3$) since the c.g. of rectangles EFLM and GHJK are not lying on YY axis.

(iii) $\qquad I_{YY} = 2 \times$ M.I. of flanges + M.I. of web

$$= 2 \times \left(\frac{10 \times 100^3}{12}\right) + 100 \times \frac{10^3}{12} = \mathbf{1.675 \times 10^6\,mm^4}$$

(iv) Polar M.I. of section,

$$I_P = I_{ZZ} = I_{XX} + I_{YY}$$

$$= 6.9 \times 10^6 + 1.675 \times 10^6 = \mathbf{8.575 \times 10^6\,mm^4}$$

**Answer :** $\boxed{I_P = 8.575 \times 10^6\,mm^4}$

---

### Similar Example for Practice :

**Example 26 :** *A symmetrical I-section of overall depth of 300 mm, has its flanges 150 mm × 10 mm and web 10 mm thick. Find the moment of inertia about its centroidal axis, parallel to the flanges.* **(B.T.E. W-2010, S-2005/4 Marks)**

**Data :** As shown in Fig. 4.31.

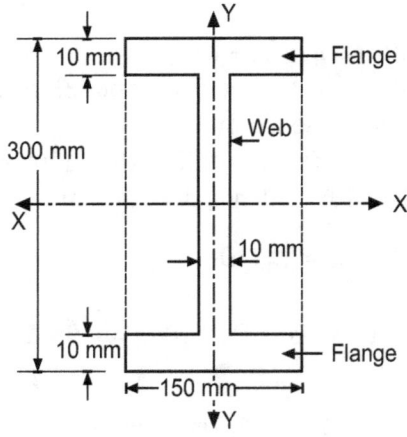

**Fig. 4.31**

**To find :** $I_{XX}$ and $I_{YY}$.

**Concept :** Same as the above example.

**Solution :**

$$I_{XX} = \frac{B \cdot D^3 - b \cdot d^3}{12} = \frac{150\,(300)^3 - (150 - 10)\,(300 - 2 \times 10)^3}{12}$$

$$= \mathbf{8.14 \times 10^7\,mm^4}$$

$$I_{YY} = 2 \times \text{M.I. of flange} + \text{M.I. of web}$$

$$= 2 \times \left(\frac{10 \times 150^3}{12}\right) + \frac{(300 - 2 \times 10)\,(10)^3}{12} = \mathbf{5.6483 \times 10^6\,mm^4}$$

**Answer :** $\boxed{I_{XX} = 8.14 \times 10^7\,mm^4,\ I_{YY} = 5.6483 \times 10^6\,mm^4}$

## Type 2.2 : Solved examples on M.I. of unsymmetrical I section.

Refer to Fig. 4.32.

$$I_{XX} = I_{XX_1} + I_{XX_2} + I_{XX_3}$$

$$= (I_{G_1} + a_1 h_1^2) + (I_{G_2} + a_2 h_2^2) + (I_{G_3} + a_3 h_3^2) \text{ where } h = |y - \bar{y}|$$

$$I_{YY} = I_{YY_1} + I_{YY_2} + I_{YY_3} = \sum \frac{db^3}{12} = \frac{d_1 b_1^3}{12} + \frac{d_2 b_2^3}{12} + \frac{d_3 b_3^3}{12}$$

where, $d_1, d_2, d_3 \rightarrow$ depth of rectangles 1, 2 and 3 respectively.

$b_1, b_2, b_3 \rightarrow$ width of rectangles 1, 2 and 3 respectively.

**Example 27 :** *Determine the M.I. of an unsymmetrical I section having the following details.*

*Top flange 160 mm $\times$ 12 mm, Bottom flange 240 mm $\times$ 12 mm, Web 200 mm $\times$ 10 mm*

**(B.T.E. W-1989/4 Marks)**

**Data :** An unsymmetrical I section as shown in Fig. 4.32.

**To find :** $I_{XX}$ and $I_{YY}$.

**Concept :** (i)     $I_{XX} = I_{XX_1} + I_{XX_2} + I_{XX_3}$

$$= (I_{G_1} + a_1 h_1^2) + (I_{G_2} + a_2 h_2^2) + (I_{G_3} + a_3 h_3^2)$$

(ii)     $I_{YY} = I_{YY_1} + I_{YY_2} + I_{YY_3}$

$$= \frac{d_1 b_1^3}{12} + \frac{d_2 b_2^3}{12} + \frac{d_3 b_3^3}{12}$$

**Solution :**

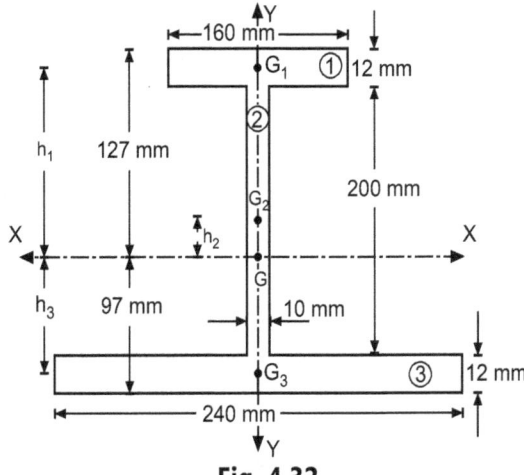

**Fig. 4.32**

**Note :**     $h = |y - \bar{y}|, \ h_1 = y_1 - \bar{y} = 218 - 97 = 121 \text{ mm} \ \ (\because y_1 > \bar{y})$

$h_2 = y_2 - \bar{y} = 112 - 97 = 15 \text{ mm} \qquad (\because y_2 > \bar{y})$

$h_3 = \bar{y} - y_3 = 97 - 6 = 91 \text{ mm} \qquad (\because \bar{y} > y_3)$

**Step 1 :** Let us divide the section into three rectangles 1, 2 and 3 as shown in Fig. 4.32. As the section is symmetrical about Y-Y axis, C.G. of the section will lie on this axis.

**Step 2 : Areas :**

$$a_1 = 160 \times 12 = 1920 \text{ mm}^2$$

$$a_2 = 200 \times 10 = 2000 \text{ mm}^2$$

$$a_3 = 240 \times 12 = 2880 \text{ mm}^2$$

Total area,     $A = a_1 + a_2 + a_3 = 1920 + 2000 + 2880 = 6800 \text{ mm}^2$

**Step 3 : Distances of the centroid from the bottom face :**

$$y_1 = 12 + 200 + \frac{12}{2} = 218 \text{ mm}$$

$$y_2 = 12 + \frac{200}{2} = 112 \text{ mm}$$

$$y_3 = \frac{12}{2} = 6 \text{ mm}$$

∴ Distance of horizontal centroidal axis from the bottom face,

$$\bar{y} = \frac{a_1 y_1 + a_2 y_2 + a_3 y_3}{A}$$

$$= \frac{1920 \times 218 + 2000 \times 112 + 2880 \times 6}{6800} = \frac{659840}{6800} = 97 \text{ mm}$$

∴ Distance of horizontal centroidal axis from the top face

$$= \text{Total depth} - \bar{y} \text{ from bottom face}$$

$$= 12 + 200 + 12 - 97 = 127 \text{ mm}$$

**Step 4 : To find $I_{XX}$ :** M.I. of the I section about the horizontal centroidal axis is given by,

$$I_{XX} = I_{XX_1} + I_{XX_2} + I_{XX_3}$$

$$I_{XX_1} = \text{M.I. of rectangle 1 about the horizontal centroidal axis X-X}$$

$$= I_{G_1} + a_1 h_1^2$$

where,     $I_{G_1}$ = M.I. of rectangle 1 about the horizontal axis passing through $G_1$

$$= \frac{160 \times 12^3}{12} = 23040 \text{ mm}^4$$

$$h_1 = \text{Distance between } G_1 \text{ and X-X axis} = 127 - \frac{12}{2} = 121 \text{ mm}$$

(or  $h_1 = y_1 - \bar{y} = 218 - 97 = 121 \text{ mm}$ )

$$I_{XX_1} = 23040 + 1920 \times (121)^2 = 28133760 \text{ mm}^4 \qquad \ldots \text{(i)}$$

$$I_{XX_2} = \text{M.I. of rectangle 2 about the horizontal centroidal axis X-X}$$

$$= I_{G_2} + a_2 h_2^2$$

where,    $I_{G_2}$ = M.I. of rectangle 2 about the horizontal axis passing through $G_2$

$$= \frac{10 \times 200^3}{12} = 6666666.67 \text{ mm}^4$$

$h_2$ = Distance between $G_2$ and X-X axis

$$= 127 - \left(12 + \frac{200}{2}\right) = 127 - 112 = 15 \text{ mm}$$

(or $h_2$ = $y_2 - \bar{y}$ = 112 - 97 = 15 mm)

∴    $I_{XX_2}$ = 6666666.67 + 2000 × (15)² = 7116666.67 mm⁴    ... (ii)

$I_{XX_3}$ = M.I. of rectangle 3 about the horizontal centroidal axis X-X

$$= I_{G_3} + a_3 h_3^2$$

where,    $I_{G_3}$ = M.I. of rectangle 3 about the horizontal axis passing through $G_3$

$$= \frac{240 \times 12^3}{12} = 34560 \text{ mm}^4$$

$h_3$ = Distance between $G_3$ and X-X axis = $97 - \dfrac{12}{2}$ = 91 mm

(Note : $h_3$ = $\bar{y} - y_3$ = 97 - 6 = 91 mm)

∴    $I_{XX_3}$ = 34560 + 2880 × (91)² = 23883840 mm⁴    ... (iii)

Adding (i), (ii) and (iii), M.I. of the whole section about X-X axis is given by,

$\mathbf{I_{XX}}$ = 28133760 + 7116666.67 + 23883840

= 59134266.67 mm⁴ = **59.13 × 10⁶ mm⁴**

**Step 5 : To find $I_{YY}$ :** M.I. of the I-section about the vertical centroidal axis is given by

$$I_{YY} = I_{YY_1} + I_{YY_2} + I_{YY_3}$$

$I_{YY_1}$ = M.I. of rectangle 1 about the vertical centroidal axis YY

$$= \frac{12 \times 160^3}{12} = 4096000 \text{ mm}^4 \qquad \text{... (iv)}$$

$I_{YY_2}$ = M.I. of rectangle 2 about the vertical centroidal axis YY

$$= \frac{200 \times 10^3}{12} = 16666.67 \text{ mm}^4 \qquad \text{... (v)}$$

$I_{YY_3}$ = M.I. of rectangle 3 about the vertical centroidal axis YY

$$= \frac{12 \times 240^3}{12} = 13824000 \text{ mm}^4 \qquad \text{... (vi)}$$

Adding (iv), (v) and (vi), M.I. of the whole section about YY axis is given by,

$\mathbf{I_{YY}}$ = 4096000 + 16666.67 + 1382400

= 17936666.67 mm⁴ = **17.93 × 10⁶ mm⁴**

**Answer :**    $\boxed{I_{XX} = 59.13 \times 10^6 \text{ mm}^4, I_{YY} = 17.93 \times 10^6 \text{ mm}^4}$

**Note :** Instead of finding $\overline{y}_{top}$ and then calculating $h_1$, $h_2$ and $h_3$, they can also be calculated as follows :

$$h_1 = y_1 - \overline{y} = 218 - 97 = 121 \text{ mm}, \quad h_2 = y_2 - \overline{y} = 112 - 97 = 15 \text{ mm}$$
$$h_3 = y_1 - y_3 = 97 - 6 = 91 \text{ mm}$$

The same procedure for calculating $h_1$, $h_2$, $h_3$ can be followed for all the solved problems.

**Example 28 :** *Find the moment of inertia of the section shown in Fig. 4.33 (i) about the centroidal X-X axis, perpendicular to the web.*　　**(B.T.E. S-2009/4 Marks)**

**Data :** An unsymmetrical I section as shown in Fig. 4.33 (i).

**To find :** $I_{XX}$.

**Concept :** Same as the above example.

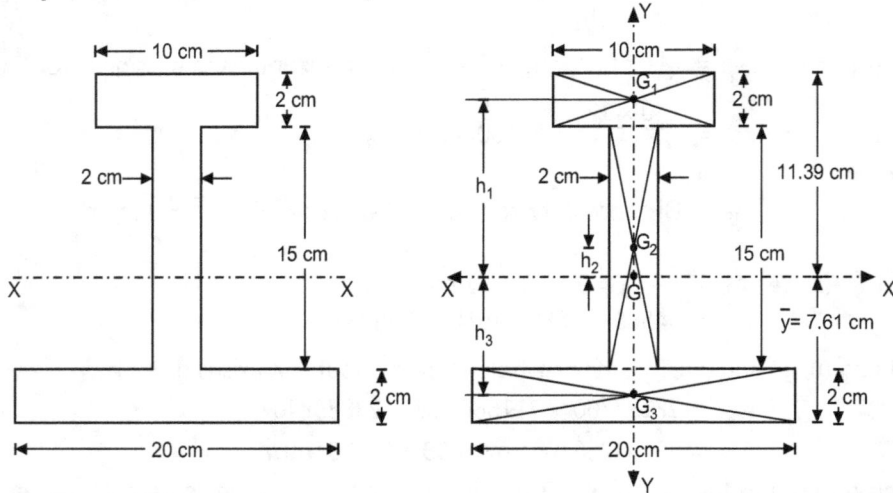

**Fig. 4.33 (i)**　　　　　　　　　　　　　**Fig. 4.33 (ii)**

**Solution : Step 1 :** Let us divide the section into three rectangles 1, 2 and 3 as shown in Fig. 4.33 (ii). As the section is symmetrical about YY axix, C.G. of the section will lie on this axis.

**Step 2 : Areas :** $a_1 = 10 \times 2 = 20 \text{ cm}^2$, $a_2 = 15 \times 2 = 30 \text{ cm}^2$, $a_3 = 20 \times 2 = 40 \text{ cm}^2$

Total area, $\quad A = a_1 + a_2 + a_3 = 20 + 30 + 40 = 90 \text{ cm}^2$

**Step 3 : Distances of centroid from the bottom face :**

$$y_1 = 2 + 15 + \frac{2}{2} = 18 \text{ cm}$$

$$y_2 = 2 + \frac{15}{2} = 9.5 \text{ cm}$$

$$y_3 = \frac{2}{2} = 1 \text{ cm}$$

Distance of X-X axis from the bottom face,

$$\overline{y}_{bottom} = \frac{a_1 y_1 + a_2 y_2 + a_3 y_3}{A} = \frac{20 \times 18 + 30 \times 9.5 + 40 \times 1}{90} = 7.61 \text{ cm}$$

$\therefore \qquad \overline{y}_{top} = (2 + 15 + 2) - 7.61 = 11.39 \text{ cm}$

**Step 4 : To find $I_{XX}$ :** M.I. of the I section about the horizontal centroidal axis is given by,

$$I_{XX} = I_{XX_1} + I_{XX_2} + I_{XX_3}$$

$$\mathbf{I_{XX_1}} = I_{G_1} + a_1 h_1^2 = \frac{10 \times 2^3}{12} + 10 \times 2 \times \left(11.39 - \frac{2}{2}\right)^2 = \mathbf{2165.71 \ cm^4} \quad \dots \text{(i)}$$

$$\mathbf{I_{XX_2}} = I_{G_2} + a_2 h_2^2$$

$$= \frac{2 \times 15^3}{12} + 2 \times 15 \times \left[11.39 - \left(2 + \frac{15}{2}\right)\right]^2 = \mathbf{669.66 \ cm^4} \quad \dots \text{(ii)}$$

$$\mathbf{I_{XX_3}} = I_{G_3} + a_3 h_3^2 = \frac{20 \times 2^3}{12} + (20 \times 2)\left(7.61 - \frac{2}{2}\right)^2 = \mathbf{1761.02 \ cm^4} \quad \dots \text{(iii)}$$

Adding (i), (ii) and (iii), we have

$$I_{XX} = 2165.71 + 669.66 + 1761.02 = \mathbf{4596.39 \ cm^4}$$

**Answer :** $\boxed{I_{XX} = 4596.39 \ cm^4}$

**Note :**

$$h_1 = y_1 - \overline{y} = 18 - 7.61 = 10.39 \ mm$$

$$h_2 = y_2 - \overline{y} = 9.5 - 7.61 = 1.89 \ mm$$

$$h_3 = \overline{y} - y_3 = 7.61 - 1 = 6.61 \ mm$$

**Example 29 :** *An I section consists of top flange 80 × 20 mm, web 120 mm deep × 20 mm thick and bottom flange 120 mm × 20 mm. Calculate moment of inertia @ X-X axis.*

**(B.T.E. S-2015, 2010/4 Marks)**

**Solution :** Exactly similar to the above solved example.

$$\overline{y} = 71.25 \ mm$$

**Answer :** $\boxed{I_{XX} = 21.1233 \times 10^6 \ mm^4}$

**Example 30 :** *Find the M.I. of the section shown in Fig. 4.34 about the centroidal axis XX perpendicular to the web.* **(B.T.E. S-2011/4 Marks)**

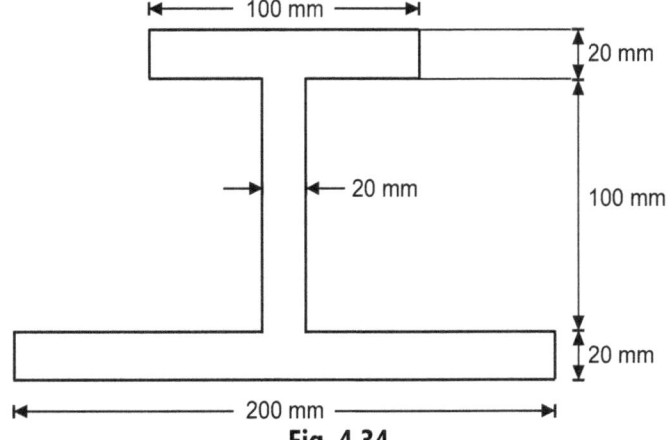

**Fig. 4.34**

**Answer :** $\boxed{I_{XX} = 2.16 \times 10^7 \ mm^4}$

**Example 31 :** *Also calculate $I_{YY}$ of Fig. 4.34.*

**Solution :**    $I_{YY} = \sum \dfrac{db^3}{12} = \dfrac{20 \times 100^3}{12} + \dfrac{100 \times 20^3}{12} + \dfrac{20 \times 200^3}{12} = \mathbf{1.51 \times 10^7 \ mm^4}$

**Answer :** $\boxed{I_{YY} = 1.51 \times 10^7 \ mm^4}$

## Type 2.3 : Solved examples on M.I. of T section.

> (i)   In this case, we get the vertical line of symmetry passing through $G_1$ and $G_2$. Hence, it is necessary to calculate only $\bar{y}$ by using standard formula $\bar{y} = \dfrac{a_1 y_1 + a_2 y_2}{A}$, where $A = a_1 + a_2$.
>
> (ii)  $I_{XX} = I_{XX_1} + I_{XX_2}$ and $I_{YY} = I_{YY_1} + I_{YY_2}$

**Example 32 :** *Find the M.I. of a T-section 200 mm × 200 mm × 20 mm about the centroidal axes.*

**(B.T.E. S-2013, W-2011/4 Marks)**

**Data :** A T-section as shown in Fig. 4.35.

**To find :** $I_{XX}$ and $I_{YY}$.

**Concept :**   (i) Use of parallel axis theorem.

(ii)            $I_{XX} = I_{XX_1} + I_{XX_2} = (I_{G_1} + a_1 h_1^2) + (I_{G_2} + a_2 h_2^2)$

$I_{YY} = I_{YY_1} + I_{YY_2} = \dfrac{d_1 b_1^3}{12} + \dfrac{d_2 b_2^3}{12}$

**Solution : Step 1 :** Fig. 4.35 shows a T-section of required dimensions. Here the overall depth of T-section is 200 mm. Therefore length of the web is 200 – 20 = 180 mm. Let us divide the section into the rectangles 1 and 2 as shown in Fig. 4.35. As the section is symmetrical about YY axis, C.G. of the section will lie on this axis. Distance of YY axis from the left face $\bar{x} = \dfrac{200}{2} = 100$ mm

**Step 2 : Areas :** $a_1 = 200 \times 20 = 4000$ mm$^2$ ;    $a_2 = 180 \times 20 = 3600$ mm$^2$

∴ Total area    $A = a_1 + a_2 = 4000 + 3600 = 7600$ mm$^2$

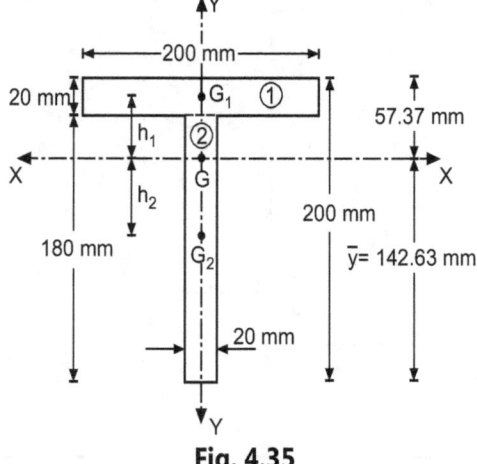

$h_1 = y_1 - \bar{y} = 190 - 142.63 = 47.37$ mm

$h_2 = \bar{y} - y_2 = 142.63 - 90 = 52.63$ mm

**Fig. 4.35**

**Step 3 : Distances of the centroid from the bottom face :**

$$y_1 = 200 - \frac{20}{2} = 190 \text{ mm} \quad \text{and} \quad y_2 = \frac{180}{2} = 90 \text{ mm}$$

Distance of X-X axis from the bottom face,

$$\bar{y} = \frac{a_1 y_1 + a_2 y_2}{A} = \frac{4000 \times 190 + 3600 \times 90}{7600} = 142.63 \text{ mm}$$

∴ Distance of X-X axis from the top face

$$= 200 - 142.63 = 57.37 \text{ mm}$$

**Step 4 : To find $I_{XX}$ :** M.I. of the section about the horizontal centroidal axis is given by,

$$I_{XX} = I_{XX_1} + I_{XX_2}$$

$$I_{XX_1} = \text{M.I. of rectangle 1 about X-X axis} = I_{G_1} + a_1 h_1^2$$

where,    $I_{G_1}$ = M.I. of rectangle 1 about the horizontal axis passing through $G_1$

$$= \frac{200 \times 20^3}{12} = 133333.33 \text{ mm}^4$$

$$h_1 = \text{Distance between } G_1 \text{ and XX axis } = 57.37 - \frac{20}{2} = 47.37 \text{ mm}$$

∴        $$I_{XX_1} = 133333.33 + 4000 \times (47.37)^2 = 9109000.93 \text{ mm}^4 \qquad \dots \text{(i)}$$

$$I_{XX_2} = \text{M.I. of rectangle 2 about X-X axis} = I_{G_2} + a_2 h_2^2$$

where,    $I_{G_2}$ = M.I. of rectangle 2 about the horizontal axis passing through $G_2$

$$= \frac{20 \times 180^3}{12} = 9720000 \text{ mm}^4$$

$$h_2 = \text{Distance between } G_2 \text{ and X-X axis} = 142.63 - \frac{180}{2} = 52.63 \text{ mm}$$

∴        $$I_{XX_2} = 9720000 + 3600 \times (52.63)^2 = 19691700.84 \text{ mm}^4 \qquad \dots \text{(ii)}$$

Adding the equations (i) and (ii),

$$\mathbf{I_{XX}} = 9109000.93 + 19691700.84 = 28800701.77 \text{ mm}^4$$
$$= \mathbf{28.8 \times 10^6 \text{ mm}^4}$$

**Step 5 : To find $I_{YY}$ :** M.I. of the section about the vertical centroidal axis is given by,

$$I_{YY} = I_{YY_1} + I_{YY_2}$$

$$I_{YY_1} = \text{M.I. of rectangle 1 about Y-Y axis} = I_{G_1} + a_1 h_1^2$$

where,    $I_{G_1}$ = M.I. of rectangle 1 about the vertical axis passing through $G_1$

$$= \frac{20 \times 200^3}{12} = 13333333.33 \text{ mm}^4$$

$$h_1 = \text{Distance between } G_1 \text{ and Y-Y axis} = 0$$

∴        $$I_{YY_1} = I_{G_1} = 13333333.33 \text{ mm}^4 \qquad \dots \text{(iii)}$$

$$I_{YY_2} = \text{M.I. of rectangle 2 about Y-Y axis} = I_{G_2} + a_2 h_2^2$$

where,          $I_{G_2}$ = M.I. of rectangle 2 about the vertical axis passing through $G_2$

$$= \frac{180 \times 20^3}{12} = 120000 \text{ mm}^4$$

$h_2$ = Distance between $G_2$ and Y-Y axis = 0

∴          $I_{YY_2} = I_{G_2} = 120000 \text{ mm}^4$          ... (iv)

Adding the equations (iii) and (iv),

$I_{YY}$ = 13333333.33 + 120000 = 13453333.33 mm$^4$

$$= \mathbf{13.45 \times 10^6 \text{ mm}^4}$$

**Answer :**  $\boxed{I_{XX} = 28.8 \times 10^6 \text{ mm}^4, I_{YY} = 13.45 \times 10^6 \text{ mm}^4}$

---

**Example 33 :** *Calculate M.I. of a T-section about the centroidal axis XX. Top flange is 1200 × 200 mm and web is 1800 mm × 200 mm. Total height is 2000 mm.*

**(B.T.E. S-2011/4 Marks)**

**Data :** A T-section as shown in Fig. 4.36.

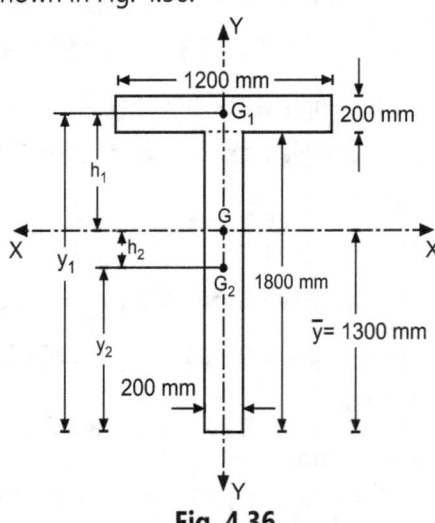

**Fig. 4.36**

**To find :** $I_{XX}$.

**Concept :** Same as the above example.

**Solution :** (i)   $a_1$ = 1200 × 200 = 2400 mm$^2$

$a_2$ = 1800 × 200 = 3600 mm$^2$

(ii)          $y_1 = 1800 + \dfrac{200}{2} = 1900$ mm

$y_2 = \dfrac{1800}{2} = 900$ mm

Now, $\qquad \bar{y} = \dfrac{a_1 y_1 + a_2 y_2}{a_1 + a_2}$

$\therefore \qquad \bar{y}_{bottom} = \dfrac{2400 \times 1900 + 3600 \times 900}{2400 + 3600} = \mathbf{1300\ mm}$

(**Note :** $h_1 = y_1 - \bar{y} = 1900 - 1300 = 600$ mm, $h_2 = \bar{y} - y_2 = 1300 - 900 = 400$ mm)

(iii) $\qquad \mathbf{I_{XX}} = I_{XX_1} + I_{XX_2} = (I_{G_1} + a_1 h_1^2) + (I_{G_2} + a_2 h_2^2)$

$$= \left[\dfrac{1200 \times 200^3}{12} + 2400 \times (1900 - 1300)^2\right] +$$

$$\left[\dfrac{200 \times 1800^3}{12} + 3600 \times (1300 - 900)^2\right]$$

$$= 1664000000 + 9.7776 \times 10^{10} = \mathbf{9.944 \times 10^{10}\ mm^4}$$

**Answer :** $\boxed{I_{XX} = 9.944 \times 10^{10}\ mm^4}$

---

**Example 34 :** *Find the M.I. of a T-section shown in Fig. 4.37 about X-X axis passing through its c.g. of the section.* **(B.T.E. W-2012/4 Marks)**

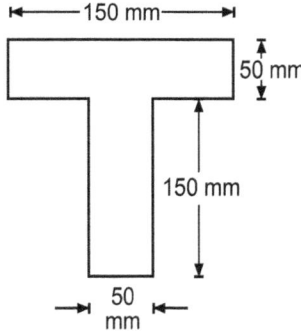

**Fig. 4.37**

**Hint :** $\qquad y_1 = 150 + \dfrac{50}{2} = 175$ mm, $\quad y_2 = \dfrac{150}{2} = 75$ mm

$\bar{y}_{bottom} = 125$ mm

$h_1 = y_1 - \bar{y} = 175 - 125 = 50$ mm , $h_2 = \bar{y} - y_2 = 125 - 75 = 50$ mm

**Answer : $I_{XX} = 53125000\ mm^4$**

---

**Example 35 :** *A symmetrical 'T' section of overall depth of 300 mm has its flanges 150 mm $\times$ 10 mm and web 10 mm thick. Find the M.I. about its centroidal axis parallel to the flanges.* **(B.T.E. S-2012/4 Marks)**

**Answer :** $\boxed{I_{XX} = 42.58 \times 10^6\ mm^4}$

## Type 2.4 : Solved examples on M.I. of an Inverted Tee section

**Example 36 :** *Calculate $I_{XX}$ of inverted T-section as shown in Fig. 4.38 (i).*

**(B.T.E. W-2014, 2009/4 Marks)**

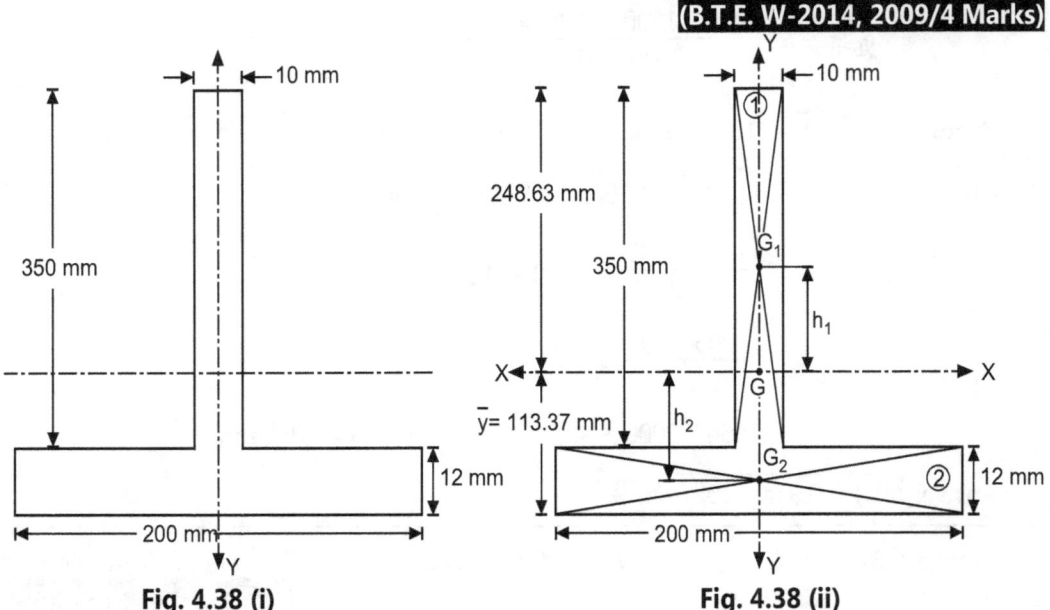

**Fig. 4.38 (i)**                **Fig. 4.38 (ii)**

**Data :** An inverted T-section as shown in Fig. 4.38 (i).

**To find :** $I_{XX}$.

**Concept :** (i) Use of parallel axis theorem.

$$\text{(ii)} \quad I_{XX} = I_{XX_1} + I_{XX_2} = (I_{G_1} + a_1h_1^2) + (I_{G_2} + a_2h_2^2)$$

**Solution : Step 1 :** Let us divide the section into two rectangles 1 and 2 as shown in Fig. 4.38 (ii). As the section is symmetrical about YY axis, C.G. of the section will lie on this axis.

**Step 2 : Areas :**  $a_1 = 10 \times 350 = 3500 \text{ mm}^2$, $a_2 = 200 \times 12 = 2400 \text{ mm}^2$

Total area,      $A = a_1 + a_2 = 3500 + 2400 = 5900 \text{ mm}^2$

**Step 3 : Distances of centroid from the bottom face :**

$$y_1 = 12 + \frac{350}{2} = 187 \text{ mm and } y_2 = \frac{12}{2} = 6 \text{ mm}$$

Distance of X-X axis from the bottom face,

$$\bar{y}_{bottom} = \frac{a_1y_1 + a_2y_2}{A} = \frac{3500 \times 187 + 2400 \times 6}{5900} = \textbf{113.37 mm}$$

$\therefore$        $\bar{y}_{top} = (350 + 12) - 113.37 = 248.63 \text{ mm}$

**Step 4 : To find $I_{XX}$ :** M.I. of the section about the horizontal centroidal axis is given by,

$$I_{XX} = I_{XX_1} + I_{XX_2}$$

$$I_{XX_1} = I_{G_1} + a_1h_1^2 = \frac{10 \times 350^3}{12} + 30 \times 350 \times \left(248.63 - \frac{350}{2}\right)^2$$

$$= 92653624.12 \text{ mm}^4 \qquad \dots \text{(i)}$$

$$I_{XX_2} = I_{G_2} + a_2 h_2^2 = \frac{200 \times 12^3}{12} + 200 \times 12 \times \left(113.37 - \frac{12}{2}\right)^2$$

$$= 27696760.56 \text{ mm}^4 \qquad \qquad \dots \text{(ii)}$$

Adding (i) and (ii), we have

$$\mathbf{I_{XX}} = 92653624.12 + 27696760.56 = \mathbf{120350384.7 \text{ mm}^4}$$

**Answer :** $\boxed{I_{XX} = 120350384.7 \text{ mm}^4}$

---

**Type 2.5 : Solved examples on M.I. of an unequal angle section.**

(i) For an unequal angle section, $\bar{x} \neq \bar{y}$. It is necessary to calculate both coordinates of C.G. by using standard formulae.

$$\bar{x} = \frac{a_1 x_1 + a_2 x_2}{A}, \quad \bar{y} = \frac{a_1 y_1 + a_2 y_2}{A}, \text{ where } A = a_1 + a_2.$$

(ii) For an unequal angle section, $I_{XX} \neq I_{YY}$. It is necessary to calculate both $I_{XX}$ and $I_{YY}$.

(iii) $I_{XX} = I_{XX_1} + I_{XX_2}$ and $I_{YY} = I_{YY_1} + I_{YY_2}$.

**Example 37 :** *Find the position of centre of gravity, $I_{XX}$ and $I_{YY}$ for an unequal angle* *125 mm $\times$ 75 mm $\times$ 10 mm thick.*        **(B.T.E. S-2015, W-2011, 1999, 1986/8 Marks)**

**Data :** An unequal angle section as shown in Fig. 4.39.

**To find :** C.G., $I_{XX}$, $I_{YY}$.

**Concept :** Use of parallel axis theorem.

**Solution : (i)** Let us divide the angle section into two rectangles 1 and 2 as shown in Fig. 4.39.

**To find c.g. :**

**(ii) Areas :**     $a_1 = (125 - 10) \times 10 = 1150 \text{ mm}^2$

$a_2 = 75 \times 10 = 750 \text{ mm}^2$

$\therefore$ Total area     $A = a_1 + a_2 = 1150 + 750 = 1900 \text{ mm}^2$

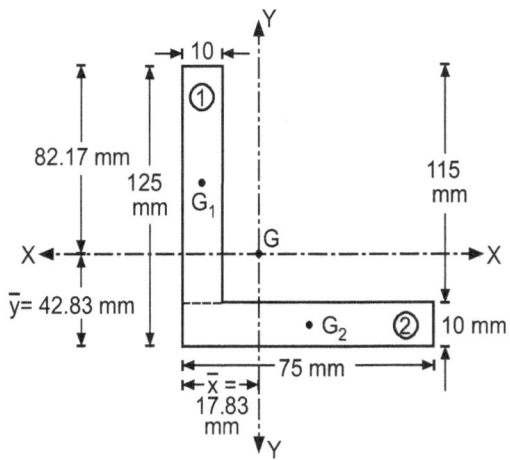

**Fig. 4.39**

**(iii) Distances of centroid from the left face :**

$$x_1 = \frac{10}{2} = 5 \text{ mm}; \quad x_2 = \frac{75}{2} = 37.5 \text{ mm}$$

**(iv) Distances of centroid from the bottom face :**

$$y_1 = 10 + \frac{115}{2} = 67.5 \text{ mm}; \quad y_2 = \frac{10}{2} = 5 \text{ mm}$$

Now,
$$\bar{x} = \frac{a_1 x_1 + a_2 x_2}{A} = \frac{1150 \times 5 + 750 \times 37.5}{1900}$$

$$= \textbf{17.83 mm (from the left face)}$$

Now,
$$\bar{y} = \frac{a_1 y_1 + a_2 y_2}{A} = \frac{1150 \times 67.5 + 750 \times 5}{1900}$$

$$= \textbf{42.83 mm (from the bottom face)}$$

The positions of X-X and YY axes are as shown in Fig. 4.39.

Now, distance of X-X axis from the top face = 125 − 42.83 = 82.17 mm.

**(v) To find $I_{XX}$ :** M.I. of the angle section about the horizontal centroidal axis is given by,

$$I_{XX} = I_{XX_1} + I_{XX_2}$$

$I_{XX_1}$ = M.I. of rectangle 1 about the horizontal centroidal axis X-X.

$$= I_{G_1} + a_1 h_1^2 \text{ where,}$$

$I_{G_1}$ = M.I. of rectangle 1 about the horizontal axis passing through $G_1$

$$= \frac{10 \times 115^3}{12} = 1267395.833 \text{ mm}^4$$

$h_1$ = Distance between $G_1$ and X-X axis

$$= 82.17 - \frac{115}{2} = 82.17 - 57.5 = 24.67 \text{ mm}$$

∴  $I_{XX_1} = 1267395.833 + 1150 \times (24.67)^2$

$$= 1967296.1 \text{ mm}^4 \qquad\qquad \text{... (i)}$$

$I_{XX_2}$ = M.I. of rectangle 2 about the horizontal centroidal axis X-X

$$= I_{G_2} + a_2 h_2^2 \text{ where,}$$

$I_{G_2}$ = M.I. of rectangle 2 about the horizontal axis passing through $G_2$

$$= \frac{75 \times 10^3}{12} = 6250 \text{ mm}^4$$

$h_2$ = Distance between $G_2$ and X-X axis

$$= 42.83 - \frac{10}{2} = 37.83 \text{ mm}$$

∴  $I_{XX_2} = 6250 + 750 \times (37.83)^2 = 1079581.675 \text{ mm}^4 \qquad\qquad \text{... (ii)}$

Adding equations (i) and (ii),

$$I_{XX} = 1967296.1 + 1079581.675 = 3046877.77 \text{ mm}^4$$

$$= \mathbf{30.47 \times 10^5 \text{ mm}^4}$$

**(vi) To find $I_{YY}$ :** M.I. of the angle section about the vertical centroidal axis is given by,

$$I_{YY} = I_{YY_1} + I_{YY_2}$$

$I_{YY_1}$ = M.I. of rectangle 1 about the vertical centroidal axis YY

$$= I_{G_1} + a_1 h_1^2 \text{ where}$$

$I_{G_1}$ = M.I. of rectangle 1 about the vertical axis passing through $G_1$

$$= \frac{115 \times 10^3}{12} = 9583.3333 \text{ mm}^4$$

$h_1$ = Distance between $G_1$ and Y-Y axis

$$= \bar{x} - \frac{10}{2} = 17.83 - 5 = 12.83 \text{ mm}$$

∴         $$I_{YY_1} = 9583.3333 + 1150 \times (12.83)^2 = 198883.57 \text{ mm}^4 \qquad \text{... (iii)}$$

$I_{YY_2}$ = M.I. of rectangle 2 about the vertical centroidal axis YY

$$= I_{G_2} + a_2 h_2^2 \text{ where}$$

$I_{G_2}$ = M.I. of rectangle 2 about the vertical axis passing through $G_2$

$$= \frac{10 \times 75^3}{12} = 351562.5 \text{ mm}^4$$

$h_2$ = Distance between $G_2$ and YY axis

$$= \frac{75}{2} - \bar{x} = 37.5 - 17.83 = 19.67 \text{ mm}$$

∴         $$I_{YY_2} = 351562.5 + 750 \times (19.67)^2 = 641744.17 \text{ mm}^4 \qquad \text{... (iv)}$$

Adding equations (iii) and (iv),

$$I_{YY} = 198883.57 + 641744.17 = 840627.74 \text{ mm}^4 = \mathbf{8.4 \times 10^5 \text{ mm}^4}$$

**Answer :** $\boxed{\begin{array}{l} \bar{x} = 17.83 \text{ mm}, \bar{y} = 42.83 \text{ mm}, \\ I_{XX} = 30.47 \times 10^5 \text{ mm}^4, I_{YY} = 8.4 \times 10^5 \text{ mm}^4 \end{array}}$

**Example 38 :** *For the lamina as shown in Fig. 4.40 (i), determine its M.I. about its X-X axis.*

(B.T.E. S-2008/4 Marks)

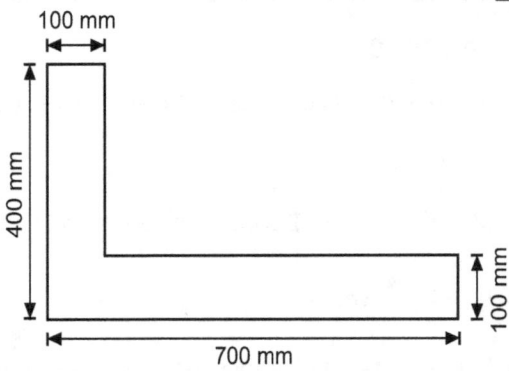

**Fig. 4.40 (i)**

**Data :** An unequal angle section as shown in Fig. 4.40 (i).

**To find :** $I_{XX}$.

**Concept :** Use of parallel axis theorem.

**Solution :** Refer to Fig. 4.40 (ii).

**Step 1 :** Divide the angle section into two areas (1) and (2) as shown in Fig. 4.40 (ii). Let OA and OB be the axes of reference.

**Step 2 : Areas** $a_1 = 100 \times 400 = 40000 \text{ mm}^2$

$$a_2 = 600 \times 100 = 60000 \text{ mm}^2$$

Net area, $A = a_1 + a_2 = 40000 + 60000 = 1 \times 10^5 \text{ mm}^2$

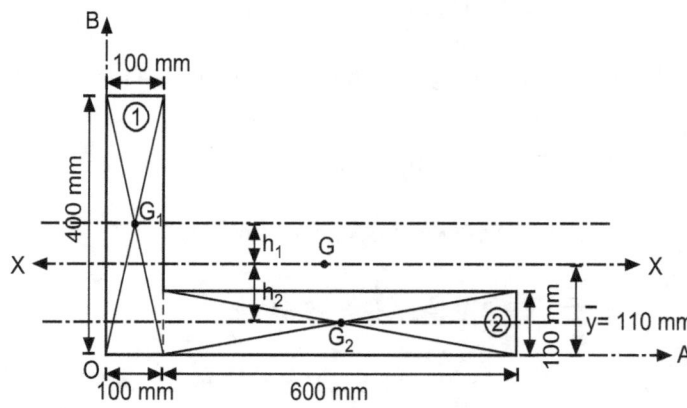

**Fig. 4.40 (ii)**

**Step 3 : Distances of C.G. from the horizontal reference axis OA :**

$$y_1 = \frac{400}{2} = 200 \text{ mm}, \ y_2 = \frac{100}{2} = 50 \text{ mm},$$

$$\overline{y}_{Base} = \frac{a_1 y_1 + a_2 y_2}{A} = \frac{40000 \times 200 + 60000 \times 50}{1 \times 10^5} = 110 \text{ mm}$$

**Step 4 :** To find $I_{xx}$.

(i)   By applying theorem of parallel axis, we have

$$I_{xx_1} = I_{G_1} + a_1 h_1^2$$

$$= \frac{100 \times 400^3}{12} + 40000 \times \left(\frac{400}{2} - 110\right)^2 = 857.33 \times 10^6 \text{ mm}^4 \qquad \dots (1)$$

(ii)   By applying theorem of parallel axis, we have

$$I_{xx_2} = I_{G_2} + a_2 h_2^2$$

$$= \frac{600 \times 100^3}{12} + 60000 \times \left(110 - \frac{100}{2}\right)^2 = 266 \times 10^6 \text{ mm}^4 \qquad \dots (2)$$

Adding (1) and (2), we get

$$\mathbf{I_{xx}} = I_{xx_1} + I_{xx_2}$$

$$= 857.33 \times 10^6 + 266 \times 10^6 = 1123.33 \times 10^6 \text{ mm}^4 = \mathbf{1.123 \times 10^9 \, mm^4}$$

**Answer :**   $\boxed{I_{xx} = 1.123 \times 10^9 \text{ mm}^4}$

---

**Example 39 :** *Find the M.I. about Y-Y axis of the angle section passing through its c.g. shown in Fig. 4.41.*                    **(B.T.E. W-2012/4 Marks)**

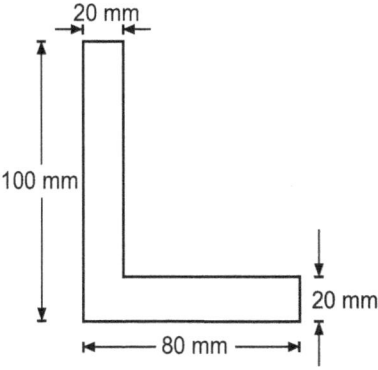

20 mm

100 mm

20 mm

80 mm

**Fig. 4.41**

**Solution :** (i)   $a_1 = 80 \times 20 = 1600 \text{ mm}^2$

$a_2 = 80 \times 20 = 1600 \text{ mm}^2$

(ii)   $x_1 = \dfrac{20}{2} = 10 \text{ mm}, \quad x_2 = \dfrac{80}{2} = 40 \text{ mm}$

$$\overline{x}_{\text{left}} = \frac{a_1 x_1 + a_2 x_2}{a_1 + a_2} = \frac{1600 \times 10 + 1600 \times 40}{1600 + 1600} = \mathbf{25 \text{ mm}}$$

[**Note :** $h_1 = \overline{x} - x_1$ and $h_2 = x_2 - \overline{x}$]

(iii)
$$I_{YY} = I_{YY_1} + I_{YY_2}$$

$$= (I_{G_1} + a_1 h_1^2) + (I_{G_2} + a_2 h_2^2)$$

$$= \left[ \frac{80 \times 20^3}{12} + 1600 \times (25 - 10)^2 \right] + \left[ \frac{20 \times 80^3}{12} + 1600 \times (40 - 25)^2 \right]$$

$$= \textbf{1626666.67 mm}^4$$

**Answer :** $\boxed{I_{YY} = 1626666.67 \text{ mm}^4}$

---

**Type 2.6 : Solved examples on M.I. of an equal angle section.**

(i) For an equal angle section, $\bar{x} = \bar{y}$ i.e. distance of c.g. from extreme left of vertical leg = distance of c.g. from extreme bottom of horizontal leg.

(ii) For an equal angle section, $I_{XX} = I_{YY}$ i.e. M.I. about horizontal centroidal axis = M.I. about vertical centroidal axis.

(iii) **Note :** (1) $\quad I_{XX} = I_{XX_1} + I_{XX_2}$

$$= (I_{G_1} + a_1 h_1^2) + (I_{G_2} + a_2 h_2^2)$$

(2) $\quad I_{YY} = I_{YY_1} + I_{YY_2}$

$$= (I_{G_1} + a_1 h_1^2) + (I_{G_2} + a_2 h_2^2)$$

**Example 40 :** *Find the moment of inertia of an equal angle section 50 mm × 50 mm × 6 mm about the horizontal axis. The distance of centroid from extreme bottom of horizontal leg is 14.70 mm (in vertical direction).* (B.T.E. W-1998/4 Marks)

**Data :** An equal angle section as shown in Fig. 4.42.

$$\bar{y} = 14.7 \text{ mm}$$

**To find :** $I_{XX}$

**Concept :** For an equal angle section, $\bar{x} = \bar{y}$ and $I_{XX} = I_{YY}$.

**Solution :** (i) Divide the angle section into two areas (1) and (2) as shown in Fig. 4.42.

(ii) **Areas :** $\quad a_1 = (50 - 6) \times 6 = 44 \times 6 = 264 \text{ mm}^2$

$$a_2 = 50 \times 6 = 300 \text{ mm}^2$$

$$A = a_1 + a_2 = 264 + 300 = 564 \text{ mm}^2$$

(iii) $\quad I_{XX} = I_{XX_1} + I_{XX_2}$

$$I_{XX_1} = \frac{6 \times 44^3}{12} + (6 \times 44) \left[ \left( 6 + \frac{44}{2} \right) - 14.7 \right]^2$$

$$= 42592 + 46698.96 = \textbf{89290.96 mm}^4$$

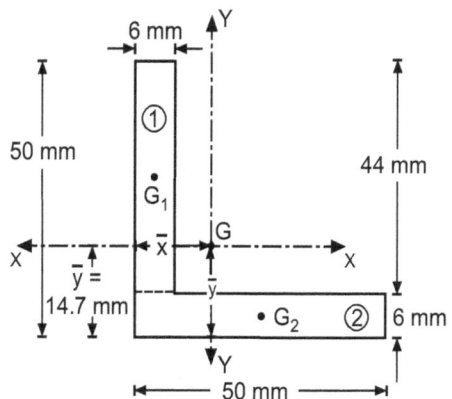

**Fig. 4.42**

$$I_{xx_2} = \frac{50 \times 6^3}{12} + (50 \times 6)\left[14.7 - \frac{6}{2}\right]^2 = 900 + 41067 = \mathbf{41967\ mm^4}$$

**Answer :** $\boxed{I_{xx} = 89290.96 + 41967 = \mathbf{131257.96\ mm^4}}$

**Example 41 :** *Calculate the moment of inertia about the centroidal axis for an angle section 200 × 200 × 20 mm size.*          **(B.T.E. S-2012, 1997/4 Marks)**

**Data :** An equal angle section as shown in Fig. 4.43.

**To find :** $I_{xx}$ and $I_{yy}$.

**Concept :** For an equal angle section, $\bar{x} = \bar{y}$ and $I_{xx} = I_{yy}$

**Solution :** (i) Divide the angle section into two areas (1) and (2) as shown in Fig. 4.43.

(ii) **Areas :**  $a_1 = 180 \times 20 = 3600\ mm^2$,  $a_2 = 200 \times 20 = 4000\ mm^2$

$A = a_1 + a_2 = 3600 + 4000 = 7600\ mm^2$

(iii) **Distances of C.G. from reference axis AB :**

$$x_1 = \frac{20}{2} = 10\ mm,\ x_2 = \frac{200}{2} = 100\ mm$$

$$\bar{x} = \frac{a_1 x_1 + a_2 x_2}{A} = \frac{3600 \times 10 + 4000 \times 100}{7600} = \mathbf{57.37\ mm}$$

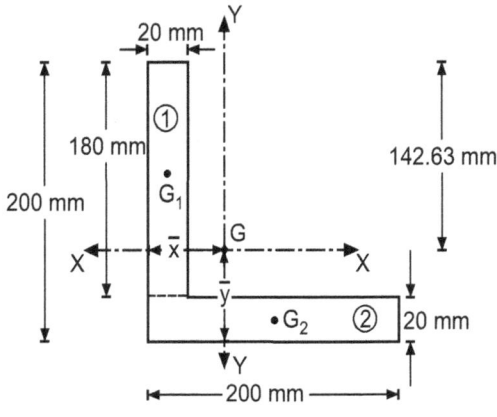

**Fig. 4.43**

For an equal angle section,

$$\bar{x} = \bar{y}$$

$$\therefore \qquad \bar{y} = 57.37 \text{ mm}$$

Here $\bar{y}$ can also be calculated by using the formula,

$$\bar{y} = \frac{a_1 y_1 + a_2 y_2}{a_1 + a_2}$$

(iv) **To find $I_{XX}$ and $I_{YY}$:**

$$I_{XX_1} = 20 \times \frac{180^3}{12} + (20 \times 180)\left(142.63 - \frac{180}{2}\right)^2 = 19691700.84 \text{ mm}^4$$

$$I_{XX_2} = \frac{200 \times 20^3}{12} + (200 \times 20)\left(57.37 - \frac{20}{2}\right)^2 = 9109000.933 \text{ mm}^4$$

$$I_{XX} = I_{XX_1} + I_{XX_2} = 19691700.84 + 9109000.933 = 28800701.77 \text{ mm}^4$$

For an equal angle section, $I_{XX} = I_{YY}$

**Answer :** $\boxed{I_{XX} = I_{YY} = 28800701.77 \text{ mm}^4}$

**Check :** [Let us calculate $I_{YY}$.

$$I_{YY} = I_{YY_1} + I_{YY_2}$$

$$I_{YY_1} = \frac{180 \times 20^3}{12} + (180 \times 20)\left(57.37 - \frac{20}{2}\right)^2 = 8198100.84 \text{ mm}^4$$

$$I_{YY_2} = \frac{20 \times 200^3}{12} + (20 \times 200)\left(\frac{200}{2} - 57.37\right)^2 = 20602600.93 \text{ mm}^4$$

$$\therefore \qquad I_{YY} = 8198100.84 + 20602600.93 = \textbf{28800701.77 mm}^4]$$

**Example 42 :** *Calculate $I_{XX}$ of an equal angle section 200 × 200 × 20 mm about the centroidal axis if the distance of the centroid from the extreme bottom of the horizontal leg is 57.37 mm.* **(B.T.E. W-2007/4 Marks)**

**Solution :** Please refer to the above solved example. It is not necessary to calculate $\bar{x}$ since its value is given. $\bar{x} = 57.37$ mm.

**Answer :** $\boxed{I_{XX} = 28800701.77 \text{ mm}^4}$

**Type 2.7 : Solved examples on M.I. of a channel section (web vertical) :**

Refer to Fig. 4.44.

(i) In this case, we get horizontal line of symmetry XX.

$$\bar{y} = \frac{\text{Total depth}}{2}$$

(ii) $\bar{x}$ can be calculated by using

$$\bar{x} = \frac{a_1 x_1 + a_2 x_2 + a_3 x_3}{A} \text{ where } A = a_1 + a_2 + a_3.$$

(iii)  $I_{XX}$ = M.I. of ABCD – M.I. of PQRS

(iv)                    $I_{YY} = I_{YY_1} + I_{YY_2} + I_{YY_3}$

$$= (I_{G_1} + a_1 h_1^2) + (I_{G_2} + a_2 h_2^2) + (I_{G_3} + a_3 h_3^2)$$

**Note :** Since $a_1 = a_3$, $I_{YY_1} = I_{YY_3}$

**Example 43 :** *A channel section has the following dimensions.*

       *Flanges    :    50 mm × 10 mm*

  *Overall depth   :   200 mm*

*Thickness of web   :   10 mm*

 *Find $I_{XX}$ and $I_{YY}$.*

**(W-2014/4 Marks)**

**Data :** A channel section as shown in Fig. 4.44.

**To find :** $I_{XX}$ and $I_{YY}$.

**Concept :** (i)   $I_{XX}$ = M.I. of outer rectangle – M.I. of inner rectangle.

                  = M.I. of ABCD – M.I. of PQRS

(ii) Since        $a_1 = a_3$, $I_{YY_1} = I_{YY_3}$

**Solution :** (i) Let us divide the channel section into three areas 1, 2 and 3 as shown in Fig. 4.44. As the section is symmetrical about X-X axis, C.G. of the section will lie on this axis.

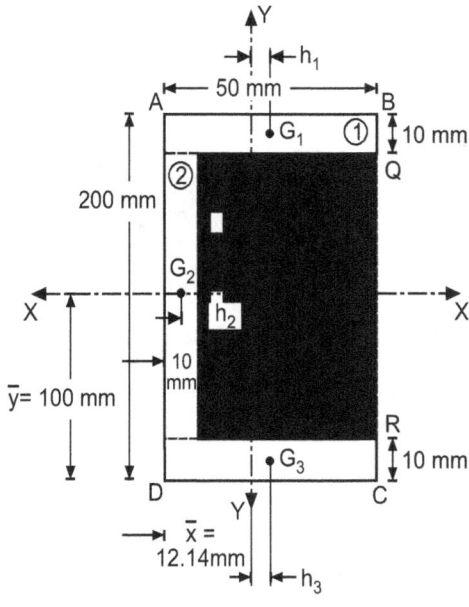

**Fig. 4.44**

Distance of X-X axis from the bottom face

$$= \frac{200}{2} = 100 \text{ mm}$$

(ii) **Areas :**     $a_1 = a_3 = 50 \times 10 = 500 \text{ mm}^2$

                  $a_2 = (200 - 10 - 10) \times (10) = 180 \times 10 = 1800 \text{ mm}^2$

Total area,      A = $a_1 + a_2 + a_3$ = 500 + 1800 + 500 = 2800 mm²

(iii) **Distances of the centroid from the left face :**

$$x_1 = x_3 = \frac{50}{2} = 25 \text{ mm}$$

$$x_2 = \frac{10}{2} = 5 \text{ mm}$$

∴ Distance of the vertical centroidal axis from the left face,

$$\bar{x} = \frac{a_1 x_1 + a_2 x_2 + a_3 x_3}{A} = \frac{500 \times 25 + 1800 \times 5 + 500 \times 25}{2800} = 12.14 \text{ mm}$$

The positions of X-X and Y-Y axis are as shown in Fig. 4.44.

(iv) In this case, $I_{XX}$ = M.I. of ABCD – M.I. of PQRS

$$= \frac{50 \times 200^3}{12} - \frac{(50 - 10) \times 180^3}{12} = \frac{1}{12}[50 \times 200^3 - 40 \times 180^3]$$

$$= \frac{1}{12} \times [4 \times 10^8 - 2.3328 \times 10^8] = 13893333.33 \text{ mm}^4$$

$$= \mathbf{13.89 \times 10^6 \text{ mm}^4}$$

(v) **To find $I_{YY}$ :**    $I_{YY} = I_{YY_1} + I_{YY_2} + I_{YY_3}$

$I_{YY_1}$ = M.I. of rectangle 1 about YY axis

$$= I_{G_1} + a_1 h_1^2$$

where,    $I_{G_1}$ = M.I. of rectangle 1 about the vertical axis passing through $G_1$

$$= \frac{10 \times 50^3}{12} = 104166.67 \text{ mm}^4$$

$h_1$ = Distance between $G_1$ and YY axis

$$= \frac{50}{2} - \bar{x} = 25 - 12.14 = 12.86 \text{ mm}$$

∴      $I_{YY_1} = 104166.67 + 500 \times (12.86)^2 = 186856.47 \text{ mm}^4$      ... (i)

Now,    $I_{YY_2}$ = M.I. of rectangle 2 about YY axis

$$= I_{G_2} + a_2 h_2^2$$

where,    $I_{G_2}$ = M.I. of rectangle 2 about the vertical axis passing through $G_2$

$$= \frac{180 \times 10^3}{12} = 15000 \text{ mm}^4$$

$h_2$ = Distance between $G_2$ and YY axis

$$= 12.14 - \frac{10}{2} = 7.14 \text{ mm}$$

∴      $I_{YY_2} = 15000 + 1800 \times (7.14)^2 = 106763.28 \text{ mm}^4$      ... (ii)

Now,    $I_{YY_3}$ = M.I. of rectangle 3 about YY axis

Since  $a_3 = a_1, I_{YY_3} = I_{YY_1} = 186856.47 \text{ mm}^4$      ... (iii)

Adding the equations (i), (ii) and (iii),

$$I_{YY} = 186856.47 + 106763.28 + 186856.47$$

$$= 480476.22 \text{ mm}^4 = \mathbf{48.05 \times 10^4 \text{ mm}^4}$$

**Answer :**   $\boxed{I_{YY} = 48.05 \times 10^4 \text{ mm}^4}$

---

### Type 2.8 : Solved examples on M.I. of a channel section (web horizontal) :

Refer to Fig. 4.45 (ii).

(i)    In this case, we get vertical line of symmetry YY.

(ii)   $\bar{y}$ can be calculated by using $\bar{y} = \dfrac{a_1 y_1 + a_2 y_2 + a_3 y_3}{A}$ where $A = a_1 + a_2 + a_3$.

(iii)           $I_{YY}$ = M.I. of rectangle ABCD about YY axis

            − M.I. of rectangle PQRS about YY axis

(iv)           $I_{XX} = I_{XX_1} + I_{XX_2} + I_{XX_3}$

            $= (I_{G_1} + a_1 h_1^2) + (I_{G_2} + a_2 h_2^2) + (I_{G_3} + a_3 h_3^2)$

**Note :** Since $a_1 = a_3$, $I_{XX_1} = I_{XX_3}$

---

**Example 44 :** *Determine the M.I. about X-X and YY axes of the channel as shown in* Fig. 4.45 (i).                                                    **(B.T.E. S-1989/8 Marks)**

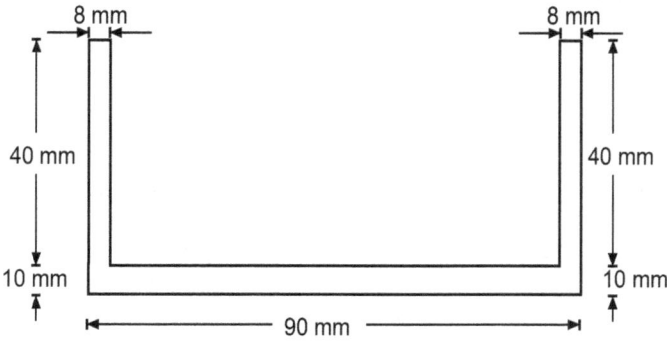

**Fig. 4.45 (i)**

**Data :** A channel section (with web horizontal) as shown in Fig. 4.45 (i).

**To find :** $I_{XX}$ and $I_{YY}$.

**Concept :** (i)       $I_{XX} = I_{XX_1} + I_{XX_2} + I_{XX_3}$

        (ii) Since $a_1 = a_3$, $I_{XX_1} = I_{XX_3}$

        (iii)       $I_{YY}$ = M.I. of rectangle ABCD about YY axis

            − M.I. of rectangle PQRS about YY axis

**Solution :**

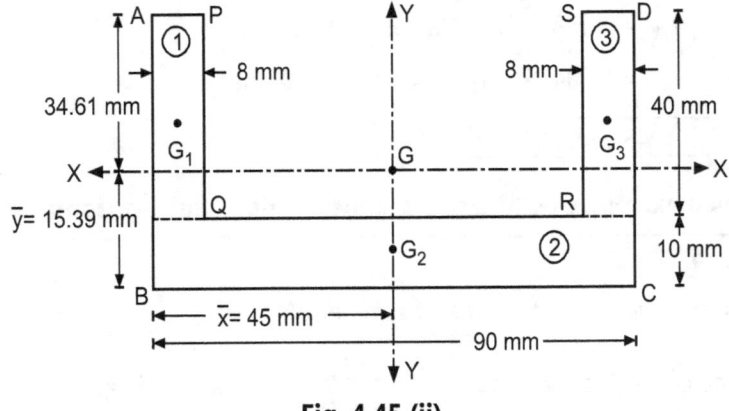

**Fig. 4.45 (ii)**

**(i)** Let us divide the section into three rectangles 1, 2 and 3 as shown in Fig. 4.45 (ii). As the section is symmetrical about YY axis, c.g. of the section will lie on this axis.

$$\therefore \quad \bar{x} = \frac{90}{2} = 45 \text{ mm (from the left face)}$$

**(ii) Areas :**  $a_1 = a_3 = 40 \times 8 = 320 \text{ mm}^2$

$$a_2 = 90 \times 10 = 900 \text{ mm}^2$$

$\therefore$  Total area A $= a_1 + a_2 + a_3 = 320 + 900 + 320 = 1540 \text{ mm}^2$

**(iii) Distances of the centroid from the base :**

$$y_1 = y_3 = 10 + \frac{40}{2} = 30 \text{ mm}$$

$$y_2 = \frac{10}{2} = 5 \text{ mm}$$

Let $\bar{y}$ be the distance of the centroid of the section from the base.

Then  $\bar{y} = \dfrac{a_1 y_1 + a_2 y_2 + a_3 y_3}{A} = \dfrac{320 \times 30 + 900 \times 5 + 320 \times 30}{1540} = 15.39 \text{ mm}$

$\therefore$  Distance of XX axis from the base = 15.39 mm

$\therefore$  Distance of XX axis from the top = 50 – 15.39 = 34.61 mm

**(iv) To find $I_{XX}$ :**

$$I_{XX} = I_{XX_1} + I_{XX_2} + I_{XX_3}$$

$$I_{XX_1} = I_{G_1} + a_1 h_1^2 \qquad \qquad \qquad \text{... (A)}$$

$$I_{G_1} = \frac{8 \times 40^3}{12} = 42666.67 \text{ mm}^4$$

$$h_1 = 34.61 - \frac{40}{2} = 14.61 \text{ mm}$$

∴  From the equation (A), we have

$$I_{XX_1} = 42666.67 + 320 \times (14.61)^2 = 110971.342 \text{ mm}^4 \qquad \text{... (i)}$$

$$I_{XX_2} = I_{G_2} + a_2 h_2^2 \qquad \text{... (B)}$$

$$I_{G_2} = \frac{90 \times 10^3}{12} = 7500 \text{ mm}^4$$

$$h_2 = 15.39 - \frac{10}{2} = 10.39 \text{ mm}$$

From the equation (B), we have

$$I_{XX_2} = 7500 + 900 \times (10.39)^2 = 104656.89 \text{ mm}^4 \qquad \text{... (ii)}$$

Since $a_3 = a_1$, $I_{XX_3}$ and $I_{XX_1}$ are equal.

∴          $$I_{XX_3} = I_{XX_1} = 110971.342 \text{ mm}^4 \qquad \text{... (iii)}$$

Adding the equations (i), (ii) and (iii), we have

$$\mathbf{I_{XX}} = 110971.342 + 104656.89 + 110971.342 = 326599.574 \text{ mm}^4$$

$$= \mathbf{32.66 \times 10^4 \text{ mm}^4}$$

**(v) To find $I_{YY}$ :** Since c.g. of the two rectangles ABCD and PQRS lies on the same line i.e. on Y-Y axis, M.I. about YY axis is given by,

$$\mathbf{I_{YY}} = \text{M.I. of rectangle ABCD about YY axis}$$

$$- \text{M.I. of rectangle PQRS about YY axis}$$

$$= \frac{50 \times 90^3}{12} - \frac{40 \times 74^3}{12} = 3037500 - 1350746.67 = 1686753.33 \text{ mm}^4$$

$$= \mathbf{16.87 \times 10^5 \text{ mm}^4}$$

**Answer :**  $\boxed{I_{XX} = 32.66 \times 10^4 \text{ mm}^4, \ I_{YY} = 16.87 \times 10^5 \text{ mm}^4}$

**Example 45 :** *Find the radius of gyration of the channel section about centroidal axis XX as shown in Fig. 4.45 (ii).*          **(B.T.E. W-2004/4 Marks)**

**Solution :** Find $I_{XX}$ as explained above.

$$\mathbf{K_{XX}} = \sqrt{\frac{I_{XX}}{A}} = \sqrt{\frac{32.66 \times 10^4}{1540}} = \sqrt{212.077} = \mathbf{14.56 \text{ mm}}$$

## Type 2.9 : Miscellaneous examples on M.I. of composite sections :

**Example 46 :** *Obtain the M.I. about both the centroidal axes for a section shown in Fig. 4.46 (i).*          **(B.T.E. W-1988/4 Marks)**

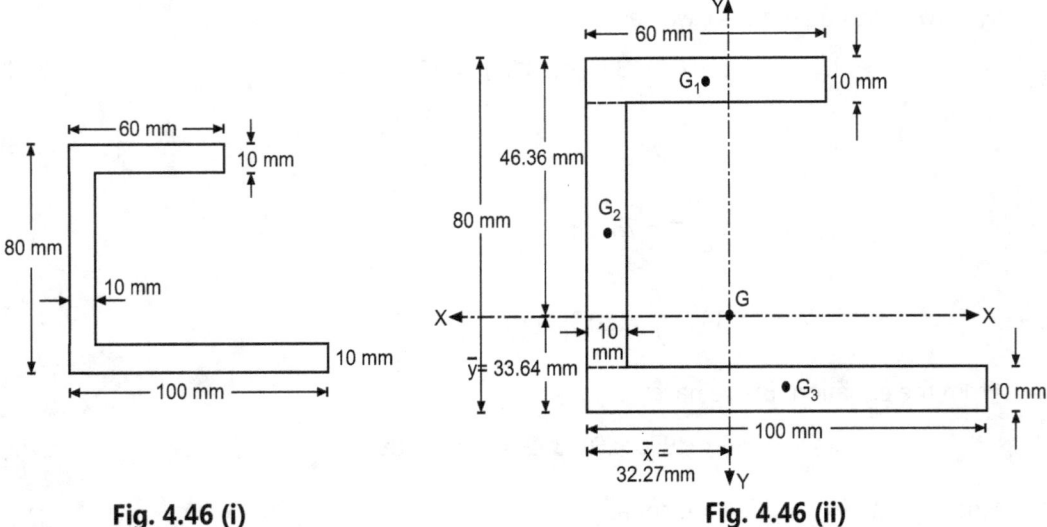

**Fig. 4.46 (i)**                 **Fig. 4.46 (ii)**

**Data :** A composite section as shown in Fig. 4.46 (i).

**To find :** $I_{XX}$ and $I_{YY}$.

**Concept :** Use of parallel axis theorem.

**Solution :** (i) Let us divide the section into three rectangles 1, 2 and 3 as shown in Fig. 4.46 (ii).

(ii) **Areas :** $a_1 = 60 \times 10 = 600$ mm²; $a_2 = 60 \times 10 = 600$ mm²; $a_3 = 100 \times 10 = 1000$ mm²

∴ Total area    $A = a_1 + a_2 + a_3 = 600 + 600 + 1000 = 2200$ mm²

(iii) **Distances of the centroid from the left face :**

$$x_1 = \frac{60}{2} = 30 \text{ mm}; \quad x_2 = \frac{10}{2} = 5 \text{ mm}; \quad x_3 = \frac{100}{2} = 50 \text{ mm}$$

∴      $$\overline{x} = \frac{a_1 x_1 + a_2 x_2 + a_3 x_3}{A} = \frac{600 \times 30 + 600 \times 5 + 1000 \times 50}{2200}$$

$$= 32.27 \text{ mm (from the left face)}$$

(iv) **Distances of the centroid from the base :**

$$y_1 = 80 - \frac{10}{2} = 75 \text{ mm}$$

$$y_2 = 10 + \frac{60}{2} = 40 \text{ mm}$$

$$y_3 = \frac{10}{2} = 5 \text{ mm}$$

∴      $$\overline{y} = \frac{a_1 y_1 + a_2 y_2 + a_3 y_3}{A} = \frac{600 \times 75 + 600 \times 40 + 1000 \times 5}{2200}$$

$$= 33.64 \text{ mm (from the base)}$$

The positions of X-X and YY axes are as shown in Fig. 4.46 (ii).

Distance of X-X axis from the top = 80 − 33.64 = 46.36 mm

(v) **To find $I_{XX}$:**   $I_{G_1} = \dfrac{60 \times 10^3}{12} = 5000 \text{ mm}^4$

$h_1 = 46.36 - \dfrac{10}{2} = 41.36 \text{ mm}$

$\therefore$     $I_{XX_1} = I_{G_1} + a_1 h_1^2 = 5000 + 600 \times (41.36)^2 = 1031389.76 \text{ mm}^4$     ... (i)

$I_{G_2} = \dfrac{10 \times 60^3}{12} = 180000 \text{ mm}^4$

$h_2 = 46.36 - \left(10 + \dfrac{60}{2}\right) = 46.36 - 40 = 6.36 \text{ mm}$

$\therefore$     $I_{XX_2} = I_{G_2} + a_2 h_2^2 = 180000 + 600 \times (6.36)^2 = 204269.76 \text{ mm}^4$     ... (ii)

$I_{G_3} = \dfrac{100 \times 10^3}{12} = 8333.33 \text{ mm}^4$

$h_3 = 33.64 - \dfrac{10}{2} = 28.64 \text{ mm}$

$\therefore$     $I_{XX_3} = I_{G_3} + a_3 h_3^2 = 8333.33 + 1000 \times (28.64)^2 = 828582.93 \text{ mm}^4$     ... (iii)

Now,     $\mathbf{I_{XX}} = I_{XX_1} + I_{XX_2} + I_{XX_3} = 1031389.76 + 204269.76 + 828582.93$

$= 2065242.45 \text{ mm}^4 = \mathbf{20.65 \times 10^5 \text{ mm}^4}$

(vi) **To find $I_{YY}$:**   $I_{G_1} = \dfrac{10 \times 60^3}{12} = 180000 \text{ mm}^4$

$h_1 = 32.27 - 30 = 2.27 \text{ mm}$

$\therefore$     $I_{YY_1} = I_{G_1} + a_1 h_1^2 = 180000 + 600 \times (2.27)^2 = 183091.74 \text{ mm}^4$     ... (iv)

$I_{G_2} = \dfrac{60 \times 10^3}{12} = 5000 \text{ mm}^4$

$h_2 = 32.27 - \dfrac{10}{2} = 27.27 \text{ mm}$

$\therefore$     $I_{YY_2} = I_{G_2} + a_2 h_2^2 = 5000 + 600 \times (27.27)^2 = 451191.74 \text{ mm}^4$     ... (v)

$I_{G_3} = \dfrac{10 \times 100^3}{12} = 833333.33 \text{ mm}^4$

$h_3 = \dfrac{100}{2} - 32.27 = 17.73 \text{ mm}$

Now,     $I_{YY_3} = I_{G_3} + a_3 h_3^2 = 833333.33 + 1000 \times (17.73)^2 = 1147686.23 \text{ mm}^4$   ... (vi)

$\therefore$     $\mathbf{I_{YY}} = I_{YY_1} + I_{YY_2} + I_{YY_3} = 183091.74 + 451191.74 + 1147686.23$

$= 1781969.71 \text{ mm}^4 = \mathbf{17.81 \times 10^5 \text{ mm}^4}$

**Answer :**   $\boxed{I_{XX} = 20.65 \times 10^5 \text{ mm}^4,\ I_{YY} = 17.81 \times 10^5 \text{ mm}^4}$

**Example 47 :** *Find the M.I. of the section shown in Fig. 4.47 (i) about the vertical and horizontal axis passing through centre of gravity. Also find the polar moment of inertia of the section.* **(B.T.E. S-2012/4 Marks)**

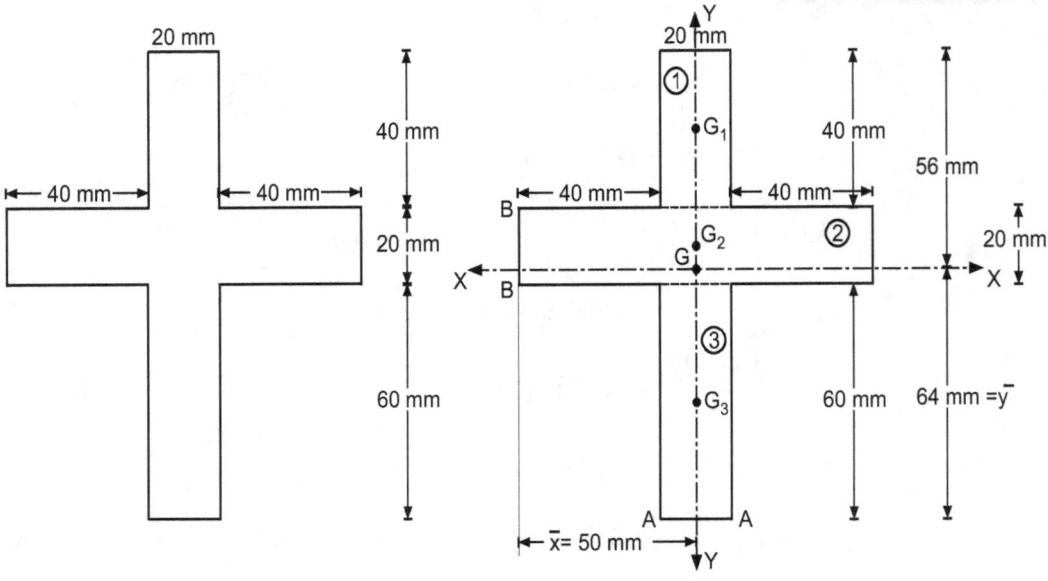

**Fig. 4.47 (i)**　　　　　　**Fig. 4.47 (ii)**

**Data :** A composite section as shown in Fig. 4.47 (i).

**To find :** $I_{XX}$, $I_{YY}$ and $I_P$.

**Concept :** (i) Use of parallel axis theorem, (ii) $I_P = I_{XX} + I_{YY}$.

**Solution :** (i) Let us divide the section into three rectangles 1, 2 and 3 as shown in Fig. 4.47 (ii). As the section is symmetrical about YY axis, c.g. of the section will lie on this axis.

(ii) **Areas :** $a_1 = 20 \times 40 = 800$ mm$^2$; $a_2 = 100 \times 20 = 2000$ mm$^2$; $a_3 = 60 \times 20 = 1200$ mm$^2$

∴　Total area　$A = a_1 + a_2 + a_3 = 800 + 2000 + 1200 = 4000$ mm$^2$

Distance of YY axis from the left edge BB, $\bar{x} = 50$ mm.

Let $\bar{y}$ be the distance of c.g. from the bottom edge AA.

(iii) **Distances of the centroid from the base AA :**

$$y_1 = 60 + 20 + \frac{40}{2} = 100 \text{ mm}$$

$$y_2 = 60 + \frac{20}{2} = 70 \text{ mm}$$

$$y_3 = \frac{60}{2} = 30 \text{ mm}$$

∴　　　　$$\bar{y} = \frac{a_1 y_1 + a_2 y_2 + a_3 y_3}{A} = \frac{800 \times 100 + 2000 \times 70 + 1200 \times 30}{4000} = 64 \text{ mm}$$

∴　Centroid will lie within the middle rectangle as shown in Fig. 4.47 (ii).

(iv) **To find $I_{XX}$ :**   $I_{G_1} = \dfrac{20 \times 40^3}{12} = 10.66 \times 10^4$

$$h_1 = 56 - \dfrac{40}{2} = 36 \text{ mm}$$

$\therefore$     $I_{XX_1} = I_{G_1} + a_1 h_1^2 = 10.66 \times 10^4 + 800 \times (36)^2 = 11.43 \times 10^5 \text{ mm}^4$     ... (i)

$$I_{G_2} = \dfrac{100 \times 20^3}{12} = 6.67 \times 10^4 \text{ mm}^4$$

$$h_2 = 56 - \left(40 + \dfrac{20}{2}\right) = 56 - 50 = 6 \text{ mm}$$

$I_{X_2} = I_{G_2} + a_2 h_2^2 = 6.67 \times 10^4 + 2000 \times 6^2 = 1.387 \times 10^5 \text{ mm}^4$     ... (ii)

$$I_{G_3} = \dfrac{20 \times 60^3}{12} = 36 \times 10^4 \text{ mm}^4$$

$$h_3 = 64 - \dfrac{60}{2} = 64 - 30 = 34 \text{ mm}$$

$\therefore$     $I_{XX_3} = I_{G_3} + a_3 h_3^2 = 36 \times 10^4 + 1200 \times (34)^2 = 17.47 \times 10^5 \text{ mm}^4$     ... (iii)

Now,     $\mathbf{I_{XX}} = I_{XX_1} + I_{XX_2} + I_{XX_3} = 11.43 \times 10^5 + 1.387 \times 10^5 + 17.47 \times 10^5$

$$= \mathbf{30.287 \times 10^5 \ mm^4}$$

(v) **To find $I_{YY}$ :**   $I_{YY_1} = \dfrac{40 \times 20^3}{12} = 2.67 \times 10^4 \text{ mm}^4$

$$I_{YY_2} = \dfrac{20 \times 100^3}{12} = 1.67 \times 10^6 \text{ mm}^4$$

$$I_{YY_3} = \dfrac{60 \times 20^3}{12} = 4 \times 10^4 \text{ mm}^4$$

$\therefore$     $\mathbf{I_{YY}} = I_{YY_1} + I_{YY_2} + I_{YY_3} = 2.67 \times 10^4 + 1.67 \times 10^6 + 4 \times 10^4$

$$= \mathbf{17.36 \times 10^5 \ mm^4}$$

(vi) Now, polar moment of inertia is given by,

$$\mathbf{I_P} = I_{ZZ} = I_{XX} + I_{YY} = 30.287 \times 10^5 + 17.36 \times 10^5$$

$$= \mathbf{47.65 \times 10^5 \ mm^4}$$

**Answer :** $\boxed{I_{XX} = 30.287 \times 10^5 \text{ mm}^4,\ I_{YY} = 17.36 \times 10^5 \text{ mm}^4,\ I_P = 47.65 \times 10^5 \text{ mm}^4}$

**Example 48 :** *A lamina consists of a semicircle and a triangle as shown in Fig. 4.48 (i). Calculate its moment of inertia about reference axis AB.* **(B.T.E. W-2010, S-2003/4 Marks)**

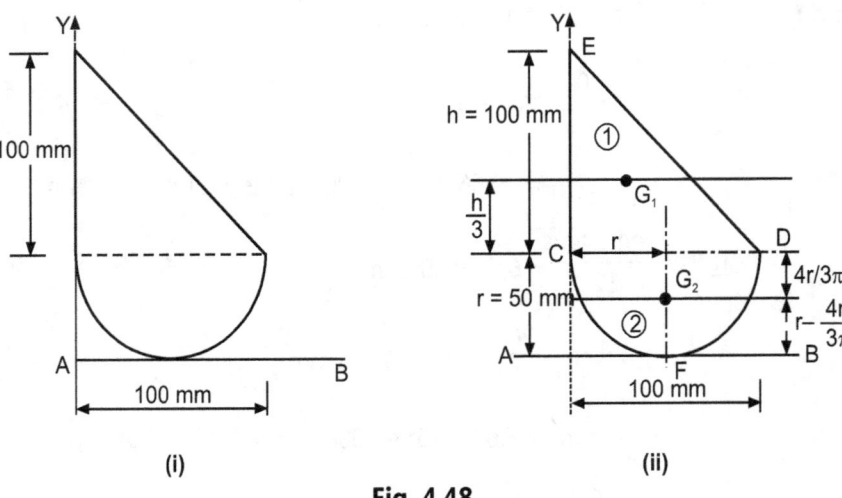

(i)          (ii)

**Fig. 4.48**

**Data**      : As shown in Fig. 4.48 (i).

**To find**   : $I_{AB}$.

**Concept**   : Use of parallel axis theorem.

**Solution**  : Let us divide the lamina into two areas as shown in Fig. 4.48 (ii).

**Areas**     : $a_1$ = area of triangle = $\frac{1}{2} \times 100 \times 100$ = 5000 mm².

$a_2$ = area of semicircle = $\frac{\pi r^2}{2} = \frac{\pi (50)^2}{2}$ = 3926.9908 mm²

M.I. of triangle ECD about its own centroidal axis passing through $G_1$,

$$I_{G_1} = I_{XX_1} = \frac{bh^3}{36} = \frac{100 \times 100^3}{36} = 2777777.78 \text{ mm}^4$$

Distance between c.g. of triangle and AB axis,

$$h_1 = \frac{h}{3} + 50 = \frac{100}{3} + 50 = 83.33 \text{ mm}$$

∴   M.I. of Δ ECD about AB, using parallel axis theorem,

$$I_{AB_1} = I_{G_1} + a_1 h_1^2 = 2777777.78 + 5000 \times 83.33^2 = 37500000 \text{ mm}^4 \qquad ... \text{(i)}$$

M.I. of semi-circle about its own centroidal axis passing through $G_2$,

$$I_{G_2} = I_{XX_2} = 0.11 \, r^4 = 0.11 \times 50^4 = 687500 \text{ mm}^4$$

Distance between c.g. of semi-circle and AB axis,

$$h_2 = r - \frac{4r}{3\pi} = 50 - \frac{4 \times 50}{3\pi} = 50 - 21.22 = 28.78 \text{ mm}$$

∴   M.I. of semi-circle about AB, using parallel axis theorem,

$$I_{AB_2} = I_{G_2} + a_2 h_2^2 = 687500 + 3926.9908 \times (28.78)^2$$

$$= 687500 + 3252680.927 = 3940180.927 \text{ mm}^4$$

Now,          $I_{AB} = I_{AB_1} + I_{AB_2}$

$\qquad\qquad = 37500000 + 3940180.927 = \mathbf{41440180.93\ mm^4}$

**Answer :** $\boxed{I_{AB} = 41440180.93\ mm^4}$

---

**Example 49 :** *Find $I_{XX}$ and $I_{YY}$ of the uniform lamina as shown in Fig. 4.49. The diameter of a semi-circle is 100 mm.* **(V.V. Imp./4 Marks)**

**Data :** A uniform lamina as shown in Fig. 4.49.

**To find :** $I_{XX}$ and $I_{YY}$.

**Concept :** Use of parallel axis theorem.

**Solution :** (i) Divide the whole section into two parts 1 and 2 as shown in Fig. 4.49.

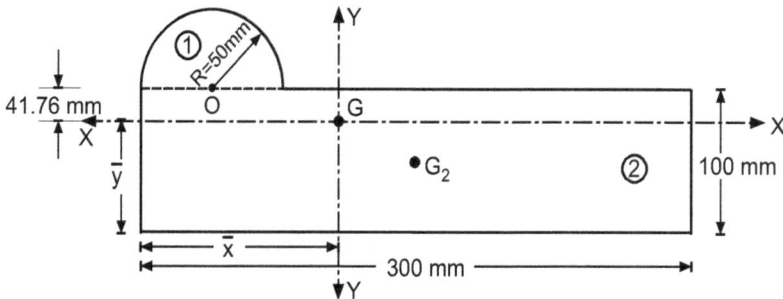

**Fig. 4.49**

(ii) **Areas :** $\qquad a_1 = $ area of semi-circle $= \dfrac{\pi r^2}{2} = \dfrac{\pi \times (50)^2}{2} = 3926.99\ mm^2$

$\qquad\qquad a_2 = $ area of rectangle $= 100 \times 300 = 30000\ mm^2$

∴ Total area $= A = a_1 + a_2 = 3926.99 + 30000 = 33926.99\ mm^2$

(iii) **Distances of the centroid from the left face :**

$\qquad\qquad x_1 = R = 50\ mm; \qquad x_2 = \dfrac{300}{2} = 150\ mm$

(iv) **Distances of the centroid from the base :**

$\qquad\qquad y_1 = 100 + \dfrac{4R}{3\pi} = 100 + \dfrac{4 \times 50}{3\pi} = 121.221\ mm$

$\qquad\qquad y_2 = \dfrac{100}{2} = 50\ mm$

Now, $\qquad \bar{x} = \dfrac{a_1 x_1 + a_2 x_2}{A} = \dfrac{3926.99 \times 50 + 30000 \times 150}{33926.99}$

$\qquad\qquad = 138.43\ mm$ (from the left face)

$\qquad\qquad \bar{y} = \dfrac{a_1 y_1 + a_2 y_2}{A} = \dfrac{3926.99 \times 121.221 + 30000 \times 50}{33926.99} = 58.24\ mm$

**(v) To find $I_{XX}$ :**

Now,

$$I_{XX_1} = I_{G_1} + a_1 h_1^2 = 0.11\,R^4 + 3926.99 \times \left(\frac{4R}{3\pi} + 41.76\right)^2$$

$$= 0.11 \times 50^4 + 3926.99\,(21.22 + 41.76)^2 = 1.626 \times 10^7\,mm^4$$

$$I_{XX_2} = I_{G_2} + a_2 h_2^2 = \frac{300 \times 100^3}{12} + 30000\left(58.24 - \frac{100}{2}\right)^2 = 2.703 \times 10^7\,mm^4$$

$\therefore$

$$\mathbf{I_{XX}} = I_{XX_1} + I_{XX_2} = 1.626 \times 10^7 + 2.703 \times 10^7$$

$$= \mathbf{4.329 \times 10^7\,mm^4}$$

**(vi) To find $I_{YY}$ :**

Now,

$$I_{YY_1} = I_{G_1} + a_1 h_1^2 = \frac{\pi}{128}\,D^4 + 3926.99\,(138.43 - 50)^2$$

$$= \frac{\pi}{128}\,(100)^4 + 3926.99\,(88.43)^2 = 3.316 \times 10^7\,mm^4$$

$$I_{YY_2} = I_{G_2} + a_2 h_2^2 = \frac{100 \times 300^3}{12} + (30000)\left(\frac{300}{2} - 138.43\right)^2 = 22.9 \times 10^7\,mm^4$$

$\therefore$

$$\mathbf{I_{YY}} = I_{YY_1} + I_{YY_2} = 3.316 \times 10^7 + 22.9 \times 10^7$$

$$= \mathbf{26.216 \times 10^7\,mm^4}$$

**Answer :** $\boxed{I_{XX} = 4.329 \times 10^7\,mm^4,\ I_{YY} = 26.216 \times 10^7\,mm^4}$

## Type 3 : Examples on M.I. of cut-out sections :

**Example 50 :** *Find the second moment of area about the indicated axis OX for the lamina as shown in Fig. 4.50 (i), if quarter circle is removed.* **(B.T.E. S-2004/4 Marks)**

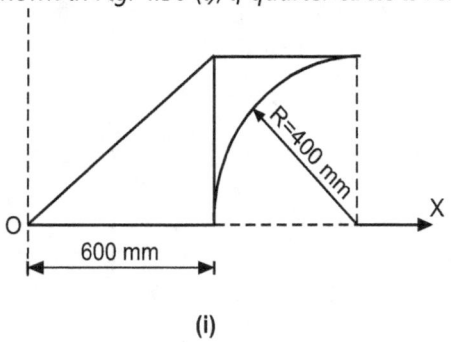
(i)

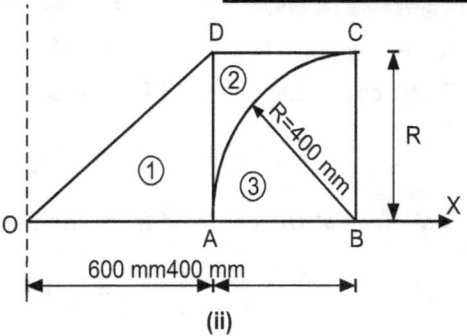
(ii)

**Fig. 4.50**

**Data** : As shown in Fig. 4.50 (i).

**To find** : $I_{OX}$.

**Concept** : $I_{OX} = I_{XX_1} + I_{XX_2} - I_{XX_3}$

**Solution** : (i) M.I. of $\triangle$ OAD about the horizontal axis through $G_1$,

$$I_{G_1} = \frac{bh^3}{36} = \frac{600 \times 400^3}{36} = 1.06 \times 10^9\,mm^4$$

(ii)  Distance between $G_1$ and OX axis,  $h_1 = \dfrac{400}{3} = 133.33$ mm.

(iii)  M.I. of square ABCD about the horizontal axis through $G_2$,

$$I_{G_2} = \frac{bh^3}{12} = \frac{400 \times 400^3}{12} = 2.133 \times 10^9 \text{ mm}^4$$

(iv)  Distance between $G_2$ and OX axis,

$$\mathbf{h_2} = \frac{400}{2} = \mathbf{200\ mm}$$

(v)  M.I. of quarter circle about the horizontal axis through $G_3$,

$$\mathbf{I_{G_3}} = 0.055\ R^4 = 0.055 \times (400)^4 = \mathbf{1.408 \times 10^9\ mm^4}$$

(vi)  Distance between $G_3$ and OX axis,

$$h_3 = \frac{4R}{3\pi} = \frac{4 \times 400}{3\pi} = 169.765 \text{ mm}$$

(vii)　　$I_{OX} = I_{XX_1} + I_{XX_2} - I_{XX_3}$

$$\mathbf{I_{OX}} = (I_{G_1} + a_1 h_1^2) + (I_{G_2} + a_2 h_2^2) - (I_{G_3} + a_3 h_3^2)$$

$$= \left[ 1.06 \times 10^9 + \frac{1}{2} \times 600 \times 400 \times (133.33)^2 \right] +$$

$$\left[ 2.133 \times 10^9 + 400 \times 400 \times (200)^2 \right] -$$

$$\left[ 1.408 \times 10^9 + \frac{\pi \times 400^2}{4} \times (169.765)^2 \right]$$

$$= 3.19 \times 10^9 + 8.533 \times 10^9 - 5.029 \times 10^9$$

$$= (3.19 + 8.533 - 5.029) \times 10^9 = \mathbf{6.694 \times 10^9\ mm^4}$$

**Answer :**　$\boxed{I_{OX} = 6.694 \times 10^9 \text{ mm}^4}$

**Example 51 :** *Calculate the M.I. of the section about the centroidal axes as shown in* Fig. 4.51 (i).　　**(B.T.E. S-2013, 1987/4 Marks)**

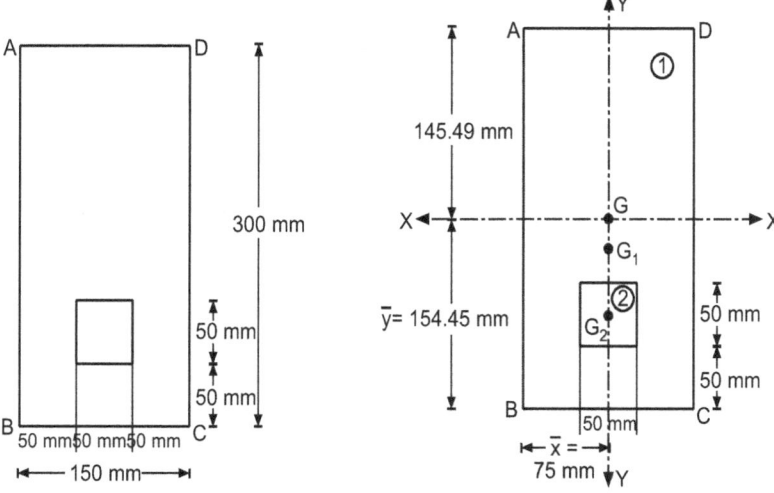

**Fig. 4.51 (i)**　　　　　　　**Fig. 4.51 (ii)**

**Data :** As shown in Fig. 4.51 (i).

**To find :** $I_{XX}$ and $I_{YY}$.

**Concept :**　　$I_{XX} = I_{XX_1} - I_{XX_2}$

　　　　　　　　$I_{YY} = I_{YY_1} - I_{YY_2}$

**Solution :** (i) As the section is symmetrical about the vertical line of symmetry (i.e. YY axis), c.g. of the section will lie on this axis.

$$\therefore \qquad \bar{x} = \frac{150}{2} = 75 \text{ mm (from AB)}$$

**To find $\bar{y}$ :** Divide the section into two areas (1) and (2) as shown in Fig. 4.51 (ii).

(ii) **Areas :**　　$a_1$ = area of rectangle ABCD = $150 \times 300$ = 45000 mm²

　　　　　　　　$a_2$ = area of square = $50 \times 50$ = 2500 mm²

$\therefore$　Total area　　A = $a_1 - a_2$ = 45000 - 2500 = 42500 mm²

(iii) **Distances of the centroid from the base BC :**

$y_1$ = 300/2 = 150 mm, $y_2$ = 50 + 50/2 = 75 mm

$$\therefore \qquad \bar{y} = \frac{a_1 y_1 - a_2 y_2}{A} = \frac{45000 \times 150 - 2500 \times 75}{42500}$$

$$= 154.41 \text{ mm (from the base BC)}$$

$\therefore$　Distance of X-X axis from the base = 154.41 mm

$\therefore$　Distance of X-X axis from the top = 300 - 154.41 = 145.59 mm

(iv) **To find $I_{XX}$ :**

Now,　　$I_{XX_1} = I_{G_1} + a_1 \cdot h_1^2 = \dfrac{150 \times 300^3}{12} + 45000 \left[ 154.45 - \dfrac{300}{2} \right]^2$

　　　　　$= 3375 \times 10^5 + 891112.5 = 3.38 \times 10^8$ mm⁴

　　　　$I_{XX_2} = I_{G_2} + a_2 \cdot h_2^2 = \dfrac{50 \times 50^3}{12} + 2500 \left[ 154.45 - \left( 50 + \dfrac{50}{2} \right) \right]^2$

　　　　　$= 52.08 \times 10^4 + 1578.07 \times 10^4 = 1630.15 \times 10^4$ mm⁴

Now,　　$\mathbf{I_{XX}} = I_{XX_1} - I_{XX_2} = 3.38 \times 10^8 - 1630.15 \times 10^4 = \mathbf{3.21 \times 10^8 \ mm^4}$

(v) **To find $I_{YY}$ :**

Now,　　$I_{YY_1} = \dfrac{300 \times 150^3}{12} = 84375 \times 10^3$ mm⁴

　　　　$I_{YY_2} = \dfrac{50 \times 50^3}{12} = 520833.33$ mm⁴

$\therefore$　　　$\mathbf{I_{YY}} = I_{YY_1} - I_{YY_2} = 84375 \times 10^3 - 520833.33 = \mathbf{8.38 \times 10^7 \ mm^4}$

**Answer :**　$\boxed{I_{XX} = 3.21 \times 10^8 \ \text{mm}^4, \ I_{YY} = 8.38 \times 10^7 \ \text{mm}^4}$

**Example 52 :** *Find the M.I. of a hollow section shown in Fig. 4.52 about an axis passing through its c.g. or parallel to X-X axis.* **(B.T.E. W-2012/4 Marks)**

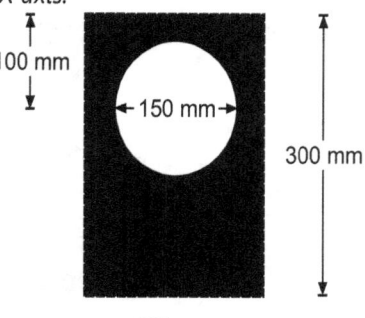

100 mm

←150 mm→

300 mm

←— 200 mm —→

**Fig. 4.52**

**Data :** A circular hole removed from a rectangular plate as shown in Fig. 4.52.

**To find :** $I_{XX}$.

**Concept :** $I_{XX} = I_{XX_1} - I_{XX_2} = I_{XX_{rectangle}} - I_{XX_{circle}}$

**Solution :** (i)   $a_1 = 200 \times 300 = 60000$ mm$^2$

$$a_2 = \frac{\pi}{4} \times (150)^2 = 17671.46 \text{ mm}^2$$

(ii)          $y_1 = \frac{300}{2} = 150$ mm , $y_2 = 300 - 100 = 200$ mm

$$\overline{y}_{bottom} = \frac{a_1 y_1 - a_2 y_2}{a_1 - a_2} = \frac{60000 \times 150 - 17671.46 \times 200}{60000 - 17671.46} = \textbf{129.126 mm}$$

(iii)        $\mathbf{I_{XX}} = \left[ \frac{200 \times 300^3}{12} + (200 \times 300)(150 - 129.126)^2 \right]$

$$- \left[ \frac{\pi}{64} \times (150)^4 + \frac{\pi}{4} \times (150)^2 \times (200 - 129.126)^2 \right]$$

$$= 476143432.6 - 113616414.8 = \textbf{362527017.8 mm}^4$$

**Answer :** $\boxed{I_{XX} = 362527017.8 \text{ mm}^4}$

---

**Example 53 :** *A rectangular hole is made in a triangular section as shown in Fig. 4.53. Determine the M.I. of the section at the base.* **(B.T.E. W-2012/4 Marks)**

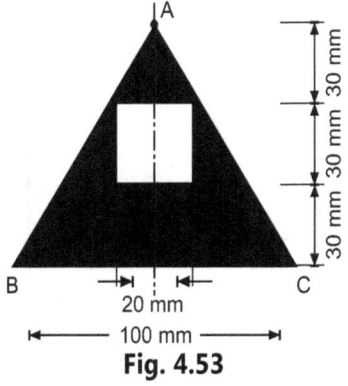

A

30 mm

30 mm   30 mm

30 mm   30 mm

B          C

20 mm

←— 100 mm —→

**Fig. 4.53**

**Data :** A rectangular portion removed from a triangular plate as shown in Fig. 4.53.

**To find :** $I_{BC}$.

**Concept :**  $I_{BC}$ = M.I. of $\Delta$ about base BC – MI of $\square$ @ base BC

$$= I_{BC_1} - I_{BC_2}$$

**Solution :**  $\mathbf{I_{BC}} = \dfrac{100 \times 90^3}{12} - \left[\dfrac{20 \times 30^3}{12} + (20 \times 30)\left(30 + \dfrac{30}{2}\right)^2\right]$

$$= \dfrac{100 \times 90^3}{12} - \left[\dfrac{20 \times 30^3}{12} + (20 \times 30)(45)^2\right]$$

$$= 6075000 - 1260000 = \mathbf{4815000\ mm^4}$$

**Answer :** $\boxed{I_{BC} = 4815000\ mm^4}$

---

**Example 54 :** *For the lamina shown in Fig. 4.54 (i), calculate moment of inertia about the axis AA.*    **(B.T.E. S-2008/4 Marks)**

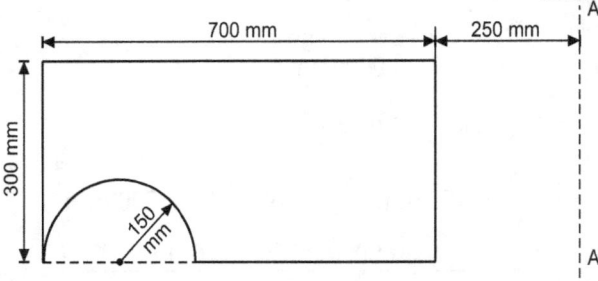

**Fig. 4.54 (i)**

**Data :** A semi-circle removed from a rectangle as shown in Fig. 4.54 (i).

**To find :** $I_{AA}$.

**Concept :** Axis AA is parallel to vertical axis passing through $G_1$ and $G_2$. Using parallel axis theorem, $I_{AA}$ can be calculated.

$$I_{AA} = I_{AA_1} - I_{AA_2}$$

**Note :** Here it is not necessary to calculate $\bar{x}$ and $I_{YY}$.

**Solution :** Refer to Fig. 4.54 (ii).

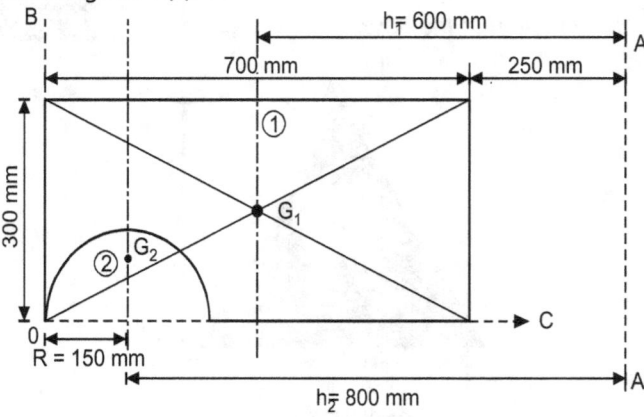

**Fig. 4.54 (ii)**

**Step 1 :** Split up the whole section into two areas 1 and 2 as shown in Fig. 4.54 (ii). Let OB and OC be the axes of reference.

**Step 2 : Areas :** $a_1$ = area of rectangle = $700 \times 300 = 210000 \text{ mm}^2$

$$a_2 = \text{area of semi-circle} = \frac{\pi R^2}{2} = \frac{\pi (150)^2}{2} = 35342.92 \text{ mm}^4$$

**Step 3 :** Find $I_{G_1}$ and $I_{G_2}$.

$I_{G_1}$ = M.I. of rectangle about the vertical axis passing through $G_1$

$$= \frac{300 \times 700^3}{12} = 8575 \times 10^6 \text{ mm}^4$$

$I_{G_2}$ = M.I. of semi-circle about the vertical axis passing through $G_2$

$$= \frac{\pi}{8} R^4 = \frac{\pi}{8} \times (150)^4 = 198803910.1 \text{ mm}^4$$

**Step 4 :** Find $I_{AA}$.　$I_{AA} = I_{AA_1} - I_{AA_2}$

By applying the theorem of parallel axis, we have

$I_{AA_1}$ = M.I. of rectangle about AA axis

$$= I_{G_1} + a_1 h_1^2 = 8575 \times 10^6 + 210000 \times 600^2 = 8.4175 \times 10^{10} \text{ mm}^4$$

By applying theorem of parallel axis, we have

$I_{AA_2}$ = M.I. of semi-circle about AA axis

$$= I_{G_2} + a_2 h_2^2 = 198803910.1 + 35342.92 \times 800^2 = 2.2818 \times 10^{10}$$

∴　　　$\mathbf{I_{AA} = 8.4175 \times 10^{10} - 2.2818 \times 10^{10} = 6.1357 \times 10^{10} \text{ mm}^4}$

**Answer :**　　$\boxed{I_{AA} = 6.1357 \times 10^{10} \text{ mm}^4}$

---

**Example 55 :** *A semi-circular portion of diameter 4 cm is cut from a plate 4 cm $\times$ 8 cm as shown in Fig. 4.55 (i). O is the centre of the semi-circle. Find $I_{XX}$ and $I_{YY}$.*

**(B.T.E. W-2006/4 Marks)**

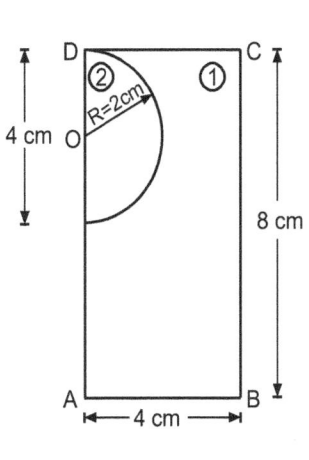

Fig. 4.55 (i)

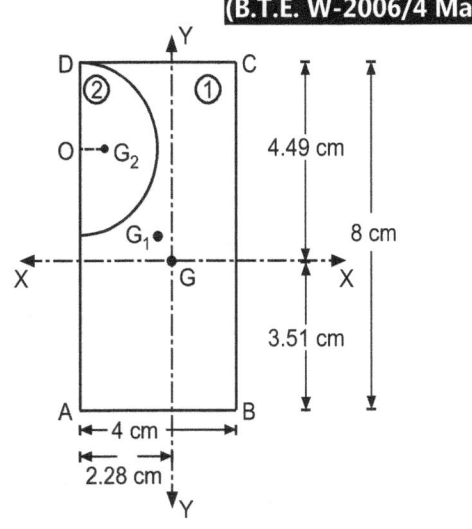

Fig. 4.55 (ii)

**Data :** A semi-circle removed from a rectangle as shown in Fig. 4.55 (i).

**To find :** $I_{XX}$ and $I_{YY}$.

**Concept :**

$$I_{XX} = I_{XX_1} - I_{XX_2} = (I_{G_1} + a_1 h_1^2) - (I_{G_2} + a_2 h_2^2)$$

$$I_{YY} = I_{YY_1} - I_{YY_2} = (I_{G_1} + a_1 h_1^2) - (I_{G_2} + a_2 h_2^2)$$

**Solution :** (i) Split up the whole section into two areas 1 and 2 as shown in Fig. 4.55 (ii). Let AB and AD be the areas of reference.

(ii) **Areas :**     $a_1$ = area of rectangle ABCD = $4 \times 8$ = 32 cm²

$a_2$ = area of semi-circle = $\dfrac{\pi R^2}{2} = \dfrac{\pi (2)^2}{2}$ = 6.28 cm²

∴   Total area = A = $a_1 - a_2$ = 32 − 6.28 = 25.72 cm²

(iii) **Distances of the centroid from AD :**

$$x_1 = \frac{4}{2} = 2 \text{ m}; \qquad x_2 = \frac{4R}{3\pi} = \frac{4 \times 2}{3\pi} = 0.85 \text{ cm}$$

(iv) **Distances of the centroid from AB :**

$$y_1 = \frac{8}{2} = 4 \text{ cm}; \qquad y_2 = 4 + R = 4 + 2 = 6 \text{ cm}$$

∴

$$\bar{x} = \frac{a_1 x_1 - a_2 x_2}{A} = \frac{32 \times 2 - 6.28 \times 0.85}{25.72} = 2.28 \text{ cm (from AD)}$$

and

$$\bar{y} = \frac{a_1 y_1 - a_2 y_2}{A} = \frac{32 \times 4 - 6.28 \times 6}{25.72} = 3.51 \text{ cm (from AB)}$$

The positions of X-X and Y-Y axes are as shown in Fig. 4.55 (ii).

(v) **To find $I_{XX}$ :**

$$I_{XX_1} = I_{G_1} + a_1 h_1^2 = \frac{4 \times 8^3}{12} + 32 \left[ \frac{8}{2} - 3.51 \right]^2 = 170.67 + 32 \times (0.49)^2$$

$$= 170.67 + 7.6832 = 178.35 \text{ cm}^4$$

$$I_{XX_2} = I_{G_2} + a_2 h_2^2 = \frac{\pi}{128} D^4 + 6.28 (4.49 - 2)^2 = \frac{\pi}{128} (4)^4 + 6.28 \times (2.49)^2$$

$$= 6.28 + 38.94 = 45.22 \text{ cm}^4$$

∴          $I_{XX} = I_{XX_1} - I_{XX_2} = 178.35 - 45.22 =$ **133.13 cm⁴**

(vi) **To find $I_{YY}$ :**

$$I_{YY_1} = I_{G_1} + a_1 h_1^2 = \frac{8 \times 4^3}{12} + (32) \left( 2.28 - \frac{4}{2} \right)^2 = 42.67 + 2.51 = 45.18 \text{ cm}^4$$

$$I_{YY_2} = I_{G_2} + a_2 h_2^2 = 0.11 R^4 + (6.28) \left( 2.28 - \frac{4R}{3\pi} \right)^2$$

$$= 0.11 \times 2^4 + 6.28 \times (2.28 - 0.85)^2 = 1.76 + 6.28 \times (1.43)^2$$

$$= 1.76 + 12.84 = 14.6 \text{ cm}^4$$

∴          $I_{YY} = I_{YY_1} - I_{YY_2} = 45.18 - 14.6 =$ **30.58 cm⁴**

**Answer :**   $\boxed{I_{XX} = 133.13 \text{ cm}^4, \; I_{YY} = 30.58 \text{ cm}^4}$

**Example 56 :** *From a plate 4 cm × 8 cm, a triangular portion CDE is cut. Determine the M.I. of the remainder about the horizontal axis passing through its c.g. Refer to Fig. 4.56 (i).*

**(V.V. Imp./4 Marks)**

**Data :** A triangular portion removed from a rectangular plate as shown in Fig. 4.56 (i).

**To find :** $I_{XX}$.

**Concept :**     $I_{XX} = I_{XX_1} - I_{XX_2} = (I_{G_1} + a_1 h_1^2) - (I_{G_2} + a_2 h_2^2)$

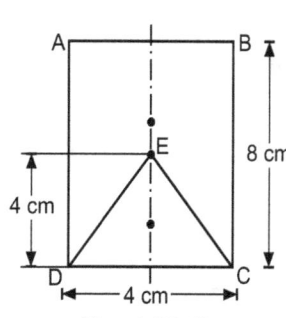

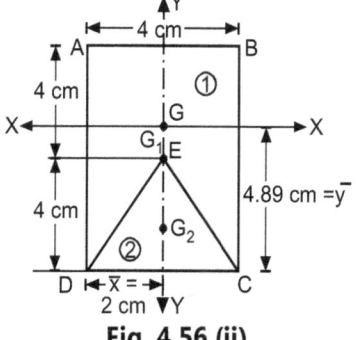

Fig. 4.56 (i)               Fig. 4.56 (ii)

**Solution :** (i) Spilt-up the whole section into two areas 1 and 2 as shown in Fig. 4.56 (ii). AD and DC are the axes of reference.

(ii) **Areas :**     $a_1$ = area of rectangle ABCD = $4 \times 8$ = 32 cm²

$$a_2 = \text{area of triangle CDE} = \frac{1}{2} \times 4 \times 4 = 8 \text{ cm}^2$$

Total area,     A = $a_1 - a_2$ = 32 – 8 = 24 cm²

(iii) The section is symmetrical about YY axis,

∴          $\bar{x} = \dfrac{4}{2}$ = 2 cm (from AD)

(iv) **Distances of the centroid from the base CD :**

$$y_1 = \frac{8}{2} = 4 \text{ cm}; \qquad y_2 = \frac{h}{3} = \frac{4}{3} = 1.33 \text{ cm}$$

∴          $\bar{y} = \dfrac{a_1 y_1 - a_2 y_2}{A} = \dfrac{32 \times 4 - 8 \times 1.33}{24}$ = 4.89 cm (from CD)

The positions of X-X and Y-Y axes are as shown in Fig. 4.56 (ii).

(v) **To find $I_{XX}$ :**

$$I_{XX_1} = I_{G_1} + a_1 h_1^2 = \frac{4 \times 8^3}{12} + (32)\left[4.89 - \frac{8}{2}\right]^2 = 170.67 + 32 \times (0.89)^2$$

$$= 170.67 + 25.35 = 196.02 \text{ cm}^4$$

$$I_{XX_2} = I_{G_2} + a_2 h_2^2 = \frac{bh^3}{36} + (8)\left(4.89 - \frac{h}{3}\right)^2 = \frac{4 \times 4^3}{36} + 8 \times \left(4.89 - \frac{4}{3}\right)^2$$

$$= 7.11 + 8 \times (3.56)^2 = 7.11 + 101.39 = 108.5 \text{ cm}^4$$

∴          $\mathbf{I_{XX}} = I_{XX_1} - I_{XX_2}$ = 196.02 – 108.5 = **87.52 cm⁴**

**Answer :**     $\boxed{I_{XX} = 87.52 \text{ cm}^4}$

**Example 57 :** *A hole of 7 cm diameter is punched from a plate of uniform thickness as shown in Fig. 4.57 (i). Calculate $I_{XX}$ and $I_{YY}$.*

**Data :** A circular hole punched from a rectangular plate as shown in Fig. 4.57 (i).

**To find :** $I_{XX}$ and $I_{YY}$.

**Concept :**
$$I_{XX} = I_{XX_1} - I_{XX_2}$$
$$I_{YY} = I_{YY_1} - I_{YY_2}$$

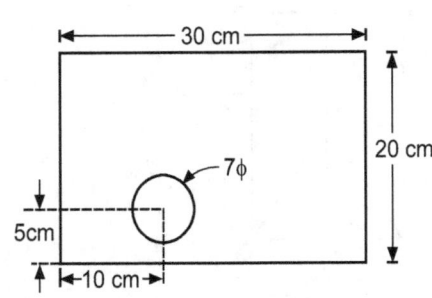

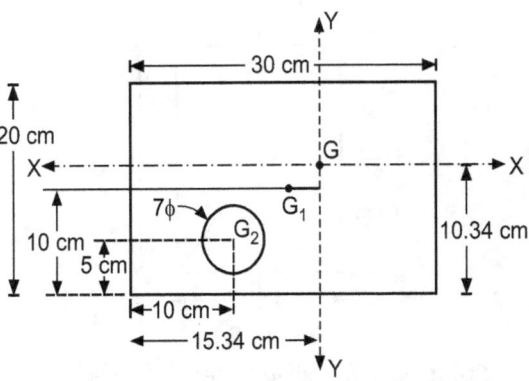

**Fig. 4.57 (i)**　　　　　　　　　　**Fig. 4.57 (ii)**

**Solution :** (i) Split up the whole section into two areas, a rectangle and a hole as shown in Fig. 4.57 (ii).

(ii) **Areas :**　　$a_1$ = area of rectangle = $30 \times 20 = 600$ cm$^2$

$$a_2 = \text{area of circle} = \frac{\pi}{4} D^2 = \frac{\pi}{4} (7)^2 = 38.48 \text{ cm}^2$$

Total area,　　$A = a_1 - a_2 = 600 - 38.48 = 561.52$ cm$^2$

(iii) **Distances of the centroid from the left face :**

$$x_1 = \frac{30}{2} = 15 \text{ cm}; \qquad x_2 = 10 \text{ cm}$$

(iv) **Distances of the centroid from the base :**

$$y_1 = \frac{20}{2} = 10 \text{ cm}; \qquad y_2 = 5 \text{ cm}$$

$\therefore$　　　　$$\bar{x} = \frac{a_1 x_1 - a_2 x_2}{A} = \frac{600 \times 15 - 38.48 \times 10}{561.62} = 15.34 \text{ cm (from the left face)}$$

$$\bar{y} = \frac{a_1 y_1 - a_2 y_2}{A} = \frac{600 \times 10 - 38.48 \times 5}{561.62} = 10.34 \text{ cm (from the base)}$$

The positions of X-X and Y-Y axes are as shown in Fig. 4.57 (ii).

(v) **To find $I_{XX}$ :**

$$I_{XX_1} = I_{G_1} + a_1 h_1^2 = \frac{30 \times 20^3}{12} + (600)\left[10.34 - \frac{20}{2}\right]^2$$

$$= 20000 + 69.36 = 20069.36 \text{ cm}^4$$

$$I_{XX_2} = I_{G_2} + a_2 h_2^2 = \frac{\pi}{64}(7)^4 + 38.48(10.34 - 5)^2$$

$$= 117.86 + 1097.28 = 1215.14 \text{ cm}^4$$

∴          $\mathbf{I_{XX}} = I_{XX_1} - I_{XX_2} = 20069.36 - 1215.14 = \mathbf{18854.22 \text{ cm}^4}$

(vi) **To find $I_{YY}$ :**

$$I_{YY_1} = I_{G_1} + a_1 h_1^2 = \frac{20 \times 30^3}{12} + (600)\left(15.34 - \frac{30}{2}\right)^2$$

$$= 45000 + 69.36 = 45069.36 \text{ cm}^4$$

$$I_{YY_2} = I_{G_2} + a_2 h_2^2 = \frac{\pi}{64}(7)^4 + 38.48(15.34 - 10)^2$$

$$= 117.86 + 1097.28 = 1215.14 \text{ cm}^4$$

∴          $\mathbf{I_{YY}} = I_{YY_1} - I_{YY_2} = 45069.36 - 1215.14 = \mathbf{43854.22 \text{ cm}^4}$

**Answer :** $\boxed{I_{XX} = 18854.22 \text{ cm}^4,\ I_{YY} = 43854.22 \text{ cm}^4}$

---

**Example 58 :** *Find the M.I. of the section about the horizontal centroidal axis as shown in Fig. 4.58 (i). The radius of semi-circle is 2 cm.*          **(V.V. Imp./4 Marks)**

**Data :** A semi-circle removed from a triangle as shown in Fig. 4.58 (i).

**To find :** $I_{XX}$.

**Concept :** $I_{XX} = I_{XX_1} - I_{XX_2}$.

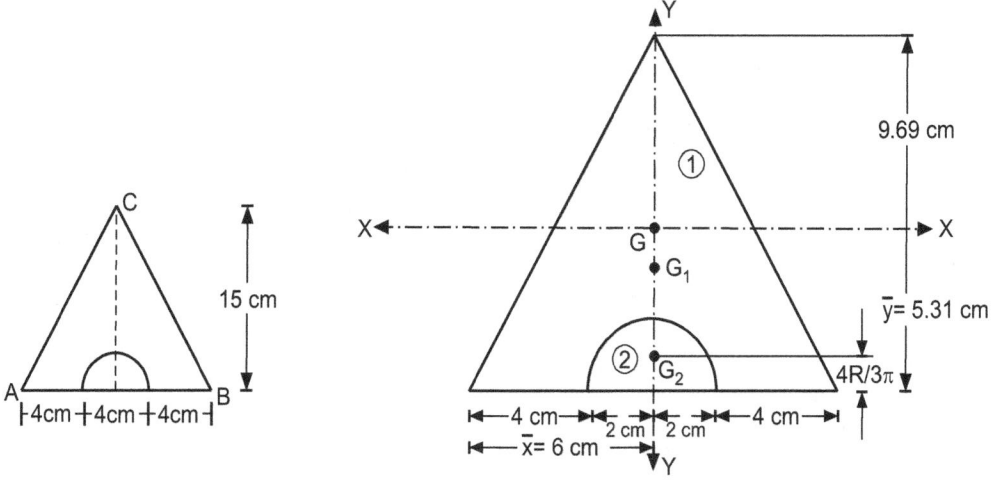

Fig. 4.58 (i)          Fig. 4.58 (ii)

**Solution :** As the section is symmetrical about the vertical axis YY, c.g. of the section will lie on this axis.

∴          $\bar{x} = 6 \text{ cm (from A)}$

Divide the section into two areas 1 and 2 as shown in Fig. 4.58 (ii).

(ii) **Areas :**    $a_1$ = area of triangle = $\frac{1}{2} \times 12 \times 15$ = 90 cm²

$$a_2 = \text{area of semi-circle} = \frac{\pi R^2}{2} = \frac{\pi \times 2^2}{2} = 6.28 \text{ cm}^2$$

$\therefore$ Total area   A = $a_1 - a_2$ = 90 − 6.28 = 83.72 cm²

Let $\bar{y}$ be the distance of c.g. of the section from the base AB.

(iii) **Distances of the centroid from the base :**

$$y_1 = \frac{h}{3} = \frac{15}{3} = 5 \text{ cm}; \qquad y_2 = \frac{4R}{3\pi} = \frac{4 \times 2}{3\pi} = 0.85 \text{ cm}$$

$\therefore$      $\bar{y} = \dfrac{a_1 y_1 - a_2 y_2}{A} = \dfrac{90 \times 5 - 6.28 \times 0.85}{83.72}$ = 5.31 cm (from the base AB)

$\therefore$ Position of X-X axis from the top = 15 − 5.31 = 9.69 cm

(iv) **To find $I_{XX}$ :**

$$I_{XX_1} = I_{G_1} + a_1 h_1^2 = \frac{bh^3}{36} + 90 \times \left(5.31 - \frac{h}{3}\right)^2 = \frac{12 \times 15^3}{36} + 90 \times \left(5.31 - \frac{15}{3}\right)^2$$

$$= 1125 + 8.649 = 1133.65 \text{ cm}^4$$

$$I_{XX_2} = I_{G_2} + a_2 h_2^2 = 0.11 \, R^4 + (6.28)\left(5.31 - \frac{4R}{3\pi}\right)^2$$

$$= 0.11 \times 2^4 + 6.28 \times \left(5.31 - \frac{4 \times 2}{3\pi}\right)^2 = 1.76 + 124.985 = 126.74 \text{ cm}^4$$

$\therefore$      $I_{XX} = I_{XX_1} - I_{XX_2}$ = 1133.65 − 126.74 = **1006.9 cm⁴**

**Answer :**   $\boxed{I_{XX} = 1006.9 \text{ cm}^4}$

---

## Type 4 : Miscellaneous Examples

**Example 59 :** *Find the M.I. of a circular lamina of diameter 'd' about any tangent to it.*

**Data :** A circular lamina of diameter d as shown in Fig. 4.59.

**To find :** $I_{AB}$.

**Concept :** Use of parallel axis theorem.

**Solution :**   We know that, $I_G = I_{XX} = \dfrac{\pi}{64} d^4$

Using the parallel axis theorem,

$\mathbf{I_{AB}}$ = M.I. about the tangent AB

= $I_G + Ah^2$

$= \dfrac{\pi}{64} d^4 + \dfrac{\pi}{4} d^2 \cdot \left(\dfrac{d}{2}\right)^2 = \dfrac{5\pi}{64} d^4 =$ **0.245 d⁴**

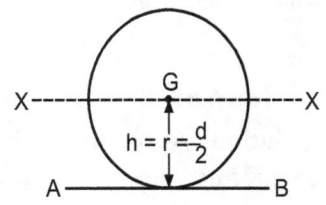

**Fig. 4.59**

**Answer :** $\boxed{I_{AB} = 0.245 \text{ d}^4}$

**Example 60 :** *Find the M.I. of a square section having a diagonal of 400 mm about its diagonal.* **(B.T.E. W-2010/4 Marks)**

**OR**

*Find M.I. of a square section about its diagonal resting on one of its corner having diagonal of 400 mm in length.* **(B.T.E. W-2010/4 Marks)**

**Data :** A square having diagonal 400 mm as shown in Fig. 4.60.

**To find :** $I_{BC}$.

**Concept :** M.I. of one triangle about its base = $\dfrac{bh^3}{12}$.

**Solution :** Refer to Fig. 4.60.

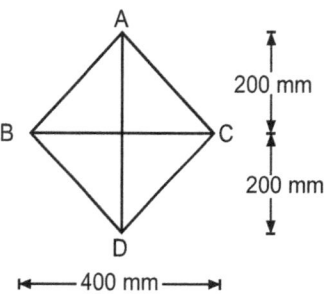

$$I_{BC} = \text{M.I. of a square section about diagonal BC}$$

$$= \text{M.I. of two triangles ABC and BCD about base BC}$$

$$= 2 \times \text{M.I. of one triangle about base BC}$$

$$= 2 \times \frac{bh^3}{12} = 2 \times \left(\frac{400 \times 200^3}{12}\right) = \mathbf{5.33 \times 10^8 \ mm^4}$$

**Answer :** $\boxed{I_{BC} = 5.33 \times 10^8 \ mm^4}$

**Fig. 4.60**

## Practice Questions

### Questions of 2 marks

1. State the parallel axis theorem of moment of inertia.

    **(B.T.E. S-2013, 2008, 1998; W-2008, 2000, 1997)**

2. State the theorem of parallel axis.          **(B.T.E. W-2012, 2011, 2010; S-2009)**

3. Define radius of gyration. State its S.I. unit.          **(B.T.E. S-2012, 2010, 2009)**

4. Define polar moment of inertia.          **(B.T.E. S-2012, 2008; W-2009)**

5. Define 'moment of inertia'. State its S.I. unit.          **(B.T.E. S-2011)**

6. State perpendicular axis theorem of moment of inertia.     **(B.T.E. W-2009, S-2000)**

7. Explain the theorem of mutually perpendicular axis for M.I.          **(B.T.E. S-2009)**

8. State the value of M.I. of a semi-circle of radius 'R' about centroidal XX and YY axes.

    **(B.T.E. W-2008)**

9. State the value of M.I. of a triangle about its base.          **(B.T.E. W-2007)**

10. What is the M.I. of a semi-circle about the base ?          **(B.T.E. S-1997)**

11. State the values of moment of inertia of -

    (i) triangle about its base, (ii) circle about its diameter.          **(B.T.E. S-1999)**

12. State the values of M.I. of a triangular section about -

    (i) its apex, (ii) horizontal axis passing through its C.G.

13. State the value of M.I. of a quarter circle about the centroidal axis.

## Problems of 2 marks

14. Find the radius of gyration of a rectangle of breadth 'b' and depth 'd' about an axis passing through its centroid and parallel to the breadth. (**Ans. :** $K_{XX} = d/2\sqrt{3}$)

15. An equilateral triangle has a side of 150 mm. Find the moment of inertia about its any one of the sides. (**B.T.E. W-2010**)

16. Find M.I. of an equilateral triangle of side 2 m about its base. (**B.T.E. W-2011**)

17. Find polar moment of inertia of a circle of 50 mm diameter. (**B.T.E. W-2012, 1998**)

18. Calculate the M.I. about any tangent of a circle having 990 mm diameter.

    (**B.T.E. S-2000**)

19. A triangular lamina is having base 100 mm and height 225 mm. Calculate its M.I. about an axis passing through its centroid and parallel to the base.

20. Find the moment of inertia of a right angled triangle 90 mm height and 120 mm base about an horizontal axis passing through the apex. (**B.T.E. W-1997**)

21. Find the radius of gyration of a circle of diameter 'd'. (**Ans. :** K = d/4)

## Questions of 4 marks

22. Define : (i) moment of inertia, (ii) radius of gyration. (**B.T.E. S-2013, W-2011**)

23. State and explain parallel axis theorem. (**B.T.E. S-2011**)

24. State and explain perpendicular axis theorem. (**B.T.E. S-2011**)

25. Write a short note on centre of gravity. (**B.T.E. S-2011**)

26. Define radius of gyration and polar moment of inertia. (**B.T.E. S-2010**)

27. State the parallel axis theorem and perpendicular axis theorem of moment of inertia.

    (**B.T.E. S-2010, W-2007**)

28. Find the M.I. of an angle section 120 mm × 80 mm × 10 mm as shown in Fig. 4.61.

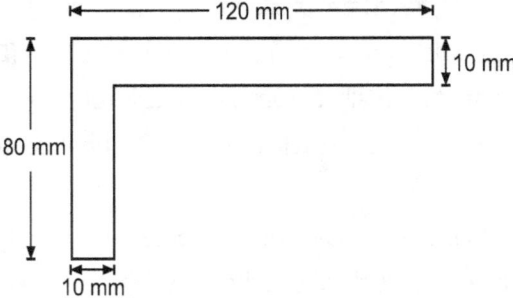

**Fig. 4.61**

(**Ans. :** $I_{XX} = 1 \times 10^6$ mm⁴, $I_{YY} = 2.783 \times 10^6$ mm⁴)

29. Find the M.I. of an inverted Tee section having the flange 100 mm × 30 mm and the web 120 mm × 30 mm as shown in Fig. 4.62.                    **(B.T.E. W-2010/4 Marks)**

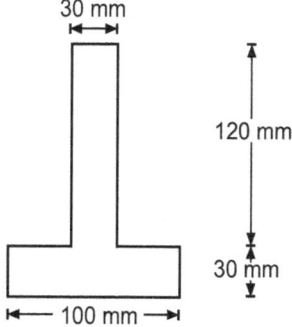

**Fig. 4.62**

(**Ans :** $I_{XX} = 13.75 \times 10^6$ mm$^4$, $I_{YY} = 2.77 \times 10^6$ mm$^4$)

30. A channel section 30 cm × 15 cm is thick. The web is vertical. Find the centroid of the section from the back of the web and calculate $I_{XX}$ and $I_{YY}$.

(**Ans :** $\bar{x}$ = 4.48 cm, $I_{XX}$ = 14709.33 mm$^4$, $I_{YY}$ = 2319.29 mm$^4$)

31. An unsymmetrical I section consists of a top flange 200 mm × 20 mm, web 10 mm × 300 mm and bottom flange 300 mm × 20 mm. Overall height is 340 mm. Find the M.I. of the section about the horizontal centroidal axis and that about the lower edge of the section.                    **(B.T.E. S-1995)**

(**Ans :** Refer to Fig. 4.63)

$\bar{y}$ = 145.38 mm  and $I_{XX}$ = 2.70956 × 10$^8$ mm$^4$)

**Hint :** $I_{AB} = I_{XX} + Ah^2 = 2.70956 \times 10^8 + 13000 \times (145.38)^2 = 5.45715 \times 10^8$ mm$^4$

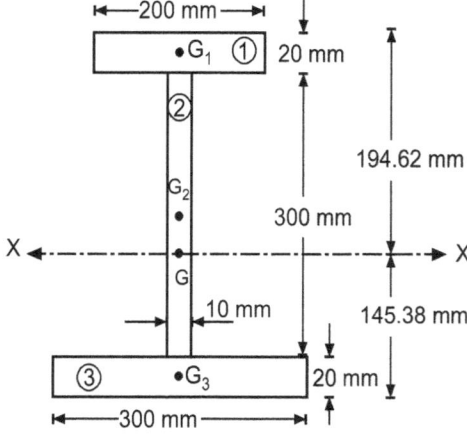

**Fig. 4.63**

32. A square section of each side equal to 'b' is kept with one of the diagonals horizontal as shown in Fig. 4.64. Find $I_{XX}$ of this section.

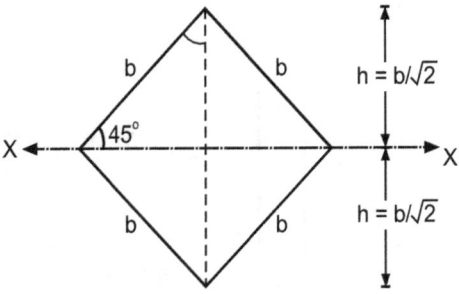

**Fig. 4.64**

**Hint :** $\sin 45° = \dfrac{h}{b}$   $\therefore$  $h = b \sin 45° = \dfrac{b}{\sqrt{2}}$                    (**Ans :** $I_{XX} = b^4/12$)

## Important Points

- **Moment of Inertia :** Moment of inertia of a body about any axis is defined as the sum of second moment of all elementary areas about that axis. It is denoted by I.

    The moment of inertia about X-X axis is denoted by $I_{XX}$.

    Mathematically, $I_{XX} = \sum ay^2$

    The moment of inertia about Y-Y axis is denoted by $I_{YY}$.

    Mathematically, $I_{YY} = \sum ax^2$

  **Unit of M.I. :** $m^4$, $mm^4$, $cm^4$ etc.

- **Radius of Gyration :** The radius of gyration of a given area about any axis is that distance from the given axis at which the entire area is assumed to be concentrated without changing the moment of inertia about the given axis. It is denoted by K and is calculated by the relation $I = AK^2$. The radius of gyration about X-X axis is generally denoted by $K_{XX}$ and that about Y-Y axis as $K_{YY}$.

    Mathematically, $K_{XX} = \sqrt{\dfrac{I_{XX}}{A}}$ and $K_{YY} = \sqrt{\dfrac{I_{YY}}{A}}$

  **Unit of K :** mm, cm, m, etc.

  Least radius of gyration,

  $$K_{least} = \sqrt{\dfrac{I_{least}}{A}}$$

- **M.I. of some standard sections :**

  **(i) Rectangular section of size b × d :**

  $$I_{XX} = \dfrac{bd^3}{12}, \qquad I_{YY} = \dfrac{db^3}{12}$$

(ii) **Hollow rectangular section of outer dimensions B, D and inner dimensions b, d :**

$$I_{XX} = \frac{1}{12}(BD^3 - b\,d^3) \quad \text{and} \quad I_{YY} = \frac{1}{12}(DB^3 - db^3)$$

(iii) **Triangular section of base 'b' and height 'h' :**

$$I_{XX} = \frac{bh^3}{36}, \; I_{Base} = \frac{bh^3}{12} \; \text{and} \; I_{Apex} = \frac{bh^3}{4}$$

(iv) **Solid circular section of diameter D :**

$$I = I_{XX} = I_{YY} = \frac{\pi}{64}D^4$$

(v) **Hollow circular section of external diameter 'D' and internal diameter 'd' :**

$$I = I_{XX} = I_{YY} = \frac{\pi}{64}(D^4 - d^4)$$

(vi) **Semi-circular section of radius 'R' :**

$$I_{XX} = 0.11\,R^4, \; I_{YY} = \frac{\pi}{128}D^4$$

(vii) **Quarter circle (Quadrant of a circle of radius 'R') :**

$$I = I_{XX} = I_{YY} = \frac{1}{2} \times 0.11\,R^4 = 0.055\,R^4$$

- **Parallel axis theorem :** It states, "The moment of inertia of a plane section about any axis parallel to the centroidal axis is equal to the moment of inertia of the section about the centroidal axis plus the product of the area of the section and the square of the distance between the two axes."

    Mathematically,

$$\begin{bmatrix} \text{M.I. about} \\ \text{parallel axis} \end{bmatrix} = \begin{bmatrix} \text{M.I. about the} \\ \text{centroidal axis} \end{bmatrix} + \text{Area} \times (\text{Distance})^2$$

∴      $I_{AB} = I_G + Ah^2$

∴      $I_{AB} = (I_{xx} \text{ or } I_{yy}) + Ah^2$

- **Perpendicular axis theorem :** It states, "If $I_{XX}$ and $I_{YY}$ are the moments of inertia of a plane section about the two mutually perpendicular axes meeting at O, then the moment of inertia $I_{ZZ}$ about the third axis ZZ perpendicular to the plane and passing through the intersection of X-X and Y-Y axes is given by,

$$I_{ZZ} = I_{XX} + I_{YY}$$

    $I_{ZZ}$ is also called as polar moment of inertia and is denoted by $I_P$.

∴      $I_P = I_{ZZ} = I_{XX} + I_{YY}$

    The theorem is also called as **polar axis theorem.**

- **Polar moment of inertia :** The moment of inertia of a plane area about an axis perpendicular to the plane of the figure is called polar moment of inertia with respect to the point, where the axis intersects the plane.

  For a solid circular shaft of diameter 'd',

  $$I_P = \frac{\pi}{32} D^4$$

  For a hollow circular shaft of external diameter D and internal diameter d,

  $$I_P = \frac{\pi}{32} (D^4 - d^4)$$

# BENDING STRESSES

Weightage of Marks = 12, Teaching Hours = 06

## Objectives

Specific Objectives :
- Acquire and apply knowledge of bending stresses and shear stresses.

## Contents

5.1 Theory of Simple Bending :
- Assumptions in the theory of bending, Moment of resistance, Section modulus, Neutral axis. Stress distribution diagram for cantilever and simply supported beam. Equation of bending (Simple numericals based on formula). **(6 Marks)**

5.2 Concept of Direct and Transverse Shear Stresses :
- Transverse shear stress equation (No derivation).
- Shear stress distribution diagrams, Average shear stress and Maximum shear stress for rectangular and circular sections **(6 Marks)**

### SUB-TOPIC 5.1 : THEORY OF SIMPLE BENDING (BENDING STRESSES) (6 Marks)

## Synopsis

Introduction, Concept of pure bending, Theory of simple (pure) bending, Assumptions in the theory of simple bending, Derivation of flexural formula, Moment of resistance ($M_r$), Bending stress distribution diagrams for symmetrical sections, Bending stress distribution diagrams for asymmetrical (unsymmetrical) sections, Section modulus (Z), Practical applications of flexural formula, Solved examples, Practice questions, Important points.

## 5.1 INTRODUCTION

In chapter 3 we have seen that shear forces and bending moments are produced at each cross-section of a beam when it is subjected to external loads. A beam gets bent-up or deformed when subjected to B.M. and S.F. As it undergoes the deformation, internal resistances are set up and the process of deformation (bending) stops when every cross-section sets up full resistance (stress) to the shear force and bending moment acting on it. *The stresses induced to resist the bending moment are called bending stresses. The stresses induced to resist the shear force are called shear stresses or shearing stresses.*

*Bending action in a beam is called flexure.* In this topic, we shall study the flexural formula (bending stress equation) and its applications to symmetrical and unsymmetrical sections.

(5.1)

## 5.2 CONCEPT OF PURE BENDING

Let us consider a simply supported beam of span L carrying two equal point loads W placed at a distance 'a' from each support as shown in Fig. 5.1 (a). The S.F. and B.M. diagrams for the beam are as shown in Fig. 5.1 (b) and 5.1 (c) respectively.

From the shear force diagram, it can be seen that there is no shear force at all sections between C and D. From the bending moment diagram, it can be seen that there is a constant B.M. between C and D equal to W.a. **In this case, the portion 'CD' of the beam between the two downward point loads is subjected to pure bending or simple bending.**

When the beam is subjected to pure bending, it bends or deflects into an arc of a circle. A beam subjected to pure bending has only normal (bending) stresses of tensile or compressive nature set up in it. A beam subjected to ordinary bending has both normal (bending) and shear stresses set up in it.

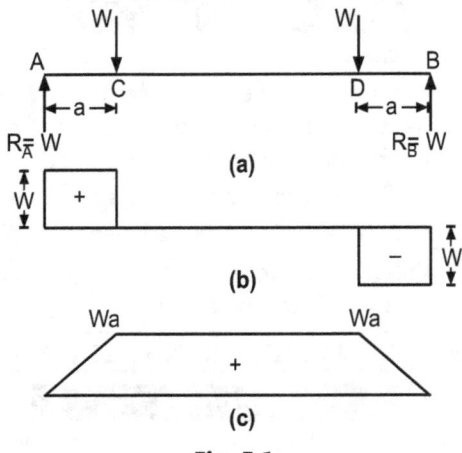

**Fig. 5.1**

1.  Differentiate between pure bending and ordinary bending.

   **(B.T.E. W-2005, S-1998/2 Marks)**

   **(Most Likely and Asked in Previous B.T.E. Exam.)**

## 5.3 THEORY OF SIMPLE (PURE) BENDING

We know that the beam bends under the action of transverse (vertical) loading on it. A simply supported beam bends in a sagging pattern whereas a cantilever beam bends in a hogging pattern, as shown in Fig. 5.2.

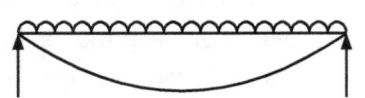
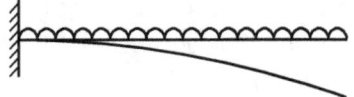

| **(a) Bending pattern of sagging type for a simply supported beam** | **(b) Bending pattern of hogging type for a cantilever beam** |

**Fig. 5.2**

Let us consider the bending pattern of a simply supported beam under the action of transverse loading on it as shown in Fig. 5.3.

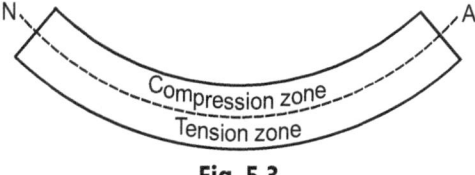

**Fig. 5.3**

The fibres in the lower part of the beam undergo elongation while those in the upper part are shortened. These changes in the lengths of the fibres set up tensile and compressive stresses in the fibres. The fibres in the dotted centroidal layer are neither shortened nor elongated. This centroidal layer which do not undergo any extension (elongation) or compression is called neutral layer or neutral surface. **The intersection of the neutral layer with any normal cross-section of a beam is called neutral axis (N.A.).** All the layers above the neutral axis are under compression while those below the neutral axis are under tension. Hence the compressive stresses are developed in the layers above the N.A. and the tensile stresses are developed in the layers below the N.A. At the N.A. there is no stress of any kind i.e. **the bending stress at the N.A. is zero.**

In short, for a simply supported beam, the tension zone is below the N.A. while the compression zone is above the N.A. The bending pattern of a cantilever beam is exactly opposite to that of a simply supported beam. Hence for a cantilever beam the tension zone is above the N.A. whereas the compression zone is below the N.A., as shown in Fig. 5.4.

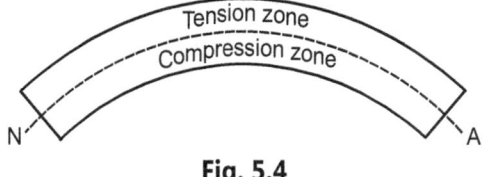

**Fig. 5.4**

| | | |
|---|---|---|
| 1. | Define neutral axis in the theory of simple bending. | **(B.T.E. W-2011/2 Marks)** |
| 2. | Define neutral axis. | **(B.T.E. S-2015, 1998/2 Marks)** |
| 3. | Explain the theory of simple bending. | **(B.T.E. S-2011/4 Marks)** |

**(Most Likely and Asked in Previous B.T.E. Exam.)**

## 5.4 ASSUMPTIONS IN THE THEORY OF SIMPLE BENDING

The following assumptions are made in the theory of simple bending while deriving the flexural formula.

(i) The material of the beam is homogeneous and isotropic. i.e. the beam is made up of the same material throughout and it has the same elastic properties in all the directions.

(ii) The beam is straight before loading and is of uniform cross-section throughout.

(iii) The beam material is stressed within its elastic limit and thus obeys Hooke's law.

(iv) The transverse sections which were plane before bending remain plane after bending.

(v) The beam is subjected to **pure bending** i.e. the effect of shear stresses is totally neglected.

(vi) Each layer of the beam is free to expand or contract independently of the layer above or below it.

(vii) Young's modulus E for the beam material has the same value in tension and compression.

---

1. State any four assumptions in the theory of simple (pure) bending.

   **(B.T.E. S-2015, 2014, 2012, 2011, 2010, 2006; W-2014, 2011, 2010, 2009, 2008, 2007/4 Marks)**

2. State two assumptions made in the theory of bending.     **(B.T.E. W-2012/2 Marks)**

---

**(Most Likely and Asked in Previous B.T.E. Exam.)**

## 5.5 DERIVATION OF FLEXURAL FORMULA (Equation of Bending)

**Note :** The derivation of flexural formula is not expected in the examination.

Consider a slice ABCD of small length dx of a simply supported beam subjected to bending moment 'M' as shown in Fig. 5.5 (a). EF is the neutral axis. It is obvious that AB = CD = EF = dx (before bending). A bent up beam is as shown in Fig. 5.5 (d). The new lengths of AB and CD are $A_1B_1$ and $C_1D_1$ respectively. For a neutral layer EF, $E_1F_1$ = EF = dx. The bent up curved portion is assumed as small arc of the circle, with O as centre. Let θ be the angle subtended at the centre by the arc. Let R be the radius of curvature of the bent up beam. The neutral axis $E_1F_1$ lies at a radius R of the circle.

Length of the arc $E_1F_1$ = R θ

Now, consider a layer GH at a distance 'y' from the neutral axis EF. Let this layer be compressed to $G_1H_1$ after bending.

Since there is no change in the length of the neutral layer, we have

$$E_1 F_1 \ = \ EF = GH = R \cdot \theta \tag{i}$$

Naturally, length of the arc $G_1H_1$ = (R – y) θ     ... (ii)

Now, decrease in the length of layer GH is given by,

$$\delta L \ = \ \text{Initial length – Final length} = GH - G_1H_1$$

$$= \ R\theta - (R - y)\,\theta = y\cdot\theta$$

∴ Strain in the layer GH is given by,

$$e \ = \ \frac{\delta L}{L} = \frac{y\cdot\theta}{R\theta} = \frac{y}{R} \tag{iii}$$

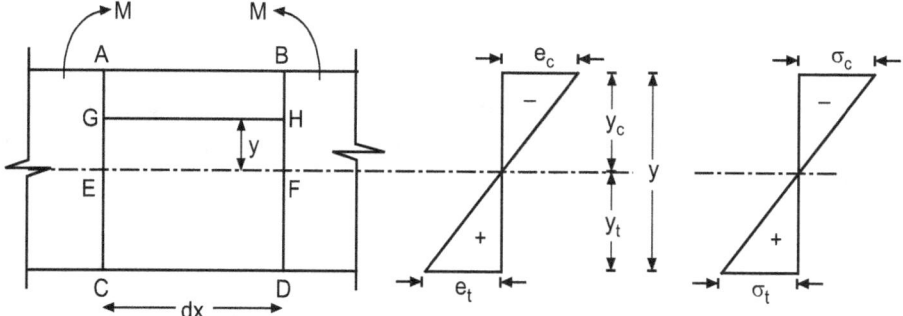

**(a) Beam before loading**    **(b) Strain distribution diagram**    **(c) Stress distribution diagram**

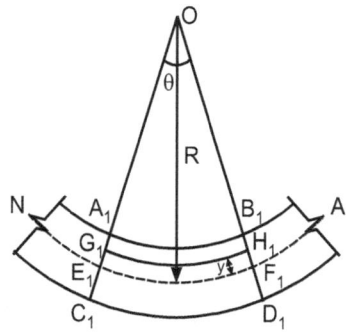

**(d) Beam after bending**

**Fig. 5.5**

But

$$\text{Strain} = \frac{\text{Stress}}{\text{Young's modulus}}$$

i.e.

$$e = \frac{\sigma}{E}$$

Substituting the value of 'e' in the equation (iii), we have

$$\frac{\sigma}{E} = \frac{y}{R}$$

∴

$$\boxed{\frac{\sigma}{y} = \frac{E}{R}}$$        ... (A)

Now, from the equation (iii), we have

$$\boxed{e \propto y}$$

i.e. the strain of any layer is proportional to its distance from the N.A.

At N.A.,      $y = 0$

∴ Strain at N.A. is always zero.

All the layers above the N.A. are compressed and those below the N.A. are elongated. The maximum compressive strain ($e_c$) occurs at the topmost layer $A_1B_1$ and the maximum tensile strain occurs at the bottommost layer $C_1D_1$. The bending strain distribution diagram is as shown in Fig. 5.5 (b).

**[Since compression causes decrease in the length and tension causes increase in the length of the layer, compressive strain is generally taken as negative and tensile strain as positive.]**

Now, consider a small area '$\delta A$' at a distance 'y' from the neutral axis as shown in Fig. 5.6.

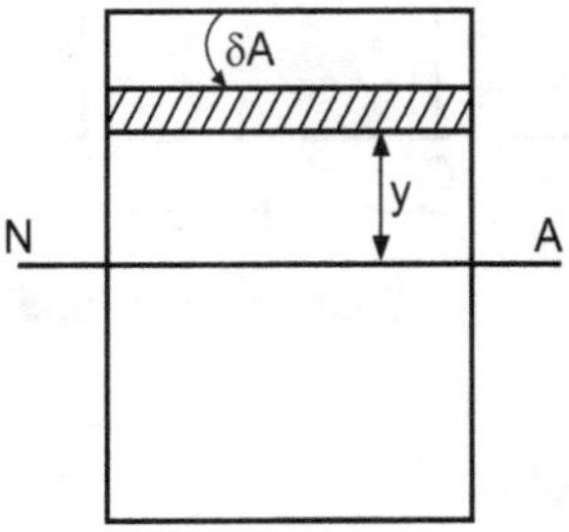

From the equation (i),

Stress on this small area,

$$\sigma = \frac{E}{R} \times y$$

∴  Small force on this area

$$\delta F = \text{Stress} \times \text{Area}$$

$$= \sigma \times \delta A = \left(\frac{E}{R} \times y\right) \times \delta A$$

**Fig. 5.6**

Moment of this small force about N.A.

$$\delta M = \delta F \times y = \left(\frac{E}{R} \times y\right) \delta A \times y = \frac{E}{R} \times \delta A \times y^2$$

∴  Total moment,     $M = \sum \delta M = \sum \frac{E}{R} \times \delta A \times y^2$

$$= \frac{E}{R} \sum \delta A \cdot y^2$$

$$= \frac{E}{R} \times I \qquad\qquad \dots (\because \sum \delta A \cdot y^2 = I)$$

∴
$$\boxed{\frac{M}{I} = \frac{E}{R}} \qquad\qquad \dots (B)$$

Combining the two equations (A) and (B), we have

$$\boxed{\frac{M}{I} = \frac{\sigma}{y} = \frac{E}{R}}$$

This is known as **flexural formula (i.e. bending stress equation).**

Now, consider the equation,

$$\frac{M}{I} = \frac{\sigma}{y}$$

∴
$$\sigma = \left(\frac{M}{I}\right) \times y$$

Since, M and I are constant, σ varies with y i.e. the bending stress at a point is directly proportional to its distance from the neutral axis.

At N.A.,　　　　　　　　$y = 0$

∴　　　　　　　　　　$\sigma = 0$

i.e. **bending stress at the N.A. is always zero.** As the distance from the N.A. increases, the bending stress also increases. The maximum bending stress occurs at the outermost layer. The bending stress distribution diagram is as shown in Fig. 5.5 (c). The maximum compressive stress ($\sigma_c$) occurs at the topmost layer $A_1B_1$ and the maximum tensile stress ($\sigma_t$) occurs at the bottommost layer $C_1D_1$.

**Note (1) :** $y_c$ *indicates depth in compression and* $y_t$ *indicates depth in tension.*

*Total depth of section,* $y = y_c + y_t$

**Note (2) :** *For a cantilever beam, the maximum compressive stress occurs at the bottom and the maximum tensile stress at the top. The bending stress and the bending strain distribution diagram for a cantilever beam is as shown in Fig. 5.7.*

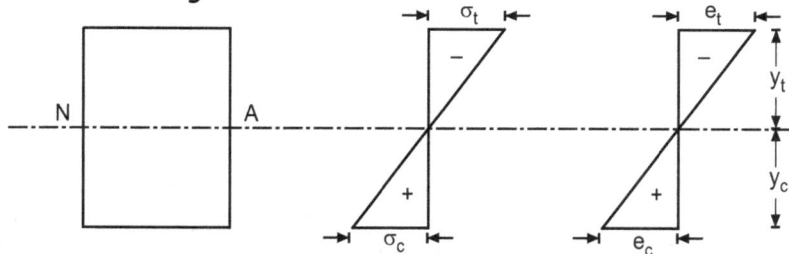

**(a) Section(b) Stress distribution(c) Strain distribution**

**Fig. 5.7**

**Note (3) :** **Flexural formula and the meaning of symbols used :**

$$\frac{M}{I} = \frac{\sigma}{y} = \frac{E}{R}$$

M = *Maximum bending moment which is equal to moment of resistance of a beam.*

I = *Moment of inertia of the beam section about the neutral axis. Since N.A. always lies at the centroid of the section,*

$$I = I_{NA} = I_{XX}$$

σ = *Bending stress in a layer at a distance 'y' from N.A.*
y = *Distance of the layer from the N.A. of the beam cross-section.*
E = *Modulus of elasticity of the beam material.*
R = *Radius of curvature of the bent up beam.*
*Sometimes the flexural formula can also be written as*

$$\frac{M_r}{I} = \frac{\sigma_{max}}{y_{max}} = \frac{E}{R}$$

*where* $M_r$ *is equal to the moment of resistance of the beam. Generally, the maximum values of* σ *and y are considered. Sometimes, the suffix 'max' is omitted while writing the formula.*

**Note (4)** : *Many times, the last term $\dfrac{E}{R}$ is not required and the flexural formula can be written as,*

$$\frac{M}{I} = \frac{\sigma}{y}$$

*To calculate the maximum compressive stress, the maximum depth in compression i.e. $y_c$ is considered.*

$\therefore$
$$\frac{M}{I} = \frac{\sigma_c}{y_c}$$

$\therefore$
$$\boxed{\sigma_c = \frac{M}{I} \times y_c}$$

*To calculate the maximum tensile stress, the maximum depth in tension i.e. $y_t$ is considered.*

$\therefore$
$$\frac{M}{I} = \frac{\sigma_t}{y_t}$$

$\therefore$
$$\boxed{\sigma_t = \frac{M}{I} \times y_t}$$

---

1. Write the flexural formula. State the meaning of symbols used in it.
**(B.T.E. W-2013, S-2012, 2010/2 Marks)**

**(Most Likely and Asked in Previous B.T.E. Exam.)**

## 5.6 MOMENT OF RESISTANCE ($M_r$)

Refer to the bending stress distribution diagram of a simply supported beam as shown in Fig. 5.8.

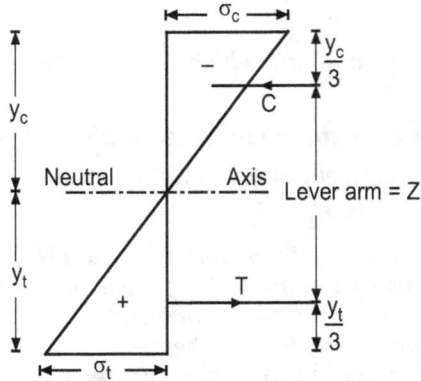

**Fig. 5.8**

On one side of N.A., there is a compressive stress and on the other side tensile stress. The compressive stress diagram is a upper triangle and the tensile stress diagram is a lower triangle as shown in Fig. 5.8. The centroid of the compressive stress diagram is at a distance of $\dfrac{y_c}{3}$ from the top and the centroid of the tensile stress diagram is at a distance of $\dfrac{y_t}{3}$ from the bottom. The total compressive force 'C' acts at the c.g. of upper triangle and the total tensile force 'T' acts at the c.g. of the lower triangle.

For the beam to be in equilibrium, the resultant force on the section must be zero.

i.e.                $T - C = 0$                                  $(\rightarrow +, \leftarrow -)$

$\therefore$                  $T = C$

C and T are the two equal, unlike parallel and non-collinear forces. Hence they form a couple. The distance between the two forces of a couple is called lever arm. It is denoted by Z.

Moment of couple = $C \times Z$ or $T \times Z$. This moment is called the moment of resistance of the beam and is denoted by $M_r$.

**Definition :** *Moment of resistance of the beam is the moment of couple formed by the total compressive force acting at the c.g. of the compressive stress diagram and the total tensile force acting at the c.g. of the tensile stress diagram. It resists the external bending moment. In the equilibrium condition, the moment of resistance must be equal to the external bending moment, i.e.* **$M_r = M$.**

1. What is meant by moment of resistance and neutral axis ?

**(B.T.E. W-2014, 2012/4 Marks)**

2. Differentiate between moment of resistance and bending moment.

**(B.T.E. W-2000; S-1999, 1997/2 Marks)**

**(Most Likely and Asked in Previous B.T.E. Exam.)**

## 5.7 BENDING STRESS DISTRIBUTION DIAGRAMS FOR SYMMETRICAL SECTIONS

For sections symmetrical about N.A. its c.g. lies at the middle of its depth i.e. $y_c = y_t$ and hence $\sigma_c = \sigma_t$. The bending stress variation diagrams for such sections are as shown in Fig. 5.9.

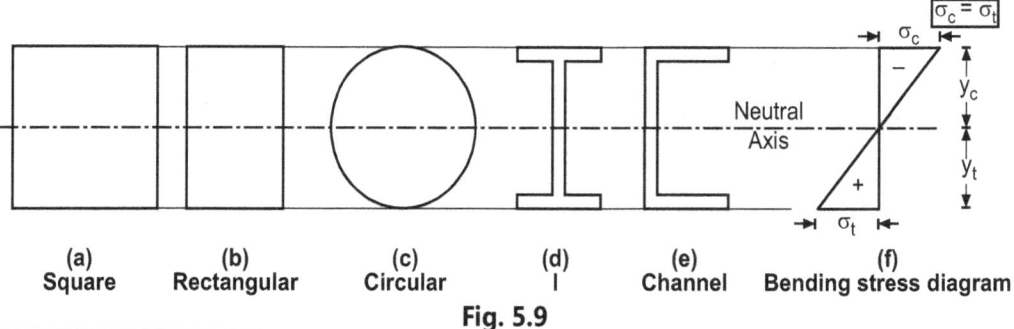

| (a) | (b) | (c) | (d) | (e) | (f) |
| Square | Rectangular | Circular | I | Channel | Bending stress diagram |

**Fig. 5.9**

1. Show the nature of stresses in the bending stress distribution diagram, if the rectangular beam is of cantilever type. The loading is downward.

**(B.T.E. S-1997/2 Marks)**

**(Most Likely and Asked in Previous B.T.E. Exam.)**

## 5.8 BENDING STRESS DISTRIBUTION DIAGRAMS FOR ASYMMETRICAL (UNSYMMETRICAL) SECTIONS

For sections unsymmetrical about N.A., $y_c \neq y_t$ and hence $\sigma_c \neq \sigma_t$. The bending stress variation diagrams for such sections are as shown in Fig. 5.10. The depth in tension or compression can be calculated by using the well known equation,

$$\bar{y} = \frac{a_1\,y_1 + a_2\,y_2 + a_3\,y_3 + \dots}{a_1 + a_2 + a_3 + \dots}$$

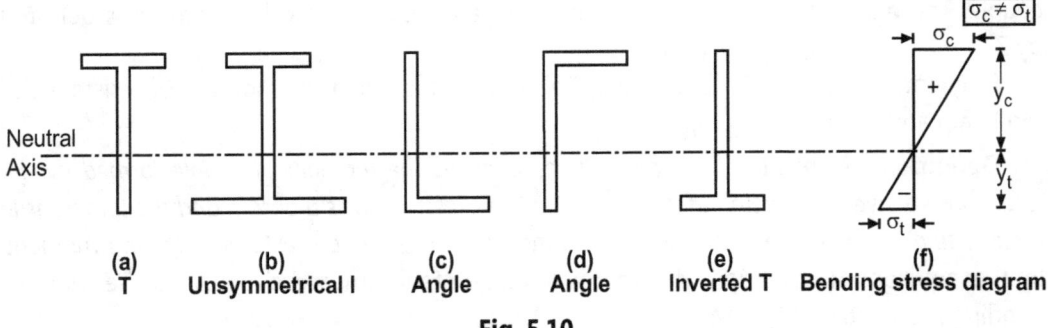

| (a)<br>T | (b)<br>Unsymmetrical I | (c)<br>Angle | (d)<br>Angle | (e)<br>Inverted T | (f)<br>Bending stress diagram |

**Fig. 5.10**

## 5.9 SECTION MODULUS (Z)

The flexural formula $\dfrac{M}{I} = \dfrac{\sigma}{y}$, can be written as

$$M = \sigma \times \left(\frac{I}{y}\right) = \sigma \times Z$$

where $Z = \dfrac{I}{y}$ is called as modulus of section or section modulus.

**Definition :** *Section modulus is the ratio of M.I. of the section about the N.A. and the distance of the most extreme fibre from the N.A.*

For sections symmetrical about N.A., Z in tension and compression has the same value. For sections which are unsymmetrical about N.A., Z will have the two different values in tension and compression.

**Unit :** Since $Z = \dfrac{I}{y}$, the unit of Z is $\dfrac{mm^4}{mm} = mm^3$.

**Other units :** $m^3$, $cm^3$, etc.

**Note (1) :** *$Z_{xx}$ denotes the section modulus about the horizontal centroidal axis.*

*i.e.* $\qquad Z_{xx} = \dfrac{I_{xx}}{y_{max}}$

**Note (2) :** *$Z_{yy}$ denotes the section modulus about the vertical centroidal axis.*

*i.e.* $\qquad Z_{yy} = \dfrac{I_{yy}}{y_{max}}$

*Let us calculate $Z_{xx}$ and $Z_{yy}$ for a rectangular and circular section.*

**(i) Rectangular section :** Consider a rectangular section of width 'b' and depth 'd' as shown in Fig. 5.11.

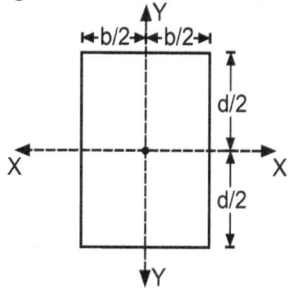

$$Z_{xx} = \frac{I_{xx}}{y_{max}} = \frac{bd^3/12}{d/2} = \frac{bd^2}{6}$$

$$Z_{yy} = \frac{I_{yy}}{y_{max}} = \frac{db^3/12}{b/2} = \frac{db^2}{6}$$

**Fig. 5.11**

**(ii) Solid circular section :** Consider a solid circular section of diameter 'D' as shown in Fig. 5.12.

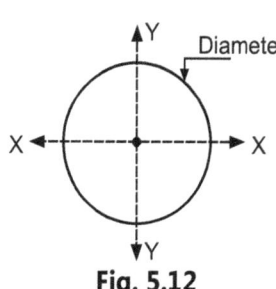

Here $y_{max} = \dfrac{D}{2} = R$

and $I = I_{xx} = I_{yy} = \dfrac{\pi}{64} D^4$

$\therefore \quad Z_{xx} = Z_{yy} = \dfrac{I}{y_{max}}$

$$= \frac{\frac{\pi}{64} D^4}{D/2} = \frac{\pi}{32} D^3$$

**Fig. 5.12**

**(iii) Hollow circular section :** Consider a hollow circular section of external diameter 'D' and internal diameter 'd' as shown in Fig. 5.13.

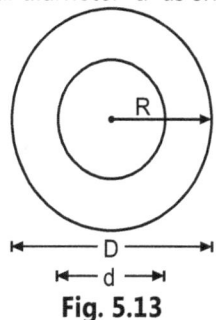

Here $y_{max} = \dfrac{D}{2} = R$

and $I = I_{xx} = I_{yy} = \dfrac{\pi}{64} (D^4 - d^4)$

$\therefore Z_{xx} = Z_{yy} = \dfrac{I}{y_{max}}$

$$= \frac{\frac{\pi}{64}(D^4 - d^4)}{D/2} = \frac{\pi}{32} \frac{(D^4 - d^4)}{D}$$

**Fig. 5.13**

1. Define section modulus and neutral axis. **(B.T.E. W-2013, S-2013/2 Marks)**
2. State the formula of section modulus for hollow circular section having external diameter D and internal diameter d. **(B.T.E. W-2010/2 Marks)**
3. Define section modulus. Write the equations of section modulus for hollow rectangular section and hollow circular section. **(B.T.E. S-2008/4 Marks)**
4. What is section modulus ? Write the expression for section modulus for (i) rectangular section, (ii) circular section. **(B.T.E. S-2009/4 Marks)**

**(Most Likely and Asked in Previous B.T.E. Exam.)**

## 5.10 PRACTICAL APPLICATIONS OF FLEXURAL FORMULA

The flexural formula $\dfrac{M}{I} = \dfrac{\sigma}{y} = \dfrac{E}{R}$ is based on the theory of pure bending. We have seen that S.F. is zero where the B.M. is maximum. Since we are interested to calculate the maximum bending stress, we have to consider the maximum B.M. Hence flexural formula gives fairly correct stresses if applied at a cross-section where S.F. is zero and the B.M. is maximum.

The maximum values of B.M. for different loading conditions are tabulated below.

**Table 5.1**

| Sr. No. | Loading condition | $M_{max}$ |
|:---:|:---|:---:|
| 1. | Simply supported beam carrying a central point load 'W'. 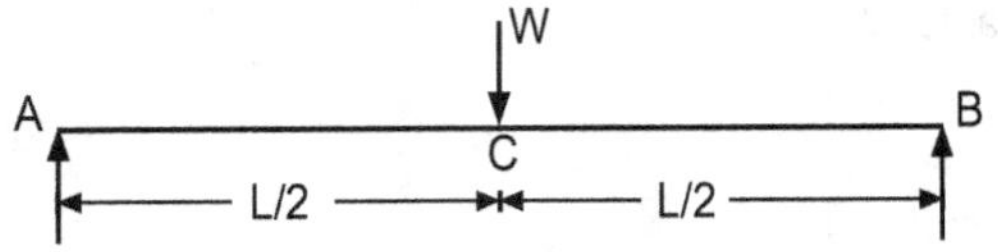 <br><br> <br> **Fig. 5.14** | $M_C = \dfrac{WL}{4}$ <br><br> (Sagging) |
| 2. | Simply supported beam carrying u.d.l. w/unit length on the entire span. 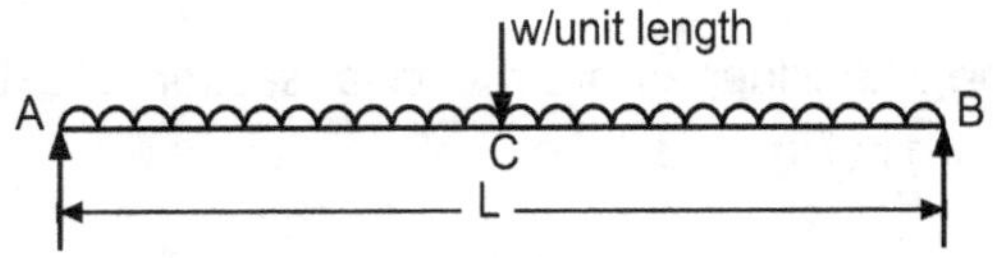 <br><br> <br> **Fig. 5.15** | $M_C = \dfrac{wL^2}{8}$ <br><br> (Sagging) |
| 3. | Cantilever beam carrying point load W at its free end. 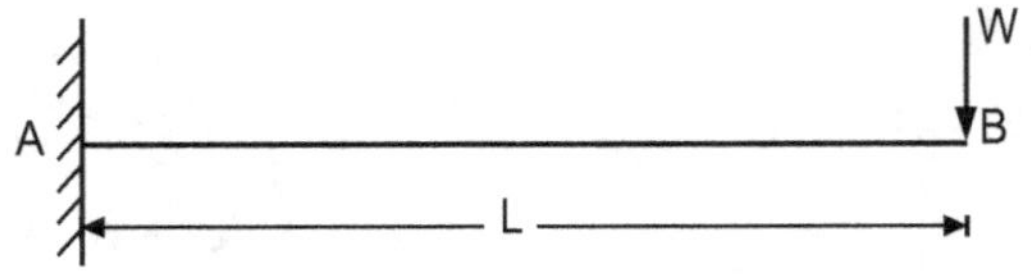 <br><br> <br> **Fig. 5.16** | $M_A = WL$ <br><br> (Hogging) |
| 4. | Cantilever carrying u.d.l. w/unit length over the entire span. 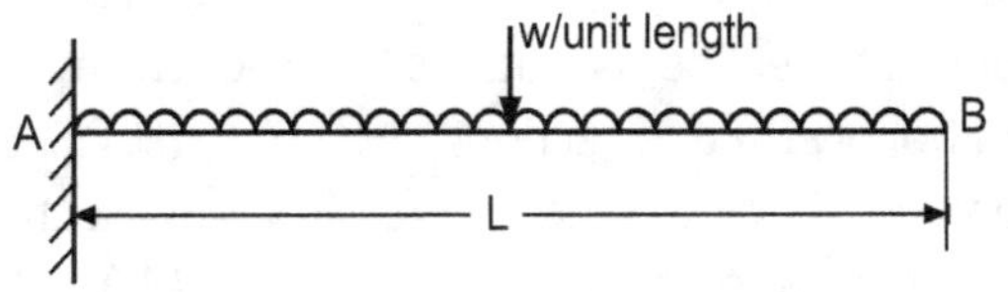 <br><br> <br> **Fig. 5.17** | $M_A = \dfrac{wL^2}{2}$ <br><br> (Hogging) |

## SOLVED EXAMPLES

### Type 1 : Given the loadings on the beam, to find the stresses produced.

#### Important Steps and Formulae

**Step (i) :** Find $M_{max}$ i.e. maximum bending moment (use table 1 to find $M_{max}$).

**Step (ii) :** Find I i.e. moment of inertia about neutral axis.

**Step (iii) :** Find y i.e. distance of extreme fibre from N.A.

**Step (iv) :** Use the bending stress equation $\dfrac{M}{I} = \dfrac{\sigma}{y}$ and find the maximum bending stress σ.

**Example 1 :** *A circular beam of 120 mm diameter is simply supported over a span of 10 m and carries a u.d.l. of 1000 N/m. Find the maximum bending stress produced.*

**(B.T.E . S-2012, W-1986/4 Marks)**

**Data**　　: A beam of circular cross-section as shown in Fig. 5.18 (b),
　　　　　　diameter d = 120 mm, L = 10 m, w = 1000 N/m

**To find**　: σ.

**Concept**　: Use of bending stress equation $\dfrac{M}{I} = \dfrac{\sigma}{y}$.

**Solution**　:

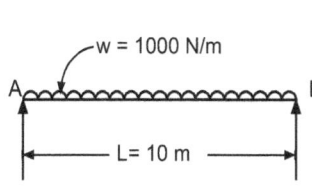

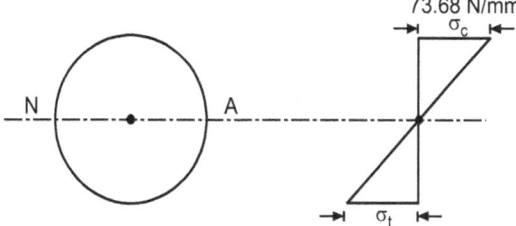

(a) Loading on beam　　　　(b) Cross-section(c) Bending stress variation diagram

**Fig. 5.18**

**Step (i) :**　　　$M_{max} = \dfrac{wL^2}{8} = \dfrac{1000 \times 10^2}{8} = 12500$ N-m $= 125 \times 10^5$ N-mm

**Step (ii) :**　　　$I = \dfrac{\pi}{64} d^4 = \dfrac{\pi}{64} (120)^4 = 10178760.2$ mm⁴

**Step (iii) :**　　　$y = \dfrac{d}{2} = \dfrac{120}{2} = 60$ mm

**Step (iv) :** Using the relation,

$$\frac{M}{I} = \frac{\sigma}{y}$$

∴　　　　　　　$\sigma = \dfrac{M}{I} \times y = \dfrac{125 \times 10^5}{10178760.2} \times 60 = \mathbf{73.68 \ N/mm^2}$

**Answer :** $\boxed{\sigma = 73.68 \ N/mm^2}$

The bending stress variation diagram is as shown in Fig. 5.18 (c).

**Example 2 :** *Determine the maximum bending stress developed in a beam of rectangular cross-section 50 mm × 150 mm when a bending moment of 600 N.m is applied about X-X axis.*

**(B.T.E. W-1998/4 Marks)**

**Data**      : A rectangular section as shown in Fig. 5.19,

b = 50 mm, d = 150 mm, M = 600 N.m = 600 × 10³ N.mm

**To find**   : σ

**Concept** : Use of bending stress equation $\dfrac{M}{I} = \dfrac{\sigma}{y}$.

**Solution** :

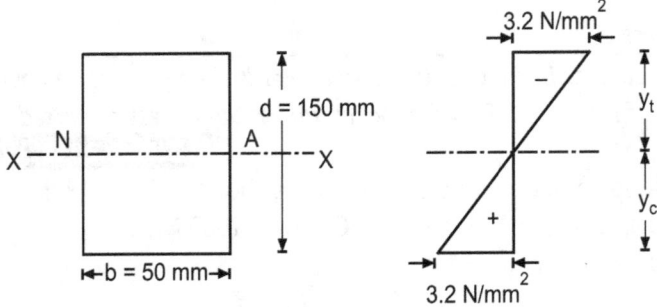

(i) Section          (ii) Bending stress distribution

**Fig. 5.19**

**Step (i) :**          $I_{XX} = \dfrac{bd^3}{12} = \dfrac{50 \times 150^3}{12} = 14062500 \ mm^4$

**Step (ii) :**          $y = \dfrac{d}{2} = \dfrac{150}{2} = 75 \ mm$

**Step (iii) :** Using the relation,

$$\dfrac{M}{I} = \dfrac{\sigma}{y}$$

∴          $\dfrac{600 \times 10^3}{14062500} = \dfrac{\sigma}{75}$

∴          $\sigma = \dfrac{600 \times 10^3 \times 75}{14062500} = \mathbf{3.2 \ N/mm^2}$

**Answer :** $\boxed{\sigma = 3.2 \ N/mm^2}$

---

**Example 3 :** *A rectangular beam section 300 mm wide and 500 mm deep is simply supported over a span of 4 m. It carries a full span uniformly distributed load of 10 kN/m. Find the maximum bending stress induced in the section. Draw the bending stress distribution diagram.*

**(B.T.E. S-2013, W-2005/4 Marks)**

**Data**      : A rectangular section, b = 300 mm, d = 500 mm, L = 4 m = 4000 mm,

w = 10 kN/m = 10 × 10³ N/m.

**To find**   : (i) σ, (ii) Bending stress distribution diagram.

**Concept** : (i) For a simply supported beam carrying u.d.l. over the entire span,

$$M_{max} = \frac{wL^2}{8}$$

(ii) Use of bending stress equation $\frac{M}{I} = \frac{\sigma}{y}$.

**Solution** : Refer to Fig. 5.20.

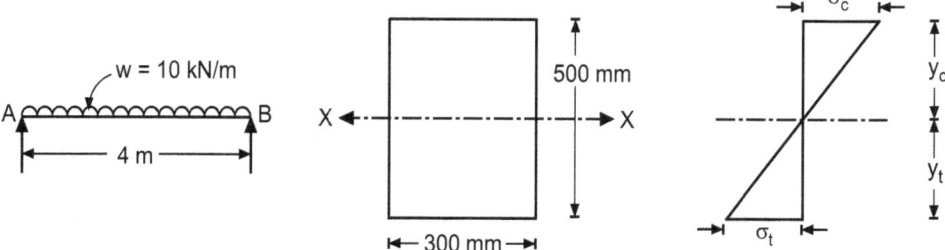

| (a) Beam | (b) Section | (c) Bending stress distribution |

**Fig. 5.20**

**Step (i) :**        $M_{max} = \frac{wL^2}{8} = \frac{10 \times 4^2}{8} = 20 \text{ kN·m} = 20 \times 10^6 \text{ N·mm}$

**Step (ii) :**        $I_{xx} = \frac{bd^3}{12} = \frac{300 \times 500^3}{12} = 3.125 \times 10^9 \text{ mm}^4$

**Step (iii) :**        $y = \frac{d}{2} = \frac{500}{2} = 250 \text{ mm}$

**Step (iv) :** Using the relation,

$$\frac{M}{I} = \frac{\sigma}{y}$$

∴        $\frac{20 \times 10^6}{3.125 \times 10^9} = \frac{\sigma}{250}$

∴        $\sigma = \mathbf{1.6 \ N/mm^2}$

**Answer :**
(i) $\sigma = \sigma_c = \sigma_t = 1.6 \text{ N/mm}^2$
(ii) The bending stress distribution diagram is as shown in Fig. 5.20 (c).

**Example 4 :** *A cantilever is 2 m long and is subjected to a u.d.l. of 2 kN/m. The cross-section of a cantilever is a tee section with flange of 80 mm × 10 mm and web of 10 mm × 120 mm such that its total depth is 130 mm. The flange is at the top and the web is vertical. Determine the maximum tensile and compressive stresses developed and their position.* **(B.T.E. S-1985/4 Marks)**

**Data :** A beam of cross-section as shown in Fig. 5.21 (b), L = 2 m, u.d.l. = 2 kN/m

**To find :** $\sigma_{max}$ and their position.

**Concept :**   (i)   For a cantilever beam, tension zone will be above N.A., and compression zone will be below N.A.

(ii)   Find $\bar{y}$ from bottom. $\bar{y}_{bottom} = y_c = y_{compression}$.

∴ $y_{tension} = y_t =$ Total depth $- y_c$

(iii)   Knowing $y_c$ and $y_t$, $\sigma_c$ and $\sigma_t$ can be calculated by using bending stress equation.

**Solution :   Step (i) :** Since the N.A. passes through the centroid of the section, let us calculate $\bar{y}$ from the base.

$$\bar{y}_{base} = \frac{a_1\,y_1 + a_2\,y_2}{a_1 + a_2} = \frac{(80 \times 10) \times 125 + (120 \times 10) \times (60)}{(80 \times 10) + (120 \times 10)} = 86 \text{ mm}$$

As the beam is cantilever, tension zone will be above N.A. and compression zone will be below N.A.

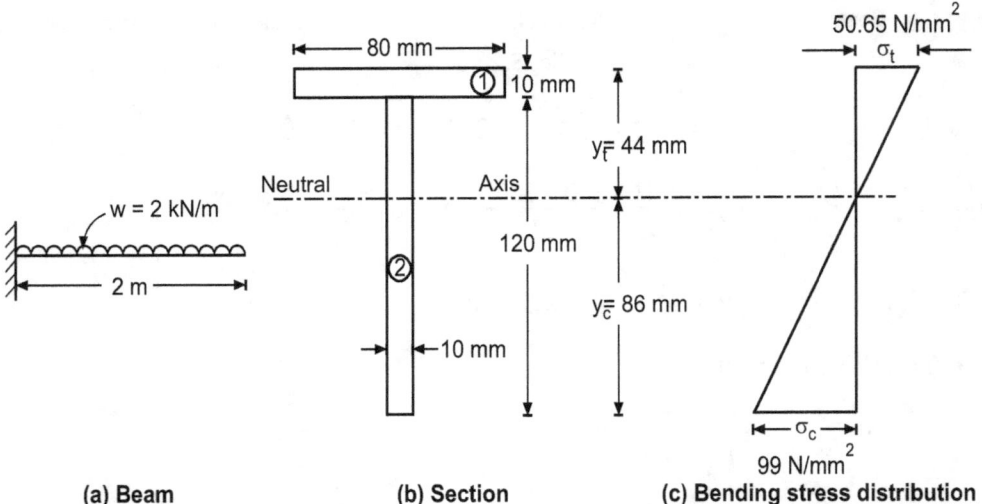

|  |  |  |
|---|---|---|
| (a) Beam | (b) Section | (c) Bending stress distribution |

**Fig. 5.21**

∴        $\bar{y}_{base} = y_c = 86 \text{ mm}$

∴        $y_t = 130 - y_c = 130 - 86 = 44 \text{ mm}.$

The position of N.A. i.e. X-X axis is as shown in Fig. 5.21 (b).

**M.I. of the section about the N.A. :**

**Step (ii) :**  $I_{NA} = I_{XX} = \dfrac{80 \times 10^3}{12} + (80 \times 10)\,[44 - 5]^2 + \dfrac{10 \times 120^3}{12} + (10 \times 120)\,[86 - 60]^2$

$= 347.4666 \times 10^4 \text{ mm}^4$

**Step (iii) :** For a cantilever beam carrying u.d.l. over the entire span,

$$M_{max} = \frac{w \cdot L^2}{2} = \frac{2 \times 2^2}{2} = 4 \text{ kN·m} = 4 \times 10^6 \text{ N·mm}$$

**Step (iv) :** Now, using the bending stress equation,

$$\frac{M}{I} = \frac{\sigma_c}{y_c} = \frac{\sigma_t}{y_t}$$

$$\frac{4 \times 10^6}{347.4666 \times 10^4} = \frac{\sigma_c}{86} = \frac{\sigma_t}{44}$$

$\therefore$　　　　$\sigma_c = \dfrac{4 \times 10^6}{347.4666 \times 10^4} \times 86 = \mathbf{99 \ N/mm^2}$

and　　　　$\sigma_t = \dfrac{4 \times 10^6}{347.4666 \times 10^4} \times 44 = \mathbf{50.65 \ N/mm^2}$

**Answer :**
(i) Maximum compressive stress at bottom fibre = 99 N/mm²
(ii) Maximum tensile stress at top fibre = 50.65 N/mm²

**The maximum compressive stress 99 N/mm² occurs at the bottom layer at a distance 86 mm from the N.A. and the maximum tensile stress 50.65 N/mm² occurs at the top layer at a distance of 44 mm from the N.A.**

The bending stress variation diagram is as shown in Fig. 5.21 (c).

**Example 5 :** *A beam of cross-section 100 mm × 200 mm is simply supported at each end as shown in Fig. 5.22 (a). It carries two concentrated loads of 100 kN each acting at the points 250 mm from both the ends. Determine the maximum bending stress induced in the beam.*

**(B.T.E. W-1985/4 Marks)**

**Data**　　: As shown in Fig. 5.22 (a).

**To find**　: σ.

**Concept**　: (i)　Beam reactions, moments at C and D are equal due to symmetry of loading.

　　　　　　(ii)　Use of bending stress equation $\dfrac{M}{I} = \dfrac{\sigma}{y}$.

**Solution** :

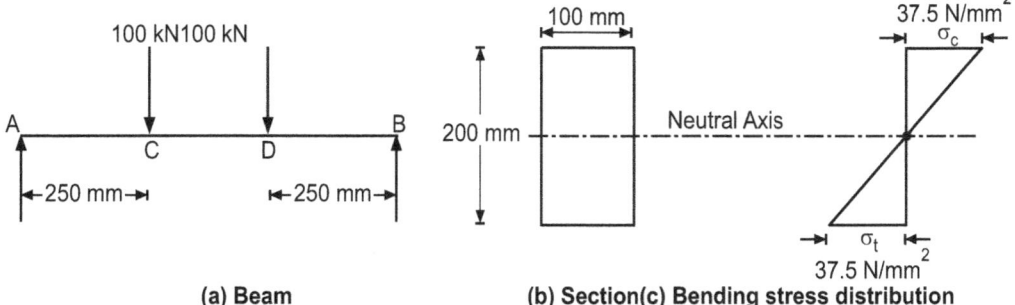

(a) Beam　　　　　(b) Section(c) Bending stress distribution

**Fig. 5.22**

**Step (i) : Reactions :** Since the loads on the beam are symmetrically placed, the reactions are equal.

$\therefore$　　　　　　　　$R_A = R_B = 100 \ kN$

**Step (ii) :** 
$$M_{max} = M_C = M_D = 100 \times 250 = 25000 \text{ kN-mm}$$
$$= 25000 \times 10^3 \text{ N-mm}$$

**Step (iii) :** 
$$I = \frac{b \cdot d^3}{12} = \left(\frac{100 \times 200^3}{12}\right) = 6.66 \times 10^7 \text{ mm}^4$$

**Step (iv) :** 
$$y = \frac{d}{2} = \frac{200}{2} = 100 \text{ mm}$$

**Step (v) :** Using the relation,

$$\frac{M}{I} = \frac{\sigma}{y}$$

$$\therefore \quad \sigma = \frac{M}{I} \times y = \frac{25000 \times 10^3}{6.66 \times 10^7} \times 100 = \mathbf{37.5 \ N/mm^2}$$

**Answer :** The maximum bending stress induced in the beam is 37.5 N/mm².

**The bending stress variation diagram is as shown in Fig. 5.22 (c).**

**Type 2 : Given the value of bending stress, dimensions of the section, to find the load on the beam :**

### Important Steps and Formulae

**Step (i) :** Find M in terms of w or W.

**Step (ii) :** Find y.

**Step (iii) :** Find I.

**Step (iv) :** Use the bending stress equation $\frac{M}{I} = \frac{\sigma}{y}$ and find the unknown load.

**Example 6 :** *A rectangular beam 120 mm wide and 300 mm deep is simply supported over a span of 4 m. What u.d.l. the beam may carry if the bending stress is not to exceed 120 MPa ? The width of the beam is 120 mm.* **(B.T.E. S-2008/4 Marks)**

**Data**      : A simply supported beam of rectangular cross-section,

         L = 4 m, b = 120 mm, d = 300 mm, $\sigma$ = 120 MPa = 120 N/mm².

**To find**      : w.

**Concept**      : (i)    Use of bending stress equation $\frac{M}{I} = \frac{\sigma}{y}$.

               (ii)    For a simply supported beam carrying u.d.l. over the entire span,

$$M_{max} = \frac{wL^2}{8}.$$

**Solution**      : Refer to Fig. 5.23.

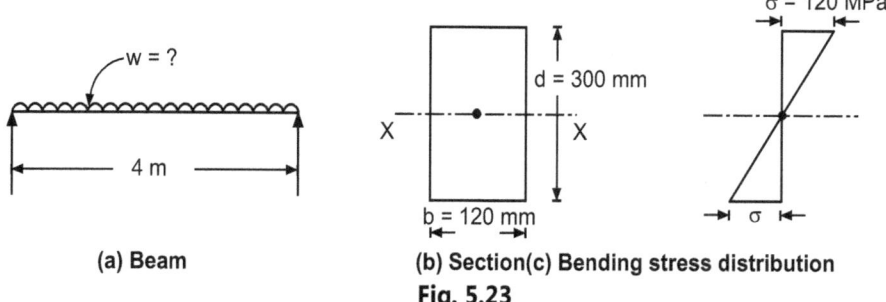

**(a) Beam**　　　**(b) Section(c) Bending stress distribution**

**Fig. 5.23**

**(i)** Let 'w' be the intensity of u.d.l. in N/m. For a simply supported beam carrying u.d.l. over the entire span, maximum B.M. at centre of span,

$$M = \frac{wL^2}{8} = \frac{w \times 4^2}{8} = (2w) \text{ N.m} = (2000\ w) \text{ N.mm}$$

**(ii)** Distance of extreme fibre from N.A. (X-X axis),

$$y = \frac{d}{2} = \frac{300}{2} = 150 \text{ mm}$$

**(iii)** M.I. about N.A.,　$I_{XX} = \frac{bd^3}{12} = \frac{120 \times 300^3}{12} = \mathbf{27 \times 10^7 \ mm^4}$

**(iv)** Using bending stress equation,

$$\frac{M}{I} = \frac{\sigma}{y}$$

$$\frac{2000\ w}{27 \times 10^7} = \frac{120}{150}$$

∴　　　　　$w = 108000 \text{ N/m} = \mathbf{108 \ kN/m}$

**Answer :** $\boxed{w = 108 \text{ kN/m}}$

---

**Example 7 :** *A rectangular beam 300 mm deep is simply supported over a span of 4 m. What uniformly distributed load per metre the beam may carry, if the bending stress is not to exceed 120 N/mm² ? Take I = 8 ×10⁶ mm⁴.* **(B.T.E. W-2012, S-2009/4 Marks)**

**Data**　　: Rectangular beam d = 300 mm, L = 4 m = 4000 mm,
　　　　　　$\sigma = 120 \text{ MPa} = 120 \text{ N/mm}^2$, $I = 8 \times 10^6 \text{ mm}^4$

**To find**　: w.

**Concept**　: Same as the above example.

**Solution**　: **(i)** Let 'w' be the intensity of u.d.l. in N/m. For a simply supported beam carrying u.d.l. over the entire span, maximum B.M. at centre of span.

$$M = \frac{wL^2}{8} = \frac{w \times 4^2}{8} = (2w) \text{ N.m} = (2000\ w) \text{ N.mm}$$

**(ii)**　　　　$y = \frac{d}{2} = \frac{300}{2} = 150 \text{ mm}$

**(iii)**　　　　$I = 8 \times 10^6 \text{ mm}^4$ (given)

**(iv)** Using bending stress equation,

$$\frac{M}{I} = \frac{\sigma}{y}$$

∴        $\dfrac{2000\,w}{8 \times 10^6} = \dfrac{120}{150}$

∴        $w = 3200\ \text{N/m} = \mathbf{3.2\ kN/m}$

**Answer :** $\boxed{w = 3.2\ \text{kN/m}}$

**Note :** *In the bending stress equation, even though all dimensions are given in N and mm, but as per our assumption, we get 'w' in N/m and not in N/mm.*

**Example 8 :** *A timber joist of 100 mm width and 200 mm depth is used as a cantilever beam of 3 metres length and loaded with a concentrated load at its free end in addition to its self weight, so that the bending stress is not to exceed 7 N/mm². Find out the maximum value of applied load. Unit weight of timber is 5 kN/m³.*        **(B.T.E. S-2009/4 Marks)**

**Data**        : Timber joist b = 100 mm, d = 200 mm, L = 3 m = 3000 m,

$\sigma = 7\ \text{N/mm}^2$, unit weight of timber = 5 kN/m³ (density)

**To find**    : W

**Concept**   : For a cantilever beam carrying u.d.l. over the entire span,

$M_{max}$ due to u.d.l. $= \dfrac{wL^2}{2}$.

For a cantilever beam carrying point load W at its free end, $M_{max} = wL$.

Hence for a given loading carrying both u.d.l. and point load,

$$M_{max} = \frac{wL^2}{2} + wL$$

**Solution   :**

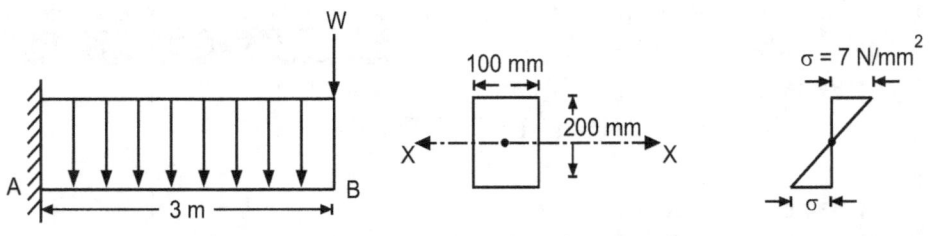

(a) Loading            (b) Cross-section(c) Bending stress variation diagram

**Fig. 5.24**

**(i)**        $I = \dfrac{bd^3}{12} = \dfrac{100 \times 200^3}{12} = 6.67 \times 10^7\ \text{mm}^4$

**(ii)**       $y = \dfrac{d}{2} = \dfrac{200}{2} = 100\ \text{mm}$

**(iii)**  w = U.D.L. on beam  = width × thickness × density

$$= 0.1 \text{ (m)} \times 0.2 \text{ (m)} \times 5 \text{ (kN/m}^3) = 0.1 \text{ kN/m} = 100 \text{ N/m}$$

∴  Maximum B.M. at fixed end A,

**(iv)**      $M_A = M_{max} = \dfrac{wL^2}{2} + WL = \dfrac{100 \times 3^2}{2} + W \times 3$

$$= (450 + 3W) \text{ N.m} = (450 + 3W) \times 10^3 \text{ N.mm}$$

**(v)**  Using the relation, $\dfrac{M}{I} = \dfrac{\sigma}{y}$

∴          $\dfrac{(450 + 3W) \, 10^3}{6.67 \times 10^7} = \dfrac{7}{100}$

∴          $450 + 3W = 0.4669 \times 10^4$

∴          $450 + 3W = 4669$

∴          $3W = 4219$

∴          **W = 1406.33 N = 1.41 kN**

**Answer :**  $\boxed{W = 1.41 \text{ kN}}$

---

**Example 9 :** *A cast iron pipe of external diameter 800 mm and internal diameter 700 mm is used to pass the hydraulic oil. The pipe is simply supported at its ends by keeping them on end bearings having span 7.5 m. Find the intensity of uniformly distributed load that pipe can carry. Bending stress in pipe material is limited to 140 N/mm².*

**(B.T.E. W-2010, 2003/4 Marks)**

**Data**    :   Outer diameter D = 800 mm, internal diameter d = 700 mm,
               span L = 7.5 m, bending stress σ = 140 N/mm².

**To find**  :   'w'.

**Concept :**  Use of bending stress equation $\dfrac{M}{I} = \dfrac{\sigma}{y}$.

**Solution :**   **Step (i) :** Let 'w' be the intensity of u.d.l. in N/m.

For a simply supported beam carrying u.d.l. over the entire span maximum bending moment,

$$M_{max} = \dfrac{w \cdot L^2}{8} = \dfrac{w \times 7.5^2}{8} = (7.03 \text{ w}) \text{ N.m} = (7.03 \text{ w} \times 10^3) \text{ N.mm}$$

**Step (ii) :**    M.I. of pipe, $I = \dfrac{\pi}{64}(D^4 - d^4) = \dfrac{\pi}{64}(800^4 - 700^4) = 83.203 \times 10^8 \text{ mm}^4$

**Step (iii) :**   Distance of extreme fibre from N.A.  $= y = \dfrac{D}{2} = \dfrac{800}{2} = 400 \text{ mm}$

**Step (iv) :** Using bending stress equation,

$$\dfrac{M_{max}}{I} = \dfrac{\sigma}{y}$$

∴          $\dfrac{7.03 \text{ w} \times 10^3}{83.203 \times 10^8} = \dfrac{140}{(400)}$

∴          **w = 409261 N/m**

**Answer :**  $\boxed{w = 409.261 \text{ kN/m}}$

**Example 10 :** *A cantilever beam of span 6.5 m is having cross-section of 400 mm wide and 700 mm deep. If the bending stress is not allowed to exceed 280 N/mm², calculate the magnitude of point load which can be applied at the free end of this cantilever beam.*

**(B.T.E. S-2012, 2000/4 Marks)**

**Data** : A cantilever beam of rectangular cross-section,

b = 400 mm, d = 700 mm, L = 6.5 m, σ = 280 N/mm²

**To find** : W at free end.

**Concept :** **Use of bending stress equation :**

**Solution : Step (i) :** Let 'W' be in 'N'. For a cantilever beam carrying a point load 'W' at free end,

$$M = W \times L = W \times 6.5 = (6.5\ W)\ \text{N.m} = (6500\ W)\ \text{N-mm}$$

**Step (ii) :**
$$I = \frac{bd^3}{12} = \frac{400 \times (700)^3}{12} = 1.143 \times 10^{10}\ \text{mm}^4$$

**Step (iii) :**
$$y = \frac{d}{2} = \frac{700}{2} = 350\ \text{mm}$$

**Step (iv) :** Using the bending stress equation,

$$\frac{M}{I} = \frac{\sigma}{y}$$

$$\frac{6500\ W}{1.143 \times 10^{10}} = \frac{280}{350}$$

**Answer :** $\boxed{W = 1406769.23\ \text{N} = \textbf{1406.769 kN = 1.4 MN}}$

---

**Example 11 :** *A rectangular section is used as a simply supported beam over a span of 5 m. Calculate the downward point at the mid-span the beam can carry, if the maximum tensile stress is not to exceed 8 N/mm². Width = 120 mm, depth = 200 mm.*

**(B.T.E. S-1987/4 Marks)**

**Data** : A simply supported beam of rectangular cross-section as shown in Fig. 5.25 (b), b = 120 mm, d = 200 mm, L = 5 m, $\sigma = \sigma_c = \sigma_t = 8$ N/mm².

**To find :** Central point load W.

**Concept :** Use of bending stress equation $\dfrac{M}{I} = \dfrac{\sigma}{y}$.

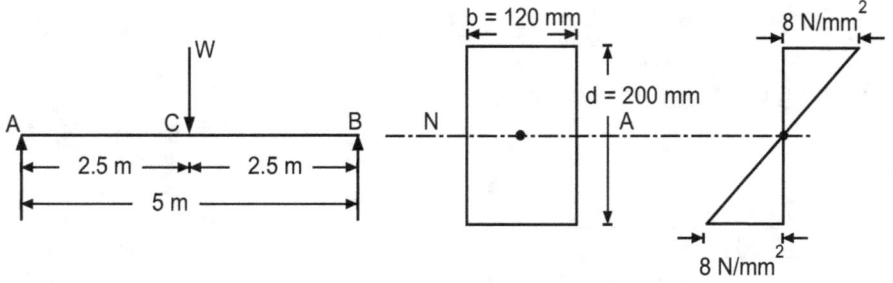

**(a) Beam**　　　　**(b) Section(c) Bending stress distribution**

**Fig. 5.25**

**Solution : Step (i) :** To find maximum B.M.

Let 'W' be in N.

Maximum B.M. at the mid-span of a beam,

$$M = M_C = \frac{WL}{4} = \frac{W \times 5}{4} = (1.25 \, W) \, \text{N-m} = (1.25 \, W \times 10^3) \, \text{N-mm}$$

**Step (ii) :**

$$I = \frac{b \, d^3}{12} = \frac{120 \times 200^3}{12} = 8 \times 10^7 \, \text{mm}^4$$

**Step (iii) :**

$$y = \frac{d}{2} = \frac{200}{2} = 100 \, \text{mm}$$

**Step (iv) :** Using the relation, $\dfrac{M}{I} = \dfrac{\sigma}{y}$

$\therefore \qquad\qquad M = \dfrac{I}{y} \times \sigma$

$\therefore \qquad 1.25 \times 10^3 \, W = \dfrac{8 \times 10^7}{100} \times 8$

**Answer :** $\boxed{\text{W} = 5120 \, \text{N} = \textbf{5.12 kN}}$

---

**Type 3 : Given the value of bending stress, to find the span of the beam :**

**Example 12 :** *A symmetrical section 300 mm deep has a moment of inertia of 22.6 $\times 10^6$ mm$^4$ about its neutral axis. Determine the longest simply supported span of the beam to carry a uniformly distributed load of 4 kN/m run without exceeding the bending stress of 125 MPa.* **(B.T.E. S-2005/4 Marks)**

**Data** : d = 300 mm, I = 22.6 $\times 10^6$ mm$^4$, w = 4 kN/m, $\sigma$ = 125 MPa = 125 N/mm$^2$

**To find :** L.

**Concept :** Use of bending stress equation $\dfrac{M}{I} = \dfrac{\sigma}{y}$.

**Solution : Step (i) :** Let 'L' be in metres.

For a simply supported beam of span L carrying u.d.l. w/unit length over the entire span,

$$M_{max} = \frac{wL^2}{8} = \frac{4 \times L^2}{8} = (0.5 \, L^2) \, \text{kN.m} = 0.5 \, L^2 \times 10^6 \, \text{N·mm}$$

**Step (ii) :**

$$y = \frac{d}{2} = \frac{300}{2} = 150 \, \text{mm}$$

**Step (iii) :** Using the relation,

$$\frac{M}{I} = \frac{\sigma}{y}$$

$$\frac{0.5 \, L^2 \times 10^6}{22.6 \times 10^6} = \frac{125}{150}$$

**Answer :** $\boxed{\text{L} = \textbf{6.13 m}}$

**Example 13 :** *A 100 × 100 × 10 mm 'T' section is used as a simply supported beam with a flange at top. It carries a u.d.l. of 10 kN/m. If the maximum stress is not to exceed 150 N/mm², calculate the maximum span.*   **(B.T.E. S-2010/4 Marks)**

**Solution :**

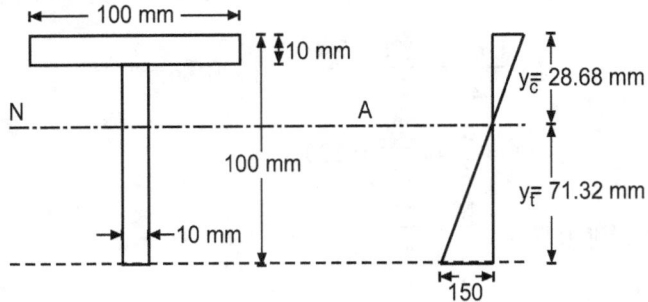

**(i) Section(ii) Bending stress distribution (N/mm²)**

**Fig. 5.26**

**Hint :** (i) Find $\bar{y}_{bottom}$.

$$\bar{y}_{bottom} = 71.32 \text{ mm}$$

(ii)  Find $I_{xx}$.     $I_{xx} = 1.7996 \times 10^6 \text{ mm}^4$

(iii)     $$\frac{M \cdot R}{I} = \frac{\sigma_{max}}{y_{max}}$$

∴     $$\frac{M \cdot R}{1.7996 \times 10^6} = \frac{150}{71.32}$$

∴     $$M \cdot R = 3.785 \times 10^6 \text{ N.mm} = 3.785 \times 10^3 \text{ N.m}$$

Let 'w' be in N/m.

(iv)     $$M \cdot R = M_{max} = \frac{wL^2}{8}$$

$$3.785 \times 10^3 = \frac{(10 \times 10^3) L^2}{8}$$

**Answer :** $\boxed{L = 1.74 \text{ m}}$

## Type 4 : Examples on moment of resistance of the beam :

**Important Steps and Formulae**

**(a) For symmetrical sections :**

   (i)   Knowing the dimensions of the section, find I.

   (ii)  Find y.

   (iii)  Knowing σ, $M_r$ can be calculated as $\frac{M_r}{I} = \frac{\sigma}{y}$.

**(b) For unsymmetrical sections :**

(i) Knowing the dimensions of the sections, locate c.g. and find $\bar{y}$, $y_c$ and $y_t$.

(ii) Find I.

(iii) Knowing $\sigma_c$, $M_r$ can be calculated as $\dfrac{M_r}{I} = \dfrac{\sigma_c}{y_c}$.

(iv) Knowing $\sigma_t$, $M_r$ can be calculated as $\dfrac{M_r}{I} = \dfrac{\sigma_t}{y_t}$.

(v) The moment of resistance of the cross-section = Minimum of (iii) and (iv).

**Example 14 :** *A rectangular beam of 400 mm × 200 mm size is of wood material. If the permissible bending stress in wood is 2 N/mm², calculate the moment of resistance of beam.*

**(B.T.E. S-1997/4 Marks)**

**Data**     :     A rectangular beam as shown in Fig. 5.27, $\sigma$ = 2 N/mm².

**To find**   :     $M_r$.

**Concept :**     For symmetric sections with same allowable stress in bending compression and tension ($\sigma_c = \sigma_t$), $M_r = Z_{XX} \cdot \sigma = \dfrac{I}{y} \cdot \sigma$.

**Solution :**    **Step (i) :**     $I = \dfrac{bd^3}{12} = \dfrac{400 \times 200^3}{12} = 266666666.7 \text{ mm}^4$

**Step (ii) :**            $y = \dfrac{d}{2} = \dfrac{200}{2} = 100 \text{ mm}$

**Step (iii) :**          $\sigma = \sigma_c = \sigma_t = 2 \text{ N/mm}^2 \text{ ... (given)}$

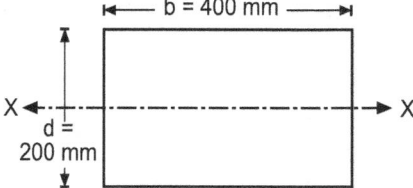

**Fig. 5.27**

Using the relation $\dfrac{M_r}{I} = \dfrac{\sigma}{y}$

$\therefore$          $M_r = \dfrac{I}{y} \times \sigma = \dfrac{266666666.7}{100} \times 2 = 5.333 \times 10^6 \text{ N-mm}$

**Answer :**   $\boxed{M_r = 5.333 \text{ kN-m}}$

**Example 15 :** *A cast iron channel shown in Fig. 5.28 (b) is used as a simply supported beam over a span of 3 m. If the permissible stress in tension is 35 MPa and in compression is 90 MPa, find the maximum safe uniformly distributed load carrying capacity.*

**(B.T.E. S-2004/4 Marks)**

**Data**     :     A simply supported beam as shown in Fig. 5.28.

               L = 3 m, $\sigma_t$ = 35 MPa = 35 N/mm², $\sigma_c$ = 90 MPa = 90 N/mm²

**To find :**  w.

**Concept :**   (i)   For unsymmetric sections with different allowable stresses in bending compression and tension ($\sigma_t \neq \sigma_c$),

$$(M_r)_{compression} = I \times \frac{\sigma_c}{y_c} \qquad \text{... (i)}$$

$$(M_r)_{tension} = I \times \frac{\sigma_t}{y_t} \qquad \text{... (ii)}$$

Governing $M_r$ = least of $(M_r)_{compression}$ and $(M_r)_{tension}$

(ii)   For a s.s. beam carrying u.d.l. over the entire span, $M = \dfrac{wL^2}{8}$.

(iii)   Equate M and $M_r$ to find 'w'.

**Solution :**

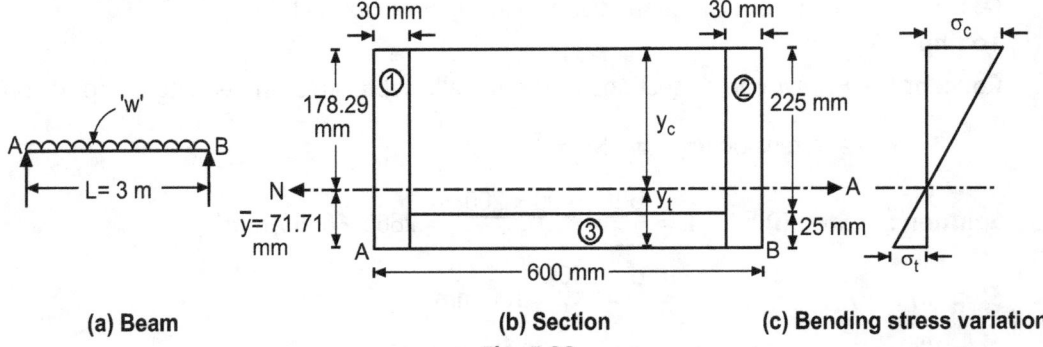

**(a) Beam**              **(b) Section**              **(c) Bending stress variation**

**Fig. 5.28**

**Step (i) :** Let us calculate the moment of inertia about the neutral axis, $I_{NA}$ i.e. $I_{XX}$.

$$I_{XX_1} = I_{XX_2} = \frac{30 \times 250^3}{12} + (30 \times 250)\left[\frac{250}{2} - 71.71\right]^2$$

$$= 39062500 + 21298680.75 = 60361180.75 \text{ mm}^4$$

$$I_{XX_3} = \frac{540 \times 25^3}{12} + (540 \times 25)\left(71.71 - \frac{25}{2}\right)^2$$

$$= 703125 + 47328625.35 = 48031750.35 \text{ mm}^4$$

$$\mathbf{I_{XX}} = I_{NA} = I_{XX_1} + I_{XX_2} + I_{XX_3} = 2 \times 60361180.75 + 48031750.35$$

$$= 168754111.9 \text{ mm}^4 \cong \mathbf{1.68 \times 10^8 \text{ mm}^4}$$

**Step (ii) : To find M :** Let 'w' be the u.d.l. in N/m.

$$\mathbf{M} = \frac{wL^2}{8} = \frac{w \times 3^2}{8} = (1.125 \text{ w}) \text{ N.m} = \mathbf{(1.125 \text{ w} \times 10^3) \text{ N·mm}} \qquad \text{... (A)}$$

**Step (iii) : Moment of resistance in compression :**

$$\frac{M_r}{I} = \frac{\sigma_c}{y_c}$$

$\therefore$

$$M_r = I \times \frac{\sigma_c}{y_c} = 1.68 \times 10^8 \times \frac{90}{178.29} = 8.4 \times 10^7 \text{ N.mm} \qquad \text{... (1)}$$

**Step (iv) : Moment of resistance in tension,**

$$\frac{M_r}{I} = \frac{\sigma_t}{y_t}$$

∴                $M_r = I \times \dfrac{\sigma_t}{y_t} = 1.68 \times 10^8 \times \dfrac{35}{71.71} = 8.19 \times 10^7 \, \text{N.mm}$          ... (2)

**Step (v) :** Safe moment of resistance which the beam can resist = least of (1) and (2).

∴                **$M_r = 8.19 \times 10^7 \, \text{N·mm}$**          ... (B)

**Step (vi) :** Equating M and $M_r$ from equations (A) and (B),

$$M = M_r$$

∴          $1.125 \, w \times 10^3 = 8.19 \times 10^7$

**Answer :**          $\boxed{w = 72800 \, \text{N/m} = \textbf{72.8 kN/m}}$

---

**Example 16 :** *The cross-section of a simply supported beam of span 5 m is symmetrical I-section having width of flange 125 mm, overall depth 220 mm and uniform thickness 10 mm. If the maximum permissible bending stress is 125 MPa, find the moment of resistance of the beam. Also find the maximum intensity of u.d.l. over the entire span.*

**(B.T.E. S-2001/ 4 Marks)**

**Data**          :     Symmetrical I-section as shown in Fig. 5.29,

                            L = 5 m, σ = 125 MPa = 125 N/mm².

**To find**     :     (i) $M_r$, (ii) w.

**Concept** :     (i)     For symmetric sections with same allowable stress in bending

                            compression and tension, $M_r = Z_{XX} \cdot \sigma = \dfrac{I}{y} \cdot \sigma$.

                    (ii)    For a s.s. beam carrying u.d.l. over the entire span,

                            maximum B.M., $M = \dfrac{wL^2}{8}$.

                    (iii)   Equate M and $M_r$ to find 'w'.

**Solution :**

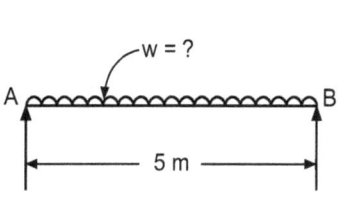

(a) Beam

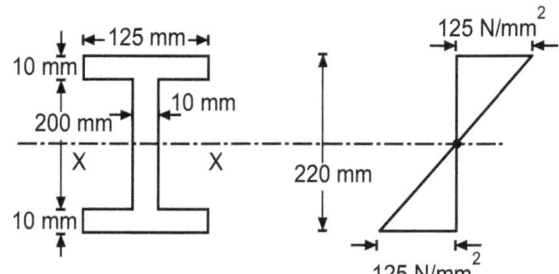

(b) Section    (c) Bending stress distribution

**Fig. 5.29**

**Step (i) :** Since the section is symmetrical about N.A. (X-X axis),

$$y = y_c = y_t = \frac{\text{Total depth}}{2} = \frac{220}{2} = 110 \text{ mm}$$

**Step (ii) :**

$$I_{XX} = \frac{125 \times 220^3}{12} - \frac{(125 - 10)(200)^3}{12} = 3425 \times 10^4 \text{ mm}^4$$

**Step (iii) :**

$$\sigma = \sigma_c = \sigma_t = 125 \text{ N/mm}^2 \text{ ... (given)}$$

**Step (iv) :** Using the relation,

$$\frac{M_r}{I} = \frac{\sigma}{y}$$

$$\therefore \quad \mathbf{M_r} = \frac{I}{y} \times \sigma = \frac{3425 \times 10^4}{110} \times 125 = \mathbf{38909090.91 \text{ N-mm}}$$

**Step (v) : To find M :** Let 'w' be in N/m.

Maximum B.M., $\quad M = \frac{wL^2}{8} = \frac{w \times 5^2}{8} = 3.125 \text{ w N-m} = (3.125 \text{ w} \times 10^3) \text{ N-mm}$

**Step (vi) :** Equating M and $M_r$, we have

$$3.125 \text{ w} \times 10^3 = 38909090.91$$

$$\therefore \quad w = 12450.9 \text{ N/m} = \mathbf{12.45 \text{ kN/m}}$$

**Answer :** | (i) $M_r$ = 38909090.91 N.m = 38.9 kN.m,　(ii) w = 12.45 kN/m |

---

**Type 5 : Examples based on bending stresses at intermediate layers :**

**Example 17 :** *Find the bending stress at 25 mm below the top edge of rectangular section 80 mm wide and 200 mm deep, if maximum bending moment is 4 kN.m*

**(B.T.E. W-2009/4 Marks)**

**Data**　　: A beam of rectangular section as shown in Fig. 5.30 (i),

b = 80 mm, d = 200 mm, M = 4 kN.m = $4 \times 10^6$ N.mm

**To find**　: Bending stress in layer AB, 25 mm below top edge i.e. 75 mm from X-X axis (neutral axis).

**Concept** : Consider similarity of triangles in bending stress variation diagram.

**Solution** : Using bending stress equation,

$$\frac{M}{I_{XX}} = \frac{\sigma_{max}}{y_{max}}$$

$$\therefore \quad \frac{4 \times 10^6}{\dfrac{80 \times 200^3}{12}} = \frac{\sigma_{max}}{\left(\dfrac{200}{2}\right)}$$

$$\therefore \quad \frac{12 \times 4 \times 10^6}{80 \times 200^3} = \frac{\sigma_{max}}{100}$$

$$\therefore \quad \sigma_{max} = 7.5 \text{ N/mm}^2$$

Let　　　　　$\sigma_1$ = stress in layer AB which is 25 mm below the top edge

The bending stress variation diagram is as shown in Fig. 5.30 (ii).

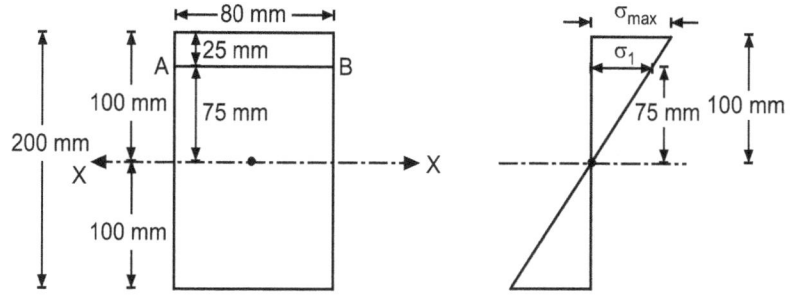

(i) Section (ii) Bending stress variation diagram

**Fig. 5.30**

From the similar triangles in stress diagram,

$$\frac{\sigma_{max}}{100} = \frac{\sigma_1}{75}$$

∴
$$\frac{7.5}{100} = \frac{\sigma_1}{75}$$

**Answer :**　　$\boxed{\sigma_1 = 5.625 \text{ N/mm}^2}$

---

**Type 6 : Given the loads on the beam and the bending stress, to find the size of the beam :**

| Important Steps and Formulae |
|---|
| (i)　Find M. |
| (ii)　Find I in terms of b or d (for rectangular section) and D (for circular section). |
| (iii)　Find y in terms of b or d (for rectangular section) and D (for circular section). |
| (iv)　Use the bending stress equation $\dfrac{M}{I} = \dfrac{\sigma}{y}$ and find the size of the beam. |

**Example 18 :** *A cantilever beam of 4 m span carries a u.d.l. of 5 kN/m and permissible stress in the material of the beam is 5 N/mm². Design the section of beam if depth to width ratio is 2.* **(B.T.E. S-1998/4 Marks)**

**Data**　　:　A cantilever beam of rectangular cross-section $\dfrac{d}{b} = 2$

　　　　　　i.e. d = 2 b, L = 4 m, w = 5 kN/m

**To find**　:　b and d.

**Concept**　:　Use of bending stress equation $\dfrac{M}{I} = \dfrac{\sigma}{y}$.

**Solution :**　(i)　For a cantilever beam carrying u.d.l. over the entire span,

$$M = \frac{wL^2}{2} = \frac{5 \times 4^2}{2} = 40 \text{ kN-m} = 40 \times 10^6 \text{ N-mm}$$

(ii)
$$I = \frac{bd^3}{12} = \frac{b\,(2b)^3}{12} = \frac{8}{12} \cdot b^4 = \frac{2}{3} \cdot b^4 \qquad \dots (\because d = 2\,b)$$

(iii) $\qquad y = \dfrac{d}{2} = \dfrac{2b}{2} = b$

(iv) Using the relation, $\dfrac{M}{I} = \dfrac{\sigma}{y}$

$\therefore \qquad \dfrac{40 \times 10^6}{\dfrac{2}{3} \times b^4} = \dfrac{5}{b}$

$\therefore \qquad \dfrac{40 \times 10^6 \times 3}{2 \times 5} = \dfrac{b^4}{b}$

$\therefore \qquad b^3 = 12 \times 10^6$

$\therefore \qquad \mathbf{b} = 228.94 \text{ mm say } \mathbf{230 \text{ mm}}$

$\therefore \qquad \mathbf{d} = 2b = 2 \times 230 = \mathbf{460 \text{ mm}}$

**Answer :** $\boxed{b = 230 \text{ mm}, d = 460 \text{ mm}}$

**Example 19 :** *A cantilever rectangular mild steel section is 4 m in length. It carries load due to its self weight of 5 kN/m and the permissible bending stress in the mild steel material is 5 N/mm². Find the size of the section, if depth to width ratio is 2.* **(B.T.E. W-2004/4 Marks)**

**Data** : $L = 4 \text{ m}, \ w = 5 \text{ kN/m} = \dfrac{5 \times 10^3}{10^3} \text{ N/mm} = 5 \text{ N/mm},$

$\sigma = 5 \text{ N/mm}^2, \dfrac{d}{b} = 2 \Rightarrow d = 2b$

**To find** : b, d.

**Concept** : (i) For given loading conditions, $M = \dfrac{wL^2}{2}$ and for rectangular cross-section, $I = \dfrac{bd^3}{12}$.

(ii) Use of bending stress equation $\dfrac{M}{I} = \dfrac{\sigma}{y}$.

**Solution :** Let b and d be in 'mm'.

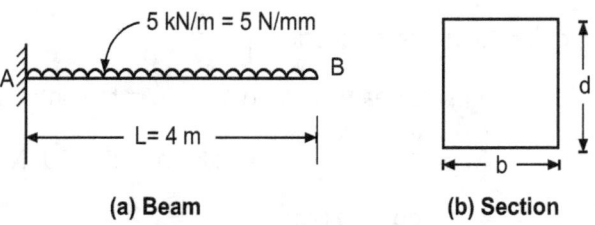

(a) Beam    (b) Section

**Fig. 5.31**

Using the relation,　　　　$\dfrac{M}{I} = \dfrac{\sigma}{y}$

$$\dfrac{\dfrac{wL^2}{2}}{\dfrac{bd^3}{12}} = \dfrac{5}{\left(\dfrac{d}{2}\right)}$$

$\therefore$　　　　$\dfrac{\dfrac{5 \times (4000)^2}{2}}{\dfrac{b\,(2b)^3}{12}} = \dfrac{5 \times 2}{(2b)}$　　　... ($\because$ L = 4 m = 4000 mm, d = 2b)

$\therefore$　　　　**b = 228.94 mm**

$\therefore$　　　　**d** = 2 × 228.94 = **457.88 mm**

**Answer :** $\boxed{\text{b = 228.94 mm, d = 457.88 mm}}$

**Example 20 :** *Find the diameter of circular section of a simply supported shaft 6 m span which carries a 81 kN weight due to pulley mounted at the centre of span, if permissible bending stress of the shaft material is limited to 8.4 MPa.* **(B.T.E. S-2003/4 Marks)**

**Data**　　:　L = 6 m = $6 \times 10^3$ mm, W = 81 kN = $81 \times 10^3$ N, $\sigma_b$ = 8.4 MPa = 8.4 N/mm².

**To find**　:　Diameter of solid circular section (d).

**Concept**　:　(i) $M_{max} = \sigma_b \cdot Z$, (ii) For circular section $Z = \dfrac{\pi}{32} d^3$.

**Solution :** (i)　For a simply supported beam carrying a point load W at the centre,

$$M_{max} = \dfrac{WL}{4} = \dfrac{(81 \times 10^3)\,(6 \times 10^3)}{4} = 121.5 \times 10^6 \text{ N·mm}$$

(ii)　　　　$M_{max} = \sigma_b \cdot Z$

$\therefore$　　　　$121.5 \times 10^6 = 8.4 \times \dfrac{\pi}{32} d^3$

**Answer :**　　　　$\boxed{\textbf{d = 528.16 mm}}$

**Example 21 :** *A cantilever beam of solid circular cross-section and 3 m long carries a concentrated load of 35 kN at its free end. If the maximum bending stress in tension or compression is not to exceed 125 N/mm², determine the diameter of the beam.*

**(B.T.E. S-1985/4 Marks)**

**Data**　　:　A beam of circular cross-section as shown in Fig. 5.32 (b), $\sigma_{max}$ = 125 N/mm²

**To find**　:　D.

**Concept**　:　(i)　For a cantilever beam carrying point load at free end, $M_{max}$ = W.L.

　　　　(ii)　Use of bending stress equation, $\dfrac{M}{I} = \dfrac{\sigma}{y}$.

**Solution :** (i)  Maximum B.M. at the fixed end of a cantilever,

$$M = M_A = W \times L = 35000 \times 3 = 105000 \text{ N-m} = 1.05 \times 10^8 \text{ N-mm}$$

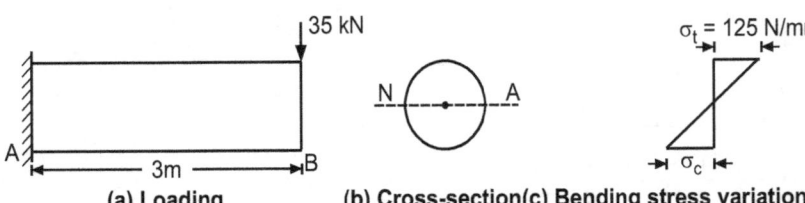

(a) Loading          (b) Cross-section(c) Bending stress variation diagram

**Fig. 5.32**

(ii) $$I_{NA} = \frac{\pi}{64} D^4 \quad \text{and} \quad y = \frac{D}{2}$$

(iii) $$\sigma = \sigma_c = \sigma_t = 125 \text{ N/mm}^2$$

(iv) Using the relation, $$\frac{M}{I} = \frac{\sigma}{y}$$

$$M = \left(\frac{I}{y}\right) \sigma$$

$\therefore$ $$1.05 \times 10^8 = \left(\frac{\frac{\pi}{64} D^4}{\frac{D}{2}}\right) \times 125$$

$\therefore$ $$1.05 \times 10^8 = \frac{\pi}{32} D^3 \times 125$$

$\therefore$ $$D^3 = 8556169.741$$

**Answer :** $\boxed{D = 204.53 \text{ mm}}$

**Example 22 :** *A cantilever beam of solid circular cross-section and 3 m long carries a concentrated load of 35 kN at its free end. If the maximum bending stress in tension or compression is not to exceed 120 N/mm², determine the diameter of beam.*

**(B.T.E. W-2008/4 Marks)**

**Answer :** $\boxed{D = 207.33 \text{ mm}}$

## Type 7 : Examples based on modulus of section of the beam :

| Important Formulae |
|---|
| (i)  For a rectangular section of size b × d, $Z_{XX} = \dfrac{bd^2}{6}$, $Z_{YY} = \dfrac{db^2}{6}$ |
| (ii)  $Z = \dfrac{M}{\sigma}$ |

**Example 23 :** *Find the section modulus of a rectangular section 200 mm × 500 mm about X-axis.*                                                                **(B.T.E. W-2011/2 Marks)**

**Data**     : b = 200 mm, d = 500 mm.
**To find**  : $Z_{xx}$.

**Concept :** Use of basic formula $Z_{xx} = \dfrac{bd^2}{6}$

**Solution :**                 $\mathbf{Z_{xx}} = \dfrac{I_{xx}}{y_{max}} = \dfrac{bd^3/12}{d/2} = \dfrac{bd^2}{6} = \dfrac{200 \times 500^2}{6} = \mathbf{8.33 \times 10^6\ mm^3}$

**Answer   :** $\boxed{Z_{xx} = 8.33 \times 10^6\ mm^3}$

---

**Example 24 :** *A simply supported beam of span 3 m carries a u.d.l. of 1000 N/m throughout the span. Calculate the modulus of section if the permissible bending stress for the material is 9 MPa.*                                             **(B.T.E. S-1999/4 Marks)**

**Data**     : Simply supported beam, L = 3 m, w = 1000 N/m, σ = 9 MPa = 9 N/mm²
**To find**  : Section modulus Z.

**Concept :** $Z = \dfrac{M}{\sigma}$.

**Solution :** For a simply supported beam carrying u.d.l. over the entire span,

$$\mathbf{M_{max}} = \frac{wL^2}{8} = \frac{1000 \times 3^2}{8} = 1.125 \times 10^3\ \text{N-m} = \mathbf{1.125 \times 10^6\ N\text{-}mm}$$

Using the bending stress equation,

$$\frac{M}{I} = \frac{\sigma}{y}$$

$\therefore$                         $\sigma = \dfrac{M}{I} \times y = \dfrac{M}{\left(\dfrac{I}{y}\right)} = \dfrac{M}{Z}$                     $\dots\left(\because\ Z = \dfrac{I}{y}\right)$

**Answer :**                $\boxed{Z = \dfrac{M}{\sigma} = \dfrac{1.125 \times 10^6}{9} = \mathbf{0.125 \times 10^6\ mm^3}}$

---

**Example 25 :** *A simply supported beam of span 8 m carries a point load of 50 kN at the centre of the span. Calculate the modulus of section required, if bending stress is not to exceed 150 MPa.*                                                            **(B.T.E. W-1999/4 Marks)**

**Data**     : Simply supported beam, L = 8 m,
              W = 50 kN = 50 × 10³ N, σ = 150 MPa = 150 N/mm²
**To find**  : Section modulus Z.

**Concept :** $Z = \dfrac{M}{\sigma}$.

**Solution :** For a simply supported beam carrying a point load W at the centre,

$$M_{max} = \frac{WL}{4} = \frac{50 \times 10^3 \times 8}{4} = 100 \times 10^3\ \text{N-m} = 100 \times 10^6\ \text{N-mm}$$

**Answer :** $\boxed{Z = \dfrac{M}{\sigma} = \dfrac{100 \times 10^6}{150} = \mathbf{0.67 \times 10^6\ mm^3}}$

### Type 8 : Examples based on the radius of curvature of the beam :

| Important Formulae |
|---|
| (i) $\dfrac{M}{I} = \dfrac{E}{R}$, (ii) $\dfrac{\sigma}{y} = \dfrac{E}{R}$ |

**Example 26 :** *A steel strip 40 mm wide and 6 mm thick is subjected to end couples 20 N-m. Find the radius of curvature of the bent up strip if E = 2 ×10⁵ MPa.*

**(B.T.E. S-1988/2 Marks)**

**Data**          : Steel strip, b = 40 mm, d = 6 mm,

B.M. or couple, M = 20 N-m = $20 \times 10^3$ N-mm,

E = $2 \times 10^5$ MPa = $2 \times 10^5$ N/mm²

**To find**     : R.

**Concept**   : Use of bending stress equation $\dfrac{M}{I} = \dfrac{E}{R}$.

**Solution**   : For a rectangular strip of size b × d,

$$I_{NA} = I_{XX} = \frac{b\,d^3}{12} = \frac{40 \times 6^3}{12} = 720 \text{ mm}^4$$

Using the relation,          $\dfrac{M}{I} = \dfrac{E}{R}$

∴          $\dfrac{20 \times 10^3}{720} = \dfrac{2 \times 10^5}{R}$

**Answer :**   $\boxed{\text{R} = 7200 \text{ mm} = \textbf{7.2 m}}$

**Example 27 :** *Determine the radius to which a bar 20 mm diameter will be required to bend so that the maximum stress induced reaches 100 N/mm². Take E = 2 ×10⁵ N/mm².*

**(B.T.E. S-1989/2 Marks)**

**Data**          : Circular bar, d = 20 mm, σ = 100 N/mm²,

E = $2 \times 10^5$ N/mm², y = radius of circle = $\dfrac{20}{2}$ = 10 mm

**To find**   : R.

**Concept**   : Use of bending stress equation, $\dfrac{\sigma}{y} = \dfrac{E}{R}$.

**Solution** : Using the relation, $\dfrac{\sigma}{y} = \dfrac{E}{R}$

∴          $\dfrac{100}{10} = \dfrac{2 \times 10^5}{R}$

**Answer:**          $\boxed{\text{R} = 20,000 \text{ mm} = \textbf{20 m}}$

**Example 28 :** *Find the bending stress induced in the steel flat 40 mm wide and 5 mm thick if it is required to bend into an arc of a circle of radius 2.5 m. Also calculate the moment required to bend the flat. Take E = 2 × 10$^5$ MPa.* **(B.T.E. S-2012, W-2007/4 Marks)**

**Data** : Steel flat b = 40 mm, d = 5 mm,

radius of curvature R = 2.5 m = 2.5 × 10$^3$ mm,

E = 2 × 10$^5$ MPa = 2 × 10$^5$ N/mm$^2$

**To find** : (i) σ, (ii) M.

**Solution** : For a steel flat of size b × d,

$$I_{NA} = I_{XX} = \frac{bd^3}{12} = \frac{40 \times 5^3}{12} = 416.67 \text{ mm}^4$$

Using the relation, $\dfrac{M}{I} = \dfrac{E}{R}$

$$\frac{M}{416.67} = \frac{2 \times 10^5}{2.5 \times 10^3}$$

∴ **M = 33333.33 N.mm = 33.33 N.m**

Using the relation, $\dfrac{\sigma}{y} = \dfrac{E}{R}$

∴ $\dfrac{\sigma}{(5/2)} = \dfrac{2 \times 10^5}{2.5 \times 10^3}$  $\quad ... (\because y = \dfrac{d}{2} = \dfrac{5}{2})$

∴ $\dfrac{\sigma}{2.5} = 80$

∴ **σ = 200 N/mm$^2$**

**Answer :** (i) M = 33.33 N.m, (ii) σ = 200 N/mm$^2$

---

## Type 9 : Miscellaneous Examples :

**Example 29 :** *A beam having modulus of elasticity of 2.8 × 10$^5$ N/mm$^2$ is bent with radius of curvature of 28 m under the effect of bending moment of 5000 N·mm. Calculate the moment of inertia of the cross-section of the beam.* **(B.T.E. S-2000/2 Marks)**

**Data** : E = 2.8 × 10$^5$ N/mm$^2$, R = 28 m = 28 × 10$^3$ mm, M = 5000 N.mm

**To find** : I.

**Concept** : Use of bending stress equation, $\dfrac{M}{I} = \dfrac{E}{R}$.

**Solution :** Using the bending stress equation,

$$\frac{M}{I} = \frac{E}{R}$$

∴ $\dfrac{5000}{I} = \dfrac{2.8 \times 10^5}{28 \times 10^3}$

**Answer :** I = 500 mm$^4$

**Example 30 :** *A solid circular compression member 60 mm in diameter is to be replaced by a hollow circular section of the same material. Find the size of the hollow section if the internal diameter is 0.6 times the external diameter.* **(B.T.E. S-2003/4 Marks)**

**Data**     :  Solid circular section D = 60 mm,

hollow circular section $d_2 = 0.6\, d_1$

where $d_1$ = external diameter and $d_2$ = internal diameter.

**To find**  :  $d_1$ and $d_2$.

**Concept** :  As the two columns have same material and strength, their M.I. must be equal.

**Solution** :  As the two columns have same material and strength,

$$I_{solid} = I_{hollow}$$

$$\frac{\pi}{64} \cdot D^4 = \frac{\pi}{64}(d_1^4 - d_2^4)$$

$$\frac{\pi}{64} \cdot D^4 = \frac{\pi}{64}[d_1^4 - (0.6\, d_1)^4]$$

$\therefore$ $\qquad\qquad D^4 = d_1^4(1 - 0.6^4) = d_1^4(1 - 0.13)$

$\therefore$ $\qquad\qquad D^4 = 0.87\, d_1^4$

$\therefore$ $\qquad\qquad 60^4 = 0.87\, d_1^4$

$\therefore$ $\qquad\qquad \mathbf{d_1 = 62.13\ mm}$

$\therefore$ $\qquad\qquad \mathbf{d_2} = 0.6 \times 62.13 = \mathbf{37.28\ mm}$

**Answer :**  $\boxed{d_1 = 62.13 \text{ mm}, d_2 = 37.28 \text{ mm}}$

**Practice Questions**

---

### Questions of 2 Marks

1. Define section modulus and neutral axis.                            **(B.T.E. S-2013)**
2. State two assumptions made in the theory of bending.               **(B.T.W. W-2012)**
3. State any four assumptions made in the theory of simple (pure) bending.

    **(B.T.E. S-2012, 2006)**

4. Write the flexural formula.

    State the meaning of symbols used in it.                          **(B.T.E. S-2012, 2010)**

5. Differentiate between pure bending and ordinary bending.      **(B.T.E. W-05, S-98)**

6. Differentiate between moment of resistance and bending moment.

    **(B.T.E. W-2000; S-1999, 1997)**

7. Define neutral axis in the theory of simple bending.              **(B.T.E. W-2011)**

8. Draw a bending stress distribution diagram for the following cases.    **(2 Marks each)**

    (i) A simply supported beam of circular cross-section subjected to a sagging moment.

(ii) A simply supported beam of rectangular cross-section subjected to a hogging moment.

(iii) A simply supported beam of T section subjected to a sagging bending moment.

(iv) A simply supported beam of unsymmetrical I section subjected to a hogging bending moment.

9. Define neutral axis. **(B.T.E. S-1998)**

10. Show the nature of stresses in bending stress distribution diagram, if the rectangular beam is of cantilever type. The loading is downward. **(B.T.E. S-1997)**

11. A beam having modulus of elasticity of $2.8 \times 10^5$ N/mm$^2$ is bent with radius of curvature of 28 mm under the effect of B.M. of 5000 N-mm. Calculate the M.I. of cross-section of the beam. **(B.T.E. S-2000)**

## Questions of 4 Marks

12. What is meant by moment of resistance and neutral axis ? **(B.T.E. W-2012)**

13. Explain the theory of simple bending. **(B.T.E. S-2011)**

14. State any four assumptions in the theory of simple bending. **(B.T.E. W-2010, S-2010)**

## Problems of 4 Marks

15. Find the bending stress induced in the steel flat 40 mm wide and 5 mm thick if it is required to bend into an arc of a circle of radius 2.5 m. Also calculate the moment required to bend the flat. Take E = $2 \times 10^5$ MPa.

**Hint :** $I = bd^3 / 12 = 416.67$ mm$^4$, $y = \dfrac{d}{2} = 2.5$ mm.

(**Ans.** M = 33333.33 N-mm and $\sigma$ = 200 N/mm$^2$)

16. State any four assumptions in the theory of simple bending.

**(B.T.E. W-2009, 2008, 2007/4 Marks)**

17. Define the section modulus. Write the equations of section modulus for hollow rectangular section and hollow circular section. **(B.T.E. S-2008/4 Marks)**

18. What is section modulus ? Write expression for section modulus for (i) rectangular section, (ii) circular section. **(B.T.E. S-2009/4 Marks)**

19. A timber beam is of circular cross-section of diameter 200 mm. The maximum bending stress produced at a section is 100 N/mm$^2$. Find the bending stress at a layer 50 mm from the N.A.

(**Hint :** Use the concept of similar triangles.) (**Ans.** 50 N/mm$^2$)

20. A rectangular timber beam is used for a simply supported span of 3.2 m. It carries u.d.l. of 30 kN/m throughout the span and a downward point load of 40 kN at the mid-span. Assume width of the beam as two-third of depth and determine the size of the beam assuming the permissible bending stress in timber as 6 N/mm$^2$.

$\left(\text{**Hint :** Here } M_{max} = \dfrac{wL^2}{8} + \dfrac{WL}{4} \text{ and } b = \dfrac{2}{3}d\right)$ (**Ans.** d = 472.6 mm, b = 315 mm)

21. Determine the moment of resistance of a Tee section having top flange 80 mm wide and 10 mm thick and a rib (web) 10 mm thick × 120 mm deep. Take the permissible bending stress = 160 N/mm$^2$.

$\left(\textbf{Hint :} \text{ Use } \dfrac{M_r}{I} = \dfrac{\sigma_{max}}{y_{max}}, \ \sigma_{max} = 160 \text{ N/mm}^2 \text{ (given)}\right)$  **(Ans.** $M_r$ = 6.46 kN·m)

22. Determine the moment of resistance of an unsymmetrical I section having the following details.

    Top flange      :   100 mm × 15 mm
    Bottom flange  :   200 mm × 20 mm
    Web                :   250 mm × 10 mm

    Take the permissible bending stress in tension 150 N/mm$^2$ and in compression 100 N/mm$^2$.

    **(Ans.** $M_r$ is the least of 53.57 kN-m and 143.43 kN-m i.e. $M_r$ = 53.57 kN-m)

23. A T-section is used as a beam simply supported over a span of 4 m. Calculate the safe u.d.l. the beam can carry without exceeding bending stress 165 N/mm$^2$.

    Properties of T – section :

    Flange width = 72 mm, flange thickness = 11.6 mm, overall depth of section = 150 mm, thickness of web = 8 mm, $I_{xx}$ = 4.5 × 10$^6$ mm$^4$, $C_{xx}$ = 47.5 mm from top, weight of section = 157 N/m.

    **(Hint :** Here $y_{max}$ = 150 – 47.5 = 102.5 mm

    **Let w be in N/m.** $M = \dfrac{wL^2}{8} = \dfrac{w \times 4^2}{8}$ = (2 w) N-m = (2000 w) N-mm)

    **(Ans.** w = 3.62 kN/m. This is u.d.l. on the beam including self weight of 157 N/m = 0.157 kN/m.

    ∴   Actual u.d.l. carried by beam = 3.62 – 0.157 = 3.46 kN/m.

24. A beam of 5 m span is simply supported at its ends and carries a u.d.l. of 3 kN/m over the entire span. If the bending stress is limited to 110 N/mm$^2$, find the section modulus of the beam.

    **(Hint :** $M = \dfrac{wL^2}{8} = \dfrac{3 \times 5^2}{8}$ kN-m = 9.375 × 10$^6$ N-mm

    Use M = σ × Z ... (where Z = I/y = section modulus)   **(Ans.** Z = 85227.27 mm$^3$)

25. A simply supported beam of span 4 m carries a u.d.l. of 4 kN/m over the entire span. Find the B.M. at a section 1 m from the left support. The beam has a cross-section of 120 mm × 200 mm. Find the bending stress at a level 80 mm above the neutral axis.

    **(Ans.** B.M. at 1 m from left support = 6 × 10$^6$ N-mm, $\sigma_{max}$ = 7.5 N/mm$^2$.

    Use the concept of similar triangles to find the stress at 80 mm above N.A., $\sigma_c$ = 6 N/mm$^2$)

26. A timber beam has a cross-section 120 mm × 200 mm. It is simply supported over a span of 4 m and carries a u.d.l. 1 kN/m over the entire span. Calculate the maximum bending stress induced in the beam and the radius of curvature to which the beam will bend at that section.　　(**Ans.** $\sigma$ = 2.5 N/mm², R = 400 mm)

27. A T-section is used as a beam over a simply supported span of 4 m with the flange at top. Beam carries a 40 kN concentrated load at the centre. Find the maximum tensile and compressive stresses developed in the beam due to bending.

    Properties of T section ISNT – 150 (depth of section), $I_{xx}$ = 5.41 × 10⁶ mm⁴, $C_{xx}$ = 36.1 mm

    (**Hint :** ISNT 150 means Indian Standard Normal Tee with overall depth 150 mm. $C_{xx}$ means the distance of c.g. from the top.)

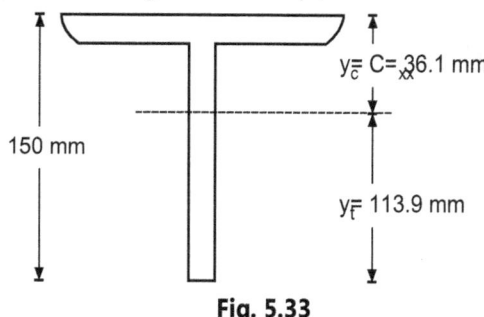

**Fig. 5.33**

(**Ans.** $\sigma_c$ = 266.91 N/mm², $\sigma_t$ = 842.14 N/mm²)

28. A beam of 4.75 m span has a cross-section of T shape. The flange is 180 mm × 12 mm and the web is 16 mm × 240 mm. Calculate the u.d.l. this beam can support if the allowable tensile stress is 100 N/mm². Assume that the beam is simply supported.

    $\left(\textbf{Hint :}\ \text{Use}\ \dfrac{M}{I} = \dfrac{\sigma_t}{y_t},\ \text{where}\ M = \dfrac{wL^2}{8}\right)$　　(**Ans.** w = 8.66 kN/m)

29. A timber beam 100 mm wide and 150 mm deep is simply supported over a span of 4 m. Find the maximum central point load the beam can carry if the bending stress in compression or tension is not to exceed 80 N/mm².　　(**Ans.** W = 30 kN)

30. A simply supported beam of 4 m span carries a u.d.l. of 2 kN/m over the entire span. If the bending stress is not to exceed 165 N/mm², find the value of Z for the beam and diameter if the beam is circular.　　(**Ans.** Z = 24242.42 mm³, d = 62.73 mm)

31. A timber specimen was tested for flexure (bending) using U.T.M. and the following observations were noted.

    (i)　Width b = 40 mm, (ii) Depth d = 80 mm,

    (iii) Span L = 360 mm, (iv) Central point load at flexure, W = 21.1 kN.

    Calculate the bending strength (stress) of the timber specimen.

    (**Ans.** $\sigma$ = 44.5 N/mm²)

## Important Points

- **Bending stresses :**

    The stresses induced to resist the B.M. are called as bending stresses or flexural stresses.

- **Difference between pure bending and ordinary bending :**

    A beam subjected to pure bending has only bending stresses of tensile or compressive nature induced in it. A beam subjected to ordinary bending has both bending stresses and shear stresses set up in it. When the beam is subjected to pure bending, it bends into an arc of a circle.

- **Tension and compression zones for beams :**

    For a simply supported beam, the tension zone is below the neutral axis and the compression zone above the neutral axis. For a cantilever beam, the tension zone is above the neutral axis and the compression zone is below the neutral axis.

- **Neutral axis :**

    The intersection of a neutral layer with any normal cross-section of a beam is called as neutral axis. The bending stress at the N.A. is always zero.

- **Flexural formula :**

    $$\frac{M}{I} = \frac{\sigma}{y} = \frac{E}{R}, \text{ where}$$

    $M$ = Maximum B.M. which is equal to the moment of resistance of the beam.

    $I$ = Moment of inertia of the beam section about the N.A. or X-X axis.

    $\sigma$ = Bending stress in a layer at a distance y from N.A.

    $y$ = Distance of the layer from the N.A.

    $E$ = Young's modulus for the beam material.

    $R$ = Radius of curvature of the bent up beam.

- **Bending stress / strain diagrams :**

    Bending stress / strain variation diagram for symmetrical and asymmetrical sections always follows the straight line law. For symmetrical sections, $\sigma_c = \sigma_t$ and $y_c = y_t$. For asymmetrical sections, $\sigma_c \neq \sigma_t$ and $y_c \neq y_t$.

- **Section modulus :**

    The ratio of M.I. of the section about the N.A. and the distance of the most extreme layer from the N.A. is called the **section modulus** or **modulus of section.** It is denoted by Z.

    Mathematically, $Z = \dfrac{I}{y}$.

    **Units of Z :** $mm^3$, $cm^3$, $m^3$ etc.

- **Moment of resistance :**

    It is the moment of couple formed by C and T forces. It resists the external B.M. In the equilibrium condition, $M_r = M$.

- **Assumptions in the theory of pure (simple) bending :**

  (i)    Beam material is homogeneous and isotropic.

  (ii)   The beam is straight before loading and is of the same cross-section throughout.

  (iii)  Hooke's law is obeyed.

  (iv)   The transverse sections which were plane before bending remain plane after bending.

  (v)    Beam is subjected to pure bending and hence the effect of shear stresses is neglected.

  (vi)   Each layer of the beam is free to expand or contract independently of the layer above or below it.

  (vii)  E has the same value in tension and compression.

## SUB-TOPIC 5.2 : CONCEPT OF DIRECT AND TRANSVERSE SHEAR STRESS  (6 Marks)

### Synopsis

Introduction, Definition of single shear and double shear, Derivation of shear stress equation, Shear stress distribution for a rectangular section, Solved examples on shear stress distribution diagram for a rectangular section, Shear stress distribution for a circular section, Solved examples on shear stress distribution diagram for a circular section, Shear stress distribution diagram for a hollow rectangular section, Solved examples on shear stress distribution diagram for a hollow rectangular section, Miscellaneous examples. Practice questions, Important points.

## 5.11 INTRODUCTION

*The internal stresses induced in the beam section which resist the shear force are called as shear stresses.* In this topic, we shall study the distribution of shear stress for various sections and the relation between the maximum and the average shear stress.

## 5.12 DEFINITION OF SINGLE SHEAR AND DOUBLE SHEAR

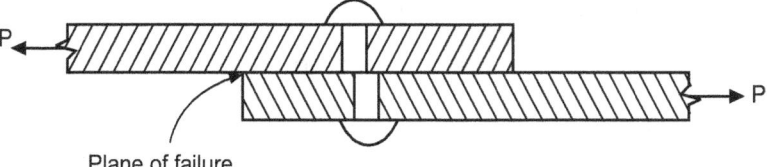

**Fig. 5.34 : Single shear failure of lap joint**

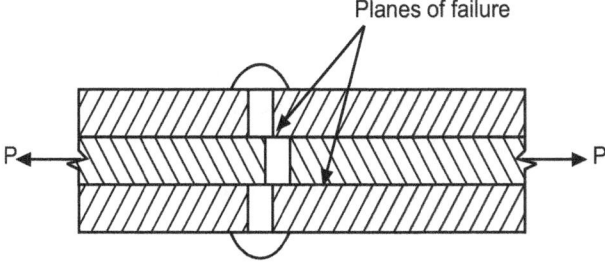

**Fig. 5.35 : Double shear failure of butt joint**

A rivet is a shear member. The rivets fail by shearing if the shearing stress exceeds their shearing strength.

*Let us consider failure of a lap joint as shown in Fig. 5.34. Since a rivet connects two plates there will be only one plane of shear failure and the cross-sectional area subjected to shear is $\frac{\pi}{4} d^2$, where d is diameter of a rivet. This is called single shear failure.*

$$\text{Single shear stress} = \frac{\text{Shear load}}{\text{Area subjected to shear}} = \frac{P}{\frac{\pi}{4} d^2}$$

*Let us consider failure of a butt joint as shown in Fig. 5.35. Since a rivet connects three plates, there will be two planes of shear failure and the cross-sectional area subjected to shear is $2 \times \frac{\pi}{4} d^2$. This is called double shear failure.*

$$\text{Double shear stress} = \frac{\text{Shear load}}{\text{Area subjected to shear}} = \frac{P}{2 \times \frac{\pi}{4} d^2}$$

1.  Differentiate between single shear and double shear.          **(B.T.E. S-2013/2 Marks)**

**(Most Likely and Asked in Previous B.T.E. Exam.)**

## 5.13 DERIVATION OF SHEAR STRESS EQUATION

(**Note :** The derivation of shear stress equation is not expected in the examination.)

Let us consider a simply supported beam of span L carrying a u.d.l. as shown in Fig. 5.36 (a). Fig. 5.36 (b) shows the longitudinal section of a loaded beam. AB and CD are the two sections very near to each other and separated by a distance 'δx'.

Let                              M  = B.M. at section AB

M + δM  = B.M. at section CD

Since the beam is subjected to a sagging B.M., the compression zone will be above the N.A. Let $y_c$ be the distance of the top compression layer from the N.A. Now, consider only the portion of the beam above the N.A. in the compression zone. This part consists of infinite number of layers of length 'δx' and area 'δa'. Let us consider a layer GH at a distance y from the N.A. having length δx, width b and thickness δy. The cross-section of a beam is as shown in Fig. 5.36 (c). Area δa = b·δy. The bending moments M and M + δM will cause the bending stresses. The bending stress variation diagram for the compression zone is also shown in Fig. 5.36 (b).

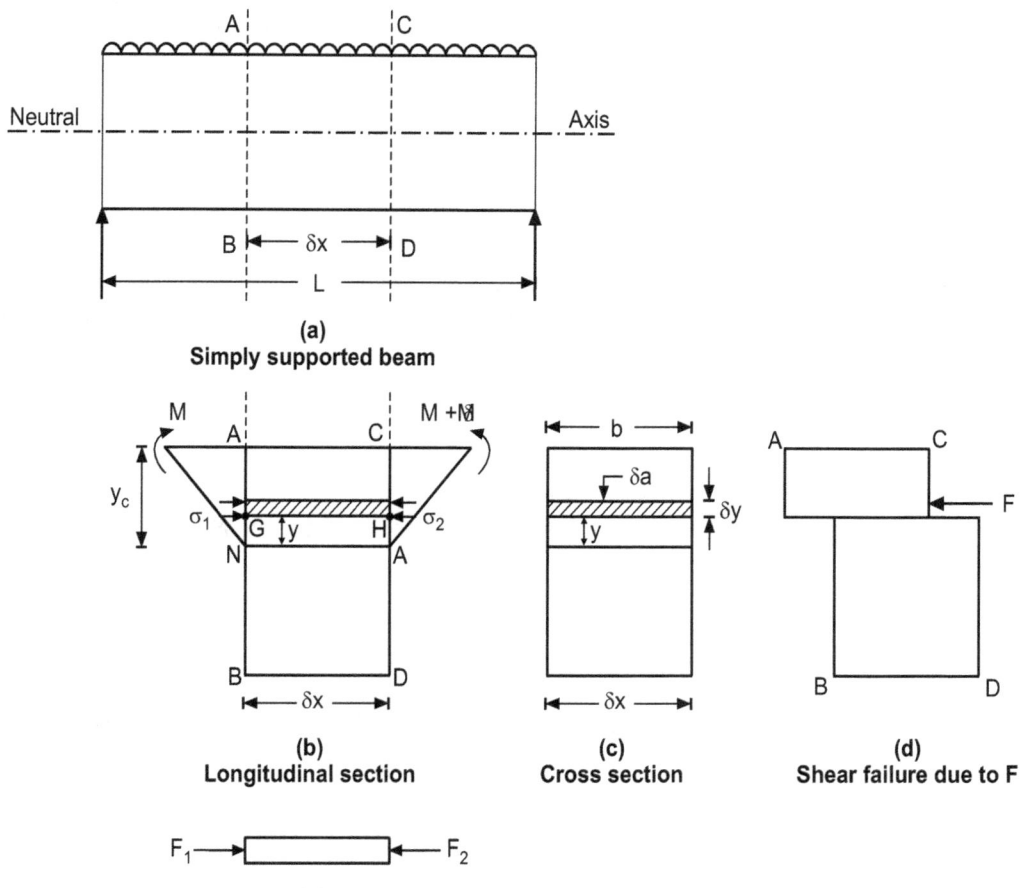

**Fig. 5.36**

Let　$\sigma_1$ = Bending stress at the layer GH at a distance y from the N.A. on section AB.

$\sigma_2$ = Bending stress at the layer GH at a distance y from the N.A. on section CD.

Using the bending stress equation, we have

$$\frac{M}{I} = \frac{\sigma_1}{y} \quad \text{and} \quad \frac{M + \delta M}{I} = \frac{\sigma_2}{y}$$

$$\therefore \qquad \sigma_1 = \frac{M}{I} \times y \text{ and } \sigma_2 = \frac{M + \delta M}{I} \times y$$

These compressive bending stresses will cause the longitudinal compressive forces acting as shear forces as shown in Fig. 5.36 (e).

Let　　　　　　　　　　$F_1$ = S.F. on the layer GH at section AB

$F_2$ = S.F. on the layer GH at section CD.

Now,　　　　since Force = Stress × Area

$$F_1 = \sigma_1 \times \delta a = \frac{M}{I} \times y \times \delta a$$

and　　　　　　　　$$F_2 = \sigma_2 \times \delta a = \frac{M + \delta M}{I} \times y \times \delta a$$

The resultant shear force F acting on the layer GH assuming that $\delta M$ is positive, is given by,

$$F = F_2 - F_1 = \frac{M + \delta M}{I} \times y \times \delta a - \frac{M}{I} \times y \times \delta a$$

$$\boxed{F = \frac{\delta M}{I} \times y \times \delta a}$$

Now, instead of considering a single layer GH of area $\delta a$, if we consider the entire block above the layer GH between the two sections AB and CD, then the resultant force on this area is given by,

$$F = \int_{y}^{y_c} \frac{\delta M}{I} \times y \times \delta a = \frac{\delta M}{I} \int_{y}^{y_c} y \cdot \delta a$$

But $y \cdot \delta a$ represents the moment of area '$\delta a$' of layer GH about the N.A.

$\int_{y}^{y_c} y \cdot \delta a$ represents the moment of entire area above the layer GH about N.A. $= A \times \bar{y}$.

where A = Area above the layer GH, $\bar{y}$ = Distance of c.g. of the area A about the N.A.

$$\therefore \qquad \int_{y}^{y_c} y \cdot \delta a = A \times \bar{y}$$

$$\therefore \qquad F = \frac{\delta M}{I} A \times \bar{y} \qquad \qquad \dots \text{(i)}$$

This horizontal force is resisted by the beam by inducing the horizontal shear stress q at the layer GH. Area subjected to shear is $b \times \delta x$.

Now, $$q = \frac{F}{b \times \delta x}$$

$$\therefore \qquad F = q \times b \times \delta x \qquad \qquad \dots \text{(ii)}$$

Equating the equations (i) and (ii), we have

$$q \times b \times \delta x = \frac{\delta M}{I} A \times \bar{y}$$

$$\therefore \qquad q = \frac{\delta M}{\delta x} \frac{A\bar{y}}{I b}$$

$$\therefore \qquad \boxed{q = S \frac{A\bar{y}}{I b}}$$

$$\left( \because \frac{\delta M}{\delta x} = \text{rate of change of B.M.} = \text{shear force at the section} = S \right)$$

Now, q is the intensity of horizontal shear stress at the layer GH at a distance y from the N.A. We know that the shear stress across a plane is always accompanied by a balancing shear stress across the plane and normal to it. Therefore, a horizontal shear stress is equal to the vertical shear stress.

∴ Vertical shear stress,

$$q = \frac{S A \bar{y}}{I b}$$

This equation gives the shear stress induced in a layer at a distance y from the N.A.

1. Explain the concept of shear stress with neat sketch.          **(B.T.E. W-2008/2 Marks)**

**(Most Likely and Asked in Previous B.T.E. Exam.)**

## 5.13.1 Shear Stress Equation and the Meaning of Symbols Used

In a simply supported beam subjected to some loading, $q = \dfrac{S A \bar{y}}{I b}$, where

q = Intensity of shear stress induced in a layer at a distance y from the neutral axis.

A = Area of the beam above the layer under consideration

$\bar{y}$ = Distance of the c.g. of the area considered from the neutral axis

$A\bar{y}$ = Moment of the area above the layer considered about the neutral axis.

I = Moment of inertia of the whole cross section about the neutral axis = $I_{NA} = I_{XX}$

b = Width of the section at a distance y from the N.A.

**Note :**

*(1) If the layer is considered above the N.A., take the moment of area above the layer considered about the N.A.*

*(2) If the layer is considered below the N.A., take the moment of area below the layer considered about the N.A.*

*(3) For the top layer at a distance $y_c$ from the N.A., there is no area above this layer. Similarly for the bottom layer at a distance $y_t$ from the N.A., there is no area below this layer. Therefore, $A \bar{y} = 0$.*

*Now,          $q = \dfrac{S A \bar{y}}{I b}$*

*Since          $A\bar{y} = 0, q = 0$*

*i.e. at the top and bottom layer, shear stress is always zero.*

*(4) Shear stress is inversely proportional to the width 'b'. If the width decreases, q increases and vice versa. Sometimes at a certain layer there are two values of width 'b'. Accordingly there will be the two values of shear stress 'q.' For example in case of channel, Tee, I and other sections at the junction of the flange and the web, there are two values of 'b.' For calculating the two values of 'q', first we have to consider the width of flange and then the width of web.*

1. State the shear stress equation and explain meaning of each term.
   **(B.T.E. S-2013/4 Marks)**
2. State the shear stress formula and write the meaning of symbols used.
   **(B.T.E. S-2010/4 Marks)**

**(Most Likely and Asked in Previous B.T.E. Exam.)**

## 5.14 SHEAR STRESS DISTRIBUTION FOR A RECTANGULAR SECTION
## (Average Shear Stress and Maximum Shear Stress for Rectangular Section)

Let us consider a rectangular section of width b and depth d as shown in Fig. 5.37 (a). N.A. represents neutral axis of the beam. The distance of extreme layer from the N.A. is d/2.

Now, consider a layer EF at a distance 'y' from the N.A. To find the intensity of shear stress 'q' at this layer, we have to consider the area above this layer i.e. shaded area *ABFE*.

Now,          $BF = \left(\dfrac{d}{2} - y\right)$

∴ Area ABFE,          $A = b\left(\dfrac{d}{2} - y\right)$

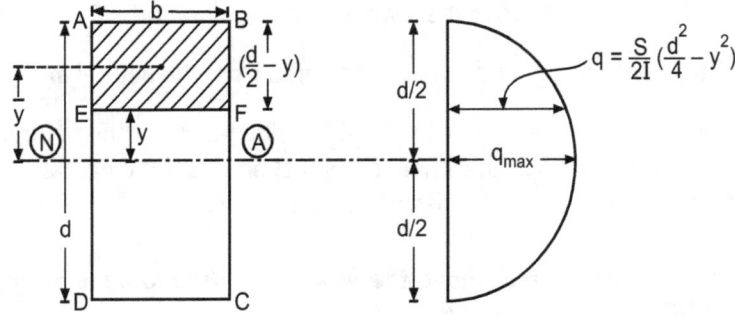

**(a) Cross-section          (b) Shear stress distribution**

**Fig. 5.37**

Distance of c.g. of this area from the N.A.,

$$\bar{y} = y + \frac{1}{2}\left(\frac{d}{2} - y\right) = y + \frac{d}{4} - \frac{y}{2} = \frac{y}{2} + \frac{d}{4} = \frac{1}{2}\left(y + \frac{d}{2}\right)$$

We know that, shear stress at a distance 'y' from the N.A. is given by,

$$q = \frac{S\,A\bar{y}}{I\,b} = \frac{S \cdot b\left(\dfrac{d}{2} - y\right)\dfrac{1}{2}\left(y + \dfrac{d}{2}\right)}{I\,b}$$

∴          $$\boxed{q = \frac{S}{2\,I}\left(\frac{d^2}{4} - y^2\right)}$$          ... (i)

From the equation (i) it is clear that, since the power of y is two, the variation of shear stress is of *parabolic nature*.

Now, y is measured from the N.A. At the N.A., y = 0 and q is maximum.

$$I = \text{M.I. of the section about the N.A.} = \frac{bd^3}{12}$$

∴ From the equation (i), we have

$$q_{max} = \frac{S}{2\,(bd^3/12)}\left(\frac{d^2}{4} - 0\right) = \frac{3}{2}\left(\frac{S}{bd}\right)$$

But      $\dfrac{S}{bd} = \dfrac{\text{Shear force}}{\text{Area}} = \text{Average shear stress}$

∴      $$\boxed{q_{max} = \frac{3}{2}\,(q_{av}) = 1.5\,q_{av}}$$

*Therefore, for a rectangular section, the maximum shear stress is 1.5 times the average shear stress.*

At the top and bottom layer, $y = \dfrac{d}{2}$

Substituting this value in the equation (i), we have

$$q = \frac{S}{2I}\left(\frac{d^2}{4} - \frac{d^2}{4}\right) = 0.$$

i.e. the shear stress at the top and the bottom layer is zero.

From the equation (i), it is clear that as y increases, q decreases. The shear stress distribution diagram is a parabolic curve as shown in Fig. 5.37 (b).

1. Draw shear stress distribution diagram for a rectangular (solid) section.
   **(S-2015) (2 Marks)**
2. State the relation between maximum shear stress and average shear stress for a rectangular section.      **(S-2015) (2 Marks)**

**(Most Likely and Asked in Previous B.T.E. Exam.)**

**Type 10 : Solved examples on shear stress distribution diagram for a rectangular section**

**Important Formulae**

(i)  Area A = b × d.

(ii)  Average shear stress,  $q_{average} = \dfrac{S}{bd}$.

(iii)  Maximum shear stress, $q_{max} = 1.5 \times q_{average}$.

**Example 31 :** *A rectangular section 100 mm wide having moment of inertia 6.67 × 10⁷ mm⁴ is subjected to a shear force of 100 kN. Find the moment of area of section under consideration corresponding to a shear stress of 4 MPa.* **(B.T.E. W-2004/2 Marks)**

**Data**      : Rectangular section, b = 100 mm, $I = 6.67 \times 10^7$ mm⁴,

S = 100 kN = $100 \times 10^3$ N,  q = 4 MPa = 4 N/mm²

**To find** $: A\bar{y}$.

**Concept :** Use of shear stress equation.

**Solution :**

$$q = \frac{SA\bar{y}}{Ib}$$

$$4 = \frac{(100 \times 10^3)\,(A\bar{y})}{(6.67 \times 10^7)\,(100)}$$

**Answer :**

$$\boxed{A\bar{y} = 266800 \text{ mm}^3}$$

---

**Example 32 :** *A rectangular section 230 mm wide and 400 mm deep is subjected to a S.F. of 40 kN. Find the maximum shear stress across the section.* **(B.T.E. S-2004/2 Marks)**

**Data** : Rectangular section b = 230 mm, d = 400 mm, S = 40 kN = $40 \times 10^3$ N

**To find** : $q_{max}$.

**Concept :** Relation between $q_{max}$ and $q_{av}$ ($q_{max} = 1.5\, q_{av}$).

**Solution :**

$$\mathbf{q_{av}} = \frac{S}{A} = \frac{S}{bd} = \frac{40 \times 10^3}{230 \times 400} = \mathbf{0.43 \text{ N/mm}^2}$$

$$\mathbf{q_{max}} = 1.5\, q_{av} = 1.5 \times 0.43 = \mathbf{0.65 \text{ N/mm}^2}$$

**Answer :**

$$\boxed{\mathbf{q_{max} = 0.65 \text{ N/mm}^2}}$$

---

**Example 33 :** *Find the maximum and average shear stress for a rectangular section 60 mm $\times$ 150 mm subjected to a shear force of 5 kN.* **(B.T.E. W-1998/4 Marks)**

**Data** : Rectangular section b = 60 mm, d = 150 mm, S = 5 kN = $5 \times 10^3$ N.

**To find** : $q_{max}$ and $q_{av}$.

**Concept :** Relation between $q_{max}$ and $q_{average}$.

**Solution :**

$$\mathbf{q_{av}} = \frac{S}{A} = \frac{S}{bd} = \frac{5 \times 10^3}{60 \times 150} = \mathbf{0.55 \text{ N/mm}^2}$$

For a rectangular section,

$$\mathbf{q_{max}} = 1.5 \times q_{av} = 1.5 \times 0.55 = \mathbf{0.83 \text{ N/mm}^2}$$

**Answer :** $\boxed{q_{av} = 0.55 \text{ N/mm}^2,\ q_{max} = 0.83 \text{ N/mm}^2}$

---

**Example 34 :** *The average shear stress across rectangular cross-section is 190 N/mm². Calculate the maximum shear stress at this section.* **(B.T.E. S-2000/4 Marks)**

**Answer :**

$$\boxed{q_{max} = 285 \text{ N/mm}^2}$$

---

**Example 35 :** *Sketch the shear stress distribution diagram for a rectangular beam of 600 $\times$ 200 mm (deep) subjected to a shear force of 20 kN.* **(B.T.E. S-1998/4 Marks)**

**Data** : Rectangular section b = 600 mm, d = 200 mm,

shear force S = 20 kN = $20 \times 10^3$ N.

**To find** : Shear stress distribution diagram.

**Concept :** The shear stress distribution diagram is of parabolic nature.

**Solution :** We know that for a rectangular section of size b × d,

$$q_{average} = \frac{S}{b\,d} = \frac{20 \times 10^3}{600 \times 200} = 0.17 \text{ N/mm}^2$$

$$q_{max} = 1.5 \times q_{average} = 1.5 \times 0.17 = 0.255 \text{ N/mm}^2$$

**Answer :** The shear stress distribution diagram is as shown in Fig. 5.41 (b).

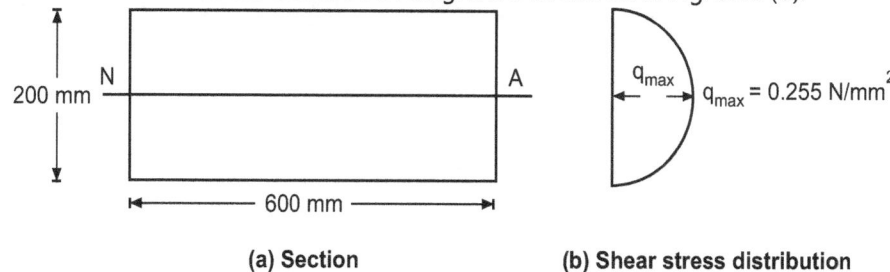

**(a) Section**　　　　　　**(b) Shear stress distribution**

**Fig. 5.38**

**Example 36 :** *A beam of rectangular cross-section 100 × 100 mm is subjected to a shear force = 30 kN. Calculate the shear stress induced across the section at a layer 20 mm away from the neutral axis.* **(B.T.E. W-2011/4 Marks)**

**Solution :**

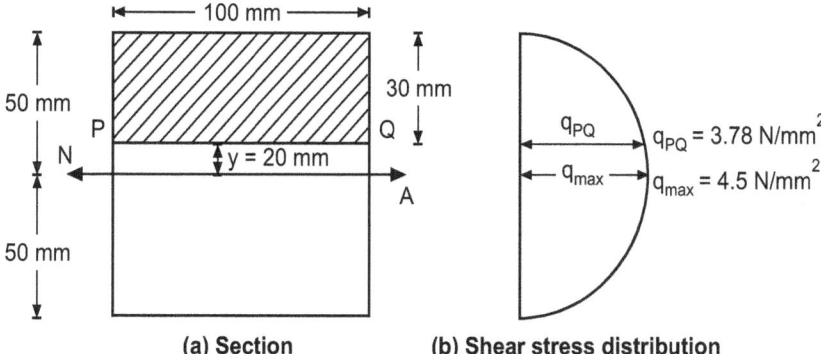

**(a) Section**　　　　　　**(b) Shear stress distribution**

**Fig. 5.39**

Here b = 100 mm, d = 100 mm, S = 30 kN = 30 × 10³ N.

M.I. of whole section about N.A. = $I = \frac{bd^3}{12} = \frac{100 \times 100^3}{12} = 8333333.33 \text{ mm}^4$

$A$ = Shaded area above layer PQ = 100 × 30 = 3000 mm²

$\bar{y}$ = Distance of C.G. of this area from the N.A. = $\frac{30}{2} + 20 = 35$ mm

b = Width at layer PQ = 100 mm

Shear stress at layer PQ is given by

$$q_{PQ} = \frac{SA\bar{y}}{Ib} = \frac{(30 \times 10^3)\,(3000)\,(35)}{(8333333.33) \times (100)} = \textbf{3.78 N/mm}^2$$

**Note :** Maximum shear stress at N.A. is given by

$$q_{max} = 1.5 \times q_{av} = 1.5\left(\frac{S}{bd}\right) = 1.5 \times \left(\frac{30 \times 10^3}{100 \times 100}\right) = 4.5 \text{ N/mm}^2$$

The shear stress distribution diagram is as shown in Fig. 5.39 (b).

**Answer :** $\boxed{q_{PQ} = 3.78 \text{ N/mm}^2}$

## 5.15 SHEAR STRESS DISTRIBUTION FOR A CIRCULAR SECTION
### (Average Shear Stress and Maximum Shear Stress for a Circular Section)

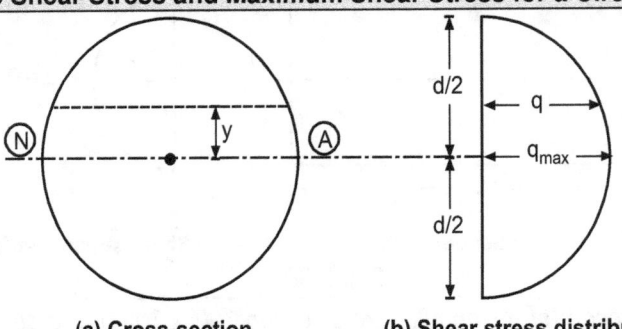

**(a) Cross-section**    **(b) Shear stress distribution**

**Fig. 5.40**

Consider a circular section of diameter 'd' as shown in Fig. 5.40 (a). The shear stress intensity at a distance y from the N.A. is given by,

$$q = S\left(\frac{r^2 - y^2}{3 I}\right), \text{ where } r = \text{radius of the circle}$$

When y = r i.e. at top and bottom,

$$q = S\left(\frac{r^2 - r^2}{3 I}\right) = 0$$

At the N.A., y = 0 and q is maximum.

$$\therefore \qquad q_{max} = S\left(\frac{r^2}{3 I}\right) = \frac{S \times \left(\frac{d}{2}\right)^2}{3 \frac{\pi}{64} d^4} \qquad \qquad \ldots\left(\because r = \frac{d}{2}, I = \frac{\pi}{64} d^4\right)$$

$$= \frac{16}{3}\frac{S}{\pi d^2} = \frac{4}{3}\frac{S}{\left(\frac{\pi}{4} d^2\right)} = \frac{4}{3} q_{av}$$

where $q_{av}$ = Average shear stress = $\dfrac{\text{S.F.}}{\text{Area}} = \dfrac{S}{\frac{\pi}{4} d^2}$

*Therefore, for a circular section, the maximum shear stress is 4/3 times the average shear stress.* The shear stress distribution diagram for a circular section is as shown in Fig. 5.40 (b).

1. Draw shear stress distribution diagram for a circular section and locate the position of maximum shear stress. **(B.T.E. S-2013/4 Marks)**

2. State the relation between $q_{max}$ and $q_{average}$ for a circular section. **(Imp./2 Marks)**

**(Most Likely and Asked in Previous B.T.E. Exam.)**

### Type 11 : Solved examples on shear stress distribution diagram for a circular section

**Important Formulae**

(i)   Area $A = \dfrac{\pi}{4} d^2$

(ii)  Average shear stress, $q_{av} = \dfrac{S}{A} = \dfrac{\text{Shear force}}{\text{Area}}$

(iii) Maximum shear stress, $q_{max} = \dfrac{4}{3} \times q_{av}$.

**Example 37 :** *A beam of circular section, 300 mm in diameter is subjected to a shear force of 40 kN. Determine the maximum shear stress induced.* **(B.T.E. S-2003/2 Marks)**

**Data**      : Diameter d = 300 mm, shear force S = 40 kN = $40 \times 10^3$ N.

**To find**   : $q_{max}$.

**Concept :** $q_{max} = \dfrac{4}{3} q_{average}$ for circular section.

**Solution :** Area $A = \dfrac{\pi}{4} d^2 = \dfrac{\pi}{4} (300)^2 = 7.068 \times 10^4 \text{ mm}^2$

Average shear stress,   $q_{av} = \dfrac{S}{A} = \dfrac{40 \times 10^3}{7.068 \times 10^4} = 0.566 \text{ N/mm}^2$

For a circular section,

$$q_{max} = \dfrac{4}{3} q_{av} = \dfrac{4}{3} \times 0.566 = \textbf{0.75 N/mm}^2$$

**Answer :** $\boxed{q_{max} = 0.75 \text{ N/mm}^2}$

**Example 38 :** *Determine the concentrated load, when placed at the free end of a cantilever beam of length 1 m will produce a shear stress 1.5 N/mm². The cross-section is circular of diameter 100 mm.* **(B.T.E. S-2010/4 Marks)**

**Data :** A cantilever carrying point load W at free end,

L = 1 m, $q_{max} = 1.5 \text{ N/mm}^2$, d = 100 mm

**To find :** W.

**Concept :** $q_{max} = \dfrac{4}{3} q_{av} = \dfrac{4}{3} \times \dfrac{W}{A} = \dfrac{4}{3} \times \dfrac{W}{\dfrac{\pi}{4} d^2}$.

**Solution :** For a cantilever beam, maximum SF = W.

Maximum shear stress $= \dfrac{4}{3} \times$ Average shear stress

$$\therefore \qquad q_{max} = \frac{4}{3} \times \frac{W}{A}$$

$$\therefore \qquad 1.5 = \frac{4}{3} \times \frac{W}{\frac{\pi}{4} \times (100)^2}$$

$$\therefore \qquad W = 1.5 \times \frac{3}{4} \times \frac{\pi}{4} \times (100)^2 = 8831.25 \text{ N} = \textbf{8.831 kN}$$

**Answer :** $\boxed{W = 8.831 \text{ kN}}$

---

**Example 39 :** *A circular cross-section of beam, 200 mm in diameter carries a shear force of 20 kN. Find the maximum and average shear stress.* (B.T.E. W-2009/4 Marks)

**Answer :** $\boxed{q_{av} = 0.64 \text{ N/mm}^2, q_{max} = 0.85 \text{ N/mm}^2}$

---

**Example 40 :** *A circular beam of 105 mm diameter is subjected to a shear force of 10 kN. Calculate the maximum value of shear.* (B.T.E. S-1997/4 Marks)

**Answer :** $\boxed{q_{max} = 1.54 \text{ N/mm}^2}$

---

**Example 41 :** *A beam of circular cross-section 100 mm diameter is subjected to a shear force of 25 kN. Calculate the maximum shear stress at the neutral axis.* (B.T.E. W-1999/4 Marks)

**Answer :** $\boxed{q_{max} = 4.24 \text{ N/mm}^2}$

---

**Example 42 :** *A circular beam of 100 mm diameter is subjected to a shear force of 12.5 kN. Calculate the value of maximum shear stress and sketch the variation of shear stress along the depth of the beam.* (B.T.E. S-2005/4 Marks)

**Data** : Circular beam diameter d = 100 mm, shear force S = 12.5 kN = $12.5 \times 10^3$ N.

**To find** : $q_{max}$, shear stress variation diagram.

**Concept :** $q_{max} = \frac{4}{3} q_{av}$.

**Solution :** $\qquad$ Area A $= \frac{\pi}{4} d^2 = \frac{\pi}{4}(100)^2 = 7853.98$ mm²

Average shear stress, $\quad q_{av} = \frac{S}{A} = \frac{12.5 \times 10^3}{7853.98} = 1.59$ N/mm²

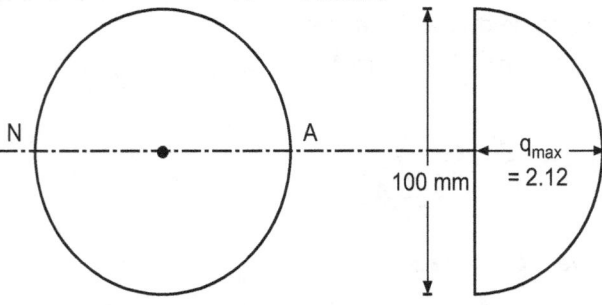

(a) Cross-section $\qquad$ (b) Shear stress distribution (N/mm²)

**Fig. 5.41**

For a circular section,

$$q_{max} = q_{NA} = \frac{4}{3} q_{av} = \frac{4}{3} \times 1.59 = \textbf{2.12 N/mm}^2$$

**Answer :** The shear stress distribution diagram is as shown in Fig. 5.41 (b). $q_{max} = 2.12$ N/mm$^2$

## 5.16 SHEAR STRESS DISTRIBUTION DIAGRAM FOR A HOLLOW RECTANGULAR SECTION

A hollow rectangular section is symmetrical about the N.A. So the shear stress distribution diagram is also symmetrical about the N.A. as shown in Fig. 5.42.

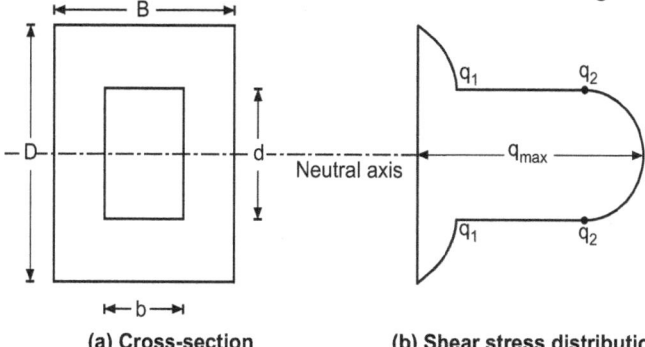

(a) Cross-section　　　　(b) Shear stress distribution

**Fig. 5.42**

After studying the shear stress distribution diagrams, it can be seen that, shear stress variation for any section is of parabolic nature. Shear stress at the extreme layers (i.e. at the top and bottom) is zero. Shear stress at the N.A. is maximum.

At the junction of the flange and the web, there is a sudden change in the width. Hence there is a sudden change in the shear stress at this junction. Since these two shear stresses are at the same distance from the N.A., the *shear stress distribution diagram at the junction is a straight line. For the remaining portion, it follows the usual parabolic variation.*

1. Draw shear stress distribution diagram for a hollow rectangular section.

**(B.T.E. W-2010/2 Marks)**

**(Most Likely and Asked in Previous B.T.E. Exam.)**

**Type 12 : Solved examples on shear stress distribution diagram for a hollow rectangular section**

| Important Formulae |
| --- |

**Steps :**

(i) Find I, $\quad I = \frac{1}{12}(BD^3 - bd^3)$.

(ii) Find A, $\quad A = BD - bd$.

(iii) Find $q_{av}$, $\quad q_{av} = \frac{S}{A}$.

Refer to Fig. 5.42.

(iv)   Find $q_1$,       $q_1$ = shear stress at bottom of flange by taking width as B.

(v)    Find $q_2$,       $q_2$ = shear stress at bottom of flange by taking width as B-b or 2t

where       t = thickness of rectangle

(vi)   Find $q_{NA}$ or $q_{max}$,

$$q_{max} = q_2 + q_{additional}$$

where $q_{additional}$ is the additional shear stress due to web area above (or below) N.A.

(vii)  Knowing $q_1$, $q_2$ and $q_{max}$, shear stress distribution diagram can be drawn as shown in Fig. 5.42.

**Example 43 :** *A hollow rectangular beam section square in size having outer dimensions 120 mm × 120 mm with thickness of material 20 mm is carrying a shear force of 125 kN. Calculate the maximum shear stress induced in the section.* (B.T.E. W-2010, 2005/4 Marks)

**Data**     : B = D = 120 mm, t = 20 mm, b = d = 120 – 2t = 120 – 2 × 20 = 80 mm,
S = 125 kN = 125 × 10³ N

**To find** : $q_{max}$.

**Concept :** (i)    Calculating $q_1$, $q_2$, $q_{additional}$ and $q_{max}$.

(ii)   $q_{max} = q_2 + q_{additional}$

**Solution :** Refer to Fig. 5.43.

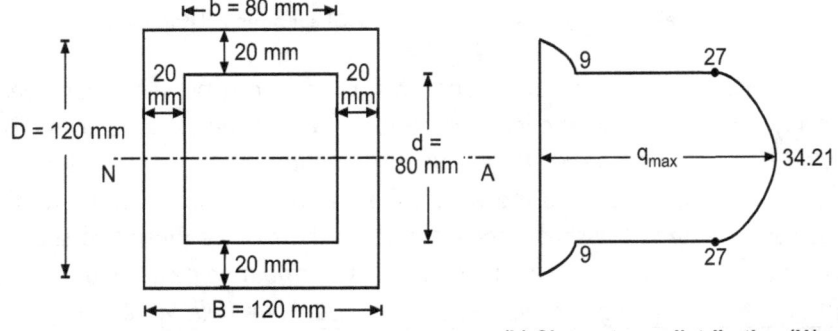

(a) Cross section

(b) Shear stress distribution (N/mm²)

**Fig. 5.43**

(i)   M.I. of section about its neutral axis,

$$I = \frac{1}{12}(BD^3 - bd^3) = \frac{1}{12}(120 \times 120^3 - 80 \times 80^3)$$

$$= 13866666.67 \text{ mm}^4$$

(ii)       Area of section, A = BD – bd = 120 × 120 – 80 × 80 = 8000 mm²

(iii)      $$q_{av} = \frac{S}{A} = \frac{125 \times 10^3}{8000} = 15.625 \text{ N/mm}^2$$

(iv) Now, let us consider the area above N.A.

$q_1$ = Shear stress at the bottom of flange by taking width (b = 120 mm)

$$= \frac{S\,A\bar{y}}{I\,b} = \frac{(125 \times 10^3)\,(120 \times 20)\left(60 - \dfrac{20}{2}\right)}{13866666.67 \times 120} = \textbf{9 N/mm}^2$$

(v)          $q_2$ = Shear stress at the bottom of flange by taking width (20 + 20 = 40 mm)

$$= q_1 \times \frac{120}{40} = \textbf{27 N/mm}^2$$

(vi) Width at N.A. = 20 + 20 = 40 mm

Now, web area above the N.A.,

$$A = 2 \times (40 \times 20) = 1600 \text{ mm}^2$$

C.G. of this area from the N.A.,

$$\bar{y} = \frac{40}{2} = 20 \text{ mm}$$

∴   Additional shear stress due to web area above the N.A. is given by,

$$q_{additional} = \frac{S\,A\bar{y}}{Ib} = \frac{(125 \times 10^3)\,(1600)\,(20)}{13866666.67\,(40)} = 7.21 \text{ N/mm}^2$$

∴   $\textbf{q}_{NA} = \textbf{q}_{max} = q_2 + q_{additional}$

$$= 27 + 7.21 = \textbf{34.21 N/mm}^2$$

The shear stress distribution diagram is symmetrical about the N.A. as shown in Fig. 5.43 (b).

$$\frac{q_{max}}{q_{av}} = \frac{34.21}{15.625} = 2.19$$

**Answer :**   $\boxed{q_{max} = q_{NA} = 34.21 \text{ N/mm}^2}$

---

### Type 13 : Miscellaneous examples

**Example 44 :** *A rectangular beam 100 mm wide is subjected to a maximum shear force of 50 kN. The maximum shear stress induced is 4 N/mm². Find the depth of the beam.*

**(B.T.E. S-2001/4 Marks)**

**Data**      : Rectangular section b = 100 mm, S = $50 \times 10^3$ N, $q_{max}$ = 4 N/mm²

**To find**   : d.

**Concept :**   Find $q_{av}$ in terms of d (depth of beam) and use the relation between $q_{max}$ and $q_{av}$.

**Solution :**          $q_{av} = \dfrac{S}{A} = \dfrac{S}{b\,d} = \dfrac{50 \times 10^3}{100 \times d}$

For a rectangular section,

$$q_{max} = 1.5 \times q_{av}$$

∴                $4 = 1.5 \times \dfrac{50 \times 10^3}{100 \times d}$

**Answer :**      $\boxed{\textbf{d} = \textbf{187.5 mm}}$

**Example 45 :** *A circular beam is subjected to a maximum shear force of 5 kN. The maximum shear stress induced is 0.8 N/mm². Find the diameter of the beam.*　　**(4 Marks)**

**Data**　　　: Circular beam, $S = 5 \times 10^3$ N, $q_{max} = 0.8$ N/mm²

**To find** : d.

**Concept :** Find $q_{av}$ in terms of d (diameter of circular beam) and use the relation between $q_{max}$ and $q_{av}$.

**Solution :**
$$q_{av} = \frac{S}{A} = \frac{5 \times 10^3}{(\pi/4)\, d^2}$$

For a circular section, $q_{max} = \frac{4}{3} \times q_{av}$

∴
$$0.8 = \frac{4}{3} \times \frac{5 \times 10^3}{\frac{\pi}{4} d^2}$$

**Answer :** $\boxed{d = 103 \text{ mm}}$

## Practice Questions

### Questions of 2 Marks

1. Draw a shear stress distribution diagram for a hollow rectangular section.

   **(B.T.E. W-2010)**

2. Explain the concept of shear stress with neat sketch.　　**(B.T.E. W-2008)**

3. Draw shear stress distribution diagram for T section and locate the position of maximum shear stress.　　**(B.T.E. W-2006, 2003)**

4. Differentiate between single shear and double shear.　　**(B.T.E. S-2013, 1997)**

5. Explain with sketch single shear failure in rivetted joint.　　**(B.T.E. S-1999)**

6. Explain by giving example, the double shear failure in case of rivetted joint.

   **(B.T.E. W-1999)**

7. What is shear stress distribution formula ? Write the meaning of symbols used.

   **(B.T.E. S-1998)**

8. Draw a shear stress distribution diagram for a circular section.　　**(B.T.E. S-1997)**

9. Draw a shear stress distribution diagram for a triangular section.　　**(B.T.E. S-1998)**

10. Draw a shear stress distribution diagram for a solid rectangular section.

11. What is the relation between maximum shear stress and average shear stress for a rectangular section ?　　**(B.T.E. W-1998)**

12. What is the relation between maximum shear stress and average shear stress for a circular section ?　　**(B.T.E. W-1997)**

13. The average shear stress across certain rectangular cross-section is 190 N/mm². Calculate the maximum shear stress at this section. **(B.T.E. S-2000)**

14. The maximum shear stress across certain circular cross-section is 200 N/mm². Calculate its average shear stress. **(B.T.E. W-2000)**

### Questions of 4 Marks

15. State the shear stress equation and explain meaning of each term. **(B.T.E. S-2013)**

16. Draw shear stress distribution diagram for circular section and locate the position of maximum shear stress. **(B.T.E. S-2013)**

### Problems of 4 Marks

17. The cross-section of a beam is a rectangle 50 mm × 150 mm. The maximum shear stress is 10 MPa. Calculate the shear stress at

    (i)  75 mm above the N.A.      (ii)  50 mm below the N.A.

    **(Ans.** (i) At 75 mm above the N.A. i.e. at the top, q = 0

    (ii) At 50 mm below the N.A., q = 5.55 N/mm²)

18. A beam 100 mm wide and 250 mm deep is subjected to a S.F. of 40 kN at a certain section. Find the maximum shear stress and draw the shear stress variation diagram.

    **(Ans.** $q_{max}$ = 2.4 N/mm²)

19. A beam of solid circular section 25 cm diameter is subjected to a S.F. of 5 kN at a certain section. Determine the maximum shear stress induced and draw the shear stress variation diagram. **(Ans.** $q_{max}$ = 0.136 N/mm²)

20. A hollow square section 100 mm × 100 mm outside dimensions and 20 mm thick is subjected to a S.F. of 75 kN. Draw the shear stress distribution diagram and find the ratio of maximum shear stress to average shear stress.

    $$\left( \textbf{Ans. } q_{max} = 25.33 \text{ N/mm}^2 , \frac{q_{max}}{q_{av}} = 2.16 \text{ N/mm}^2 \right)$$

21. A simply supported beam of span 3 m and cross-section 150 mm × 300 mm carries a central point load W. If the maximum value of shear stress is 3 N/mm², find the value of W. **(Ans.** W = 180 kN)

22. A rectangular beam 200 mm wide is subjected to a maximum S.F. of 30 kN. If the maximum shear stress induced is 1 N/mm², find the depth of the beam.

    **(Ans.** d = 225 mm)

23. A cantilever beam of solid circular section of diameter 150 mm is subjected to a point load W at its free end. If the maximum shear stress is 4 N/mm$^2$, find the value of W. **(Ans.** W = 53 kN)

24. A circular beam is subjected to a maximum S.F. of 6 kN. If the maximum shear stress is 0.24 N/mm$^2$, find the diameter of the beam. **(Ans.** d = 206 mm)

## Important Points

- **Shear stresses :**

  The internal stresses induced in the beam section which resist the shear force are called as shear stresses.

- **Shear stress equation :**

  In a simply supported beam subjected to some loading,

  $$q = \frac{S\,A\,\bar{y}}{I\,b}, \text{ where}$$

  q = Intensity of shear stress induced in a layer at a distance y from the N.A.

  A = Area of the beam above (or below) the layer under consideration.

  $\bar{y}$ = Distance of the c.g. of the area considered from the N.A.

  $A\,\bar{y}$ = Moment of area above (or below) the layer considered about the N.A.

  I = Moment of inertia of the whole cross-section about the N.A. = $I_{xx}$

  b = Width of the section at a distance y from the N.A.

- **Average shear stress :**

  It is calculated by the formula,

  $$q_{average} = \frac{S}{A}$$

  where,          S = S.F. at a section

  A = Area of the beam cross-section

- **Relation between q$_{max}$ and q$_{av}$ for some standard sections :**

  (a) For a rectangular section of size b × d : $q_{max} = 1.5 \times q_{av}$

  (b) For a circular section of diameter D : $q_{max} = 1.33\ q_{av}$

  ❑❑❑

# Chapter 6

# DIRECT AND BENDING STRESSES

| Weightage of Marks = 16, Teaching Hours = 07 |

## *Objectives*

Specific Objectives :

Acquire and apply knowledge of bending stresses and direct stresses.

## *Contents*

6.1 Concept of Axial load, Eccentric load, Direct stresses, Bending stresses, Maximum and Minimum stresses.

Stress distribution diagram. (4 Marks)

6.2 Problems on the above concepts for strut, Machine parts such as offset links, C-clamp, Bench vice, Drilling machine frame, etc. (8 Marks)

6.3 Condition for no tension in the section, Core of a section. (4 Marks)

| SUB-TOPIC 6.1 : CONCEPT OF AXIAL LOAD, ECCENTRIC LOAD, DIRECT STRESSES, BENDING STRESSES, MAXIMUM AND MINIMUM STRESSES, STRESS DISTRIBUTION DIAGRAM (4 Marks) |

## *Synopsis*

Introduction, Concept of direct load, Concept of an eccentric load, Analysis of an eccentric load, Resultant stress, Stress distribution at base, Uniaxial bending for short compression member, Uniaxial bending for tension member, Condition for no tension, Section modulus, Middle third rule, Core of a section, Core of a circular section.

## 6.1 INTRODUCTION

If a force passes through the centroid of the section then direct stress alone is produced in the body. But if the force is eccentric, it will cause direct as well as bending stresses in the section. As the direct and bending stresses act normal to a cross-section, the resultant stress at any point in the section can be calculated by taking the algebraic sum of direct and bending stresses.

## 6.2 CONCEPT OF DIRECT LOAD

**Definition :** *A load whose line of action coincides with the axis of a member is called an axial load or direct load.*

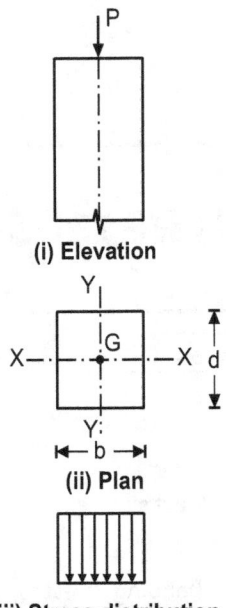

**(i) Elevation**

**(ii) Plan**

**(iii) Stress distribution**

**Fig. 6.1**

Let us consider a column of rectangular section of width b and thickness d carrying an axial compressive load P as shown in Fig. 6.1 (i). The load P acts exactly over the centroid G of the section. The load P causes a direct stress of compressive nature whose intensity is uniform throughout the cross-section i.e. the stress at any point in the cross-section is P/A. Hence the stress distribution diagram at the base of a column is a rectangle as shown in Fig. 6.1 (iii). Direct stress is denoted by $\sigma_o$.

Cross-sectional area of column, A = b × d

$$\text{Direct stress } \sigma_o = \frac{P}{A} = \frac{P}{b \times d} \text{ (Compressive)}$$

1.  Define the term direct load with formula.          **(B.T.E. S-2014, 2012/2 Marks)**
2.  Define the term direct stress with formula.

**(Most Likely and Asked in Previous B.T.E. Exam.)**

## 6.3 CONCEPT OF AN ECCENTRIC LOAD

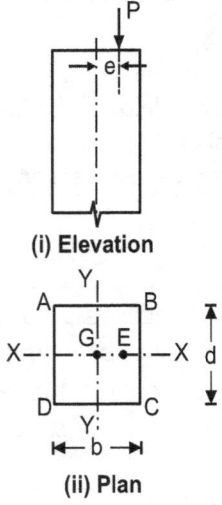

**(i) Elevation**

**(ii) Plan**

**Fig. 6.2**

**Definition :** *A load whose line of action does not coincide with the axis of a member is called an eccentric load. The distance between the geometric axis of the body and the point of loading is called an eccentric limit or limit of eccentricity. It is denoted by 'e'.*

Axial load causes only direct stress whereas an eccentric load causes direct as well as bending stresses.

Fig. 6.2 shows a column ABCD subjected to an eccentric compressive load P. The load P acts at point E in a plane bisecting the thickness i.e. on X-X axis i.e. it is eccentric with respect to Y-Y axis. The distance GE is called eccentricity.

*Note :*

(i) *X-X and Y-Y axes passing through the centroid G of the section are called principle axes.*

(ii) *The load may be eccentric w.r.t. Y-Y axis, w.r.t. X-X axis or w.r.t. both the axes.*

(iii) *If the load is eccentric w.r.t. Y-Y axis, bending of a member will occur about Y-Y axis. In such a case, Y-Y axis is taken as neutral axis and the moment of inertia of the section should be taken about Y-Y axis.*

(iv) *If the load is eccentric w.r.t. X-X axis, bending of a member will occur about X-X axis. In such a case, X-X axis is taken as neutral axis and the moment of inertia of the section should be taken about X-X axis.*

| | | |
|---|---|---|
| 1. | Define eccentric load and axial load. | **(B.T.E. W-2013, S-2013/2 Marks)** |
| 2. | Define the term limit of eccentricity. | **(B.T.E. S-2013, 2012; W-2008, 2000/2 Marks)** |
| 3. | Define an eccentric load. | **(B.T.E. S-2014, W-2012/2 Marks)** |
| 4. | What do you understand by an eccentric load ? | **(B.T.E. W-2009/2 Marks)** |
| 5. | What is eccentric loading ? State two examples of eccentric loading. | |
| | | **(B.T.E. S-2009/2 Marks)** |

**(Most Likely and Asked in Previous B.T.E. Exam.)**

## 6.4 ANALYSIS OF AN ECCENTRIC LOAD
## (Direct Stresses and Bending Stresses)

Let us consider a column ABCD subjected to an eccentric load P at point E. Let G be the centroid of the section. Distance GE = e.

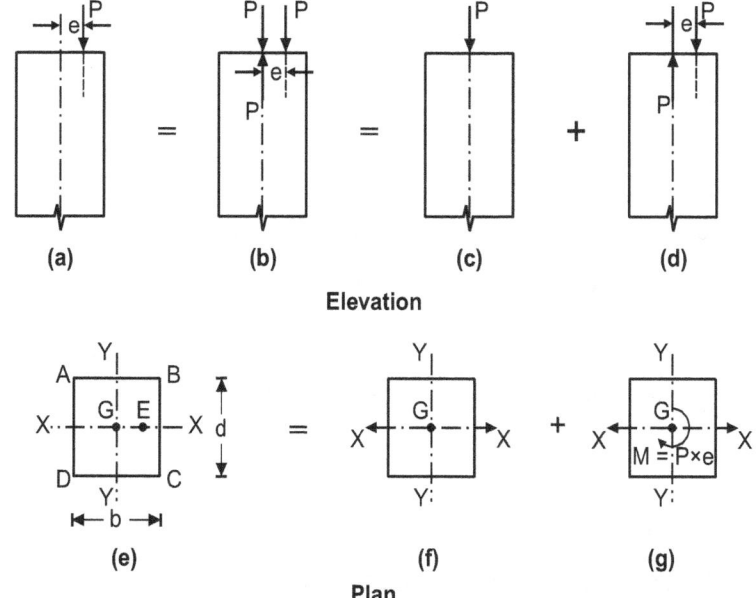

Eccentric load at E ≡ Direct load at G  +  Moment at G

**Fig. 6.3**

Introduce two equal and opposite forces P along the axis of the column as shown in Fig. 6.3 (b). Application of these equal, opposite and collinear forces does not change the loading pattern of the column as their resultant is zero. The three forces can be split up into a downward axial force P [Fig. 6.3 (c)] and a couple [Fig. 6.3 (d)]. The downward force P acting at the centroid G [Fig. 6.3 (f)] will cause a *direct stress*. The remaining two forces viz. a downward eccentric force P and an upward axial force P will form a clockwise couple whose moment at the centroid G will be M = P × e. This moment acting at the centroid G [Fig. 6.3 (g)] will cause a bending stress. *Thus a body subjected to an eccentric loading causes direct as well as bending stresses.*

---

1. Explain with diagram, how direct and bending stresses are developed in a column due to an eccentric load.                    **(B.T.E. S-2008/2 Marks)**

---

**(Most Likely and Asked in Previous B.T.E. Exam.)**

## 6.4.1 Resultant Stress (Maximum and Minimum Stress)

*Direct stress due to eccentric load P,*

$$\boxed{\sigma_o = \frac{P}{A}}$$                    ... (i)

### Bending stress due to eccentric load P :

This can be calculated by using bending stress equation i.e. flexural formula.

$$\frac{M}{I} = \frac{\sigma_b}{y}$$

∴                    $$\sigma_b = \frac{M}{I} \times y = \frac{M}{(I/y)}$$

∴                    $$\boxed{\sigma_b = \frac{M}{Z}}$$                    ... (ii)

where          I = M.I. of the column section about the neutral axis Y-Y = $db^3/12$

y = Distance of the layer from the neutral axis Y-Y

$\sigma_b$ = Bending stress in a layer at a distance y from the neutral axis

Z = Section modulus = $\dfrac{I}{y}$

**The resultant stress at any layer at a distance y from the neutral axis Y-Y is given by,**

$\sigma_r$ = **Direct stress ± Bending stress**

= $\sigma_o \pm \sigma_b$

$\sigma_{max} = \sigma_o + \sigma_b$

$\sigma_{min} = \sigma_o - \sigma_b$

## 6.4.2 Stress Distribution at Base (Stress Distribution Diagrams)

Refer to Fig. 6.3. Due to bending moment M = P × e, acting at the centroid G, the portion to the right of Y-Y axis will be subjected to compressive stress and the portion to the left of Y-Y axis will be subjected to tensile stress. Hence, $\sigma_b$ will be compressive for BC and tensile for AD. Since the corners B and C are nearer to the load P, the maximum stress will be produced at the corners B and C. Since the corners A and D are away from the load P, the minimum stress will be produced at the corners A and D.

Resultant stress on side BC,

$$\sigma_{max} = \text{Direct stress + Bending stress} = \sigma_o + \sigma_b = \frac{P}{A} + \frac{M}{Z} \text{ (Compressive)}$$

Resultant stress on side AD,

$$\sigma_{min} = \text{Direct stress − Bending stress} = \sigma_o - \sigma_b = \frac{P}{A} - \frac{M}{Z}$$

Nature of $\sigma_{min}$ depends upon the magnitudes of $\sigma_o$ and $\sigma_b$.

**Note : For calculating the bending stress at the extreme layers BC and AD, y should be taken as $y_{max}$. Here $y_{max} = b/2$.**

For calculating the resultant stress due to eccentric loading as shown in Fig. 6.3, three cases are possible.

(i) If $\sigma_o > \sigma_b$, the stress throughout the section will be of the same nature i.e. compressive.

(ii) If $\sigma_o = \sigma_b$, then also the stress throughout the section will be of the same nature i.e. compressive.

In this case, $\sigma_{max} = 2\sigma_o$ and $\sigma_{min} = 0$.

(iii) If $\sigma_o < \sigma_b$, the stress will be partly tensile and partly compressive.

The stress distribution diagrams for the above three cases are as shown in Fig. 6.4.

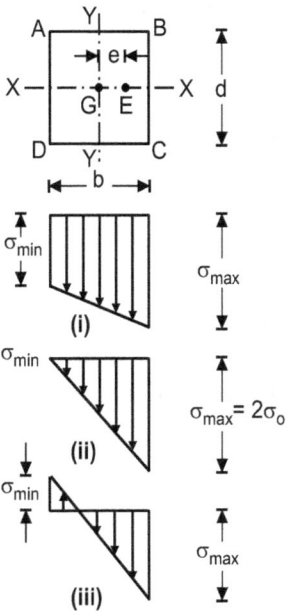

Eccentric compressive load at E

Stress distribution totally compressive
$\sigma_o > \sigma_b$

Stress distribution totally compressive
$\sigma_o = \sigma_b$

Stress distribution partly tensile
and partly compressive
$\sigma_o < \sigma_b$

**Fig. 6.4**

1.  Define direct and bending stresses. Draw the stress distribution diagram if a rectangular section is subjected to direct and bending stresses.
    **(B.T.E. S-2014, W-2012, 2011/4 Marks)**

2.  Sketch the resultant stress distribution at the base section for the condition that direct stress is equal to bending stress.    **(B.T.E. W-2013, 2008, 1998/2 Marks)**

    **OR**

    In case of combined stress, direct stress is equal to bending stress. Draw the nature of total stress distribution diagram across the section.
    **(B.T.E. W-2010, 2000; S-2000/2 Marks)**

3.  Draw the nature of total stress variation diagram if direct stress is less than bending stress.    **(B.T.E. S-2008/2 Marks)**

4.  Draw the nature of total stress variation diagram if direct stress is more than bending stress.    **(VV Imp/2 Marks)**

**(Most Likely and Asked in Previous B.T.E. Exam.)**

## 6.5 UNIAXIAL BENDING FOR SHORT COMPRESSION MEMBER

Bending of a member about one principle axis i.e. X-X or Y-Y is called uniaxial bending. In the previous article, we have seen bending of a compressive member carrying load P on X-X axis.

Now, let us assume that the compressive load P acts at point E on the Y-Y axis i.e. it is eccentric w.r.t. X-X axis as shown in Fig. 6.5.

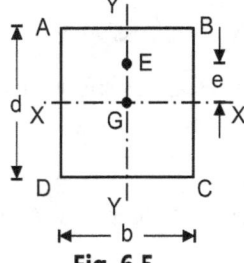

**Fig. 6.5**

In this case,

$$\sigma_o = P/A \text{ (compressive)}$$

$$\sigma_b = \pm \frac{M}{I_{xx}} \cdot y_{max}$$

$$= \pm \frac{P \cdot e}{bd^3/12} \times \left(\frac{d}{2}\right)$$

... (compressive for AB and tensile for CD)

$$\sigma_r \text{ on side AB} = \sigma_{max} = \sigma_o + \sigma_b \text{ (Compressive)}$$

$$\sigma_r \text{ on side CD} = \sigma_{min} = \sigma_o - \sigma_b$$

Nature of $\sigma_{min}$ depends upon the magnitudes of $\sigma_o$ and $\sigma_b$.

In this case, side AB will be subjected to maximum stress since it is nearer to the load and side CD will be subjected to minimum stress being away from the load.

## 6.6 UNIAXIAL BENDING FOR TENSION MEMBER

Refer to Fig. 6.4. *Let us assume that load P at E is tensile.*

Then
$$\sigma_o = \frac{P}{A} \text{ (tensile)},$$

$$\sigma_b = \pm \frac{M}{I_{YY}} \times y_{max}$$

$$= \pm \frac{P \cdot e}{I_{YY}} \times \frac{b}{2}$$

... (tensile for BC and compressive for AD)

$\sigma_r$ on side BC $= \sigma_{max} = \sigma_o + \sigma_b$ (tensile)

$\sigma_r$ on side AD $= \sigma_{min} = \sigma_o - \sigma_b$

Nature of $\sigma_{min}$ depends upon the magnitudes of $\sigma_o$ and $\sigma_b$. Stress distribution diagram will be totally tensile if $\sigma_o > \sigma_b$ and $\sigma_o = \sigma_b$. If $\sigma_o < \sigma_b$, stress will be partly tensile and partly compressive.

Now, refer to Fig. 6.5. *Let us assume that the load P at E is tensile.*

Then $\qquad \sigma_o = \dfrac{P}{A}$ (tensile) ,

$$\sigma_b = \pm \dfrac{M}{I_{xx}} \times y_{max}$$

$$= \pm \dfrac{P \cdot e}{I_{xx}} \times \dfrac{d}{2} \qquad \text{... (tensile for AB and compressive for CD)}$$

$\sigma_r$ on side AB $= \sigma_{max} = \sigma_o + \sigma_b$ (tensile)

$\sigma_r$ on side CD $= \sigma_{min} = \sigma_o - \sigma_b$

Nature of $\sigma_{min}$ depends upon the magnitudes of $\sigma_o$ and $\sigma_b$.

## SOLVED EXAMPLES

### Type 1 : Examples based on compression member

**Note :** In such type of examples, compressive stress is taken as positive and tensile stress as negative.

---

**Important Formulae**

(i)   Direct stress, $\qquad \sigma_o = \dfrac{P}{A}$

(ii)  Bending stress, $\qquad \sigma_b = \dfrac{M}{Z_{YY}}$ (if the load is eccentric w.r.t. YY axis)

       Bending stress, $\qquad \sigma_b = \dfrac{M}{Z_{XX}}$ (if the load is eccentric w.r.t. XX axis)

(iii)               $\sigma_{max} = \sigma_o + \sigma_b$ (compressive)

                $\sigma_{min} = \sigma_o - \sigma_b$ (compressive if $\sigma_o > \sigma_b$ and tensile if $\sigma_o < \sigma_b$)

(iv)  If $\sigma_o > \sigma_b$, the stress distribution diagram is totally compressive.

     If $\sigma_o = \sigma_b$, the stress distribution diagram is totally compressive

                $\sigma_{max} = 2\sigma_o$ and $\sigma_{min} = 0$.

     If $\sigma_o < \sigma_b$, the stress distribution diagram is partly tensile and partly compressive.

---

To calculate $\sigma_o$, we require values of A for different sections.

## Note : Values of A for different sections :

(a) For a rectangular column of size $b \times d$, $A = b \times d$.

(b) For a column of hollow rectangular section $A = BD - bd$.

(c) For a column of solid circular section, $A = \dfrac{\pi}{4} D^2$.

(d) For a column of hollow circular section, $A = \dfrac{\pi}{4} (D^2 - d^2)$.

To calculate $\sigma_b$ we require values of Z for different sections.

## Note : Values of Z for different sections :

1. For a column of rectangular section of width b and depth d,

$$Z_{XX} = \frac{I_{XX}}{y_{max}} = \frac{bd^3/12}{d/2} = \frac{bd^2}{6}$$

$$Z_{YY} = \frac{I_{YY}}{y_{max}} = \frac{db^3/12}{b/2} = \frac{db^2}{6}$$

2. For a column of hollow rectangular section having external dimensions B and D and internal dimensions b and d,

$$Z_{XX} = \frac{I_{XX}}{y_{max}} = \frac{\dfrac{BD^3 - bd^3}{12}}{\dfrac{D}{2}} = \frac{BD^3 - bd^3}{6D}, \quad Z_{YY} = \frac{I_{YY}}{y_{max}} = \frac{\dfrac{DB^3 - db^3}{12}}{\dfrac{B}{2}} = \frac{DB^3 - db^3}{6B}$$

3. For a column of solid circular section of diameter D,

$$Z = Z_{XX} = Z_{YY} = \frac{I}{y_{max}} = \frac{\dfrac{\pi}{64} D^4}{\dfrac{D}{2}} = \frac{\pi}{32} D^3$$

4. For a column of hollow circular section of external diameter D and internal diameter d,

$$Z = Z_{XX} = Z_{YY} = \frac{1}{y_{max}} = \frac{\dfrac{\pi}{64} (D^4 - d^4)}{\left(\dfrac{D}{2}\right)} = \frac{\pi}{32} \left(\frac{D^4 - d^4}{D}\right)$$

## Type 1.1 : Examples on column of solid rectangular section :

**Example 1 :** *A column section 200 mm wide and 150 mm thick is subjected to a load of 200 kN at an eccentricity of 20 mm in a plane bisecting the thickness. Find the maximum and minimum intensities of stress in the section.* **(B.T.E. S-2013/4 Marks)**

**Data**     :     Width b = 200 mm, thickness d = 150 mm,

P = 200 kN, eccentricity e = 20 mm, load P = $200 \times 10^3$ N

**To find** :     $\sigma_{max}$ and $\sigma_{min}$

**Concept :**    Axis of bending is YY axis. The load is eccentric w.r.t. YY axis. So we have to consider $Z_{YY}$ (or $I_{YY}$).

**Solution :**   Area of section,

$$A = b \times d = 200 \times 150 = 3 \times 10^4 \text{ mm}^2$$

Direct stress,    $\sigma_o = \dfrac{P}{A}$

$$= \dfrac{200 \times 10^3}{3 \times 10^4}.$$

$$= 6.67 \text{ N/mm}^2 \text{ (Compressive)}$$

Bending stress,  $\sigma_b = \dfrac{M}{Z_{YY}} = \dfrac{P \times e}{db^2/6} = \dfrac{6\,Pe}{db^2}$

$$= \dfrac{6 \times 200 \times 10^3 \times 20}{150 \times 200^2}$$

$$= 4 \text{ N/mm}^2$$

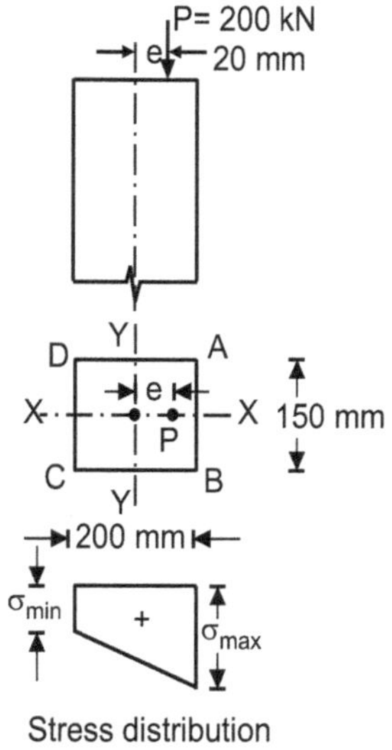

Fig. 6.6

**Answer :**

$\sigma_{\textbf{max}} = \sigma_o + \sigma_b = 6.67 + 4$

$\qquad = \textbf{10.67 N/mm}^2 \textbf{ (Compressive on face AB)}$

$\sigma_{\textbf{min}} = \sigma_o - \sigma_b = 6.67 - 4$

$\qquad = \textbf{2.67 N/mm}^2 \textbf{ (Compressive on face CD)}$

The stress distribution diagram is totally compressive as shown in Fig. 6.6.

***Note : While solving problem on direct and bending stresses, compressive stresses are plotted below the base line and tensile stresses above the base line.***

**Example 2 :** *A rectangular column is 200 mm wide and 100 mm thick. It is subjected to a load of 180 kN at an eccentricity of 100 mm in the plane bisecting the thickness. Draw the combined stress distribution diagram showing their values.* **(B.T.E. S-2008/4 Marks)**

**Data**      :   Width b = 200 mm, thickness d = 100 mm, load P = 180 kN = $180 \times 10^3$ N,

eccentricity e = 100 mm.

**To find**   :   $\sigma_{max}$ and $\sigma_{min}$, to draw combined stress distribution diagram.

**Concept**  :   Axis of bending is YY axis. The load is eccentric w.r.t. YY axis. So we have to consider $Z_{YY}$ (or $I_{YY}$).

**Solution** :   Area of section,

$$A = b \times d = 200 \times 100 = 2 \times 10^4 \text{ mm}^2$$

Direct stress, $\sigma_o = \dfrac{P}{A}$

$$= \frac{180 \times 10^3}{2 \times 10^4}$$

$$= 9 \text{ N/mm}^2 \text{ (Compressive)}$$

Bending stress, $\sigma_b = \dfrac{M}{Z_{YY}}$

$$= \frac{P \times e}{db^2/6}$$

$$= \frac{6 P \times e}{db^2}$$

$$= \frac{6 \times 180 \times 10^3 \times 100}{100 \times 200^2}$$

$$= 27 \text{ N/mm}^2$$

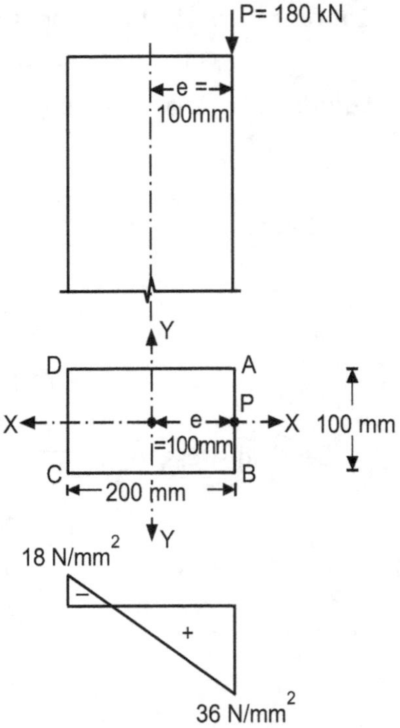

**Fig. 6.7 : Stress distribution**

$$\sigma_{max} = \sigma_o + \sigma_b = 9 + 27$$

$$= \textbf{36 N/mm}^2 \textbf{ (Compressive on face AB)}$$

$$\sigma_{min} = \sigma_o - \sigma_b = 9 - 27 = -18 \text{ N/mm}^2$$

$$= \textbf{18 N/mm}^2 \textbf{ (Tensile on face CD)}$$

Since $\sigma_o < \sigma_b$, the stress distribution diagram is partly tensile and partly compressive as shown in Fig. 6.7.

**Answer :** $\boxed{\sigma_{max} = 36 \text{ N/mm}^2 \text{ (Compressive on face AB)}, \sigma_{min} = 18 \text{ N/mm}^2 \text{ (Tensile on face CD)}}$

**Example 3 :** *A rectangular column 150 mm wide and 100 mm thick carries a load of 150 kN at an eccentricity of 50 mm in the plane bisecting the thickness. Find $\sigma_{max}$ and $\sigma_{min}$.*

**(B.T.E. S-2015, 2012, W-2007/4 Marks)**

**Data** : Width b = 150 mm, thickness d = 100 mm, load P = 150 kN = $150 \times 10^3$ N, eccentricity e = 50 mm.

**To find** : $\sigma_{max}$ and $\sigma_{min}$.

**Concept** : Same as the above example.

**Solution** : Area of section,

$$A = b \times d = 150 \times 100 = 15 \times 10^3 \text{ mm}^2$$

Direct stress, $\sigma_o = \dfrac{P}{A}$

$= \dfrac{150 \times 10^3}{15 \times 10^3}$

$= 10 \text{ N/mm}^2 \text{ (Compressive)}$

Bending stress, $\sigma_b = \dfrac{M}{Z_{YY}}$

$= \dfrac{P \times e}{db^2/6}$

$= \dfrac{6 \, P \cdot e}{db^2}$

$= \dfrac{6 \times (150 \times 10^3) \times 50}{100 \times 150^2}$

$= 20 \text{ N/mm}^2$

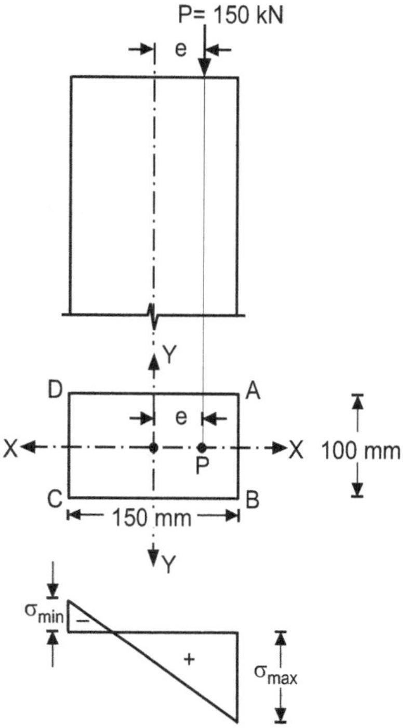

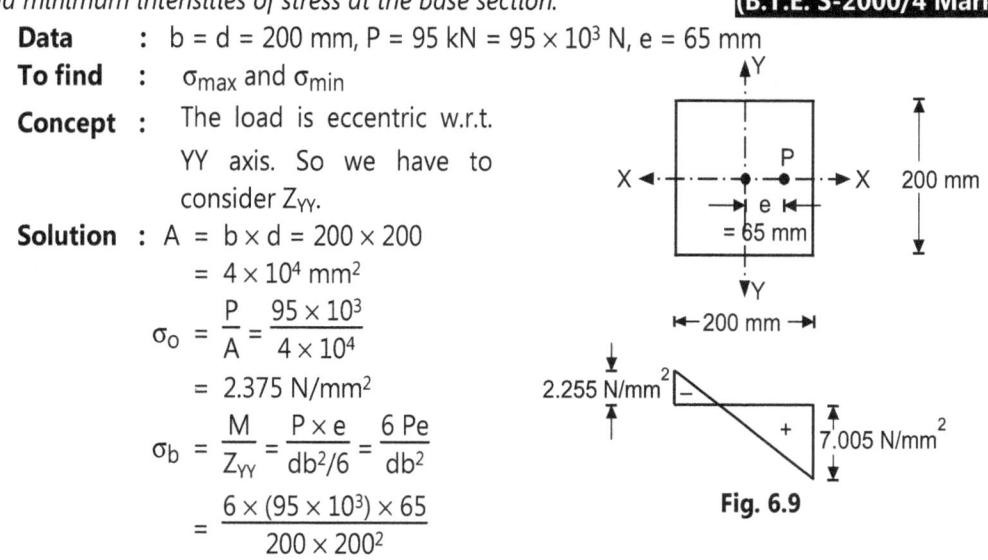

**Fig. 6.8 : Stress distribution**

**Answer :** $\boxed{\begin{array}{l} \sigma_{max} = \sigma_o + \sigma_b = 10 + 20 = \textbf{30 N/mm}^2 \textbf{ (Compressive on face AB)} \\ \sigma_{min} = \sigma_o - \sigma_b = 10 - 20 = -10 \text{ N/mm}^2 = \textbf{10 N/mm}^2 \textbf{ (Tensile on face CD)} \end{array}}$

**Note :** Since $\sigma_o < \sigma_b$, the stress distribution diagram is partly tensile and partly compressive as shown in Fig. 6.8.

**Example 4 :** *A short column 200 mm × 200 mm is subjected to an eccentric load of 95 kN at an eccentricity of 65 mm in the plane bisecting the two opposite faces. Find the maximum and minimum intensities of stress at the base section.* **(B.T.E. S-2000/4 Marks)**

**Data**     :  b = d = 200 mm, P = 95 kN = 95 × 10³ N, e = 65 mm

**To find**  :  $\sigma_{max}$ and $\sigma_{min}$

**Concept**  :  The load is eccentric w.r.t. YY axis. So we have to consider $Z_{YY}$.

**Solution** :  A = b × d = 200 × 200

$= 4 \times 10^4 \text{ mm}^2$

$\sigma_o = \dfrac{P}{A} = \dfrac{95 \times 10^3}{4 \times 10^4}$

$= 2.375 \text{ N/mm}^2$

$\sigma_b = \dfrac{M}{Z_{YY}} = \dfrac{P \times e}{db^2/6} = \dfrac{6 \, Pe}{db^2}$

$= \dfrac{6 \times (95 \times 10^3) \times 65}{200 \times 200^2}$

$= 4.63 \text{ N/mm}^2$

**Fig. 6.9**

**Answer :**

$$\sigma_{max} = \sigma_o + \sigma_b = 2.375 + 4.63 = \textbf{7.005 N/mm}^2 \textbf{ (Compressive)}$$

$$\sigma_{min} = \sigma_o - \sigma_b = 2.375 - 4.63 = \textbf{– 2.255 N/mm}^2 \textbf{ (Tensile)}$$

**Example 5 :** *A short column 200 mm × 100 mm is subjected to an eccentric load of 60 kN at an eccentricity of 40 mm in the plane bisecting the 100 mm side. Find the maximum and minimum intensities of stresses at the base.* **(B.T.E. W-2014, 2011, S-1998/4 Marks)**

**Data** : $b = 200$ mm, $d = 100$ mm, $P = 60$ kN, $e = 40$ mm

**To find** : $\sigma_{max}$ and $\sigma_{min}$

**Concept :** The load is eccentric w.r.t. YY axis.
So we have to consider $Z_{YY}$.

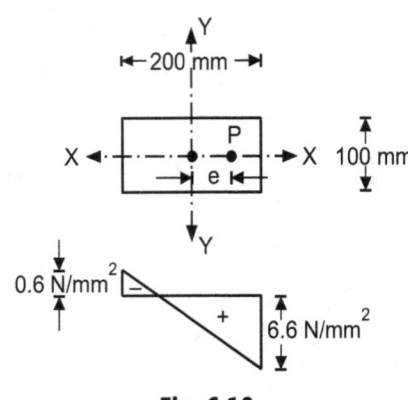

**Solution :** $A = b \times d = 200 \times 100$

$$= 2 \times 10^4 \text{ mm}^2$$

$$\sigma_o = \frac{P}{A} = \frac{60 \times 10^3}{2 \times 10^4} = 3 \text{ N/mm}^2$$

$$\sigma_b = \frac{M}{Z_{YY}} = \frac{P \times e}{db^2/6} = \frac{6 \, Pe}{db^2}$$

$$= \frac{6 \times (60 \times 10^3) \times 40}{100 \times 200^2}$$

$$= 3.6 \text{ N/mm}^2$$

**Fig. 6.10**

**Answer :**

$$\sigma_{max} = \sigma_o + \sigma_b = 3 + 3.6 = \textbf{6.6 N/mm}^2 \textbf{ (Compressive)}$$

$$\sigma_{min} = \sigma_o - \sigma_b = 3 - 3.6 = \textbf{– 0.6 N/mm}^2 \textbf{ (Tensile)}$$

## Type 1.2 : Examples on column of hollow rectangular section :

**Example 6 :** *A short column of hollow rectangular cross-section has external dimensions 2.4 m × 1.8 m and is 20 mm thick. It carries a vertical load of 500 kN at an eccentricity of 30 mm from the geometric axis of the section bisecting the longer side. Find $\sigma_{max}$ and $\sigma_{min}$.*

**(V.V. Imp.)**

**Data** : **Outer dimensions :** $B = 1800$ mm, $D = 2400$ mm

**Inner dimensions :** $b = 1800 – 20 – 20 = 1760$ mm, $d = 2400 – 20 – 20 = 2360$ mm,

Area $A = BD – bd = 1800 \times 2400 – 1760 \times 2360 = 166400$ mm$^2$,

Eccentricity $e = 30$ mm,  Load $P = 500$ kN $= 500 \times 10^3$ N

**To find** : $\sigma_{max}$ and $\sigma_{min}$

**Concept :** The load is eccentric w.r.t. YY axis. So we have to consider $Z_{YY}$ or $I_{YY}$.

**Solution :**   Section modulus,

$$Z_{YY} = \frac{I_{YY}}{y_{max}}$$

$$= \frac{\frac{1}{12}(DB^3 - db^3)}{B/2}$$

$$= \frac{1}{6}\frac{DB^3 - db^3}{B}$$

$$= \frac{1}{6}\frac{2400 \times 1800^3 - 2360 \times 1760^3}{1800}$$

$$= 104685985.2 \text{ mm}^3$$

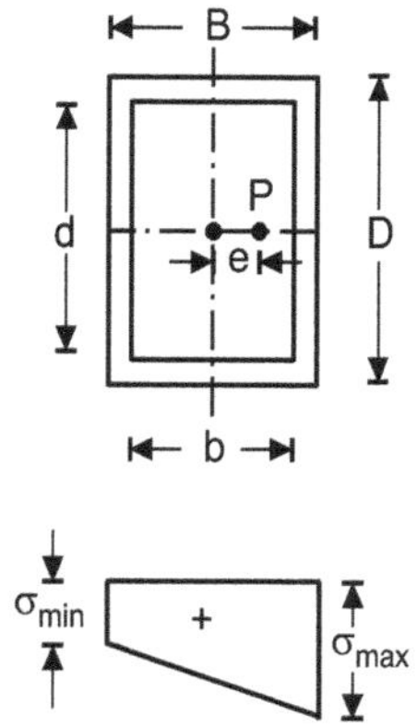

$$\sigma_o = \frac{P}{A} = \frac{500 \times 10^3}{166400}$$

$$= 3 \text{ N/mm}^2 \text{ (Compressive)}$$

$$\sigma_b = \frac{M}{Z_{YY}} = \frac{P \cdot e}{Z_{YY}} = \frac{500 \times 10^3 \times 30}{104685985.2} = 0.14 \text{ N/mm}^2$$

**Fig. 6.11**

**Answer :**

$$\boxed{\begin{array}{l} \sigma_{\textbf{max}} = \sigma_o + \sigma_b = 3 + 0.14 = \textbf{3.14 N/mm}^2 \textbf{ (Compressive)} \\ \sigma_{\textbf{min}} = \sigma_o - \sigma_b = 3 - 0.14 = \textbf{2.86 N/mm}^2 \textbf{ (Compressive)} \end{array}}$$

**Example 7 :** *A hollow column of rectangular section 600 mm × 300 mm overall and 500 mm × 250 mm internally carries a load of 15 kN which is of the geometric axis by 100 mm in the vertical plane bisecting the thickness i.e. 300 mm side. Calculate the extreme intensities of stress induced in the section.*    **(B.T.E. W-2005/4 Marks)**

**Data**    :    Hollow rectangle B = 600 mm, D = 300 mm, b = 500 mm, d = 250 mm,

P = 15 kN = $15 \times 10^3$ N, $e_y$ = 100 mm.

**To find**   :   $\sigma_{max}$, $\sigma_{min}$.

**Concept :**   The load is eccentric w.r.t. YY axis. So we have to calculate $I_{YY}$ and $Z_{YY}$.

**Solution :**   Area, A = BD − bd = 600 × 300 − 500 × 250 = 55000 mm².

Direct stress, $\sigma_o = \dfrac{P}{A} = \dfrac{15 \times 10^3}{55000} = \textbf{0.27 N/mm}^2 \textbf{ (Compressive)}$

The load is eccentric w.r.t. YY axis.

$$\therefore \quad I_{YY} = \frac{DB^3 - db^3}{12} = \frac{300 \times 600^3 - 250 \times 500^3}{12} = 2795833333 \text{ mm}^4$$

$$y_{max} = \frac{600}{2} = 300 \text{ mm}$$

$$Z_{YY} = \frac{I_{YY}}{y_{max}} = \frac{2795833333}{300} = 9319444.44 \text{ mm}^3$$

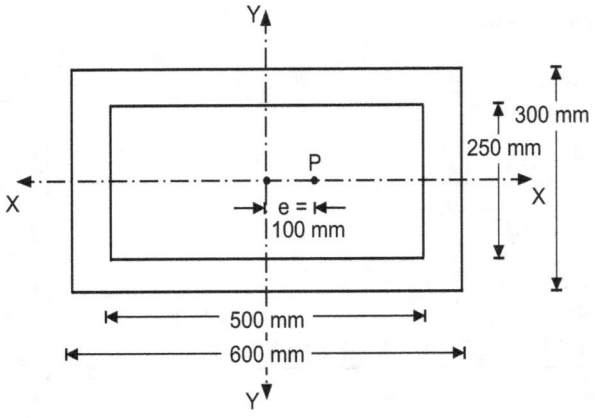

**Fig. 6.12**

Bending stress, $\sigma_b = \dfrac{M_{YY}}{Z_{YY}} = \dfrac{P \cdot e_y}{Z_{YY}} = \dfrac{(15 \times 10^3)\,(100)}{9319444.44} = \textbf{0.16 N/mm}^2$

**Answer :**

$$\sigma_{max} = \sigma_0 + \sigma_b = 0.27 + 0.16 = \textbf{0.43 N/mm}^2 \textbf{ (Compressive)}$$
$$\sigma_{min} = \sigma_0 - \sigma_b = 0.27 - 0.16 = \textbf{0.11 N/mm}^2 \textbf{ (Compressive)}$$

## Type 1.3 : Examples on column of solid circular section :

**Example 8 :** *A solid circular column of diameter 150 mm carries a vertical load of 50 kN at outer edge of the column. Calculate $\sigma_{max}$ and $\sigma_{min}$.* **(B.T.E. W-2004/8 Marks)**

**Data**     :    Diameter D = 150 mm, load P = 50 kN = $50 \times 10^3$ N,
                eccentricity e = R = D/2 = 150/2 = 75 mm

**To find**   :    $\sigma_{max}$ and $\sigma_{min}$.

**Concept**   :    The load acts at the outer edge of the column. So $e = \dfrac{D}{2} = \dfrac{150}{2} = 75$ mm.

**Solution :**

$\sigma_0 = \dfrac{P}{A} = \dfrac{50 \times 10^3}{\dfrac{\pi}{4} \times 150^2}$

     $= 2.83$ N/mm$^2$ (Compressive)

$Z = \dfrac{I}{y} = \dfrac{\dfrac{\pi}{64}D^4}{\dfrac{D}{2}} = \dfrac{\pi}{32}D^3$

     $= \dfrac{\pi}{32}150^3 = 331339.85$ mm$^3$

$\sigma_b = \dfrac{M}{Z} = \dfrac{Pe}{Z} = \dfrac{50 \times 10^3 \times 75}{331339.85}$

     $= 11.31$ N/mm$^2$

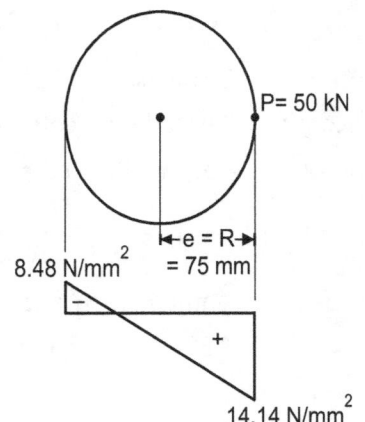

**Fig. 6.13 : Stress distribution diagram**

**Answer :**

$$\sigma_{max} = \sigma_0 + \sigma_b = 2.83 + 11.31 = \textbf{14.14 N/mm}^2 \textbf{ (Compressive)}$$
$$\sigma_{min} = \sigma_0 - \sigma_b = 2.83 - 11.31 = \textbf{– 8.48 N/mm}^2 \textbf{ (Tensile)}$$

### Type 1.4 : Examples on column of hollow circular section :

**Example 9 :** *A hollow circular column having external and internal diameters of 40 cm and 30 cm respectively, carries a vertical load of 150 kN at the outer edge of the column. Calculate the maximum and minimum intensities of stress in the section.*

**(B.T.E. S-2015, 2009/4 Marks)**

**Data** : $D = 40$ cm $= 400$ mm, $d = 30$ cm $= 300$ mm, $P = 150$ kN $= 150 \times 10^3$ N,

$e = \dfrac{D}{2} = 200$ mm (since load acts at outer edge of the column)

**To find** : $\sigma_{max}, \sigma_{min}$.

**Concept** : Direct and bending stresses; axis of bending = diameter normal to the diameter on which load acts ($Z_{XX} = Z_{YY}$).

**Solution** : $A = \dfrac{\pi}{4}(D^2 - d^2) = \dfrac{\pi}{4}(400^2 - 300^2) = 54977.87$ mm$^2$

$$Z = \frac{I}{y} = \frac{\dfrac{\pi}{64}(D^4 - d^4)}{\dfrac{D}{2}} = \frac{\pi}{32}\left(\frac{D^4 - d^4}{D}\right)$$

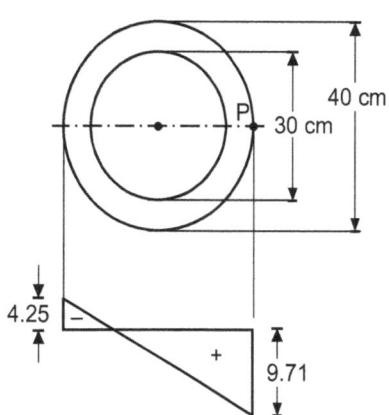

$$= \frac{\pi}{32}\left[\frac{400^4 - 300^4}{400}\right]$$

$$= 4295146.21 \text{ mm}^3$$

$$\sigma_o = \frac{P}{A}$$

$$= \frac{150 \times 10^3}{54977.87} = 2.73 \text{ N/mm}^2$$

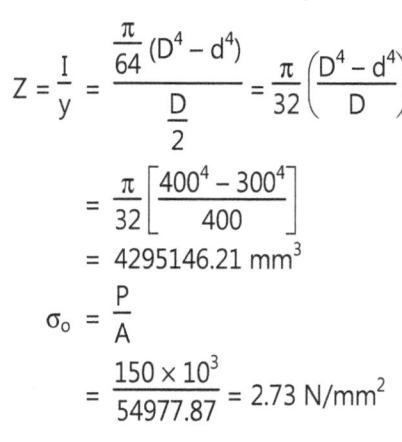

**Fig. 6.14 : Stress distribution diagram**

$$\sigma_b = \frac{M}{Z} = \frac{P \times e}{Z} = \frac{150 \times 10^3 \times 200}{4295146.21} = 6.98 \text{ N/mm}^2$$

**Answer :** $\boxed{\begin{array}{l} \sigma_{max} = \sigma_o + \sigma_b = 2.73 + 6.98 = \textbf{9.71 N/mm}^2 \textbf{ (Compressive)} \\ \sigma_{min} = \sigma_o - \sigma_b = 2.73 - 6.98 = \textbf{– 4.25 N/mm}^2 \textbf{ (Tensile)} \end{array}}$

**Example 10 :** *A hollow circular column having external and internal diameters of 300 mm and 250 mm respectively carries a vertical load of 100 kN at the outer edge of the column. Calculate the maximum and minimum intensities of stresses in the section.*

**(B.T.E. W-2012/4 Marks)**

**Data** : $D = 300$ mm, $d = 250$ mm, $P = 100$ kN $= 100 \times 10^3$ N,

$e = \dfrac{300}{2} = 150$ mm (load acting at outer edge of the column)

**To find** : $\sigma_{max}, \sigma_{min}$.

**Concept** : Same as the above example.

**Solution** : $A = \dfrac{\pi}{4}(D^2 - d^2) = \dfrac{\pi}{4}(300^2 - 250^2) = 21598.45$ mm$^2$

$$\sigma_o = \frac{P}{A} = \frac{100 \times 10^3}{21598.45} = 4.63 \text{ N/mm}^2$$

$$M = P \times e = (100 \times 10^3) \times 150 = 1.5 \times 10^7 \text{ N.mm}$$

$$I = \frac{\pi}{64}(D^4 - d^4) = \frac{\pi}{64}(300^4 - 250^4) = 0.20586 \times 10^9 \text{ mm}^4$$

$$y = \frac{D}{2} = \frac{300}{2} = 150 \text{ mm}$$

$$\sigma_b = \frac{M}{I} \times y = \frac{1.5 \times 10^7}{0.20586 \times 10^9} \times 150 = 10.93 \text{ N/mm}^2$$

**Answer :**
$$\sigma_{max} = \sigma_o + \sigma_b = 4.63 + 10.93 = \mathbf{15.56 \text{ N/mm}^2 \textbf{ (Compressive)}}$$
$$\sigma_{min} = \sigma_o - \sigma_b = 4.63 - 10.93 = \mathbf{-6.3 \text{ N/mm}^2 \textbf{ (Tensile)}}$$

**Example 11 :** *A C.I. hollow circular stanchion has external diameter of 250 mm and internal diameter of 200 mm. It is subjected to a vertical load of 20 kN at a distance of 400 mm from the vertical axis of the stanchion. Calculate the maximum and minimum stresses at the base of stanchion.* **(B.T.E. W-2014, 2008/4 Marks)**

**Data** : C.I. column, D = 250 mm, d = 200 mm, P = 20 kN = $20 \times 10^3$ N, e = 400 mm.

**To find** : $\sigma_{max}, \sigma_{min}$.

**Concept :** $Z = Z_{XX} = Z_{YY} = \dfrac{I}{y} = \dfrac{\dfrac{\pi}{64}(D^4 - d^4)}{\dfrac{D}{2}} = \dfrac{\pi}{32}\left(\dfrac{D^4 - d^4}{D}\right)$

**Solution :** Cross-sectional area of column,

$$A = \frac{\pi}{4}(D^2 - d^2)$$

$$= \frac{\pi}{4}(250^2 - 200^2)$$

$$= 17671.46 \text{ mm}^2$$

Direct stress,

$$\sigma_o = \frac{P}{A} = \frac{20 \times 10^3}{17671.46}$$

$$= 1.13 \text{ N/mm}^2 \text{ (Compressive)}$$

Bending stress,

$$\sigma_b = \pm\frac{M}{Z} = \pm\frac{P \times e}{\frac{\pi}{32}\left(\frac{D^4 - d^4}{D}\right)}$$

$$= \pm\frac{(20 \times 10^3) \times 400}{\frac{\pi}{32}\left(\frac{250^4 - 200^4}{250}\right)}$$

$$= \pm\frac{8 \times 10^6}{105662.26}$$

$$= \pm 8.83 \text{ N/mm}^2$$

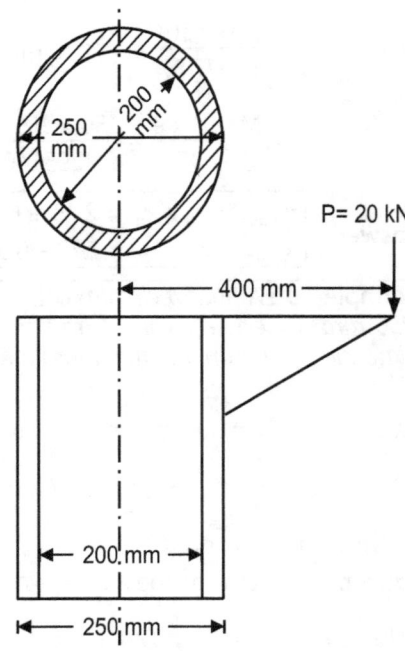

P= 20 kN

400 mm

200 mm

250 mm

**Fig. 6.15**

**Answer :**

$$\therefore \quad \sigma_{max} = \sigma_o + \sigma_b = 1.13 + 8.83 = \textbf{9.96 N/mm}^2 \textbf{ (Compressive)}$$

$$\sigma_{min} = \sigma_o - \sigma_b = 1.13 - 8.83 = \textbf{– 7.7 N/mm}^2$$

Minus sign indicates tensile nature

$$\therefore \quad \sigma_{min} = \textbf{7.7 N/mm}^2 \textbf{ (Tensile)}$$

**Example 12 :** *A short column of hollow cylindrical section 250 mm outside diameter and 150 mm inside diameter carries a vertical load of 390 kN along one of the diameter planes 95 mm away from the axis of the column. Find the extreme intensities of stresses and state their nature.* **(B.T.E. W-2007, S-2001/4 Marks)**

**Data    :**   D = 250 mm, d = 150 mm, P = 390 kN = 390 × 10³ N, e = 95 mm

**To find  :**   $\sigma_{max}$, $\sigma_{min}$ and their nature.

**Concept :**   $Z = Z_{XX} = Z_{YY} = \dfrac{I}{y}$ .

**Solution :**        $A = \dfrac{\pi}{4}(D^2 - d^2) = \dfrac{\pi}{4}(250^2 - 150^2) = 31415.93 \text{ mm}^2$

$$Z = \frac{I}{y} = \frac{\frac{\pi}{64}(D^4 - d^4)}{\frac{D}{2}}$$

$$= \frac{\pi}{32}\left(\frac{D^4 - d^4}{D}\right)$$

$$= \frac{\pi}{32}\left[\frac{250^4 - 150^4}{250}\right]$$

$$= 1335176.88 \text{ mm}^3$$

$$\sigma_O = \frac{P}{A} = \frac{390 \times 10^3}{31415.93}$$

$$= 12.41 \text{ N/mm}^2$$

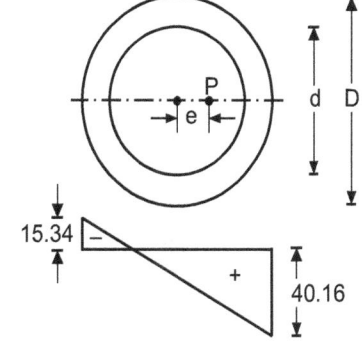

**Fig. 6.16**

$$\sigma_b = \frac{M}{Z} = \frac{P \times e}{Z} = \frac{390 \times 10^3 \times 95}{1335176.88} = 27.75 \text{ N/mm}^2$$

**Answer :**

$$\sigma_{max} = \sigma_O + \sigma_b = 12.41 + 27.75 = \textbf{40.16 N/mm}^2 \textbf{ (Compressive)}$$

$$\sigma_{min} = \sigma_O - \sigma_b = 12.41 - 27.75 = \textbf{– 15.34 N/mm}^2 \textbf{ (Tensile)}$$

## Type 1.5 : Miscellaneous Examples :

**Example 13 :** *A rectangular column 300 mm wide and 200 mm thick carries an axial load of 180 kN and a clockwise moment of 2.8 kN-m in the plane bisecting 200 mm side. Calculate the resultant stresses induced at the base.* **(B.T.E. S-2007/8 Marks)**

**Data**     :   b = 300 mm,  d = 200 mm, P = 180 kN = $180 \times 10^3$ N,
                 M = 2.8 kN-m = $2.8 \times 10^6$ N.mm

**To find**  :   $\sigma_{max}$ and $\sigma_{min}$.

**Concept** :   Bending stress due to M, $\sigma_b = \dfrac{M}{Z_{YY}}$.

**Solution** : Area A = b × d  = 300 × 200 = $6 \times 10^4$ mm²

$$\sigma_o = \frac{P}{A} = \frac{180 \times 10^3}{6 \times 10^4} = \textbf{3 N/mm}^2 \textbf{ (Compressive)}$$

$$\sigma_b = \frac{M}{Z_{YY}} = \frac{M}{db^2/6} = \frac{6M}{db^2} = \frac{6 \times 2.8 \times 10^6}{200 \times 300^2} = \textbf{0.93 N/mm}^2$$

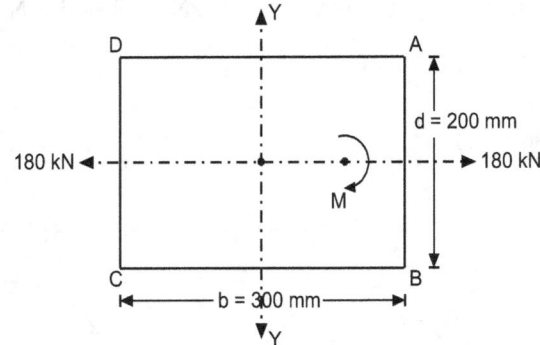

**Fig. 6.17**

**Answer :**
$$\boxed{\begin{array}{l} \sigma_{max} = \sigma_o + \sigma_b = 3 + 0.93 = \textbf{3.93 N/mm}^2 \textbf{ (Compressive)} \\ \sigma_{min} = \sigma_o - \sigma_b = 3 - 0.93 = \textbf{2.07 N/mm}^2 \textbf{ (Compressive)} \end{array}}$$

**Example 14 :** *A rectangular pier 1000 mm × 1500 mm is subjected to a compressive load of 500 kN with an eccentricity of 250 mm along the axis bisecting 1000 mm side. Find the resultant stress intensities at the base cross-section of the pier.*          **(B.T.E. S-2005/8 Marks)**

**Data :** B = 1000 mm, D = 1500 mm, P = 500 kN = $500 \times 10^3$ N, e = 250 mm.

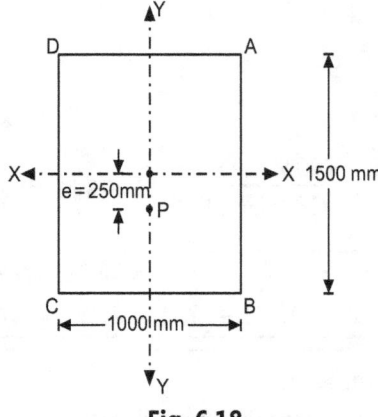

**Fig. 6.18**

**To find :** $\sigma_{max}$ and $\sigma_{min}$.

**Concept :** The load is eccentric w.r.t. XX axis. Hence we have to consider $I_{XX}$ and $Z_{XX}$.

**Solution :**

Area of section,     $A = B \times D = 1000 \times 1500 = 15 \times 10^5 \ \text{mm}^4$

Direct stress,     $\sigma_0 = \dfrac{P}{A} = \dfrac{500 \times 10^3}{15 \times 10^5} = 0.33 \ \text{N/mm}^2$

The load is eccentric w.r.t. XX axis. So we have to consider $Z_{XX}$.

$$Z_{XX} = \frac{BD^2}{6} = \frac{1000 \times 1500^2}{6} = 375 \times 10^6$$

Bending stress,     $\sigma_b = \dfrac{M}{Z_{XX}} = \dfrac{P \cdot e}{Z_{XX}} = \dfrac{500 \times 10^3}{375 \times 10^6} = 1.33 \times 10^{-3} \ \text{N/mm}^2$

**Answer :**

$$\sigma_{max} = \sigma_0 + \sigma_b = 0.33 + 1.33 \times 10^{-3}$$

$$= \textbf{0.33 N/mm}^2 \textbf{ (Compressive on face BC)}$$

$$\sigma_{min} = \sigma_0 - \sigma_b = 0.33 - 1.33 \times 10^{-3}$$

$$= \textbf{0.33 N/mm}^2 \textbf{ (Compressive on face AD)}$$

**Example 15 :** *A diamond shaped pier with diagonals 3 m and 6 m is subjected to an eccentric load of 1500 kN at a distance of 1 m from centroid and on the longer diagonal. Calculate the maximum stress induced in the section.*     **(B.T.E. S-1999/4 Marks)**

**Data**     :     Diamond shaped pier as shown in Fig. 6.19, $P = 1500 \ \text{kN} = 1500 \times 10^3 \ \text{N}$.

**To find**     :     $\sigma_{max}$

**Concept :**     The load $P = 1500$ kN acts at 1 m from centroid E on the longer diagonal AC.

The load is eccentric w.r.t. shorter diagonal BD (i.e. X-X axis). Hence we have to consider $I_{XX}$ and $Z_{XX}$.

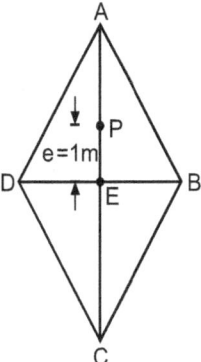

**Solution :**     Area, $A = 2 \times \left( \dfrac{1}{2} \times 3 \times 3 \right)$

$$= 9 \ \text{m}^2 = 9 \times 10^6 \ \text{mm}^2$$

**Fig. 6.19**

Eccentricity, $e = 1 \ \text{m} = 1000 \ \text{mm}$

Direct stress, $\sigma_0 = \dfrac{P}{A} = \dfrac{1500 \times 10^3}{9 \times 10^6} = 0.167 \ \text{N/mm}^2$

Bending moment,     $M = P \times e = 1500 \times 10^3 \times 1000 = 15 \times 10^8 \ \text{N-mm}$

$$\mathbf{I_{XX}} = I_{DB} = 2 \left( \frac{bb^3}{12} \right) = 2 \times \left( \frac{3 \times 3^3}{12} \right) = 13.5 \ \text{m}^4$$

$$= \textbf{13.5} \times \textbf{10}^{12} \ \textbf{mm}^4$$

Distance of extreme point A or C from X-X axis,

$$y = \frac{6}{2} = 3 \text{ m} = 3000 \text{ mm}$$

Section modulus,          $$Z_{XX} = \frac{I_{XX}}{y} = \frac{13.5 \times 10^{12}}{3000} = 45 \times 10^8 \text{ mm}^3$$

Bending stress,          $$\sigma_b = \frac{M}{Z_{XX}} = \frac{15 \times 10^8}{45 \times 10^8} = 0.33 \text{ N/mm}^2$$

**Answer :**

> $\sigma_{max} = \sigma_0 + \sigma_b = 0.167 + 0.33 =$ **0.497 N/mm² say 0.5 N/mm² (Compressive)**
>
> $\sigma_{min} = \sigma_0 - \sigma_b = 0.167 - 0.33 = -$ **0.163 N/mm² = 0.163 N/mm² (Tensile)**

**Example 16 :** *The cross-section through a rectangular pre-stressed concrete beam at mid span is shown in Fig. 6.20 (a). At this section, a thrust of 270 kN occurs at point A normal to cross-section due to prestressing force. Calculate the stress at the top and bottom of the beam.*

**(B.T.E. W-2010, 1998/4 Marks)**

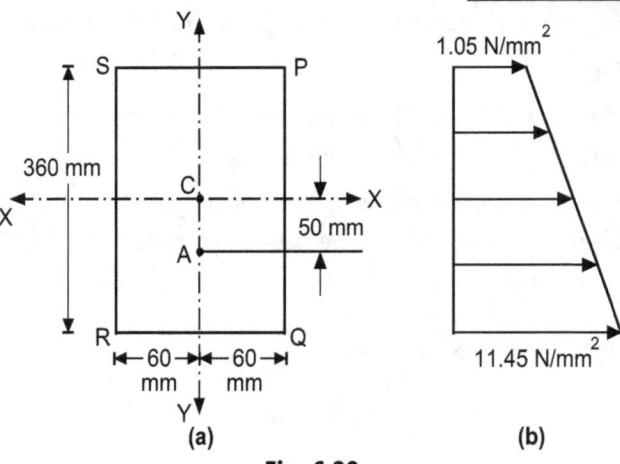

**Fig. 6.20**

**Data**     :     Thrust P = 270 kN = $270 \times 10^3$ N,  width b = 120 mm,

depth d = 360 mm, eccentricity about X-axis $e_x$ = 50 mm

**To find** :     Stress at top, stress at bottom.

**Concept** :     The load is eccentric w.r.t. XX axis. So we have to calculate $M_{XX}$ and $Z_{XX}$.

**Solution** :     Direct stress,

$$\sigma_0 = \frac{P}{A} = \frac{270 \times 10^3}{120 \times 360} = \text{6.25 N/mm}^2 \text{ (Compressive)}$$

Load is eccentric w.r.t. X-axis.

Bending moment, $M_{XX} = P \times e_x = 270 \times 10^3 \times 50 = 13.5 \times 10^6$ N.mm

Section modulus, $Z_{XX} = \dfrac{bd^2}{6} = \dfrac{120 \times 360^2}{6} = 2.592 \times 10^6 \, mm^3$

Bending stress, $\sigma_b = \dfrac{M_{XX}}{Z_{XX}} = \dfrac{13.5 \times 10^6}{2.592 \times 10^6} = $ **5.2 N/mm²**

**(Compressive for bottom and tensile for top)**

**Answer :**

$\sigma_{max} = \sigma_0 + \sigma_b = 6.25 + 5.2 = $ **11.45 N/mm² (Compressive)**

**Stress at bottom = 11.45 N/mm² (Compressive)**

$\sigma_{min} = \sigma_0 - \sigma_b = 6.25 - 5.2 = $ **1.05 N/mm² (Compressive)**

**Stress at top = 1.05 N/mm² (Compressive)**

**Example 17 :** *A rectangular beam 300 mm wide and 500 mm deep is simply supported on a span of 3 m. It carries a central load of 50 kN and an axial pull of 100 kN acting longitudinally. Find the resultant stresses induced at top and bottom of the beam for the mid-span section. Neglect the self-weight of the beam.* **(B.T.E. S-2005/4 Marks)**

**Data** : b = 300 mm, d = 500 mm, L = 3 m = 3000 mm,
central load W = 50 kN = $50 \times 10^3$ N, axial pull P = 100 kN = $100 \times 10^3$ N

**To find :** $\sigma_{max}$, $\sigma_{min}$.

**Concept :** An axial pull of 100 kN will cause direct stress $\sigma_0$ and a vertical central load of 50 kN will cause bending stress $\sigma_b$.

**Solution :**

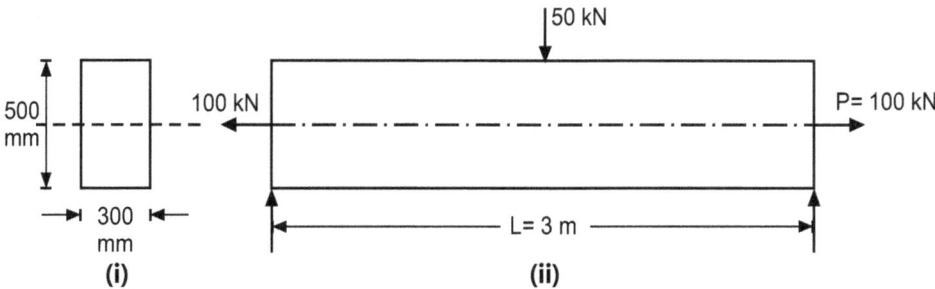

**Fig. 6.21**

**Direct stress,** $\sigma_0 = \dfrac{P}{A} = \dfrac{100 \times 10^3}{300 \times 500}$

$= 0.66 \, N/mm^2$ (Tensile)

$M = \dfrac{WL}{4} = \dfrac{50 \times 10^3 \times 3000}{4} = 37.5 \times 10^6 \, N.mm$

$Z = \dfrac{I}{y} = \dfrac{300 \times 500^3/12}{500/2} = 12.5 \times 10^6 \, mm^3$

**Bending stress,** $\sigma_b = \dfrac{M}{Z} = \dfrac{37.5 \times 10^6}{12.5 \times 10^6} = 3 \, N/mm^2$

Bending stress will be compressive at top fibre i.e. –3 N/mm² and it will be tensile at bottom fibre i.e. 3 N/mm².

**Resultant stresses :**

**Answer :**

| | |
|---|---|
| At bottom fibre, $\sigma_{max}$ | $= \sigma_0 + \sigma_b = 0.66 + 3 =$ **3.66 N/mm² (Tensile)** |
| At top fibre, $\sigma_{min}$ | $= \sigma_0 - \sigma_b = 0.66 - 3 =$ **−2.67 N/mm² (Compressive)** |

### Type 2 : Examples based on Tension member

**Note :** In such types of examples, tensile stress is taken as positive and compressive stress as negative.

> **Important Formulae**
>
> $\sigma_{max} = \sigma_0 + \sigma_b$ (Tensile)
>
> $\sigma_{min} = \sigma_0 - \sigma_b$ (Tensile if $\sigma_0 > \sigma_b$ and Compressive if $\sigma_0 < \sigma_b$)

**Example 18 :** *A steel flat 200 mm wide and 20 mm thick is subjected to a pull of 200 kN at an eccentricity of 10 mm in a plane bisecting the thickness. Find $\sigma_{max}$ and $\sigma_{min}$.*

**(B.T.E. W-2010/4 Marks)**

**Data** : $b = 200$ mm, $d = 20$ mm, Pull $P = 200 \times 10^3$ N, $e = 10$ mm

**To find** : $\sigma_{max}$ and $\sigma_{min}$.

**Concept :** (i) Since the load is tensile on the right side of YY axis, maximum resultant stress will occur on right face.

(ii) The load is eccentric w.r.t. YY axis. Hence we have to calculate $Z_{YY}$.

**Solution :** Refer to Fig. 6.22.

$A = b \times d = 200 \times 20 = 4000$ mm²

$\sigma_0 = \dfrac{P}{A} = \dfrac{200 \times 10^3}{4000}$

$\quad = 50$ N/mm² (Tensile)

$\sigma_b = \dfrac{M}{Z_{YY}} = \dfrac{P \cdot e}{db^2/6}$

$\quad = \dfrac{6Pe}{db^2} = \dfrac{6 \times 200 \times 10^3 \times 10}{20 \times 200^2}$

$\quad = 15$ N/mm²

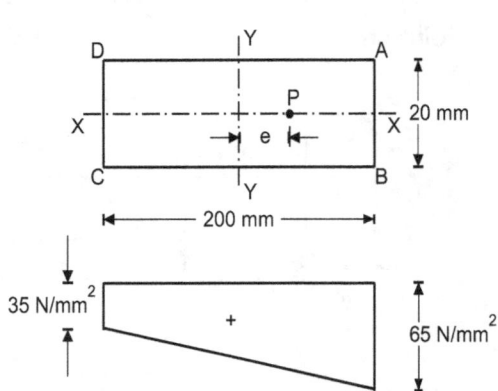

**Fig. 6.22 : Stress distribution diagram**

**Answer :**

| |
|---|
| $\sigma_{max} = \sigma_0 + \sigma_b = 50 + 15 =$ **65 N/mm² (Tensile on face AB)** |
| $\sigma_{min} = \sigma_0 - \sigma_b = 50 - 15 =$ **35 N/mm² (Tensile on face CD)** |

**Example 19 :** *A tie member 150 mm wide carries an eccentric load of 150 kN at an eccentricity of 5 mm in a plane bisecting the thickness. Find out the minimum thickness of the tie if the permissible tensile stress is 100 N/mm². Also calculate the minimum value of stress.*

**(Imp.)**

**Data** : $b = 150$ mm, $P = 150$ kN $= 150 \times 10^3$ N,

$e = 5$ mm, $\sigma_{max} = 100$ N/mm² (tensile) on face BC.

**To find** : (i) d, (ii) $\sigma_{min}$.

**Concept :** Since the load is tensile on the right side of Y-Y axis, the maximum resultant stress will occur on the right face (BC).

**Solution :** Refer to Fig. 6.23. Let d be the thickness of the tie member.

If the load is eccentric about Y-Y axis,

$$\sigma_{max} = \frac{P}{A} + \frac{M}{Z_{YY}} = \frac{P}{A} + \frac{Pe}{db^2/6}$$

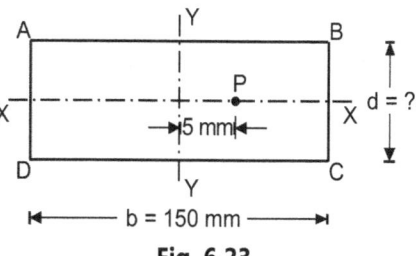

$$\therefore \quad 100 = \frac{150 \times 10^3}{150 \times d} + \frac{150 \times 10^3 \times 5}{d \times 150^2/6}$$

$$\therefore \quad 100 = \frac{10^3}{d} + \frac{200}{d} = \frac{1200}{d}$$

**Fig. 6.23**

$$\therefore \quad \mathbf{d = 12 \ mm}$$

$$\sigma_{min} = \frac{P}{A} - \frac{M}{Z_{YY}} = \frac{P}{A} - \frac{Pe}{db^2/6} = \frac{150 \times 10^3}{150 \times 12} - \frac{150 \times 10^3 \times 5}{12 \times 150^2/6} = 83.33 - 16.67$$

$$= \mathbf{66.67 \ N/mm^2 \ (Tensile \ on \ face \ AD)}$$

**Answer :** $\boxed{\text{(i) d = 12 mm, (ii) } \sigma_{min} = 66.67 \ N/mm^2 \text{ (Tensile on face AD)}}$

**Example 20 :** *A mild steel flat 50 mm wide and 5 mm thick is subjected to load 'P' acting in the plane bisecting thickness at a point 10 mm away from the centroid of the section. If the tensile stress is not to exceed 150 MPa, calculate the magnitude of P.*

**(B.T.E. W-1999/4 Marks)**

**Data**　：　b = 50 mm, d = 5 mm, e = 10 mm, $\sigma_{max}$ = 150 MPa = 150 N/mm² (tensile)

**To find**　：　P.

**Concept :**　The load is eccentric w.r.t. YY axis. So we have to calculate $Z_{YY}$.

**Solution :**　A　= b × d = 50 × 5 = 250 mm²

$$\sigma_0 = \frac{P}{A} = \frac{P}{250}$$

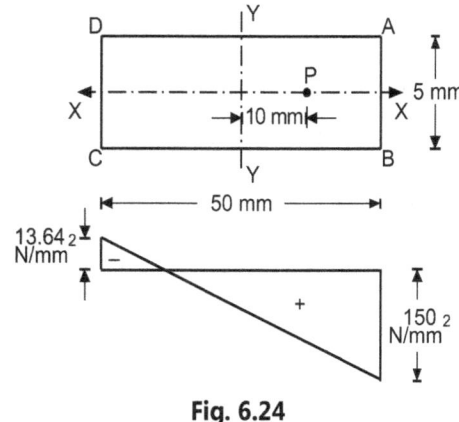

$$\sigma_b = \frac{M}{Z_{yy}} = \frac{P \times e}{db^2/6} = \frac{6 \ Pe}{db^2}$$

$$= \frac{6 \times P \times 10}{5 \times 50^2} = 0.0048 \ P$$

$$\sigma_{max} = \sigma_0 + \sigma_b$$

$$150 = \frac{P}{250} + 0.0048 \ P$$

$$= P \left( \frac{1}{250} + 0.0048 \right)$$

**Fig. 6.24**

$$= 0.0088 \ P$$

**Answer :**　$\boxed{P = \dfrac{150}{0.0048} = 17045.45 \ N = \mathbf{17.045 \ kN}}$

**Extension to the example :**

**Example 21 :** *Also calculate $\sigma_{min}$ and draw stress distribution diagram.*

**Solution :**　　$\sigma_O = \dfrac{P}{250} = \dfrac{17045.45}{250} = 68.18$ N/mm$^2$

$\sigma_b = 0.0048 P = 0.0048 \times 17045.45 = 81.82$ N/mm$^2$

$\sigma_{min} = \sigma_O - \sigma_b = 68.18 - 81.82 = $ **–13.64 N/mm$^2$ (Compressive)**

The stress distribution diagram is as shown in Fig. 6.24.

---

## SUB-TOPIC 6.2 : PROBLEMS ON THE ABOVE CONCEPTS FOR STRUT, MACHINE PARTS SUCH AS OFFSET LINKS, C-CLAMP, BENCH VICE, DRILLING MACHINE FRAME ETC.
### (8 Marks)

### Type 3 : Miscellaneous Examples [C-clamp, hook, offset link, masonry wall, etc.]

**Example 22 :** *A C-clamp made up of rectangular cross section 30 × 10 mm as shown in Fig. 6.25 is subjected to a force of 2.5 kN. Find the stresses induced at section AB.*

**(B.T.E. S-2012; W-2013, 2011, 2004/4 Marks)**

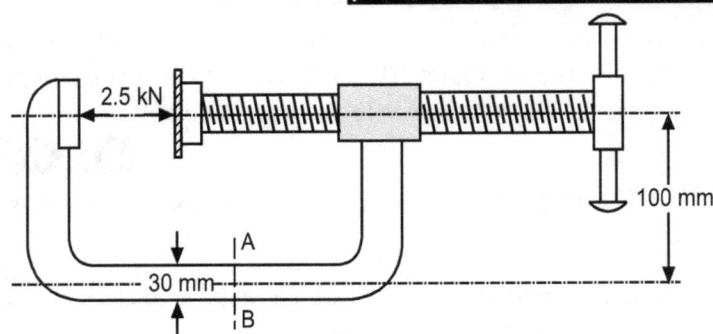

**Fig. 6.25**

**Data** 　:　$P = 2.5$ kN $= 2.5 \times 10^3$ N, $b = 10$ mm, $d = 30$ m, $e_x = 100$ mm.

**To find** 　:　$\sigma_{max}$ and $\sigma_{min}$.

**Concept :**　$M_{XX} = P \cdot e_x$ and $\sigma_b = \dfrac{M_{XX}}{Z_{XX}}$ where $Z_{XX} = \dfrac{bd^2}{6}$ .

**Solution :**

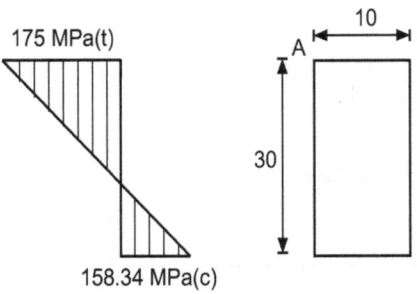

**(i)Stress diagram(ii)Cross-section**

**Fig. 6.26**

$$\text{Direct stress, } \sigma_o = \frac{P}{A} = \frac{2.5 \times 10^3}{10 \times 30} = \textbf{8.33 N/mm}^2 \textbf{ (Tensile)}$$

$$\text{Section modulus, } Z_{xx} = \frac{bd^2}{6} = \frac{10 \times 30^2}{6} = 1500 \text{ mm}^3$$

$$\text{Bending moment, } M_{xx} = P \cdot e_x = (2.5 \times 10^3)(100) = 250000 \text{ N.mm}$$

$$\text{Bending stress, } \sigma_b = \frac{M_{xx}}{Z_{xx}} = \frac{250000}{1500} = \textbf{166.67 N/mm}^2$$

**Answer :**

> **Stress at top fibre (A) :**
> $$\sigma_{max} = \sigma_o + \sigma_b = 8.33 + 166.67$$
> $$= \textbf{175 N/mm}^2 \textbf{ (Tensile)}$$
> **Stress at bottom fibre (B) :**
> $$\sigma_{min} = \sigma_o - \sigma_b = 8.33 - 166.67$$
> $$= \textbf{-158.34 N/mm}^2 \textbf{ (Compressive)}$$

**Example 23 :** *A C-clamp as shown in Fig. 6.27, carries a load P = 25 kN. The cross-section of the clamp at X-X is rectangular, having width equal to twice the thickness. Assuming that the C-clamp is made of steel casting with an allowable stress of 100 N/mm², find its dimensions.*　　　　**(B.T.E. W-2012/4 Marks)**

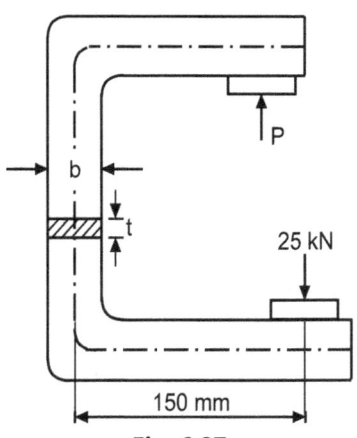

**Fig. 6.27**

**Data** : b = 2t, σ = 100 N/mm², e = 150 mm, P = 25 kN = 25 × 10³ N.

**To find** : b and t.

**Concept :** Same as the above example.

**Solution :**
$$A = b \times t = 2t \times t = (2t^2) \text{ mm}^2$$
$$\sigma_o = \frac{25 \times 10^3}{2t^2} = \frac{12500}{t^2} \text{ N/mm}^2$$
$$M = (25 \times 10^3) \times 150 = 3750 \times 10^3 \text{ N.mm}$$
$$Z = \frac{t \times b^2}{6} = \frac{t \times (2t)^2}{6} = \frac{2}{3} t^3 \text{ mm}^3$$
$$\sigma_b = \frac{M}{Z} = \frac{3750 \times 10^3}{\left(\frac{2}{3} t^3\right)} = \frac{5625 \times 10^3}{t^3} \text{ N/mm}^2$$

$$\sigma_{max} = \sigma_o + \sigma_b = \frac{12500}{t^2} + \frac{5625 \times 10^3}{t^3}$$

$$\therefore \qquad 100 = \frac{12500}{t^2} + \frac{5625 \times 10^3}{t^3}$$

$$\therefore \qquad 100t^3 = 12500t + 5625 \times 10^3$$

$$\therefore \quad 100t^3 - 12500t - 5625 \times 10^3 = 0$$

$$\therefore \quad t^3 - 125t - 56250 = 0$$

By trial and error,    $t = 39.4$ mm **say 40 mm**

$$\therefore \qquad b = 2t = 2 \times 39.4 = 78.8 \text{ mm } \textbf{say 80 mm}$$

**Answer :** $\boxed{b = 80 \text{ mm}, t = 40 \text{ mm}}$

---

**Example 24 :** *A M.S. link as shown in Fig. 6.28 by full lines, transmits a pull of 80 kN. Find the dimensions b and t if b = 3t. Assume the permissible tensile stress as 70 MPa.*

**(B.T.E. W-2014, 2012/4 Marks)**

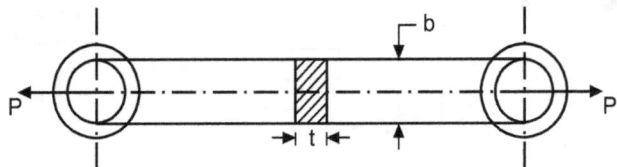

**Fig. 6.28**

**Solution :** Let b and t be in 'mm'.

$$A = t \times b = t \times 3t = 3t^2$$

$$\sigma = \frac{P}{A} = \left( \frac{80 \times 10^3}{3t^2} \right) \text{N/mm}^2$$

But    $\sigma = 70 \text{ MPa} = 70 \text{ N/mm}^2$

$$\therefore \qquad \frac{80 \times 10^3}{3t^2} = 70$$

$$\therefore \qquad t^2 = \frac{80 \times 10^3}{3 \times 70} = 380.95$$

$$t = 19.52 \text{ mm } \textbf{say 20 mm}$$

$$\therefore \qquad b = 3t = 3 \times 20 = \textbf{60 mm}$$

**Answer :** $\boxed{b = 60 \text{ mm}, t = 20 \text{ mm}}$

---

**Example 25 :** *A rectangular rod of size 50 mm × 100 mm is bent into C-shape and a load of 40 kN is applied at a distance of 40 mm from the centre of vertical side (eccentricity). Calculate the resultant stresses developed at section XX.*    **(B.T.E. S-2013/4 Marks)**

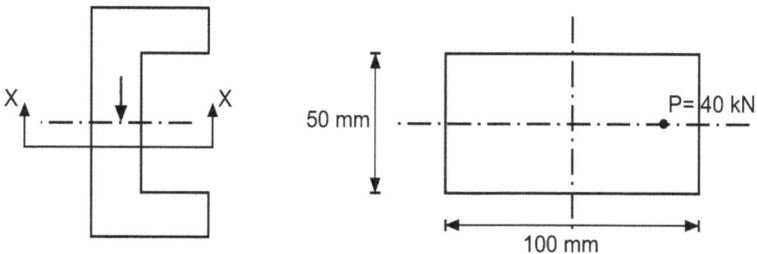

**Fig. 6.29**

**Data**    :    As shown in Fig. 6.29, P = 40 kN = $40 \times 10^3$ N, $e_y$ = 40 mm, b = 100 mm, d = 50 mm.

**To find** :    Resultant stress at section XX.

**Concept :**    $M_{YY} = P \cdot e_y$,    $\sigma_b = \dfrac{M_{YY}}{Z_{YY}}$ where $Z_{YY} = \dfrac{db^2}{6}$

**Solution :**    Direct stress,    $\sigma_o = \dfrac{P}{A} = \dfrac{40 \times 10^3}{100 \times 50}$ = **8 N/mm²**

Bending stress, $\sigma_b = \dfrac{M_{YY}}{Z_{YY}} = \dfrac{P \cdot e_y}{db^2/6} = \dfrac{6P \cdot e_y}{db^2} = \dfrac{6 \times (40 \times 10^3) \times 40}{50 \times 100^2}$ = **19.2 N/mm²**

Now resultant stresses developed at section XX are given by

$$\sigma_{max} = \sigma_o + \sigma_b$$
$$\sigma_{min} = \sigma_o - \sigma_b$$

**Answer :**

| **Resultant stresses :** |
| --- |
| $\sigma_{max}$ = 8 + 19.2 = **27.2 N/mm² (Tensile)** |
| $\sigma_{min}$ = 8 – 19.2 = **– 11.2 N/mm² (Compressive)** |

**Example 26 :** *A rectangular rod of size 50 mm × 100 mm is bent into 'C' shape as shown in Fig. 6.30 and applied load of 40 kN at point A. Calculate the resultant stresses developed at section XX.*          **(B.T.E. S-2015, 2012, 2006; W-2011/4 Marks)**

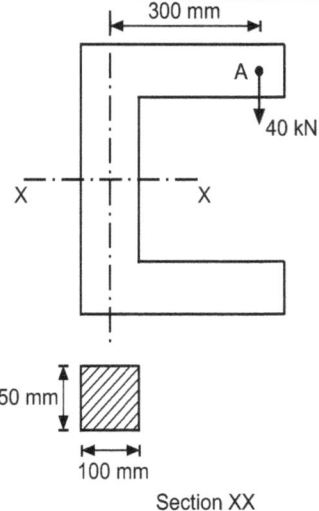

Section XX

**Fig. 6.30**

**Data** : As shown in Fig. 6.30, P = 40 kN = $40 \times 10^3$ N, $e_y$ = 300 mm, b = 100 mm, d = 50 mm.

**To find** : Resultant stresses at section XX

**Concept :** $M_{YY} = P \cdot e_y$ and $\sigma_b = \dfrac{M_{YY}}{Z_{YY}}$ where $Z_{YY} = \dfrac{db^2}{6}$.

**Solution :** Direct stress, $\sigma_o = \dfrac{P}{A} = \dfrac{40 \times 10^3}{100 \times 50}$ = **8 N/mm²**

Bending stress, $\sigma_b = \dfrac{M_{YY}}{Z_{YY}} = \dfrac{P \cdot e_y}{db^2/6} = \dfrac{6P \cdot e_y}{db^2} = \dfrac{6 \times 40 \times 10^3 \times 300}{50 \times 100^2}$ = **144 N/mm²**

**Answer :**

> **Resultant stresses :**
>
> $\sigma_{max}$ = 8 + 144 = **152 N/mm² (T)**
>
> $\sigma_{min}$ = 8 − 144 = **−136 N/mm² (C)**

**Example 27 :** *A mild steel tube of 50 mm external diameter and 10 mm thickness is bent in the form of hook as shown in Fig. 6.31. What maximum load P the hook can lift if the stresses on the cross-section AB should not exceed 100 MPa in tension and 25 N/mm² in compression ?* （B.T.E. W-2010, 2003; S-2007/4 Marks)

**Data** : D = 50 mm, t = 10 mm, d = D − 2t = 50 − 2 × 10 = 30 mm,

　　　　$\sigma_r$ = 100 MPa = 100 N/mm² (tensile), $\sigma_r$ = 25 N/mm² (compressive),

　　　　e = 100 mm

**To find** : Safe load P.

**Concept :** (i)　Find $\sigma_o$ and $\sigma_b$ in terms of P.

　　　　(ii)　From equations $\sigma_r = \sigma_o + \sigma_b$ and $\sigma_r = \sigma_o - \sigma_b$, find the two values of P.

　　　　(iii)　Safe load to satisfy the required stress criteria is the minimum of two values of P.

**Solution :** Cross-sectional area,

$$A = \frac{\pi}{4}(D^2 - d^2) = \frac{\pi}{4}(50^2 - 30^2) = 1256.64 \text{ mm}^2$$

$$I = \frac{\pi}{64}(D^4 - d^4) = \frac{\pi}{64}(50^4 - 30^4) = 267035.376 \text{ mm}^4$$

$$y_{max} = \frac{D}{2} = \frac{50}{2} = 25 \text{ mm}$$

$$Z = \frac{I}{y_{max}} = \frac{267035.376}{25} = 10681.415 \text{ mm}^3$$

Direct stress, $\sigma_o = \dfrac{P}{A} = \dfrac{P}{1256.64}$ = **0.000796 · P (Tensile)**

Bending stress, $\sigma_b = \pm\dfrac{M}{Z} = \pm\dfrac{P \cdot e}{Z} = \pm\dfrac{P \times 100}{10681.415}$ = **± 0.00936 · P**

**Resultant stresses in tension are**

$$\sigma_r = \sigma_o + \sigma_b \text{ (tensile)}$$

$$100 = 0.000796\,P + 0.00936\,P$$

$$= (0.000796 + 0.00936)\,P$$

$$= 0.010156\,P$$

$$P = \frac{100}{0.010156} = 9846.4 \text{ N}$$

$$= \mathbf{9.85 \text{ kN}} \qquad \text{... (1)}$$

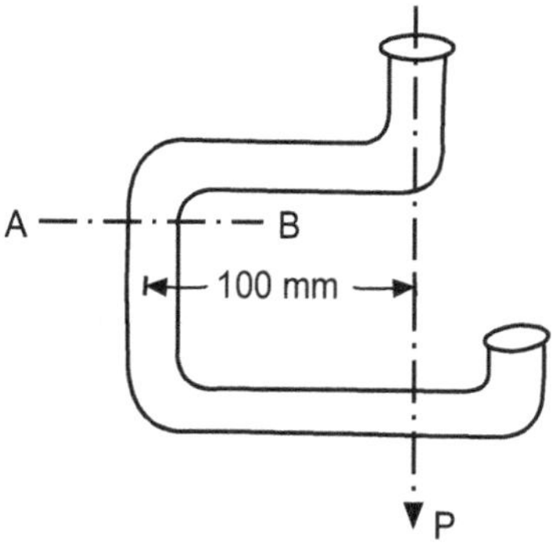

**Fig. 6.31**

**Resultant stresses in compression are**

$$\sigma_r = \sigma_o - \sigma_b$$

$$-25 = 0.000796\,P - 0.00936\,P = (0.000796 - 0.00936)\,P$$

∴          $$-25 = -0.000564\,P$$

∴          $$P = 2919.2 \text{ N} = \mathbf{2.92 \text{ kN}} \qquad \text{... (2)}$$

∴   Safe load to satisfy the required stress criteria is the lesser of (1) and (2).

**Answer :** |Safe load, P  = 2.92 kN|

---

**Example 28 :** *A 30 mm diameter rod is bent up to form an offset link as shown in Fig. 6.32. If permissible tensile stress is 80 MPa, determine the maximum value of P.*

**(B.T.E. S-2012, W-2009/4 Marks)**

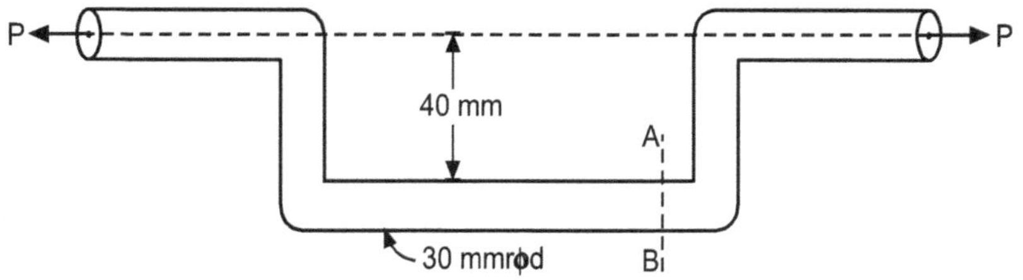

**Fig. 6.32**

**Data**     : D = 30 mm, $e_x = 40 + \dfrac{30}{2} = 55$ mm , $\sigma_{max} = 80$ MPa (tensile).

**To find**   : P.

**Concept** : $M_{xx} = P \cdot e_x$ and $\sigma_b = \dfrac{M_{xx}}{Z_{xx}}$ where $Z_{xx} = \dfrac{\pi}{32} D^3$

**Solution** : Direct stress, $\sigma_o = \dfrac{P}{A} = \dfrac{P}{\dfrac{\pi}{4}(30)^2} = 0.001415\,P$

$$\text{Section modulus, } Z_{xx} = \frac{\dfrac{\pi}{64}(D^4)}{\left(\dfrac{D}{2}\right)} = \frac{\pi}{32} D^3 = \frac{\pi}{32}(30^3) = 2650.72 \text{ mm}^3$$

Bending moment, $M_{XX} = P \cdot e_x = P \times 55$ N.mm

Bending stress, $\sigma_b = \dfrac{M_{XX}}{Z_{XX}} = \dfrac{P \times 55}{2650.72} = \mathbf{0.020749\ P}$

$\sigma_{max} = \sigma_o + \sigma_b$

$80 = 0.001415\ P + 0.020749\ P = 0.022164\ P$

$\therefore \quad P = \dfrac{80}{0.022164} = 3609.46\ N = \mathbf{3.6\ kN}$

**Answer :** $\boxed{P = 3.6\ kN}$

---

**Example 29 :** *A masonry wall 6 m high, 2 m thick and 1 m wide is subjected to a horizontal wind pressure of 5 kN/m² on 1 m face. Find the value of net stresses at base of the wall. Masonry weighs 20 kN/m³.* **(B.T.E. W-2009/4 Marks)**

**Data** : Masonry wall height H = 6 m, thickness t = 2 m, width b = 1 m,

horizontal wind pressure $p = 5$ kN/m² $= 5 \times 10^3$ N/m²,

weight of masonry $\rho = 20$ kN/m³ $= 20 \times 10^3$ N/m³

**To find** : $\sigma_{max}, \sigma_{min}.$

**Concept** : Total wind load $P = p \times (b \times H)$ and it acts at $\dfrac{H}{2}$ from the base.

**Solution** : (i) Weight of wall,

$W = A \times H \times \rho$

$= 2 \times 1 \times 6 \times 20 \times 10^3 = 24 \times 10^4$ N

(ii) Cross-sectional area,

$A = 2 \times 1 = 2$ m²

(iii) Direct stress,

$\sigma_o = \dfrac{W}{A} = \dfrac{24 \times 10^4}{2} = 12 \times 10^4$ N/m²

(iv) Total wind load,

$P = p \times$ projected area

$= p \times (b \times H) = (5 \times 10^3) \times (1 \times 6)$

$= 30 \times 10^3$ N

(v) Moment of P about the base,

$M = P \times \dfrac{H}{2} = 30 \times 10^3 \times \dfrac{6}{2}$

$= 90 \times 10^3$ N.m

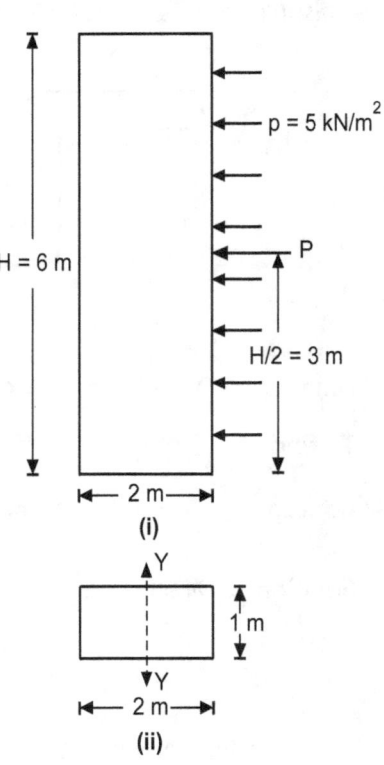

Fig. 6.33

(vi) Section modulus of the base section about YY axis of bending,

$$Z = \frac{b \times t^2}{6} = \frac{1 \times 2^2}{6} = 0.67 \text{ m}^3$$

(vii) Bending stress,      $\sigma_b = \dfrac{M}{Z} = \dfrac{90 \times 10^3}{0.67} = 134328.36 \text{ N/m}^2$

**Answer :**

$$\sigma_{max} = \sigma_0 + \sigma_b = 12 \times 10^4 + 134328.36$$
$$= \mathbf{254328.36 \ N/m^2 \ (Compressive)}$$
$$\sigma_{min} = \sigma_0 - \sigma_b = 12 \times 10^4 - 134328.36$$
$$= \mathbf{-14328.36 \ N/m^2 \ (Tensile)}$$

**Example 30 :** *A rectangular masonry wall 8 m high is 4 m wide and 2 m thick. A horizontal wind pressure of 1500 N/m² acts on 4 m side. Find the maximum and minimum intensities of stress induced on the base if the density of masonry is 20,000 N/m³.*

**(B.T.E. S-2010/4 Marks)**

**Solution :** Very similar to the above solved example.

(i)   Weight of wall
$$W = A \times H \times \rho = (2 \times 4) \times 8 \times 20000$$
$$= 128 \times 10^4 \text{ N}$$

(ii) Cross-sectional area,
$$A = 2 \times 4 = 8 \text{ m}^2$$

(iii) Direct stress,
$$\sigma_0 = \frac{W}{A} = \frac{128 \times 10^4}{8} = 16 \times 10^4 \text{ N/m}^2$$

(iv) Total wind load,
$$P = p \times \text{projected area} = p \times (b \times H)$$
$$= 1500 \times (4 \times 8) = 48000 \text{ N}$$

(v)  Moment of P about base
$$M = P \times \frac{H}{2} = 48000 \times \frac{8}{2}$$
$$= 19.2 \times 10^4 \text{ N.m}$$

(vi) Section modulus of base section about YY axis of bending,
$$Z = \frac{b \times t^2}{6} = \frac{4 \times 2^2}{6} = \frac{8}{3} \text{ m}^3$$

(vii) Bending stress,
$$\sigma_b = \frac{M}{Z} = \frac{19.2 \times 10^4}{\left(\frac{8}{3}\right)} = 72000 \text{ N/m}^2$$

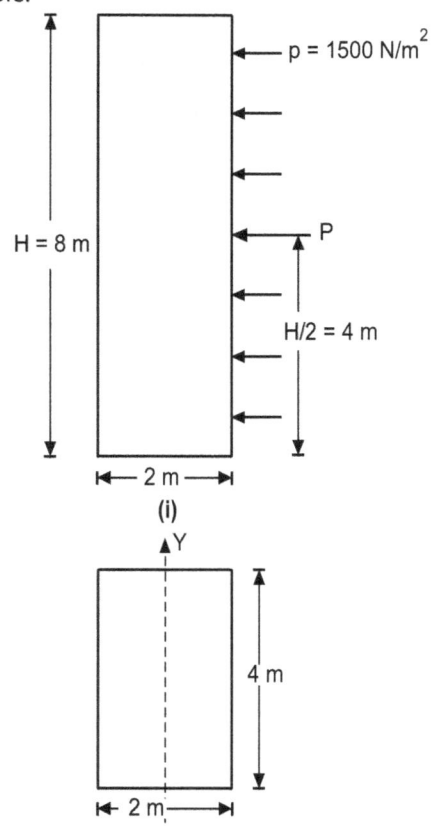

**Fig. 6.34**

**Answer :**
$$\sigma_{max} = \sigma_0 + \sigma_b = 16 \times 10^4 + 72000 = \mathbf{232000 \ N/m^2 \ (Compressive)}$$
$$\sigma_{min} = \sigma_0 - \sigma_b = 16 \times 10^4 - 72000 = \mathbf{88000 \ N/m^2 \ (Compressive)}$$

**Example 31 :** *A masonry pillar 8 m high is 1.5 × 2.5 m². A horizontal wind pressure of 1400 N/m² acts on 2.5 m × 8 m face. Find the maximum and minimum stresses induced on the base section. ρ = 22500 N/m³.* **(B.T.E. 2011/4 Marks)**

**Answer :**
$$\sigma_{max} = 180 + 119.5 = \textbf{229.5 kN/m}^2 \textbf{ (C)}$$
$$\sigma_{min} = 180 - 119.5 = \textbf{60.5 kN/m}^2 \textbf{ (C)}$$

**Example 32 :** *A steel plate 15 mm × 50 mm is pulled by a tensile force of 45 kN, line of action of the loading being 35 mm from one edge as shown in Fig. 6.35. Extension of 0.055 mm over a gauge length of 125 mm. Determine the extreme stresses for plate section and Young's modulus of steel.* **(B.T.E. S-2011/4 Marks)**

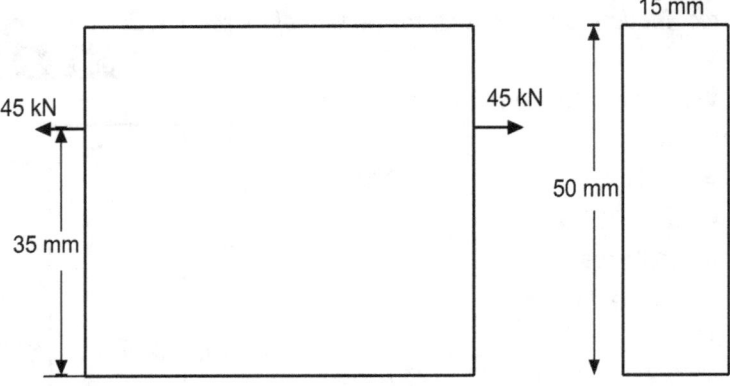

**Fig. 6.35**

**Solution :** (i)
$$A = 15 \times 50 = 750 \text{ mm}^2$$

$$I = \frac{15 \times 50^3}{12} = 156250 \text{ mm}^4$$

$$y = \frac{50}{2} = 25 \text{ mm}$$

$$Z = \frac{I}{y} = 6250 \text{ mm}^3$$

(ii) $\text{Direct stress} = \sigma_o = \frac{P}{A} = \frac{-45 \times 10^3}{750} = -60 \text{ N/mm}^2 \text{ (Tensile)}$

$$\text{Eccentricity, } \mathbf{e} = 35 - \frac{50}{2} = 35 - 25 = \textbf{10 mm}$$

$$M = P \times e = 45 \times 10^3 \times 10 = 450 \times 10^3 \text{ N.mm}$$

(iii) $\text{Bending stress, } \sigma_b = \pm\frac{M}{Z} = \pm\frac{450 \times 10^3}{6250} = \pm 72 \text{ N/mm}^2$

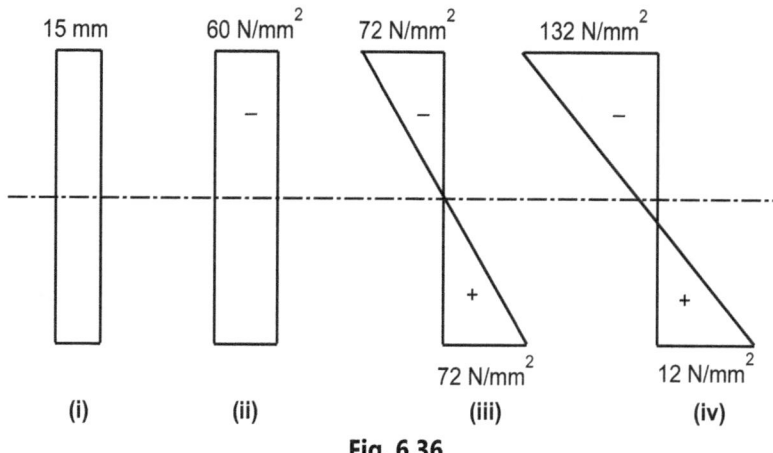

**Fig. 6.36**

(iv) Extreme stresses,

**Resultant stress at top** $= -60 - 72 = $ **−132 N/mm² (Tensile)**

**Resultant stress at bottom** $= -60 + 72 = $ **12 N/mm² (Compressive)**

(v)  Using,                $\delta L = \dfrac{PL}{AE}$

$$0.055 = \dfrac{45 \times 10^3 \times 125}{(750)\, E}$$

$$E = 1.36 \times 10^5 \text{ N/mm}^2$$

**Answer :** (i) $\sigma_{top} = -132$ N/mm² (Tensile), (ii) $\sigma_{bottom} = 12$ N/mm² (Compressive), (iii) $E_{for\ steel} = 1.36 \times 10^5$ N/mm²

## SUB-TOPIC 6.3 : CONDITION FOR NO TENSION IN THE SECTION, CORE OF A SECTION
### (4 Marks)

## 6.8 CONDITION FOR NO TENSION

We have seen that when an eccentric compressive load acts on a column, it produces direct as well as bending stress. If $\sigma_o > \sigma_b$, the resultant stress is compressive. If $\sigma_o = \sigma_b$, the minimum stress is zero and the maximum stress is $2\sigma_o$ and the stress distribution is compressive. But if $\sigma_o < \sigma_b$, the stress is partly compressive and partly tensile. A small tensile stress at the base of a structure may develop tension cracks. *Hence, for no-tension condition, direct stress should be greater than or equal to bending stress.*

Mathematically,                $\sigma_o \geq \sigma_b$

$$\dfrac{P}{A} \geq \dfrac{M}{Z}$$

$$\dfrac{P}{A} \geq \dfrac{P \cdot e}{Z}$$

$\therefore$                $\dfrac{1}{A} \geq \dfrac{e}{Z}$

i.e.
$$\frac{e}{Z} \le \frac{1}{A}$$

i.e.
$$\boxed{e \le \frac{Z}{A}}$$

*Hence, for no-tension condition, eccentricity should be less than Z/A, or maximum it should be equal to Z/A.*

---

1. What is the condition for no tension in section ?　　**(B.T.E. S-2013/2 Marks)**
2. State the condition for no tension at the base of a column.
   　　　　　　　　　　　**(B.T.E. W-2009, 2007, 1997/2 Marks)**
3. State the condition for no tension anywhere in the cross-section of a column.
   　　　　　　　　　　　**(B.T.E. S-2008/2 Marks)**

---

**(Most Likely and Asked in Previous B.T.E. Exam.)**

## 6.9 SECTION MODULUS

*It is the ratio of M.I. of the section about the neutral axis and the distance of the most extreme layer from the neutral axis.*

$$Z_{XX} = \text{Section modulus about X-X axis} = \frac{I_{XX}}{y_{max}}$$

$$Z_{YY} = \text{Section modulus about Y-Y axis} = \frac{I_{YY}}{y_{max}}$$

## 6.10 MIDDLE THIRD RULE

Let us consider a rectangular section of width b and thickness d as shown in Fig. 6.37.

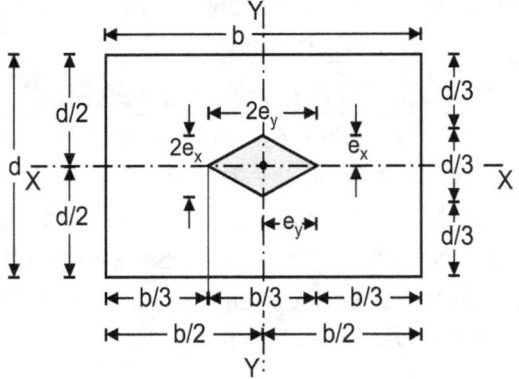

**Fig. 6.37**

Area of section,　　　$A = b \times d.$

$$Z_{XX} = \frac{I_{XX}}{y_{max}} = \frac{bd^3/12}{d/2} = \frac{bd^2}{6}$$

$$Z_{YY} = \frac{I_{YY}}{y_{max}} = \frac{db^3/12}{b/2} = \frac{db^2}{6}$$

For no tension or zero tensile stress condition,

$$e \leq \frac{Z_{XX}}{A} \quad \text{and} \quad e \leq \frac{Z_{YY}}{A}$$

$$\therefore \quad e \leq \frac{bd^2/6}{bd} \quad \therefore \quad e \leq \frac{db^2/6}{bd}$$

$$\therefore \quad \boxed{e \leq d/6} \quad \therefore \quad \boxed{e \leq b/6}$$

i.e. $\quad e_x = d/6 \quad$ and $\quad e_y = b/6$

$$\therefore \quad 2\,e_x = \frac{d}{3} \quad \text{and} \quad 2\,e_y = \frac{b}{3}$$

*For no-tension condition, the load must lie within the middle third shaded area of eccentricity 2e as shown in Fig. 6.37. This is known as middle third rule. The central shaded portion is also called core or Kernel of a section.*

1. Draw a neat sketch to show core of a rectangular section.

   **(B.T.E. W-2011/2 Marks)**

2. State middle third rule with diagram　**(B.T.E. W-2014, 2010, S-2010/2 Marks)**

3. What is limit of eccentricity ? State its value for rectangular section.

   **(B.T.E. S-2009/2 Marks)**

4. State middle third rule regarding direct and bending stresses.

   **(B.T.E. W-2005, S-2005/2 Marks)**

5. What is middle third rule for a rectangular section ?

   **(B.T.E. W-1998, S-1998/2 Marks)**

6. Calculate the limit of eccentricity of a rectangular cross-section of size 1000 mm × 2000 mm and sketch it.　**(B.T.E. S-2000/2 Marks)**

7. Obtain the core of a section for a rectangular section.　**(B.T.E. S-2007/2 Marks)**

   **(Most Likely and Asked in Previous B.T.E. Exam.)**

## 6.10.1 Core of a Section

*The centrally located portion of a section within which the load must act so as to produce only compressive stress is called a core or kernel of a section.*

1. Define core of a section. Obtain the core section for a rectangular section.

   **(B.T.E. S-2013/4 Marks)**

2. Define the core of a section.　**(B.T.E. W-2014, 2011/2 Marks)**

3. What is core or kernel of a section ?

   **(B.T.E. W-2008, 2007, 1997; S-1999, 1997/2 Marks)**

   **(Most Likely and Asked in Previous B.T.E. Exam.)**

## 6.10.2 Core of a Circular Section

Let us consider a solid circular section of diameter D as shown in Fig. 6.38.

Section modulus, $Z = Z_{XX} = Z_{YY}$

$$= \frac{I}{y} = \frac{\frac{\pi}{64} D^4}{D/2} = \frac{\pi}{32} D^3$$

Area of section, $A = \frac{\pi}{4} D^2$

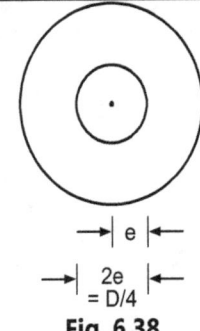

**Fig. 6.38**

**For no-tension condition,** $e \leq \dfrac{Z}{A}$

$\therefore$ $\qquad e \leq \dfrac{\frac{\pi}{32} D^3}{\frac{\pi}{4} D^2}$

$\therefore$ $\qquad \boxed{e \leq \dfrac{D}{8}}$

$\therefore$ $\qquad e_{max} = \dfrac{D}{8}$

$\therefore$ $\qquad 2\,e_{max} = 2 \times \dfrac{D}{8} = \dfrac{D}{4}$

*For no-tension condition, the load must lie within a circle of diameter 2e i.e. D/4 as shown in Fig. 6.38. In this case, core of a section is a circle of diameter D/4.*

1. Calculate the maximum eccentricity for a circular section of diameter D for no tension at base. **(B.T.E. W-2012/2 Marks)**
2. What is core of a section ? Sketch it for a circular section. **(B.T.E. W-2010/4 Marks)**
3. What is core of a section ? Write its value for a circular section.
   **(B.T.E. W-2014, S-2015, 2009/2 Marks)**
4. Sketch the core of a section for a circular section. Show its size.
   **(B.T.E. W-2014, 2007, 1999/2 Marks)**
5. State the core of solid circular column having diameter 200 mm.
   **(B.T.E. W-2009, S-2015/2 Marks)**
6. Find the limit of eccentricity of a hollow circular column of external diameter D and internal diameter d. **(B.T.E. S-1999, 1997; W-1997/2 Marks)**

**(Most Likely and Asked in Previous B.T.E. Exam.)**

**Type 4 : Examples based on zero stress condition at one extreme layer**

**Working rule :** Equate direct stress to bending stress.

$$\sigma_o = \sigma_b \text{ i.e. } \frac{P}{A} = \frac{M}{Z}$$

## Type 4.1 : Examples on calculating e :

**Example 33 :** *A short masonry pillar 400 mm × 400 mm in section is subjected to an eccentric load of 5000 kN about one axis. Find eccentricity of the load so as to produce compression only at the section.* **(B.T.E. W-1997/4 Marks)**

**Data** : b = d = 400 mm, P = 5000 kN = 5000 × 10³ N

**To find** : e.

**Concept :** For no-tension condition, direct stress = bending stress.

**Solution :** For no-tension condition (only compression condition),

$$\sigma_0 = \sigma_b$$

$$\therefore \quad \frac{P}{A} = \frac{M}{Z} = \frac{P \times e}{db^2/6} = \frac{6\,P.e}{db^2}$$

$$\therefore \quad \frac{1}{A} = \frac{6\,e}{db^2}$$

$$\therefore \quad \frac{1}{400 \times 400} = \frac{6 \times e}{400 \times 400^2}$$

$$\therefore \quad e = \frac{400}{6} = \mathbf{66.67\ mm}$$

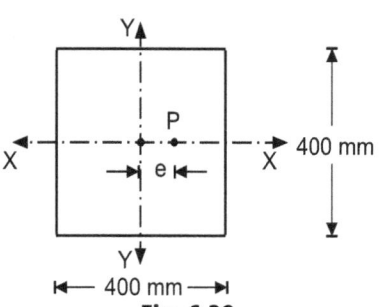

Fig. 6.39

**Answer :** **Therefore, the load must be placed at an eccentricity of 66.67 mm on X-X or Y-Y axis so as to produce only compression at the section.**

---

**Example 34 :** *A short masonry pillar is 500 mm × 500 mm in section. At what eccentricity a point load of 9500 kN be placed on one of the centroidal axis of the section so as to produce no tension in the section ?* **(B.T.E. S-2008/4 Marks)**

**Data** : b = d = 500 mm, P = 9500 kN = 9500 × 10³ N.

**To find** : e

**Concept :** For no-tension condition, direct stress = bending stress.

**Solution :** For no-tension condition (only compression condition),

$$\sigma_0 = \sigma_b$$

$$\frac{P}{A} = \frac{M}{Z} = \frac{P \times e}{db^2/6} = \frac{6P \times e}{db^2}$$

Dividing both sides by P,

$$\frac{1}{A} = \frac{6 \times e}{db^2}$$

$$\therefore \quad \frac{1}{500 \times 500} = \frac{6 \times e}{500 \times 500^2}$$

$$\therefore \quad 1 = \frac{6e}{500}$$

$$\therefore \quad e = \frac{500}{6} = \mathbf{83.33\ mm}$$

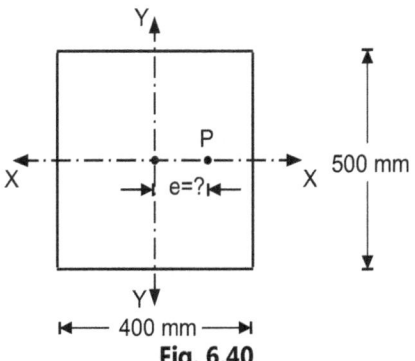

Fig. 6.40

**Answer :** Therefore, a point load of 9500 kN must be placed at an eccentricity of 83.33 mm on X-X or Y-Y axis so as to produce no tension in the section.

**Example 35 :** *A circular section of diameter 'd' is subjected to load 'P' eccentric to the axis YY (vertical). The eccentricity of load is 'e'. Obtain the limit of eccentricity such that no tension is induced at the section.* **(B.T.E. W-1999/4 Marks)**

**OR**

*A mild steel column of circular cross-section is subjected to a force P parallel to the axis but at a distance of 'e' from axis. Show that if there is no tension produced in column, the value of 'e' must not exceed $\frac{1}{8}$ of the diameter of column. Also draw core of the section.*

**(B.T.E. W-2010, S-2004/4 Marks)**

**Data** : A circular section carrying an eccentric load.

**To find** : e.

**Concept :** For no-tension condition, $\sigma_o = \sigma_b$.

**Solution :** Direct stress, $\sigma_0 = \dfrac{P}{A}$ and bending stress, $\sigma_b = \dfrac{M}{Z}$

For circular section, $\qquad I = \dfrac{\pi}{64} d^4$ and $y = \dfrac{d}{2}$

∴ Section modulus, $\qquad Z = \dfrac{I}{y} = \dfrac{\dfrac{\pi}{64} d^4}{\dfrac{d}{2}} = \dfrac{\pi}{32} d^3$

For no-tension condition, $\sigma_0 = \sigma_b$

∴ $\qquad \dfrac{P}{A} = \dfrac{M}{Z}$

∴ $\qquad \dfrac{P}{A} = \dfrac{P \times e}{Z}$

∴ $\qquad \dfrac{1}{A} = \dfrac{e}{Z}$

∴ $\qquad \mathbf{e} = \dfrac{Z}{A} = \dfrac{\dfrac{\pi}{32} d^3}{\dfrac{\pi}{4} d^2} = \dfrac{\mathbf{d}}{\mathbf{8}}$

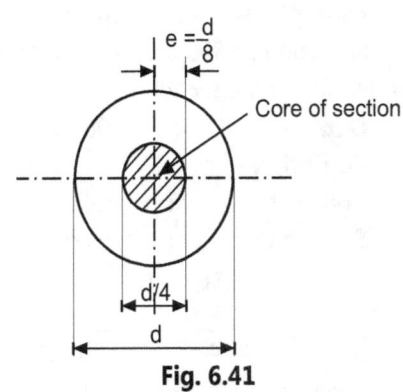

**Fig. 6.41**

**Answer :** The core of a section is a circle of radius $e = \dfrac{d}{8}$ or diameter $\dfrac{d}{4}$ .

---

**Example 36 :** *Calculate the limit of eccentricity of a rectangular cross-section of size 1000 mm × 2000 mm and sketch it.* **(B.T.E. S-2015, 2013, 2000/4 Marks)**

**Data** : Rectangular section b = 1000 mm, d = 2000 mm

**To find** : $e_x$ and $e_y$.

**Concept :** For no-tension condition, $\sigma_o = \sigma_b$.

**Solution :** **Case 1 : When the load P acts at D on X-X axis i.e. it is eccentric w.r.t. YY axis :**

Direct stress, $\sigma_0 = \dfrac{P}{A} = \dfrac{P}{b.d}$

**Since the load is eccentric w.r.t. YY axis, we have to consider $M_{YY}$ and $Z_{YY}$.**

$$M_{YY} = P \times e_y$$

$$Z_{YY} = \frac{I_{YY}}{y_{max}} = \frac{db^3/12}{b/2} = \frac{db^2}{6}$$

Bending stress, $\sigma_b = \dfrac{M_{YY}}{Z_{YY}} = \dfrac{P \cdot e_y}{db^2/6} = \dfrac{6P \cdot e_y}{db^2}$

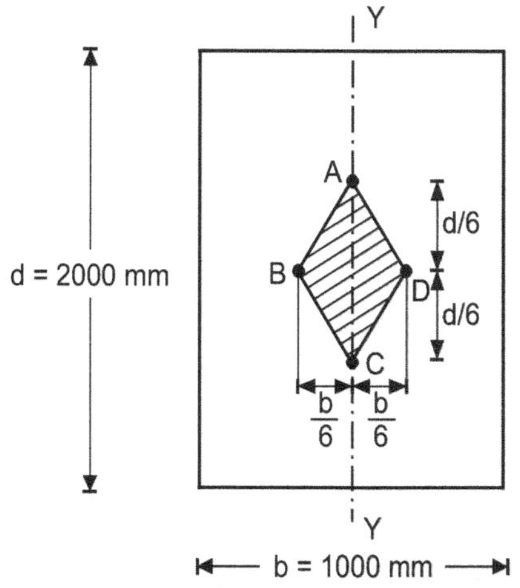

**Fig. 6.42**

For no-tension condition,

$$\sigma_o = \sigma_b$$

$$\frac{P}{b \cdot d} = \frac{6P \cdot e_y}{db^2}$$

$\therefore \qquad e_y = \dfrac{b}{6} = \dfrac{1000}{6} = \textbf{166.67 mm}$

**Case 2 : When the load P acts at A on YY axis, i.e. it is eccentric w.r.t. XX axis :**

**Since the load is eccentric w.r.t. XX axis, here we have to consider $M_{XX}$ and $Z_{XX}$.**

$$M_{XX} = P_X e_x$$

$$Z_{XX} = \frac{I_{XX}}{y_{max}} = \frac{bd^3/12}{d/2} = \frac{bd^2}{6}$$

Bending stress, $\qquad \sigma_b = \dfrac{M_{XX}}{Z_{XX}} = \dfrac{P \cdot e_x}{bd^2/6} = \dfrac{6P \cdot e_x}{bd^2}$

For no-tension condition,

$$\sigma_o = \sigma_b$$

$$\frac{P}{b \cdot d} = \frac{6P \cdot e_x}{b \cdot d^2}$$

$\therefore \qquad e_x = \dfrac{d}{6} = \dfrac{2000}{6} = \textbf{333.33 mm}$

**Answer :** $\boxed{e_x = 333.33 \text{ mm}, \ e_y = 166.67 \text{ mm}}$

**Example 37 :** *A short mild steel column of external diameter 200 mm and internal diameter 150 mm carries an eccentric load. Find the greatest eccentricity which the load can have without producing tension in the section of column.*

**(B.T.E. S-2012, 2010, 2003/4 Marks)**

**Data** : Hollow M.S. column, external diameter D = 200 mm,
internal diameter d = 150 mm subjected to eccentric load P.

**To find** : e.

**Concept** : For no-tension condition, direct stress = bending stress.

**Solution** : For no-tension condition,

$$\sigma_o = \sigma_b$$

$$\therefore \quad \frac{P}{A} = \frac{M}{Z}$$

$$\therefore \quad \frac{P}{A} = \frac{P \cdot e}{Z}$$

$$\therefore \quad e = \frac{Z}{A} = \frac{\dfrac{\pi}{32}\left(\dfrac{D^4 - d^4}{D}\right)}{\dfrac{\pi}{4}(D^2 - d^2)} = \frac{\dfrac{\pi}{32}\left(\dfrac{200^4 - 150^4}{200}\right)}{\dfrac{\pi}{4}(200^2 - 150^2)} = \textbf{39.06 mm}$$

**Answer :** $\boxed{e = 39.06 \text{ mm}}$

---

**Type 4.2 : Examples on calculating dimensions of core of a section :**

**Example 38 :** *Calculate the diameter of core for a hollow circular section having external diameter twice that of internal diameter.* **(B.T.E. S-1997/8 Marks)**

**Data :** Hollow circular section D = 2 d

**To find :** Diameter of core.

**Concept :** For no-tension condition, $e \leq \dfrac{Z}{A}$.

**Solution :** For a hollow circular section of external diameter D and internal diameter d,

$$I = \frac{\pi}{64}(D^4 - d^4)\ , y = \frac{D}{2}, A = \frac{\pi}{4}(D^2 - d^2)$$

$$Z = \frac{I}{y} = \frac{\dfrac{\pi}{64}(D^4 - d^4)}{D/2} = \frac{\pi}{32}\frac{(D^4 - d^4)}{D}$$

**For no-tension condition,**

$$e \leq \frac{Z}{A}$$

$$\therefore \quad e \leq \frac{\dfrac{\dfrac{\pi}{32}(D^4 - d^4)}{D}}{\dfrac{\pi}{4}(D^2 - d^2)}$$

$$\therefore \quad e \le \frac{1}{8} \frac{(D^2 - d^2)\,(D^2 + d^2)}{D\,(D^2 - d^2)}$$

$$\therefore \quad e \le \frac{D^2 + d^2}{8D}$$

Hence for no-tension condition, the load can be placed anywhere but not farther than $\frac{D^2 + d^2}{8D}$ from the centre of the section. The diameter of a circle within which the load can be applied is

$$2\,e = 2 \times \frac{D^2 + d^2}{8D} = \frac{D^2 + d^2}{4\,D}$$

Thus core of a section is a circle of diameter $\frac{D^2 + d^2}{4D}$.

$$\therefore \quad \textbf{Diameter of core} = \frac{D^2 + d^2}{4D} = \frac{(2d)^2 + d^2}{4 \times 2\,d} \qquad \dots (\because D = 2\,d)$$

$$= \frac{4\,d^2 + d^2}{8\,d} = \frac{5\,d^2}{8\,d} = \frac{5\,d}{8} = \textbf{0.625 d}$$

**Answer :** $\boxed{\textbf{Thus diameter of core = 0.625} \times \textbf{internal diameter.}}$

---

**Example 39 :** *Calculate the limit of eccentricity for a circular section having diameter 50 mm.* **(B.T.E. W-2012/4 Marks)**

**Data :** Solid circular section, D = 50 mm.

**To find :** e.

**Concept :** For no-tension condition, $e = \dfrac{Z}{A}$

**Solution :**

$$e = \frac{Z}{A}$$

$$Z = \frac{I}{y} = \frac{\frac{\pi}{64} D^4}{D/2} = \frac{\pi}{32} D^3$$

$$A = \frac{\pi}{4} D^2$$

$$e = \frac{Z}{A} = \frac{\frac{\pi}{32} D^3}{\frac{\pi}{4} D^2} = \frac{D}{8}$$

$$\therefore \quad e = \frac{50}{8} = \textbf{6.25 mm}$$

**Answer :** $\boxed{e = 6.25 \text{ mm}}$

## Type 4.3 : Examples on calculating W for no-tension condition :

**Example 40 :** *A hollow C.I. column of external diameter 250 mm and internal diameter 200 mm carries an axial load 'W' kN and a load of 100 kN at an eccentricity of 175 mm. Calculate the minimum value of W so as to avoid the tensile stresses.*

**(B.T.E. W-2005/4 Marks)**

**Data :** D = 250 mm, d = 200 mm, axial load = W,

eccentric load = 100 kN = $100 \times 10^3$ N, e = 175 mm

**To find :** W for no-tension condition.

**Concept :** For no-tension condition, $\sigma_o = \sigma_b$.

**Solution :** $A = \dfrac{\pi}{4}(D^2 - d^2) = \dfrac{\pi}{4}(250^2 - 200^2) = 17671.46$ mm$^2$

$$Z = \dfrac{I}{y} = \dfrac{\dfrac{\pi}{64}(D^4 - d^4)}{\left(\dfrac{D}{2}\right)} = \dfrac{\pi}{32}\left(\dfrac{D^4 - d^4}{D}\right)$$

$$= \dfrac{\pi}{32}\left(\dfrac{250^4 - 200^4}{250}\right) = 905662.26 \text{ mm}^2$$

Let 'W' be in N.

$$\sigma_o = \dfrac{\text{Total load}}{A} = \left[\dfrac{W + (100 \times 10^3)}{17671.46}\right] \text{N/mm}^2 \text{ (Compressive)}$$

$$\sigma_b = \dfrac{M}{Z} = \dfrac{P \times e}{Z} = \dfrac{(100 \times 10^3) \times 175}{905662.26} = 19.32 \text{ N/mm}^2$$

For no-tension condition, $\sigma_o = \sigma_b$.

$\therefore \qquad \dfrac{W + (100 \times 10^3)}{17671.46} = 19.32$

$\therefore \qquad W + (100 \times 10^3) = 341412.6$

$\therefore \qquad$ **W** $= 341412.6 - (100 \times 10^3) = 241412.6$ N = **241.4 kN**

**Answer :** $\boxed{W = 241.4 \text{ kN}}$

## Type 4.4 : Miscellaneous examples on no-tension condition :

**Example 41 :** *A pier of 2 m $\times$ 2 m in section and having its weight 385 kN, carries a compressive load P which is acting at 75 mm from its edge bisecting one of its axis. What is the value of P for no-tension conditions ?* **(B.T.E. W-2011, 2006, 2004; S-2004, 2003/4 Marks)**

**Data :** Pier b = 2 m, d = 2 m, own weight W = 385 kN = $385 \times 10^3$ N,

eccentric load P at 75 mm from edge

i.e. e = 1000 mm – 75 mm = 925 mm = 0.925 m.

**To find :** P for no-tension condition.

**Concept :** For no-tension condition, $\sigma_o = \sigma_b$.

**Solution :** The load P acts at 0.925 m from centroid G on the Y-Y axis i.e. it is eccentric w.r.t. XX axis. Hence, we have to consider $I_{XX}$ and $Z_{XX}$.

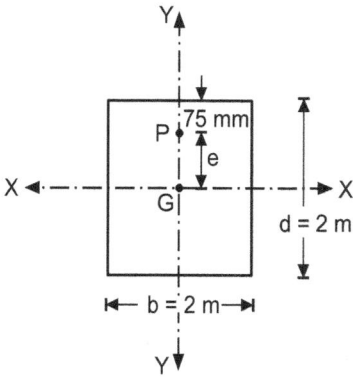

**Fig. 6.43**

Area :  $A = 2 \times 2 = 4 \text{ m}^2$

Direct stress due to own weight W,

$$\sigma_{O_1} = \frac{W}{A} = \frac{385 \times 10^3}{4} = 96250 \text{ N/m}^2 \qquad \dots \text{(i)}$$

Direct stress due to eccentric compressive load P,

$$\sigma_{O_2} = \frac{P}{A} = \frac{P}{4} = (0.25 \text{ P}) \text{ N/m}^2 \qquad \dots \text{(ii)}$$

Total direct stress,  $\boldsymbol{\sigma_O} = \sigma_{O_1} + \sigma_{O_2} = \boldsymbol{96250 + 0.25\ P}$ $\qquad \dots \text{(1)}$

$$I_{XX} = \frac{bd^3}{12}, \quad y_{max} = \frac{d}{2}$$

$\therefore$  $\boldsymbol{Z_{XX}} = \dfrac{I_{XX}}{y_{max}} = \dfrac{bd^3/12}{d/2} = \dfrac{bd^2}{6} = \dfrac{1 \times 1^2}{6} = \boldsymbol{1.333\ m^3}$

Bending moment, $\boldsymbol{M} = P \times e_x = P \times 0.925 = \boldsymbol{0.925\ P}$

Bending stress, $\boldsymbol{\sigma_b} = \dfrac{M}{Z_{XX}} = \dfrac{0.925\ P}{1.333} = \boldsymbol{(0.6939\ P)\ N/m^2}$ $\qquad \dots \text{(2)}$

For no-tension condition,  $\sigma_o = \sigma_b$

$\therefore$  $96250 + 0.25\ P = 0.6939\ P$

$96250 = (0.6939 - 0.25)\ P = 0.4439\ P$

$\therefore$  $\boldsymbol{P} = \dfrac{96250}{0.4439} = \boldsymbol{216828.11\ N}$

**Answer :**  $\boxed{P = 216.83 \text{ kN (Compressive)}}$

## *Practice Questions*

### Questions of 2 marks

1. Calculate the maximum eccentricity for circular section of diameter D for no tension at base. **(B.T.E. W-2012)**

2. Define eccentric load. **(B.T.E. W-2012)**

3. Define the term direct load with formula. **(B.T.E. S-2012)**

4. Define the term limit of eccentricity. **(B.T.E. S-2013, 2012; W-2008, 2000)**

5. Define the core of a section. **(B.T.E. W-2011)**

6. Draw a neat sketch to show core of a rectangular section. **(B.T.E. W-2011)**

7. State middle third rule with diagram **(B.T.E. W-2010, S-2010)**

8. Sketch the resultant stress distribution at the base section for the condition that direct stress is equal to bending stress. **(B.T.E. W-2008, 1998)**

**OR**

In case of combined stress, direct stress is equal to bending stress. Draw the nature of total stress distribution diagram across the section. **(B.T.E. W-2010, 2000; S-2000)**

9. Define eccentric load and axial load. **(B.T.E. S-2013)**

10. Define the term direct stress with formula.

11. What do you understand by an eccentric load ? **(B.T.E. W-2009)**

12. What is eccentric loading ? State two examples of eccentric loading.

**(B.T.E. S-2013, 2009)**

13. Explain with diagram how direct and bending stresses are developed in a column due to an eccentric load. **(B.T.E. S-2008)**

14. Draw the nature of total stress distribution diagram if direct stress is less than bending stress. **(B.T.E. S-2008)**

15. Draw the nature of total stress variation diagram if direct stress is more than bending stress.

16. State the condition for no tension at the base of a column.

**(B.T.E. W-2009, 2007, 1997)**

**OR**

What is the condition for no tension in section ? **(B.T.E. S-2013)**

17. State the condition for no tension anywhere in the cross-section of a column.

**(B.T.E. S-2008)**

18. What is limit of eccentricity ? State its value for rectangular section. **(B.T.E. S-2009)**

19. State middle third rule regarding direct and bending stresses.**(B.T.E. W-2005, S-2005)**

20. What is middle third rule for a rectangular section ?          **(B.T.E. W-1998, S-1998)**

21. Calculate the limit of eccentricity for a rectangular cross-section of size 1000 mm × 2000 mm and sketch it.          **(B.T.E. S-2000)**

22. Obtain the core of a section for a rectangular section.          **(B.T.E. S-2007)**

23. What is core or Kernal of a section ?     **(B.T.E. S-2008, 1999, 1997; W-2007, 1997)**

24. What is core of a section ? Write its value for a circular section.          **(B.T.E. S-2009)**

25. Sketch the core of a section for a circular section. Show its size. **(B.T.E. W-2007, 1999)**

26. Sketch the core of solid circular column having diameter 200 mm.          **(B.T.E. W-2009)**

27. Find the limit of eccentricity of a hollow circular column of external diameter D and internal diameter d.          **(B.T.E. S-1999, 1997; W-1997)**

## Questions of 4 marks

28. Define core of a section. Obtain the core section for a rectangular section.
          **(B.T.E. S-2013)**

29. Define direct and bending stress. Draw the stress distribution diagram if a rectangular section is subjected to direct and bending stresses.**(B.T.E. W-2012, 2011)**

30. What is core of a section ? Sketch it for a circular section.          **(B.T.E. W-2010)**

## Problems of 4 marks

31. A short column of external diameter 200 mm and internal diameter 150 mm carries an eccentric load. Find the eccentricity which the load can have without producing tension in the section of a column.          **(B.T.E. S-86) (Ans.** e = 39.1 mm)

32. A square pillar is 600 mm × 600 mm in section. At what eccentricity a point load of 6000 kN be placed on one of the centroidal axis of the section so as to produce no tension in the section ?          **(Ans.** e = 100 mm)

33. A rectangular column 150 mm wide and 100 mm thick carries a load of 150 kN at an eccentricity of 50 mm in the plane bisecting the thickness. Find $\sigma_{max}$ and $\sigma_{min}$.
          **[Ans.** $\sigma_{max}$ = 30 N/mm$^2$ (Compressive), $\sigma_{min}$ = 10 N/mm$^2$ (Tensile)**]**

34. A hollow circular steel column having external diameter 300 mm and internal diameter 250 mm carries an eccentric load of 100 kN acting at an eccentricity of 100 mm. Calculate the maximum and minimum stresses.          **(B.T.E. W-85)**
          **[Ans.** $\sigma_{max}$ = 11.92 N/mm$^2$ (Compressive), $\sigma_{min}$ = 2.66 N/mm$^2$ (Tensile)**]**

35. A C.I. hollow circular column section has external diameter 250 mm and internal diameter 200 mm. It is subjected to a vertical force of 20 kN at a distance of 400 mm from the vertical axis of the bar. Calculate the maximum and minimum stresses at the base of the column and draw stress diagram.          **(B.T.E. W-88)**
          **[Ans.** $\sigma_{max}$ = 9.96 N/mm$^2$ (Compressive),  $\sigma_{min}$ = 7.7 N/mm$^2$ (Tensile)**]**

36. The cross-section through a rectangular pressed concrete beam at mid-span is shown in Fig. 6.44. At this section a thrust of 270 kN occurs at point A normal to the cross-section due to prestressing force. Calculate stress at top and bottom of the beam.          **(B.T.E. W-89)**

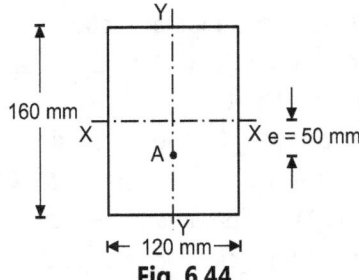

**Fig. 6.44**

**Hint :** Since the load is eccentric about X-X axis, $Z_{xx}$ should be considered for calculating $\sigma_b$.

(In this case, $y_{max}$ = 360/2 = 180 mm)

[**Ans.** $\sigma_{max}$ = 11.46 N/mm² (Compressive at bottom),

$\sigma_{min}$ = 1.04 N/mm² (Compressive at top)]

37. A square column 300 mm × 300 mm carries an axial load of 200 kN. Find the position of 30 kN load along the axis bisecting the width of the cross-section so that the stresses developed at the other extreme of the column will be zero.     **(B.T.E. S-91)**

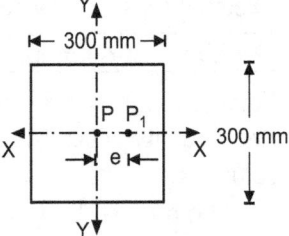

**Fig. 6.45**

**Hint :** Refer to Fig. 6.45. P = 200 kN; $P_1$ = 30 kN

Only a load of $P_1$ = 30 kN will cause bending stress.

$$\text{Direct stress} = \frac{P + P_1}{A} = \frac{\text{Total load}}{\text{Area}} \quad \text{and} \quad \text{Bending stress} = \frac{M}{Z_{yy}} = \frac{P_1 \cdot e}{db^2/6}$$

Equate direct stress to bending stress.     (**Ans.** e = 383.81 mm)

**Important Points**

- Axial load causes only direct stress whereas an eccentric load causes direct as well as bending stresses.

    Direct stress,     $\sigma_0$ = P/A

    Bending stress,     $\sigma_b = \frac{M}{I} \times y = \frac{M}{I/y} = \frac{M}{Z}$

- The resultant stress at a distance y from the neutral axis is given by,

    $\sigma_r = \sigma_0 \pm \sigma_b$

    Use positive sign for calculating $\sigma_{max}$ and negative sign for $\sigma_{min}$.

- If the load is eccentric about X-X axis, $Z_{xx}$ should be considered for calculating $\sigma_b$ and if it is eccentric about Y-Y axis, $Z_{yy}$ should be considered for calculating $\sigma_b$.

- For no-tension condition, $e_{max} = \frac{Z}{A}$.

□□□

# TORSION

| Weightage of Marks = 16, Teaching Hours = 06 |

## Objectives

**Specific Objectives :**

Understand and apply the concept of pure torsion and stresses due to power transmission.

## Contents

7.1 Concept of Pure Torsion :
  - Assumptions in the theory of pure torsion, Torsion equation for solid and hollow circular shafts, stress distribution across solid circular shaft (No derivation).
  - Power transmitted by a shaft.                    **(10 Marks)**
7.2 Comparison between solid and hollow shafts subjected to pure torsion (No problems on composite and non-homogeneous shaft)      **(06 Marks)**

### SUB-TOPIC 7.1 : CONCEPT OF PURE TORSION (10 Marks)

## Synopsis

Torsion, Concept of Pure Torsion, Assumptions in the Theory of Torsion, Derivation of Torsional formula, Torsional Formula and the Meaning of Symbols used, Polar Modulus, Strength of a Shaft, Torsional Rigidity, Power Transmitted by a Shaft, H.P. Transmitted by a Shaft.

## 7.1 TORSION

*When a tangential force is applied to a shaft at the circumference, in the plane of its transverse cross-section, the shaft is said to be subjected to a twisting moment or a torque which is equal to the product of the force and the radius.*

### S.I. Unit of Torque :

Since Torque = Force × Radius

| S.I. unit of torque = N.m |

1. Define torque or twisting moment. State its S.I. unit.

                    **(B.T.E. S-2013, 2012; W-2007/2 Marks)**

                    **(Most Likely and Asked in Previous B.T.E. Exam.)**

## 7.1.1 Concept of Pure Torsion

If the shaft is subjected to two equal and opposite torques at its two ends, it is said to be under pure torsion. Due to torsion, shearing stresses are developed in the material of the shaft. A shaft is subjected to pure torsion if it is subjected to only twisting moment and no other bending moment or thrust acts on the shaft.

| | |
|---|---|
| 1.　Explain the theory of pure torsion. | **(B.T.E. S-2014, 11/4 Marks)** |

**(Most Likely and Asked in Previous B.T.E. Exam.)**

## 7.2 ASSUMPTIONS IN THE THEORY OF TORSION

In deriving the torsional formula, we make the following assumptions :

(1) The shaft is straight having uniform circular cross-section.

(2) The shaft is homogeneous and isotropic.

(3) Circular sections remain circular even after twisting.

(4) Plain sections before twisting remain plain after twisting and do not twist or warp.

(5) A diameter in the section before deformation remains a diameter or straight line after deformation.

(6) Stresses do not exceed the proportional limit.

(7) Shaft is loaded by twisting couples in the planes that are perpendicular to the axis of the shaft.

(8) Twist along the shaft is uniform.

1.　State the assumptions in the theory of torsion.
**(B.T.E. W-2013, S-2015, 2013/4 Marks)**

2.　State any four assumptions made in the theory of pure torsion.
**(B.T.E. S-2014, 2008, 2005, 1997; W-2014, 2011, 1997/2 Marks)**

3.　State any four assumptions in the theory of torsion in solid circular shaft.
**(B.T.E. S-2012, 2010/4 Marks)**

**(Most Likely and Asked in Previous B.T.E. Exam.)**

## 7.3 DERIVATION OF TORSIONAL FORMULA
### [Stress Distribution Across a Solid Circular Shaft]
### No Derivation is Expected in the Examination

Consider a solid shaft of length L and radius R fixed at one end and subjected to a torque T at the other end as shown in Fig. 7.1. As a result of the application of torque T, the shaft will get twisted and every cross-section of the shaft will be subjected to some shear stress.

Let the line AB on the surface of the shaft be deformed to AB' and OB to OB'.

$$\angle \, BAB' \; = \; \phi = \frac{BB'}{AB} \text{ is called shear strain}$$

$$\angle \, BOB' \; = \; \theta \text{ is called angle of twist.}$$

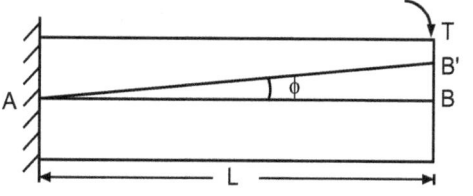 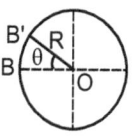

**(a) Longitudinal section**          **(b) Cross section**

**Fig. 7.1**

Now, in triangle ABB',

$$\tan \phi = \frac{BB'}{L}$$

∴ $\quad BB' = L \cdot \tan \phi$

∴ $\quad BB' = L \cdot \phi$ $\qquad$ ... (since $\phi$ is small, $\tan \phi = \phi$)

But $\quad BB' = R\,\theta$

∴ $\quad L\phi = R\,\theta$

∴ $\quad \phi = \dfrac{R\,\theta}{L}$ $\qquad$ ... (i)

Let '$f_s$' be the shear stress at the outermost surface of the shaft and 'C' be the modulus of rigidity of the shaft material.

Then $\qquad C = \dfrac{f_s}{\phi}$

∴ $\qquad \phi = \dfrac{f_s}{C}$ $\qquad$ ... (ii)

Equating (i) and (ii), we have

$$\frac{R\,\theta}{L} = \frac{f_s}{C}$$

∴ $\qquad \boxed{\dfrac{C\,\theta}{L} = \dfrac{f_s}{R}}$ $\qquad$ ... (A)

Now from the equation (A), we have

$$f_s = \left(\frac{C\,\theta}{L}\right) R$$

As C, $\theta$ and L are constants,

$$f_s \propto R$$

i.e. *the shear stress at any point is directly proportional to its distance from the axis of the shaft.*

If $\quad R = 0,\ f_s = 0$

i.e. at the centre of the shaft, the shear stress is zero. The maximum shear stress $f_s$ will occur at the outermost layer at a distance R from the centre of the shaft.

Let '$q$' be the shear stress at any intermediate layer at a distance '$r$' from the centre of the shaft.

Then $$q = \left(\frac{C\,\theta}{L}\right) \cdot r$$

The variation of shear stress for a solid and hollow shaft is as shown in Fig. 7.2.

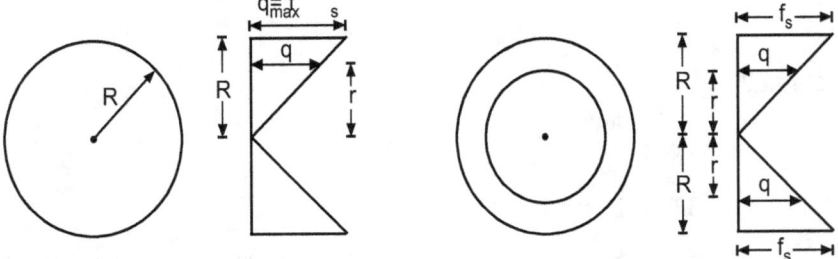

   **(a) Solid shaft radius R**          **(b) Hollow shaft outer radius R, inner radius r**

**Fig. 7.2**

Now, the applied torque T is resisted by the balancing torque $T_r$. $T_r$ is called the torque of resistance or resistive torque. In equilibrium, T and $T_r$ are equal in magnitude but opposite in direction.

**To find $T_r$ :**

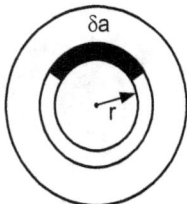

Let us consider an elementary area '$\delta a$' at a distance '$r$' from the axis of the shaft, as shown in Fig. 7.3.

**Fig. 7.3**

The shear stress at the elementary area '$\delta a$',

$$q = \left(\frac{C\,\theta}{L}\right) \cdot r = \frac{f_s}{R} \cdot r \qquad\qquad \ldots\left(\because \frac{C\theta}{L} = \frac{f_s}{R}\right)$$

The total shear resistance offered by the area $\delta a$

$$= q \times \delta a = \left(\frac{f_s}{R}\,r\right)\delta a$$

Moment of resistance about the centre of the shaft

$$= \text{Force} \times \text{Radius} = \left(\frac{f_s}{R}\,r\,\delta a\right) \times r = \frac{f_s}{R}\,r^2\,\delta a$$

∴ Total moment of resistance offered by the whole sections,

$$T_r = \sum \frac{f_s}{R} r^2 \, \delta a = \frac{f_s}{R} \sum r^2 \, \delta a$$

∴ $\quad T_r = \dfrac{f_s}{R} I_p \qquad$ ... ($\because \sum r^2 \, \delta a$ = Polar M.I. of the section and is denoted by $I_p$ or J)

∴ $\quad \dfrac{T_r}{I_p} = \dfrac{f_s}{R}$

In equilibrium, Resistive torque = Applied torque

i.e. $\qquad\qquad\qquad T_r = T$

∴ $\qquad\qquad \boxed{\dfrac{T}{I_p} = \dfrac{f_s}{R}} \qquad\qquad\qquad$ ... (B)

Equating (A) and (B), we have $\boxed{\dfrac{T}{I_p} = \dfrac{C\,\theta}{L} = \dfrac{f_s}{R}}$

This is known as torsional formula.

## 7.3.1 Torsional Formula and the Meaning of Symbols Used

When a shaft is subjected to pure torsion,

$$\frac{T}{I_p} = \frac{C\,\theta}{L} = \frac{f_s}{R}$$

where　T = Torque or turning moment (N·mm)

$I_p$ = Polar moment of inertia of the shaft section

= $I_{XX} + I_{YY}$ (mm⁴)

C = Modulus of rigidity of the shaft material (N/mm²)

θ = Angle through which the shaft is twisted due to torque i.e. angle of twist (radians)

L = Length of the shaft (mm)

$f_s$ = Maximum shear stress induced at the outermost layer of the shaft (N/mm²)

R = Radius of the shaft (mm)

1. State the torsional formula and explain meaning of each term.

**(B.T.E. S-2013/4 Marks)**

2. State the torsional formula and explain the meaning and units of each term.

**(B.T.E. W-2011, 1998; S-1999, 1997/2 Marks)**

3. State the equation of torsion. **(B.T.E. S-2010/2 Marks)**

4. Write torsion equation along with meaning of symbols used there in.

**(B.T.E. S-2008/2 Marks)**

5. State the equation of torsion giving meaning of each term used in it.

**(B.T.E. S-2011; W-2010, 2008/2 Marks)**

6. Sketch the shear stress variation across circular cross-section of shaft subjected to torsion. **(B.T.E. W-2013, S-2006/2 Marks)**

**(Most Likely and Asked in Previous B.T.E. Exam.)**

## 7.3.2 Polar Modulus

We know that,　　　　$\dfrac{T}{I_p} = \dfrac{f_s}{R}$

∴　　　　　　　　$T = \left(\dfrac{I_p}{R}\right) \cdot f_s$

For a given shaft, $I_p$ and R are constants. Therefore, $\dfrac{I_p}{R}$ is constant and is known as polar modulus of the shaft section and is denoted by $Z_p$.

**Definition :** *Polar modulus is the ratio of the polar moment of inertia of the section and the radius of the shaft.*

### Case I : Solid circular shaft of diameter D :

$$I_p = I_{XX} + I_{YY} = \frac{\pi}{64} D^4 + \frac{\pi}{64} D^4 = \frac{\pi}{32} D^4$$

∴　　　　$Z_p = \dfrac{I_p}{R} = \dfrac{\frac{\pi}{32} D^4}{D/2} = \dfrac{\pi}{16} D^3$

### Case II : Hollow circular shaft of external diameter 'D' and internal diameter 'd' :

$$I_p = I_{XX} + I_{YY} = \frac{\pi}{64} (D^4 - d^4) + \frac{\pi}{64} (D^4 - d^4)$$

$$= 2 \times \frac{\pi}{64} (D^4 - d^4) = \frac{\pi}{32} (D^4 - d^4)$$

∴　　　　$Z_p = \dfrac{I_p}{R} = \dfrac{\frac{\pi}{32} (D^4 - d^4)}{D/2} = \dfrac{\pi}{16} \left(\dfrac{D^4 - d^4}{D}\right)$

**S.I. unit :** Since　　　$Z_p = \dfrac{I_p}{R}$ ,

$$\text{S.I. unit of } Z_p = \frac{\text{Unit of } I_p}{\text{Unit of } R} = \frac{mm^4}{mm} = mm^3$$

**Other units :** $m^3$, $cm^3$, etc.

1. Define polar modulus of section. **(B.T.E. S-2008/2 Marks)**
2. Define polar modulus of section. State its S.I. unit.
   **(B.T.E. W-2008, 2007, 1999, 1997; S-2000/2 Marks)**
3. Write torsion equation for hollow shaft. State assumptions made in the theory of pure torsion. **(B.T.E. S-2009/2 Marks)**
4. Differentiate between polar modulus and section modulus. **(V.V. Imp./2 Marks)**
5. Calculate the polar modulus of circular shaft of 100 mm diameter.
   **(B.T.E. S-1999/2 Marks)**

**(Most Likely and Asked in Previous B.T.E. Exam.)**

## 7.4 STRENGTH OF A SHAFT
### (Torsion Equation for Solid and Hollow Circular Shafts)

*The ability of a shaft to resist the action of twisting moment is called the strength of the shaft.*

### (i) Strength of a solid shaft in terms of $Z_p$ :

We know that,

$$\frac{T}{I_p} = \frac{f_s}{R}$$

$\therefore$

$$T = \frac{I_p}{R} f_s = Z_p \cdot f_s$$

For a solid shaft,

$$Z_p = \frac{\pi}{16} D^3$$

$\therefore$

$$\boxed{T = \frac{\pi}{16} D^3 \cdot f_s} \qquad \text{... (A)}$$

This is the equation of torsion for a solid circular shaft.

### Strength of a hollow shaft in terms of $Z_p$ :

For a hollow shaft,

$$Z_p = \frac{\pi}{16} \left( \frac{D^4 - d^4}{D} \right)$$

Now,

$$T = Z_p \cdot f_s \text{ gives}$$

$$\boxed{T = \frac{\pi}{16} \left( \frac{D^4 - d^4}{D} \right) f_s} \qquad \text{... (B)}$$

This is the equation of torsion for a hollow circular shaft.

**Note :** For a shaft instead of applying torsional formula $\frac{T}{I_p} = \frac{f_s}{R}$, it is convenient to use the modified form as shown in equation (A) or (B).

---

1. Write the equation of torsion for a hollow shaft of outside diameter ($d_o$) and inside diameter ($d_i$). **(B.T.E. W-2012/2 Marks)**

2. Compare solid shaft and hollow shaft. **(B.T.E. S-2012/2 Marks)**

3. Calculate the torque exerted by a solid shaft of 40 mm diameter if the maximum shearing stress is 20 N/mm². **(B.T.E. W-1998/2 Marks)**

---

**(Most Likely and Asked in Previous B.T.E. Exam.)**

## 7.5 TORSIONAL RIGIDITY

Consider the equality,

$$\frac{T}{I_p} = \frac{C\theta}{L}$$

$\therefore$

$$\theta = \frac{TL}{C I_p}$$

Since C, $I_p$ and L are constants for a given shaft, $\theta \propto T$ i.e. the angle of twist is directly proportional to the twisting moment.

Now, if L and $\theta$ be unity, then, $T = C \cdot I_p$

**The quantity $C \cdot I_p$ is called torsional rigidity.**

**Definition :** *Torsional rigidity is the torque that produces a twist of one radian in a shaft of unit length.*

**S.I. unit :** Unit of torsional rigidity = Unit of C × Unit of $I_p$

$$= \frac{N}{m^2} \times m^4 = N\text{-}m^2$$

**Other units :** N-mm², kN·mm², etc.

**Note :** In case of flexure (i.e. bending), the product of E and I is called *flexural rigidity.*

i.e. $\boxed{\text{Flexural rigidity} = E.I}$

---

1. State formula for torsional rigidity and write the unit.     **(B.T.E. W-2007/2 Marks)**

2. Define the term torsional rigidity.     **(B.T.E. W-2013, 2000/2 Marks)**

**(Most Likely and Asked in Previous B.T.E. Exam.)**

---

## 7.6 POWER TRANSMITTED BY A SHAFT

The main purpose of the shaft is to transmit power from one shaft to another. *If a shaft is subjected to an average torque T (N·m) and rotates at N (rpm) and transmits power P (watts), then*

$$P = \left( \frac{2\pi N T}{60} \right) watts,$$

where   P = Power in watts

        T = Average (or mean) torque in N·m

        N = Number of revolutions of shaft per minute (rpm)

### 7.6.1 H.P. Transmitted by a Shaft

$$P = \left( \frac{2\pi N T}{4500} \right) H.P.$$

where      P = Horse power (metric)

           T = Average (mean) torque in kg·m

**Remember :** $\boxed{\textit{1 (metric) H.P. = 75 kg·m/sec = 75} \times \textit{9.81 N·m/sec = 735.75 W}}$

**Note :** *In power formula, T is average or mean torque. Generally, the maximum torque is 20 to 30 % higher over the average value. If the maximum torque exceeds 20 % over the mean value, then*

$$T_{max} = T_{mean} + \left(\frac{20}{100}\right) T_{mean} = T_{mean} + 0.2 \, T_{mean} = T_{mean} (1 + 0.2)$$

∴　　$\boxed{T_{max} = 1.2 \times T_{mean}}$

*When nothing is mentioned, the average torque is taken equal to the maximum torque.*

*i.e.* $\boxed{T_{average} = T_{max}}$

---

1. How the power of shaft can be calculated ?　　**(B.T.E. S-2013, 1998/2 Marks)**

2. State the expression for power transmitted by a shaft giving meaning of each term used.　　**(B.T.E. S-2014, W-2012/2 Marks)**

3. State the expression for power transmitted by a shaft at N rpm giving meaning of each term.　　**(B.T.E. W-2008/2 Marks)**

4. Write the expression for power transmitted by a shaft.　　**(B.T.E. S-2009/2 Marks)**

5. A circular shaft is rotating at 200 rpm. Calculated the power developed if the torque is 40000 N.mm.　　**(B.T.E. W-1999/2 Marks)**

---

**(Most Likely and Asked in Previous B.T.E. Exam.)**

## SOLVED EXAMPLES

**Type 1 : Examples based on torsion of solid shafts**

**Type 1.1 : Examples on strength of a solid shaft :**

**Important Formula**

---

$T = \dfrac{\pi}{16} f_s D^3$ where

T = Torque or twisting moment (N.mm)

$f_s$ = Maximum shear stress induced at the outermost layer of the shaft (N/mm$^2$)

D = Diameter of the solid shaft (mm)

---

**Example 1 :** *What is the torque induced in a solid circular shaft of 50 mm diameter rotating at 100 r.p.m., if the permissible shear stress is not to exceed 75 MPa ?*

**(B.T.E. W-2011, 2005/2 Marks)**

**Data**　:　Diameter D = 50 mm, shear stress $f_s$ = 75 MPa = 75 N/mm², 

　　　　　speed N = 100 r.p.m.

**To find**　:　Torque T.

**Concept :** Use of torsional formula (strength of a solid shaft)

**Solution :** Using the relation,

$$T = \frac{\pi}{16} f_s D^3 = \frac{\pi}{16} \times 75 \times 50^3$$

$$= 1840776.945 \text{ N.mm}$$

**Answer :** $\boxed{T = 1840.777 \text{ N.m}}$

---

**Example 2 :** *Find the torque which a solid shaft 50 mm diameter can safely transmit if the shear stress is not to exceed 80 MPa.* **(B.T.E. W-2010/2 Marks)**

**Data** : Diameter D = 50 mm, shear stress $f_s$ = 80 MPa = 80 N/mm$^2$.

**To find** : Torque T.

**Concept :** Use of standard formula.

**Solution :** Using the relation, $T = \frac{\pi}{16} f_s D^3 = \frac{\pi}{16} \times 80 \times 50^3 = 1963495.4 \text{ N·mm}$

**Answer :** $\boxed{T = 1963.495 \text{ N·m}}$

---

**Example 3 :** *Find the diameter of a solid shaft if it transmits a torque of $15 \times 10^6$ N·mm. The maximum shearing stress is not to exceed 45 N/mm$^2$.* **(Imp./2 Marks)**

**Data** : Torque T = $15 \times 10^6$ N·mm, Shear stress $f_s$ = 45 N/mm$^2$

**To find** : Diameter D.

**Concept :** Use of torsional formula (strength of a solid shaft)

**Solution :** Using the relation, $T = \frac{\pi}{16} f_s D^3$

$$15 \times 10^6 = \frac{\pi}{16} \times 45 \times D^3$$

**Answer :** $\boxed{D = 119.3 \text{ mm say 120 mm.}}$

---

**Type 1.2 : Examples based on the torsional formula :**

| Important Formulae |
|---|
| $$\frac{f_s}{R} = \frac{G\theta}{L}$$ $$\frac{T}{I_p} = \frac{G\theta}{L}$$ where, $f_s$ = Maximum shear stress at the outermost layer of the shaft (N/mm$^2$)<br>R = Radius of the shaft (mm)<br>G = Modulus of rigidity of shaft material (N/mm$^2$)<br>$\theta$ = Angle of twist (radians)<br>L = Length of shaft (mm)<br>T = Torque or turning moment (N.mm)<br>$I_p$ = Polar moment of inertia of shaft section (mm$^4$) |

**Example 4 :** *A solid circular shaft of 30 mm diameter is subjected to a torque of 0.25 kN·m causing an angle of twist of 3.74° in a 2 m length. Determine the modulus of rigidity for the material of the shaft.* **(B.T.E. W-2011/4 Marks)**

**Data**  : Solid shaft D = 30 mm, T = 0.25 kN·m = $0.25 \times 10^6$ N·mm,

$$\theta = 3.74° = \left(3.74 \times \frac{\pi}{180}\right) \text{rad}, \text{L} = 2 \text{ m} = 2000 \text{ mm}.$$

**To find**  : C.

**Concept :** Use of torsional formula.

**Solution :** Using the relation,     $\dfrac{T}{I_p} = \dfrac{C\theta}{L}$

∴          $$\frac{0.25 \times 10^6}{\dfrac{\pi}{32}(30)^4} = \frac{C \times \left(3.74 \times \dfrac{\pi}{180}\right)}{2000}$$

**Answer :** $\boxed{\text{C} = 96324.36 \text{ N/mm}^2 \cong \mathbf{0.96 \times 10^5 \text{ N/mm}^2}}$

---

**Example 5 :** *What must be the length of a 8 mm diameter aluminium wire so that it can be twisted through one complete revolution without exceeding a shearing stress of 45 MPa ? Consider the modulus of rigidity as 27 GPa.* **(V.V.Imp., B.T.E. S-2005/4 Marks)**

**Data**  :  D = 8 mm, i.e. R = 8/2 = 4 mm, $\theta$ = 1 rev = $2\pi$ radian,

$f_s$ = 45 MPa = 45 N/mm², G = 27 GPa = $27 \times 10^3$ N/mm²

**To find**  :  L.

**Concept :**  Use of torsional formula.

**Solution :**  We know that,

$$\frac{f_s}{R} = \frac{G \cdot \theta}{L}$$

∴          $$L = \frac{G \cdot \theta \cdot R}{f_s} = \frac{27 \times 10^3 \times 2\pi \times 4}{45}$$

**Answer :**    $\boxed{\text{L} = 15079.6 \text{ mm} = \mathbf{15.0796 \text{ m}}}$

---

**Example 6 :** *A shaft of 3 m length and 75 mm diameter is fixed at one end and twisted at free end by a force of 2 kN acting at mean radius of 0.6 m. Find the angle of twist. Assume, G = 90 GN/m².* **(V.V.Imp., B.T.E. W-2014, 2006/4 Marks)**

**Data**  :  Solid shaft, L = 3 m = $3 \times 10^3$ mm, D = 75 mm, force at free end F = 2 kN,

R = 0.6 m,  G = 90 GN/m² = $90 \times 10^3$ N/mm²

**To find**  :  $\theta$.

**Concept :**  Use of torsional formula.

**Solution :**   Here,      $T = F \times R = 2 \times 0.6 = 1.2$ kN.m $= 1.2 \times 10^6$ N-mm

Using the relation,

$$\frac{T}{I_p} = \frac{G\theta}{L}$$

$$\frac{1.2 \times 10^6}{\frac{\pi}{32}(75)^4} = \frac{(90 \times 10^3)\,\theta}{3 \times 10^3}$$

**Answer :**   $\boxed{\theta = 0.01287 \text{ rad} = \left(0.01287 \times \frac{180}{\pi}\right)^{\circ} = \mathbf{0.74°}}$

---

**Example 7 :** *Find the torque that can be applied to a shaft of 100 mm in diameter, if the permissible angle of twist is 2.75° in a length of 6 m. Take C = 80 kN/mm².*

(B.T.E. W-2014, 1997/4 Marks)

**Data**      : Solid shaft, D = 100 mm, $\theta = 2.75° = \left(2.75 \times \frac{\pi}{180}\right)$ rad,

L = 6 m = $6 \times 10^3$ mm, C = 80 kN/mm² = $80 \times 10^3$ N/mm²

**To find**   : T.

**Concept :** Use of torsional formula.

**Solution :** Using the relation,

$$\frac{T}{I_p} = \frac{C\theta}{L}$$

$\therefore$
$$\frac{T}{\frac{\pi}{32}D^4} = \frac{C\theta}{L}$$

$\therefore$
$$\frac{T}{\frac{\pi}{32}(100)^4} = \frac{(80 \times 10^3)\left(2.75 \times \frac{\pi}{180}\right)}{6 \times 10^3}$$

**Answer :** $\boxed{T = 6282734.283 \text{ N·mm} = \mathbf{6282.734 \text{ N·m} = 6.282 \text{ kN·m}}}$

---

**Example 8 :** *A 200 mm diameter shaft is subjected to a twisting moment. If the angle of twist is to be restricted to 2° in a length of 8 m, find the maximum twisting moment that can be applied. Consider C = 0.8 × 10⁵ MPa.*   (B.T.E. S-2008/4 Marks)

**Data**     :   Solid shaft, D = 200 mm, $\theta = 2° = \left(2 \times \frac{\pi}{180}\right)$ rad,

L = 8 m = $8 \times 10^3$ mm, C = $0.8 \times 10^5$ MPa = $0.8 \times 10^5$ N/mm²

**To find :**   T.

**Concept :** Use of torsional formula or torque based on angle of twist criteria (stiffness criteria)

**Solution :** Using the relation,

$$\frac{T}{I_p} = \frac{C\theta}{L}$$

$\therefore$

$$\frac{T}{\frac{\pi}{32}D^4} = \frac{C\theta}{L}$$

$\therefore$

$$\frac{T}{\frac{\pi}{32}(200)^4} = \frac{(0.8 \times 10^5)\left(2 \times \frac{\pi}{180}\right)}{8 \times 10^3}$$

**Answer :** $\boxed{T = 54831135.56 \text{ N.mm} = \textbf{54.83 kN.m}}$

## Type 2 : Examples based on design of solid shafts

**Strength and stiffness criteria :** For the design of circular shafts (solid or hollow), following are the two criteria.

**(i) Strength criteria :** It means, with the designed diameter, shear stress shall not exceed the allowable value.

**(ii) Stiffness criteria :** It means, with the designed diameter, angle of twist shall not exceed the allowable value.

Diameter of the shaft is obtained by using above two conditions and the greater of the two is to be used.

---

### Important Formulae

**(i) Diameter based on strength criteria :** This can be calculated by using the relation,

$$T = \frac{\pi}{16}f_s D^3$$

**(ii) Diameter based on stiffness criteria :** This can be calculated by using the relation,

$$\frac{T}{I_p} = \frac{C\theta}{L}$$

---

**Example 9 :** *A solid shaft is to transmit a torque of $45 \times 10^5$ N·mm. If the maximum shearing stress is not to exceed 80 N/mm² and angle of twist is not to exceed one degree in 20 diameters length of the shaft, determine the diameter of the shaft.*

*Take C = $0.8 \times 10^5$ N/mm².* **(V.V. Imp./4 Marks)**

**Data** : Solid shaft, $T = 45 \times 10^5$ N·mm, $f_s = 80$ N/mm²,

$\theta = 1° = \dfrac{\pi}{180}$ rad $= 0.0174532$ rad; Length $= 20 \times$ Diameter of shaft,

i.e. $L = 20$ D, $C = 0.8 \times 10^5$ N/mm²

**To find　:** D.

**Concept :** Design of cross-section of shaft based on strength and stiffness criteria.

Diameter to be used is greater of that obtained from above two conditions.

**Solution :**

**Case 1　: Diameter based on shear stress**

**(Diameter based on strength criteria) :**

Using the relation,　　　$T = \dfrac{\pi}{16} f_s D^3$

$\therefore$　　　　　$45 \times 10^5 = \dfrac{\pi}{16} \times 80 \times D^3$

$\therefore$　　　　　**D = 65.92 mm**

**Case 2 : Diameter based on angle of twist**

**(Diameter based on stiffness criteria) :**

Using the relation,　　　$\dfrac{T}{I_p} = \dfrac{C\theta}{L}$

$\therefore$　　　$\dfrac{45 \times 10^5}{\dfrac{\pi}{32} D^4} = \dfrac{(0.8 \times 10^5)\,(0.0174532)}{20\,D}$

$\therefore$　　　　　$D^3 = 656564.7504$

$\therefore$　　　　　**D = 86.91 mm**

**Check :** Now, if we select D = 86.91 mm i.e. diameter based on angle of twist, the shear stress must be within the limit.

$$T = \dfrac{\pi}{16} f_s D^3$$

$\therefore$　　　　　$45 \times 10^5 = \dfrac{\pi}{16} f_s (86.91)^3$

$\therefore$　$f_s = 34.91$ N/mm$^2$ < 80 N/mm$^2$ $\therefore$ O. K.

If we select D = 65.92 mm i.e. diameter based on shear stress, the angle of twist must be within the limit i.e. less than 1°.

$$\dfrac{T}{I_p} = \dfrac{C\theta}{L}$$

$$\dfrac{45 \times 10^5}{\dfrac{\pi}{32}(65.92)^4} = \dfrac{(0.8 \times 10^5)\,(\theta)}{20 \times 65.92}$$

$\therefore$　　　　　$\theta = 0.04000378$ rad

　　　　　$\boldsymbol{\theta = 2.29° > 1°}$

Since the angle of twist exceeds 1°, D = 65.92 mm is not possible.

**Answer : The required diameter of the shaft satisfying the given conditions is 86.91 mm** (i.e. greater of the two values).

**Example 10 :** *Select a suitable diameter for a solid circular shaft to transmit 200 H.P. at 180 r.p.m. The allowable shear stress is 80 N/mm² and the allowable angle of twist is 1° in a length of 3 m. Take C = 0.82 × 10⁵ N/mm².* **(B.T.E. S-2013/4 Marks)**

**Data**    : Power P = 200 H.P., speed N = 180 rpm, shear stress $f_s$ = 80 N/mm²,

$$\theta = 1° = \frac{\pi}{180} \text{ rad; length L = 3 m = 3} \times 10^3 \text{ mm, C = 0.82} \times 10^5 \text{ N/mm}^2$$

**To find**  : D.

**Concept :**   Use equation of power first, find T and then find diameter based on strength and stiffness criteria. Diameter to be used is greater of that obtained from these two conditions.

**Solution :** If the power is given in terms of H.P.,

$$P = \left(\frac{2 \pi N T}{4500}\right) \text{H.P.}$$

$\therefore$         $200 = \dfrac{2 \pi \times 180 \times T_{kg.m}}{4500}$

$\therefore$         $T = 795.77471 \text{ kg.m}$

$\therefore$         $T = 795.77471 \times 9.81 = 7806.5499 \text{ N·m}$

**T = 7806.5499 × 10³ N·mm**

**Note :** $T_{kg\text{-}m}$ indicates torque in kg-m.

**Case 1 : Diameter based on shear stress :**

Using the relation,        $T = \dfrac{\pi}{16} f_s D^3$

$\therefore$         $7806.5499 \times 10^3 = \dfrac{\pi}{16} \times 80 \times D^3$

$\therefore$         **D = 79.21 mm**

**Case 2 : Diameter based on angle of twist :**

Using the relation,        $\dfrac{T}{I_p} = \dfrac{C \theta}{L}$

$\therefore$         $\dfrac{7806.5499 \times 10^3}{\dfrac{\pi}{32} D^4} = \dfrac{(0.82 \times 10^5)\left(\dfrac{\pi}{180}\right)}{3000}$

$\therefore$         $D^4 = 166682221.7$

$\therefore$         **D = 113.62 mm**

**Answer : The required diameter of the shaft satisfying the given conditions is 113.62 mm (i.e. the greater of the two values).**

**Example 11 :** *A shaft has to transmit 105 kW at 160 rpm. If the shear stress is not to exceed 65 N/mm² and twist in the length of 3.5 m must not exceed 1°, find the diameter of the shaft. Take C = 8 ×10⁵ N/mm².*  **(B.T.E. S-2011/4 Marks)**

**Data** : Power P = 105 kW = $105 \times 10^3$ W, Speed N = 160 rpm,

Shear stress $f_s$ = 65 N/mm², $\theta = 1° = \dfrac{\pi}{180}$ rad,

Length L = 3.5 m = $3.5 \times 10^3$ mm, Modulus of rigidity C = $8 \times 10^5$ N/mm².

**To find** : D.

**Concept** : Same as the above example.

**Solution** : (i)     $P = \dfrac{2\pi NT}{60}$ watts

$$105 \times 10^3 = \frac{2\pi \times 160 \times T_{mean}}{60}$$

∴     $T_{mean}$ = 6266.72 N.m = $6266.72 \times 10^3$ N.mm

**Note** : (i)  In power formula $P = \dfrac{2\pi NT}{60}$ watts, torque T is mean torque in N.m.

(ii)  Relation between maximum torque and mean (average) torque is not given here. Hence assume $T_{max} = T_{mean}$.

**(ii) Case 1 : Diameter based on shear stress :**

$$T_{max} = \frac{\pi}{16} f_s D^3$$

$$6266.72 \times 10^3 = \frac{\pi}{16} \times 65 \times D^3$$

∴     **D** = 78.89 ≅ **79 mm**

**(ii) Case 2 : Diameter based on angle of twist :**

$$\frac{T_{max}}{I_p} = \frac{C\theta}{L}$$

$$\frac{6266.72 \times 10^3}{\dfrac{\pi}{32} D^4} = \frac{(8 \times 10^5) \times \left(\dfrac{\pi}{180}\right)}{3.5 \times 10^3}$$

Solving this equation, we get,

$$\boxed{\text{D = 112.5 mm}}$$

**Answer : The required diameter of the shaft satisfying the given conditions is 112.5 mm (i.e. the greater of the two values).**

**Example 12 :** *A steel shaft of solid circular section has to transmit 375 kW at 210 rpm. The maximum shear stress is not to exceed 50 MPa and the angle of twist must not be more than 1° in a length of 3 m. Take G = 80 GPa. Determine diameter of the shaft.*

**(B.T.E. W-2012/4 Marks)**

**Data**   :   Power P = 375 kW = $375 \times 10^3$ W,   Speed N = 210 rpm,

Shear stress $f_s$ = 50 MPa = 50 N/mm$^2$, Angle of twist $\theta$ = 1° = $\dfrac{\pi}{180}$ rad,

Length L = 3 m = $3 \times 10^3$ mm,

Modulus of rigidity G = 80 GPa = $80 \times 10^3$ N/mm$^2$.

**To find**   :   D.

**Concept :**   Same as the above example.

**Solution :**   (i)      $I_p = \dfrac{\pi}{32} D^4 = (0.098175\ D^4)$ mm$^4$

Using               $P = \dfrac{2\pi NT}{60}$

$$375 \times 10^3 = \dfrac{2\pi \times 210 \times T}{60}$$

$\therefore$                   T = 17052.31 N.m

In power formula, this is the mean torque.

$$T_{mean} = 17052.31\ \text{N.m}$$

Since relation between $T_{max}$ and $T_{mean}$ is not given here,

assume,        $T_{max} = T_{mean} = 17052.31$ N.m = $17052.31 \times 10^3$ N.mm

(ii)  Using         $\dfrac{T_{max}}{I_p} = \dfrac{f_s}{R} = \dfrac{G\theta}{L}$

$$\dfrac{17052.31 \times 10^3}{0.098175\ D^4} = \dfrac{50}{\dfrac{D}{2}} = \dfrac{80 \times 10^3 \times \left(\dfrac{\pi}{180}\right)}{3 \times 10^3}$$

                 (i)          (ii)        (iii)

**Case 1 : Diameter based on shear stress :** Equating (i) and (ii), we get

$$17052.31 \times 10^3 \left(\dfrac{D}{2}\right) = 50 \times 0.098175\ D^4$$

$\therefore$               $D^3 = \dfrac{17052.31 \times 10^3}{2} \times \dfrac{1}{50 \times 0.098175}$

                  = 1736929.972

$\therefore$           **D = 120.206 mm**

**Case 2 : Diameter based on angle of twist :** Equating (ii) and (iii), we get

$$\frac{50}{(D/2)} = \frac{80 \times 10^3 \times \left(\frac{\pi}{180}\right)}{3 \times 10^3}$$

$$\therefore \quad \frac{2 \times 50 \times 3 \times 10^3}{80 \times 10^3 \times \left(\frac{\pi}{180}\right)} = D$$

$$\therefore \qquad\qquad D = 214.86 \text{ mm}$$

**Answer :** Required diameter = 214.86 mm (i.e. greater of two values)

**Example 13 :** *A shaft is transmitting 100 kW at 180 r.p.m. If the allowable stress in the material is 60 N/mm², determine the suitable diameter for the shaft. The shaft is not to twist more than 1° in a length of 3 m. Take C = 80 kN/mm².* **(B.T.E. S-2009/4 Marks)**

**Answer :** Required D = 103.8 mm

**Example 14 :** *A shaft is transmitting 150 kW at 200 r.p.m. If allowable shear stress is 80 N/mm² and allowable twist is 1.5° per 4 m, find the diameter of the shaft. Take C = 0.8 × 10⁵ N/mm².* **(B.T.E. S-2015, 2010/4 Marks)**

**Solution :** Exactly similar to the above solved example.

**Answer :** Required diameter = 108.69 mm = 110 mm

**Type 3 : Examples based on power and torque formula (P and T formula)**

**Relation between $T_{max}$ and $T_{mean}$ (or $T_{average}$) is not given.**

### Important Formulae

(i)  $T_{max}$ can be calculated by using the formula $T_{max} = \frac{\pi}{16} f_s D^3$.

(ii) Power can be calculated by using the formula $P = \left(\frac{2\pi N\, T_{mean}}{60}\right)$ watts,

where,          P  =  Power in watts

T  =  Mean or average torque in N.m

N  =  Number of revolutions of shaft per minute (r.p.m.)

**Note :** If the relation between $T_{max}$ and $T_{mean}$ is not given, assume

$$T_{max} = T_{mean}$$

**Example 15 :** *Find the power that can be transmitted by a shaft 40 mm diameter rotating at 200 rpm, if the maximum permissible shear stress is 85 MPa.*

**(B.T.E. S-2015, 2013, W-2011/4 Marks)**

**Data**       : Solid shaft D = 40 mm, N = 200 rpm, $f_s$ = 85 MPa = 85 N/mm²

**To find**   : P.

**Concept :** Find the value of torque based on shear stress criteria and then use equation of power.

**Solution :** (i) Using the relation,

$$T = \frac{\pi}{16} f_s D^3 = \frac{\pi}{16} \times 85 \times 40^3 = 1068141.5 \text{ N·mm}$$

$$= 1068.1415 \text{ N·m}$$

(ii) Using the relation,    Power P $= \dfrac{2\pi N T}{60} = \dfrac{2\pi \times 200 \times 1068.1415}{60} = 22371.1 \text{ watts}$

**Answer :** $\boxed{P = 22.37 \text{ kW}}$

---

**Example 16 :** *Find the power transmitted by a shaft having 50 mm diameter rotating at 120 rpm if maximum permissible shear stress = 80 MPa.* **(B.T.E. W-2012/4 Marks)**

**Answer :** $\boxed{P = 24.674 \text{ kW}}$

---

**Example 17 :** *How the power of shaft can be calculated ? A circular shaft is rotating at 200 rpm, calculate the power developed if the torque is 40000 N.mm.* **(B.T.E. S-2012/4 Marks)**

**Data**      : Speed N = 200 rpm, torque T = 40000 N.mm = 40 N.m.

**To find**    : P.

**Concept**   : Use of power formula.

**Solution :**     **Power, P** $= \left(\dfrac{2\pi NT}{60}\right) \cdot W = \dfrac{2\pi \times 200 \times 40}{60} = \mathbf{837.76\ W}$

**Answer**    : $\boxed{P = 837.76 \text{ W}}$

---

**Example 18 :** *A solid circular shaft of 100 mm diameter is transmitting power 100 kW at 150 r.p.m. Find the intensity of the induced shear stress in the shaft.*

**(V.V. Imp., B.T.E. S-1998/4 Marks)**

**Data**      : Solid shaft, D = 100 mm, P = 100 kW = $100 \times 10^3$ W, N = 150 r.p.m.

**To find**   : $f_s$.

**Concept :** Use equation of power first, find T and then use equation of T to find $f_s$.

**Solution :** (i) Using the relation,    $P = \dfrac{2\pi NT}{60}$

$$100 \times 10^3 = \frac{2\pi \times 150 \times T}{60}$$

$\therefore$            $T = 6366.1977 \text{ N·m} = 6366.1977 \times 10^3 \text{ N·mm}$

(ii) Now, using the relation,      $T = \dfrac{\pi}{16} f_s D^3$

$\therefore$       $6366.1977 \times 10^3 = \dfrac{\pi}{16} \times f_s \times (100)^3$

**Answer :** $\boxed{f_s = 32.42 \text{ N/mm}^2}$

**Example 19 :** *Calculate the suitable diameter of the solid shaft to transmit 220 kW at 150 r.p.m. if the permissible shear is 68 MPa.* **(B.T.E. W-2000/4 Marks)**

**Data**     : Power, P = 220 kW = $220 \times 10^3$ W, speed N = 150 r.p.m.,
              shear stress, $f_s$ = 68 MPa = 68 N/mm$^2$

**To find**  : Diameter D.

**Concept :** Use equation of power first, find T and then use equation of T to find D.

**Solution :** (i) Using the relation,

$$\text{Power, P} = \left(\frac{2\pi\,NT}{60}\right)W$$

$$220 \times 10^3 = \frac{2\pi \times 150 \times T}{60}$$

$$T = 14005.63499 \text{ N·m} = 14005.63499 \times 10^3 \text{ N·mm}$$

(**Note :** Relation between maximum torque and average torque is not given.)

(ii)  Using the relation,      $T = \dfrac{\pi}{16} f_s D^3$

$\therefore$          $14005.63499 \times 10^3 = \dfrac{\pi}{16} \times 68 \times D^3$

$\therefore$                    $D^3 = 1048972.254$

**Answer :** $\boxed{\text{D} = 101.6 \text{ mm}}$

---

**Example 20 :** *A solid circular shaft is to transmit power of 1000 kW at 150 r.p.m. If the shear stress in the material is not to exceed 80 N/mm$^2$, calculate the diameter of the shaft.*

**(B.T.E. S-2006/4 Marks)**

**Solution** : Exactly similar to the above solved example.

**Answer :** $\boxed{\text{D} = 159.44 \text{ mm}}$

---

**Type 4 : Example on calculating H.P.**

**Example 21 :** *A steel shaft 10 mm diameter rotates at the speed of 9900 r.p.m. Calculate the maximum power in H.P. that the shaft can transmit without exceeding the shear stress of 40 MPa.* **(B.T.E. S-2000/4 Marks)**

**Data**     : Solid shaft, D = 10 mm, N = 9900 r.p.m., $f_s$ = 40 MPa = 40 N/mm$^2$

**To find**  : H.P. of the shaft.

**Concept :** Find the value of torque in kg.m units by using strength equation and then use equation of power.

**Solution :** (i) Using the relation,

$$T = \frac{\pi}{16} f_s D^3 = \frac{\pi}{16} \times 40 \times (10)^3 = 7853.98 \text{ N·mm}$$

$$= 7.85398 \text{ N·m} = \frac{7.85398}{9.81} \text{ kg·m} = 0.8 \text{ kg·m}$$

(ii)  Now,          **H.P.** $= \dfrac{2\pi \times N \times T_{(kg.m)}}{4500} = \dfrac{2\pi \times 9900 \times 0.8}{4500} = \mathbf{11.05}$

**Answer :** $\boxed{\text{H.P.} = 11.05}$

## Type 5 : Examples based on P and T formula. Relation between $T_{max}$ and $T_{mean}$ is given

| **Important Formulae** |
|---|
| (i) $\quad T_{max} = \dfrac{\pi}{16} f_s D^3$ |
| (ii) $\quad P = \left(\dfrac{2\pi N\, T_{mean}}{60}\right)$ watts |
| (iii) If maximum torque exceeds 40% over mean value, |
| $\qquad T_{max} = T_{mean} + \left(\dfrac{40}{100}\right) T_{mean}$ |
| $\qquad\quad = T_{mean}(1 + 0.4)$ |
| $\qquad T_{max} = 1.4\, T_{mean}$ |

**Example 22 :** *A shaft is required to transmit 20 kW at 150 r.p.m. The maximum torque may exceed average torque by 40 %. Determine the diameter of shaft, if the shear stress is not to exceed 50 MPa.*　　**(B.T.E. S-2015, 1999/4 Marks)**

**Data**　　: Solid shaft; P = 20 kW = $20 \times 10^3$ W, N = 150 r.p.m.,

$\qquad T_{max} = 1.4\, T_{mean},\ f_s = 50$ MPa $= 50$ N/mm$^2$

**To find**　: D.

**Concept :**　(i)　Use equation of power first and find $T_{mean}$.

$\qquad\qquad$ (ii)　Knowing $T_{mean}$ find $T_{max}$.

$\qquad\qquad$ (iii)　Use equation of $T_{max}$ to find D.

**Solution :** (i) Using the relation, $\quad P = \dfrac{2\pi NT}{60}$

$\therefore \qquad\qquad 20 \times 10^3 = \dfrac{2\pi \times 150 \times T_{mean\,(N.m)}}{60}$

$\therefore \qquad\qquad T_{mean} = 1273.239545$ N.m

(ii) Now, $\qquad\qquad T_{max} = 1.4\, T_{mean} = 1.4 \times 1273.239545 = 1782.535363$ N.m

$\qquad\qquad\qquad\qquad = 1782.535363 \times 10^3$ N.mm

(iii) Now, using the relation, $\quad T_{max} = \dfrac{\pi}{16} f_s D^3$

$\therefore \qquad 1782.535363 \times 10^3 = \dfrac{\pi}{16} \times 50 \times D^3$

$\therefore \qquad\qquad\qquad D^3 = 181567.5611$

**Answer :**　$\boxed{\text{D} = 56.62 \text{ mm}}$

**Example 23 :** *A solid circular shaft of 120 mm diameter is transmitting power of 100 kW at 150 rpm. Find the intensity of the shear stress induced in the shaft. Take $T_{max} = 1.4\ T_{avg}$.*

**(B.T.E. W-2012/4 Marks)**

**Data** : Solid shaft D = 120 mm, power P = 100 kW = $100 \times 10^3$ W,

speed N = 150 rpm, $T_{max} = 1.4\ T_{avg} = 1.4\ T_{mean}$.

**To find** : $f_s$.

**Concept** : (i)　Use equation of power first to find $T_{mean}$.

(ii)　Find $T_{max}$ by knowing $T_{mean}$.

(iii)　Use equation of $T_{max}$ to find $f_s$.

**Solution** : (i)　　Power P $= \left(\dfrac{2\pi N\ T_{mean}}{60}\right)$ W

$$100 \times 10^3 = \frac{2\pi \times 150 \times T_{mean}}{60}$$

$\therefore$　　　　　　$T_{mean} = 6366.197$ N.m

(ii)　　$\mathbf{T_{max}} = 1.4\ T_{mean} = 1.4 \times 6366.197 = 8912.68$ N.m

$$= \mathbf{8912.68 \times 10^3\ N.mm}$$

(iii)　　$T_{max} = \dfrac{\pi}{16}\ f_s\ D^3$

$$8912.68 \times 10^3 = \frac{\pi}{16} \times f_s \times (120)^3$$

$\therefore$　　　　　　$f_s = 26.268$ N/mm$^2$

**Note :** $f_s$ can also be calculated by using the relation,

$$\frac{T}{I_p} = \frac{f_s}{R}$$

$$\frac{8912.68 \times 10^3}{\dfrac{\pi}{32}(120)^4} = \frac{f_s}{\left(\dfrac{120}{2}\right)}$$

$\therefore$　　　　　　$\mathbf{f_s = 26.268\ N/mm^2}$

**Answer :** $\boxed{f_s = 26.268\ \text{N/mm}^2}$

---

**Example 24 :** *Calculate the power a shaft of 300 mm can transmit with a speed of 200 r.p.m. if the permissible shear stress is 120 N/mm². Take maximum torque as 30% more than the average torque.*　　**(B.T.E. W-2010, 2006/4 Marks)**

**Data** : Solid shaft, D = 300 mm, N = 200 r.p.m., $f_s = 120$ N/mm², $T_{max} = 1.30\ T_{mean}$.

**To find** : P.

**Concept :** (i) Find $T_{max}$ by using standard formula.

(ii) Since relation between $T_{max}$ and $T_{mean}$ is given, find $T_{mean}$.

(iii) Knowing $T_{mean}$, use equation of power to find P.

**Solution :** (i) We know that, $T_{max}$ = $\dfrac{\pi}{16} f_s D^3$

$$= \dfrac{\pi}{16} \times 120 \times (300)^3 = 636172512.4 \text{ N.mm}$$

$$= 636172.5124 \text{ N.m}$$

(ii) Now, $\qquad\qquad\qquad T_{max}$ = $1.3\ T_{mean}$

$\therefore \qquad\qquad\qquad\qquad T_{mean}$ = $\dfrac{T_{max}}{1.3} = \dfrac{636172.5124}{1.3} = 489363.471 \text{ N.m}$

(iii) Now, $\qquad\qquad$ Power, **P** = $\left[\dfrac{2\pi N\ T_{mean}\ (\text{N.m})}{60}\right] W$

$$= \dfrac{2\pi \times 200 \times 489363.471}{60} = \mathbf{10249204.57\ W}$$

**Answer :** $\boxed{P = 10249.2 \text{ kW}}$

---

## Similar examples for practice :

**Example 25 :** *Calculate the power transmitted by a shaft 40 mm in diameter, rotating at 120 rpm if permissible shear stress is 80 N/mm². $T_{max} = 1.2\ T_{av}$.* **(B.T.E. S-2011/4 Marks)**

**Answer :** $\boxed{P = 10.53 \text{ kW}}$

---

**Example 26 :** *Find the power transmitted by a solid shaft of diameter 60 mm running at 220 r.p.m. if the permissible shear stress is 68 MPa. The maximum torque is likely to exceed the mean torque by 25 %.* **(B.T.E. S-2012, 2001/4 Marks)**

**Answer :** $\boxed{P = 51.109 \text{ kW}}$

---

**Example 27 :** *Determine the safe diameter of solid shaft which transmits 500 kW at 100 r.p.m. The value of shear stress and the angle of twist are restricted to 100 MN/m² and 1° in 1.5 m length respectively. The shaft is likely to have a maximum torque 40% more than the mean. Take G = 8.5 ×10⁴ MN/m².* **(B.T.E. W-2004/4 Marks)**

**Data** : Solid shaft P = 500 kW = $500 \times 10^3$ W, N = 100 r.p.m.,

$f_s$ = 100 MN/m² = 100 N/mm², $\theta$ = 1° = $\left(\dfrac{\pi}{180}\right)$ rad = 0.0174532 rad,

L = 1.5 m = $1.5 \times 10^3$ mm, $T_{max} = 1.40\ T_{mean}$,

G = $8.5 \times 10^4$ MN/m² = $8.5 \times 10^4$ N/mm².

**To find** : Safe diameter D satisfying both strength and stiffness considerations.

**Concept :** (i) Use power formula to find $T_{mean}$.

(ii) Since relation between $T_{mean}$ and $T_{max}$ is given, find $T_{max}$.

(iii) Find the diameter based on strength and stiffness criteria. Diameter to be used is greater of that obtained from these two conditions.

**Solution** : (i) Using the relation,

$$P = \frac{2\pi N\, T_{mean\,(N.m)}}{60}$$

$\therefore$ $\qquad\qquad\qquad 500 \times 10^3 = \dfrac{2\pi \times 100 \times T_{mean}}{60}$

$\therefore$ $\qquad\qquad\qquad T_{mean} = 47746.5$ N.m

(ii) Now, $\qquad\qquad T_{max} = 1.40\, T_{mean} = 1.40 \times 47746.5 = 66845$ N.m

$\qquad\qquad\qquad\qquad\qquad = 66845 \times 10^3$ N.mm

**(iii) Diameter based on shear stress (strength consideration) :**

Using the relation, $\qquad T = \dfrac{\pi}{16} f_s\, D^3$

$\qquad\qquad 66845 \times 10^3 = \dfrac{\pi}{16} \times 100 \times D^3$ $\qquad\qquad$ ... (Here T = $T_{max}$)

$\therefore$ $\qquad\qquad\qquad\quad$ **D = 150.43 mm** $\qquad\qquad\qquad\qquad$ ... (1)

**(iv) Diameter based on angle of twist (stiffness consideration) :**

Using the relation, $\qquad \dfrac{T}{I_p} = \dfrac{G\theta}{L}$

$$\frac{66845 \times 10^3}{\dfrac{\pi}{32} D^4} = \frac{8.5 \times 10^4 \times 0.0174532}{1.5 \times 10^3}$$

$\qquad\qquad\qquad\qquad D^4 = 688440325.4$

$\therefore$ $\qquad\qquad\qquad$ **D = 161.982 mm** $\qquad\qquad\qquad\qquad$ ... (2)

**Answer :** The required diameter of the shaft satisfying both the considerations is **161.982 mm** i.e. greater of the two values.

**Type 6 : Examples based on torsion of hollow shafts**

**Type 6.1 : Examples based on strength of a hollow shaft :**

**Important Formulae**

$T = \dfrac{\pi}{16} f_s \left( \dfrac{D^4 - d^4}{D} \right)$, where

T = Torque or turning moment in N.mm

$f_s$ = Maximum shear stress induced at the outermost layer of the shaft N/mm$^2$

D = External diameter of hollow shaft (mm)

d = Internal diameter of hollow shaft (mm)

**Example 28 :** *Find the torsional moment of resistance for a hollow circular shaft of 225 mm external diameter and 200 mm internal diameter, if the permissible shear stress is 60 MPa.* **(B.T.E. W-1998/4 Marks)**

**Data** : Hollow shaft, D = 225 mm, d = 200 mm, $f_s$ = 60 MPa = 60 N/mm$^2$

**To find** : T.

**Concept :** Strength of a hollow shaft

**Solution :**
$$T = \frac{\pi}{16} f_s \left(\frac{D^4 - d^4}{D}\right) = \frac{\pi}{16} \times 60 \times \left(\frac{225^4 - 200^4}{225}\right)$$

**Answer :** $\boxed{T = 50416835.23 \text{ N.mm} \cong 50.42 \text{ kN.m}}$

---

## Type 6.2 : Examples based on the torsional formula :

| **Important Formulae** |
|---|
| (i) $\quad \dfrac{T}{I_p} = \dfrac{f_s}{R} = \dfrac{C\theta}{L}$ |
| (ii) $\quad \dfrac{T}{I_p} = \dfrac{f_s}{R}$ gives |
| $\quad \dfrac{T}{\dfrac{\pi}{32}(D^4 - d^4)} = \dfrac{f_s}{\dfrac{D}{2}} \Rightarrow T = \dfrac{\pi}{16} f_s \left(\dfrac{D^4 - d^4}{D}\right)$ |

**Example 29 :** *Find the maximum stress in a propeller shaft 400 mm external and 200 mm internal diameter, when subjected to a twisting moment of 4650 N.m. If the modulus of rigidity is 82 GPa, calculate the twist in a length 20 times the external diameter.*

**(B.T.E. S-2015, 2005/4 Marks)**

**Data** : Hollow shaft D = 400 mm, d = 200 mm, T = 4650 Nm = $4650 \times 10^3$ N.mm,

$\quad$ G = 82 GPa = $82 \times 10^3$ N/mm², L = 20 D = 20 × 400 = 8000 mm.

**To find** : (i) $f_s$ and (ii) $\theta$.

**Concept :** Use of torsional formula.

**Solution :** **(i) To calculate maximum shear stress ($f_s$) :**

For a hollow shaft, $\qquad T = \dfrac{\pi}{16} f_s \left(\dfrac{D^4 - d^4}{D}\right)$

$$4650 \times 10^3 = \frac{\pi}{16} \times f_s \times \left(\frac{400^4 - 200^4}{400}\right)$$

$\therefore \qquad 4650 \times 10^3 = \dfrac{\pi}{16} \times f_s \times (6 \times 10^7)$

$\therefore \qquad f_s = \dfrac{4650 \times 10^3 \times 16}{\pi \times 6 \times 10^7} = 0.3947 \text{ N/mm}^2$

**(ii) To find angle of twist ($\theta$) :** Using the relation,

$$\frac{T}{I_p} = \frac{G\theta}{L}$$

$\therefore \qquad T = I_p \cdot \left(\dfrac{G\theta}{L}\right) = \dfrac{\pi}{32}(D^4 - d^4)\left(\dfrac{G\theta}{L}\right)$

$\therefore$ $\qquad$ $4650 \times 10^3 = \dfrac{\pi}{32}(400^4 - 200^4)\left(\dfrac{82 \times 10^3 \times \theta}{8000}\right)$

$\therefore$ $\qquad$ $4650 \times 10^3 = \dfrac{\pi}{32} \times (2.4 \times 10^{10})\left(\dfrac{82 \times 10^3}{8000}\right)\theta$

$\qquad\qquad\qquad = 2.4150 \times 10^{10}\,\theta$

$\therefore$ $\qquad\qquad$ $\theta = \dfrac{4650 \times 10^3}{2.4150 \times 10^{10}} = 0.0001925$ rad.

$\qquad\qquad\qquad = \left[(0.0001925)\times\left(\dfrac{180}{\pi}\right)\right]^\circ = \mathbf{0.011°}$

**Answer :** $\boxed{\text{(i) } f_s = 0.3947 \text{ N/mm}^2,\ \text{(ii) } \theta = 0.0001925 \text{ rad} = 0.011°}$

---

**Example 30 :** *A shaft of hollow circular cross-section has outer diameter 120 mm, inner 90 mm. It is subjected to a torsional moment of 18 kN/m. For this shaft compute shear stress at the outer surface.* **(B.T.E. W-2012/4 Marks)**

**Data** : Hollow shaft D = 120 mm, d = 90 mm, T = 18 kN.m = $18 \times 10^6$ N.mm,

$\qquad$ $R = \dfrac{D}{2} = \dfrac{120}{2} = 60$ mm.

**To find** : $f_{s\,max}$ i.e. shear stress at outer surface.

**Concept :** (i) Use of torsional formula, (ii) maximum shear stress will occur at outermost layer at a distance R from the centre of the shaft.

**Solution :** (i) $\qquad$ Polar M.I. $= I_p = \dfrac{\pi}{32}(D^4 - d^4)$

$\qquad\qquad\qquad\qquad = \dfrac{\pi}{32}(120^4 - 90^4) = 13916273.71 \text{ mm}^4$

$\qquad$ (ii) $\qquad$ Using, $\dfrac{T}{I_p} = \dfrac{f_{s\,max}}{R}$

$\qquad\qquad\qquad \dfrac{18 \times 10^6}{13916273.71} = \dfrac{f_{s\,max}}{60}$

$\therefore$ $\qquad\qquad\qquad \mathbf{f_{s\,max} = 77.61 \text{ N/mm}^2}$

**Alternative method :**

$\qquad\qquad$ Using $T = \dfrac{\pi}{16}f_s\left(\dfrac{D^4 - d^4}{D}\right)$

$\qquad\qquad$ $18 \times 10^6 = \dfrac{\pi}{16} \times f_s \times \left(\dfrac{120^4 - 90^4}{120}\right)$

**Answer :** $\boxed{f_s = 77.61 \text{ N/mm}^2}$

**Example 31 :** *A hollow shaft is of external diameter and internal diameter 400 mm and 200 mm respectively. Find the maximum torque it can transmit, if the angle of twist is not to exceed 1.5° in a length of 10 m. Take C = 0.8 ×10⁵ N/mm².* **(B.T.E. S-1997/4 Marks)**

**Data** : Hollow shaft, D = 400 mm, d = 200 mm, $\theta = 1.5° = \left(1.5 \times \dfrac{\pi}{180}\right)$ rad = 0.026 rad,

L = 10 m = $10 \times 10^3$ mm, C = $0.8 \times 10^5$ N/mm²

**To find** : T.

**Concept :** Use of torsional formula.

**Solution :** Using the relation,

$$\frac{T}{I_p} = \frac{C\,\theta}{L}$$

∴

$$T = I_p \cdot \left(\frac{C\,\theta}{L}\right) = \frac{\pi}{32}(D^4 - d^4)\left(\frac{C\,\theta}{L}\right)$$

$$= \frac{\pi}{32}(400^4 - 200^4)\frac{(0.8 \times 10^5) \times 0.026}{10 \times 10^3}$$

$$= \frac{\pi}{32} \times 2.4 \times 10^{10} \times 0.208 = 4.9 \times 10^8 \text{ N.mm}$$

**Answer :** $\boxed{\text{T = 490 kN.m}}$

---

**Type 7 : Examples based on design of hollow shafts**
　　　**(strength and stiffness criteria)**

| **Important Formulae** |
| --- |
| **(i) Diameter based on strength criteria :** |
| $$T = \frac{\pi}{16}\,f_s\left(\frac{D^4 - d^4}{D}\right)$$ |
| **(ii) Diameter based on stiffness criteria :** |
| $$\frac{T}{I_p} = \frac{G\theta}{L}\ \text{where,}$$ |
| $$I_p = \frac{\pi}{32}(D^4 - d^4)$$ |
| Required diameter to satisfy both the conditions is maximum of the two values. |

**Example 32 :** *A hollow shaft is required to transmit a torque of 24 kN.m. The inside diameter is 0.6 times the external diameter. Calculate both the diameters if the allowable shear stress is　80 MPa.* **(B.T.E. S-2012; W-2009/4 Marks)**

**Data** : Hollow shaft T = 24 kN.m = $24 \times 10^6$ N.mm, d = 0.6 D,
　　　　$f_s$ = 80 MPa = 80 N/mm²

**To find**　　: d and D.

**Concept**　　: Diameter based on strength criteria.

**Solution**　　: Using the relation,

$$T = \frac{\pi}{16} f_s \left( \frac{D^4 - d^4}{D} \right)$$

$$24 \times 10^6 = \frac{\pi}{16} \times 80 \times \left[ \frac{D^4 - (0.6\,D)^4}{D} \right]$$

$$24 \times 10^6 = \frac{\pi}{16} \times 80 \times \left[ \frac{D^4 - 0.1296\,D^4}{D} \right] = \frac{\pi}{16} \times 80 \times \left[ \frac{D^4\,(1 - 0.1296)}{D} \right]$$

$$= \frac{\pi}{16} \times 80 \times 0.8704\,D^3$$

∴ $$D^3 = \frac{24 \times 10^6 \times 16}{\pi \times 80 \times 0.8704} = 1755385$$

∴ $$D = \sqrt[3]{1755385} = \textbf{120.63 mm}$$

∴ $$d = 0.6 \times 120.63 = \textbf{72.38 mm}$$

**Answer :** $\boxed{D = 120.63 \text{ mm}, \ d = 72.38 \text{ mm}}$

---

### Similar example for practice :

**Example 33 :** *A hollow shaft is required to transmit a torque of 36 kN.m. The inside diameter is 0.6 times the external diameter. Calculate both the diameters, if the allowable shear stress is 80 MPa.*　　**(B.T.E. W-1999/4 Marks)**

**Answer :** $\boxed{D = 138 \text{ mm}, d = 0.6 \times 138 = 82.8 \text{ mm}}$

---

**Example 34 :** *A hollow shaft of diameter ratio $\frac{3}{5}$ is required to transmit maximum torque of 61465 N.m. The shear stress is not to exceed 63 MPa and twist in a length of 3 meters is not to exceed 1.4°. Calculate the minimum external diameter satisfying these conditions.*

*Take G = 84 GPa.*　　**(B.T.E. W-2010, 2008/4 Marks)**

**Data**　　: Let D = external diameter, d = internal diameter

$$\frac{d}{D} = \frac{3}{5} \text{ (given)} \Rightarrow d = \frac{3}{5} D = 0.6\,D.$$

Torque T = 61465 N.m = 61465 × 10³ N.mm, $f_s$ = 63 MPa = 63 N/mm²,

length L = 3 m = 3 × 10³ mm, twist θ = 1.4° = $\left( 1.4 \times \dfrac{\pi}{180} \right)$ rad,

G = 84 GPa = 84 × 10³ N/mm²

**To find**　　: D.

**Concept**　　: Design based on strength and stiffness criteria.

**Solution　: (i) Case-1 :** Diameter based on shear stress (strength criteria).

Using the relation,　　$T = \dfrac{\pi}{16} f_s \left( \dfrac{D^4 - d^4}{D} \right)$

$$61465 \times 10^3 = \dfrac{\pi}{16} \times 63 \times \left[ \dfrac{D^4 - (0.6\,D)^4}{D} \right]$$

∴　　　$61465 \times 10^3 = \dfrac{\pi}{16} \times 63 \times \dfrac{D^4\,(1 - 0.1296)}{D}$

∴　　　$61465 \times 10^3 = \dfrac{\pi}{16} \times 63 \times 0.8704\,D^3$

∴　　　　**D = 178.72 mm**

**(ii) Case-2 : Diameter based on angle of twist (stiffness criteria) :**

Using the relation,　　$\dfrac{T}{I_p} = \dfrac{G\theta}{L}$

Now,　　$I_p = \dfrac{\pi}{32}(D^4 - d^4) = \dfrac{\pi}{32}[D^4 - (0.6\,D)^4]$

$$= \dfrac{\pi}{32} \times 0.8704\,D^4 = 0.085\,D^4$$

∴　　　$\dfrac{61465 \times 10^3}{0.085\,D^4} = \dfrac{(84 \times 10^3)\left(1.4 \times \dfrac{\pi}{180}\right)}{3 \times 10^3}$

∴　　　　**D = 180.31 mm**

---

**Answer :** Minimum external diameter to satisfy both the conditions is **180.31 mm (Maximum of the two values).**

---

## SUB-TOPIC 7.2 : COMPARISON BETWEEN SOLID AND HOLLOW SHAFTS SUBJECTED TO PURE TORSION (4 Marks)

**(No problems on composite and non-homogeneous shaft)**

**Type 8 : Examples on comparison between solid and hollow shafts subjected to pure torsion (Replacement of shaft and % saving in material cost) :**

**Example 35 :** *A solid wrought iron shaft is to be replaced by a hollow steel shaft whose diameter is equal to external diameter of hollow steel shaft. Determine the ratio of external and internal diameter of hollow steel shaft, if maximum shear stress in steel is 1.3 times the maximum shear stress in wrought iron.* **(B.T.E. W-2010, 2004/4 Marks)**

**Data :** Diameter of solid wrought iron shaft = external diameter of hollow steel shaft = D

　　　　Let d = internal diameter of hollow steel shaft

　　　　$(f_s)_{steel} = 1.3\,(f_s)_{wrought\ iron}.$

**To find :**　$\dfrac{D}{d}$.

**Concept :** Torque transmitted by both the shafts must be the same.

**Solution :**   (i) Torque transmitted by steel,

$$T_{steel} = \left[ I_p \left( \frac{f_s}{R} \right) \right]_{steel} = \frac{\pi}{32} (D^4 - d^4) \frac{(f_s)_{steel}}{\left( \frac{D}{2} \right)} \qquad \qquad ... (1)$$

(ii)  Torque transmitted by wrought iron,

$$T_{W.I.} = \left( I_p \cdot \frac{f_s}{R} \right)_{W.I.} = \frac{\pi}{32} D^4 \cdot \frac{(f_s)_{W.I.}}{\left( \frac{D}{2} \right)} \qquad \qquad ... (2)$$

(iii)  Torque transmitted must be the same by both the shafts. Hence, equating (1) and (2), we have

$$T_{steel} = T_{W.I.}$$

$$\frac{\pi}{32} \frac{(D^4 - d^4)}{\left( \frac{D}{2} \right)} (f_s)_{steel} = \frac{\frac{\pi}{32} D^4}{\left( \frac{D}{2} \right)} (f_s)_{W.I.}$$

$$(D^4 - d^4)\,[1.3\,(f_s)_{W.I.}] = D^4\,(f_s)_{W.I.}$$

$$\frac{D^4 - d^4}{D^4} = \frac{1}{1.3}$$

$$1.3\,(D^4 - d^4) = D^4$$

∴        $$1.3\,D^4 - 1.3\,d^4 = D^4$$

∴        $$1.3\,D^4 - D^4 = 1.3\,d^4$$

∴        $$(1.3 - 1)\,D^4 = 1.3\,d^4$$

∴        $$0.3\,D^4 = 1.3\,d^4$$

∴        $$\frac{D^4}{d^4} = \frac{1.3}{0.3} = 4.33$$

∴        $$\left( \frac{D}{d} \right)^4 = 4.33$$

**Answer :**        $$\boxed{\left( \frac{D}{d} \right) = 1.4428}$$

---

**Example 36 :** *Two shafts of same material are subjected to same torque. If first shaft is solid and the other one is hollow having I.D. = 2/3 O.D., compare the weights of two shafts.*

**(B.T.E. S-2011/4 Marks)**

**Data**    :  Let        $D$ = Diameter of solid shaft

$D_1$ = Outer diameter of hollow shaft

$d$ = Inner diameter of hollow shaft = $\frac{2}{3} D_1$

**To find** : Compare weights of two shafts.

**Concept :** (i) $Z_p$ for solid shaft = $Z_p$ for hollow shaft.

(ii) $\dfrac{\text{Weight of hollow shaft}}{\text{Weight of solid shaft}} = \dfrac{\text{Area of h.s.}}{\text{Area of s.s.}}$

**Solution : Polar modulus for hollow shaft :**

$$Z_p = \frac{\pi}{16}\left(\frac{D_1^4 - d^4}{D}\right)$$

$$= \frac{\pi}{16}\left[\frac{D_1^4 - \left(\frac{2}{3}D_1\right)^4}{D_1}\right] = \frac{\pi}{16}\times\left[D_1^3 \times\left(1 - \frac{16}{81}\right)\right]$$

$$= \frac{\pi}{16}\times\frac{65}{81}D_1^3 \qquad\qquad \text{... (i)}$$

**Polar modulus for solid shaft :**

$$Z_p = \frac{\pi}{16}D^3 \qquad\qquad \text{... (ii)}$$

Equating (i) and (ii), we get

$$\frac{\pi}{16}\times\frac{65}{81}D_1^3 = \frac{\pi}{16}D^3$$

$$\frac{D_1^3}{D^3} = \frac{81}{65} = 1.246$$

$\therefore$     $\dfrac{D_1}{D} = \sqrt[3]{1.246} = 1.076$

$$\frac{\text{Weight of hollow shaft}}{\text{Weight of solid shaft}} = \frac{\text{Area of h.s.}}{\text{Area of s.s.}}$$

$$= \frac{\frac{\pi}{4}\left[D_1^2 - \left(\frac{2}{3}D_1\right)^2\right]}{\frac{\pi}{4}D^2} = \frac{5}{9}\left(\frac{D_1}{D}\right)^2 = \frac{5}{9}(1.076)^2 = \mathbf{0.643}$$

**Answer :** $\boxed{\dfrac{\text{Weight of solid shaft}}{\text{Weight of hollow shaft}} = 0.643}$

---

**Example 37 :** *A hollow circular shaft of 180 mm external diameter and 120 mm internal diameter is to be replaced by a solid shaft of the same material having same twisting moment and stiffness. Determine the equivalent diameter of solid shaft. Also calculate the ratio of maximum shear stresses induced in the shafts.* **(B.T.E. S-2004/4 Marks)**

**Data :**

|  |  | Hollow shaft | Solid shaft |
|---|---|---|---|
| (i) | Diameters | $d_o = 180$ mm, $d_i = 120$ mm | $d$ |
| (ii) | Material is same | G | G |
| (iii) | Twisting moment is same | T | T |
| (iv) | Stiffness is same | $\dfrac{T}{\theta}$ | $\dfrac{T}{\theta}$ |

**To find :** (i) d, (ii) $\dfrac{(f_s)_h}{(f_s)_s}$.

**Concept :** (i) Stiffness of the shaft is the ratio of torque to angle of twist.

From torsion equation, $\dfrac{T}{I_p} = \dfrac{G\theta}{L}$

$\therefore$ Stiffness, $\dfrac{T}{\theta} = \dfrac{GI_p}{L}$

(ii) Since the stiffness of both the hollow and solid shaft is same i.e. $\dfrac{G}{L} I_p$ is same for both the shafts. But material and length of the shaft is also same, hence $I_p$ for both the shafts must be equal.

$$(I_p)_{\text{hollow shaft}} = (I_p)_{\text{solid shaft}}$$

**Solution : (i) Diameter of solid shaft :**

$$(I_p)_{\text{hollow shaft}} = (I_p)_{\text{solid shaft}}$$

$$\frac{\pi}{32}(d_o^4 - d_i^4) = \frac{\pi}{32} d^4$$

$\therefore$ $$\frac{\pi}{32}(180^4 - 120^4) = \frac{\pi}{32} d^4$$

$\therefore$ $$d^4 = 180^4 - 120^4 = 8.424 \times 10^8 \text{ mm}^4$$

$\therefore$ $$\mathbf{d = 170.36 \text{ mm}}$$

**(ii) Ratio of maximum shear stresses :**

From torsion equation, $\dfrac{T}{I_p} = \dfrac{f_s}{R}$

Since T and $I_p$ are same for both shafts,

$$\left(\frac{f_s}{R}\right)_{\text{hollow shaft}} = \left(\frac{f_s}{R}\right)_{\text{solid shaft}}$$

$$\frac{(f_s)_{\text{hollow shaft}}}{(f_s)_{\text{solid shaft}}} = \frac{(R)_{\text{hollow shaft}}}{(R)_{\text{solid shaft}}} = \frac{180/2}{170.36/2}$$

$\therefore$ $$\frac{(f_s)_h}{(f_s)_s} = \frac{180}{170.36} = \mathbf{1.056}$$

**Answer :** $\boxed{d = 170.36 \text{ mm}, \dfrac{(f_s)_h}{(f_s)_s} = 1.056}$

**Example 38 :** *A solid aluminium shaft 1 m long and 50 mm diameter is replaced by a tubular steel shaft of the same length and outside diameter. What must be the inner diameter of the tubular shaft for the same torque ?*

Take : $G_S = 8.5 \times 10^4$ N/mm² for steel and $G_A = 2.8 \times 10^4$ N/mm² for aluminium

**(B.T.E. W-2003, S-2003/4 Marks)**

**Data :**

| | Solid aluminium shaft | Tubular steel shaft |
|---|---|---|
| Length | 1 m = 1000 mm | 1 m = 1000 mm |
| Diameter | d = 50 mm | Outer diameter, $d_o$ = 50 mm, Inner diameter, $d_i$ = ? |
| Modulus of rigidity | $G_A = 2.8 \times 10^4$ N/mm² | $G_S = 8.5 \times 10^4$ N/mm² |
| Torque | T | T |

**To find :** Inner diameter of tubular steel shaft ($d_i$).

**Concept :** (i) Torsion equation is $\dfrac{T}{I_p} = \dfrac{G \cdot \theta}{L}$

$\therefore$ $\qquad\qquad\qquad T = \dfrac{G \cdot \theta}{L} \cdot I_p$ $\qquad\qquad$ ... (1)

(ii) Since the torque is same and external diameter is same both for solid aluminium and tubular steel shaft,

$$\boxed{\theta_A = \theta_S} \qquad\qquad ... (2)$$

**Solution :** (i) From equation (1),

Since, $\qquad\qquad (T)_{Aluminium} = (T)_{Steel}$

$$\frac{G_A \cdot \theta_A}{L_A} \cdot (I_p)_A = \frac{G_S \cdot \theta_S}{L_S} \cdot (I_p)_S$$

(ii) Since, $\qquad\qquad \theta_A = \theta_S, \; L_A = L_S$

$\therefore$ $\qquad\qquad\qquad G_A (I_p)_A = G_S (I_p)_S$

$$(2.8 \times 10^4)\left[\frac{\pi}{32}(50)^4\right] = (8.5 \times 10^4)\left[\frac{\pi}{32}(50^4 - d_i^4)\right]$$

Dividing both sides by $10^4 \times \dfrac{\pi}{32}$,

$$2.8 \times 50^4 = 8.5\,(50^4 - d_i^4)$$

$$\frac{2.8 \times 50^4}{8.5} = 50^4 - d_i^4$$

$$2058823.529 = 6250000 - d_i^4$$

$$d_i^4 = 4191176.471$$

Inner diameter of steel shaft,

$$d_i = \textbf{45.25 mm}$$

**Answer :** $\boxed{d_i = 45.25 \text{ mm}}$

**Example 39 :** *A solid circular shaft is replaced by a hollow circular shaft of the same material to transmit the same power. If the inside diameter of the hollow shaft is $\frac{2}{3}$ of outside diameter, find the saving in material, if any, by this replacement.* **(B.T.E. W-1988/4 Marks)**

**Data** : For hollow shaft, $d = \frac{2}{3} D$.

Let d' = diameter of solid shaft. Material for both shafts is same, power is same.

**To find** : % saving in material.

**Concept** : The maximum torque a shaft can resist is given by,
$$T = f_s \times Z_p$$

In order that the solid and hollow shaft should have same strength to resist the torque, the polar modulli of the shaft must be equal.

**Solution :** $(Z_p)_{\text{Solid shaft}} = (Z_p)_{\text{Hollow shaft}}$

$$\frac{\pi}{16} (d')^3 = \frac{\pi}{16} \left( \frac{D^4 - d^4}{D} \right)$$

∴ $$\frac{\pi}{16} (d')^3 = \frac{\pi}{16} \left[ \frac{D^4 - \left( \frac{2}{3} D \right)^4}{D} \right]$$

∴ $$(d')^3 = \frac{65}{81} D^3$$

∴ $$\left( \frac{d'}{D} \right)^3 = \frac{65}{81} \quad \therefore \quad \frac{d'}{D} = \mathbf{0.929}$$

**% saving in material** $= \left[ \dfrac{\text{Area of solid shaft} - \text{Area of hollow shaft}}{\text{Area of solid shaft}} \right] \times 100$

$$= \left[ \frac{\frac{\pi}{4} (d')^2 - \frac{\pi}{4} (D^2 - d^2)}{\frac{\pi}{4} (d')^2} \right] \times 100 = \frac{\frac{\pi}{4} (d')^2 - \frac{\pi}{4} \left[ D^2 - \left( \frac{2}{3} D \right)^2 \right]}{\frac{\pi}{4} (d')^2} \times 100$$

$$= \left[ \frac{\frac{\pi}{4} (d')^2 - \frac{\pi}{4} D^2 \left( 1 - \frac{4}{9} \right)}{\frac{\pi}{4} (d')^2} \right] \times 100 = \left[ 1 - \left( \frac{D}{d'} \right)^2 \left( 1 - \frac{4}{9} \right) \right] \times 100$$

$$= \left[ 1 - \left( \frac{1}{0.929} \right)^2 \left( \frac{5}{9} \right) \right] \times 100 = 0.3566 \times 100 = \mathbf{35.66\ \%}$$

**Answer :** | % saving in material = 35.66 % |

---

**Example 40 :** *To transmit the same torque, a solid circular shaft 80 mm in diameter is to be replaced by a hollow circular shaft having external diameter 1.5 times the internal diameter. The material for solid and hollow shaft is the same. Determine the diameters of the hollow shaft. How much is the percentage saving in the material cost ?* **(B.T.E. S-1990/4 Marks)**

**Data** : Solid shaft d' = 80 mm, Hollow shaft D = 1.5 d.

Material for both the shafts is same, torque is same.

**To find** : (i)  D, d.,  (ii) % saving in material.

**Concept** : Torque for both the shafts is same. Hence,

$$\left(\frac{T}{f_s}\right)_{solid\ shaft} = \left(\frac{T}{f_s}\right)_{hollow\ shaft}$$

**Solution :** (i) For a solid shaft,

$$T = \frac{\pi}{16} f_s (d')^3$$

$$\frac{T}{f_s} = \frac{\pi}{16} (80)^3 = 100530.96 \text{ mm}^3$$

(ii)  For a hollow shaft,    $T = \frac{\pi}{16} f_s \left(\frac{D^4 - d^4}{D}\right)$

$\therefore$    $\frac{T}{f_s} = \frac{\pi}{16} \left[\frac{(1.5\ d)^4 - d^4}{1.5\ d}\right]$

$\therefore$    $100530.96 = \frac{\pi}{16} \left(\frac{5.0625\ d^4 - d^4}{1.5\ d}\right) = \frac{\pi}{16} \frac{d^4 (5.0625 - 1)}{1.5\ d}$

$\therefore$    $100530.96 = 0.53178\ d^3$

$\therefore$    $d^3 = 189046.1469$

$\therefore$    $\mathbf{d = 57.39 \text{ mm}}$

$\mathbf{D} = 1.5 \times 57.39 = \mathbf{86.08 \text{ mm}}$

**% saving in material** $= \left[\frac{\text{Area of solid shaft} - \text{Area of hollow shaft}}{\text{Area of solid shaft}}\right] \times 100$

$$= \left[\frac{\frac{\pi}{4} \times 80^2 - \frac{\pi}{4} (86.08^2 - 57.39^2)}{\frac{\pi}{4} \times 80^2}\right] \times 100 = \mathbf{35.66 \ \%}$$

**Answer :** $\boxed{\text{% saving in material} = 35.66 \ \%}$

---

## Practice Questions

### Questions of 2 marks

1. State the expression for power transmitted by a shaft giving meaning of each term used.        **(B.T.E. W-2012)**

2. Write the equation of torsion for a hollow shaft of outside diameter ($d_o$) and inside diameter ($d_i$).        **(B.T.E. W-2012)**

3. Define torque or twisting moment. State its S.I. unit.  **(B.T.E. S-2013, 2012; W-2007)**

4. State the torsional formula and explain the meaning and units of each term.
        **(B.T.E. W-2011, 1998; S-1999, 1997)**

5. State the expression for power transmitted by a shaft.        **(B.T.E. W-2011, S-2009)**

6. State the equation of torsion giving meaning of each term used in it.
**(B.T.E. S-2011, 2010; W-2010, 2008)**

7. Write torsion equation along with meaning of symbols used there in. **(B.T.E. S-2008)**

8. Write torsion equation of hollow shaft. State the assumptions made for theory of pure torsion. **(B.T.E. S-2009)**

9. State the expression for power transmitted by a shaft at N rpm giving meaning of each term. **(B.T.E. W-2008)**

10. State any four assumptions made in theory of pure torsion. **(B.T.E. S-2008, 2005)**

11. Sketch the shear stress variation across circular cross-section of shaft subjected to torsion. **(B.T.E. S-2006)**

12. What are the assumptions in the theory of pure torsion ? **(B.T.E. W-1997, S-1997)**

13. Define polar modulus of section and state its S.I. unit.
**(B.T.E. W-2008, 2007, 1999, 1997; S-2000, 2008)**

14. Differentiate between the polar modulus and section modulus.

15. Define the term 'torsional rigidity'. **(B.T.E. W-2000)**

16. State the formula of torsional rigidity and write the unit. **(B.T.E. W-2007)**

17. How the power of shaft can be calculated ? **(B.T.E. S-2013, 1998)**

18. Calculate the polar modulus of solid circular shaft of 100 mm diameter.
**(B.T.E. S-1999)**

19. Calculate the torque exerted by solid shaft of 40 mm diameter if the maximum shearing stress is 20 N/mm$^2$. **(B.T.E. W-1998)**

20. A circular shaft is rotating at 200 rpm. Calculate power developed if the torque is 40000 N-mm. **(B.T.E. W-1999)**

## Questions of 4 marks

21. State the assumptions in the theory of torsion. **(B.T.E. S-2013)**

**OR**

State any four assumptions in the theory of pure torsion in solid circular shaft.
**(B.T.E. S-2012, 2010; W-2011)**

22. State the torsional formula and explain meaning of each term. **(B.T.E. S-2013)**

23. Explain the theory of pure torsion. **(B.T.E. S-2011)**

## Problems of 4 marks

24. Find the polar modulus of a solid circular shaft of diameter 200 mm.
**(Ans.** $Z_p$ = 1570796.33 mm$^3$)

25. Find the polar modulus of a hollow circular shaft of external diameter 400 mm and internal diameter 300 mm. **(Ans.** $Z_p$ = 8590292.41 mm$^3$)

26. A solid shaft of 100 mm diameter is subjected to a torque of 6 kN·m. Find the maximum shear stress induced in the shaft. **(Ans.** $f_s$ = 30.56 N/mm$^2$)

27. A solid shaft has to transmit a power of 800 kW at 200 rpm. The maximum torque is likely to exceed the mean torque by 30 %. Find the diameter of the shaft if the maximum shearing stress is limited to 80 N/mm$^2$. **(Ans.** D = 146.76 mm)

28. A hollow shaft 2.5 m long has external diameter 400 mm and thickness of 50 mm. Find the torque that can be resisted by the shaft if the maximum shearing stress is not to exceed 60 N/mm$^2$ and the angle of twist is not to exceed 1/2° per metre length of the shaft. Take G = 80 kN/mm$^2$.

> **[Ans.** Torque based on shear stress = 5.1541 × 10$^8$ N·mm
> Torque based on angle of twist = 1.1994 × 10$^9$ N·mm
> Suitable torque = 5.1541 × 10$^8$ N·mm (Minimum of the two values)]

29. A solid circular shaft has to develop 120 kW power at 180 r.p.m. If the maximum permissible shear stress is not to exceed 84 N/mm$^2$ and the angle of twist is not to exceed 2° per 2 m length, find the diameter of the shaft. Take G = 80 kN/mm$^2$.

> **[Ans.** Diameter based on shear stress = 72.8 mm,
> Diameter based on angle of twist = 82.5 mm,
> Suitable diameter = 82.5 mm (Greater of the two values)]

30. A hollow shaft has to transmit 60 kW at 150 rpm. The maximum torque may exceed mean torque by 50 %. If the permissible shear stress is 80 N/mm$^2$, calculate the external diameter of the shaft. The internal diameter is 0.8 times the external diameter. What will be the external diameter if the angle of twist is limited to 1.5° in 6 m ? Take C = 8 × 10$^4$ N/mm$^2$.          **(Ans.** (i) D = 71.45 mm, (ii) D = 129.72 mm)

31. A hollow circular shaft has internal diameter 3/4$^{th}$ of the external diameter and transmits 500 kW at 120 rpm. If the shear stress is limited to 80 N/mm$^2$ and the angle of twist is not to exceed 1.4° in 3 m length, calculate the external and internal diameter. Take C = 84 kN/mm$^2$.          **(Ans.** D = 171.6 mm, d = 128.7 mm)

32. A solid shaft 54 mm diameter has to transmit a torque of 1100 N·m. The maximum torque is 1.3 times the average value. The twist observed is 1.2° per metre. Calculate the maximum shear stress induced and the modulus of rigidity.

    **Hint :** Given torque is the average torque.

    $T_{max}$ = 1.3 × 1100 = 1430 N·m.          **(Ans.** $f_s$ = 46.25 N/mm$^2$, C = 0.8 × 10$^5$ N/mm$^2$)

33. A hollow shaft 120 mm external diameter and 100 mm internal diameter is running at 200 rpm. The maximum torque is 20 % more than the average torque. The permissible shear stress is 90 N/mm$^2$ and the angle of twist is 1° per 3 m length. Calculate the power transmitted.

    **Hint :** Find the average torque from the shear stress and the angle of twist consideration.          **(Ans.** P = 87.5 kW)

## Important Points

- A product of the circumferential force and the radius of the shaft is called twisting moment or torque. It is denoted by T. S.I. unit of torque is N·m.
- **Torsional formula :**

  When a shaft is subjected to pure torsion,

  $$\frac{T}{I_p} = \frac{C\theta}{L} = \frac{f_s}{R}$$

where　T = Torque or turning moment (N-mm)

$I_p$ = Polar moment of inertia (mm$^4$)

C = Modulus of rigidity of the shaft material (N/mm$^2$)

θ = Angle of twist in radians

L = Length of the shaft

$f_s$ = Intensity of shear stress at the outermost layer of the shaft (N/mm$^2$)

R = Radius of the shaft (mm)

- **Strength of a solid shaft :**

For a solid shaft,

$$I_p = \frac{\pi}{32} d^4$$

Now,

$$\frac{T}{I_p} = \frac{f_s}{R} \text{ gives}$$

$$\frac{T}{\frac{\pi}{32} d^4} = \frac{f_s}{\frac{d}{2}}$$

∴

$$\boxed{T = \frac{\pi}{16} f_s d^3}$$

... (A)

- **Strength of a hollow shaft :**

For a hollow shaft,

$$I_p = \frac{\pi}{32} (D^4 - d^4)$$

Now,

$$\frac{T}{I_p} = \frac{f_s}{R} \text{ gives}$$

$$\frac{T}{\frac{\pi}{32} (D^4 - d^4)} = \frac{f_s}{\frac{D}{2}}$$

∴

$$\boxed{T = \frac{\pi}{16} f_s \left( \frac{D^4 - d^4}{D} \right)}$$

... (B)

- **Power transmitted by a shaft :**

$$P = \frac{2\pi N T}{60} \text{ watts}$$

where　　　　N = Number of revolutions of the shaft per minute

T = Mean (or average) torque in N·m

- **Horse-power transmitted by a shaft :**

$$H.P. = \frac{2\pi N T}{4500}$$

where　　　　N = Number of revolutions of the shaft per minute

T = Mean (or average) torque in kg·m.

□□□

# STRENGTH OF MATERIALS
## Winter 2013

Time : 3 Hours        Subject Code : 17304        Marks : 100

1. (a) **Attempt any Six of the following :**      (12 Marks)
   - (i) State Hook's law.
   - (ii) Define – Principal plane and principal stress.
   - (iii) State perpendicular axes theorem.
   - (iv) Define axial load and eccentric load.
   - (v) Draw stress distribution across solid circular shaft subjected to pure torsion.
   - (vi) Define – Bulk modulus.
   - (vii) State the relation between hoop stress and longitudinal stress, for thin cylinder.
   - (viii) A point in a strained material is subjected to tensile stress of 60 $N/mm^2$ along horizontal direction and compressive stress of 40 $N/mm^2$ along vertical direction. Draw a Mohr's circle for the stress system.

   (b) **Attempt any Two of the following :**      (08 Marks)
   - (i) A metal rod, 500 mm long and 20 mm in diameter, is subjected to an axial pull of 40 kN. Under this load, elongation of rod is 0.5 mm and decrease in diameter of rod is 0.006 mm. Calculate modulus of elasticity and Poisson's ratio.
   - (ii) A simply supported beam of 5 m span is subjected to UDL of 20 kN/m over 3 m length from left support. Draw shear force diagram for the beam.
   - (iii) A circular beam of 300 mm diameter is simply supported over a span of 4 m. Calculate UDL the beam can carry if the maximum bending stress is not to exceed 16 $N/mm^2$.

2. **Attempt any Four of the following :**      (16 Marks)
   - (a) (i) Define – Elasticity and Plasticity.
     (ii) State Rankine's formula for columns giving meaning of each terms used in it.
   - (b) A column 2.2 m long is 30 mm in diameter. It is fixed at one end and hinged at other. Calculate buckling load for column using Euler's formula. Take $E = 2 \times 10^5$ $N/mm^2$.
   - (c) A steel rod, 1.2 m long and 25 mm in diameter is held between rigid grips. The rod is heated through 60°C. Calculate stress and strain developed in the rod due to temperature change. Take $\alpha = 12 \times 10^{-6}/°C$ and $E = 2.1 \times 10^5$ $N/mm^2$.
   - (d) A composite bar of length 500 mm consists of a mild steel circular rod of 20 mm diameter enclosed in a brass tube of 30 mm external and 22 mm internal diameter. The composite bar is subjected to an axial pull of 60 kN. Find stresses in mild steel rod and brass tube. $E_s$ = 210 GPa and $E_{br}$ = 100 GPa.
   - (e) At a point in material, stresses of 500 $N/mm^2$ (Tensile) and 200 $N/mm^2$ (Compressive) are acting along two mutually perpendicular directions. Find the normal and tangential stresses on an oblique plane making an angle of 40° with the plane carrying 500 $N/mm^2$ stress.
   - (f) Find hoop stress and longitudinal stress induced in a cylindrical boiler 1.5 m internal diameter subjected to an internal pressure of 2.4 MPa. Thickness of the wall is 30 mm.

3. **Attempt any Four of the following :**      (16 Marks)
   - (a) A cantilever beam of span 'L' is subjected to point load of 'W' at free end. Draw S.F. and B.M. diagrams.
   - (b) A simply supported beam of span 'L' is subjected to UDL of 'w/unit length' over the entire span. Draw S.F. and B.M. diagrams.
   - (c) A simply supported beam of 6 m span is subjected to two point loads of 100 kN and 200 kN at 1 m and 4 m from left end support respectively. Draw S.F. diagram.

(d)    A cantilever beam of span 2 m is subjected to UDL of 10 kN/m over the entire span. Draw S.F. and B.M. diagrams.

(e)    Beam ABC is supported at A and B. Portion BC is overhang. UDL of 6 kN/m is acting over the entire length of ABC. AB = 4 m and BC = 1 m. Taking 'A' as origin write B.M. equation for portion AB and locate the position of point of contraflexure.

(f)    An element of triangular cross-section has base of 50 mm and height 60 mm. Calculate M.I. @ centroidal axis parallel to its base.

4.  **Attempt any Four of the following :**                                                   **(16)**

(a)    State parallel axis theorem. Draw related sketch and write mathematical expression.

(b)    A 'T' section has flange 120 mm × 20 mm, web 120 × 10 mm, overall depth 140 mm. Find M.I. about centroidal XX axis parallel to the flange.

(c)    A rectangular beam section has width of 200 mm and depth of 300 mm. Using parallel axis theorem calculate M.I. @ its base.

(d)    A hollow circular cross section has external diameter 100 mm with 10 mm wall thickness. Calculate its polar M.I.

(e)    Draw nature of bending stress distribution diagram for a cantilever beam having rectangular cross-section b × d and subjected to downward point load 'W' at free end. Also state maximum value of bending moment if span = 'L'.

(f)    Draw shear stress distribution diagram for circular section. Also state relation between maximum shear stress and average shear stress for this distribution.

5.  **Attempt any Four of the following :**                                          **(16 Marks)**

(a)    The cross-section of beam is symmetrical I-section having flange width 100 mm, overall depth 180 mm and thickness 10 mm. If the maximum permissible bending stress is 120 N/mm$^2$, find the moment of resistance of the beam section.

(b)    Calculate limit of eccentricity for a circular section having diameter 100 mm.

(c)    Draw core section for a rectangular section having dimensions 600 mm × 450 mm. Show the dimensions of core section in it.

(d)    A C-clamp made up of rectangular cross-section 30 mm × 10 mm as shown in Fig. 1, is subjected to a force of 2.5 kN. Find the stresses induced at section AB.

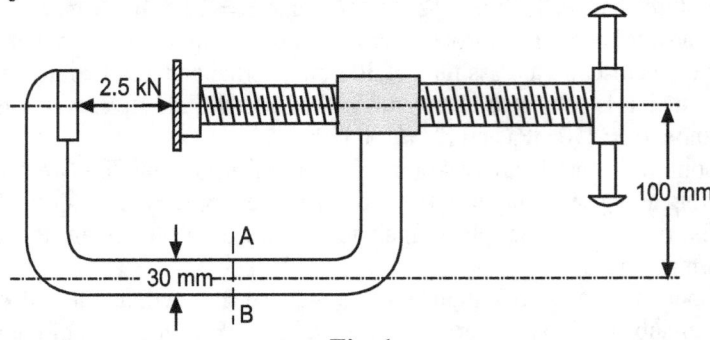

**Fig. 1**

(e)    Draw resultant stress distribution diagram for following conditions :
(i)  Direct stress > Bending stress.
(ii) Direct stress < Bending stress.

(f)    A rectangular strut is 120 mm × 80 mm thick. It carries a load of 100 kN at an eccentricity of 10 mm in a plane bisecting the thickness. Find the maximum and minimum intensities of stress in the strut section.

**6.** **Attempt any Four of the following :**                                      **(16 Marks)**

(a)  State assumptions in the theory of pure torsion.

(b)  Find the power that can be transmitted by a shaft 40 mm diameter rotating at 200 rpm if the maximum permissible shear stress is 85 N/mm$^2$. Take $T_{max} = 1.4\ T_{average}$.

(c)  A shaft is required to transmit 22 kW power at 160 rpm. The maximum torque may exceed the average torque by 40%. Calculate diameter of solid circular shaft if shear stress is not to exceed 50 N/mm$^2$.

(d)  A hollow shaft is required to transmit a torque of 40 kN/m. The inside diameter is 0.5 times the external diameter. Calculate both diameters if allowable stress is 80 MPa.

(e)  A solid circular shaft is replaced by a hollow circular shaft of same material whose external diameter is twice the internal diameter. Both the shafts are required to transmit same power at same speed. Calculate percentage saving in weight, if both shafts have same strength.

(f)  (i) Define – Section modulus.

(ii) Define – Torsional stiffness.

## ANSWERS

**1.**  (a)  (i)  Please refer to section 1.23.

(ii)  Please refer to section 2.3.

(iii)  Please refer to section 4.8.

(iv)  Please refer to sections 6.2 and 6.3.

(v)  Please refer to section 7.3, Fig. 7.2 (a).

(vi)  Please refer to section 1.38.

(vii)  $\sigma_L = \dfrac{1}{2}(\sigma_c) = \dfrac{1}{2}\left(\dfrac{pd}{2t}\right) = \dfrac{pd}{4t}$

(b)  (i)  $E = 127.323 \times 10^3$ N/mm$^2$, $\mu = 0.3$

(ii)  $F_A = 42$ kN, $F_C = F_B = -18$ kN

(iii)  $w = 21.205$ kN/m

**2.**  (a)  (i)  Please refer to section 1.6 (ii) and (iii).

(ii)  Please refer to section 1.53.

(b)  $P = 32.43 \times 10^3$ N

(c)  $\sigma = 151.2$ N/mm$^2$, $e = 7.2 \times 10^{-4}$

(d)  $\sigma_s = 126$ N/mm$^2$, $\sigma_b = 60$ N/mm$^2$

(e)  $\sigma_n = 210.76$ N/mm$^2$ (tensile), $\sigma_t = 344.68$ N/mm$^2$

(f)  $\sigma_c = 60$ N/mm$^2$, $\sigma_L = 30$ N/mm$^2$

**3.**  (a)  $F_x = W$   i.e. $F_A = F_B = W$

$M_A = -WL$, $M_B = 0$

(b)  $F_A = \dfrac{wL}{2}$, $F_B = -\dfrac{wL}{2}$, $F_C = 0$

$M_A = M_B = 0$, $M_C = \dfrac{wL^2}{8}$

(c)  $F_A = 150$ kN, $F_{C_L} = 150$ kN, $F_{C_R} = 50$ kN,

$F_{D_L} = 50$ kN, $F_{D_R} = -150$ kN, $F_B = -150$ kN

(d)  $F_A = 20$ kN, $F_B = 0$, $M_A = -20$ kN·m, $M_B = 0$

(e)  For AB portion,

$$M_X = R_A \times x - 6 \times x \times \frac{x}{2} = 11.25x - \frac{6x^2}{2}$$

Point of contraflexure, $M_x = 0$ gives,

$$11.25x - \frac{6x^2}{2} = 0 \Rightarrow x = 3.75 \text{ m from A.}$$

(f)  $$I_{XX} = \frac{bh^3}{36} = \frac{50 \times 60^3}{36} = 300 \times 10^3 \text{ mm}^4$$

**4.**  (a)  Please refer to section 4.7.

(b)  $$I_{XX} = 5.43999 \times 10^6 \text{ mm}^4$$

(c)  $$I_{Base} = 1.8 \times 10^9 \text{ mm}^4$$

(d)  $$I_{XX} = I_{YY} = 2.898 \times 10^6 \text{ mm}^4$$

$$I_P = 2I_{XX} = 5.796 \times 10^6 \text{ mm}^4$$

(e)  Please refer to section 5.5, Fig. 5.7 (a) and (b).

$$M_{max} = -wL \text{ at fixed end.}$$

(f)  Please refer to section 5.15, Fig. 5.40.

$$q_{max} = \frac{4}{3} q_{av}$$

**5.**  (a)  $$M_r = 23.84 \times 10^6 \text{ N·mm} = 23.84 \text{ kN·m}$$

(b)  $$e = 12.5 \text{ mm}$$

(c)  $$e_x = 75 \text{ mm}, \ e_y = 100 \text{ mm}$$

(d)  Please refer to the solved example 22, page 6.24.

$$\sigma_{max} = 175 \text{ N/mm}^2 \text{ (Tensile, on upper side)}$$

$$\sigma_{min} = -158.34 \text{ N/mm}^2 \text{ (Compressive, on lower side)}$$

(e)  Please refer to section 6.4.2, Fig. 6.4 (i) and (iii).

(f)  $$\sigma_{max} = 15.61 \text{ N/mm}^2 \text{ (Compressive)},$$

$$\sigma_{min} = 5.21 \text{ N/mm}^2 \text{ (Compressive)}.$$

**6.**  (a)  Please refer to section 7.2.

(b)  $$P = 16.39 \text{ kW}$$

(c)  $$D = 57.123 \text{ mm}$$

(d)  $$D = 139.526 \text{ mm}, \ d = 69.763 \text{ mm}$$

(e)  % saving in weight = 21.699%

(f)  (i)  Please refer to section 5.9 for section modulus.

(ii)  Please refer to section 7.5 for torsional rigidity (Torsional stiffness).

□□□

# STRENGTH OF MATERIALS
## Summer 2014

Time : 3 Hours       Subject Code : 17304       Marks : 100

1. (A) **Attempt any Six of the following :**       **(12 Marks)**
   (a) Define Poisson's ratio and state relation between modulus of elasticity and bulk modulus.
   (b) Define principal plane and stress.
   (c) Write equation of M.I. for semi-circle about its base.
   (d) Define direct load and eccentric load.
   (e) Give the equation for power transmitted by shaft with meaning of each term.
   (f) Define the terms ductility and malleability.
   (g) State Hoop stress with its expression.
   (h) Sketch the resultant stress distribution at the base section for the condition that direct stress is equal to bending stress.

   (B) **Attempt any Two of the following :**       **(8 Marks)**
   (a) A rod is 2 m long at 10°C, find the expansion of the rod when the temperature is raised to 80°C, if this expansion is prevented, find the stress in the material.
      Take $E = 1 \times 10^5$ N/mm$^2$ and $\alpha = 0.000012$/°C.
   (b) A simply supported beam of span 'L' carrying a concentrated load 'W' at midpoint, draw SFD and BMD for the beam.
   (c) A simply supported beam of 4 m span, carries a udl of 2 kN/m over the entire span. If the bending stress is not to exceed 165 N/mm$^2$, find the value of section modulus for the beam and diameter when beam is circular.

2. **Attempt any Four of the following :**       **(16 Marks)**
   (a) (i) State the principle of superposition.
      (ii) Give the effective length for :
         (a) when both ends are hinged, (ii) when both ends are fixed.
   (b) Draw and explain stress-strain curve for brittle material.
   (c) Give any four assumptions made in Euler's theory.
   (d) A brass bar having a cross-sectional area of 1000 mm$^2$ is subjected to axial forces as shown in Fig. 1. Find the total change in length of the bar. Take $E = 1.05 \times 10^5$ N/mm$^2$.

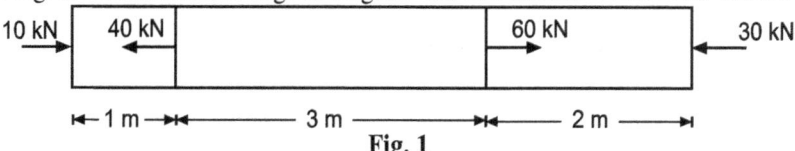

**Fig. 1**

   (e) At a certain point in a beam there is a tensile bending stress of 120 N/mm$^2$ in the horizontal direction accompanied by a shear stress of 40 N/mm$^2$. Find :
      (i) Principal stresses.
      (ii) Position of principal planes. Use Mohr's circle method.
   (f) A thin cylinder contains fluid at pressure of 3 N/mm$^2$. The inside diameter of the cylinder is 500 mm and the tensile stress in the material is to be limited to 80 N/mm$^2$. What is the wall thickness required ?

3. **Attempt any Four of the following :**       **(16 Marks)**
   (a) A cantilever beam of span 'L' carrying a point load 'W' at the free end. Draw SFD and BMD. Also state the maximum shear force and bending moment values.
   (b) A simply supported beam of span 6 m carries a UDL of 3 kN/m spread over 2 m from left support and a point load of 6 kN at 4 m from left support. Draw SFD and BMD.
   (c) Draw B.M. and S.F. diagrams for the beam shown in Fig. 2.

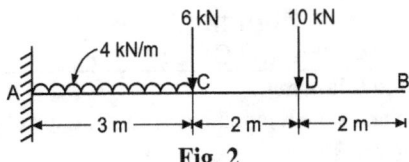

**Fig. 2**

(d) A simply supported beam of span 6 m carries a UDL of 1.6 kN/m over entire span and a point load of 3 kN at 2 m from right support. Draw SFD and also calculate point of contraflexure.

(e) Draw the bending moment diagram for the beam shown in Fig. 3.

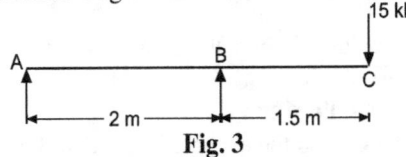

**Fig. 3**

(f) Explain perpendicular and parallel axis theorem for moment of inertia.

**4. Attempt any Four of the following :**                                      **(16 Marks)**

(a) Find M.I. of an equilateral triangle of side 3 m about its apex point and base line.

(b) Find the M.I. of a T-section of 150 mm × 150 mm × 10 mm about the centroidal axes.

(c) A lamina consists of a semicircle and a triangle shown in Fig. 4. Calculate its M.I. about reference axis AB.

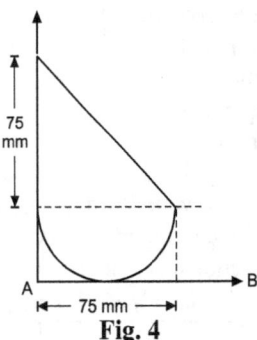

**Fig. 4**

(d) A hollow C.I. pipe with external diameter 100 mm and thickness of metal 10 mm is used as a strut. Calculate the moment of inertia and radius of gyration about its diameter.

(e) State any four assumptions of theory of simple bending.

(f) A beam of circular cross-section 100 mm diameter is subjected to a shear force of 25 kN. Calculate the maximum shear stress at the neutral axis.

**5. Attempt any Four of the following :**                                      **(16 Marks)**

(a) A timber beam is of circular cross-section of diameter 200 mm. The maximum bending stress produced at a section is 100 N/mm$^2$. Find the bending stress at a layer 50 mm from the neutral axis.

(b) A square pillar is 600 mm × 600 mm in section. At what eccentricity a point load of 6000 kN be placed on one of the centroidal axis of the section so as to produce no tension in the section ?

(c) A M.S. link as shown in Fig. 5 transmits a pull of 85 kN. Find the dimensions 'b' and 't' if b = 3.5t. Assume the permissible tensile stress as 60 MPa.

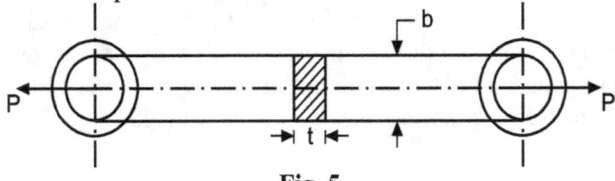

**Fig. 5**

(d) A circular section of diameter 'd' is subjected to load 'p' eccentric to the axis Y-Y. The eccentricity of the load is 'e'. Obtain the limit of eccentricity such that no tension is induced at the section.

(e) Define core of a section and obtain core of section for a rectangular section.

(f) Calculate the limit of eccentricity for a rectangular cross-section of size 1000 mm × 2000 mm and sketch it.

**6. Attempt any Four of the following :**                                 **(16 Marks)**

(a) Explain the theory of pure torsion.

(b) A solid shaft has to transmit a power of 800 kW at 200 rpm. The maximum torque is likely to exceed the mean torque by 30%. Find the diameter of the shaft if the maximum shearing stress is limited to 80 N/mm$^2$.

(c) Select a suitable diameter for a solid circular shaft to transmit 200 HP at 180 rpm. The allowable shear stress is 90 N/mm$^2$ and the allowable angle of twist is 1° in a length of 5 m. Take C/G = $0.82 \times 10^5$ N/mm$^2$.

(d) A hollow shaft is of external diameter and internal diameter 400 mm and 200 mm respectively. Find the maximum torque it can transmit, if the angle of twist is not to exceed 1.5° in a length of 10 m. Take C or G = $0.85 \times 10^5$ N/mm$^2$.

(e) A hollow shaft is required to transmit a torque of 36 kN·m. The inside diameter is 0.6 times the external diameter. Calculate both the diameters if the allowable shear stress is 83 MPa.

(f) Define section modulus with its unit. Write equation for strength of hollow shaft with their meaning of each term.

$$\boxed{\textbf{ANSWERS}}$$

**1.** (A) (a)    Please refer to sections 1.30. and 1.39.

        (b)    Please refer to section 2.3.

        (c)    Please refer to section 4.5, Fig. 4.9.

        (d)    Please refer to sections 6.2 and 6.3.

        (e)    Please refer to section 7.6.

        (f)    Please refer to section 1.6 (iv) and (vi).

        (g)    Please refer to section 2.7.

        (h)    Please refer to section 6.4.2, Fig. 6.4 (ii).

   (B) (a)    $\delta L$ = 1.68 mm, $\sigma$ = 84 N/mm$^2$ (Compressive)

        (b)    $F_A = \dfrac{W}{2}$, remains constant from A to C

               $F_B = -\dfrac{W}{2}$, remains constant from C to B

               $M_{max} = M_C = \dfrac{WL}{4}$, $M_A = M_B = 0$

        (c)    Z = 21621.621 mm$^3$, d = 60.389 mm

**2.** (a) (i)   Please refer to section 1.25.1. (ii) Please refer to section 1.47 (Figs. 1.62 and 1.63).

      (b)    Please refer to section 1.27, Fig. 1.23.

      (c)    Please refer to section 1.48.1.

      (d)    **Hint :** $P_1$ = − 10 kN, $P_2$ = + 30 kN, $P_3$ = − 30 kN, $\delta L$ = 0.1905 mm (increase)

      (e)   (i)    $\sigma_{n_1}$ = 132 N/mm$^2$ (Tensile), $\sigma_{n_2}$ = − 12 N/mm$^2$ (Compressive)

           (ii)    $\theta_1$ = 16.5°, $\theta_2$ = 106.5°

      (f)    t = 9.375 mm

**3.** (a)      $F_A = F_B = W$, $F_{max} = W$, $M_A = M_{max} = - WL$, $M_B = 0$

      (b)    Assuming A as left end and D as right end,

             $F_A = R_A = 7$ kN, $F_B = 7 - 3 \times 2 = 1$ kN,

$$F_{C_L} = 1 \text{ kN}, \ F_{C_R} = 1 - 6 = -5 \text{ kN}, \ F_D = -5 \text{ kN} = -R_D$$

$$M_A = 0, \ M_B = 1 \times 2 - 3 \times 2 \times \frac{2}{2} = 8 \text{ kN·m}$$

$$M_C = 7 \times 4 - 3 \times 2 \times \left( \frac{2}{2} + 2 \right) = 10 \text{ kN·m}, \ M_D = 0$$

(c)      $F_B = F_{D_R} = 0, \ F_{D_L} = 10 \text{ kN}, \ F_{C_R} = 10 \text{ kN}, \ F_{C_L} = 10 + 6 = 16 \text{ kN},$

$$F_A = 16 + 4 \times 3 = 28 \text{ kN}, \ M_B = M_D = 0, \ M_C = -10 \times 2 = -20 \text{ kN·m}$$

$$M_A = -10 \times 5 - 6 \times 3 - 4 \times 3 \times \frac{3}{2} = -86 \text{ kN·m}$$

(d)      $R_A = 5.8 \text{ kN}, \ R_B = 6.8 \text{ kN}, \ F_A = 5.8 \text{ kN}, \ F_{C_L} = 5.8 - 1.6 \times 4 = -0.6 \text{ kN·m}$

$$F_{C_R} = -0.6 - 3 = -3.6 \text{ kN·m}$$

$$F_B = -3.6 - (1.6 \times 2) = -6.8 \text{ kN}$$

$$M_A = M_B = 0, \ M_C = 10.4 \text{ kN·m}$$

Point of zero shear,

$$x = 0.375 \text{ m from C} = 3.625 \text{ m from A}$$

$$M_{max} = 10.515 \text{ kN·m}$$

**Note :** There is no point of contraflexure, but there is a point of zero shear.

(e)      $M_A = 0, \ M_B = -22.5 \text{ kN·m}, \ M_C = 0$

(f)      Please refer to sections 4.8 and 4.7.

**4.**    (a)      $I_{apex} = 13.1516 \text{ m}^4, \ I_{Base} = 4.38386 \text{ m}^4$

     (b)      $I_{XX} = 6.3724 \times 10^6 \text{ mm}^4, \ I_{YY} = 2.824 \times 10^6 \text{ mm}^4$

     (c)      $I_{AB} = 13.1109 \times 10^6 \text{ mm}^4$

     (d)      $I_{dia} = 2.898 \times 10^6 \text{ mm}^4, \ K = 32.015 \text{ mm}$

     (e)      Please refer to section 5.4.

     (f)      $q_{max} = 4.244 \text{ N/mm}^2$

**5.**    (a)      $\sigma_b = 50 \text{ N/mm}^2$

     (b)      $e = 100 \text{ mm}$

     (c)      $t = 20.11 \text{ mm}, \ b = 70.38 \text{ mm}$

     (d)      $e_{max} = \dfrac{d}{8}, \ 2e_{max} = \dfrac{d}{4}.$

For no-tension condition, the load must lie within a circle of diameter $\dfrac{d}{4}$.

     (e)      $e_x = \dfrac{d}{6}, \ e_y = \dfrac{b}{6} \Rightarrow 2e_x = \dfrac{d}{3}, \ 2e_y = \dfrac{b}{3}$

     (f)      $e_x = \dfrac{d}{6} \Rightarrow 2e_x = \dfrac{d}{3} = \dfrac{2000}{3} = 666.67 \text{ mm}$

$$e_y = \dfrac{b}{6} \Rightarrow 2e_y = \dfrac{b}{3} = \dfrac{1000}{3} = 383.33 \text{ mm}$$

Size of core of section is $2e_x \times 2e_y$.

**6.**    (a)      Please refer to sections 7.1.1 and 7.2 and draw Fig. 7.1.

     (b)      $d = 146.76 \text{ mm}$

     (c)      $d_1 = 76.16 \text{ mm}, \ d_2 = 129.32 \text{ mm}$

Suitable diameter satisfying given conditions = 129.32 mm.

     (d)      $T = 524.32 \text{ kN·m}$

     (e)      $D = 131.36 \text{ mm}, \ d = 78.82 \text{ mm}$

# STRENGTH OF MATERIALS
## Winter 2014

Time : 3 Hours        Subject Code : 17304        Marks : 100

1. **(A)** **Attempt any six of the following :**      $(2 \times 6 = 12)$
   - (a) Define malleability and state names of any two malleable metals.
   - (b) Write an equation of tangential stress on an inclined plane making an angle $\theta°$ with the plane subjected to stress in uniaxial stress system.
   - (c) State the theorem of mutually perpendicular axis for moment of inertia.
   - (d) State middle third rule with diagram.
   - (e) State four assumptions made in the theory of pure torsion.
   - (f) Define lateral and longitudinal strain.
   - (g) Distinguish between circumferential stress and longitudinal stress in a thin cylindrical shell, when subjected to an internal pressure.
   - (h) Define core of a section. Write its value for a circular section.

   **(B)** **Attempt any two of the following :**      $(4 \times 2 = 8)$
   - (a) A bar of cross-section 20 mm × 20 mm is axially pulled by a force 'P' kN. If the maximum stress induced in the bar is 50 MPa, determine 'P'. If elongation of 1.2 mm is observed over a gauge length of 3 m, determine Young's modulus.
   - (b) Draw shear force and bending moment diagram of a simply supported beam AB, 4 metres long, loaded with uniformly distributed load of 10 kN/m utpo 2 metres from B and a concentrated load of 12 kN at 1 meter from A.
   - (c) A rectangular beam of 120 mm wide and 300 mm deep is simply supported over a span of 4 m. Determine uniformly distributed load the beam may carry, if the bending stress is not to exceed 120 MPa.

2. **Attempt any four of the following :**      $(4 \times 4 = 16)$
   - (a) (i) Define composite section and modular ratio.
     - (ii) Write Rankine's formula. State the meaning of each symbol used.
   - (b) State the values of effective length of column for the following end conditions :
     - (i) Both ends hinged. (ii) Both ends fixed. (iii) One end fixed and other end hinged.
     - (iv) One end fixed and other end free.
   - (c) For a certain meterial, E = 2.8 K (where E = modulus of elasticity and K = bulk modulus) calculate Poisson's ratio. Also calculate the ratio of Young's modulus to the modulus of rigidity.
   - (d) A steel tube of 40 mm inside diameter and 4 mm metal thickness is filled with concrete. Determine the stresses in each material due to an axial thrust of 120 kN. Take modulus of elasticity for steel and concrete as $2.1 \times 10^5$ N/mm$^2$ and $0.14 \times 10^5$ N/mm$^2$ respectively.
   - (e) The principal stresses at a point in the section of a member are 100 N/mm$^2$ and 50 N/mm$^2$ both tensile. Find the normal and tangential stresses across a plane passing through that point inclined at 60° to the plane having 100 N/mm$^2$ stress.
   - (f) A hydraulic main of 1 m diameter and 10 mm thick has to carry water under a head of 200 m. Calculate (i) Hoop stress, (ii) Longitudinal stress. Assume, density of water as $10 \times 10^3$ N/m$^3$.

3. **Attempt any four of the following :**      $(4 \times 4 = 16)$
   - (a) Draw shear force and bending moment diagram for a cantilever beam of span 4 m carrying :
     - (i) a point load 20 kN at the free end.
     - (ii) a uniform distributed load of 10 kN/m length over the entire span.
     - Also state the maximum shear force and bending moment values.
   - (b) Draw shear force and bending moment diagram for simply supported beam of span 4 m with overhangs of 2 m on both sides and carrying uniformly distributed load of 10 kN/m over the whole length and point load of 20 kN at 1 m from left hand support.

(c)    Fig. 1 shows a simply supported beam carrying loads. Draw shear force diagram and BMD.

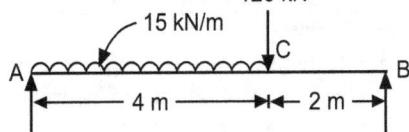

**Fig. 1**

(d)    Find the support reaction for the following sketch (refer Fig. 2) and draw shear force and bending moment diagram. Find the point of contraflexure if any.

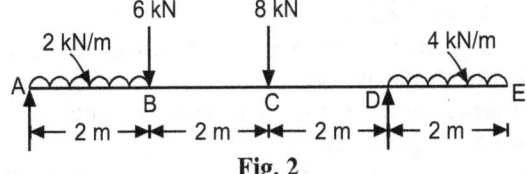

**Fig. 2**

(e)    Draw shear force and bending moment diagram for a cantilever beam AB of 4 m long having its fixed end at A and loaded with uniformly distributed load of 2 kN/m over entire span and point load of 3 kN acting upward at the free end of the cantilever. Find point of contraflexure if any.

(f)    A hollow square has inner dimensions 80 × 80 mm and outer dimensions 120 mm × 120 mm. Find the moment of inertia about the outer size.

**4.    Attempt any four of the following :**                                            **(4 × 4 = 16)**

(a)    Define : (i) Moment of inertia and (ii) Radius of gyration.

(b)    Calculate moment of inertia ($I_{xx}$) of inverted 'T'-section as shown in Fig. 3.

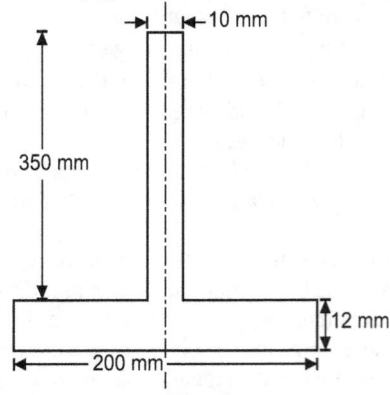

**Fig. 3**

(c)    A hollow circular section with 220 mm external diameter and 110 mm internal diameter. Calculate the moment of inertia of the section about any of its tangent. Also, find polar moment of inertia.

(d)    A channel section has the following dimensions :
    −    Flanges : 50 mm × 10 mm  − Overall depth : 200 mm  − Thickness of web : 10 mm.
    Find moment of inertia about X-X and Y-Y axis.

(e)    State four assumptions made in the theory of simple (pure) bending.

(f)    A symmetrical I-section has flanges 100 mm × 20 mm and web 300 mm × 20 mm. Draw shear stress distribution diagram for above section. Take shear force at section 100 kN.

**5.    Attempt any four of the following :**                                            **(4 × 4 = 16)**

(a)    Explain the meaning of moment of resistance and neutral axis in the theory of simple bending.

(b)　A short column of 200 mm × 100 mm is subjected to an eccentric load of 60 kN at an eccentricity of 40 mm in the plane bisecting the 100 mm side. Find the maximum and minimum intensities of stresses at the base.

(c)　A C.I. hollow circular stanchion has external diameter of 250 mm and internal diameter of 200 mm. It is subjected to vertical load of 20 kN at a distance of 400 mm from the vertical axis of the stanchion. Calculate maximum and minimum stresses at the base of stanchion.

(d)　Fig. 4 shows the frame of a screw clamp carrying a load of 4 kN. The cross-section of the frame is rectangular having width 60 mm and thickness 20 mm. Determine the resultant stresses for the frame material.

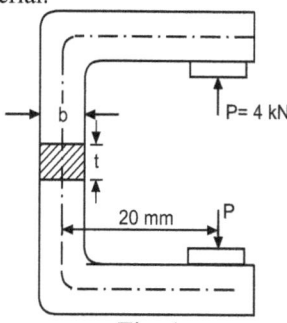

**Fig. 4**

(e)　Fig. 5 shows a M.S. offset link subjected to a pull of 80 kN. The cross-section of the link is rectangular having b = 120 mm, t = 40 mm. Find the resultant stresses produced in the link.

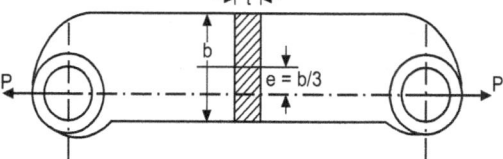

**Fig. 5**

(f)　Determine the limit of eccentricity for a hollow circular section having D = 300 mm and d = 100 mm.

## 6.　Attempt any four of the following :　　　　　　　　　　　　　　　　(4 × 4 = 16)

(a)　To transmit the same torque, a solid circular shaft of 80 mm in diameter is to be replaced by a hollow circular shaft having external diameter 1.5 times the internal diameter. The material for solid and hollow shaft is same. Determine the diameter of the hollow shaft. Also calculate the percentage saving in the material.

(b)　A shaft of 3 m length and 75 mm diameter is fixed at one end and twisted at free end, by a force of 2 kN acting at mean radius of 0.6 m. Find the angle of twist. Assume modulus of rigidity, $G = 90$ GN/m$^2$.

(c)　A solid shaft in the rolling mill transmits 20 kW at 2 revolutions per second. Determine the diameter of shaft, if shear stress is not to exceed 40 MN/m$^2$. The shaft is likely to have a maximum torque 40% more than mean torque.

(d)　Find the torque that can be applied to a shaft of 100 mm in diameter, if the permissible angle of twist is 2.75° in a length of 6 m. Assume modulus of rigidity, $G = 80$ kN/mm$^2$.

(e)　A hollow shaft is required to transmit the maximum torque to 62 kN.m. The shear stress is not to exceed 63 MPa and the twist in a length of 3 m is not to exceed 1.4°. Calculate the minimum external diameter satisfying these conditions.

(f)　(i)　Draw a shear stress distribution diagram for a T section.

　　(ii)　Sketch the shear stress variation across circular cross-section of shaft subjected to torsion.

**ANSWERS**

**1.** **(A)** (a) Please refer to section 1.6 (vi).

(b) $\sigma_t = \dfrac{\sigma_x}{2} \cdot \sin 2\theta$ .

(c) Please refer to section 4.8.

(d) Please refer to section 6.10.

(e) Please refer to section 7.2.

(f) Please refer to sections 1.28 and 1.29.

(g) Please refer to section 2.6 (i) and (ii).

In a thin cylindrical shell when subjected to an internal pressure

(i) The longitudinal stress is equal to half the circumferential stress.

(ii) Circumferential stress acts along the circumference and longitudinal stress acts along the length of shell.

(h) Please refer to sections 6.10.1 and 6.10.2.

The value of diameter of core of section for circular section is d/4 and d/8 for an either side from centre of section.

**(B)** (a) Similar to example 7, page 1.18.

$P = 20$ kN, $E = 125 \times 10^3$ N/mm$^2$

(b)

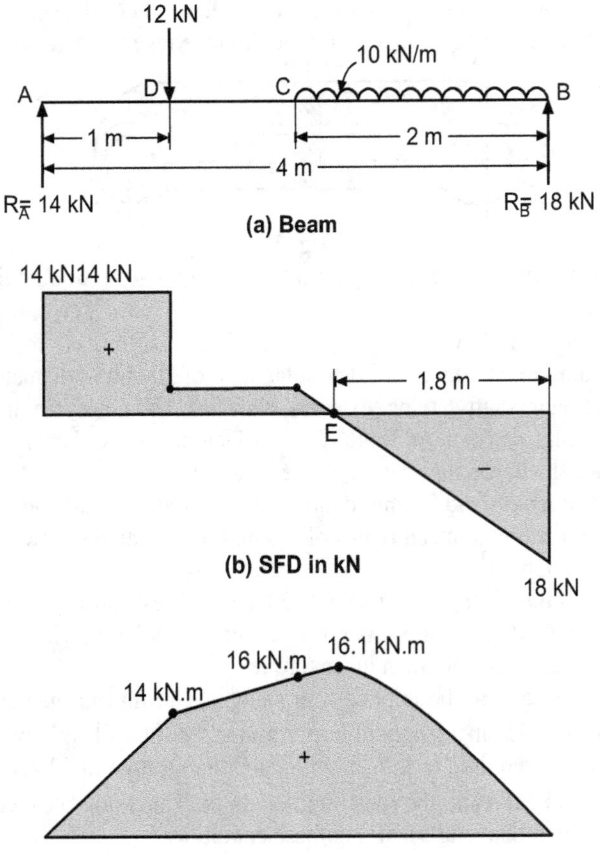

**(a) Beam**

**(b) SFD in kN**

**(c) BMD in kN.m**

**Fig. 6**

(c) Please refer to the solved example 6, page 5.18. w = 108 kN/m.

**2.** (a) (i) Please refer to section 1.44. (ii) Please refer to section 1.53.

(b) Please refer to section 1.45 (vi).

    (i) Both ends hinged, $L_e = L$. (ii) Both ends fixed, $L_e = \dfrac{L}{2}$.

    (iii) One end fixed and other end hinged, $L_e = \dfrac{L}{\sqrt{2}}$.

    (iv) One end fixed and other end free, $L_e = 2L$.

(c) Please refer to the solved example 18, page 1.39. $\mu = 0.035$, $E/G = 2.07$.

(d) Similar to example 92, page 1.86. $\sigma_c = 12.56$ N/mm$^2$, $\sigma_s = 188.47$ N/mm$^2$.

(e) Please refer to the solved example 11, page 2.18.
$\sigma_n = 62.5$ N/mm$^2$ (tensile), $\sigma_t = 21.65$ N/mm$^2$.

(f) Please refer to the solved example 11, page 2.47. $\sigma_c = 100$ N/mm$^2$, $\sigma_L = 50$ N/mm$^2$.

**3.** (a) (i)

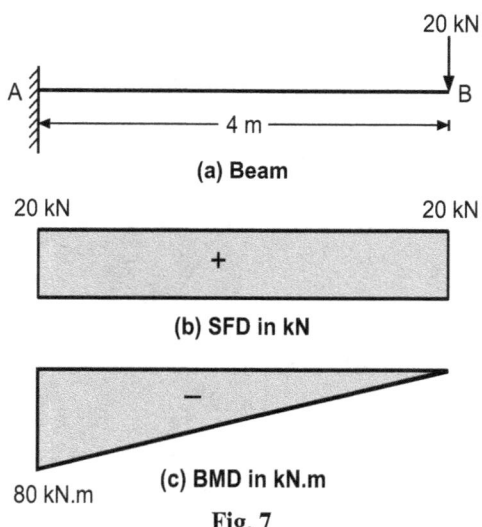

Fig. 7

(ii)

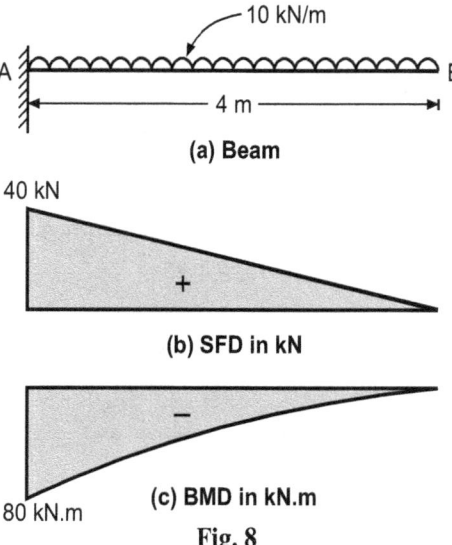

Fig. 8

(b)

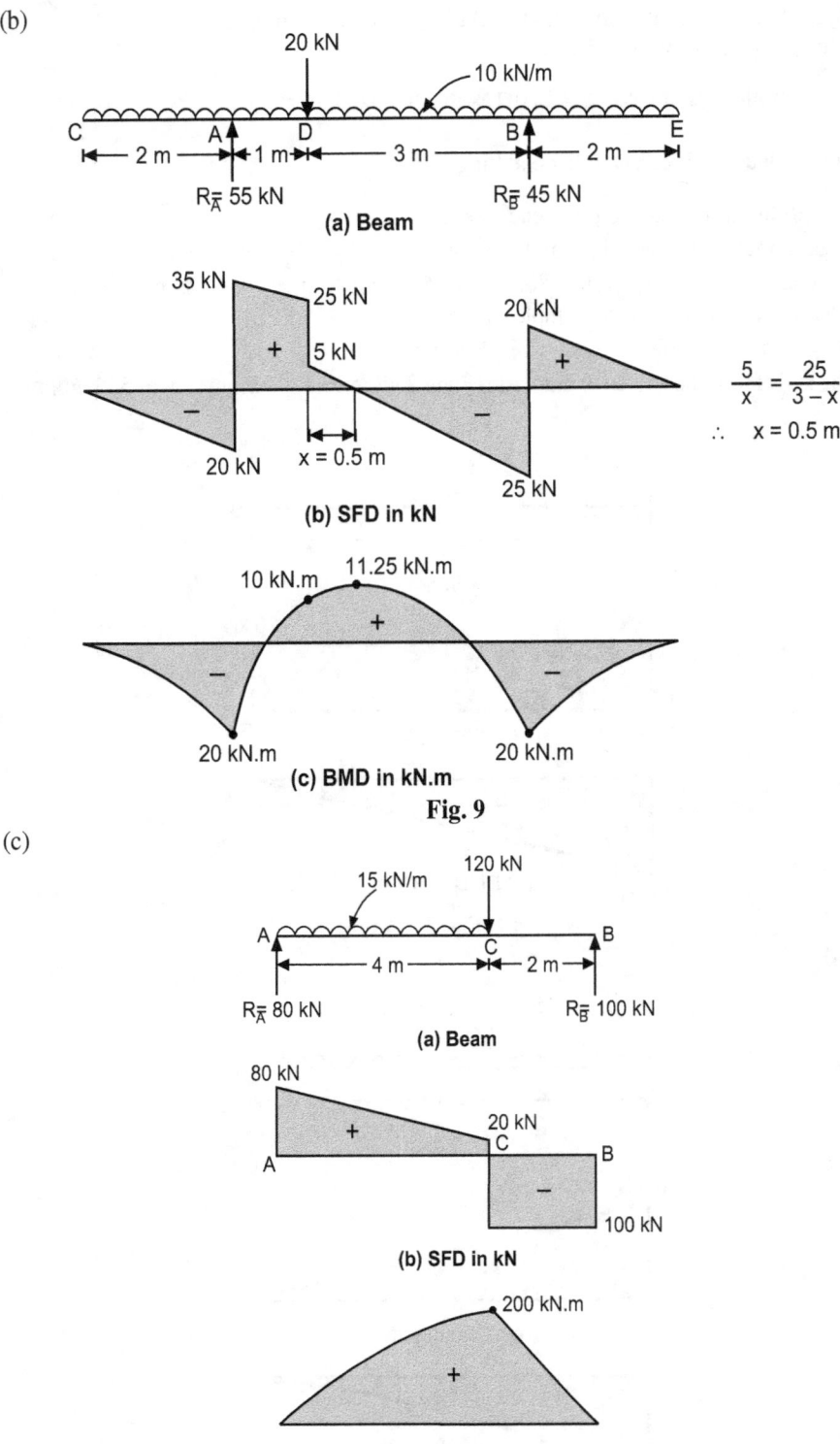

$\dfrac{5}{x} = \dfrac{25}{3-x}$

$\therefore \quad x = 0.5$ m

(a) Beam

(b) SFD in kN

(c) BMD in kN.m

**Fig. 9**

(c)

(a) Beam

(b) SFD in kN

(c) BMD in kN.m

**Fig. 10**

(d)

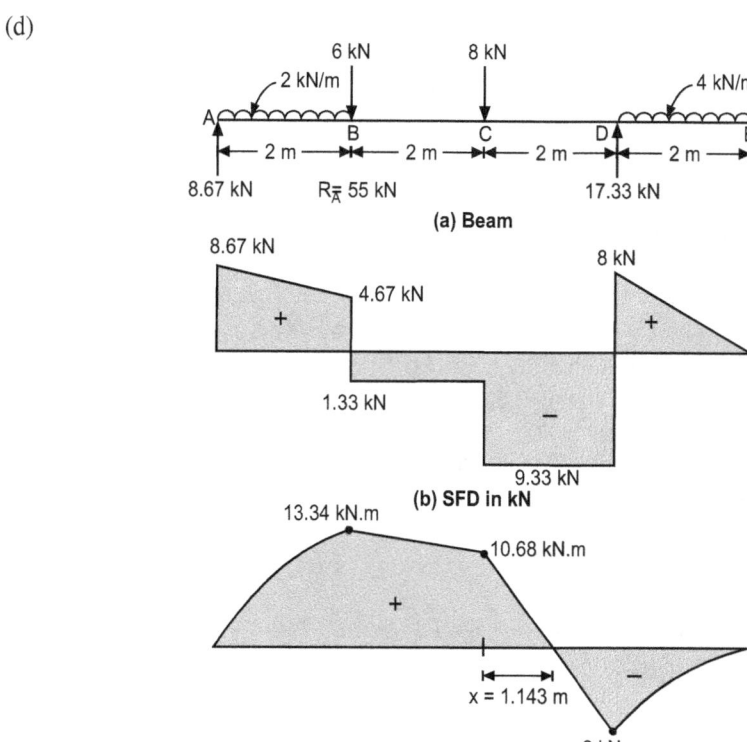

**(a) Beam**

**(b) SFD in kN**

**(c) BMD in kN.m**

**Fig. 11**

(e)   Very similar to example 32, page 3.54.

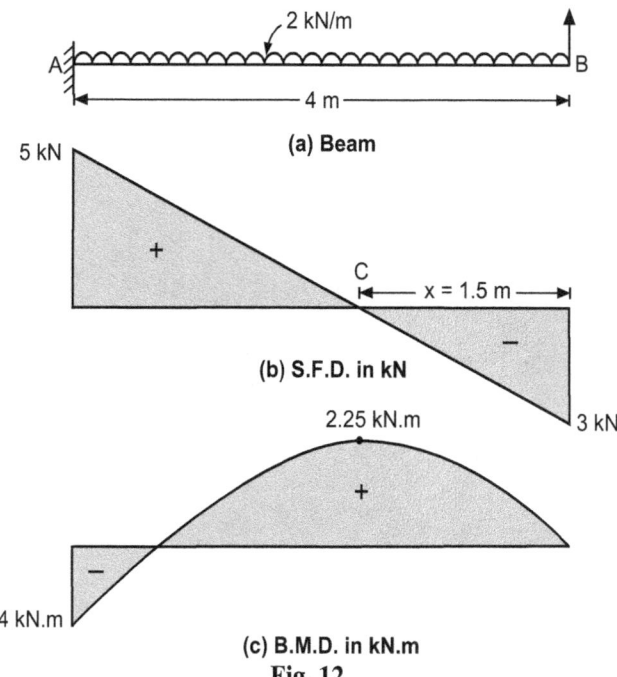

**(a) Beam**

**(b) S.F.D. in kN**

**(c) B.M.D. in kN.m**

**Fig. 12**

(f)   Similar to example 4, page 4.16. $I_{AB} = 42.667 \times 10^6$ mm$^4$.

**4.** (a) (i) Please refer to section 4.2. (ii) Please refer to section 4.3.

(b) Please refer to the solved example 36, page 4.40.

$I_{xx} = 120350384.7$ mm$^4$. $I_{tangent} = 45.27 \times 10^7$ mm$^4$, $I_p = 215.60 \times 10^6$ mm$^4$

(d) Please refer to the solved example 43, page 4.49.

$I_{xx} = 13.89 \times 10^6$ mm$^4$, $I_{yy} = 48.05 \times 10^4$ mm$^4$.

(e) Please refer to section 5.4.

(f) $q_1 = 2.169$ N/mm$^2$, $q_2 = 10.845$ N/mm$^2$, $q_{max} = 18.49$ N/mm$^2$.

**5.** (a) Please refer to section 5.6.

(b) Please refer to the solved example 5, page 6.12.

$\sigma_{max} = 6.6$ N/mm$^2$ (Compressive), $\sigma_{min} = -0.6$ N/mm$^2$ (Tensile)

(c) Please refer to the solved example 11, page 6.16.

$\sigma_{max} = 9.96$ N/mm$^2$ (Compressive), $\sigma_{min} = -7.7$ N/mm$^2$ (Tensile)

(d) Similar to example 23, page 6.25.

$\sigma_{max} = 70$ N/mm$^2$ (Compressive), $\sigma_{min} = -63.34$ N/mm$^2$ (Tensile)

(e) Please refer to similar example 24, page 6.26.

$\sigma_{max} = 50$ N/mm$^2$ (Compressive), $\sigma_{min} = -16.66$ N/mm$^2$ (Tensile)

(f) $e = 41.65$ mm $\Rightarrow 2e = 83.30$ mm.

**6.** (a) $d = 57.40$ mm, % saving $= 35.64\%$

(b) Please refer to the solved example 6, page 7.11.

$\theta = 0.01287$ rad $= 0.74°$

(c) $D = 65.68$ mm

(d) Please refer to the solved example 7, page 7.12.

$T = 6.282$ kN.m

(e) Diameter based on shear stress, D = 194.23 mm.

Diameter based on stiffness, D = 194.048 mm.

Required diameter satisfying given conditions, D = **194.23 mm**.

(f) (i)

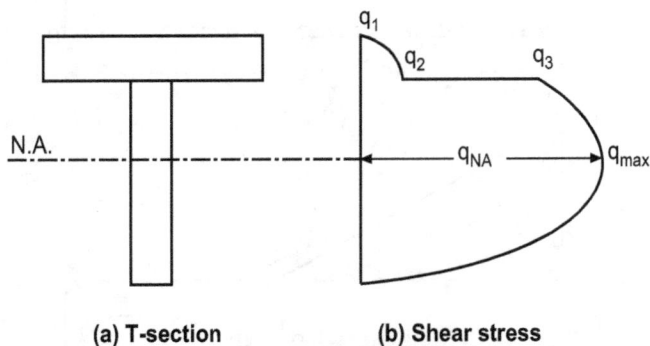

**(a) T-section**          **(b) Shear stress distribution diagram**

**Fig. 13**

(ii) Please refer to Fig. 7.2 (a) for variation of shear stress for a solid shaft subjected to torsion.

⊐⊐⊐

# STRENGTH OF MATERIALS
## Summer 2015

Time : 3 Hours                    Subject Code : 17304                    Marks : 100

**1. (A)  Attempt any six of the following :**                              **(12)**

(a)  Define fatigue and creep.

(b)  Define principal plane and principal stress.

(c)  State the relation between B.M. and S.F.

(d)  Give the four assumptions in the theory of bending.

(e)  Draw the core section for circular column of diameter 'd'.

(f)  Give the relationship between E, G and K.

(g)  State the value of two different angles of planes with principal plane where the tangential stress is maximum.

(h)  Draw stress distribution on rectangular section subjected to bending, when used as cantilever and simply supported beam.

**(B)  Attempt any two of the following :**                              **(8)**

(a)  Find the required diameter of steel rod that has to carry an axial pull of 40 kN, if the permissible stress is 150 MPa.

(b)  A seamless pipe 1 m diameter contains a fluid pressure of 1.5 N/mm$^2$. If the ultimate tensile stress is 450 N/mm$^2$, find the minimum thickness of pipe. Take factor of safety as 4.5.

(c)  A symmetrical I-section of overall depth of 300 mm, has its flanges 150 mm × 10 mm and web 10 mm thick. Find the M.I. about its centroidal axis parallel to the flanges.

**2.  Attempt any four of the following :**                              **(16)**

(a)  (i)  Draw the sketch of uniformly varying section showing axial load.

     (ii)  State the effective length for one end fixed and other end hinged column.

(b)  Write the assumptions made in the Euler's column theory.

(c)  A rod 300 mm long and 20 mm in diameter is heated through 100°C and at the same time pulley by a force 'P'. If the total extension is 0.4 mm, what is the magnitude of 'P' ?
Take E = 2 × 10$^5$ N/mm$^2$ and α = 12 × 10$^{-6}$/°C.

(d)  A member ABCD is subjected to loads as shown in Fig. 1. Find the force 'P' and net change in length of the member. Take E = 2 × 10$^5$ N/mm$^2$.

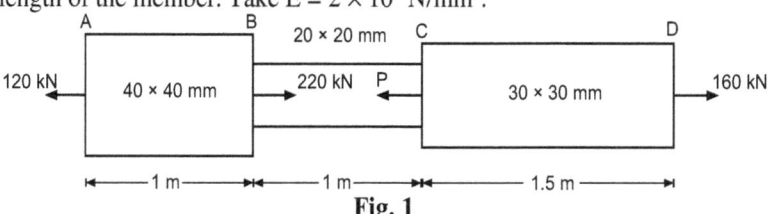

**Fig. 1**

(e)  A straight bar of uniform cross-section has a diameter of 10 mm. It is subjected to an axial pull of 20 kN. Find the normal and tangential stresses on a plane inclined at an angle of 30° to the axis of bar.

(f)  A cylindrical shell is 3 m long, 1 m internal diameter and 15 mm metal thickness. Calculate circumferential strain and longitudinal strain, if cylindrical shell is subjected to internal pressure of 1.5 N/mm$^2$. Take E = 2 × 10$^5$ N/mm$^2$ and μ = 0.25.

**3.  Attempt any four of the following :**                              **(16)**

(a)  Draw S.F. and B.M. diagrams for a simply supported beam of a span 'L' carrying a central point load 'W'. State the values of maximum S.F. and maximum B.M. and their locations.

(b)  A simply supported beam ABC is supported at A and B, 6 m apart with an overhang BC 2 m long, carries a udl of 15 kN/m over AB and a point load of 30 kN at C. Draw S.F. and B.M. diagrams.

(c) A cantilever beam 4 m long carries a udl of 2 kN/m over 2 m from free end and a point load of 4 kN at free end. Draw S.F. and B.M. diagrams.

(d) Draw S.F. and B.M. diagrams of a cantilever beam AB 4 m long having its fixed end at A and loaded a udl of 1 kN/m upto 2 m from B and with a point load of 2 kN at 1 m from A.

(e) A simply supported beam of span 4 m carries two point loads of 5 kN and 7 kN at 1.5 m and 3.5 m from the left hand support respectively. Draw SFD and BMD showing important values.

(f) A circular disc has M.I. about its any one tangent is $6.283 \times 10^5$ mm$^4$. Calculate diameter of disc.

**4. Attempt any four of the following :**　　　　　　　　　　　　　　　　　　　**(16)**

(a) Determine the M.I. of a solid rectangular section 40 mm wide and 60 mm deep about its smaller side.

(b) An I-section have the following dimensions :

Top flange – 80 mm × 20 mm, Bottom flange – 120 mm × 20 mm

Web – 120 mm × 20 mm. Calculate the M.I. about X-X axis.

(c) Find $I_{yy}$ for an unequal angle section having vertical leg of 125 × 10 mm and horizontal leg of 75 × 10 mm.

(d) An isosceles triangular section ABC has base width 80 mm and height 60 mm. Determine the M.I. of the section about the C.G. of the section and about the base BC.

(e) State bending equation and define moment of resistance.

(f) Draw shear stress distribution diagram for rectangular section. Also state the relationship between maximum and average shear stress.

**5. Attempt any four of the following :**　　　　　　　　　　　　　　　　　　　**(16)**

(a) A timber beam 100 mm wide and 150 mm deep supports a udl over a span of 2 m. If the safe stresses are 28 N/mm$^2$ in bending and 2 N/mm$^2$ in shear, calculate the maximum load which can be supported by the beam.

(b) Calculate the limit of eccentricity for a circular section having diameter 80 mm. (Not by using direct formula but from basic principle).

(c) A rectangular column 150 mm wide and 100 mm thick carries a load of 150 kN at an eccentricity of 50 mm in the plane bisecting the thickness. Find the maximum and minimum intensities of stress in the section.

(d) A hollow circular column having external and internal diameters of 40 cm and 30 cm respectively, carries a vertical load of 150 kN at the outer edge of the column. Calculate the maximum and minimum intensities of stresses in the section.

(e) A rectangular rod of size 50 mm × 100 mm is bent into "C" shape as shown in Fig. 2 and applied load of 40 kN at point A. Calculate resultant stress developed at section X-X.

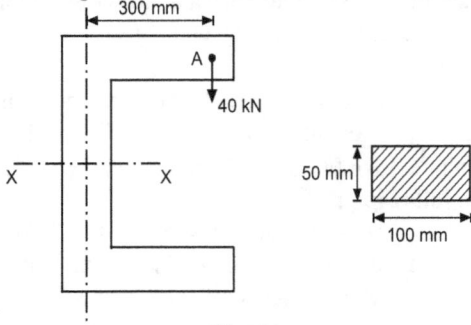

Fig. 2

(f) Calculate the limit of eccentricity of a rectangular cross-section of size 1000 mm × 2000 mm and sketch it.

**6.** **Attempt any four of the following :**                                                    **(16)**

   (a)   State the assumptions in the theory of pure torsion.

   (b)   A shaft required to transmit 20 kW power at 150 r.p.m. The maximum torque may exceed
         the average torque by 40%. Determine the diameter of the shaft if shear stress is not to
         exceed 50 MPa.

   (c)   Find the power that can be transmitted by a shaft of 40 mm diameter rotating at 200 r.p.m.,
         if maximum shear stress is not to exceed 85 MPa.

   (d)   A shaft is transmitting 150 kW at 200 r.p.m. If allowable shear stress is 80 $N/mm^2$ and
         allowable twist is 1.5° per 4 m length, find the diameter of shaft.
         Take $G = 0.8 \times 10^5 \ N/mm^2$.

   (e)   Find the maximum stress in a propeller shaft 400 mm external and 200 mm internal
         diameter, when subjected to a twisting moment of 4650 Nm. If the modulus of rigidity is
         82 GPa, calculate the twist in a length 20 times the external diameter.

   (f)   (i)  Define neutral axis.
         (ii) Compare solid shaft and hollow shaft.

**ANSWERS**

**1.**   (A)   (a)   Please refer to section 1.6 (ix) and (x).

         (b)   Please refer to section 2.3.

         (c)   Please refer to section 3.9.

         (d)   Please refer to section 5.4.

         (e)   Please refer to section 6.10.2.

         (f)   Please refer to section 1.40.

               The relation is $E = \dfrac{9\,GK}{G + 3\,K}$

         (g)   $\theta_1 = 45°$ and $\theta_2 = 135°$ are the angles where the tangential stress is maximum.

         (h)   Bending stress distribution diagram for rectangular section for simply supported and
               cantilever beam.

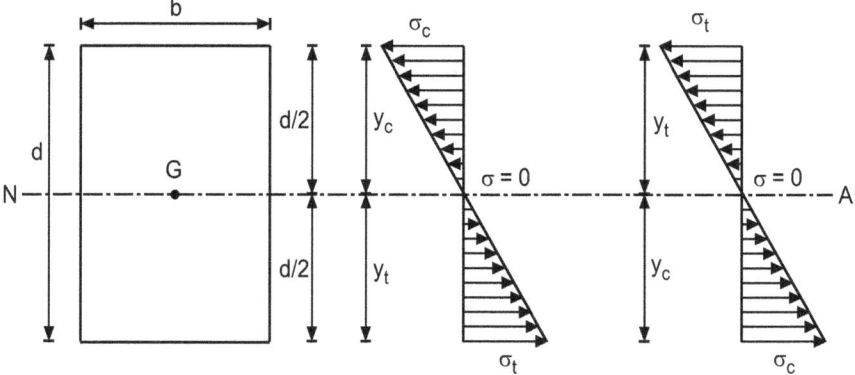

**(a) Beam section**          **(b) Bending stress**          **(c) Bending stress**
                              **variation diagram for**        **variation for**
                              **simply supported beam**        **cantilever beam**

**Fig. 3**

   (B)   (a)   Please refer to the solved example 6, page 1.18.  d = 18.43 mm.

         (b)   Please refer to the solved example 15, page 2.50.  t = 7.5 mm.

         (c)   Please refer to the solved example 26, page 4.30.  $I_{xx} = 8.14 \times 10^7 \ mm^4$.

**2.**   (a)   (i)   Please refer to Fig. 1.45, page 1.80.

        (ii)   $L_e = \dfrac{L}{\sqrt{2}}$

    (b)   Please refer to section 1.48.1.

    (c)   Please refer to example 69, page 1.68. P = 8.37 kN.

    (d)   Please refer to the solved example 84, page 1.75.

        P = 260 kN ($\leftarrow$),   $\delta L$ = 0.455 mm (increase).

    (e)   Please refer to example 3, page 2.13.

        $\sigma_n$ = 63.66 N/mm$^2$ (tensile),   $\sigma_t$ = 110.27 N/mm$^2$.

    (f)   Refer to similar example 3, page 2.44.   $e_c = 2.1875 \times 10^{-4}$, $e_L = 6.25 \times 10^{-5}$.

**3.**   (a)   Please refer to section 3.11, case 1, Fig. 3.33.

      The maximum S.F. will be developed at the supports. Due to symmetry, maximum S.F. at supports A and B are equal. Maximum S.F. = $R_A = R_B = \dfrac{W}{4}$.

      As the point of contra shear is under the point load, the maximum B.M. will be developed under the point load i.e. at C.

      Maximum B.M. at C,   $M_C = R_A \times \dfrac{L}{2} = \dfrac{W}{2} \times \dfrac{L}{2} = \dfrac{WL}{2}$

    (b)   Please refer to similar example 47, page 3.65.

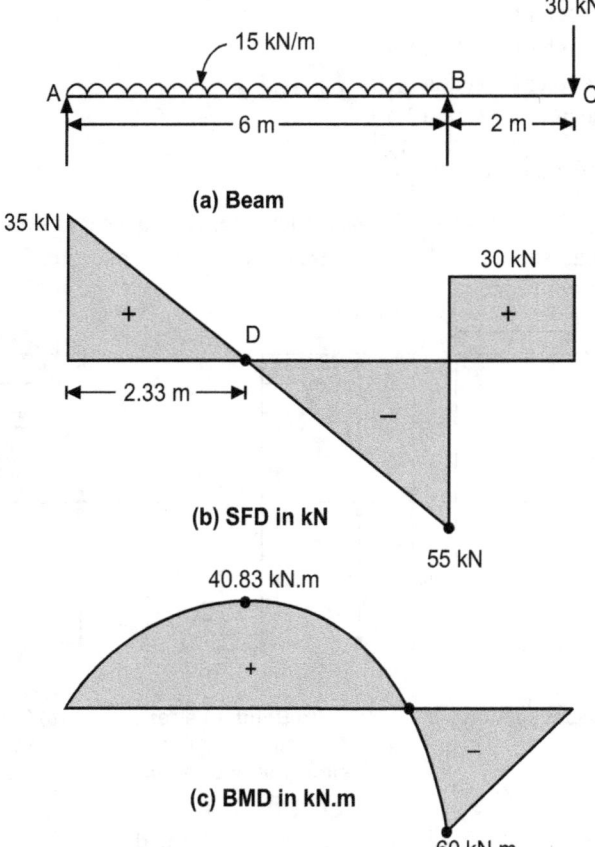

**Fig. 4**

    (c)   Please refer to the solved example 38, page 3.58.

(d)

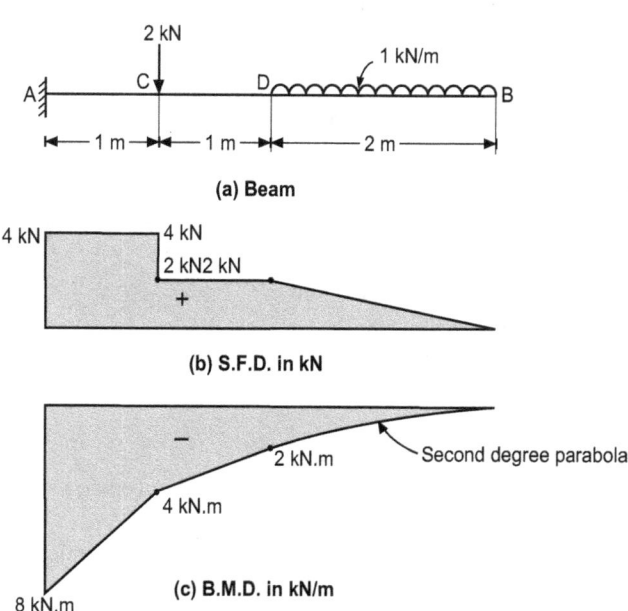

**Fig. 5**

(e)   Please refer to similar solved example 1, page 3.24.

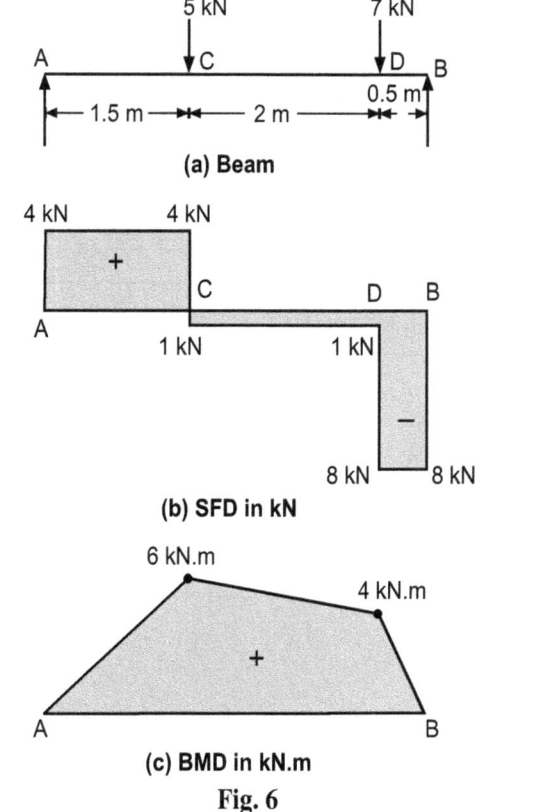

**Fig. 6**

(f)　$I_{tangent} = I_G + Ah^2 = \dfrac{\pi}{64} D^4 + \dfrac{\pi}{4} D^2 \left(\dfrac{D}{2}\right)^2 = \dfrac{\pi}{64} D^4 + \dfrac{\pi}{16} D^4 = 0.2454\, D^4$　　… (i)

But $I_{tangent} = 6.283 \times 10^5$ mm$^4$　　… (ii)

Equating (i) and (ii),　$0.2454\, D^4 = 6.283 \times 10^5$　$\therefore$　D = **40 mm**.

4. (a) $I_{smaller\ side} = 2.88 \times 10^6$ mm$^4$.
   (b) Please refer to example 29, page 4.35.　$I_{xx} = 21.1233 \times 10^6$ mm$^4$.
   (c) Please refer to the solved example 37, page 4.41. $I_{yy} = 8.4 \times 10^5$ mm$^4$.
   (d) Please refer to the solved example 16, page 4.21.
       $I_{Base} = 144 \times 10^4$ mm$^4$,　$I_{xx} = 48 \times 10^4$ mm$^4$.
   (e) Please refer to sections 5.5 and 5.6.
   (f) Please refer to Fig. 5.37, section 5.14, page 5.46.　$q_{max} = 1.5\, q_{av}$.

5. (a) w = 21 kN/m,　W = 21 × 2 = 42 kN.
   (b) e = 10 mm
   (c) Please refer to the solved example 3, page 6.10.
       $\sigma_{max} = 30$ kN/mm$^2$ (Compressive),　$\sigma_{min} = -10$ N/mm$^2$ (Tensile).
   (d) Please refer to the solved example 9, page 6.15.
       $\sigma_{max} = 9.71$ N/mm$^2$ (Compressive),　$\sigma_{min} = -4.25$ N/mm$^2$ (Tensile).
   (e) Please refer to the solved example 26, page 6.27.
       $\sigma_{max} = 152$ N/mm$^2$ (Tensile),　$\sigma_{min} = -136$ N/mm$^2$ (Compressive).
   (f) Please refer to the solved example 36, page 6.38.
       $e_x = 333.33$ mm,　$e_y = 166.67$ mm.

6. (a) Please refer to section 7.2.
   (b) Please refer to the solved example 22, page 7.21.　D = 56.62 mm.
   (c) Please refer to the solved example 15, page 7.18.　P = 22.37 kW.
   (d) Please refer to example 14, page 7.18.　D = 108.69 mm say 110 mm.
   (e) Please refer to the solved example 29, page 7.25.
       $f_s = 0.3947$ MPa,　$\theta = 0.0001925$ rad = 0.011°
   (f) (i)　Please refer to section 5.3.
       (ii)　Comparison between solid shaft and hollow shaft.

| Sr. No. | Parameter | Solid shaft | Hollow shaft |
|---|---|---|---|
| 1. | Polar MI | $I_P = \dfrac{\pi}{32} \times (D)^4$ | $\dfrac{\pi}{32} \times \dfrac{(D^4 - d^4)}{D}$ |
| 2. | Polar modulus | $Z_P = \dfrac{\pi}{16} \times D^3$ | $\dfrac{\pi}{16} \times (D^4 - d^4)$ |
| 3. | Torque transmitted | $T = \dfrac{\pi}{16} F_s\, D^3$ | $T = \dfrac{\pi}{16} F_s \left(\dfrac{D^4 - d^4}{D}\right)$ |
| 4. | Stiffness | Solid shaft has less strength and stiffness than a hollow shaft. | Hollow shaft has greater strength and stiffness than a solid shaft. |